RALPH THE HEIR

by

Anthony Trollope

With 12 Illustrations by
F. A. Fraser

DOVER PUBLICATIONS, INC.
NEW YORK

Published in Canada by General Publishing Company, Ltd., 30 Lesmill Road, Don Mills, Toronto, Ontario.

Published in the United Kingdom by Constable and Company, Ltd., 10 Orange Street, London WC2H 7EG.

This Dover edition, first published in 1978, is an unabridged republication of the work originally published by Strahan & Co., London, in 1871. An illustration to another work, erroneously bound into the original, has been omitted in the present edition. New captions have been supplied for the 12 illustrations by F. A. Fraser.

International Standard Book Number:
0-486-23642-0
Library of Congress Catalog Card Number:
78-51956

Manufactured in the United States of America
Dover Publications, Inc.
180 Varick Street
New York, N.Y. 10014

CONTENTS.

RALPH THE HEIR.

CHAPTER I.

SIR THOMAS.

THERE are men who cannot communicate themselves to others, as there are also men who not only can do so, but cannot do otherwise. And it is hard to say which is the better man of the two. We do not specially respect him who wears his heart upon his sleeve for daws to peck at, who carries a crystal window to his bosom so that all can see the work that is going on within it, who cannot keep any affair of his own private, who gushes out in love and friendship to every chance acquaintance; but then, again, there is but little love given to him who is always wary, always silent as to his own belongings, who buttons himself in a suit of close reserve which he never loosens. Respect such a one may gain, but hardly love. It is natural to us to like to know the affairs of our friends; and natural also, I think, to like to talk of our own to those whom we trust. Perhaps, after all that may be said of the weakness of the gushing and indiscreet babbler, it is pleasanter to live with such a one than with the self-constrained reticent man of iron, whose conversation among his most intimate friends is solely of politics, of science, of literature, or of some other subject equally outside the privacies of our inner life.

Sir Thomas Underwood, whom I, and I hope my readers also, will have to know very intimately, was one of those who are not able to make themselves known intimately to any. I am speaking now of a man of sixty, and I am speaking also of one who had never yet made a close friend,—who had never by unconscious and slow degrees of affection fallen into that kind of intimacy with another man which justifies and renders necessary mutual freedom of intercourse in all the affairs of life. And yet he was possessed of warm affections, was by no means misanthropic in his nature, and would, in truth, have given much to be able to be free and jocund as are other men. He lacked the power that way, rather than the will. To himself it seemed to be a weakness in him rather than a strength that he should always be silent, always guarded, always secret and dark. He had lamented it as an acknowledged infirmity ;—as a man grieves that he should be short-sighted, or dull of hearing; but at the age of sixty he had taken no efficient steps towards curing himself of the evil, and had now abandoned all idea of any such cure.

Whether he had been, upon the whole, fortunate or unfortunate in life shall be left to the reader's judgment. But he certainly had not been happy. He had suffered cruel disappointments ; and a disappointment will crush the spirit worse than a realised calamity. There is no actual misfortune in not being Lord Mayor of London ;— but when a man has set his heart upon the place, has worked himself into a position within a few feet of the Mansion House, has become alderman with the mayoralty before him in immediate rotation, he will suffer more at being passed over by the liverymen than if he had lost half his fortune. Now Sir Thomas Underwood had become Solicitor-General in his profession, but had never risen to the higher rank or more assured emoluments of other legal offices.

We will not quite trace our Meleager back to his egg, but we will explain that he was the only son of a barrister of moderate means, who put him to the Bar, and who died leaving little or nothing behind him. The young barrister had an only sister, who married an officer in the army, and who had passed all her latter life in distant countries to which her husband had been called by the necessity of living on the income which his profession gave him. As a Chancery barrister, Mr. Underwood,—our Sir Thomas,—had done well, living on the income he made, marrying at thirty-five, going into Parliament at forty-five, becoming Solicitor-General at fifty,— and ceasing to hold that much-desired office four months after his appointment. Such cessation, however, arising from political causes, is no disappointment to a man. It will doubtless be the case that a man so placed will regret the weakness of his party, which has been unable to keep the good things of Government in its hands ; but he will recognise without remorse or sorrow the fact that the Ministry to which he has attached himself must cease to be a Ministry ;—and there will be nothing in his displacement to gall his pride, or to create that inner feeling of almost insupportable mortification which comes from the conviction of personal failure. Sir Thomas Underwood had been Solicitor-General for a few months under a Conservative

Prime Minister; and when the Conservative Minister went out of office, Sir Thomas Underwood followed him with no feeling of regret that caused him unhappiness. But when afterwards the same party came back to power, and he, having lost his election at the borough which he had represented, was passed over without a word of sympathy or even of assumed regret from the Minister, then he was wounded. It was true, he knew, that a man, to be Solicitor-General, should have a seat in Parliament. The highest legal offices in the country are not to be attained by any amount of professional excellence, unless the candidate shall have added to such excellence the power of supporting a Ministry and a party in the House of Commons. Sir Thomas Underwood thoroughly understood this;— but he knew also that there are various ways in which a lame dog may be helped over a stile,—if only the lame dog be popular among dogs. For another ex-Solicitor-General a seat would have been found,—or some delay would have been granted,—or at least there would have been a consultation, with a suggestion that something should be tried. But in this case a man four years his junior in age, whom he despised, and who, as he was informed, had obtained his place in Parliament by gross bribery, was put into the office without a word of apology to him. Then he was unhappy, and acknowledged to himself that his spirit was crushed.

But he acknowledged to himself at the same time that he was one doomed by his nature to such crushing of the spirit if he came out of the hole of his solitude, and endeavoured to carry on the open fight of life among his fellow-men. He knew that he was one doomed to that disappointment, the bitterest of all, which comes from failure when the prize has been all but reached. It is much to have become Solicitor-General, and that he had achieved;—but it is worse than nothing to have been Solicitor-General for four months, and then to find that all the world around one regards one as having failed, and as being, therefore, fit for the shelf. Such were Sir Thomas Underwood's feelings as he sat alone in his chambers during those days in which the new administration was formed,—in which days he was neither consulted nor visited, nor communicated with either by message or by letter. But all this, — this formation of a Ministry, in which the late Solicitor-General was not invited to take a part,—occurred seven years before the commencement of our story.

During those years in which our lawyer sat in Parliament as Mr. Underwood,—at which time he was working hard also as a Chancery barrister, and was, perhaps, nearer to his fellow-men than he had ever been before, or was ever destined to be afterwards,—he resided, as regarded himself almost nominally, at a small but pretty villa, which he had taken for his wife's sake at Fulham. It was close upon the river, and had well-arranged, though not extensive, shrubbery walks, and a little lawn, and a tiny conservatory, and a charming opening down to the Thames. Mrs. Underwood had found herself unable to live in Half-moon Street; and Mr. Underwood, not unwillingly, had removed his household gods to this retreat. At that time his household gods consisted of a wife and two daughters;—but the wife had died before the time came at which she could have taken on herself the name of Lady Underwood. The villa at Fulham was still kept, and there lived the two girls, and there also Sir Thomas, had he been interrogated on the subject, would have declared that he also was domiciled. But if a man lives at the place in which he most often sleeps, Sir Thomas in truth lived at his chambers at Southampton Buildings. When he moved those household gods of his to the villa, it was necessary, because of his duties in Parliament, that he should have some place in town wherein he might lay his head, and therefore, I fear not unwillingly, he took to laying his head very frequently in the little bedroom which was attached to his chambers.

It is not necessary that we should go back to any feelings which might have operated upon him during his wife's lifetime, or during the period of his parliamentary career. His wife was now dead, and he no longer held a seat in Parliament. He had, indeed, all but abandoned his practice at the Bar, never putting himself forward for the ordinary business of a Chancery barrister. But, nevertheless, he spent the largest half of his life in his chambers, breakfasting there, reading there, writing there, and sleeping there. He did not altogether desert the lodge at Fulham, and the two girls who lived there. He would not even admit to them, or allow them to assert that he had not his home with them. Sometimes for two nights together, and sometimes for three, he would be at the villa,— never remaining there, however, during the day. But on Sundays it may almost be said that he was never at home. And hence arose the feeling that of all went the nearest to create discord between the father and the daughters. Sir Thomas was always in Southampton Buildings on Sundays. Did Sir Thomas go to church? The Miss Underwoods did go to church very regularly, and thought much of the propriety and necessity of such Sunday exercises. They could remember that in their younger days their father always had been there with them. They could remember, indeed, that he, with something of sternness, would require from them punctuality and exactness in this duty. Now and again,—perhaps four times in the year,—he would go to the Rolls Chapel. So much they could learn. But they believed that beyond that his Sundays were kept holy by no attendance at divine service. And it may be said at once that they believed aright.

Sir Thomas's chambers in Southampton Buildings, though they were dull and dingy of aspect from the outside, and were reached by a staircase which may be designated as lugubrious,—so much did its dark and dismantled condition tend to melancholy,—were in themselves large and commodious. His bedroom was small, but he had two spacious sitting-rooms, one of which was fitted up as a library, and the other as a dining-room. Over and beyond these there was a clerk's room;—for Sir Thomas, though he had given up the greater part of his business, had not given up his clerk; and here the old man, the clerk, passed his entire time, from half-past eight in the morning till ten at night, waiting upon his employer in various capacities with a sedulous personal attention to which he had probably not intended to devote himself when he first took upon himself the duties of clerk to a practising Chancery barrister. But Joseph Stemm and Sir Thomas were not unlike in character, and had grown old together with too equal a step to admit of separation and of new alliance. Stemm had but one friend in the world, and Sir Thomas was that friend. I have already said that Sir Thomas had no friend;—but perhaps he felt more of that true intimacy, which friendship produces, with Stemm than with any other human being.

Sir Thomas was a tall thin man, who stooped considerably,—though not from any effect of years, with a face which would perhaps have been almost mean had it not been rescued from that evil condition by the assurance of intelligence and strength which is always conveyed by a certain class of ugliness. He had a nose something like the great Lord Brougham's,—thin, long, and projecting at the point. He had quick grey eyes, and a good forehead;—but the component parts of his countenance were irregular and roughly put together. His chin was long, as was also his upper lip;—so that it may be taken as a fact that he was an ugly man. He was hale, however, and strong, and was still so good a walker that he thought nothing of making his way down to the villa on foot of an evening, after dining at his club.

It was his custom to dine at his club,—that highly respectable and most comfortable club situated at the corner of Suffolk Street, Pall Mall;—the senior of the two which are devoted to the well-being of scions of our great Universities. There Sir Thomas dined, perhaps four nights in the week, for ten months in the year. And it was said of him in the club that he had never been known to dine in company with another member of the club. His very manner as he sat at his solitary meal,—always with a pint of port on the table,—was as well known as the figure of the old king on horseback outside in the street, and was as unlike the ordinary manner of men as is that unlike the ordinary figures of kings. He had always a book in

his hand,—not a club book, nor a novel from Mudie's, nor a magazine, but some ancient and hard-bound volume from his own
library, which he had brought in his pocket, and to which his
undivided attention would be given. The eating of his dinner, which
always consisted of the joint of the day and of nothing else, did not
take him more than five minutes ;—but he would sip his port wine
slowly, would have a cup of tea which he would also drink very
slowly,—and would then pocket his book, pay his bill, and would go.
It was rarely the case that he spoke to any one in the club. He
would bow to a man here and there,—and if addressed would
answer ; but of conversation at his club he knew nothing, and hardly
ever went into any room but that in which his dinner was served to
him.

In conversing about him men would express a wonder how such
a one had ever risen to high office,—how, indeed, he could have
thriven at his profession. But in such matters we are, all of us,
too apt to form confident opinions on apparent causes which are
near the surface, but which, as guides to character, are fallacious.
Perhaps in all London there was no better lawyer, in his branch of
law, than Sir Thomas Underwood. He had worked with great
diligence ; and though he was shy to a degree quite unintelligible to
men in general in the ordinary intercourse of life, he had no feeling of diffidence when upon his legs in Court or in the House of
Commons. With the Lord Chancellor's wife or daughters he could
not exchange five words with comfort to himself,—nor with his
lordship himself in a drawing-room ; but in Court the Lord Chancellor was no more to him than another lawyer whom he believed to
be not so good a lawyer as himself. No man had ever succeeded in
browbeating him when panoplied in his wig and gown ; nor had
words ever been wanting to him when so arrayed. It had been
suggested to him by an attorney who knew him in that way in which
attorneys ought to know barristers, that he should stand for a certain borough ;—and he had stood and had been returned. Thrice he
had been returned for the same town ; but at last, when it was discovered that he would never dine with the leading townsmen, or call
on their wives in London, or assist them in their little private views,
the strength of his extreme respectability was broken down,—and he
was rejected. In the meantime he was found to be of value by the
party to which he had attached himself. It was discovered that he
was not only a sound lawyer, but a man of great erudition, who had
studied the experience of history as well as the wants of the present
age. He was one who would disgrace no Government,—and he was
invited to accept the office of Solicitor-General by a Minister who had
never seen him out of the House of Commons. " He is as good a
lawyer as there is in England," said the Lord Chancellor. " He

always speaks with uncommon clearness," said the Chancellor of the Exchequer. "I never saw him talking with a human being," said the Secretary to the Treasury, deprecating the appointment. "He will soon get over that complaint with your assistance," said the Minister, laughing. So Mr. Underwood became Solicitor-General and Sir Thomas ;—and he so did his work that no doubt he would have returned to his office had he been in Parliament when his party returned to power. But he had made no friend, he had not learned to talk even to the Secretary of the Treasury ;—and when the party came back to power he was passed over without remorse, and almost without a regret.

He never resumed the active bustle of his profession after that disappointment. His wife was then dead, and for nearly a twelve-month he went about, declaring to attorneys and others that his professional life was done. He did take again to a certain class of work when he came back to the old chambers in Southampton Buildings ; but he was seen in Court only rarely, and it was understood that he wished it to be supposed that he had retired. He had ever been a moderate man in his mode of living, and had put together a sum of money sufficient for moderate wants. He possessed some twelve or fourteen hundred a year independent of anything that he might now earn ; and, as he had never been a man greedy of money, so was he now more indifferent to it than in his earlier days. It is a mistake, I think, to suppose that men become greedy as they grow old. The avaricious man will show his avarice as he gets into years, because avarice is a passion compatible with old age,—and will become more avaricious as his other passions fall off from him. And so will it be with the man that is open-handed. Mr. Underwood, when struggling at the Bar, had fought as hard as any of his compeers for comfort and independence ;—but money, as money, had never been dear to him ;— and now he was so trained a philosopher that he disregarded it altogether, except so far as it enabled him to maintain his independence.

On a certain Friday evening in June, as he sat at dinner at his club, instead of applying himself to his book, which according to his custom he had taken from his pocket, he there read a letter, which as soon as read he would restore to the envelope, and would take it out again after a few moments of thought. At last, when the cup of tea was done and the bill was paid, he put away letter and book together and walked to the door of his club. When there he stood and considered what next should he do that evening. It was now past eight o'clock, and how should he use the four, five, or perhaps six hours which remained to him before he should go to bed ? The temptation to which he was liable prompted him to return to his solitude in Southampton Buildings. Should he do so, he would

sleep till ten in his chair,—then he would read, and drink more tea,
or perhaps write, till one ; and after that he would prowl about the
purlieus of Chancery Lane, the Temple, and Lincoln's Inn, till two
or even three o'clock in the morning ;—looking up at the old dingy
windows, and holding, by aid of those powers which imagination gave
him, long intercourse with men among whom a certain weakness in
his physical organisation did not enable him to live in the flesh.
Well the policemen knew him as he roamed about, and much they
speculated as to his roamings.　But in these night wanderings he
addressed no word to any one ; nor did any one ever address a word
to him.　Yet the world, perhaps, was more alive to him then than at
any other period in the twenty-four hours.

But on the present occasion the temptation was resisted.　He had
not been at home during the whole week, and knew well that he
ought to give his daughters the countenance of his presence.
Whether that feeling alone would have been sufficient to withdraw
him from the charms of Chancery Lane and send him down to the
villa may be doubted ; but there was that in the letter which he
had perused so carefully which he knew must be communicated to
his girls.　His niece, Mary Bonner, was now an orphan, and would
arrive in England from Jamaica in about a fortnight.　Her mother
had been Sir Thomas's sister, and had been at this time dead about
three years.　General Bonner, the father, had now died, and the girl
was left an orphan, almost penniless, and with no near friend unless
the Underwoods would befriend her.　News of the General's death
had reached Sir Thomas before ;—and he had already made inquiry
as to the fate of his niece through her late father's agents.　Of the
General's means he had known absolutely nothing,—believing,
however, that they were confined to his pay as an officer.　Now
he was told that the girl would be at Southampton in a fortnight,
and that she was utterly destitute.　He declared to himself as
he stood on the steps of the club that he would go home and
consult his daughters ;—but his mind was in fact made up as to
his niece's fate long before he got home,—before he turned out of
Pall Mall into St. James's Park.　He would sometimes talk to
himself of consulting his daughters ; but in truth he very rarely
consulted any human being as to what he would do or leave undone.
If he went straight, he went straight without other human light
than such as was given to him by his own intellect, his own heart,
and his own conscience.　It took him about an hour and a half to
reach his home, but of that time four-fifths were occupied, not in
resolving what he would do in this emergency, but in deep grumblings
and regrets that there should be such a thing to be done at all.
All new cares were grievous to him.　Nay ;—old cares were grievous,
but new cares were terrible.　Though he was bold in deciding, he

was very timid in looking forward as to the results of that decision. Of course the orphan girl must be taken into his house;— and of course he must take upon himself the duty of a father in regard to her.

CHAPTER II.

POPHAM VILLA.

POPHAM VILLA was the name of the house at Fulham,—as was to be seen by all men passing by, for it was painted up conspicuously on the pillars through which the gate led into the garden. Mr. Underwood, when he had first taken the place, had wished to expunge the name, feeling it to be cockneyfied, pretentious, and unalluring. But Mrs. Underwood had rather liked it, and it remained. It was a subject of ridicule with the two girls; but they had never ventured to urge its withdrawal, and after his wife's death Sir Thomas never alluded to the subject. Popham Villa it was, therefore, and there the words remained. The house was unpretentious, containing only two sitting-rooms besides a small side closet,—for it could hardly be called more,—which the girls even in their mother's lifetime had claimed as their own. But the drawing-room was as pretty as room could be, opening on to the lawn with folding windows, and giving a near view of the bright river as it flowed by, with just a glimpse of the bridge. That and the dining-room and the little closet were all on the ground floor, and above were at any rate as many chambers as the family required. The girls desired no better house,—if only their father could be with them. But he would urge that his books were all in London; and that, even were he willing to move them, there was no room for them in Popham Villa.

It was sad enough for the two girls,—this kind of life. The worst of it, perhaps, was this; that they never knew when to expect him. A word had been said once as to the impracticability of having dinner ready for a gentleman, when the gentleman would never say whether he would want a dinner. It had been an unfortunate remark, for Sir Thomas had taken advantage of it by saying that when he came he would come after dinner, unless he had certified to the contrary beforehand. Then, after dinner, would come on him the temptation of returning to his chambers, and so it would go on with him from day to day.

On this Friday evening the girls almost expected him, as he rarely let a week pass without visiting them, and still more rarely came to them on a Saturday. He found them out upon the lawn, or rather on the brink of the river, and with them was standing a young man whom he knew well. He kissed each of the girls, and then gave his hand to the young man. " I am glad to see you, Ralph," he said. " Have you been here long ? "

" As much as an hour or two, I fear. Patience will tell you. I meant to have got back by the 9.15 from Putney ; but I have been smoking, and dreaming, and talking, till now it is nearly ten."

" There is a train at 10.30," said the eldest Miss Underwood.

" And another at 11.15," said the young man.

Sir Thomas was especially anxious to be alone with his daughters, but he could not tell the guest to go. Nor was he justified in feeling any anger at his presence there,—though he did experience some prick of conscience in the matter. If it was wrong that his daughters should be visited by a young man in his absence, the fault lay in his absence, rather than with the young man for coming, or with the girls for receiving him. The young man had been a ward of his own, and for a year or two in former times had been so intimate in his house as to live with his daughters almost as an elder brother might have done. But young Ralph Newton had early in life taken rooms for himself in London, had then ceased to be a ward, and had latterly,—so Sir Thomas understood,—lived such a life as to make him unfit to be the trusted companion of his two girls. And yet there had been nothing in his mode of living to make it necessary that he should be absolutely banished from the villa. He had spent more money than was fitting, and had got into debt, and Sir Thomas had had trouble about his affairs. He too was an orphan,—and the nephew and the heir of an old country squire whom he never saw. What money he had received from his father he had nearly spent, and it was rumoured of him that he had raised funds by post-obits on his uncle's life. Of all these things more will be told here-after ;—but Sir Thomas,—though he had given no instruction on the subject, and was averse even to allude to it,—did not like to think that Ralph Newton was at the villa with the girls in his absence. His girls were as good as gold. He was sure of that. He told himself over and over again that were it not so, he would not have left them so constantly without his own care. Patience, the elder, was a marvel among young women for prudence, con-duct, and proper feeling ; and Clarissa, whom he had certainly ever loved the better of the two, was as far as he knew faultless ;— a little more passionate, a little warmer, somewhat more fond of pleasure than her sister ; but on that account only the more to be loved. Nothing that he could do would make them safer than

sisters had occupied separate bedrooms, but now, as one chamber must be given up to the stranger, it would be necessary that they should be together. But there are sacrifices which entail so little pain that the pleasant feeling of sacrificial devotion much more than atones for the consequences.

Patience Underwood, the elder and the taller of the two girls, was certainly not pretty. Her figure was good, her hands and feet were small, and she was in all respects like a lady; but she possessed neither the feminine loveliness which comes so often simply from youth, nor that other, rarer beauty, which belongs to the face itself, and is produced by its own lines and its own expression. Her countenance was thin, and might perhaps have been called dry and hard. She was very like her father,—without, however, her father's nose, and the redeeming feature of her face was to be found in that sense of intelligence which was conveyed by her bright grey eyes. There was the long chin, and there was the long upper lip, which, exaggerated in her father's countenance, made him so notoriously plain a man. And then her hair, though plentiful and long, did not possess that shining lustre which we love to see in girls, and which we all recognise as one of the sweetest graces of girlhood. Such, outwardly, was Patience Underwood; and of all those who knew her well there was not one so perfectly satisfied that she did want personal attraction as was Patience Underwood herself. But she never spoke on the subject,—even to her sister. She did not complain; neither, as is much more common, did she boast that she was no beauty. Her sister's loveliness was very dear to her, and of that she would sometimes break out into enthusiastic words. But of herself, externally, she said nothing. Her gifts, if she had any, were of another sort; and she was by no means willing to think of herself as one unendowed with gifts. She was clever, and knew herself to be clever. She could read, and understood what she read. She saw the difference between right and wrong, and believed that she saw it clearly. She was not diffident of herself, and certainly was not unhappy. She had a strong religious faith, and knew how to supplement the sometimes failing happiness of this world, by trusting in the happiness of the next. Were it not for her extreme anxiety in reference to her father, Patience Underwood would have been a happy woman.

Clarissa, the younger, was a beauty. The fact that she was a beauty was acknowledged by all who knew her, and was well known to herself. It was a fact as to which there had never been a doubt since she was turned fifteen. She was somewhat shorter than her sister, and less slender. She was darker in complexion, and her hair, which was rich in colour as brown hair can be, was lustrous, silky, and luxuriant. She wore it now, indeed, according to the fashion of the day, with a chignon on her head; but beneath that there were curls which escaped, and over her forehead it was clipped short, and was wavy, and impertinent,—as is also the fashion of the day. Such as it was, she so wore it that a man could hardly wish it to be otherwise. Her eyes, unlike those of her father and sister, were blue; and in the whole contour of her features there was nothing resembling theirs. The upper lip was short, and the chin was short and dimpled. There was a dimple on one cheek too, a charm so much more maddening than when it is to be seen on both sides alike. Her nose was perfect;—not Grecian, nor Roman, nor Egyptian,—but simply English, only just not retroussé. There were those who said her mouth was a thought too wide, and her teeth too perfect,—but they were of that class of critics to whom it is a necessity to cavil rather than to kiss. Added to all this there was a childishness of manner about her of which, though she herself was somewhat ashamed, all others were enamoured. It was not the childishness of very youthful years,—for she had already reached the mature age of twenty-one; but the half-doubting, half-pouting, half-yielding, half-obstinate, soft, loving, lovable childishness, which gives and exacts caresses, and which, when it is genuine, may exist to an age much beyond that which Clarissa Underwood had reached.

But with all her charms, Clarissa was not so happy a girl as her sister. And for this lack of inward satisfaction there were at this time two causes. She believed herself to be a fool, and was in that respect jealous of her sister;—and she believed herself to be in love, and in love almost without hope. As to her foolishness, it seemed to her to be a fact admitted by every one but by Patience herself. Not a human being came near her who did not seem to imply that any question as to wisdom or judgment or erudition between her and her sister would be a farce. Patience could talk Italian, could read German, knew, at least by name, every poet that had ever written, and was always able to say exactly what ought to be done. She could make the servants love her and yet obey her, and could always dress on her allowance without owing a shilling. Whereas Clarissa was obeyed by no one, was in debt to her bootmaker and milliner, and, let her struggles in the cause be as gallant as they might, could not understand a word of Dante, and was aware that she read the "Faery Queen" exactly as a child performs a lesson. As to her love,—there was a sharper sorrow. Need the reader be told that Ralph Newton was the hero to whom its late owner believed that her heart had been given? This was a sore subject, which had never as yet been mentioned frankly even between the two sisters. In truth, though Patience thought that there was a fancy, she did not think that there was much more than fancy. And, as far as she could see, there was not even fancy on the young man's part. No word had been spoken that could be accepted as an expression of avowed love. So at least Patience believed. And she would have been very unhappy had it been otherwise, for Ralph Newton was not,—in her opinion,—a man to whose love her sister could be trusted with confidence. And yet, beyond her father and sister, there was no one whom Patience loved as she did Ralph Newton.

There had, however, been a little episode in the life of Clarissa Underwood, which had tended to make her sister uneasy, and which the reader may as well hear at once. There was a second Newton, a younger brother,—but, though younger, not only in orders but in the possession of a living, Gregory Newton,—the Rev. Gregory Newton,—who in the space of a few weeks' acquaintance had fallen into a fury of love for Clarissa, and in the course of three months had made her as many offers, and had been as often refused. This had happened in the winter and spring previous to the opening of our story,—and both Patience and Sir Thomas had been well disposed towards the young man's suit. He had not been committed to Sir Thomas's charge, as had Ralph, having been brought up under the care of the uncle whose heir Ralph was through the obligation of legal settlements. This uncle, having quarrelled with his own brother, since dead, and with his heir, had nevertheless taken his other nephew by the hand, and had bestowed upon the young clergyman the living of Newton. Gregory Newton had been brought to the villa by his brother, and had at once fallen on his knees before the beauty. But the beauty would have none of him, and he had gone back to his living in Hampshire a broken-hearted priest and swain. Now, Patience, though she had never been directly so informed, feared that some partiality for the unworthy Ralph had induced her sister to refuse offers from the brother, who certainly was worthy. To the thinking of Patience Underwood, no lot in life could be happier for a woman than to be the wife of a zealous and praiseworthy parson of an English country parish;—no lot in life, at least, could be happier for any woman who intended to become a wife.

Such were the two girls at Popham Villa who were told on that evening that a new sister was to be brought home to them. When the next morning came they were of course still full of the subject. Sir Thomas was to go into London after breakfast, and he intended to walk over the bridge and catch an early train. He was as intent on being punctual to time as though he were bound to be all day in Court: and, fond as he might be of his daughters, had already enjoyed enough of the comforts of home to satisfy his taste. He did love his daughters;—but even with them he was not at his ease.

The only society he could enjoy was that of his books or of his own thoughts, and the only human being whom he could endure to have long near him with equanimity was Joseph Stemm. He had risen at nine, as was his custom, and before ten he was bustling about with his hat and gloves. "Papa," said Clarissa, "when shall you be home again?"

"I can't name a day, my dear."

"Papa, do come soon."

"No doubt I shall come soon." There was a slight tone of anger in his voice as he answered the last entreaty, and he was evidently in a hurry with his hat and gloves.

"Papa," said Patience, "of course we shall see you again before you go to Southampton." The voice of the elder was quite different from that of the younger daughter; and Sir Thomas, though the tone and manner of the latter question was injurious to him, hardly dared to resent it. Yet they were not, as he thought, justified. It now wanted twelve days to the date of his intended journey, and not more than three or four times in his life had he been absent from home for twelve consecutive days.

"Yes, my dear," he said, "I shall be home before that."

"Because, papa, there are things to be thought of."

"What things?"

"Clarissa and I had better have a second bed in our room,—unless you object."

"You know I don't object. Have I ever objected to anything of the kind?" He now stood impatient, with his hat in his hand.

"I hardly like to order things without telling you, papa. And there are a few other articles of furniture needed."

"You can get what you want. Run up to town and go to Barlow's. You can do that as well as I can."

"But I should have liked to have settled something about our future way of living before Mary comes," said Patience in a very low voice.

Sir Thomas frowned, and then he answered her very slowly. "There can be nothing new settled at all. Things will go on as they are at present. And I hope, Patience, you will do your best to make your cousin understand and receive favourably the future home which she will have to inhabit."

"You may be sure, papa, I shall do my best," said Patience;—and then Sir Thomas went.

He did return to the villa before his journey to Southampton, but it was only on the eve of that journey. During the interval the two girls together had twice sought him at his chambers,—a liberty on their part which, as they well knew, he did not at all approve. "Sir Thomas is very busy," old Stemm would say, shaking his head,

even to his master's daughters, "and if you wouldn't mind——"
Then he would make a feint as though to close the door, and would
go through various manoeuvres of defence before he would allow
the fort to be stormed. But Clarissa would ridicule old Stemm to his
face, and Patience would not allow herself to be beaten by him. On
their second visit they did make their way into their father's sanctum,
—and they never knew whether in truth he had been there when
they called before. " Old Stemm doesn't in the least mind what lies
he tells," Clarissa had said. To this Patience made no reply, feeling
that the responsibility for those figments might not perhaps lie
exclusively on old Stemm's shoulders.

"My dears, this is such an out-of-the-way place for you," Sir
Thomas said, as soon as the girls had made good their entrance.
But the girls had so often gone through all this before, that they
now regarded but little what ejaculations of that nature were made
to them.

"I have come to show you this list, papa," said Patience. Sir
Thomas took the list, and found that it contained various articles for
bedroom and kitchen use,—towels, sheets, pots and pans, knives and
forks, and even a set of curtains and a carpet.

"I shouldn't have thought that a girl of eighteen would have
wanted all these things,—a new corkscrew, for instance,—but if she
does, as I told you before, you must get them."

"Of course they are not all for Mary," said Patience.

"The fact is, papa," said Clarissa, "you never do look to see how
things are getting worn out."

"Clarissa!" exclaimed the angry father.

"Indeed, papa, if you were more at home and saw these things,"
began Patience——

"I have no doubt it is all right. Get what you want. Go to
Barlow's and to Green's, and to Block and Blowhard. Don't let
there be any bills, that's all. I will give you cheques when you
get the accounts. And now, my dears,—I am in the middle of
work which will not bear interruption." Then they left him, and
when he did come to the villa on the evening before his journey,
most of the new articles,—including the corkscrew,—were already in
the house.

CHAPTER III.

WHAT HAPPENED ON THE LAWN AT POPHAM VILLA.

SIR THOMAS started for Southampton on a Friday, having understood that the steamer from St. Thomas would reach the harbour
on Saturday morning. He would then immediately bring Mary
Bonner up to London and down to Fulham;—and there certainly had
come to be a tacit understanding that he would stay at home on the
following Sunday. On the Friday evening the girls were alone at the
villa; but there was nothing in this, as it was the life to which they
were accustomed. They habitually dined at two, calling the meal
lunch,—then had a five or six o'clock tea,—and omitted altogether
the ceremony of dinner. They had local acquaintances, with whom
occasionally they would spend their evenings; and now and then an
old maid or two,—now and then also a young maid or two would drop
in on them. But it was their habit to be alone. During these days
of which we are speaking Clarissa would take her "Faery Queen,"
and would work hard perhaps for half an hour. Then the "Faery
Queen" would be changed for a novel, and she would look up from
her book to see whether Patience had turned upon her any glance of
reprobation. Patience, in the meantime, would sit with unsullied
conscience at her work. And so the evenings would glide by; and in
these soft summer days the girls would sit out upon the lawn, and
would watch the boats of London watermen as they passed up and
down below the bridge. On this very evening, the last on which
they were to be together before the arrival of their cousin,—Patience
came out upon the lawn with her hat and gloves. "I am going
across to Miss Spooner's," she said; "will you come?" But Clarissa
was idle, and making some little joke, not very much to the honour
of Miss Spooner, declared that she was hot and tired, and had a
headache, and would stay at home. "Don't be long, Patty," she
said; "it is such a bore to be alone." Patience promised a speedy
return, and, making her way to the gate, crossed the road to Miss
Spooner's abode. She was hardly out of sight when the nose of a
wager boat was driven up against the bank, and there was Ralph
Newton, sitting in a blue Jersey shirt, with a straw hat and the
perspiration running from his handsome brow. Clarissa did not
see him till he whistled to her, and then she started, and laughed,
and ran down to the boat, and hardly remembered that she was quite
alone till she had taken his hand. "I don't think I'll come out, but
you must get me some soda-water and brandy," said Ralph. "Where's
Patience?"

"Patience has gone out to see an old maid; and we haven't got any brandy."

"I am so hot," said Ralph, carefully extricating himself from the boat. "You have got sherry?"

"Yes, we've got sherry, and port wine, and Gladstone;" and away she went to get him such refreshment as the villa possessed.

He drank his sherry and soda-water, and lit his pipe, and lay there on the lawn, as though he were quite at home; and Clarissa ministered to him,—unconscious of any evil. He had been brought up with them on terms of such close intimacy that she was entitled to regard him as a brother,—almost as a brother,—if only she were able so to regard him. It was her practice to call him Ralph, and her own name was as common to him as though she were in truth his sister. "And what do you think of this new cousin?" he asked.

"I can think nothing as yet;—but I mean to like her."

"I mean to hate her furiously," said Ralph.

"That is nonsense. She will be nothing to you. You needn't even see her unless you please. But, Ralph, do put your jacket on. I'm sure you'll catch cold." And she went down, and hooked his jacket for him out of the boat, and put it over his shoulders. "I won't have you throw it off," she said; "if you come here you must do as you're told."

"You needn't have knocked the pipe out of my mouth all the same. What is she like, I wonder?"

"Very,—very beautiful, I'm told."

"A kind of tropical Venus,—all eyes, and dark skin, and black hair, and strong passions, and apt to murder people;—but at the same time so lazy that she is never to do anything either for herself or anybody else;—wouldn't fetch a fellow's jacket for him, let him be catching cold ever so fast."

"She wouldn't fetch yours, I dare say."

"And why shouldn't she?"

"Because she doesn't know you."

"They soon get to know one,—girls of that sort. I'm told that in the West Indies you become as thick as thieves in half a morning's flirtation, and are expected to propose at the second meeting."

"That is not to be your way with our cousin, I can assure you."

"But these proposals out there never mean much. You may be engaged to half a dozen girls at the same time, and be sure that each of them will be engaged to half-a-dozen men. There's some comfort in that, you know."

"Oh, Ralph!"

"That's what they tell me. I haven't been there. I shall come and look at her, you know."

" Of course you will."

" And if she is very lovely ——"

" What then ?"

" I do like pretty girls, you know."

" I don't know anything about it."

"I wonder what uncle Gregory would say if I were to marry a West Indian! He wouldn't say much to me, because we never speak, but he'd lead poor Greg a horrid life. He'd be sure to think she was a nigger, or at least a creole. But I shan't do that."

" You might do worse, Ralph."

" But I might do much better." As he said this, he looked up into her face, with all the power of his eyes, and poor Clarissa could only blush. She knew what he meant, and knew that she was showing him that she was conscious. She would have given much not to blush, and not to have been so manifestly conscious, but she had no power to control herself. " I might do much better," he said. " Don't you think so ?"

As far as she could judge of her own feelings at this moment, in the absolute absence of any previous accurate thought on the subject, she fancied that a real, undoubted, undoubting, trustworthy engagement with Ralph Newton would make her the happiest girl in England. She had never told herself that she was in love with him ; she had never flattered herself that he was in love with her ;—she had never balanced the matter in her mind as a contingency likely to occur ; but now, at this moment, as he lay there smoking his pipe and looking full into her blushing face, she did think that to have him for her own lover would be joy enough for her whole life. She knew that he was idle, extravagant, fond of pleasure, and,—unsteady, as she in her vocabulary would be disposed to describe the character which she believed to be his. But in her heart of hearts she liked unsteadiness in men, if it were not carried too far. Ralph's brother, the parson, as to whom she was informed that he possessed every virtue incident to humanity, and who was quite as good-looking as his brother, had utterly failed to touch her heart. A black coat and a white cravat were antipathetic to her. Ralph, as he lay on the green sward, hot, with linen trousers and a coloured flannel shirt, with a small straw hat stuck on the edge of his head, with nothing round his throat, and his jacket over his shoulder, with a pipe in his mouth and an empty glass beside him, was to her, in externals, the beau-ideal of a young man. And then, though he was unsteady, extravagant, and idle, his sins were not so deep as to exclude him from her father's and her sister's favour. He was there, on the villa lawn, not as an interloper, but by implied permission. Though she made for herself no argument on the matter,—not having much time just now for arguing,—she felt that it was her undoubted privilege to be made love to by Ralph Newton, if he and she pleased so to amuse themselves. She had never been told not to be made love to by him. Of course she would not engage herself without her father's permission. Of course she would tell Patience if Ralph should say anything very special to her. But she had a right to be made love to if she liked it;—and in this case she would like it. But when Ralph looked at her, and asked her whether he might not do better than marry her West Indian cousin, she had not a word with which to answer him. He smoked on for some seconds in silence still looking at her, while she stood over him blushing. Then he spoke again. "I think I might do a great deal better." But still she had not a word for him.

"Ah;—I suppose I must be off," he said, jumping up on his legs, and flinging his jacket over his arm. "Patience will be in soon."

"I expect her every minute."

"If I were to say,—something uncivil about Patience, I suppose you wouldn't like it?"

"Certainly, I shouldn't like it."

"Only just to wish she were at,—Jericho?"

"Nonsense, Ralph."

"Yes; that would be nonsense. And the chances are, you know, that you would be at Jericho with her. Dear, dear Clary,—you know I love you." Then he put his right arm round her waist, pipe and all, and kissed her.

She certainly had expected no such assault,—had not only not thought of it, but had not known it to be among the possibilities that might occur to her. She had never been so treated before. One other lover she had had,—as we know; but by him she had been treated with the deference due by an inferior to a superior being. It would have been very nice if Ralph would have told her that he loved her,—but this was not nice. That had been done which she would not dare to tell to Patience,—which she could not have endured that Patience should have seen. She was bound to resent it;—but how? She stood silent for a moment, and then burst into tears. "You are not angry with me, Clary?" he said.

"I am angry;—very angry. Go away. I will never speak to you again."

"You know how dearly I love you."

"I don't love you at all. You have insulted me, and I will never forgive you. Go away." At this moment the step of Patience coming up from the gate was heard upon the gravel. Clarissa's first thought when she heard it was to hide her tears. Though the man had injured her,—insulted her,—her very last resource would be to complain to others of the injury or the insult. It must be hidden in

her own breast,—but remembered always. Forgotten it could not
be,—nor, as she thought at the moment, forgiven. But, above all,
it must not be repeated. As to any show of anger against the sinner,
that was impossible to her,—because it was so necessary that the
sin should be hidden.

"What;—Ralph? Have you been here long?" asked Patience,
looking with somewhat suspicious eyes at Clarissa's back, which was
turned to her.

"About half an hour,—waiting for you, and smoking and drinking
soda-water. I have a boat here, and I must be off now."

"You'll have the tide with you," said Clarissa, with an effort.

"There is a tide in the affairs of men," said Ralph, with a forced
laugh. "My affairs shall at once take advantage of this tide. I'll
come again very soon to see the new cousin. Good-bye, girls."
Then he inserted himself into his boat, and took himself off, without
bestowing even anything of a special glance upon Clarissa.

"Is there anything the matter?" Patience asked.

"No;—only why did you stay all the evening with that stupid old
woman, when you promised me that you would be back in ten
minutes?"

"I said nothing about ten minutes, Clary; and, after all, I haven't
been an hour gone. Miss Spooner is in trouble about her tenant,
who won't pay the rent, and she had to tell me all about it."

"Stupid old woman!"

"Have you and Ralph been quarrelling, Clary?"

"No;—why should we quarrel?"

"There seems to have been something wrong."

"It's so stupid being found all alone here. It makes one feel that
one is so desolate. I do wish papa would live with us like other
girls' fathers. As he won't, it would be much better not to let people
come at all."

Patience was sure that something had happened,—and that that
something must have reference to the guise of lover either assumed
or not assumed by Ralph Newton. She accused her sister of no
hypocrisy, but she was aware that Clarissa's words were wild, not
expressing the girl's thoughts, and spoken almost at random. Something must be said, and therefore these complaints had been made.
"Clary, dear; don't you like Ralph?" she asked.

"No. That is;—oh yes, I like him, of course. My head aches
and I'll go to bed."

"Wait a few minutes, Clary. Something has disturbed you. Has
it not?"

"Everything disturbs me."

"But if there is anything special, won't you tell me?" There had
been something very special, which Clarissa certainly would not tell.

He drank his sherry and soda-water, and lit his pipe, and lay there on the lawn, as though he were quite at home; and Clarissa ministered to him.

(*See page 19*)

The doctor was at her elbow to the last;— and her boxes and trunks seemed to extricate themselves from the general mass.

(*See page 28*)

"What has he said to you? I don't think he would be simply cross to you."

"He has not been cross at all."

"What is it then? Well;—if you won't tell me, I think that you are afraid of me. We never yet have been afraid of each other." Then there was a pause. "Clary, has he said that,—he loves you?" There was another pause. Clarissa thought it all over, and for a moment was not quite certain whether any such sweet assurance had or had not been given to her. Then she remembered his words;— "You know how dearly I love you." But ought they to be sweet to her now? Had he not so offended her that there could never be forgiveness? And if no forgiveness, how then could his love be sweet to her? Patience waited, and then repeated her question. "Tell me, Clary; what has he said to you?"

"I don't know."

"Do you love him, Clary?"

"No. I hate him."

"Hate him, Clary? You did not use to hate him. You did not hate him yesterday? You would not hate him without a cause. My darling, tell me what it means! If you and I do not trust each other what will the world be to us? There is no one else to whom we can tell our troubles." Nevertheless Clarissa would not tell this trouble. "Why do you say that you hate him?"

"I don't know why. Oh, dear Patty, why do you go on so? Yes; he did say that he loved me;—there."

"And did that make you unhappy? It need not make you unhappy, though you should refuse him. When his brother asked you to marry him, that did not make you unhappy."

"Yes it did;—very."

"And is this the same?"

"No;—it is quite different."

"I am afraid, Clary, that Ralph Newton would not make a good husband. He is extravagant and in debt, and papa would not like it."

"Then papa should not let him come here just as he pleases and whenever he likes. It is papa's fault;—that is to say it would be if there were anything in it."

"Is there nothing in it, Clary? What answer did you make when he told you that he loved you?"

"You came, and I made no answer. I do so wish that you had come before." She wanted to tell her sister everything but the one thing, but was unable to do so because the one thing affected the other things so vitally. As it was, Patience, finding that she could press her questions no further, was altogether in the dark. That Ralph had made a declaration of love to her sister she did know;

but in what manner Clarissa had received it she could not guess.
She had hitherto feared that Clary was too fond of the young man,
but Clary would now only say that she hated him. But the matter
would soon be set at rest. Ralph Newton would now, no doubt,
go to their father. If Sir Thomas would permit it, this new-fangled
hatred of Clary's would, Patience thought, soon be overcome. If,
however,—as was more probable,—Sir Thomas should violently
disapprove, then there would be no more visits from Ralph Newton
to the villa. As there had been a declaration of love, of course
their father would be informed of it at once. Patience, having
so resolved, allowed her sister to go to her bed without further
questioning.

In Clarissa's own bosom the great offence had been forgiven,—or
rather condoned before the morning. Her lover had been very cruel
to her, very wicked, and most unkind;—especially unkind in this,
that he had turned to absolute pain a moment of life which might
have been of all moments the fullest of joy; and especially cruel in
this, that he had so treated her that she could not look forward to
future joy without alloy. She could forgive him;—yes. But she
could not endure that he should think that she would forgive him.
She was willing to blot out the offence, as a thing by itself, in an
island of her life,—of which no one should ever think again. Was
she to lose her lover for ever because she did not forgive him! If
they could only come to some agreement that the offence should be
acknowledged to be heinous, unpardonable, but committed in temporary madness, and that henceforward it should be buried in oblivion!
Such agreement, however, was impossible. There could be no speech
about the matter. Was she or was she not to lose her lover for
ever because he had done this wicked thing? During the night she
made up her mind that she could not afford to pay such a price for the
sake of avenging virtue. For the future she would be on her guard!
Wicked and heartless man, who had robbed her of so much! And
yet how charming he had been to her as he looked into her eyes, and
told her that he could do very much better than fall in love with her
West Indian cousin. Then she thought of the offence again. Ah, if
only a time might come in which they should be engaged together as
man and wife with the consent of everybody! Then there would be
no more offences.

CHAPTER IV.

MARY BONNER.

WHILE Clarissa Underwood was being kissed on the lawn at Popham Villa, Sir Thomas was sitting, very disconsolate, in a private room at the Dolphin, in Southampton. It had required no great consideration to induce him to resolve that a home should be given by him to his niece. Though he was a man so weak that he could allow himself to shun from day to day his daily duty,—and to do this so constantly as to make up out of various omissions, small in themselves, a vast aggregate of misconduct,—still he was one who would certainly do what his conscience prompted him to be right in any great matter as to which the right and the wrong appeared to him to be clearly defined. Though he loved his daughters dearly, he could leave them from day to day almost without protection,—because each day's fault in so doing was of itself but small. This new niece of his he certainly did not love at all. He had never seen her. He was almost morbidly fearful of new responsibilities. He expected nothing but trouble in thus annexing a new unknown member to his family. And yet he had decided upon doing it, because the duty to be done was great enough to be clearly marked,—demanding an immediate resolve, and capable of no postponement. But, as he thought of it, sitting alone on the eve of the girl's coming, he was very uneasy. What was he to do with her if he found her to be one difficult to manage, self-willed, vexatious, or,—worse again,—ill-conditioned as to conduct, and hurtful to his own children? Should it even become imperative upon him to be rid of her, how should riddance be effected? And then what would she think of him and his habits of life?

And this brought him to other reflections. Might it not be possible utterly to break up that establishment of his in Southampton Buildings, so that he would be forced by the necessity of things to live at his home,—at some home which he would share with the girls? He knew himself well enough to be sure that while those chambers remained in his possession, as long as that bedroom and bed were at his command, he could not extricate himself from the dilemma. Day after day the temptation was too great for him. And he hated the villa. There was nothing there that he could do. He had no books at the villa; and,—so he averred,—there was something in the air of Fulham which prevented him from reading books when he brought them there. No! He must break altogether fresh ground, and set up a new establishment. One thing was clear; he could not now do this before Mary Bonner's arrival, and therefore there was nothing to create any special urgency. He had hoped that his girls would marry, so that he might be left to live alone in his chambers,—waited upon by old Stemm,—without sin on his part; but he was beginning to discover that girls do not always get married out of the way in their first bloom. And now he was taking to himself another girl! He must, he knew, give over all hope of escape in that direction. He was very uneasy; and when quite late at night,—or rather, early in the morning,—he took himself to bed, his slumbers were not refreshing. The truth was that no air suited him for sleeping except the air of Southampton Buildings.

The packet from St. Thomas was to be in the harbour at eight o'clock the next morning,—telegrams from Cape Clear, The Lizard, Eddystone Lighthouse, and where not, having made all that as certain as sun-rising. At eight o'clock he was down on the quay, and there was the travelling city of the Royal Atlantic Steam Mail Packet Company at that moment being warped into the harbour. The ship as he walked along the jetty was so near to him that he could plainly see the faces of the passengers on deck,—men and women, girls and children, all dressed up to meet their friends on shore, crowding the sides of the vessel in their eagerness to be among the first to get on shore. He anxiously scanned the faces of the ladies that he might guess which was to be the lady that was to be to him almost the same as a daughter. He saw not one as to whom he could say that he had a hope. Some there were in the crowd, some three or four, as to whom he acknowledged that he had a fear. At last he remembered that his girl would necessarily be in deep mourning. He saw two young women in black;—but there was nothing to prepossess him about either of them. One of them was insignificant and very plain. The other was fat and untidy. They neither of them looked like ladies. What if fate should have sent to him as a daughter,—as a companion for his girls,—that fat, untidy, ill-bred looking young woman! As it happened, the ill-bred looking young woman whom he feared, was a cook who had married a ship-steward, had gone out among the islands with her husband, had found that the speculation did not answer, and was now returning in the hope of earning her bread in her old vocation. Of this woman Sir Thomas Underwood was in great dread.

But at last he was on board, and whispered his question to the purser. Miss Bonner! Oh, yes; Miss Bonner was on board. Was he Sir Thomas Underwood, Miss Bonner's uncle? The purser evidently knew all about it, and there was something in his tone which seemed to assure Sir Thomas that the fat, untidy woman and his niece could not be one and the same person. The purser had just raised his cap to Sir Thomas, and had turned towards the cabin-stairs to go in search of the lady herself; but he was stopped immediately by Miss Bonner herself. The purser did his task very well,—said some slightest word to introduce the uncle and the niece together, and then vanished. Sir Thomas blushed, shuffled with his feet, and put out both his hands. He was shy, astonished, and frightened,—and did not know what to say. The girl came up to him, took his hand in hers, holding it for a moment, and then kissed it. "I did not think you would come yourself," she said.

"Of course I have come myself. My girls are at home, and will receive you to-night." She said nothing further then, but again raised his hand and kissed it.

It is hardly too much to say that Sir Thomas Underwood was in a tremble as he gazed upon his niece. Had she been on the deck as he walked along the quay, and had he noted her, he would not have dared to think that such a girl as that was coming to his house. He declared to himself at once that she was the most lovely young woman he had ever seen. She was tall and somewhat large, with fair hair, of which now but very little could be seen, with dark eyes, and perfect eyebrows, and a face which, either for colour or lines of beauty, might have been taken as a model for any female saint or martyr. There was a perfection of symmetry about it,—and an assertion of intelligence combined with the loveliness which almost frightened her uncle. For there was something there, also, beyond intelligence and loveliness. We have heard of "an eye to threaten and command." Sir Thomas did not at this moment tell himself that Mary Bonner had such an eye, but he did involuntarily and unconsciously acknowledge to himself that over such a young lady as this whom he now saw before him, it would be very difficult for him to exercise parental control. He had heard that she was nineteen, but it certainly seemed to him that she was older than his own daughters. As to Clary, there could be no question between the two girls as to which of them would exercise authority over the other,—not by force of age,—but by dint of character, will, and fitness. And this Mary Bonner, who now shone before him as a goddess almost, a young woman to whom no ordinary man would speak without that kind of trepidation which goddesses do inflict on ordinary men, had proposed to herself,—to go out as a governess! Indeed, at this very moment such, probably, was her own idea. As yet she had received no reply to the letter she had written other than that which was now conveyed by her uncle's presence.

A few questions were asked as to the voyage. No ;—she had not been at all ill. "I have almost feared," she said, "to reach England, thinking I should be so desolate." "We will not let you be desolate," said Sir Thomas, brightening up a little under the graciousness of the goddess's demeanour. "My girls are looking forward to your coming with the greatest delight." Then she asked some question as to her cousins, and Sir Thomas thought that there was majesty even in her voice. It was low, soft, and musical ; but yet, even in that as in her eye, there was something that indicated a power of command.

He had no servant with him to assist in looking after her luggage. Old Stemm was the only man in his employment, and he could hardly have brought Stemm down to Southampton on such an errand. But he soon found that everybody about the ship was ready to wait upon Miss Bonner. Even the captain came to take a special farewell of her, and the second officer seemed to have nothing to do but to look after her. The doctor was at her elbow to the last;—and all her boxes and trunks seemed to extricate themselves from the general mass with a readiness which is certainly not experienced by ordinary passengers. There are certain favours in life which are very charming,—but very unjust to others, and which we may perhaps lump under the name of priority of service. Money will hardly buy it. When money does buy it, there is no injustice. When priority of service is had, like a coach-and-four, by the man who can afford to pay for it, industry, which is the source of wealth, receives its fitting reward. Rank will often procure it ; most unjustly,—as we, who have no rank, feel sometimes with great soreness. Position other than that of rank, official position or commercial position, will secure it in certain cases. A railway train is stopped at a wrong place for a railway director, or a post-office manager gets his letters taken after time. These, too, are grievances. But priority of service is perhaps more readily accorded to feminine beauty, and especially to unprotected feminine beauty, than to any other form of claim. Whether or no this is ever felt as a grievance, ladies who are not beautiful may perhaps be able to say. There flits across our memory at the present moment some reminiscence of angry glances at the too speedy attendance given by custom-house officers to pretty women. But this priority of service is, we think, if not deserved, at least so natural, as to take it out of the catalogue of evils of which complaint should be made. One might complain with as much avail that men will fall in love with pretty girls instead of with those who are ugly ! On the present occasion Sir Thomas was well contented. He was out of the ship, and through the Custom House, and at the railway station, and back at the inn before the struggling mass of passengers had found out whether their longed-for boxes had or had not come with them in the ship. And then Miss Bonner took it all,—not arrogantly, as though it were her due ; but just as the grass takes rain or the flowers sunshine. These good things came to her from heaven, and no doubt she was thankful. But they came to her so customarily, as does a man's dinner to him, or his bed, that she could not manifest surprise at what was done for her.

Sir Thomas hardly spoke to her except about her journey and her luggage till they were down together in the sitting-room at the inn. Then he communicated to her his proposal as to her future life. It was right, he thought, that she should know at once what he intended. Two hours ago, before he had seen her, he had thought of telling her simply where she was to live, and of saying that he would find a home for her. Now he found it expedient to place the matter in a different light. He would offer her the shelter of his roof as though she were a queen who might choose among her various palaces. "Mary," he said, "we hope that you will stay with us altogether."

"To live with you,—do you mean?"

"Certainly to live with us."

"I have no right to expect such an offer as that."

"But every right to accept it, my dear, when it is made. That is if it suits you."

"I had not dreamed of that. I thought that perhaps you would let me come to you for a few weeks,—till I should know what to do."

"You shall come and be one of us altogether, my dear, if you think that you will like it. My girls have no nearer relative than you. And we are not so barbarous as to turn our backs on a new-found cousin." She again kissed his hand, and then turned away from him and wept. "You feel it all strange now," he said, "but I hope we shall be able to make you comfortable."

"I have been so lonely," she sobbed out amidst her tears.

He had not dared to say a word to her about her father, whose death had taken place not yet three months since. Of his late brother-in-law he had known little or nothing, except that the General had been a man who always found it difficult to make both ends meet, and who had troubled him frequently, not exactly for loans, but in regard to money arrangements which had been disagreeable to him. Whether General Bonner had or had not been an affectionate father he had never heard. There are men who, in Sir Thomas's position, would have known all about such a niece after a few hours' acquaintance; but our lawyer was not such a man. Though the girl seemed to him to be everything that was charming, he did not dare to question her; and when they arrived at the station in London, no word had as yet been said about the General.

As they were having the luggage piled on the top of a cab, the fat cock passed along the platform. "I hope you are more comfortable now, Mrs. Woods," said Mary Bonner, with a smile as sweet as May, while she gave her hand to the woman.

"Thank'ee, Miss; I'm better; but it's only a moil of trouble, one thing as well as t'other." Mrs. Woods was evidently very melancholy at the contemplation of her prospects.

"I hope you'll find yourself comfortable now." Then she whispered to Sir Thomas;—"She is a poor young woman whose husband has ill used her, and she lost her only child, and has now come here to earn her bread. She isn't nice looking, but she is so good!" Sir

Thomas did not dare to tell Mary Bonner that he had already noticed
Mrs. Wood, and that he had conceived the idea that Mrs. Wood was
the niece of whom he had come in search.

They made the journey at once to Fulham in the cab, and Sir
Thomas found it to be very long. He was proud of his new niece,
but he did not know what to say to her. And he felt that she,
though he was sure that she was clever, gave him no encouragement
to speak. It was all very well while, with her beautiful eyes full of
tears, she had gone through the ceremony of kissing his hand in
token of her respect and gratitude ;—but that had been done often
enough, and could not very well be repeated in the cab. So they
sat silent, and he was rejoiced when he saw those offensive words,
Popham Villa, on the posts of his gateway. "We have only a
humble little house, my dear," he said, as they turned in. She
looked at him and smiled. "I believe you West Indians generally
are lodged very sumptuously."

"Papa had a large straggling place up in the hills, but it was
anything but sumptuous. I do love the idea of an English home,
where things are neat and nice. Oh, dear ;—how lovely ! That is
the River Thames ;—isn't it ? How very beautiful !" Then the
two girls were at the door of the cab, and the newcomer was
enveloped in the embraces of her cousins.

Sir Thomas, as he walked along the banks of the river while the
young ladies prepared each other for dinner, reflected that he had
never in his life done such a day's work before as he had just accomplished. When he had married a wife, that indeed had been a great
piece of business ; but it had been done slowly,—for he had been
engaged four years,—and he had of course been much younger at
that period. Now he had brought into his family a new inmate who
would force him in his old age to change all his habits of life. He
did not think that he would dare to neglect Mary Bonner, and to
stay in London while she lived at the villa. He was almost sorry
that he had ever heard of Mary Bonner, in spite of her beauty, and
although he had as yet been able to find in her no cause of complaint. She was ladylike and quiet ;—but yet he was afraid of her.
When she came down into the drawing-room with her hand clasped
in that of Clarissa, he was still more afraid of her. She was dressed
all in black, with the utmost simplicity,—with nothing on her by
way of ornament beyond a few large black beads ; but yet she
seemed to him to be splendid. There was a grace of motion about
her that was almost majestic. Clary was very pretty,—very pretty,
indeed ; but Clary was just the girl that an old gentleman likes to
fetch him his slippers and give him his tea. Sir Thomas felt that,
old as he was, it would certainly be his business to give Mary Bonner
her tea.

The two girls contrived to say a few words to their father that night before they joined Mary amidst her trunks in her bedroom. "Papa, isn't she lovely?" said Clarissa.

"She certainly is a very handsome young woman."

"And not a bit like what I expected," continued Clary. "Of course I knew she was good-looking. I had always heard that. But I thought that she would have been a sort of West Indian girl, dark, and lazy, and selfish. Ralph was saying that is what they are out there."

"I don't suppose that Ralph knows anything about it," said Sir Thomas. "And what do you say of your new cousin, Patience?"

"I think I shall love her dearly. She is so gentle and sweet."

"But she is not at all what you expected?" demanded Clarissa.

"I hardly know what I expected," replied the prudent Patience. "But certainly I did not expect anything so lovely as she is. Of course, we can't know her yet; but as far as one can judge, I think I shall like her."

"But she is so magnificently beautiful!" said the energetic Clarissa.

"I think she is," said Sir Thomas. "And I quite admit that it is a kind of beauty to surprise one. It did surprise me. Had not one of you better go up-stairs to her?" Then both the girls bounded off to assist their cousin in her chamber.

CHAPTER V.

MR. NEEFIT AND HIS FAMILY.

MR. NEEFIT was a breeches-maker in Conduit Street, of such repute that no hunting man could be said to go decently into the hunting field unless decorated by a garment made in Mr. Neefit's establishment. His manipulation of leather was something marvellous; and in latter years he had added to his original art,—an art which had at first been perfect rather than comprehensive,—an exquisite skill in cords, buckskins, and such like materials. When his trade was becoming prosperous he had thought of degenerating into a tailor, adding largely to his premises, and of compensating his pride by the prospects of great increase to his fortune; but an angel of glory had whispered to him to let well alone, and he was still able to boast that all his measurements had been confined to the legs of sportsmen. Instead of extending his business he had simply extended his price, and had boldly clapped on an extra half-guinea to every pair that he supplied. The experiment was altogether successful, and when it was heard by the riding men of the City that Mr. Neefit's prices were

undoubtedly higher than those of any other breeches-maker in
London, and that he had refused to supply breeches for the grooms
of a Marquis because the Marquis was not a hunting man, the riding
men of the City flocked to him in such numbers, that it became quite
a common thing for them to give their orders in June and July, so
that they might not be disappointed when November came round.
Mr. Neefit was a prosperous man, but he had his troubles. Now, it
was a great trouble to him that some sporting men would be so very
slow in paying for the breeches in which they took pride !

Mr. Neefit's fortune had not been rapid in early life. He had
begun with a small capital and a small establishment, and even now
his place of business was very limited in size. He had been clever
enough to make profit even out of its smallness,—and had contrived
that it should be understood that the little back room in which men
were measured was so diminutive because it did not suit his special
business to welcome a crowd. It was his pride, he said, to wait
upon hunting men,—but with the garments of the world at large he
wished to have no concern whatever. In the outer shop, looking
into Conduit Street, there was a long counter on which goods were
unrolled for inspection ; and on which an artist, the solemnity of
whose brow and whose rigid silence betokened the nature of his
great employment, was always cutting out leather. This grave man
was a German, and there was a rumour among young sportsmen that
old Neefit paid this highly-skilled operator £600 a year for his
services ! Nobody knew as he did how each morsel of leather would
behave itself under the needle, or could come within two hairbreadths
of him in accuracy across the kneepan. As for measuring, Mr.
Neefit did that himself,—almost always: To be measured by Mr.
Neefit was as essential to perfection as to be cut out for by the German.
There were rumours, indeed, that from certain classes of customers
Mr. Neefit and the great foreigner kept themselves personally aloof.
It was believed that Mr. Neefit would not condescend to measure a
retail tradesman. Latterly, indeed, there had arisen a doubt whether
he would lay his august hand on a stockbroker's leg ; though little
Wallop, one of the young glories of Capel Court, swears that he is
handled by him every year. "Confound 'is impudence," says
Wallop ; "I'd like to see him sending a foreman to me. And as for
cutting, d' you think I don't know Bawwah's 'and !" The name of
the foreign artist is not exactly known ; but it is pronounced as we
have written it, and spelt in that fashion by sporting gentlemen when
writing to each other.

Our readers may be told in confidence that up to a very late date
Mr. Neefit lived in the rooms over his shop. This is certainly not
the thing for a prosperous tradesman to do. Indeed, if a tradesman
be known not to have a private residence, he will hardly become
prosperous. But Neefit had been a cautious man, and till two years

before the commencement of our story, he had actually lived in Conduit Street,—working hard, however, to keep his residence a deep secret from his customers at large. Now he was the proud possessor of a villa residence at Hendon, two miles out in the country beyond the Swiss Cottage ; and all his customers knew that he was never to be found before 9.30 A.M., or after 5.15 P.M.

As we have said, Mr. Neefit had his troubles, and one of his great troubles was our young friend, Ralph Newton. Ralph Newton was a hunting man, with a stud of horses,—never less than four, and sometimes running up to seven and eight,—always standing at the Moonbeam, at Barnfield. All men know that Barnfield is in the middle of the B. B. Hunt,—the two initials standing for those two sporting counties, Berkshire and Buckinghamshire. Now, Mr. Neefit had a very large connexion in the B. B., and, though he never was on horseback in his life, subscribed twenty-five pounds a year to the pack. Mr. Ralph Newton had long favoured him with his custom ; but, we are sorry to say, Mr. Ralph Newton had become a thorn in the flesh to many a tradesman in these days. It was not that he never paid. He did pay something ; but as he ordered more than he paid, the sum-total against him was always an increasing figure. But then he was a most engaging, civil-spoken young man, whose order it was almost impossible to decline. It was known, moreover, that his prospects were so good ! Nevertheless, it is not pleasant for a breeches-maker to see the second hundred pound accumulating on his books for leather breeches for one gentleman. " What does he do with 'em ? " old Neefit would say to himself ; but he didn't dare to ask any such question of Mr. Newton. It isn't for a tradesman to complain that a gentleman consumes too many of his articles. Things, however, went so far that Mr. Neefit found it to be incumbent on him to make special inquiry about those prospects. Things had gone very far indeed,—for Ralph Newton appeared one summer evening at the villa at Hendon, and absolutely asked the breeches-maker to lend him a hundred pounds ! Before he left he had taken tea with Mr. and Mrs. and Miss Neefit on the lawn, and had received almost a promise that the loan should be forthcoming if he would call in Conduit Street on the following morning. That had been early in May, and Ralph Newton had called, and, though there had been difficulties, he had received the money before three days had passed.

Mr. Neefit was a stout little man, with a bald head and somewhat protrusive eyes, whose manners to his customers contained a combination of dictatorial assurance and subservience, which he had found to be efficacious in his peculiar business. On general subjects he would rub his hands, and bow his head, and agree most humbly with every word that was uttered. In the same day he would be a Radical and a Conservative, devoted to the Church and a scoffer at parsons, animated on behalf of staghounds and a loud censurer of aught in the way of hunting other than the orthodox fox. On all trivial outside subjects he considered it to be his duty as a tradesman simply to ingratiate himself; but in a matter of breeches he gave way to no man, let his custom be what it might. He knew his business, and was not going to be told by any man whether the garments which he made did or did not fit. It was the duty of a gentleman to come and allow him to see them on while still in a half-embryo condition. If gentlemen did their duty, he was sure that he could do his. He would take back anything that was not approved without a murmur;—but after that he must decline further transactions. It was, moreover, quite understood that to complain of his materials was so to insult him that he would condescend to make no civil reply. An elderly gentleman from Essex once told him that his buttons were given to breaking. "If you have your breeches,—washed,—by an old woman,—in the country,"—said Mr. Neefit, very slowly, looking into the elderly gentleman's face, "and then run through the mangle,—the buttons will break." The elderly gentleman never dared even to enter the shop again.

Mr. Neefit was perhaps somewhat over imperious in matters relating to his own business; but, in excuse for him, it must be stated that he was, in truth, an honest tradesman;—he was honest at least so far, that he did make his breeches as well as he knew how. He had made up his mind that the best way to make his fortune was to send out good articles,—and he did his best. Whether or no he was honest in adding on that additional half guinea to the price because he found that the men with whom he dealt were fools enough to be attracted by a high price, shall be left to advanced moralists to decide. In that universal agreement with diverse opinions there must, we fear, have been something of dishonesty. But he made the best of breeches, put no shoddy or cheap stitching into them, and was, upon the whole, an honest tradesman.

From 9.30 to 5.15 were Mr. Neefit's hours; but it had come to be understood by those who knew the establishment well, that from half-past twelve to half-past one the master was always absent. The young man who sat at the high desk, and seemed to spend all his time in contemplating the bad debts in the ledger, would tell gentlemen who called up to one that Mr. Neefit was in the City. After one it was always said that Mr. Neefit was lunching at the Restaurong. The truth was that Mr. Neefit always dined in the middle of the day at a public-house round the corner, having a chop and a "follow chop," a pint of beer, a penny newspaper and a pipe. When the villa at Hendon had been first taken Mrs. Neefit had started late dinners; but that vigilant and intelligent lady had soon perceived that this simply meant, in regard to her husband, two dinners a day,—and apoplexy. She had, therefore, returned to the old ways,—an early dinner for herself and daughter, and a little bit of supper at night. Now, one day in June,—that very Saturday on which Sir Thomas Underwood brought his niece home to Fulham, the day after that wicked kiss on the lawn at Fulham, Ralph Newton walked into Neefit's shop during the hour of Mr. Neefit's absence, and ordered,—three pair of breeches. Herr "Bawwah," the cutter, who never left his board during the day for more than five minutes at a time, remained, as was his custom, mute and apparently inattentive; but the foreman came down from his perch and took the order. Mr. Neefit was out, unfortunately;—in the City. Ralph Newton remarked that his measure was not in the least altered, gave his order, and went out.

"Three pair?—leather?" asked Mr. Neefit, when he returned, raising his eyebrows, and clearly showing that the moment was not one of unmixed delight.

"Two leather;—one cord," said the foreman.

"He had four pair last year," said Mr. Neefit, in a tone so piteous that it might almost have been thought that he was going to weep.

"One hundred and eighty-nine pounds, fourteen shillings, and nine pence was the Christmas figure," said the foreman, turning back to a leaf in the book, which he found without any difficulty. Mr. Neefit took himself to the examination of certain completed articles which adorned his shop, as though he were anxious to banish from his mind so painful a subject. "Is he to 'ave 'em, Mr. Neefit?" asked the foreman. The master was still silent, and still fingered the materials which his very soul loved. "He must 'ave a matter of twenty pair by him,—unless he sells 'em," said the suspicious foreman.

"He don't sell 'em," said Mr. Neefit. "He ain't one of that sort. You can put 'em in hand, Waddle."

"Very well, Mr. Neefit. I only thought I'd mention it. It looked queer like, his coming just when you was out."

"I don't see anything queer in it. He ain't one of that sort. Do you go on." Mr. Waddle knew nothing of the hundred pounds, nor did he know that Ralph Newton had,—twice drank tea at Hendon. On both occasions Mrs. Neefit had declared that if ever she saw a gentleman, Mr. Newton was a gentleman; and Miss Neefit, though her words had been very few, had evidently approved of Mr. Newton's manners. Now Miss Neefit was a beauty and an heiress.

Mr. Waddle had hardly been silenced, and had just retired with melancholy diligence amidst the records of unsatisfactory commercial transactions, before Ralph Newton again entered the shop. He shook hands with Mr. Neefit,—as was the practice with many favourite customers,—and immediately went to work in regard to his new order, as though every Christmas and every Midsummer saw an account closed on his behalf in Mr. Neefit's books. "I did say just now, when I found you were out, that last year's lines would do ; but it may be, you know, that I'm running a little to flesh."

" We can't be too particular, Mr. Newton," said the master.

" It's all for your sake that I come," said the young sportsman, walking into the little room, while Mr. Neefit followed with his scraps of paper and tapes, and Waddle followed him to write down the figures. " I don't care much how they look myself."

" Oh, Mr. Newton ! "

" I shouldn't like 'em to wrinkle inside the knee, you know."

" That isn't likely with us, I hope, Mr. Newton."

" And I own I do like to be able to get into them."

" We don't give much trouble in that way, Mr. Newton."

" But the fact is I have such trust in you and the silent gentleman out there, that I believe you would fit me for the next twenty years, though you were never to see me."

" Oh, thank you, Mr. Newton,—2, 4, and $\frac{1}{8}$th, Waddle. I think Mr. Newton is a little stouter. But, perhaps, you may work that off before November, Mr. Newton. Thank you, Mr. Newton ;—I think that'll do. You'll find we shan't be far wrong. Three pair, Mr. Newton ? "

" Yes ;—I think three pair will see me through next season. I don't suppose I shall hunt above four days, and I have some by me."

Some by him ! There must be drawers full of them,—presses full of them, chests full of them ! Waddle, the melancholy and suspicious Waddle, was sure that their customer was playing them false,—raising money on the garments as soon as they were sent to him ; but he did not dare to say anything of this after the snubbing which he had already received. If old Neefit chose to be done by a dishonest young man it was nothing to him. But in truth Waddle did not understand men as well as did his master ;—and then he knew nothing of his master's ambitious hopes.

" The bishops came out very strong last night ;—didn't they ? " said Ralph, in the outer shop.

" Very strong, indeed, Mr. Newton ;—very strong."

" But, after all, they're nothing but a pack of old women."

" That's about what they are, Mr. Newton."

" Not but what we must have a Church, I suppose."

" We should do very badly without a Church, Mr. Newton. At least that is my opinion." Then Ralph left the shop, and the breeches-maker bowed him out of the door.

" Fifty thousand pounds ! " said Ralph Newton to himself, as he walked into Bond Street and down to his club. When a man is really rich rumour always increases his money,—and rumour had doubled the fortune which Mr. Neefit had already amassed. " That means two thousand a year ; and the girl herself is so pretty, that upon my honour I don't know which is the prettier,—she or Clary. But fancy old Neefit for one's father-in-law ! Everybody is doing it now ; but I don't think I'd do it for ten times the money. The fact is, one has got to get used to these things, and I am not used to it yet. I soon shall be,—or to something worse." Such was the nature of Ralph's thoughts as he walked away from Mr. Neefit's house to his club.

Mr. Neefit, as he went home, had his speculations also. In making breeches he was perfect, and in putting together money he had proved himself to be an adept. But as to the use of his money, he was quite as much at a loss as he would have been had he tried to wear the garments for which he measured his customers so successfully. He had almost realised the truth that from that money he himself could extract, for himself, but little delight beyond that which arose simply from the possession. Holidays destroyed him. Even a day at home at Hendon, other than Sunday, was almost more than he could endure. The fruition of life to him was in the completing of breeches, and its charm in a mutton-chop and a pipe of tobacco. He had tried idleness, and was wise enough to know almost at the first trial that idleness would not suit him. He had made one mistake in life which was irreparable. He had migrated from Conduit Street to a cold, comfortless box of a house at a place in which, in order that his respectability might be maintained, he was not allowed to show his face in a public-house. This was very bad, but he would not make bad worse by giving up so much of Conduit Street as was still left to him. He would stick to the shop. But what would he do with his money ? He had but one daughter. Thinking of this, day after day, month after month, year after year, he came slowly to the conclusion that it was his duty to make his daughter a lady. He must find some gentleman who would marry her, and then would give that gentleman all his money,—knowing as he did so that the gentleman would probably never speak to him again. And to this conclusion he came with no bitterness of feeling, with no sense of disappointment that to such an end must come the exertions of his laborious and successful life. There was nothing else for him to do. He could not be a gentleman himself. It seemed to be no more within his reach than it is for the gentleman to be an angel. He did not desire it. He would not have enjoyed it. He had that sort of sense which makes a man know so thoroughly his own limits that he has no regret at not passing them. But yet in his eyes a gentleman was so grand a thing,—a being so infinitely superior to himself,—that, loving his daughter above anything else, he did think that he could die happy if he could see her married into a station so exalted. There was a humility in this as regarded himself and an affection for his child which were admirable.

The reader will think that he might at any rate have done better than to pitch upon such a one as Ralph Newton; but then the reader hardly knows Ralph Newton as yet, and cannot at all realise the difficulty which poor Mr. Neefit experienced in coming across any gentleman in such a fashion as to be able to commence his operations. It is hardly open to a tradesman to ask a young man home to his house when measuring him from the hip to the knee. Neefit had heard of many cases in which gentlemen of money had married the daughters of commercial men, and he knew that the thing was to be done. Money, which spent in other directions seemed to be nearly useless to him, might be used beneficially in this way. But how was he to set about it? Polly Neefit was as pretty a girl as you shall wish to see, and he knew that she was pretty. But, if he didn't take care, the good-looking young gasfitter, next door to him down at Hendon, would have his Polly before he knew where he was. Or, worse still, as he thought, there was that mad son of his old friend Moggs, the bootmaker, Ontario Moggs as he had been christened by a Canadian godfather, with whom Polly had condescended already to hold something of a flirtation. He could not advertise for a genteel lover. What could he do?

Then Ralph Newton made his way down to the Hendon villa,—asking for money. What should have induced Mr. Newton to come to him for money he could not guess;—but he did know that, of all the young men who came into his back shop to be measured, there was no one whose looks and manners and cheery voice had created so strong a feeling of pleasantness as had those of Mr. Ralph Newton. Mr. Neefit could not analyse it, but there was a kind of sunshine about the young man which would have made him very unwilling to press hard for payment, or to stop the supply of breeches. He had taken a liking to Ralph, and found himself thinking about the young man in his journeys between Hendon and Conduit Street. Was not this the sort of gentleman that would suit his daughter? Neefit wanted no one to tell him that Ralph Newton was a gentleman,—what he meant by a gentleman,—and that Wallop the stockbroker was not. Wallop the stockbroker spoke of himself as though he was a very fine fellow indeed; but to the thinking of Mr. Neefit, Ontario Moggs was more like a gentleman than Mr. Wallop. He had feared much as to his daughter, both in reference to the handsome gasfitter and to Ontario Moggs, but since that second tea-drinking he had hoped that his daughter's eyes were opened.

He had made inquiry about Ralph Newton, and had found that the young man was undoubtedly heir to a handsome estate in Hampshire,—a place called Newton Priory, with a parish of Newton Peele, and lodges, and a gamekeeper, and a park. He knew from of old that Ralph's uncle would have nothing to do with his nephew's debts; but he learned now as a certainty that the uncle could not disinherit his nephew. And the debts did not seem to be very high;

—and Ralph had come into some property from his father. Upon the whole, though of course there must be a sacrifice of money at first, Neefit thought that he saw his way. Mr. Newton, too, had been very civil to his girl,—not simply making to her foolish flattering little speeches, but treating her,—so thought Neefit,—exactly as a high-bred gentleman would treat the lady of his thoughts. It was a high ambition; but Neefit thought that there might possibly be a way to success.

Mrs. Neefit had been a good helpmate to her husband,—having worked hard for him when hard work on her part was needed,—but was not altogether so happy in her disposition as her lord. He desired to shine only in his daughter,—and as a tradesman. She was troubled by the more difficult ambition of desiring to shine in her own person. It was she who had insisted on migrating to Hendon, and who had demanded also the establishment of a one-horse carriage. The one-horse carriage was no delight to Neefit, and hardly gave satisfaction to his wife after the first three months. To be driven along the same roads, day after day, at the rate of six miles an hour, though it may afford fresh air, is not an exciting amusement. Mrs. Neefit was not given to reading, and was debarred by a sense of propriety from making those beef-steak puddings for which, within her own small household, she had once been so famous. Hendon she found dull; and, though Hendon had been her own choice, she could not keep herself from complaining of its dulness to her husband. But she always told him that the fault lay with him. He ought to content himself with going to town four times a week, and take a six weeks' holiday in the autumn. That was the recognised mode of life with gentlemen who had made their fortunes in trade. Then she tried to make him believe that constant seclusion in Conduit Street was bad for his liver. But above all things he ought to give up measuring his own customers with his own hands. None of their genteel neighbours would call upon his wife and daughter as long as he did that. But Mr. Neefit was a man within whose bosom gallantry had its limits. He had given his wife a house at Hendon, and was contented to take that odious journey backwards and forwards six days a week to oblige her. But when she told him not to measure his own customers, " he cut up rough " as Polly called it. " You be blowed," he said to the wife of his bosom. He had said it before, and she bore it with majestic equanimity.

Polly Neefit was, as we have said, as pretty a girl as you shall wish to see, in spite of a nose that was almost a pug nose, and a mouth that was a little large. I think, however, that she was perhaps prettier at seventeen, when she would run up and down Conduit Street on messages for her father,—who was not as yet aware that she had ceased to be a child,—than she became afterwards at Hendon, when she was twenty. In those early days her glossy black hair hung down her face in curls. Now, she had a thing on the back of her head, and her hair was manœuvred after the usual fashion. But her laughing dark eyes were full of good-humour, and looked as though they could be filled also with feeling. Her complexion was perfect,—perfect at twenty, though from its nature it would be apt to be fixed, and perhaps rough and coarse at thirty. But at twenty it was perfect. It was as is the colour of a half-blown rose, in which the variations from white to pink, and almost to red, are so gradual and soft as to have no limits. And then with her there was a charm beyond that of the rose, for the hues would ever be changing. As she spoke or laughed, or became serious or sat thoughtless, or pored over her novel, the tint of her cheek and neck would change as this or that emotion, be it ever so slight, played upon the current of her blood. She was tall, and well made,—perhaps almost robust. She was good-humoured, somewhat given to frank coquetry, and certainly fond of young men. She had sense enough not to despise her father, and was good enough to endeavour to make life bearable to her mother. She was clever, too, in her way, and could say sprightly things. She read novels, and loved a love story. She meant herself to have a grand passion some day, but did not quite sympathise with her father's views about gentlemen. Not that these views were discussed between them, but each was gradually learning the mind of the other. It was very pleasant to Polly Neefit to waltz with the good-looking gasfitter ;—and indeed to waltz with any man was a pleasure to Polly, for dancing was her Paradise upon earth. And she liked talking to Ontario Moggs, who was a clever man and had a great deal to say about many things. She believed that Ontario Moggs was dying for her love, but she had by no means made up her mind that Ontario was to be the hero of the great passion. The great passion was quite a necessity for her. She must have her romance. But Polly was aware that a great passion ought to be made to lead to a snug house, half a dozen children, and a proper, church-going, roast-mutton, duty-doing manner of life. Now Ontario Moggs had very wild ideas. As for the gasfitter he danced well and was good-looking, but he had very little to say for himself. When Polly saw Ralph Newton,—especially when he sat out on the lawn with them and smoked cigars on his second coming, —she thought him very nice. She had no idea of being patronised by any one, and she was afraid of persons whom she called " stuck-up " ladies and gentlemen. But Mr. Newton had not patronised her, and she had acknowledged that he was——very nice. Such as she was, she was the idol of her father's heart and the apple of his eye. If she had asked him to give up measuring, he might have yielded. But then his Polly was too wise for that.

We must say a word more of Mrs. Neefit, and then we shall hope

that our readers will know the family.   She had been the daughter of
a breeches-maker, to whom Neefit had originally been apprenticed,—
and therefore regarded herself as the maker of the family.   But in
truth the business, such as it was now in its glory, had been constructed by her husband, and her own fortune had been very small.
She was a stout, round-faced, healthy, meaningless woman, in whom ill-
humour would not have developed itself unless idleness,—that root of
all evil,—had fallen in her way.   As it was, in the present condition
of their lives, she did inflict much discomfort on poor Mr. Neefit.
Had he been ill, she would have nursed him with all her care.   Had
he died, she would have mourned for him as the best of husbands.
Had he been three parts ruined in trade, she would have gone back
to Conduit Street and made beef-steak puddings almost without a
murmur.   She was very anxious for his Sunday dinner,—and would
have considered it to be a sin to be without a bit of something nice
for his supper.   She took care that he always wore flannel, and would
never let him stay away from church,—lest worse should befall him.
But she couldn't let him be quiet.   What else was there left for her
to do but to nag him?   Polly, who was with her during the long
hours of the day, would not be nagged.   "Now, mamma!" she'd
say with a tone of authority that almost overcame mamma.   And if
mamma was very cross, Polly would escape.   But during the long
hours of the night the breeches-maker could not escape;—and in
minor matters the authority lay with her.   It was only when great
matters were touched that Mr. Neefit would rise in his wrath and
desire his wife "to be blowed."

No doubt Mrs. Neefit was an unhappy woman,—more unfortunate
as a woman than was her husband as a man.   The villa at Hendon
had been heavy upon him, but it had been doubly heavy upon her.
He could employ himself.   The legs of his customers, to him, were a
blessed resource.   But she had no resource.   The indefinite idea which
she had formed of what life would be in a pretty villa residence had
been proved to be utterly fallacious,—though she had never acknowledged the fallacy either to husband or daughter.   That one-horse
carriage in which she was dragged about, was almost as odious to her
as her own drawing-room.   That had become so horrible that it was
rarely used;—but even the dining-room was very bad.   What would
she do there, poor woman?   What was there left for her to do at all
in this world,—except to nag at her husband?

Nevertheless all who knew anything about the Neefits said that
they were very respectable people, and had done very well in the
world.

CHAPTER VI.

MRS. NEEFIT'S LITTLE DINNER.

ON the Sunday morning following that remarkable Saturday on which Miss Bonner had been taken to her new home and Ralph Newton had ordered three pair of breeches, Mr. Neefit made a very ambitious proposition. "My dear, I think I'll ask that young man to come and have a bit of dinner here next Sunday." This was said after breakfast, as Mr. Neefit was being made smart in his church-going coat and his Sunday hat, which were kept together in Mrs. Neefit's big press.

"Which young man?" Now Mrs. Neefit when she asked the question knew very well that Mr. Newton was the young man to whom hospitality was to be offered. Ontario Moggs was her favourite; but Mr. Neefit would not have dreamed of asking Ontario Moggs to dinner.

"Mr. Newton, my dear," said Mr. Neefit, with his head stuck sharply up, while his wife tied a bow in his Sunday neckhandkerchief.

"Why should us ask him? He won't think nothing of his vittels when he gets 'em. He'd only turn up his nose; and as for Polly, what's the use of making her more saucy than she is? I don't want such as him here, Neefit;—that I don't. Stuck-up young men like him had better stay away from Alexandrina Cottage,"—that was the name of the happy home at Hendon. "I'm sure our Polly won't be the better for having the likes of him here."

Nothing more was said on the subject till after the return of the family from church; but, during the sermon Mr. Neefit had had an opportunity of thinking the subject over, and had resolved that this was a matter in which it behoved him to be master. How was this marriage to be brought about if the young people were not allowed to see each other? Of course he might fail. He knew that. Very probably Mr. Newton might not accept the invitation,—might never show himself again at Alexandrina Cottage; but unless an effort was made there could not be success. "I don't see why he shouldn't eat a bit of dinner here," said Mr. Neefit, as soon as his pipe was lighted after their early dinner. "It ain't anything out of the way, as I know of."

"You're thinking of Polly, Neefit?"

"Why shouldn't I be thinking of her? There ain't no more of 'em. What's the use of working for her, if one don't think of her?"

" It won't do no good, Neefit. If we had things here as we might have 'em, indeed——! "

" What's amiss ? "

" With nothing to drink out of, only common wine-glasses ; and it's my belief Jemima 'd never cook a dinner as he'd look at. I know what they are,—them sort of young men. They're worse than a dozen ladies when you come to vittels."

Nevertheless Mr. Neefit resolved upon having his own way, and it was settled that Ralph Newton should be asked to come and eat a bit of dinner on next Sunday. Then there arose a difficulty as to the mode of asking him. Neefit himself felt that it would be altogether out of his line to indite an invitation. In days gone by, before he kept a clerk for the purpose, he had written very many letters to gentlemen, using various strains of pressure as he called their atten- tion to the little outstanding accounts which stood on his books and were thorns in his flesh. But of the writing of such letters as this now intended to be written he had no experience. As for Mrs. Neefit, her skill in this respect was less even than that of her husband. She could write, no doubt. On very rare occasions she would make some expression of her thoughts with pen and ink to Polly, when she and Polly were apart. But no one else ever saw how slight was her proficiency in this direction. But Polly was always writing. Polly's pothooks, as her father called them, were pictures in her father's eyes. She could dash off straight lines of writing,—line after line,— with sharp-pointed angles and long-tailed letters, in a manner which made her father proud of the money which he had spent on her education. So Polly was told to write the letter, and after many expressions of surprise, Polly wrote the letter that evening. " Mr. and Mrs. Neefit's compliments to Mr. Newton, and hope he will do them the honour to dine with them on Sunday next at five o'clock. Alexandrina Cottage, Sunday."

" Say five sharp," said the breeches-maker.

" No, father, I won't,—say anything about sharp."

" Why not, Polly ? "

" It wouldn't look pretty. I don't suppose he'll come, and I'm sure I don't know why you should ask him. Dear me, I'm certain he'll know that I wrote it. What will he think ? "

" He'll think it comes from as pretty a young woman as he ever clapped his eyes on," said Mr. Neefit, who was not at all reticent in the matter of compliments to his daughter.

" Laws, Neefit, how you do spoil the girl ! " said his wife.

" He has about finished spoiling me now, mamma ; so it don't much signify. You always did spoil me ;—didn't you, father ? " Then Polly kissed Mr. Neefit's bald head ; and Mr. Neefit, as he sat in the centre of his lawn, with his girdle loose around him, a

glass of gin and water by his side, and a pipe in his mouth, felt that
in truth there was something left in the world worth living for. But
a thought came across his mind,—"If that chap comes I shan't be as
comfortable next Sunday." And then there was another thought,—
"If he takes my Polly away from me, I don't know as I shall ever be
comfortable again." But still he did not hesitate or repent. Of course
his Polly must have a husband.

Then a dreadful proposition was made by Mrs. Neefit. "Why not
have Moggs too?"

"Oh, mamma!"

"Are you going to turn your nose up at Ontario Moggs, Miss
Pride?"

"I don't turn my nose up at him. I'm very fond of Mr. Moggs.
I think he's the best fun going. But I am sure that if Mr. Newton
does come, he'd rather not have Mr. Moggs here too."

"It wouldn't do at all," said Mr. Neefit. "Ontario is all very
well, but Mr. Newton and he wouldn't suit."

Mrs. Neefit was snubbed, and went to sleep on the sofa for the
rest of the afternoon,—intending, no doubt, to let Mr. Neefit have
the benefit of her feelings as soon as they two should be alone
together.

Our friend Ralph received the note, and accepted the invitation.
He told himself that it was a lark. As the reader knows, he had
already decided that he would not sell himself even to so pretty
a girl as Polly Neefit for any amount of money; but not the less
might it be agreeable to him to pass a Sunday afternoon in her
company.

Ralph Newton at this time occupied very comfortable bachelor's
rooms in a small street close to St. James's Palace. He had now
held these for the last two years, and had contrived to make his
friends about town know that here was his home. He had declined
to go into the army himself when he was quite young,—or rather
had agreed not to go into the army, on condition that he should not
be pressed as to any other profession. He lived, however, very much
with military friends, many of whom found it convenient occasionally
to breakfast with him, or to smoke a pipe in his chambers. He
never did any work, and lived a useless, butterfly life,—only with
this difference from other butterflies, that he was expected to pay for
his wings.

In that matter of payment was the great difficulty of Ralph Newton's
life. He had been started at nineteen with an allowance of £250 per
annum. When he was twenty-one he inherited a fortune from his
father of more than double that amount; and as he was the undoubted
heir to a property of £7,000 a year, it may be said of him that he
was born with a golden spoon. But he had got into debt before he

was twenty, and had never got out of it. The quarrel with his uncle was an old affair, arranged for him by his father before he knew how to quarrel on his own score, and therefore we need say no more about that at present. But his uncle would not pay a shilling for him, and would have quarrelled also with his other nephew, the clergyman, had he known that the younger brother assisted the elder. But up to the moment of which we are writing, the iron of debt had not as yet absolutely entered into the soul of this young man. He had, in his need, just borrowed £100 from his breeches-maker; and this perhaps was not the first time that he had gone to a tradesman for assistance. But hitherto money had been forth-coming, creditors had been indulgent, and at this moment he pos-sessed four horses which were eating their heads off at the Moon-beam, at Barnfield.

At five o'clock, with sufficient sharpness, Ralph Newton got out of a Hansom cab at the door of Alexandrina Cottage. "He's cum in a 'Ansom," said Mrs. Neefit, looking over the blind of the drawing-room window. "That's three-and-six," said Neefit, with a sigh. "You didn't think he was going to walk, father?" said Polly. "There's the Underground within two miles, if the Midland didn't suit," said Mr. Neefit. "Nonsense, father. Of course he'd come in a cab!" said Polly. Mrs. Neefit was not able to add the stinging remark with which her tongue was laden, as Ralph Newton was already in the house. She smoothed her apron, crossed her hands, and uttered a deep sigh. There could be no more going down into the kitchen now to see whether the salmon was boiled, or to provide for the proper dishing of the lamb. "This is quite condescending of you, Mr. Newton," said the breeches-maker, hardly daring to shake hands with his guest,—though in his shop he was always free enough with his customers in this matter. Polly looked as though she thought there was no condescension whatever, held up her head, and laughed and joked, and asked some questions about the German at the shop, whom she declared she was never allowed to see now, and whose voice she swore she had never heard. "Is he dumb, Mr. Newton? Father never will tell me anything about him. You must know."

"Laws, Polly, what does it matter?" said Mrs. Neefit. And they were the only words she had spoken. Polly, from the first, had resolved that she would own to the shop. If Mr. Newton came to see her, he should come to see a girl who was not ashamed to speak of herself as the daughter of a breeches-maker.

"He don't talk much, does he, Mr. Newton?" said Mr. Neefit, laughing merrily.

"Do tell me one thing," said Ralph. "I know it's a secret, but I'll promise not to tell it. What is his real name?"

"This isn't fair," said Mr. Neefit, greatly delighted. "All trades have their secrets. Come, come, Mr. Newton!"

"I know his name," said Polly.

"Do tell me," said Ralph, coming close to her, as though he might hear it in a whisper.

"Mr. Neefit, I wish you wouldn't talk about such things here," said the offended matron. "But now here's dinner." She was going to take her guest's arm, but Mr. Neefit arranged it otherwise.

"The old uns and the young uns;—that's the way to pair them," said Mr. Neefit,—understanding nature better than he did precedence; and so they walked into the next room. Mrs. Neefit was not quite sure whether her husband had or had not done something improper. She had her doubts, and they made her uncomfortable.

The dinner went off very well. Neefit told how he had gone himself to the fishmonger's for that bit of salmon, how troubled his wife had been in mind about the lamb, and how Polly had made the salad. "And I'll tell you what I did, Mr. Newton; I brought down that bottle of champagne in my pocket myself;—gave six bob for it at Palmer's, in Bond Street. My wife says we ain't got glasses fit to drink it out of."

"You needn't tell Mr. Newton all that."

"Mr. Newton, what I am I ain't ashamed on, nor yet what I does. Let me have the honour of drinking a glass of wine with you, Mr. Newton. You see us just as we are. I wish it was better, but it couldn't be welcomer. Your health, Mr. Newton."

There are many men,—and men, too, not of a bad sort,—who in such circumstances cannot make themselves pleasant. Grant the circumstances, with all the desire to make the best of them,—and these men cannot be otherwise than stiff, disagreeable, and uneasy. But then, again, there are men who in almost any position can carry themselves as though they were to the manner born. Ralph Newton was one of the latter. He was not accustomed to dine with the tradesmen who supplied him with goods, and had probably never before encountered such a host as Mr. Neefit;—but he went through the dinner with perfect ease and satisfaction, and before the pies and jellies had been consumed, had won the heart of even Mrs. Neefit. "Laws, Mr. Newton," she said, "what can you know about custards?" Then Ralph Newton offered to come and make custards against her in her own kitchen, —providing he might have Polly to help him. "But you'd want the back kitchen to yourselves, I'm thinking," said Mr. Neefit, in high good-humour.

Mr. Neefit certainly was not a delicate man. As soon as dinner was over, and the two ladies had eaten their strawberries and cream, he suggested that the port wine should be taken out into the garden. In the farther corner of Mr. Neefit's grounds, at a distance of about twenty yards from the house, was a little recess called " the arbour," admonitory of earwigs, and without much pretension to comfort. It might hold three persons, but on this occasion Mr. Neefit was minded that two only should enjoy the retreat. Polly carried out the decanter and glasses, but did not presume to stay there for a moment. She followed her mother into the gorgeous drawing-room, where Mrs. Neefit at once went to sleep, while her daughter consoled herself with a novel. Mr. Neefit, as we have said, was not a delicate man. " That girl 'll have twenty thousand pound, down on the nail, the day she marries the man as I approves of. Fill your glass, Mr. Newton. She will;—and there's no mistake about it. There'll be more money too, when I'm dead,—and the old woman."

It might be owned that such a speech from the father of a marriageable daughter to a young man who had hardly as yet shown himself to be enamoured, was not delicate. But it may be a question whether it was not sensible. He had made up his mind, and therefore went at once at his object. And unless he did the business in this way, what chance was there that it would be done at all? Mr. Newton could not come down to Alexandrina Cottage every other day, or meet the girl elsewhere, as he might do young ladies of fashion. And, moreover, the father knew well enough that were his girl once to tell him that she had set her heart upon the gasfitter, or upon Ontario Moggs, he would not have the power to contradict her. He desired that she should become a gentleman's wife; and thinking that this was the readiest way to accomplish his wish, he saw no reason why he should not follow it. When he had spoken, he chucked off his glass of wine, and looked into his young friend's face for an answer.

" He'll be a lucky fellow that gets her," said Ralph, beginning unconsciously to feel that it might perhaps have been as well for him had he remained in his lodgings on this Sunday.

" He will be a lucky fellow, Mr. Newton. She's as good as gold. And a well bred 'un too, though I say it as shouldn't. There's not a dirty drop in her. And she's that clever, she can do a'most anything. As for her looks, I'll say nothing about them. You've got eyes in your head. There ain't no mistake there, Mr. Newton; no paint; no Madame Rachel; no made beautiful for ever! It's human nature what you see there, Mr. Newton."

" I'm quite sure of that."

" And she has the heart of an angel." By this time Mr. Neefit was alternately wiping the tears from his eyes, and taking half glasses of port wine. " I know all about you, Mr. Newton. You are a gentleman;—that's what you are."

"I hope so."

"And if you don't get the wrong side of the post, you'll come out right at last. You'll have a nice property some of these days, but you're just a little short of cash at present."

"That's about true, Mr. Neefit."

"I want nobody to tell me;—I know," continued Neefit. "Now if you make up to her, there she is,—with twenty thousand pounds down. You are a gentleman, and I want that girl to be a lady. You can make her a lady. You can't make her no better than she is. The best man in England can't do that. But you can make her a lady. I don't know what she'll say, mind; but you can ask her,—if you please. I like you, and you can ask her, —if you please. What answer she'll make, that's her look out. But you can ask her,—if you please. Perhaps I'm a little too forrard; but I call that honest. I don't know what you call it. But this I do know;—there ain't so sweet a girl as that within twenty miles round London." Then Mr. Neefit, in his energy, dashed his hand down among the glasses on the little rustic table in the arbour.

The reader may imagine that Ralph Newton was hardly ready with his answer. There are men, no doubt, who in such an emergency would have been able to damn the breeches-maker's impudence, and to have walked at once out of the house. But our young friend felt no inclination to punish his host in such fashion as this. He simply remarked that he would think of it, the matter being too grave for immediate decision, and that he would join the ladies.

"Do, Mr. Newton," said Mr. Neefit; "go and join Polly. You'll find she's all I tell you. I'll sit here and have a pipe."

Ralph did join the ladies; and, finding Mrs. Neefit asleep, he induced Polly to take a walk with him amidst the lanes of Hendon. When he left Alexandrina Cottage in the evening, Mr. Neefit whispered a word into his ear at the gate. "You know my mind. Strike while the iron's hot. There she is,—just what you see her."

CHAPTER VII.

YOU ARE ONE OF US NOW.

THE first week after Mary Bonner's arrival at Popham Villa went by without much to make it remarkable, except the strangeness arising from the coming of a stranger. Sir Thomas did stay at home on that Sunday, but when the time came for going to morning church, shuffled out of that disagreeable duty in a manner that was satisfactory neither to himself nor his daughters. "Oh, papa; I thought you would have gone with us!" said Patience at the last moment.

"I think not to-day, my dear," he said, with that sort of smile which betokens inward uneasiness. Patience reproached him with a look, and then the three girls went off together. Even Patience herself had offered to excuse Mary, on the score of fatigue, sea-sickness, and the like; but Mary altogether declined to be excused. She was neither fatigued, she said, nor sick; and of course she would go to church. Sir Thomas stayed at home, and thought about himself. How could he go to church when he knew that he could neither listen to the sermon nor join in the prayers? "I suppose people do," he said to himself; "but I can't. I'd go to church all day long, if I found that it would serve me."

He went up to London on the Monday, and returned to the villa to dinner. He did the same on the Tuesday. On the Wednesday he remained in London. On the Thursday he came home, but dined in town. After that he found himself to be on sufficiently familiar terms with his niece to fall back into his old habits of life.

Patience was very slow in speaking to their cousin of her father's peculiarities; but Clarissa soon told the tale. "You'll get to know papa soon," she said.

"He has been so kind to me."

"He is very good; but you must know, dear, that we are the most deserted and disconsolate ladies that ever lived out of a poem. Papa has been home now four days together; but that is for your beaux yeux. We are here for weeks together without seeing him;—very often for more than a week."

"Where does he go?"

"He has a place in London;—such a place! You shall go and see it some day, though he won't thank us a bit for taking you there. He has the queerest old man to wait upon him, and he never sees anybody from day to day."

"But what does he do?"

"He is writing a book. That is the great secret. He never speaks about it, and does not like to be asked questions. But the truth is, he is the most solitude-loving person in the world. He does find its charms, though Alexander Selkirk never could."

"And does nobody come here to you?"

"In the way of taking care of us? Nobody! We have to take care of ourselves. Of course it is dull. People do come and see us sometimes. Miss Spooner, for instance."

"Why should you laugh at poor Miss Spooner?" asked Patience.

"I don't laugh at her. We have other friends, you know; but not enough to make the house pleasant to you." After that, when Patience was not with them, she told something of Ralph Newton and his visits, though she said nothing to her cousin of her own cherished hopes. "I wonder what you'll think of Ralph Newton?" she said. Ralph Newton's name had been mentioned before in Mary's hearing more than once.

"Why should I think anything particular of Ralph Newton?"

"You'll have to think something particular about him as he is a sort of child of the house. Papa was his guardian, and he comes here just when he pleases."

"Who is he, and what is he, and where is he, and why is he?"

"He's a gentleman at large who does nothing. That's who he is."

"He thinks ever so much of himself, then?"

"No;—he doesn't. And he is nephew to an old squire down in Hampshire, who won't give him a penny. He oughtn't to want it, however, because when he came of age he had ever so much money of his own. But he does want it,—sometimes. He must have the property when his uncle dies."

"Dear me;—how interesting!"

"As for the where he is, and why he is,—he comes here just when it suits him, and because we were almost brought up together. He doesn't dine here, and all that kind of thing, because papa is never at home. Nobody ever does dine here."

Then there was a short pause. "This Mr. Newton isn't a lover then?" asked Miss Bonner.

There was another pause before Clarissa could answer the question. "No," she said; "no; he isn't a lover. We don't have any lovers at Popham Villa." "Only that's not quite true," she said, after a pause. "And as you are to live with us just like a sister, I'll tell you about Gregory Newton, Ralph's brother." Then she did tell the story of the clergyman's love and the clergyman's discomfiture; but she said not a word of Ralph's declaration and Ralph's great sin on that fatal evening. And the way in which she told her story about the one brother altogether disarmed Mary Bonner's suspicion as to the other.

In truth Clarissa did not know whether it was or was not her privilege to regard Ralph Newton as her lover. He had not been to the cottage since that evening; and though the words he had spoken were still sweet in her ears,—so sweet that she could not endure the thought of abandoning their sweetness,—still she had a misgiving that they were in some sort rendered nugatory by his great fault. She had forgiven the fault;—looking back at it now over the distance of eight or ten days, had forgiven it with all her heart; but still there remained with her an undefined and unpleasant feeling that the spoken words, accompanied by a deed so wicked, were absorbed, and, as it were, drowned in the wickedness of the deed. What if the words as first spoken were only a prelude to the deed,— for, as she well remembered, they had been spoken twice,—and if the subsequent words were only an excuse for it! There was a painful idea in her mind that such might possibly be the case, and that if so, the man could never be forgiven, or at least ought never to be spoken to again. Acting on this suggestion from within, she absolutely refused to tell her father what had happened when Patience urged her to do so. "He'll come and see papa himself,— if he means anything," said Clary. Patience only shook her head. She thought that Sir Thomas should be told at once; but she could not take upon herself to divulge her sister's secret, which had been imparted to her in trust.

Clarissa was obstinate. She would not tell her father, nor would she say what would be her own answer if her father were to give his permission for the match. As to this Patience had not much doubt. She saw that her sister's heart was set upon this lover. She had feared it before this late occurrence, and now she could hardly have a doubt. But if Ralph really meant it he would hardly have told her that he loved her, and then not waited for an answer,—not have come back for an answer,—not have gone to their father for an answer. And then, Patience thought, Sir Thomas would never consent to this marriage. Ralph was in debt, and a scapegrace, and quite unfit to undertake the management of a wife. Such was the elder sister's belief as to her father's mind. But she could not force upon Clary the necessity of taking any action in the matter. She was not strong enough in her position as elder to demand obedience. Clarissa's communication had been made in confidence; and Patience, though she was unhappy, would not break the trust.

At last this young Lothario appeared among them again; but, as it happened, he came in company with Sir Thomas. Such a thing had not happened before since the day on which Sir Thomas had given up all charge of his ward's property. But it did so happen now. The two men had met in London, and Sir Thomas had suggested that Ralph should come and be introduced to the new cousin.

" What are you doing now ? " Sir Thomas had asked.

" Nothing particular just at present."

" You can get away this evening ? "

" Yes,—I think I can get away." It had been his intention to dine at his club with Captain Cox; but as he had dined at the club with Captain Cox on the previous day, the engagement was not felt to be altogether binding. "I can get away for dinner that is, but I've got to go out in the evening. It's a bore, but I promised to be at Lady McMarshal's to-night. But if I show there at twelve it will do." Thus it happened that Sir Thomas and Ralph Newton went down to Popham Villa in a cab together.

It was clear, both to Patience and Clarissa, that he was much struck with the new cousin; but then it was quite out of the question that any man should not be struck with her. Her beauty was of that kind,—like the beauty of a picture,—which must strike even if it fails to charm. And Mary had a way of exciting attention with strangers, even by her silence. It was hardly intentional, and there certainly was no coquetry in it; but it was the case that she carried herself after a fashion which made it impossible for any stranger to regard her place in the room as being merely a chair with a young lady in it. She would speak hardly a word; but her very lack of speech was eloquent. At the present time she was of course in deep mourning, and the contrast between the brilliance of her complexion and the dark dress which covered her throat ;— between the black scarf and the profusion of bright hair which fell upon it, was so remarkable as of itself to excite attention. Clarissa, watching everything, though, with feminine instinct, seeming to watch nothing, could see that he was amazed. But then she had known that he would be amazed. And of what matter would be his amazement, if he were true ? If, indeed, he were not true,—then, then,—then nothing mattered ! Such was the light in which Clary viewed the circumstances around her at the present moment.

The evening did not pass very pleasantly. Ralph was introduced to the cousin, and asked some questions about the West Indies. Then there was tea. Ralph was dressed, with a black coat and white cravat, and Clary could not keep herself from thinking how very much nicer he was with a pipe in his mouth, and his neck bare, drinking soda-water and sherry out on the lawn. Ah,—in spite of all that had then happened, that was the sweetest moment in her existence, when he jumped up from the ground and told her that he might do a great deal better than marry the West Indian cousin. She thought now of his very words, and suggested to herself that perhaps

he would never say them again. Nay;—might it not be possible
that he would say the very reverse, that he would declare his wish to
marry the West Indian cousin. Clary could not conceive but that he
might have her should he so wish. Young ladies, when they are in
love, are prone to regard their lovers as being prizes so valuable as
to be coveted by all female comers.

Before Ralph had taken his leave Sir Thomas took Mary apart to
make some communication to her as to her own affairs. Everything
was now settled, and Sir Thomas had purchased stock for her with
her little fortune. " You have £20 2*s.* 4*d.* a year, quite your own,"
he said, laughing;—as he might have done to one of his own girls,
had an unexpected legacy been left to her.

" That means that I must be altogether dependent on your
charity," she said, looking into his face through her tears.

"It means nothing of the kind," he said, with almost the impetuosity
of anger. " There shall be no such cold word as charity between you
and me. You are one of us now, and of my cup and of my loaf it is
your right to partake, as it is the right of those girls there. I shall
never think of it, or speak of it again."

" But I must think of it, uncle."

"The less the better;—but never use that odious word again
between you and me. It is a word for strangers. What is given as
I give to you should be taken without even an acknowledgment. My
payment is to be your love."

" You shall be paid in full," she said as she kissed him. This was
all very well, but still on his part there was some misgiving,—some
misgiving, though no doubt. If he were to die what would become
of her ? He must make a new will,—which in itself was to him a
terrible trouble ; and he must take something from his own girls in
order that he might provide for this new daughter. That question of
adopting is very difficult. If a man have no children of his own,—
none others that are dependent on him,—he can give all, and there is
an end of his trouble. But a man feels that he owes his property to
his children ; and, so feeling, may he take it from them and give it
to others ? Had she been in truth his daughter, he would have felt
that there was enough for three ; but she was not his daughter, and
yet he was telling her that she should be to him the same as a child
of his house !

In the meantime Ralph was out on the lawn with the two sisters,
and was as awkward as men always are in such circumstances. When
he spoke those words to Clarissa he had in truth no settled purpose
in his mind. He had always liked her,—loved her after a fashion,—
felt for her an affection different to that which he entertained for her
sister. Nevertheless, most assuredly he had not come down to Fulham on that evening prepared to make her an offer. He had been

there by chance, and it had been quite by chance that he found Clarissa alone. He knew that the words had been spoken, and he knew also that he had drawn down her wrath upon his head by his caress. He was man enough also to feel that he had no right to believe himself to have been forgiven, because now, in the presence of others, she did not receive him with a special coldness which would have demanded special explanation. As it was, the three were all cold. Patience half felt inclined to go and leave them together. She would have given a finger off her hand to make Clary happy; —but would it be right to make Clary happy in such fashion as this? She had thought at first when she saw her father and Ralph together, that Ralph had spoken of his love to Sir Thomas, and that Sir Thomas had allowed him to come; but she soon perceived that this was not the case: and so they walked about together, each knowing that their intercourse was not as it always had been, and each feeling powerless to resume an appearance of composure.

"I have got to go and be at Lady McMarshal's," he said, after having suffered in this way for a quarter of an hour. "If I did not show myself there her ladyship would think that I had given over all ideas of propriety, and that I was a lost sheep past redemption."

"Don't let us keep you if you ought to go," said Clary, with dismal propriety.

"I think I'll be off. Good-bye, Patience. The new cousin is radiant in beauty. No one can doubt that. But I don't know whether she is exactly the sort of girl I admire most. By-the-bye, what do you mean to do with her?"

"Do with her?" said Patience. "She will live here, of course."

"Just settle down as one of the family? Then, no doubt, I shall see her again. Good-night, Patience. Good-bye, Clary. I'll just step in and make my adieux to Sir Thomas and the beauty." This he did;—but as he went he pressed Clary's hand in a manner that she could but understand. She did not return the pressure, but she did not resent it.

"Clarissa," said Patience, when they were together that night, "dear Clarissa!"

Clary knew that when she was called Clarissa by her sister something special was meant. "What is it?" she asked. "What are you going to say now?"

"You know that I am thinking only of your happiness. My darling, he doesn't mean it."

"How do you know? What right have you to say so? Why am I to be thought such a fool as not to know what I ought to do?"

"Nobody thinks that you are a fool, Clary. I know how clever you are,—and how good. But I cannot bear that you should be unhappy. If he had meant it, he would have spoken to papa. If you will only tell me that you are not thinking of him, that he is not making you unhappy, I will not say a word further."

"I am thinking of him, and he is making me unhappy," said Clarissa, bursting into tears. " But I don't know why you should say that he is a liar, and dishonest, and everything that is bad."

"I have neither said that, nor thought it, Clary."

"That is what you mean. He did say that he loved me."

" And you,—you did not answer him ? "

" No ;—I said nothing. I can't explain it, and I don't want to explain it. I did not say a word to him. You came ; and then he went away. If I am to be unhappy, I can't help it. He did say that he loved me, and I do love him."

" Will you tell papa ? "

" No ;—I will not. It would be out of the question. He would go to Ralph, and there would be a row, and I would not have it for worlds." Then she tried to smile. " Other girls are unhappy, and I don't see why I'm to be better off than the rest. I know I am a fool. You'll never be unhappy, because you are not a fool. But, Patience, I have told you everything, and if you are not true to me I will never forgive you." Patience promised that she would be true ; and then they embraced and were friends.

CHAPTER VIII.

RALPH NEWTON'S TROUBLES.

JULY had come, the second week in July, and Ralph Newton had not as yet given any reply to that very definite proposition which had been made to him after the little dinner by Mr. Neefit. Now the proposition was one which certainly required an answer ;—and all the effect which it had hitherto had upon our friend was to induce him not to include Conduit Street in any of his daily walks. It has already been said that before the offer was made to him, when he believed that Polly's fortune would be more than Mr. Neefit had been able to promise, he had determined that nothing should induce him to marry the daughter of a breeches-maker ; and therefore the answer might have been easy. Nevertheless he made no answer, but kept out of Conduit Street, and allowed the three pair of breeches to be sent home to him without trying them on. This was very wrong ; for Mr. Neefit, though perhaps indelicate, had at least been generous and trusting;—and a definite answer should have been given before the middle of July.

Troubles were coming thick upon Ralph Newton. He had borrowed a hundred pounds from Mr. Neefit, but this he had done under pressure of a letter from his brother the parson. He owed the parson,—we will not say how much. He would get fifty pounds or a hundred from the parson every now and again, giving an assurance that it should be repaid in a month or six weeks. Sometimes the promise would be kept,—and sometimes not. The parson, as a bachelor, was undoubtedly a rich man. He had a living of £400 a year, and some fortune of his own; but he had tastes of his own, and was repairing the Church at Peele Newton, his parish in Hampshire. It would therefore sometimes happen that he was driven to ask his brother for money. The hundred pounds which had been borrowed from Mr. Neefit had been sent down to Peele Newton with a mere deduction of £25 for current expenses. Twenty-five pounds do not go far in current expenses in London with a man who is given to be expensive, and Ralph Newton was again in want of funds.

And there were other troubles, all coming from want of money. Mr. Horsball, of the Moonbeam, who was generally known in the sporting world as a man who never did ask for his money, had remarked that as Mr. Newton's bill was now above a thousand, he should like a little cash. Mr. Newton's bill at two months for £500 would be quite satisfactory. "Would Mr. Newton accept the enclosed document?" Mr. Newton did accept the document, but he didn't like it. How was he to pay £500 in the beginning of September, unless indeed he got it from Mr. Neefit? He might raise money, no doubt, on his own interest in the Newton Priory estate. But that estate would never be his were he to die before his uncle, and he knew that assistance from the Jews on such security would ruin him altogether. Of his own property there was still a remnant left. He owned houses in London from which he still got some income. But they were mortgaged, and the title-deeds not in his possession, and his own attorney made difficulties about obtaining for him a further advance.

He was sitting one bright July morning in his own room in St. James's Street, over a very late breakfast, with his two friends, Captain Fooks and Lieutenant Cox, when a little annoyance of a similar kind fell upon him;—a worse annoyance, indeed, than that which had come from Mr. Horsball, for Mr. Horsball had not been spiteful enough to call upon him. There came a knock at his door, and young Mr. Moggs was ushered into the room. Now Mr. Moggs was the son of Booby and Moggs, the well-known bootmakers of Old Bond Street; and the boots they had made for Ralph Newton had been infinite in number, as they had also, no doubt, been excellent in make and leather. But Booby and Moggs had of late wanted money, had written many letters, and for four months had not seen the face of their customer. When a gentleman is driven by his indebtedness to go to another tradesman, it is, so to say, "all up with him" in the way of credit. There is nothing the tradesman dislikes so much as this, as he fears that the rival is going to get the ready money after he has given the credit. And yet what is a gentleman to do when his demand for further goods at the old shop is met by a request for a little ready money? We know what Ralph Newton did at the establishment in Conduit Street. But then Mr. Neefit was a very peculiar man.

Cox had just lighted his cigar, and Fooks was filling his pipe when Ontario Moggs entered the room. This rival in the regards of Polly Neefit was not at that time personally known to Ralph Newton; but the name, as mentioned by his servant, was painfully familiar to him. "Oh, Mr. Moggs,—ah;—it's your father, I suppose, that I know. Sit down, Mr. Moggs;—will you have a cup of tea;—or perhaps a glass of brandy? Take a cigar, Mr. Moggs." But Moggs declined all refreshment for the body. He was a tall, thin, young man, with long straggling hair, a fierce eye, very thick lips, and a flat nose,—a nose which seemed to be all nostril;—and then, below his mouth was a tuft of beard, which he called an imperial. It was the glory of Ontario Moggs to be a politician;—it was his ambition to be a poet;—it was his nature to be a lover;—it was his disgrace to be a bootmaker. Dependent on a stern father, and aware that it behoved him to earn his bread, he could not but obey; but he groaned under this servitude to trade, and was only happy when speaking at his debating club, held at the Cheshire Cheese, or when basking in the beauty of Polly Neefit. He was great upon Strikes, —in reference to which perilous subject he was altogether at variance with his father, who worshipped capital and hated unions. Ontario held horrible ideas about co-operative associations, the rights of labour, and the welfare of the masses. Thrice he had quarrelled with his father;—but the old man loved his son, and though he was stern, strove to bring the young man into the ways of money-making. How was he to think of marrying Polly Neefit,—as to the expediency of which arrangement Mr. Moggs senior quite agreed with Mr. Moggs junior,—unless he would show himself to be a man of business? Did he think that old Neefit would give his money to be wasted upon strikes? Ontario, who was as honest a fool as ever lived, told his father that he didn't care a straw for Neefit's money. Then Moggs the father had made a plunge against the counter with his sharp-pointed shoemaker's knife, which he always held in his hand, that had almost been fatal to himself; for the knife broke at the thrust, and the fragment cut his wrist. At this time there was no real Booby, and the firm was in truth Moggs, and Moggs only. The great question was whether it should become Moggs and Son. But what tradesman would take a partner into his firm who began by declaring that strikes were the safeguards of trade, and that he, — the proposed partner, — did not personally care for money? Nevertheless old Moggs persevered; and Ontario, alive to the fact that it was his duty to be a bootmaker, was now attempting to carry on his business in the manner laid down for him by his father.

A worse dun,—a dun with less power of dunning,—than Ontario Moggs could not be conceived. His only strength lay in his helplessness. When he found that Mr. Newton had two friends with him, his lips were sealed. To ask for money at all was very painful to him, but to ask for it before three men was beyond his power. Ralph Newton, seeing something of this, felt that generosity demanded of him that he should sacrifice himself. "I'm afraid you've come about your bill, Mr. Moggs," he said. Ontario Moggs, who on the subject of Trades' Unions at the Cheshire Cheese could pour forth a flood of eloquence that would hold the room in rapt admiration, and then bring down a tumult of applause, now stammered out a half-expressed assent. "As Mr. Newton was engaged perhaps he had better call again."

"Well;—thankee, yes. It would be as well. But what's the total, Mr. Moggs?" Ontario could not bring himself to mention the figures, but handed a paper to our friend. "Bless my soul! that's very bad," said our friend. "Over two hundred pounds for boots! How long can your father give me?"

"He's a little pressed just at present," whispered Moggs.

"Yes;—and he has my bill, which he was forced to take up at Christmas. It's quite true." Moggs said not a word, though he had been especially commissioned to instruct the debtor that his father would be forced to apply through his solicitor, unless he should receive at least half the amount due before the end of the next week. "Tell your father that I will certainly call within the next three days and tell him what I can do;—or, at least, what I can't do. You are sure you won't take a cigar?" Moggs was quite sure that he wouldn't take a cigar, and retired, thanking Ralph as though some excellent arrangement had been made which would altogether prevent further difficulties.

"That's the softest chap I ever saw," said Lieutenant Cox.

"I wish my fellows would treat me like that," said Captain Fooks. "But I never knew a fellow have the luck that Newton has. I don't suppose I owe a tenth of what you do."

"That's your idea of luck?" said Ralph.

" Well ;—yes. I owe next to nothing, but I'll be hanged if I can
get anything done for me without being dunned up to my very eyes.
You know that chap of Neefit's ? I'm blessed if he didn't ask me
whether I meant to settle last year's bill, before he should send me
home a couple of cords I ordered ! Now I don't owe Neefit twenty
pounds if all was told."

" What did you do ?" asked Lieutenant Cox.

" I just walked out of the shop. Now I shall see whether they're
sent or not. They tell me there's a fellow down at Rugby makes
just as well as Neefit, and never bothers you at all. What do you
owe Neefit, Newton ?"

" Untold sums."

" But how much really ?"

" Don't you hear me say the sums are untold ?"

" Oh ; d—n it ; I don't understand that. I'm never dark about
anything of that kind. I'll go bail it's more than five times what
I do."

" Very likely. If you had given your orders generously, as I have
done, you would have been treated nobly. What good has a man
in looking at twenty pounds on his books ? Of course he must get
in the small sums."

" I suppose there's something in that," said the captain thought-
fully. At this moment the conversation was interrupted by the
entrance of another emissary,—an emissary from that very establishment to which they were alluding. It was Ralph Newton's orders
that no one should ever be denied to him when he was really in his
rooms. He had fought the battle long enough to know that such
denials create unnecessary animosity. And then, as he said, they
were simply the resources of a coward. It was the duty of a brave
man to meet his enemy face to face. Fortune could never give him
the opportunity of doing that pleasantly, in the field, as might happen
any day to his happy friends, Captain Fooks and Lieutenant Cox ;
but he was determined that he would accustom himself to stand
fire ;—and that, therefore, he would never run away from a dun.
Now there slipped very slowly into the room, that most mysterious
person who was commonly called Herr Bawwah,—much to the
astonishment of the three young gentlemen, as the celebrated cutter
of leather had never previously been seen by either of them elsewhere than standing silent at his board in Neefit's shop, with
his knife in his hands. They looked at one another, and the two
military gentlemen thought that Mr. Neefit was very much in
earnest when he sent Bawwah to look for his money. Mr. Neefit
was very much in earnest ; but on this occasion his emissary had
not come for money. " What, Herr Bawwah ;—is that you ?"
said Ralph, making the best he could of the name. " Is there

anything wrong at the shop?" The German looked slowly round the room, and then handed to the owner of it a little note without a word.

Ralph read the note,—to himself. It was written on one of the shop bills, and ran as follows:—"Have you thought of what I was saying? If so, I should be happy to see Mr. Newton either in Conduit Street or at Alexandrina Cottage." There was neither signature nor date. Ralph knew what he was called upon to do, as well as though four pages of an elaborate epistle had been indited to him. And he knew, too, that he was bound to give an answer. He asked the "Herr" to sit down, and prepared to write an answer at once. He offered the Herr a glass of brandy, which the Herr swallowed at a gulp. He handed the Herr a cigar, which the Herr pocketed;—and in gratitude for the latter favour some inarticulate grunt of thanks was uttered. Ralph at once wrote his reply, while the two friends smoked, looked on, and wondered. "Dear Mr. Neefit, —I will be with you at eleven to-morrow morning. Yours most truly, RALPH NEWTON." This he handed, with another glass of brandy, to the Herr. The Herr swallowed the second glass,—as he would have done a third had it been offered to him,—and then took his departure.

"That was another dun;—eh, Newton?" asked the lieutenant.

"What a conjuror you are?" said Ralph.

"I never heard of his sending Bawwah out before," said the captain.

"He never does under two hundred and fifty pounds," said Ralph. "It's a mark of the greatest respect. If I wore nothing but brown cords, like you, I never should have seen the Herr here."

"I never had a pair of brown cords in my life!" said the offended captain. After this the conversation fell away, and the two warriors went off to their military occupations at the Horse Guards, where, no doubt, the Commander-in-chief was waiting for them with impatience.

Ralph Newton had much to think of, and much that required thinking of at once. Did he mean to make an offer to Clary Underwood? Did he mean to take Polly Neefit and her £20,000? Did he mean to marry at all? Did he mean to go to the dogs? Had he ever in his life seen anybody half so beautiful as Mary Bonner? What was he to say to Mr. Moggs? How was he to manage about that £500 which Horsball would demand of him in September? In what terms could he speak to Neefit of the money due both for breeches and the loan, in the event of his declining Polly? And then, generally, how was he to carry on the war? He was thoroughly disgusted with himself as he thought of all the evil that he had done, and of the good which he had omitted to do. While he was yet at college Sir Thomas had been anxious that he should be called to the Bar, and had again and again begged of him to consent to this as a commencement of his life in London. But Ralph had replied,—and had at last replied with so much decision that Sir Thomas had abandoned the subject,—that as it was out of the question that he should ever make money at the Bar, the fact of his being called would be useless to him. He argued that he need not waste his life because he was not a lawyer. It was not his intention to waste his life. He had a sufficient property of his own at once, and must inherit a much larger property later in life. He would not be called to the Bar, nor would he go into the army, nor would he go abroad for any lengthened course of travelling. He was fond of hunting, but he would keep his hunting within measure. Surely an English private gentleman might live to some profit in his own country! He would go out in honours, and take a degree, and then make himself happy among his books. Such had been his own plan for himself at twenty-one. At twenty-two he had quarrelled with the tutor at his college, and taken his name off the books without any degree. About this, too, he had argued with Sir Thomas, expressing a strong opinion that a university degree was in England, of all pretences, the most vain and hollow. At twenty-three he began his career at the Moonbeam with two horses,—and from that day to this hunting had been the chief aim of his life. During the last winter he had hunted six days a week,—assuring Sir Thomas, however, that at the end of that season his wild oats would have been sown as regarded that amusement, and that henceforth he should confine himself to two days a week. Since that he had justified the four horses which still remained at the Moonbeam by the alleged fact that horses were drugs in April, but would be pearls of price in November. Sir Thomas could only expostulate, and when he did so, his late ward and present friend, though he was always courteous, would always argue. Then he fell, as was natural, into intimacies with such men as Cox and Fooks. There was no special harm either in Cox or Fooks; but no one knew better than did Ralph Newton himself that they were not such friends as he had promised himself when he was younger.

Fathers, guardians, and the race of old friends generally, hardly ever give sufficient credit to the remorse which young men themselves feel when they gradually go astray. They see the better as plainly as do their elders, though they so often follow the worse,—as not unfrequently do the elders also. Ralph Newton passed hardly a day of his life without a certain amount of remorse in that he had not managed himself better than he had done, and was now doing. He knew that Fortune had been very good to him, and that he had hitherto wasted all her gifts. And now there came the question whether it was as yet too late to retrieve the injury which he had done. He did believe,—not even as yet doubting his power to do well,—that everything might be made right, only that his money difficulties pressed him so hardly. He took pen and paper, and made out a list of his debts, heading the catalogue with Mr. Horsball of the Moonbeam. The amount, when added together, came to something over four thousand pounds, including a debt of three hundred to his brother the parson. Then he endeavoured to value his property, and calculated that if he sold all that was remaining to him he might pay what he owed, and have something about fifty pounds per annum left to live upon till he should inherit his uncle's property. But he doubted the accuracy even of this, knowing that new and unexpected debts will always crop up when the day of settlement arrives. Of course he could not live upon fifty pounds a year. It would have seemed to him to be almost equally impossible to live upon four times fifty pounds. He had given Sir Thomas a promise that he would not raise money on post-obits on his uncle's life, and hitherto he had kept that promise. He thought that he would be guilty of no breach of promise were he so to obtain funds, telling Sir Thomas of his purpose, and asking the lawyer's assistance; but he knew that if he did this all his chance of future high prosperity would be at an end. His uncle might live these twenty years, and in that time he, Ralph, might quite as readily die. Money might no doubt be raised, but this could only be done at a cost which would be utterly ruinous to him. There was one way out of his difficulty. He might marry a girl with money. A girl with money had been offered to him, and a girl, too, who was very pretty and very pleasant. But then, to marry the daughter of a breeches-maker!

And why not? He had been teaching himself all his life to despise conventionalities. He had ridiculed degrees. He had laughed at the rank and standing of a barrister. "The rank is but the guinea stamp—the man's the gowd for a' that." How often had he declared to himself and others that that should be his motto through life. And might not he be as much a man, and would not his metal be as pure, with Polly Neefit for his wife as though he were to marry a duchess? As for love, he thought he could love Polly dearly. He knew that he had done some wrong in regard to poor Clary; but he by no means knew how much wrong he had done. A single word of love,—which had been so very much to her in her innocence,—had been so little to him who was not innocent. If he could allow himself to choose out of all the women he had ever seen, he would, he thought, instigated rather by the ambition of having the loveliest woman in the world for his wife than by any love, have endeavoured to win Mary Bonner as his own. But that was out of the question. Mary Bonner was as poor as himself; and, much as he admired her, he certainly could not tell himself that he loved her. Polly Neefit would pull him through all his difficulties. Nevertheless, he could not make up his mind to ask Polly Neefit to be his wife.

But he must make up his mind either that he would or that he would not. He must see Mr. Neefit on the morrow;—and within the next few days he must call on Mr. Moggs, unless he broke his word. And in two months' time he must have £500 for Mr. Horsball. Suppose he were to go to Sir Thomas, tell his whole story without reserve, and ask his old friend's advice! Everything without reserve he could not tell. He could say nothing to the father of that scene on the lawn with Clarissa. But of his own pecuniary difficulties, and of Mr. Neefit's generous offer, he was sure that he could tell the entire truth. He did go to Southampton Buildings, and after some harsh language between himself and Mr. Stemm,— Sir Thomas being away at the time,—he managed to make an appointment for nine o'clock that evening at his late guardian's chambers. At nine o'clock precisely he found himself seated with Sir Thomas, all among the books in Southampton Buildings. "Perhaps you'll have a cup of tea," said Sir Thomas. "Stemm, give us some tea." Ralph waited till the tea was handed to him and Stemm was gone. Then he told his story.

He told it very fairly as against himself. He brought out his little account and explained to the lawyer how it was that he made himself out to be worth fifty pounds a year, and no more. "Oh, heavens, what a mess you have made of it!" said the lawyer, holding up both his hands. "No doubt I have," said Ralph,—"a terrible mess! But as I now come to you for advice hear me out to the end. You can say nothing as to my folly which I do not know already." "Go on," said Sir Thomas. "Go on,—I'll hear you." It may, however, be remarked, by the way, that when an old gentleman in Sir Thomas's position is asked his advice under such circumstances, he ought to be allowed to remark that he had prophesied all these things beforehand. "I told you so," is such a comfortable thing to say! And when an old gentleman has taken much fruitless trouble about a young gentleman, he ought at least not to be interrupted in his remarks as to that young gentleman's folly. But Ralph was energetic, and, knowing that he had a point before him, would go on with his story. "And now," he said, "I am coming to a way of putting these things right which has been suggested to me. You won't like it, I know. But it would put me on my legs."

"Raising money on your expectations?" said Sir Thomas.

"No;—that is what I must come to if this plan don't answer."

"Anything will be better than that," said Sir Thomas.

Then Ralph dashed at the suggestion of marriage without further delay. "You have heard of Mr. Neefit, the breeches-maker!" It so happened that Sir Thomas never had heard of Mr. Neefit. "Well; —he is a tradesman in Conduit Street. He has a daughter, and he will give her twenty thousand pounds."

"You don't mean to run away with the breeches-maker's daughter?" ejaculated Sir Thomas.

"Certainly not. I shouldn't get the twenty thousand pounds if I did." Then he explained it all;—how Neefit had asked him to the house, and offered him the girl; how the girl herself was as pretty and nice as a girl could be; and how he thought,—though as to that he expressed himself with some humility,—that, were he to propose to her, the girl might perhaps take him.

"I dare say she would," said Sir Thomas.

"Well;—now you know it all. In her way, she has been educated. Neefit père is utterly illiterate and ignorant. He is an honest man, as vulgar as he can be,—or rather as unlike you and me, which is what men mean when they talk of vulgarity,—and he makes the best of breeches. Neefit mère is worse than the father,— being cross and ill-conditioned, as far as I can see. Polly is as good as gold; and if I put a house over my head with her money, of course her father and her mother will be made welcome there. Your daughters would not like to meet them, but I think they could put up with Polly. Now you know about all that I can tell you."

Ralph had been so rapid, so energetic, and withal so reasonable, that Sir Thomas, at this period of the interview, was unable to refer to any of his prophecies. What advice was he to give? Should he adjure this young man not to marry the breeches-maker's daughter because of the blood of the Newtons and the expected estate, or were he to do so even on the score of education and general unfitness, he must suggest some other mode or means of living. But how could he advise the future Newton of Newton Priory to marry Polly Neefit? The Newtons had been at Newton Priory for centuries, and the men Newtons had always married ladies, as the women Newtons had always either married gentlemen or remained unmarried. Sir Thomas, too, was of his nature, and by all his convictions, opposed to such matches. "You have hardly realised," said he, "what it would be to have such a father-in-law and such a mother-in-law;— or probably such a wife."

"Yes, I have. I have realised all that."

"Of course, if you have made up your mind——"

"But I have not made up my mind, Sir Thomas. I must make it up before eleven o'clock to-morrow morning, because I must then be with Neefit,—by appointment. At this moment I am so much in doubt that I am almost inclined to toss up."

"I would sooner cut my throat!" said Sir Thomas, forgetting his wisdom amidst the perplexities of his position.

"Not quite that, Sir Thomas. I suppose you mean to say that anything would be better than such a marriage?"

"I don't suppose you care for the girl," said Sir Thomas, crossly.

"I do not feel uneasy on that score. If I did not like her, and think that I could love her, I would have nothing to do with it. She herself is charming,—though I should lie if I were to say that she were a lady."

"And the father offered her to you?"

"Most distinctly,—and named the fortune."

"Knowing your own condition as to money?"

"Almost exactly;—so much so that I do not doubt he will go on with it when he knows everything. He had heard about my uncle's property, and complimented me by saying that I am a,—gentleman."

"He does not deserve to have a daughter," said Sir Thomas.

"I don't know about that. According to his lights, he means to do the best he can for her. And, indeed, I think myself that he might do worse. She will probably become Mrs. Newton of Newton Priory if she marries me; and the investment of Neefit's twenty thousand pounds won't be so bad."

"Nothing on earth can make her a lady."

"I'm not so sure of that," said Ralph. "Nothing on earth can make her mother a lady; but of Polly I should have hopes. You, however, are against it?"

"Certainly."

"Then what ought I to do?" Sir Thomas rubbed the calf of his leg and was silent. "The only advice you have given me hitherto was to cut my throat," said Ralph.

"No, I didn't. I don't know what you're to do. You've ruined yourself;—that's all."

"But there is a way out of the ruin. In all emergencies there is a better and a worse course. What, now, is the better course?"

"You don't know how to earn a shilling," said Sir Thomas.

"No; I don't," said Ralph Newton.

Sir Thomas rubbed his face and scratched his head; but did not know how to give advice. "You have made your bed, and you must lie upon it," he said.

"Exactly;—but which way am I to get into it, and which way shall I get out?" Sir Thomas could only rub his face and scratch his head. "I thought it best to come and tell you everything," said Ralph. That was all very well, but Sir Thomas would not advise him to marry the breeches-maker's daughter.

"It is a matter," Sir Thomas said at last, "in which you must be guided by your own feelings. I wish it were otherwise. I can say no more." Then Ralph took his leave, and wandered all round St. James's Park and the purlieus of Westminster till midnight, endeavouring to make up his mind, and building castles in the air, as to what he would do with himself, and how he would act, if he had not brought himself into so hopeless a mess of troubles.

CHAPTER IX.

ONTARIO MOGGS.

ON the following morning Ralph Newton was in Conduit Street exactly at the hour named. He had not even then made up his mind; —but he thought that he might get an extension of the time allowed him for decision. After all, it was hardly a month yet since the proposition was made to him. He found Mr. Neefit in the back shop, measuring a customer. "I'll be with you in two minutes," said Mr. Neefit, just putting his head through the open door, and then going back to his work; " 3—1—$\frac{1}{8}$, Waddle; Sir George isn't quite as stout as he was last year. Oh, no, Sir George; we won't tie you in too tight. Leave it to us, Sir George. The last pair too tight? Oh, no; I think not, Sir George. Perhaps your man isn't as careful in cleaning as he ought to be. Gentlemen's servants do get so careless, it quite sickens one!" So Mr. Neefit went on, and as Sir George was very copious in the instructions which he had to give,—all of which, by-the-bye, were absolutely thrown away,—Ralph Newton became tired of waiting. He remembered too that he was not there as a customer, but almost as a member of the family, and the idea sickened him. He bethought himself that on his first visit to Conduit Street he had seen his Polly in the shop, cutting up strips wherewith her father would measure gentlemen's legs. She must then have been nearly fifteen, and the occupation, as he felt, was not one fitting for the girl who was to be his wife. "Now, Mr. Newton," said Mr. Neefit, as Sir George at last left the little room. The day was hot, and Mr. Neefit had been at work in his shirt sleeves. Nor did he now put on his coat. He wiped his brow, put his cotton handkerchief inside his braces, and shook hands with our hero. "Well, Mr. Newton," he said, "what do you think of it? I couldn't learn much about it, but it seemed to me that you and Polly got on famous that night. I thought we'd have seen you out there again before this."

"I couldn't come, Mr. Neefit, as long as there was a doubt."

"Oh, as to doubts,—doubts be bothered. Of course you must run your chance with Polly like any other man."

"Just so."

"But the way to get a girl like that isn't not to come and see her for a month. There are others after our Polly, I can tell you;—and men who would take her with nothing but her smock on."

"I'm quite sure of that. No one can see her without admiring her."

"Then what's the good of talking of doubts? I like you because you are a gentleman;—and I can put you on your legs, which, from all I hear, is a kind of putting you want bad enough just at present. Say the word, and come down to tea this evening."

"The fact is, Mr. Neefit, this is a very serious matter."

"Serious! Twenty thousand pounds is serious. There ain't a doubt about that. If you mean to say you don't like the bargain,"—and as he said this there came a black cloud upon Mr. Neefit's brow,—"you've only got to say the word. Our Polly is not to be pressed upon any man. But don't let's have any shilly-shallying."

"Tell me one thing, Mr. Neefit."

"Well;—what's that?"

"Have you spoken to your daughter about this?"

Mr. Neefit was silent for a moment, "Well, no; I haven't," he said. "But I spoke to her mother, and women is always talking. Mind, I don't know what our Polly would say to you, but I do think she expects something. There's a chap lives nigh to us who used always to be sneaking round; but she has snubbed him terribly this month past. So my wife tells me. You come and try, Mr. Newton, and then you'll know all about it."

Ralph was aware that he had not as yet begun to explain his difficulty to the anxious father. "You see, Mr. Neefit," he said,—and then he paused. It had been much easier for him to talk to Sir Thomas than to the breeches-maker.

"If you don't like it,—say so," said Mr. Neefit;—"and don't let us have no shilly-shallying."

"I do like it."

"Then give us your hand, and come out this evening and have a bit of some'at to eat and a drop of some'at hot, and pop the question. That's about the way to do it."

"Undoubtedly;—but marriage is such a serious thing!"

"So it is serious,—uncommon serious to owe a fellow a lot of money you can't pay him. I call that very serious."

"Mr. Neefit, I owe you nothing but what I can pay you."

"You're very slow about it, Mr. Newton; that's all I can say. But I wasn't just talking of myself. After what's passed between you and me I ain't going to be hard upon you."

"I'll tell you what, Mr. Neefit," said Ralph at last,—"of course you can understand that a man may have difficulties with his family."

"Because of my being a breeches-maker?" said Neefit contemptuously.

" I won't say that ; but there may be difficulties."

" Twenty thousand pounds does away with a deal of them things."

" Just so ;—but as I was saying, you can understand that there may be family difficulties. I only say that because I ought perhaps to have given you an answer sooner. I won't go down with you this evening."

" You won't ? "

" Not to-night ;—but I'll be with you on Saturday evening, if that will suit you."

" Come and have a bit of dinner again on Sunday," said Neefit. Ralph accepted the invitation, shook hands with Neefit, and escaped from the shop.

When he thought of it all as he went to his rooms, he told himself that he had now as good as engaged himself to Polly ;—as good or as bad. Of course, after what had passed, he could not go to the house again without asking her to be his wife. Were he to do so Neefit would be justified in insulting him. And yet when he undertook to make this fourth visit to the cottage, he had done so with the intention of allowing himself a little more time for judgment. He saw plainly enough that he was going to allow himself to drift into this marriage without any real decision of his own. He prided himself on being strong, and how could any man be more despicably weak than this ? It was, indeed, true that in all the arguments he had used with Sir Thomas he had defended the Neefit marriage as though it was the best course he could adopt;—and even Sir Thomas had not ultimately ventured to oppose it. Would it not be as well for him to consider that he had absolutely made up his mind to marry Polly ?

On the Friday he called at Mr. Moggs's house ; Mr. Moggs senior was there, and Mr. Moggs junior, and also a shopman. " I was sorry," said he, " that when your son called, I had friends with me, and could hardly explain circumstances."

" It didn't signify at all," said Moggs junior.

" But it does signify, Mr. Newton," said Moggs senior, who on this morning was not in a good humour with his ledger. " Two hundred and seventeen pounds, three shillings and four-pence is a good deal of money for boots, Mr. Newton. You must allow that."

" Indeed it is, Mr. Moggs."

" There hasn't been what you may call a settlement for years. Twenty-five pounds paid in the last two years !" and Mr. Moggs as he spoke had his finger on the fatal page. " That won't do, you know, Mr. Newton ;—that won't do at all ! " Mr. Moggs, as he looked into his customer's face, worked himself up into a passion. " But I suppose you have come to settle it now, Mr. Newton ? "

" Not exactly at this moment, Mr. Moggs."

" It must be settled very soon, Mr. Newton ;—it must indeed.

My son can't be calling on you day after day, and all for nothing. We can't stand that you know, Mr. Newton. Perhaps you'll oblige me by saying when it will be settled." Then Ralph explained that he had called for that purpose, that he was making arrangements for paying all his creditors, and that he hoped that Mr. Moggs would have his money within three months at the farthest. Mr. Moggs then proposed that he should have his customer's bill at three months, and the interview ended by the due manufacture of a document to that effect. Ralph, when he entered the shop, had not intended to give a bill; but the pressure had been too great upon him, and he had yielded. It would matter little, however, if he married Polly Neefit. And had he not now accepted it as his destiny that he must marry Polly Neefit?

The Saturday he passed in much trouble of spirit, and with many doubts; but the upshot of it all was that he would keep his engagement for the Sunday. His last chance of escape would have been to call in Conduit Street on the Saturday and tell Mr. Neefit, with such apologies as he might be able to make, that the marriage would not be suitable. While sitting at breakfast he had almost resolved to do this;—but when five o'clock came, after which, as he well knew, the breeches-maker would not be found, no such step had been taken. He dined that evening and went to the theatre with Lieutenant Cox. At twelve they were joined by Fooks and another gay spirit, and they eat chops and drank stout and listened to songs at Evans's till near two. Cox and Fooks said that they had never been so jolly in their lives;—but Ralph,—though he eat and drank as much and talked more than the others,—was far from happy. There came upon him a feeling that after to-morrow he would never again be able to call himself a gentleman. Who would associate with him after he had married the breeches-maker's daughter? He laid in bed late on Sunday, and certainly went to no place of worship. Would it not be well even yet to send a letter down to Neefit, telling him that the thing could not be? The man would be very angry with him, and would have great cause to be angry. But it would at least be better to do this now than hereafter. But when four o'clock came no letter had been sent.

Punctually at five the cab set him down at Alexandrina Cottage. How well he seemed to know the place;—almost as well as though he were already one of the family. He was shown into the drawing-room, and whom should he see there, seated with Mr. and Mrs. and Miss Neefit, but Ontario Moggs. It was clear enough that each of the party was ill at ease. Neefit welcomed him with almost boisterous hospitality. Mrs. Neefit merely curtseyed and bobbed at him. Polly smiled, and shook hands with him, and told him that he was welcome;—but even Polly was a little beside herself. Ontario Moggs stood bolt upright and made him a low bow, but did not attempt to speak.

"I hope your father is well," said Ralph, addressing himself to Moggs junior.

"Pretty well, I thank you," said Mr. Moggs, getting up from his chair and bowing a second time.

Mr. Neefit waited for a moment or two during which no one except Ralph spoke a word, and then invited his intended son-in-law to follow him into the garden. "The fact is," said Neefit winking, "this is Mrs. N.'s doing. It don't make any difference, you know."

"I don't quite understand," said Ralph.

"You see we've known Onty Moggs all our lives, and no doubt he has been sweet upon Polly. But Polly don't care for him, mind you. You ask her. And Mrs. N. has got it into her head that she don't want you for Polly. But I do, Mr. Newton;—and I'm master."

"I wouldn't for the world make a family quarrel."

"There won't be no quarrelling. It's I as has the purse, and it's the purse as makes the master, Mr. Newton. Don't you mind Moggs. Moggs is very well in his way, but he ain't going to have our Polly. Well;—he come down here to-day, just by chance;—and what did Mrs. N. do but ask him to stop and eat a bit of dinner! It don't make any difference, you know. You come in now, and just go on as though Moggs weren't there. You and Polly shall have it all to yourselves this evening."

Here was a new feature added to the pleasures of his courtship! He had a rival,—and such a rival;—his own bootmaker, whom he could not pay, and whose father had insulted him a day or two since. Moggs junior would of course know why his customer was dining at Alexandrina Cottage, and would have his own feelings, too, upon the occasion.

"Don't you mind him,—no more than nothing," said Neefit, leading the way back into the drawing-room, and passing at the top of the kitchen stairs the young woman with the bit of salmon.

The dinner was not gay. In the first place, Neefit and Mrs. Neefit gave very explicit and very opposite directions as to the manner in which their guests were to walk in to dinner, the result of which was that Ralph was obliged to give his arm to the elder lady, while Ontario carried off the prize. Mrs. Neefit also gave directions as to the places, which were obeyed in spite of an attempt of Neefit's to contravene them. Ontario and Polly sat on one side of the table, while Ralph sat opposite to them. Neefit, when he saw that the arrangement was made and could not be altered, lost his temper and scolded his wife. "Law, papa, what does it matter?" said Polly. Polly's position certainly was unpleasant enough; but she made head against her difficulties gallantly. Ontario, who had begun to guess the truth, said not a word. He was not, however, long in making up his mind that a personal encounter with Mr. Ralph Newton might be good for his system. Mrs. Neefit nagged at her husband, and told him when he complained about the meat, that if he would look after the drinkables that would be quite enough for him to do. Ralph himself found it to be impossible even to look as though things were going right. Never in his life had he been in a position so uncomfortable,—or, as he thought, so disreputable. It was not to be endured that Moggs, his bootmaker, should see him sitting at the table of Neefit, his breeches-maker.

The dinner was at last over, and the port-wine was carried out into the arbour ;—not, on this occasion, by Polly, but by the maid. Polly and Mrs. Neefit went off together, while Ralph crowded into the little summer-house with Moggs and Neefit. In this way half an hour was passed,—a half hour of terrible punishment. But there was worse coming. " Mr. Newton," said Neefit, " I think I heard something about your taking a walk with our Polly. If you like to make a start of it, don't let us keep you. Moggs and I will have a pipe together."

" I also intend to walk with Miss Neefit," said Ontario, standing up bravely.

" Two's company and three's none," said Neefit.

" No doubt," said Ontario ; " no doubt. I feel that myself. Mr. Newton, I've been attached to Miss Neefit these two years. I don't mind saying it out straight before her father. I love Miss Neefit! I don't know, sir, what your ideas are ; but I love Miss Neefit! Perhaps, sir, your ideas may be money ;—my ideas are a pure affection for that young lady. Now, Mr. Newton, you know what my ideas are." Mr. Moggs junior was standing up when he made this speech, and, when he had completed it, he looked round, first upon her father and then upon his rival.

" She's never given you no encouragement," said Neefit. " How dare you speak in that way about my Polly ? "

" I do dare," said Ontario. " There ! "

" Will you tell Mr. Newton that she ever gave you any encouragement ? "

Ontario thought about it for a moment, before he replied. " No ;— I will not," said he. " To say that of any young woman wouldn't be in accord with my ideas."

" Because you can't. It's all gammon. She don't mean to have him, Mr. Newton. You may take my word for that. You go in and ask her if she do. A pretty thing indeed! I can't invite my friend, Mr. Newton, to eat a bit of dinner, and let him walk out with my Polly, but you must interfere. If you had her to-morrow you wouldn't have a shilling with her."

" I don't want a shilling with her!" said Ontario, still standing upon his legs. "I love her. Will Mr. Newton say as fair as that?"

Mr. Newton found it very difficult to say anything. Even had he been thoroughly intent on the design of making Polly his wife, he could not have brought himself to declare his love aloud, as had just been done by Mr. Moggs. "This is a sort of matter that shouldn't be discussed in public," he said at last.

"Public or private, I love her!" said Ontario Moggs with his hand on his heart.

Polly herself was certainly badly treated among them. She got no walk that evening, and received no assurance of undying affection either from one suitor or the other. It became manifest even to Neefit himself that the game could not be played out on this evening. He could not turn Moggs off the premises, because his wife would have interfered. Nor, had he done so, would it have been possible, after such an affair to induce Polly to stir from the house. She certainly had been badly used among them; and so she took occasion to tell her father when the visitors were both gone. They left the house together at about eight, and Polly at that time had not reappeared. Moggs went to the nearest station of the Midland Railway, and Ralph walked to the Swiss Cottage. Certainly Mr. Neefit's little dinner had been unsuccessful; but Ralph Newton, as he went back to London, was almost disposed to think that Providence had interposed to save him.

"I'll tell you what it is, father," said Polly to her papa, as soon as the two visitors had left the house, "if that's the way you are going to go on, I'll never marry anybody as long as I live."

"My dear, it was all your mother," said Mr. Neefit. "Now wasn't it all your mother? I wish she'd been blowed fust!"

CHAPTER X.

SIR THOMAS IN HIS CHAMBERS.

IT will be remembered that Sir Thomas Underwood had declined to give his late ward any advice at that interview which took place in Southampton Buildings;—or rather that the only advice which he had given to the young man was to cut his throat. The idle word had left no impression on Ralph Newton;—but still it had been spoken, and was remembered by Sir Thomas. When he was left alone after the young man's departure he was very unhappy. It was not only that he had spoken a word so idle when he ought to have been grave and wise, but that he felt that he had been altogether remiss in his duty as guide, philosopher, and friend. There were old sorrows, too, on this score. In the main Sir Thomas had discharged well a most troublesome, thankless, and profitless duty towards the son of a man who had not been related to him, and with whom an accidental intimacy had been ripened into friendship by letter rather than by social intercourse. Ralph Newton's father had been the younger brother of the present Gregory Newton, of Newton Priory, and had been the parson of the parish of Peele Newton,—as was now Ralph's younger brother, Gregory. The present squire of Newton had been never married, and the property, as has before been said, had been settled on Ralph, as the male heir,—provided, of course, that his uncle left no legitimate son of his own. It had come to pass that the two brothers, Gregory and Ralph, had quarrelled about matters of property, and had not spoken for years before the death of the younger. Ralph at this time had been just old enough to be brought into the quarrel. There had been questions of cutting timber and of leases, as to which the parson, acting on his son's behalf, had opposed the Squire with much unnecessary bitterness and suspicion. And it was doubtless the case that the Squire resented bitterly an act done by his own father with the view of perpetuating the property in the true line of the Newtons. For when the settlement was made on the marriage of the younger brother, the elder was already the father of a child, whom he loved none the less because that child's mother had not become his wife. So the quarrel had been fostered, and at the time of the parson's death had extended itself to the young man who was his son, and the heir to the estate. When on his death-bed, the parson had asked Mr. Underwood, who had just then entered the House of Commons, to undertake this guardianship; and the lawyer, with many doubts, had consented. He had striven, but striven in vain, to reconcile the uncle and nephew. And, indeed, he was ill-fitted to accomplish such task. He could only write letters on the subject, which were very sensible but very cold;—in all of which he would be careful to explain that the steps which had been taken in regard to the property were in strict conformity with the law. The old Squire would have nothing to do with his heir,— in which resolution he was strengthened by the tidings which reached him of his heir's manner of living. He was taught to believe that everything was going to the dogs with the young man, and was wont to say that Newton Priory, with all its acres, would be found to have gone to the dogs too when his day was done ;—unless, indeed, Ralph should fortunately kill himself by drink or evil living, in which case the property would go to the younger Gregory, the present parson. Now the present parson of Newton was his uncle's friend. Whether that friendship would have been continued had Ralph died and the young clergyman become the heir, may be matter of doubt.

This disagreeable duty of guardianship Sir Thomas had performed with many scruples of conscience, and a determination to do his best;—and he had nearly done it well. But he was a man who could not do it altogether well, let his scruples of conscience be what they might. He had failed in obtaining a father's control over the young man; and even in regard to the property which had passed through his hands,—though he had been careful with it,—he had not been adroit. Even at this moment things had not been settled which should have been settled; and Sir Thomas had felt, when Ralph had spoken of selling all that remained to him and of paying his debts, that there would be fresh trouble, and that he might be forced to own that he had been himself deficient.

And then he told himself,—and did so as soon as Ralph had left him,—that he should have given some counsel to the young man when he came to ask for it. " You had better cut your throat !" In his troubled spirit he had said that, and now his spirit was troubled the more because he had so spoken. He sat for hours thinking of it all. Ralph Newton was the undoubted heir to a very large property. He was now embarrassed,—but all his present debts did not amount to much more than half one year's income of that property which would be his,—probably in about ten years. The Squire might live for twenty years, or might die to-morrow; but his life-interest in the estate, according to the usual calculations, was not worth more than ten years' purchase. Could he, Sir Thomas, have been right to tell a young man, whose prospects were so good, and whose debts, after all, were so light, that he ought to go and cut his throat, as the only way of avoiding a disreputable marriage which would otherwise be forced upon him by the burden of his circumstances ? Would not a guardian, with any true idea of his duty, would not a friend, whose friendship was in any degree real, have found a way out of such difficulties as these?

And then as to the marriage itself,—the proposed marriage with the breeches-maker's daughter,—the more Sir Thomas thought of it the more distasteful did it become to him. He knew that Ralph was unaware of all the evil that would follow such a marriage;— relatives whose every thought and action and word would be distasteful to him; children whose mother would not be a lady, and whose blood would be polluted by an admixture so base;—and, worse still, a life's companion who would be deficient in all those attributes which such a man as Ralph Newton should look for in a wife. Sir Thomas was a man to magnify rather than lesson these evils. And now he allowed his friend,—a man for whose behalf he had bound himself to use all the exercise of friendship,—to go from him with an idea that nothing but suicide could prevent this marriage, simply because there was an amount of debt, which, when compared with the man's prospects, should hardly have been regarded as a burden! As he thought of all this Sir Thomas was very unhappy.

Ralph had left him at about ten o'clock, and he then sat brooding over his misery for about an hour. It was his custom when he remained in his chambers to tell his clerk, Stemm, between nine and ten that nothing more would be wanted. Then Stemm would go, and Sir Thomas would sleep for a while in his chair. But the old clerk never stirred till thus dismissed. It was now eleven, and Sir Thomas knew very well that Stemm would be in his closet. He opened the door and called, and Stemm, aroused from his slumbers, slowly crept into the room. "Joseph," said his master, "I want Mr. Ralph's papers."

"To-night, Sir Thomas?"

"Well;—yes, to-night. I ought to have told you when he went away, but I was thinking of things."

"So I was thinking of things," said Stemm, as he very slowly made his way into the other room, and, climbing up a set of steps which stood there, pulled down from an upper shelf a tin box,—and with it a world of dust. "If you'd have said before that they'd be wanted, Sir Thomas, there wouldn't be such a deal of dry muck," said Stemm, as he put down the box on a chair opposite Sir Thomas's knees.

"And now where is the key?" said Sir Thomas. Stemm shook his head very slowly. "You know, Stemm;—where is it?"

"How am I to know, Sir Thomas? I don't know, Sir Thomas. It's like enough in one of those drawers." Then Stemm pointed to a certain table, and after a while slowly followed his own finger. The drawer was unlocked, and under various loose papers there lay four or five loose keys. "Like enough it's one of these," said Stemm.

" Of course you knew where it was," said Sir Thomas.

" I didn't know nothing at all about it," said Stemm, bobbing his head at his master, and making at the same time a gesture with his lips, whereby he intended to signify that his master was making a fool of himself. Stemm was hardly more than five feet high, and was a wizened dry old man, with a very old yellow wig. He delighted in scolding all the world, and his special delight was in scolding his master. But against all the world he would take his master's part, and had no care in the world except his master's comfort. When Sir Thomas passed an evening at Fulham, Stemm could do as he pleased with himself ; but they were blank evenings with Stemm when Sir Thomas was away. While Sir Thomas was in the next room, he always felt that he was in company, but when Sir Thomas was away, all London, which was open to him, offered him no occupation. " That's the key," said Stemm, picking out one; " but it wasn't I as put it there ; and you didn't tell me as it was there, and I didn't know it was there. I guessed,—just because you do chuck things in there, Sir Thomas."

" What does it matter, Joseph ?" said Sir Thomas.

" It does matter when you say I knowed. I didn't know,—nor I couldn't know. There's the key anyhow."

" You can go now, Joseph," said Sir Thomas.

" Good night, Sir Thomas," said Stemm, retiring slowly, " but I didn't know, Sir Thomas,—nor I couldn't know." Then Sir Thomas unlocked the box, and gradually surrounded himself with the papers which he took from it. It was past one o'clock before he again began to think what he had better do to put Ralph Newton on his legs, and to save him from marrying the breeches-maker's daughter. He sat meditating on that and other things as they came into his mind for over an hour, and then he wrote the following letter to old Mr. Newton. Very many years had passed since he had seen Mr. Newton,—so many that the two men would not have known each other had they met ; but there had been an occasional correspondence between them, and they were presumed to be on amicable terms with each other.

"Southampton Buildings, 14th July, 186—.

" DEAR SIR,—

" I wish to consult you about the affairs of your heir and my late ward, Ralph Newton. Of course I am aware of the unfortunate misunderstanding which has hitherto separated you from him, as to which I believe you will be willing to allow that he, at least, has not been in fault. Though his life has by no means

"I love Miss Neefit! I don't know, sir, what your ideas are; but I love Miss Neefit!"

(See page 71)

The Squire paused a moment, and then asked a question. "What should you say if I proposed to sell Brownriggs?"

(*See page 85*)

been what his friends could have wished it, he is a fine young fellow; and perhaps his errors have arisen as much from his unfortunate position as from any natural tendency to evil on his own part. He has been brought up to great expectations, with the immediate possession of a small fortune. These together have taught him to think that a profession was unnecessary for him, and he has been debarred from those occupations which generally fall in the way of the heir to a large landed property by the unfortunate fact of his entire separation from the estate which will one day be his. Had he been your son instead of your nephew, I think that his life would have been prosperous and useful.

"As it is, he has got into debt, and I fear that the remains of his own property will not more than suffice to free him from his liabilities. Of course he could raise money on his interest in the Newton estate. Hitherto he has not done so; and I am most anxious to save him from a course so ruinous;—as you will be also, I am sure. He has come to me for advice, and I grieve to say, has formed a project of placing himself right again as regards money by offering marriage to the daughter of a retail tradesman. I have reason to believe that hitherto he has not committed himself; but I think that the young woman's father would accept the offer, if made. The money, I do not doubt, would be forthcoming; but the result could not be fortunate. He would then have allied himself with people who are not fit to be his associates, and he would have tied himself to a wife who, whatever may be her merits as a woman, cannot be fit to be the mistress of Newton Priory. But I have not known what advice to give him. I have pointed out to him the miseries of such a match; and I have also told him how surely his prospects for the future would be ruined, were he to attempt to live on money borrowed on the uncertain security of his future inheritance. I have said so much as plainly as I know how to say it;—but I have been unable to point out a third course. I have not ventured to recommend him to make any application to you.

"It seems, however, to me, that I should be remiss in my duty both to him and to you were I not to make you acquainted with his circumstances,—so that you may interfere, should you please to do so, either on his behalf or on behalf of the property. Whatever offence there may have been, I think there can have been none personally from him to yourself. I beg you to believe that I am far from being desirous to dictate to you, or to point out to you this or that as your duty; but I venture to think that you will be obliged to me for giving you information which may lead to the protection of interests which cannot but be dear to you. In conclusion, I will only again say that Ralph himself is clever, well-conditioned, and, as I most truly believe, a thorough gentleman. Were the intercourse

between you that of a father and son, I think you would feel proud
of the relationship.

" I remain, dear sir,
" Very faithfully yours,
" THOMAS UNDERWOOD.

" Gregory Newton, Esq., Newton Priory."

This was written on Friday night, and was posted on the Saturday
morning by the faithful hand of Joseph Stemm ;—who, however,
did not hesitate to declare to himself, as he read the address, that
his master was a fool for his pains. Stemm had never been favourable
to the cause of young Newton, and had considered from the first that
Sir Thomas should have declined the trust that had been imposed
upon him. What good was to be expected from such a guardianship?
And as things had gone on, proving Stemm's prophecies as to young
Newton's career to be true, that trusty clerk had not failed to remind
his master of his own misgivings. " I told you so," had been
repeated by Stemm over and over again, in more phrases than one,
until the repetition had made Sir Thomas very angry. Sir Thomas,
when he gave the letter to Stemm for posting, said not a word of the
contents ; but Stemm knew something of old Mr. Gregory Newton
and the Newton Priory estate. Stemm, moreover, could put two and
two together. " He's a fool for his pains ;—that's all," said Stemm,
as he poked the letter into the box.

During the whole of the next day the matter troubled Sir Thomas.
What if Ralph should go at once to the breeches-maker's daughter,—
the thought of whom made Sir Thomas very sick,—and commit himself before an answer should be received from Mr. Newton ? It was
only on Sunday that an idea struck him that he might still do something further to avoid the evil ;—and with this object he despatched a
note to Ralph, imploring him to wait for a few days before he would
take any steps towards the desperate remedy of matrimony. Then
be begged Ralph to call upon him again on the Wednesday morning.
This note Ralph did not get till he went home on the Sunday evening ;
—at which time, as the reader knows, he had not as yet committed
himself to the desperate remedy.

On the following Tuesday Sir Thomas received the following letter
from Mr. Newton :—

" Newton Priory, 17th July, 186—.

" DEAR SIR,—

" I have received your letter respecting Mr. Ralph Newton's
affairs, in regard to which, as far as they concern himself, I am free
to say that I do not feel much interest. But you are quite right in
your suggestion that my solicitude in respect of the family property

is very great. I need not trouble you by pointing out the nature of my solicitude, but may as well at once make an offer to you, which you, as Mr. Ralph Newton's friend, and as an experienced lawyer, can consider,—and communicate to him, if you think right to do so.

" It seems that he will be driven to raise money on his interest in this property. I have always felt that he would do so, and that from the habits of his life the property would be squandered before it came into his possession. Why should he not sell his reversion, and why should I not buy it? I write in ignorance, but I presume such an arrangement would be legal and honourable on my part. The sum to be given would be named without difficulty by an actuary. I am now fifty-five, and, I believe, in good health. You yourself will probably know within a few thousand pounds what would be the value of the reversion. A proper person would, however, be of course employed.

" I have saved money, but by no means enough for such an outlay as this. I would, however, mortgage the property or sell one half of it, if by doing so I could redeem the other half from Mr. Ralph Newton.

" You no doubt will understand exactly the nature of my offer, and will let me have an answer. I do not know that I can in any other way expedite Mr. Ralph Newton's course in life.

" I am, dear sir,
" Faithfully yours,
" GREGORY NEWTON, Senior."

When Sir Thomas read this he was almost in greater doubt and difficulty than before. The measure proposed by the elder Newton was no doubt legal and honourable, but it could hardly be so carried out as to be efficacious. Ralph could only sell his share of the inheritance ;—or rather his chance of inheriting the estate. Were he to die without a son before his uncle, then his brother would be the heir. The arrangement, however, if practicable, would at once make all things comfortable for Ralph, and would give him, probably, a large unembarrassed revenue,—so large, that the owner of it need certainly have recourse to no discreditable marriage as the means of extricating himself from present calamity. But then Sir Thomas had very strong ideas about a family property. Were Ralph's affairs, indeed, in such disorder as to make it necessary for him to abandon the great prospect of being Newton of Newton? If the breeches-maker's twenty thousand would suffice, surely the thing could be done on cheaper terms than those suggested by the old Squire,—and done without the intervention of Polly Neefit!

CHAPTER XI.

NEWTON PRIORY.

NEWTON PRIORY was at this time inhabited by two gentlemen,— old Gregory Newton, who for miles round was known as the Squire; and his son, Ralph Newton,—his son, but not his heir; a son, however, whom he loved as well as though he had been born with an undoubted right to inherit all those dearly-valued acres. A few lines will tell all that need be told of the Squire's early life,—and indeed of his life down to the present period. In very early days, immediately upon his leaving college, he had travelled abroad and had formed an attachment with a German lady, who by him became the mother of a child. He intended to marry her, hoping to reconcile his father to the match; but before either marriage or reconciliation could take place the young mother, whose babe's life could then only be counted by months, was dead. In the hope that the old man might yield in all things, the infant had been christened Ralph; for the old Squire's name was Ralph, and there had been a Ralph among the Newtons since Newton Priory had existed. But the old Squire had a Ralph of his own,—the father of our Ralph and of the present parson,—who in his time was rector of Peele Newton; and when the tidings of this foreign baby and of the proposed foreign marriage reached the old Squire,—then he urged his second son to marry, and made the settlement of the estate of which the reader has heard. The settlement was natural enough. It simply entailed the property on the male heir of the family in the second generation. It deprived the eldest son of nothing that would be his in accordance with the usual tenure of English primogeniture. Had he married and become the father of a family, his eldest son would have been the heir. But heretofore there had been no such entails in the Newton family; or, at least, he was pleased to think that there had been none such. And when he himself inherited the property early in life,—before he had reached his thirtieth year,—he thought that his father had injured him. His boy was as dear to him, as though the mother had been his honest wife. Then he endeavoured to come to some terms with his brother. He would do anything in order that his child might be Newton of Newton after him. But the parson would come to no terms at all, and was powerless to make any such terms as those which the elder brother required. The parson was honest, self-denying, and proud on behalf of his own children; but he was intrusive in regard to the property, and apt to claim privileges of interference beyond his right as the guardian of his own or of his children's future interests. And so the brothers had quarrelled;—and so the story of Newton Priory is told up to the period at which our story begins.

Gregory Newton and his son Ralph had lived together at the Priory for the last six-and-twenty years, and the young man had grown up as a Newton within the knowledge of all the gentry around them. The story of his birth was public, and it was of course understood that he was not the heir. His father had been too wise on the son's behalf to encourage any concealment. The son was very popular, and deserved to be so; but it was known to all the young men round, and also to all the maidens, that he would not be Newton of Newton. There had been no ill-contrived secret, sufficient to make a difficulty, but not sufficient to save the lad from the pains of his position. Everybody knew it; and yet it can hardly be said that he was treated otherwise than he would have been treated had he been the heir. In the hunting-field there was no more popular man. A point had been stretched in his favour, and he was a magistrate. Mothers were kind to him, for it was known that his father loved him well, and that his father had been a prudent man. In all respects he was treated as though he were the heir. He managed the shooting, and was the trusted friend of all the tenants. Doubtless his father was the more indulgent to him because of the injury that had been done to him. After all, his life promised well as to material prosperity; for, though the Squire, in writing to Sir Thomas, had spoken of selling half the property with the view of keeping the other half for his son, he was already possessed of means that would enable him to make the proposed arrangement without such sacrifice as that. For twenty-four years he had felt that he was bound to make a fortune for his son out of his own income. And he had made a fortune, and mothers knew it, and everybody in the county was very civil to Ralph,—to that Ralph who was not the heir.

But the Squire had never yet quite abandoned the hope that Ralph who was not the heir might yet possess the place; and when he heard of his nephew's doings, heard falsehood as well as truth, from day to day he built up new hopes. He had not expected any such overture as that which had come from Sir Thomas; but if, as he did expect, Ralph the heir should go to the Jews, why should not the Squire purchase the Jews' interest in his own estate? Or, if Ralph the heir should, more wisely, deal with some great money-lending office, why should not he redeem the property through the same? Ralph the heir would surely throw what interest he had into the market, and if so, that interest might be bought by the person to whom it must be of more value than to any other. He had said little about it even to his son;—but he had hoped; and now had come this letter from Sir Thomas. The reader knows the letter and the Squire's answer.

The Squire himself was a very handsome man, tall, broad-shouldered, square-faced, with hair and whiskers almost snow-white already, but which nevertheless gave to him but little sign of age. He was very strong, and could sit in the saddle all day without fatigue. He was given much to farming, and thoroughly understood the duties of a country gentleman. He was hospitable, too; for, though money had been saved, the Priory had ever been kept as one of the pleasantest houses in the county. There had been no wife, no child but the one, and no house in London. The stables, however, had been full of hunters: and it was generally said that no men in Hampshire were better mounted than Gregory the father and Ralph the son. Of the father we will only further say that he was a generous, passionate, persistent, vindictive, and unforgiving man, a bitter enemy and a staunch friend; a thorough-going Tory, who, much as he loved England and Hampshire and Newton Priory, feared that they were all going to the dogs because of Mr. Disraeli and household suffrage; but who felt, in spite of those fears, that to make his son master of Newton Priory after him would be the greatest glory of his life. He had sworn to the young mother on her death-bed that the boy should be to him as though he had been born in wedlock. He had been as good as his word; — and we may say that he was one who had at least that virtue, that he was always as good as his word.

The son was very like the father in face and gait and bearing,—so like that the parentage was marked to the glance of any observer. He was tall, as was his father, and broad across the chest, and strong and active, as his father had ever been. But his face was of a nobler stamp, bearing a surer impress of intellect, and in that respect telling certainly the truth. This Ralph Newton had been educated abroad, his father, with a morbid feeling which he had since done much to conquer, having feared to send him among other young men, the sons of squires and noblemen, who would have known that their comrade was debarred by the disgrace of his birth from inheriting the property of his father. But it may be doubted whether he had not gained as much as he had lost. German and French were the same to him as his native tongue; and he returned to the life of an English country gentleman young enough to learn to ride to hounds, and to live as he found others living around him.

Very little was said, or indeed ever had been said, between the father and son as to their relative position in reference to the property. Ralph,—the illegitimate Ralph,—knew well enough and had always known, that the estate was not to be his. He had known this so long that he did not remember the day when he had not known it. Occasionally the Squire would observe with a curse that this or that could not be done with the property,—such a house pulled down, or such another built, this copse grupped up, or those trees cut down,—because of that reprobate up in London. As to pulling down, there was no probability of interference now, though there had been much of such interference in the life of the old rector. "Ralph," he had once said to his brother the rector, "I'll marry and have a family yet if there is another word about the timber." "I have not the slightest right or even wish to object to your doing so," said the rector; "but as long as things are on their present footing, I shall continue to do my duty." Soon after that it had come to pass that the brothers so quarrelled that all intercourse between them was at an end. Such revenge, such absolute punishment as that which the Squire had threatened, would have been very pleasant to him;—but not even for such pleasure as that would he ruin the boy whom he loved. He did not marry, but saved money, and dreamed of buying up the reversion of his nephew's interest.

His son was just two years older than our Ralph up in London, and his father was desirous that he should marry. "Your wife would be mistress of the house,—as long as I live, at least," he had once said. "There are difficulties about it," said the son. Of course there were difficulties. "I do not know whether it is not better that I should remain unmarried," he said, a few minutes later. "There are men whom marriage does not seem to suit,—I mean as regards their position." The father turned away, and groaned aloud when he was alone. On the evening of that day, as they were sitting together over their wine, the son alluded, not exactly to the same subject, but to the thoughts which had arisen from it within his own mind. "Father," he said, "I don't know whether it wouldn't be better for you to make it up with my cousin, and have him down here."

"What cousin?" said the Squire, turning sharply round.

"With Gregory's eldest brother." The reader will perhaps remember that the Gregory of that day was the parson. "I believe he is a good fellow, and he has done you no harm."

"He has done me all harm."

"No; father; no. We cannot help ourselves, you know. Were he to die, Gregory would be in the same position. It would be better that the family should be kept together."

"I would sooner have the devil here. No consideration on earth shall induce me to allow him to put his foot upon this place. No;— not whilst I live." The son said nothing further, and they sat together in silence for some quarter of an hour,—after which the elder of the two rose from his chair, and, coming round the table, put his hand on the son's shoulder, and kissed his son's brow. "Father," said the young man, "you think that I am troubled by things which hardly touch me at all." "By God, they touch me close enough!" said the elder. This had taken place some month or two before the date of Sir Thomas's letter;—but any reference to the matter of which they were both no doubt always thinking was very rare between them.

Newton Priory was a place which a father might well wish to leave unimpaired to his son. It lay in the north of Hampshire, where that county is joined to Berkshire; and perhaps in England there is no prettier district, no country in which moorland and woodland and pasture are more daintily thrown together to please the eye, in which there is a sweeter air, or a more thorough seeming of English wealth and English beauty and English comfort. Those who know Eversley and Bramshill and Heckfield and Strathfieldsaye will acknowledge that it is so. But then how few are the Englishmen who travel to see the beauties of their own country! Newton Priory, or Newton Peele as the parish was called, lay somewhat west of these places, but was as charming as any of them. The entire parish belonged to Mr. Newton, as did portions of three or four parishes adjoining. The house itself was neither large nor remarkable for its architecture ;— but it was comfortable. The rooms indeed were low, for it had been built in the ungainly days of Queen Anne, with additions in the equally ungainly time of George II., and the passages were long and narrow, and the bedrooms were up and down stairs, as though pains had been taken that no two should be on a level; and the windows were of ugly shape, and the whole mass was uncouth and formless,— partaking neither of the Gothic beauty of the Stuart architecture, nor of the palatial grandeur which has sprung up in our days; and it stood low, giving but little view from the windows. But, nevertheless, there was a family comfort and a warm solidity about the house, which endeared it to those who knew it well. There had been a time in which the present Squire had thought of building for himself an entirely new house, on another site,—on the rising brow of a hill, some quarter of a mile away from his present residence ;—but he had remembered that as he could not leave his estate to his son, it behoved him to spend nothing on the property which duty did not demand from him.

The house stood in a park of some two hundred acres, in which the ground was poor, indeed, but beautifully diversified by rising knolls and little ravines, which seemed to make the space almost unlimited. And then the pines which waved in the Newton woods sighed and moaned with a melody which, in the ears of their owner, was equalled by that of no other fir trees in the world. And the broom was yellower at Newton than elsewhere, and more plentiful; and the heather was sweeter ;—and wild thyme on the grass more fragrant. So at least Mr. Newton was always ready to swear. And all this he could not leave behind him to his son ;—but must die with the knowledge, that as soon as the breath was out of his body, it would become the property of a young man whom he hated! He might not cut down the pine woods, nor disturb those venerable single trees which were the glory of his park;—but there were moments in which he thought that he could take a delight in plough-ing up the furze, and in stripping the hill-sides of the heather. Why should his estate be so beautiful for one who was nothing to him? Would it not be well that he should sell everything that was saleable in order that his own son might be the richer?

On the day after he had written his reply to Sir Thomas he was rambling in the evening with his son through the woods. Nothing could be more beautiful than the park was now;—and Ralph had been speaking of the glory of the place. But something had occurred to make his father revert to the condition of a certain tenant, whose holding on the property was by no means satisfactory either to him-self or to his landlord. "You know, sir," said the son, "I told you last year that Darvell would have to go."

"Where's he to go to?"

"He'll go to the workhouse if he stays here. It will be much better for him to be bought out while there is still something left for him to sell. Nothing can be worse than a man sticking on to land without a shilling of capital."

"Of course it's bad. His father did very well there."

"His father did very well there till he took to drink and died of it. You know where the road parts Darvell's farm and Brownriggs? Just look at the difference of the crops. There's a place with wheat on each side of you. I was looking at them before dinner."

"Brownriggs is in a different parish. Brownriggs is in Bostock."

"But the land is of the same quality. Of course Walker is a different sort of man from Darvell. I believe there are nearly four hundred acres in Brownriggs."

"All that," said the father.

"And Darvell has about seventy;—but the land should be made to bear the same produce per acre."

The Squire paused a moment, and then asked a question. "What should you say if I proposed to sell Brownriggs?" Now there were two or three matters which made the proposition to sell Brownriggs a very wonderful proposition to come from the Squire. In the first place he couldn't sell an acre of the property at all,—of which fact his son was very well aware; and then, of all the farms on the estate it was, perhaps, the best and most prosperous. Mr. Walker, the tenant, was a man in very good circumstances, who hunted, and was popular, and was just the man of whose tenancy no landlord would be ashamed.

"Sell Brownriggs!" said the young man. "Well, yes; I should be surprised. Could you sell it?"

"Not at present," said the Squire.

"How could it be sold at all?" They were now standing at a gate leading out of the park into a field held by the Squire in his own hands, and were both leaning on it. "Father," said the son, "I wish you would not trouble yourself about the estate, but let things come and go just as they have been arranged."

"I prefer to arrange them for myself,—if I can. It comes to this, that it may be possible to buy the reversion of the property. I could not buy it all;—or if I did, must sell a portion of it to raise the money. I have been thinking it over and making calculations. If we let Walker's farm go, and Ingram's, I think I could manage the rest. Of course it would depend on the value of my own life."

There was a long pause, during which they both were still leaning on the gate. "It is a phantom, sir!" the young man said at last.

"What do you mean by a phantom? I don't see any phantom. A reversion can be bought and sold as well as any other property. And if it be sold in this case, I am as free to buy it as any other man."

"Who says it is to be sold, sir?"

"I say so. That prig of a barrister, Sir Thomas Underwood, has already made overtures to me to do something for that young scoundrel in London. He is a scoundrel, for he is spending money that is not his own. And he is now about to make a marriage that will disgrace his family." The Squire probably did not at the moment think of the disgrace which he had brought upon the family by not marrying. "The fact is, that he will have to sell all that he can sell. Why should I not buy it!"

"If he were to die?" suggested the son.

"I wish he would," said the father.

"Don't say that, sir. But if he were to die, Gregory here, who is as good a fellow as ever lived, would come into his shoes. Ralph could sell no more than his own chance."

"We could get Gregory to join us," said the energetic Squire. "He, also, could sell his right."

"You had better leave it as it is, sir," said the son, after another pause. "I feel sure that you will only get yourself into trouble. The place is yours as long as you live, and you should enjoy it."

"And know that it is going to the Jews after me! Not if I can help it. You won't marry, as things are; but you'd marry quick enough if you knew you would remain here after my death;—if you were sure that a child of yours could inherit the estate. I mean to try it on, and it is best that you should know. Whatever he can make over to the Jews he can make over to me;—and as that is what he is about, I shall keep my eyes open. I shall go up to London about it and see Carey next week. A man can do a deal if he sets himself thoroughly to work."

"I'd leave it alone if I were you," said the young man.

"I shall not leave it alone. I mayn't be able to get it all, but I'll do my best to secure a part of it. If any is to go, it had better be the land in Bostock and Twining. I think we could manage to keep Newton entire."

His mind was always on the subject, though it was not often that he said a word about it to the son in whose behalf he was so anxious. His thoughts were always dwelling on it, so that the whole peace and comfort of his life were disturbed. A life-interest in a property is, perhaps, as much as a man desires to have when he for whose protection he is debarred from further privileges of ownership is a well-loved son;—but an entail that limits an owner's rights on behalf of an heir who is not loved, who is looked upon as an enemy, is very grievous. And in this case the man who was so limited, so cramped, so hedged in, and robbed of the true pleasures of ownership, had a son with whom he would have been willing to share everything,—whom it would have been his delight to consult as to every roof to be built, every tree to be cut, every lease to be granted or denied. He would dream of telling his son, with a certain luxury of self-abnegation, that this or that question as to the estate should be settled in the interest, not of the setting, but of the rising sun. "It is your affair rather than mine, my boy;—do as you like." He could picture to himself in his imagination a pleasant, half-mock melancholy in saying such things, and in sharing the reins of government between his own hands and those of his heir. As the sun is falling in the heavens and the evening lights come on, this world's wealth and prosperity afford no pleasure equal to this. It is this delight that enables a man to feel, up to the last moment, that the goods of the world are good. But of all this he was to be robbed,—in spite of all his prudence. It might perhaps sometimes occur to him that he by his own vice had brought this scourge upon his back;—but not the less on that account did it cause him to rebel against the rod. Then there would come upon him the idea that he might cure this evil were his energy sufficient; —and all that he heard of that nephew and heir, whom he hated, tended to make him think that the cure was within his reach. There had been moments in which he had planned a scheme of leading on that reprobate into quicker and deeper destruction, of a pretended friendship with the spendthrift, in order that money for speedier ruin might be lent on that security which the uncle himself was so anxious to possess as his very own. But the scheme of this iniquity, though it had been planned and mapped out in his brain, had never been entertained as a thing really to be done. There are few of us who have not allowed our thoughts to work on this or that villany, arranging the method of its performance, though the performance itself is far enough from our purpose. The amusement is not without its danger,—and to the Squire of Newton had so far been injurious that it had tended to foster his hatred. He would, however, do nothing that was dishonest,—nothing that the world would condemn,—nothing that would not bear the light. The argument to which he mainly trusted was this,—that if Ralph Newton, the heir, had anything to sell and was pleased to sell it, it was as open to him to buy it as to any other. If the reversion of the estate of Newton Priory was in the market, why should he not buy it?—the reversion or any part of the reversion? If such were the case he certainly would buy it.

CHAPTER XII.

MRS. BROWNLOW.

THERE was a certain old Mrs. Brownlow, who inhabited a large old-fashioned house on the Fulham Road, just beyond the fashionable confines of Brompton, but nearer to town than the decidedly rural district of Walham Green and Parson's Green. She was deeply interested in the welfare of the Underwood girls, having been a first cousin of their paternal grandmother, and was very unhappy because their father would not go home and take care of them. She was an excellent old woman, affectionate, charitable, and religious; but she was rather behindhand in general matters, and did not clearly understand much about anything in these latter days. She had heard that Sir Thomas was accustomed to live away from his daughters, and thought it very shocking;—but she knew that Sir Thomas either was or had been in Parliament, and that he was a great lawyer and a very clever man, and therefore she made excuses. She did not quite understand it all, but she thought it expedient to befriend the young ladies. She had heard, too, that Ralph Newton, who had been entrusted to the care of Sir Thomas, was heir to an enormous property; and she thought that the young man ought to marry one of the young ladies. Consequently, whenever she would ask her cousins to tea, she would also ask Mr. Ralph Newton. Sometimes he would come. More frequently he would express his deep regret that a previous engagement prevented him from having the pleasure of accepting Mrs. Brownlow's kind invitation. On all these occasions Mrs. Brownlow invited Sir Thomas;—but Sir Thomas never came. It could hardly have been expected of him that he should do so. Bolsover House was the old-fashioned name of Mrs. Brownlow's residence; and an invitation for tea had been sent for a certain Tuesday in July,—Tuesday, July the 18th. Mrs. Brownlow had of course been informed of the arrival of Mary Bonner,—who was in truth as nearly related to her as the Underwood girls,—and the invitation was given with the express intention of doing honour to

Mary. By the young ladies from Popham Villa the invitation was accepted as a matter of course.

" Will he be there ? " Clary said to her sister.

" I hope not, Clarissa."

" Why do you hope not ? We are not to quarrel; are we, Patty ? "

" No ;—we need not quarrel. But I am afraid of him. He is not good enough, Clary, for you to be unhappy about him. And I fear, —I fear, he is——"

" Is what, Patty ? Do speak it out. There is nothing I hate so much as a mystery."

" I fear he is not genuine ;—what people call honest. He would say things without quite meaning what he says."

" I don't think it. I am sure he is not like that. I may have been a fool——" Then she stopped herself, remembering the whole scene on the lawn. Alas ;—there had been no misunderstanding him. The crime had been forgiven ; but the crime had been a great fact. Since that she had seen him only once, and then he had been so cold ! But yet as he left her he had not been quite cold. Surely that pressure of her hand had meant something ;—had meant something after that great crime ! But why did he not come to her; or why,—which would have been so far, far better,—did he not go to her papa and tell everything to him ? Now, however, there was the chance that she would see him at Bolsover House. That Mrs. Brownlow would ask him was quite a matter of course.

The great event of the evening was to be the introduction of Mrs. Brownlow to the new cousin. They were to drink tea out in the old-fashioned garden behind the house, from which Mrs. Brownlow could retreat into her own room at the first touch of a breath of air. The day was one of which the world at large would declare that there was no breath of air, morning, noon, or night. There was to be quite a party. That was evident from the first to our young ladies, who knew the ways of the house, and who saw that the maids were very smart, and that an extra young woman had been brought in; but they were the first to come,—as was proper.

" My dear Mary," said the old woman to her new guest, " I am glad to see you. I knew your mother and loved her well. I hope you will be happy, my dear." Mrs. Brownlow was a very little old woman, very pretty, very grey, very nicely dressed, and just a little deaf. Mary Bonner kissed her, and murmured some word of thanks. The old woman stood for a few seconds, looking at the beauty,— astounded like the rest of the world. " Somebody told me she was good-looking," Mrs. Brownlow said to Patience ;—" but I did not expect to see her like that."

" Is she not lovely ? "

" She is a miracle, my dear! I hope she won't steal all the nice young men away from you and your sister, eh? Yes ;—yes. What does Mr. Newton say to her? " Patience, however, knew that she need not answer all the questions which Mrs. Brownlow asked, and she left this question unanswered.

Two or three elderly ladies came in, and four or five young ladies, and an old gentleman who sat close to Mrs. Brownlow and squeezed her hand very often, and a middle-aged gentleman who was exceedingly funny, and two young gentlemen who carried the tea and cakes about, but did not talk much. Such were the guests, and the young ladies, who no doubt were accustomed to Mrs. Brownlow's parties, took it all as it was intended, and were not discontented. There was one young lady, however, who longed to ask a question, but durst not. Had Ralph Newton promised that he would come? Clary was sitting between the old gentleman who seemed to be so fond of Mrs. Brownlow's hand and her cousin Mary. She said not a word,—nor, indeed, was there much talking among the guests in general. The merry, middle-aged gentleman did the talking, combining with it a good deal of exhilarating laughter at his own wit. The ladies sat round, and sipped their tea and smiled. That middle-aged gentleman certainly earned his mild refreshment ;—for the party without him must have been very dull. Then there came a breath of air,—or, as Mrs. Brownlow called it, a keen north wind; and the old lady retreated into the house. " Don't let me take anybody else in,—only I can't stand a wind like that." The old gentleman accompanied her, and then the elderly ladies. The young ladies came next, and the man of wit, with the silent young gentlemen, followed, laden with scarfs, parasols, fans, and stray teacups. " I don't think we used to have such cold winds in July," said Mrs. Brownlow. The old gentleman pressed her hand once more, and whispered into her ear that there had certainly been a great change.

Suddenly Ralph Newton was among them. Clarissa had not heard him announced, and to her it seemed as though he had come down from the heavens,—as would have befitted his godship. He was a great favourite with Mrs. Brownlow, who, having heard that he was heir to a very large property, thought that his extravagance became him. According to her views it was his duty to spend a good deal of money, and his duty also to marry Clarissa Underwood. As he was as yet unmarried to any one else, she hardly doubted that he would do his duty. She was a sanguine old lady, who always believed that things would go right. She bustled and fussed on the present occasion with the very evident intention of getting a seat for him next to Clarissa ; but Clarissa was as active in avoiding such an arrangement, and Ralph soon found himself placed between Mary Bonner and a very deaf old lady, who was always present at Mrs.

Brownlow's tea-parties. "I suppose this has all been got up in your honour," he said to Mary. She smiled, and shook her head. "Oh, but it has. I know the dear old lady's ways so well! She would never allow a new Underwood to be at the villa for a month without having a tea-party to consecrate the event."

"Isn't she charming, Mr. Newton;—and so pretty?"

"No end of charming, and awfully pretty. Why are we all in here instead of out in the garden?"

"Mrs. Brownlow thought that it was cold."

"With the thermometer at 80°! What do you think, who ought to know what hot weather means? Are you chilly?"

"Not in the least. We West Indians never find this climate cold the first year. Next year I don't doubt that I shall be full of rheumatism all over, and begging to be taken back to the islands."

Clarissa watched them from over the way as though every word spoken between them had been a treason to herself. And yet she had almost been rude to old Mrs. Brownlow in the manner in which she had placed herself on one side of the circle when the old lady had begged her to sit on the other. Certainly, had she heard all that was said between her lover and her cousin, there was nothing in the words to offend her. She did not hear them; but she could see that Ralph looked into Mary's beautiful face, and that Mary smiled in a demure, silent, self-assured way which was already becoming odious to Clarissa. Clarissa herself, when Ralph looked into her face, would blush and turn away, and feel herself unable to bear the gaze of the god.

In a few minutes there came to be a sudden move, and all the young people trooped back into the garden. It was Ralph Newton who did it, and nobody quite understood how it was done. "Certainly, my dears; certainly," said the old lady. "I dare say the moon is very beautiful. Yes; I see Mr. Ralph. You are not going to take me out, I can tell you. The moon is all very well, but I like to see it through the window. Don't mind me. Mr. Truepeny will stay with me." Mr. Truepeny, who was turned eighty, put out his hand and patted Mrs. Brownlow's arm, and assured her that he wanted nothing better than to stay with her for ever. The witty gentleman did not like the move, because it had been brought about by a new-comer, who had, as it were, taken the wind out of his sails. He lingered awhile, hoping to have weight enough to control the multitude;—in which he failed, and at last made one of the followers. And Clarissa lingered also, because Ralph had been the first to stir. Ralph had gone out with Mary Bonner, and therefore Clarissa had held back. So it came to pass that she found herself walking round the garden with the witty, exhilarating, middle-aged gentleman,— whom, for the present at least, she most cordially hated. "I am not quite sure that our dear old friend isn't right," said the witty man, whose name was Poojean ;—"a chair to sit down upon, and a wall or two around one, and a few little knick-nacks about,— carpets and tables and those sort of things,— are comfortable at times."

" I wonder you should leave them then," said Clarissa.

" Can there be a wonder that I leave them with such temptation as this," said the gallant Poojean. Clarissa hated him worse than ever, and would not look at him, or even make the faintest sign that she heard him. The voice of Ralph Newton through the trees struck her ears ; and yet the voice wasn't loud,—as it would not be if it were addressed with tenderness to Mary. And there was she bound by some indissoluble knot to,—Mr. Poojean. " That Mr. Newton is a friend of yours ? " asked Mr. Poojean.

" Yes ;—a friend of ours," said Clarissa.

" Then I will express my intense admiration for his wit, general character, and personal appearance. Had he been a stranger to you, I should, of course, have insinuated an opinion that he was a fool, a coxcomb, and the very plainest young man I had ever seen. That is the way of the world,—isn't it, Miss Underwood ? "

" I don't know," said Clarissa.

" Oh, yes,—you do. That's the way we all go on. As he is your friend, I can't dare to begin to abuse him till after the third time round the garden."

" I beg, then, that 'there may be only two turns," said Clarissa. But she did not know how to stop, or to get rid of her abominable companion.

" If I mustn't abuse him after three turns, he must be a favourite," said the persevering Poojean. " I suppose he is a favourite. By-the-bye, what a lovely girl that is with whom your favourite was,— shall I say flirting ? "

" That lady is my cousin, Mr. Poojean."

" I didn't say that she was flirting, mind. I wouldn't hint such a thing of any young lady, let her be anybody's cousin. Young ladies never flirt. But young men do sometimes ;—don't they ? After all, it is the best fun going ;—isn't it ? "

" I don't know," said Clarissa. By this time they had got round to the steps leading from the garden to the house. " I think I'll go in, Mr. Poojean." She did go in, and Mr. Poojean was left looking at the moon all alone, as though he had separated himself from all mirth and society for that melancholy but pleasing occupation. He stood there gazing upwards with his thumbs beneath his waistcoat. " Grand,—is it not ? " he said to the first couple that passed him.

" Awfully grand, and beautifully soft, and all the rest of it," said Ralph, as he went on with Mary Bonner by his side.

" That fellow has got no touch of poetry in him ! " said Poojean to himself. In the meantime Clarissa, pausing a moment as she entered through the open window, heard Ralph's cheery voice. How well she knew its tones! And she still paused, with ears erect, striving to catch some word from her cousin's mouth. But Mary's words, if they were words spoken by her, were too low and soft to be caught. " Oh,—if she should turn out to be sly ! " Clarissa said to herself. Was it true that Ralph had been flirting with her,—as that odious man had said ? And why, why, why had Ralph not come to her, if he really loved her, as he had twice told her that he did ? Of course she had not thrown herself into his arms when old Mrs. Brownlow made that foolish fuss. But still he might have come to her. He might have waited for her in the garden. He might have saved her from the " odious vulgarity " of that " abominable old wretch." For in such language did Clarissa describe to herself the exertions to amuse her which had been made by her late companion. But had the Sydney Smith of the day been talking to her, he would have been dull, or the Count D'Orsay of the day, he would have been vulgar, while the sound of Ralph Newton's voice, as he walked with another girl, was reaching her ears. And then, before she had seated herself in Mrs. Brownlow's drawing-room, another idea had struck her. Could it be that Ralph did not come to her because she had told him that she would never forgive him for that crime ? Was it possible that his own shame was so great that he was afraid of her ? If so, could she not let him know that he was,—well, forgiven ? Poor Clarissa ! In the meantime the voices still came to her from the garden, and she still thought that she could distinguish Ralph's low murmurings.

It may be feared that Ralph had no such deep sense of his fault as that suggested. He did remember well enough,—had reflected more than once or twice,—on those words which he had spoken to Clary. Having spoken them he had felt his crime to be their not unnatural accompaniment. At that moment, when he was on the lawn at Fulham, he had thought that it would be very sweet to devote himself to dear Clary,—that Clary was the best and prettiest girl he knew, that, in short, it might be well for him to love her and cherish her and make her his wife. Had not Patience come upon the scene, and disturbed them, he would probably then and there have offered to her his hand and heart. But Patience had come upon the scene, and the offer had not been, as he thought, made. Since all that, which had passed ages ago,—weeks and weeks ago,—there had fallen upon him the prosaic romance of Polly Neefit. He had actually gone down to Hendon to offer himself as a husband to the breeches-maker's daughter. It is true he had hitherto escaped in that quarter also,—or, at any rate, had not as yet committed himself. But the train of incidents and thoughts which had induced him to think seriously of marrying Polly, had made him aware that he could not propose marriage to Sir Thomas Underwood's daughter. From such delight as that he found, on calm reflection, that he had debarred himself by the folly of his past life. It was well that Patience had come upon the scene.

Such being the state of affairs with him, that little episode with Clary being at an end,—or rather, as he thought, never having quite come to a beginning,—and his little arrangement as to Polly Neefit being in abeyance, he was free to amuse himself with this new-comer. Miss Bonner was certainly the most lovely girl he had ever seen. He could imagine no beauty to exceed hers. He knew well enough that her loveliness could be nothing to him ;—but a woman's beauty is in one sense as free as the air in all Christian countries. It is a light shed for the delight, not of one, but of many. There could be no reason why he should not be among the admirers of Miss Bonner. " I expect, you know, to be admitted quite on the terms of an old friend," he said. " I shall call you Mary, and all that kind of thing."

" I don't see your claim," said Miss Bonner

" Oh yes, you do,—and must allow it. I was almost a sort of son of Sir Thomas's,—till he turned me off when I came of age. And Patience and Clarissa are just the same as sisters to me."

" You are not even a cousin, Mr. Newton."

" No ;—I'm not a cousin. It's more like a foster-brother, you know. Of course I shan't call you Mary if you tell me not. How is it to be ? "

" Just for the present I'll be Miss Bonner."

" For a week or so ? "

" Say for a couple of years, and then we'll see how it is."

" You'll be some lucky's fellow's wife long before that. Do you like living at Fulham ? "

" Very much. How should I not like it ? They are so kind to me. And you know, when I first resolved to come home, I thought I should have to go out as a governess,—or, perhaps, as a nursery-maid, if they didn't think me clever enough to teach. I did not expect my uncle to be so good to me. I had never seen him, you know. Is it not odd that my uncle is so little at home ? "

" It is odd. He is writing a book, you see, and he finds that the air of Fulham doesn't suit his brains."

" Oh, Mr. Newton ! "

" And he likes to be quite alone. There isn't a better fellow going than your uncle. I am sure I ought to say so. But he isn't just what I should call,—sociable."

" I think him almost perfection ;—but I do wish he was more at home for their sakes. We'll go in now, Mr. Newton. Patience has gone in, and I haven't seen Clarissa for ever so long."

Soon after this the guests began to go away. Mr. Truepeny gave Mrs. Brownlow's hand the last squeeze, and Mr. Poojean remarked that all terrestrial joys must have an end. "Not but that such hours as these," said he, "have about them a dash of the celestial which almost gives them a claim to eternity." " Horrible fool ! " said Clarissa to her sister, who was standing close to her.

" Mrs. Brownlow would, perhaps, prefer going to bed," said Ralph. Then every one was gone except the Underwoods and Ralph Newton. The girls had on their hats and shawls, and all was prepared for their departure ;—but there was some difficulty about the fly. The Fulham fly which had brought them, and which always took them everywhere, had hitherto omitted to return for them. It was ordered for half-past ten, and now it was eleven. " Are you sure he was told ? " said Clary. Patience had told him herself,—twice. " Then he must be tipsy again," said Clary. Mrs. Brownlow bade them to sit still and wait ; but when the fly did not arrive by half-past eleven, it was necessary that something should be done. There were omnibuses on the road, but they might probably be full. " It is only two miles,—let us walk," said Clary ; and so it was decided.

Ralph insisted on walking with them till he should meet an omnibus or a cab to take him back to London. Patience did her best to save him from such labour, protesting that they would want no such escort. But he would not be gainsayed, and would go with them at least a part of the way. Of course he did not leave them till they had reached the gate of Popham Villa. But when they were starting there arose a difficulty as to the order in which they would marshal themselves ;—a difficulty as to which not a word could be spoken, but which was not the less a difficulty. Clarissa hung back. Ralph had spoken hardly a word to her all the evening. It had better continue so. She was sure that he could not care for her. But she thought that she would be better contented that he should walk with Patience than with Mary Bonner. But Mary took the matter into her own hands, and started off boldly with Patience. Patience hardly approved, but there would be nothing so bad as seeming to disapprove. Clary's heart was in her mouth as she found her arm within his. He had contrived that it should be so, and she could not refuse. Her mind was changed again now, and once more she wished that she could let him know that the crime was forgiven.

" I am so glad to have a word with you at last," he said. " How do you get on with the new cousin ? "

" Very well ;—and how have you got on with her ? "

" You must ask her that. She is very beautiful,—what I call wonderfully beautiful."

" Indeed she is," said Clary, withdrawing almost altogether the weight of her hand from his arm.

" And clever, too,—very clever ; but——"

" But what ? " asked Clary, and the softest, gentlest half-ounce of pressure was restored.

" Well ;—nothing. I like her uncommonly ;—but is she not quite, —quite,—quite——"

" She is quite everything that she ought to be, Ralph."

" I'm sure of that ;—an angel, you know, and all the rest of it. But angels are cold, you know. I don't know that I ever admired a girl so much in my life." The pressure was again lessened,—all but annihilated. " But, somehow, I should never dream of falling in love with your cousin."

" Perhaps you may do so without dreaming," said Clary, as unconsciously she gave back the weight to her hand.

" No ;—I know very well the sort of girl that makes me spoony." This was not very encouraging to poor Clary, but still she presumed that he meant to imply that she herself was a girl of the sort that so acted upon him. And the conversation went on in this way throughout the walk. There was not much encouragement to her, and certainly she did not say a word to him that could make him feel that she wanted encouragement. But still he had been with her, and she had been happy ; and when they parted at the gate, and he again pressed her hand, she thought that things had gone well. " He must know that I have forgiven him now ! " she said to herself.

CHAPTER XIII.

MR. NEEFIT IS DISTURBED.

ON the morning following Mrs. Brownlow's little tea-party Ralph Newton was bound by appointment to call upon Sir Thomas. But before he started on that duty a certain friend of his called upon him. This friend was Mr. Neefit. But before the necessary account of Mr. Neefit's mission is given, the reader must be made acquainted with a few circumstances as they had occurred at Hendon.

It will be remembered perhaps that on the Sunday evening the two rivals left the cottage at the same moment, one taking the road to the right, and the other that to the left,—so that bloodshed, for that occasion at least, was prevented. "Neefit," said his wife to him when they were alone together, "you'll be getting yourself into trouble." "You be blowed," said Neefit. He was very angry with his wife, and was considering what steps he would take to maintain his proper marital and parental authority. He was not going to give way to the weaker vessel in a matter of such paramount importance, as to be made a fool of in his own family. He was quite sure of this, while the strength of the port wine still stood to him; and though he was somewhat more troubled in spirit when his wife began to bully him on the next morning, he still had valour enough to say that Ontario Moggs also might be—blowed.

On the Monday, when he eturned home and asked for Polly, he found that Polly was out walking. Mrs. Neefit did not at once tell him that Moggs was walking with her, but such was the fact. Just at five o'clock Moggs had presented himself at the cottage,—knowing very well, sly dog that he was, the breeches-maker's hour of return, which took place always precisely at four minutes past six,—and boldly demanded an interview with Polly. "I should like to hear what she's got to say to me," said he, looking boldly, almost savagely, into Mrs. Neefit's face. According to that matron's ideas this was the proper way in which maidens should be wooed and won ; and, though Polly had at first declared that she had nothing at all to say to Mr. Moggs, she allowed herself at last to be led forth. Till they had passed the railway station on the road leading away from London, Ontario said not a word of his purpose. Polly, feeling that silence was awkward, and finding that she was being hurried along at a tremendous pace, spoke of the weather and of the heat, and expostulated. "It is hot, very hot," said Ontario, taking off his hat and wiping his brow,—"but there are moments in a man's life when he can't go slow."

"Then there are moments in his life when he must go on by himself," said Polly. But her pluck was too good for her to desert him at such a moment, and, although he hardly moderated his pace till he had passed the railway station, she kept by his side. As things had gone so far it might be quite as well now that she should hear what he had to say. A dim, hazy idea had crossed the mind of Moggs that it would be as well that he should get out into the country before he began his task, and that the line of the railway which passed beneath the road about a quarter of a mile beyond Mr. Neefit's cottage, might be considered as the boundary which divided the town from pastoral joys. He waited, therefore, till the bridge was behind them, till they had passed the station, which was close to the bridge ;—and then he began. "Polly," said he, "you know what brings me here."

Polly did know very well, but she was not bound to confess such knowledge. "You've brought me here, Mr. Moggs, and that's all I know," she said.

"Yes ;—I've brought you here. Polly, what took place last night made me very unhappy,—very unhappy indeed."

"I can't help that, Mr. Moggs."

"Not that I mean to blame you."

"Blame me ! I should think not. Blame me, indeed ! Why are you to blame anybody because father chooses to ask whom he pleases to dinner ? A pretty thing indeed, if father isn't to have whom he likes in his own house."

"Polly, you know what I mean."

"I know you made a great goose of yourself last night, and I didn't feel a bit obliged to you."

"No, I didn't. I wasn't a goose at all. I don't say but what I'm as big a fool as most men. I don't mean to stick up for myself. I know well enough that I am foolish often. But I wasn't foolish last night. What was he there for ?"

"What business have you to ask, Mr. Moggs ? "

"All the business in life. Love ;—real love. That's why I have business. That young man, who is, I suppose, what you call a swell."

"Don't put words into my mouth, Mr. Moggs. I don't call him anything of the kind."

"He's a gentleman."

"Yes ;—he is a gentleman,—I suppose."

"And I'm a tradesman,—a bootmaker."

"So is father a tradesman, and if you mean to tell me that I turn up my nose at people the same as father is, you may just go back to London and think what you like about me. I won't put up with it from you or anybody. A tradesman to me is as good as anybody,—if he is as good. There."

" Oh, Polly, you do look so beautiful ! "

" Bother ! "

" When you say that, and speak in that way, I think you as good as you are beautiful."

" Remember,—I don't say a word against what you call—— gentlemen. I take 'em just as they come. Mr. Newton is a very nice young man."

" Are you going to take him, Polly ? "

" How can I take him when he has never asked me ? You are not my father, Mr. Moggs, not yet my uncle. What right have you to question me ? If I was going to take him, I shouldn't want your leave."

" Polly, you ought to be honest."

" I am honest."

" Will you hear me, Polly ? "

" No, I won't."

" You won't ! Is that answer to go for always ? "

" Yes, it is. You come and tease and say uncivil things, and I don't choose to be bullied. What right have you to talk to me about Mr. Newton ? Did I ever give you any right ? Honest indeed ! What right have you to talk to me about being honest ? "

" It's all true, dear."

" Very well, then. Hold your tongue, and don't say such things. Honest indeed ! If I were to take the young man to-morrow, that would not make me dishonest."

" It's all true, dear, and I· beg your pardon. If I have offended you, I will beg your pardon."

" Never mind about that ;—only don't say foolish things."

" Is it foolish, Polly, to say that I love you ? And if I love you, can I like to see a young fellow like Mr. Newton hanging about after you ? He doesn't love you. He can't love you,—as I do. Your father brings him here because he is a gentleman."

" I don't think anything of his being a gentleman."

" But think of me. Of course I was unhappy, wretched,—miserable. I knew why he was there. You can understand, Polly, that when a man really loves he must be the miserablest or the happiest of human beings."

" I don't understand anything about it."

" I wish you would let me teach you."

" I don't want to learn, and I doubt whether you'd make a good master. I really must go back now, Mr. Moggs. I came out because mother said I'd better. I don't know that it could do any good if we were to walk on to Edgeware." And so saying, Polly turned back.

He walked beside her half the way home in silence, thinking that if he could only choose the proper words and the proper tone he might yet prevail; but feeling that the proper words and the proper tone were altogether out of his reach. On those favourite subjects, the ballot, or the power of strikes, he could always find the proper words and the proper tone when he rose upon his legs at the Cheshire Cheese;—and yet, much as he loved the ballot, he loved Polly Neefit infinitely more dearly. When at the Cheshire Cheese he was a man; but now, walking with the girl of his heart, he felt himself to be a bootmaker, and the smell of the leather depressed him. It was evident that she would walk the whole way home in silence, if he would permit it. The railway station was already again in sight, when he stopped her on the pathway, and made one more attempt. "You believe me, when I say that I love you?"

"I don't know, Mr. Moggs."

"Oh, Polly, you don't know!'

"But it doesn't signify,—not the least. I ain't bound to take a man because he loves me."

"You won't take Mr. Newton;—will you?"

"I don't know. I won't say anything about it. Mr. Newton is nothing to you." Then there was a pause. "If you think, Mr. Moggs, that you can recommend yourself to a young woman by such tantrums as there were going on last night, you are very much mistaken. That's not the way to win me."

"I wish I knew which was the way."

"Mr. Newton never said a word."

"Your father told him to take you out a-walking before my very eyes! Was I to bear that? Think of it, Polly. You mayn't care for me, and I don't suppose you do; but you may understand what my feelings were. What would you have thought of me if I'd stayed there, smoking, and borne it quiet,—and you going about with that young man? I'll tell you what it is, Polly, I couldn't bear it, and I won't. There;—and now you know what I mean." At this point in his speech he took off his hat and waved it in the air. "I won't bear it. There are things a man can't bear,—can't bear,—can't bear. Oh, Polly! if you could only be brought to understand what it is that I feel!"

After all, he didn't do it so very badly. There was just a tear in the corner of Polly's eye, though Polly was very careful that he shouldn't see it. And Polly did know well enough that he was in earnest,—that he was, in fact, true. But then he was gawky and ungainly. It was not that he was a shoemaker. Could he have had his own wits, and danced like the gasfitter, he might have won her still, against Ralph Newton, with all his blood and white hands. But poor Ontario was, as regarded externals, so ill a subject for a great passion!

" And where have you been, Polly ? " said her father, as soon as she entered the house.

" I have been walking with Ontario Moggs," said Polly boldly.

" What have you been saying to him ? I won't have you walk with Ontario Moggs. I and your mother 'll have to fall out if this kind of thing goes on."

" Don't be silly, father."

" What do you mean by that, miss ? "

" It is silly. Why shouldn't I walk with him ? Haven't I known him all my life, and walked with him scores of times ? Isn't it silly, father ? Don't I know that if I told you I loved Ontario Moggs, you'd let me marry him to-morrow ? "

" He'd have to take you in what you stand up in."

" He wouldn't desire anything better. I'll say that for him. He's true and honest. I'd love him if I could,—only, somehow I don't."

" You've told him you didn't,—once and for all ? "

" I don't know about that, father. He'll come again, you may be sure. He's one of that sort that isn't easily said nay to. If you mean,—have I said yes ?—I haven't. I'll never say yes to any man unless I love him. When I do say it I shall mean it,—whether it's Onty Moggs or anybody else. I'm not going to be given away, you know, like a birthday present, out of a shop. There's nobody can give me away, father,—only myself." To all which utterances of a rebellious spirit the breeches-maker made no answer. He knew that Polly would, at least, be true to him ; and, as she was as yet free, the field was still open to his candidate. He believed thoroughly that had not his wife interfered, and asked the bootmaker to join that unfortunate dinner party, his daughter and Ralph Newton would now have been engaged together. And probably it might have been so. When first it had been whispered to Polly that that handsome and very agreeable young gentleman, Mr. Ralph Newton, might become a suitor for her hand, she had chucked up her head and declared to her mother that she didn't intend to take a husband of her father's choosing ; but as she came to know Ralph a little, she did find that he was good-looking and agreeable,—and her heart did flutter at the idea of becoming the wife of a real, undoubted gentle-man. She meant to have her grand passion, and she must be quite sure that Mr. Newton loved her. But she didn't see any reason why Mr. Newton shouldn't love her, and, upon the whole, she was inclined to obey her father rather than to disobey him. And it might still be that he should win her ;—for he had done nothing to disgrace himself in her sight. But there did lurk within her bosom some dim idea that he should have bestirred himself more thoroughly on that Sunday evening, and not have allowed himself to be driven out of the field by Ontario Moggs. She wronged him there, as indeed he had had no alternative, unless he had followed her up to her bed-room.

Mr. Neefit, when he found that no harm had as yet been done, resolved that he would return to the charge. It has been before observed that he lacked something in delicacy, but what he did so lack he made up in persistency. He had been unable to impute any blame to Ralph as to that evening. He felt that he rather owed an apology to his favourite candidate. He would make the apology, and inform the favourite candidate, at the same time, that the course was still open to him. With these views he left Conduit Street early on the Wednesday morning, and called on Ralph at his rooms. " Mr. Newton," he said, hastening at once upon the grand subject, " I hope you didn't think as I was to blame in having Moggs at our little dinner on Sunday." Ralph declared that he had never thought of imputing blame to any one. " But it was,—as awk'ard as awk'ard could be. It was my wife's doing. Of course you can see how it all is. That chap has been hankering after Polly ever since she was in her teens. But, Lord love you, Captain, he ain't a chance with her. He was there again o' Monday, but the girl wouldn't have a word to say to him." Ralph sat silent, and very grave. He was taken now somewhat by surprise, having felt, up to this moment, that he would at least have the advantage of a further interview with Sir Thomas, before he need say another word to Mr. Neefit. " What I want you to do, Captain, is just to pop it, straight off, to my girl. I know she'd take you, because of her way of looking. Not, mind, that she ever said so. Oh, no. But the way to find out is just to ask the question."

" You see, Mr. Neefit, it wasn't very easy to ask it last Sunday," said Ralph, attempting to laugh.

" Moggs has been at her again," said Neefit. This argument was good. Had Ralph been as anxious as Moggs, he would have made his opportunity.

" And, to tell you the truth, Mr. Neefit—— "

" Well, sir ? "

" There is nothing so disagreeable as interfering in families. I admire your daughter amazingly."

" She's a trump, Mr. Newton."

" She is indeed ;—and I thoroughly appreciate the great generosity of your offer."

" I'll be as good as my word, Mr. Newton. The money shall be all there,—down on the nail."

" But, you see, your wife is against me."

" Blow my wife. You don't think Polly 'd do what her mother tells her ? Who's got the money-bag ? That's the question. You go down and pop it straight. You ain't afraid of an old woman, I suppose ;—nor yet of a young un. Don't mind waiting for more dinners, or anything of that kind. They likes a man to be hot about it;—that's what they likes. You're sure to find her any time before dinner;—that's at one, you know. May be she mayn't be figged out fine, but you won't mind that. I'll go bail you'll find the flesh and blood all right. Just you make your way in, and say what you've got to say. I'll make it straight with the old woman afterwards."

Ralph Newton had hitherto rather prided himself on his happy management of young ladies. He was not ordinarily much afflicted by shyness, and conceived himself able to declare a passion, perhaps whether felt or feigned, as well as another. And now he was being taught how to go a-wooing by his breeches-maker! He did not altogether like it, and, as at this moment his mind was rather set against the Hendon matrimonial speculation, he was disposed to resent it. "I think you're making a little mistake, Mr. Neefit," he said.

"What mistake? I don't know as I'm making any mistake. You'll be making a mistake, and so you'll find when the plum's gone."

"It's just this, you know. When you suggested this thing to me—— "

"Well;—yes; I did suggest it, and I ain't ashamed of it."

"I was awfully grateful. I had met your daughter once or twice, and I told you I admired her ever so much."

"That's true;—but you didn't admire her a bit more than what she's entitled to."

"I'm sure of that. But then I thought I ought,—just to,—know her a little better, you see. And then how could I presume to think she'd take me till she knew me a little better?"

"Presume to think! Is that all you know about young women? Pop the question right out, and give her a buss. That's the way."

Newton paused a moment before he spoke, and looked very grave. "I think you're driving me a little too fast, Mr. Neefit," he said at last.

"The deuce I am! Driving you too fast. What does that mean?"

"There must be a little management and deliberation in these things. If I were to do as you propose, I should not recommend myself to your daughter; and I should myself feel that, at the most important crisis of my life, I was allowing myself to be hurried beyond my judgment." These words were spoken with a slow solemnity of demeanour, and a tone of voice so serious that for a moment they perfectly awed the breeches-maker. Ralph was almost successful in reducing his proposed father-in-law to a state of absolute subjection. Mr. Neefit was all but induced to forget that he stood there with twenty thousand pounds in his pocket. There came a drop or two of perspiration on his brow, and his large saucer eyes almost quailed before those of his debtor. But at last he rallied himself,—though not entirely. He could not quite assume that self-assertion which he knew that his position would have warranted; but he did keep his flag up after a fashion. "I dare say you know your own business best, Mr. Newton;—only them's not my ideas; that's all. I come to you fair and honest, and I repeats the same. Good morning, Mr. Newton." So he went, and nothing had been settled.

To say that Ralph had even yet made up his mind would be to give him praise which was not his due. He was still doubting, though in his doubts the idea of marrying Polly Neefit became more indistinct, and less alluring than ever. By this time he almost hated Mr. Neefit, and most unjustly regarded that man as a persecutor, who was taking advantage of his pecuniary ascendancy to trample on him. "He thinks I must take his daughter because I owe him two or three hundred pounds." Such were Ralph Newton's thoughts about the breeches-maker,—which thoughts were very unjust. Neefit was certainly vulgar, illiterate, and indelicate; but he was a man who could do a generous action, and having offered his daughter to this young aristocrat would have scorned to trouble him afterwards about his "little bill." Ralph sat trying to think for about an hour, and then walked to Southampton Buildings. He had not much hope as he went. Indeed hope hardly entered into his feelings. Sir Thomas would of course say unpleasant words to him, and of course he would be unable to answer them. There was no ground for hoping anything,—unless indeed he could make himself happy in a snug little box in a hunting country, with Polly Neefit for his wife, living on the interest of the breeches-maker's money. He was quite alive to the fact that in this position he would in truth be the most miserable dog in existence,—that it would be infinitely better for him to turn his prospects into cash, and buy sheep in Australia, or cattle in South America, or to grow corn in Canada. Any life would be better than one supported in comfortable idleness on Mr. Neefit's savings. Nevertheless he felt that that would most probably be his doom. The sheep or the cattle or the corn required an amount of energy which he no longer possessed. There were the four horses at the Moonbeam;—and he could ride them to hounds as well as any man. So much he could do, and would seem in doing it to be full of life. But as for selling the four horses, and changing altogether the mode of his life,—that was more than he had vitality left to perform. Such was the measure which he took of himself, and in taking it he despised himself thoroughly,—knowing well how poor a creature he was.

Sir Thomas told him readily what he had done, giving him to read a copy of his letter to Mr. Newton and Mr. Newton's reply. "I can do nothing more," said Sir Thomas. "I hope you have given up the sad notion of marrying that young woman." Ralph sat still and listened. "No good, I think, can come of that," continued Sir Thomas. "If you are in truth compelled to part with your reversion to the Newton estate,—which is in itself a property of great value,—I do not doubt but your uncle will purchase it at its worth. It is a thousand pities that prospects so noble should have been dissipated by early imprudence."

"That's quite true, Sir Thomas," said Ralph, in a loud ringing tone, which seemed to imply that let things be as bad as they might he did not mean to make a poor mouth of them. It was his mask for the occasion, and it sufficed to hide his misery from Sir Thomas.

"If you think of selling what you have to sell," continued Sir Thomas, "you had better take Mr. Newton's letter and put it into the hands of your own attorney. It will be ten times better than going to the money-lending companies for advances. If I had the means of helping you myself, I would do it."

"Oh, Sir Thomas!"

"But I have not. I should be robbing my own girls, which I am sure you would not wish."

"That is quite out of the question, Sir Thomas."

"If you do resolve on selling the estate, you had better come to me as the thing goes on. I can't do much, but I may perhaps be able to see that nothing improper is proposed for you to do. Good-bye, Ralph. Anything will be better than marrying that what-d'ye-callem's daughter."

Ralph, as he walked westwards towards the club, was by no means sure that Sir Thomas had been right in this. By marrying Polly he would, after all, keep the property.

Just by the lions in Trafalgar Square he met Ontario Moggs. Ontario Moggs scowled at him, and cut him dead.

CHAPTER XIV

THE REV. GREGORY NEWTON.

IT was quite at the end of July, in the very hottest days of a very hot summer, that Squire Newton left Newton Priory for London, intent upon law business, and filled with ambition to purchase the right of leaving his own estate to any heir whom he might himself select. He left his son alone at the Priory; but his son and the parson were sure to be together on such an occasion. Ralph,—the country Ralph,—dined at the Rectory on the day that his father started; and on every succeeding day, Gregory, the parson, dined up at the large house. It was a thing altogether understood at the Priory that the present parson Gregory was altogether exempted from the anathema which had been pronounced against the heir and against the memory of the heir's father. Gregory simply filled the place which might have been his had there been no crushing entail, and was, moreover, so sweet and gentle-hearted a fellow that it was impossible not to love him. He was a tall, slender man, somewhat narrow-chested, bright-eyed, with a kind-looking sweet mouth, a small well-cut nose, dark but not black hair, and a dimple on his chin. He always went with his hands in his pockets, walking quick, but shuffling sometimes in step as though with hesitation, stooping somewhat, absent occasionally, going about with his chin stuck out before him, as though he were seeking something,—he knew not what. A more generous fellow, who delighted more in giving, hesitated more in asking, more averse to begging though a friend of beggars, less self-arrogant, or self-seeking, or more devoted to his profession, never lived. He was a man with prejudices,—kindly, gentlemanlike, amiable prejudices. He thought that a clergyman should be a graduate from one of the three universities,—including Trinity, Dublin ; and he thought, also, that a clergyman should be a gentleman. He thought that Dissenters were,—a great mistake. He thought that Convocation should be potential. He thought that the Church had certain powers and privileges which Parliament could not take away except by spoliation. He thought that a parson should always be well-dressed,—according to his order. He thought that the bishop of his diocese was the purest, best, and noblest peer in England. He thought that Newton Churchyard was, of all spots on earth, the most lovely. He thought very little of himself. And he thought that of all the delights given by God for the delectation of his creatures, the love of Clarissa Underwood would be the most delightful. In all these thinkings he was astray, carried away by prejudices which he was not strong enough to withstand. But the joint effect of so many faults in judgment was not disagreeable ; and, as one result of that effect, Gregory Newton was loved and respected and believed in by all men and women, poor and rich, who lived within knowledge of his name. His uncle Gregory, who was wont to be severe in his judgment on men, would declare that the Rev. Gregory,—as he was called,—was perfect. But then the Squire was a man who was himself very much subject to prejudices.

There was now, and ever had been, great freedom of discussion between Ralph Newton of the Priory and his cousin Gregory,—if under the circumstances the two young men may be called cousins, —respecting the affairs of the property. There was naturally much to check or to prevent such freedom. Their own interests in regard to the property were, as far as they went, adverse. The young parson might possibly inherit the whole of the estate, whereas he was aware that the present Squire would move heaven and earth to leave it, or a portion of it, to his own son. Gregory had always taken his brother's part before the Squire ; and the Squire, much as he liked the parson, was never slow in abusing the parson's brother. It would have been no more than natural had the question of the property been, by tacit agreement, always kept out of sight between the two young men. But they had grown up from boyhood together as firm friends, and there was no reticence between them on this all-important subject. The Squire's son had never known his mother; and could therefore speak of his own position as would hardly have been possible to him had any memory of her form or person remained with him. And then, though their interests were opposite, nothing that either could say would much affect those interests.

The two men were sitting on the lawn at the Priory after dinner, smoking cigars, and Ralph,—this other Ralph,—had just told the parson of his intention of joining his father in London. " I don't see that I can do any good," said Ralph, " but he wishes it, and of course I shall go."

" You won't see my brother, I suppose ? "

" I should think not. You know what my father's feelings are, and I certainly shall not go out of my way to offend them. I have no animosity against Ralph ; but I could do no good by opposing my father."

" No," said the parson, " not but what I wish it were otherwise. It is a trouble to me that I cannot have Ralph here ;—though perhaps he would not care to come."

" I feel it hard too, that he should not be allowed to see a place which, in a measure, belongs to him. I wish with all my heart that my father did not think so much about the estate. Much as I love the old place, I can hardly think about it without bitterness. Had my father and your brother been on good terms together, there would have been none of that. Nothing that he could do,—no success in his efforts,—can make me be as I should have been had I been born his heir. It is a misfortune, and of course one feels it ; but I think I should feel it less were he not so fixed in his purpose to undo what can never be undone."

" He will never succeed," said Gregory.

" Probably not ;—though, for that matter, I suppose Ralph will be driven to raise money on his inheritance."

" He will never sell the property."

" It seems that he does spend money faster than he can get it."

" He may have done so."

" Is he not always in debt to you yourself ? Is he not now thinking of marrying some tradesman's daughter to relieve him of his embarrassments ? We have to own, I suppose, that Master Ralph has made a mess of his money matters ? " The parson, who couldn't deny the fact, hardly knew what to say on his brother's behalf. " I protest to you, Greg., that if my father were to tell me that he had changed his mind, and paid your brother's debts out of sheer kindness and uncleship, and the rest of it, I should be well pleased. But he won't do that, and it does seem to me probable that the estate will get into the hands of Jews, financiers, and professional money-dealers, unless my father can save it. You wouldn't be glad to see some shopkeeper's daughter calling herself Mrs. Newton of Newton."

"A shopkeeper's daughter need not necessarily be a—a—a bad sort of woman," said Gregory.

"The chances are that a shopkeeper's daughter will not be an educated lady. Come, Greg.;—you cannot say that it is the kind of way out of the mess you would approve."

"I am so sorry that there should be any mess at all!"

"Just so. It is a pity that there should be any mess;—is not it? Come, old fellow, drink your coffee, and let us take a turn across the park. I want to see what Larkin is doing about those sheep. I often feel that my coming into the world was a mess altogether; though, now that I am here, I must make the best of it. If I hadn't come, my father would have married, and had a score of children, and Master Ralph would have been none the better for it."

"You'll go and see the Underwoods," said the parson, as they were walking across the park.

"If you wish it, I will."

"I do wish it. They know all tne nistory as a matter of course. It cannot be otherwise. And they have so often heard me talk of you. The girls are simply perfect. I shall write to Miss Underwood, and tell her that you will call. I hope, too, that you will see Sir Thomas. It would be so much better that he should know you."

That same night Gregory Newton wrote the two following letters before he went to bed;—the first written was to Miss Underwood, and the second to his brother; but we will place the latter first;—

"Newton, 4th August, 186—.

"MY DEAR RALPH,—

"No doubt you know by this time that my uncle, Gregory, is in London, though you will probably not have seen him. I understand that he has come up with the express purpose of making some settlement in regard to the property, on account of your embarrassments. I need not tell you how sorry I am that the state of your affairs should make this necessary. Ralph goes up also to-morrow;—and though he does not purpose to hunt you up, I hope that you may meet. You know what I think of him, and how much I wish that you two could be friends. He is as generous as the sun, and as just as he is generous. Every Newton ought to make him welcome as one of the family.

"As to money, I do not know what may be the state of your affairs.

I only hear from him what he hears from his father. Sooner than that you should endanger your inheritance here I will make any sacrifice,—if there be anything that I can do. You are welcome to sell my share of the Holborn property, and you can pay me after my uncle's death. I can get on very well with my living, as it is not probable that I shall marry. At any rate, understand that I should infinitely prefer to lose every shilling of the London property to hearing that you had imperilled your position here at Newton. I do not suppose that what I have can go far;—but as far as it will go it is at your service. You can show this letter to Sir Thomas if you think fit.

"I could say ever so much more, only that you will know it all without my saying it. And I cannot bear that you should think that I would preach sermons to you. Never mind what I said before about the money that I wanted then. I can do without it now. My uncle will pay for the entire repair of the chancel out of his own pocket. Ever so much must be left undone till more money comes in. Money does come in from this quarter or from that, by God's help. As for the church rates, of course I regret them. But we have to take things in a lump, and it is certainly the fact that we spend ten times as much on the churches as was spent fifty years ago.

"Your most affectionate brother,

"GREGORY NEWTON."

The other letter was much shorter, and was addressed to Patience Underwood;—

"Newton Peele Parsonage, 4th August, 186—.

"MY DEAR MISS UNDERWOOD,—

"My cousin, Mr. Ralph Newton, of whom you have heard me speak so often, is going up to London, and I have asked him to call at Popham Villa, because I am desirous that so very dear a friend of mine should know other friends whom I love so dearly. I am sure you will receive him kindly for my sake, and that you will like him for his own. There are reasons why I wish that your father should know him.

"Give my most affectionate love to your sister. I can send her no other message, and I do not think she will be angry with me for sending that. It cannot hurt her; and she and you at least know how honest and how true it is. Distance and time make no difference. It is as though I were on the lawn with her now.

"Most sincerely yours,

"GREGORY NEWTON."

When he had written this in the little book-room of his parsonage he opened the window, and, crossing the garden, seated himself on a low brick wall, which divided his small domain from the churchyard. The night was bright with stars, but there was no moon in the heavens, and the gloom of the old ivy-coloured church tower was complete. But all the outlines of the place were so well known to him that he could trace them all in the dim light. After a while he got down among the graves, and with slow steps walked round and round the precincts of his church. Here, at least, in this spot, close to the house of God which was his own church, within this hallowed enclosure, which was his own freehold in a peculiar manner, he could, after a fashion, be happy, in spite of the misfortunes of himself and his family. His lines had been laid for him in very pleasant places. According to his ideas there was no position among the children of men more blessed, more diversified, more useful, more noble, than that which had been awarded to him,—if only, by God's help, he could perform with adequate zeal and ability the high duties which had been entrusted to him. Things outside were dark,—at least, so said the squires and parsons around him, with whom he was wont to associate. His uncle, Gregory, was sure that all things were going to the dogs, since a so-called Tory leader had become an advocate for household suffrage, and real Tory gentlemen had condescended to follow him. But to our parson it had always seemed that there was still a fresh running stream of water for him who would care to drink from a fresh stream. He heard much of unbelief, and of the professors of unbelief, both within and without the great Church ;—but in that little church with which he was personally concerned there were more worshippers now than there had ever been before. And he heard, too, how certain well-esteemed preachers and prophets of the day talked loudly of the sins of the people, and foretold destruction such as was the destruction of Gomorrah ;—but to him it seemed that the people of his village were more honest, less given to drink, and certainly better educated than their fathers. In all which thoughts he found matter for hope and encouragement in his daily life. And he set himself to work diligently, placing all this as a balance against his private sorrows, so that he might teach himself to take that world, of which he himself was the centre, as one whole,—and so to walk on rejoicing.

The one great sorrow of his life, the thorn in the flesh which was always festering, the wound which would not be cured, the grief for which there was no remedy, was his love for Clarissa Underwood. He had asked her thrice to be his wife,—with very little interval, indeed, between the separate prayers,—and had been so answered that he entertained no hope. Had there been any faintest expectation in his mind that Clarissa would at last become his wife he would have been deterred by a sense of duty from making to his brother that generous offer of all the property he owned. But he had no such hope. Clarissa had given thrice that answer, which of all answers is the most grievous to the true-hearted lover. "She felt for him unbounded esteem, and would always regard him as a friend." A short decided negative, or a doubtful no, or even an indignant repulse, may be changed,—may give way to second convictions, or to better acquaintance, or to altered circumstances, or even simply to per-severance. But an assurance of esteem and friendship means, and only can mean, that the lady regards her lover as she might do some old uncle or patriarchal family connection, whom, after a fashion, she loves, but who can never be to her the one creature to be worshipped above all others.

Such were Gregory Newton's ideas as to his own chance of success, and, so believing, he had resolved that he would never press his suit again. He endeavoured to conquer his love ;—but that he found to be impossible. He thought that it was so impossible that he had determined to give up the endeavour. Though he would have advised others that by God's mercy all sorrows in this world could be cured, he told himself,—without arraigning God's mercy,—that for him this sorrow could not be cured. He did not scruple, therefore, to assure his brother that he would not marry,—nor did he hesitate, in writing to Patience Underwood, to assure her that his love for her sister was unchangeable. In saying so he urged no suit ;—but it was impossible that he should write to the house without some message, and none other from him to her could be a true message. It could not hurt her. It would not even give her the trouble to think whether she had decided well. He quite understood the nature of the love he wanted, —a love that would have felt it to be all happiness to lean upon his bosom. Without this love he would not have wished to take her ;— and with such love as that he knew he could not fill her heart. Therefore it was that he would satisfy himself with walking round the churchyard of Newton Peele, and telling himself that the pleasure of this world was best to be found in the pursuit of the joys of the next.

CHAPTER XV.

CLARISSA WAITS.

WHEN Patience and Clarissa had got to their own room on the night on which they had walked back from Mrs. Brownlow's house to Popham Villa,—during all which long walk Clarissa's hand had lain gently upon Ralph Newton's arm,—the elder sister looked painfully and anxiously into the younger's face, in order that, if it were possible, she might learn without direct enquiry what had been said during that hour of close communion. Had Ralph meant to speak there could have been no time more appropriate. And Patience hardly knew what she herself wished,—except that she wished that her sister might have everything that was good and joyous and prosperous. There was never a look of pain came across Clary's face, but Patience suffered some touch of inner agony. This feeling was so strong that she sympathised even with Clary's follies, and with Clary's faults. She almost knew that it would not be well that Ralph Newton should be encouraged as a lover,—brilliant as were his future prospects, and dear. as he was personally to them all. He was a spendthrift, and it might be that his fine prospects would all be wasted before they were matured. And then their father would so probably disapprove! And then, again, it was so wrong that Clary's peace should have been disturbed and yet no word said to their father. There was much that was wrong;—but still so absolute was her clinging love for Clary that she longed above all things that Clary should be made happy. When Ralph's brother had declared himself as a suitor,—which he had done boldly to Sir Thomas, after but a short intimacy with the family,— Patience had given him all her sympathy. Sir Thomas, having looked at his circumstances, had made him welcome to the house, and to his daughter's hand,—if he could win her heart. The stage had been open to him, and Patience had been his most eager friend. But all that had passed away,—and Clary had been obstinate. "Patty," she had said, with some little arrogance, " he has made a mistake. He should have fallen in love with you." " Clergymen are as fond of pretty girls as other men," Patty had said, with a smile. " And isn't my Patty as pretty and as delicate as a primrose ? " Clary had said, embracing her sister. Pretty Patience Underwood was not ;— but for delicacy,—that with which Patience Underwood was gifted transcended poor Clarissa's powers of comparison. So it was between them, and now there was this acknowledged passion for the spendthrift!

Patience could see that her sister was not unhappy when she came in from her walk,—was not moody,—was not heart-broken. And yet it had seemed to her, before the walk began, while they were sauntering about Mrs. Brownlow's garden, that Ralph had devoted himself entirely to the new cousin, and that Clarissa had been miserable. Surely if he had spoken during the walk,—if he had renewed his protestations of love, if he were now regarded by Clary as her accepted lover, Clary would not keep all this as a secret ! It could not be that Clary should have surrendered herself to a lover, and that their father was to be allowed to remain in ignorance that it was so ! And yet how could it be otherwise if Clary was happy now,—Clary who had acknowledged that she loved this man, and had now been leaning on his arm for an hour beneath the moonlight ? But Patience said not a word. She could not bring herself to speak when speech might pain her sister.

When they had been some half hour in bed, there stole a whisper across the darkness of the chamber from one couch to the other; "Patty, are you asleep?" Patience declared that she was wide awake. "Then I'll come to you,"—and Clary's naked feet pattered across the room. "I've just something to say, and I'll say it better here." Patience made glad way for the intruder, and knew that now she would hear it all. "Patty, it is better to wait."

"What do you mean, dear?"

"I mean this. I think he does like me; I'm almost sure he does."

"He said nothing to-night?"

"He said a great deal,—of course; but nothing about that;—nothing about that exactly."

"Oh, Clary, I'm afraid of him."

"What is the good of fear? The evil is, dear, I think he likes me, but it may so well be that he cannot speak out. He is in debt, and all that;—and he must wait."

"But that is so terrible. What will you do?"

"I will wait too. I have thought about it, and have determined. What's the good of loving a man if one won't go through something for him? I do love him,—with all my heart. I pray God I may never have a husband, if I cannot be his wife." Patience shuddered in her sister's embrace, as these bold words were spoken with energy. "I tell you, Patty, just as I tell myself, because you love me so dearly."

"I do love you;—oh, I do love you."

"I do not think it can be unmaidenly to tell the truth to you and to myself. How can I help telling it to myself? There it is. I feel that I could kiss the very ground on which he stands. He is my hero, my Paladin, my heart, my soul. I have given myself to him for everything. How can I help myself?"

"But, Clary,—you should repress this, not encourage it."

"It won't be repressed,—not in my own heart. But I will never, never, never let him know that it has been so,—till he is all my own. There may be a day when,—oh,—I shall tell him everything; how wretched I was when he did not speak to me;—how broken-hearted when I heard his voice with Mary; how fluttered, and half-happy, and half-wretched when I found that I was to have that long walk with him;—and then how I determined to wait. I will tell him all,—perhaps,—some day. Good-night, dear, dear Patty. I could not sleep without letting you know everything." Then she sprang out from her sister's arms, and pattered back across the room to her own bed. In two minutes Clarissa was asleep, but Patience lay long awake, and before she slept her pillow was damp with her tears.

In the course of the following week Ralph was again at the villa. Sir Thomas, as a matter of course, was away, but the three girls were at home ; and, as it happened, Miss Spooner had also come over to take her tea with her friends. The hour that he spent there was passed half indoors and half out, and certainly Ralph's attentions were chiefly paid to Miss Bonner. Miss Bonner herself, however, was so discreet in her demeanour, that no one could have suggested that any approach had been made to flirtation. To tell the truth, Mary, who had received no confidence from her cousin,—and who was a girl slow to excite or give a confidence,—had seen some sign, or heard some word which had created on her mind a suspicion of the truth. It was not that she thought that Clary's heart was irrecoverably given to the young man, but that there seemed to be just something with which it might be as well that she herself should not interfere. She was there on sufferance,—dependent on her uncle's charity for her daily bread, let her uncle say what he might to the contrary. As yet she hardly knew her cousins, and was quite sure that she was not known by them. She heard that Ralph Newton was a man of fashion, and the heir to a large fortune. She knew herself to be utterly destitute,—but she knew herself to be possessed of great beauty. In her bosom, doubtless, there was an ambition to win by her beauty, from some man whom she could love, those good things of which she was so destitute. She did not lack ambition, and had her high hopes, grounded on the knowledge of her own charms. Her beauty, and a certain sufficiency of intellect,—of the extent of which she was in a remarkable degree herself aware,—were the gifts with which she had been endowed. But she knew when she might use them honestly and when she ought to refrain from using them. Ralph had looked at her as men do look who wish to be allowed to love. All this to her was much more clearly intelligible than to Clarissa, who was two years her senior. Though she had seen Ralph but thrice, she already felt that she might have him on his knees before her, if she cared so to place him. But there was that suspicion of something which had gone before, and a feeling that honour and gratitude,—perhaps, also, self-interest,—called upon her to be cold in her manner to Ralph Newton. She had purposely avoided his companionship in their walk home from Mrs. Brownlow's house ; and now, as they wandered about the lawn and shrubberies of Popham Villa, she took care not to be with him out of earshot of the others. In all of which there was ten times more of womanly cleverness,—or cunning, shall we say,—than had yet come to the possession of Clarissa Underwood.

Cunning she was ;—but she did not deserve that the objectionable epithet should be applied to her. The circumstances of her life had made her cunning. She had been the mistress of her father's house since her fifteenth year, and for two years of her life had had a succession of admirers at her feet. Her father had eaten and drunk

There was now, and ever had been, great freedom of discussion between Ralph Newton of the Priory and his cousin Gregory.

(See page 106)

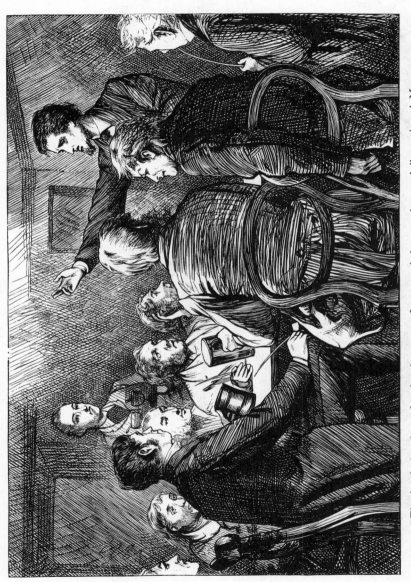

"The battle has been fought since man first crawled upon the earth," continued Moggs, stretching himself to his full height and pointing to the farthest confines of the inhabited globe.

(*See page 122*)

and laughed, and had joked with his child's lovers about his child.
It had been through no merit of his that she had held her own among
them all without soiling either her name or her inner self. Captains
in West Indian regiments, and lieutenants from Queen's ships lying
at Spanish Point, had been her admirers. Proposals to marry are as
ready on the tongues of such men, out in the tropics, as offers to
hand a shawl or carry a parasol. They are soft-hearted, bold to face
the world, and very confident in circumstances. Then, too, they are
ignorant of any other way to progress with a flirtation which is all-
engrossing. In warm latitudes it is so natural to make an offer after
the fifth dance. It is the way of the people in those latitudes, and
seems to lead to no harm. Men and women do marry on small
incomes ; but they do not starve, and the world goes on wagging.
Mary Bonner, however, whose father's rank had, at least, been higher
than that of her adorers, and who knew that great gifts had been
given to her, had held herself aloof from all this, and had early
resolved to bide her time. She was still biding her time,—with
patience sufficient to enable her to resist the glances of Ralph
Newton.

Clarissa Underwood behaved very well on this evening. She gave
a merry glance at her sister, and devoted herself to Miss Spooner.
Mary was so wise and so prudent that there was no cause for any
great agony. As far as Clary could see, Ralph had quite as much to
say to Patience as to Mary. For herself she had resolved that she
would wait. Her manner to him was very pretty,—almost the
manner of a sister to a brother. And then she stayed resolutely with
Miss Spooner, while Ralph was certainly tempting Mary down by the
river-side. It did not last long. He was soon gone, and Miss Spooner
had soon followed him.

"He is very amusing," Mary said, as soon as they were alone.

"Very amusing," said Patience.

"And uncommonly good-looking. Isn't he considered a very
handsome man here ?"

"Yes ;—I suppose he is," said Patience. "I don't know that I
ever thought much about that."

"Of course he is," said Clarissa. "Nobody can doubt about it.
There are some people as to whom it is as absurd not to admit that
they are handsome as it would be to say that a fine picture is
not beautiful. Ralph is one such person,—and of course I know
another."

Mary would not seem to take the allusion, even by a smile. "I
always thought Gregory much nicer looking," said Patience.

"That must be because you are in love with him," said Clarissa.

"There is a speaking brightness, an eloquence, in his eyes ; and a
softness of feeling in the expression of his face, which is above all
beauty," continued Patience, with energy.

"Here's poetry," said Clarissa. "Eloquence, and softness, and eyes, and feeling, and expressive and speaking brightness! You'd better say at once that he's a god."

"I wish I knew him," said Mary Bonner.

"You'll know him before long, I don't doubt. And when you do, you'll know one of the best fellows in the world. I'll admit as much as that; but I will not admit that he can be compared to his brother in regard to good looks." In all which poor Clarissa, who had nothing to console her but her resolve to wait with courage, bore herself well and gallantly.

Soon after this there arrived at Popham Villa the note from Gregory Newton. As it happened, Sir Thomas was at home on that morning, and heard the tidings. "If young Mr. Newton does come, get him to dine, and I will take care to be at home," said Sir Thomas. Patience suggested that Ralph,—their own Ralph,—should be asked to meet him; but to this Sir Thomas would not accede. "It is not our business to make up a family quarrel," he said. "I have had old Mr. Newton with me once or twice lately, and I find that the quarrel still exists as strong as ever. I asked him to dine here, but he refused. His son chooses to come. I shall be glad to see him."

Gregory's letter had not been shown to Sir Thomas, but it was, of course, shown to Clarissa. "How could I help it?" said she. From which it may be presumed that Patience had looked as though Gregory had been hardly treated. "One doesn't know how it is, or why it comes, or what it is ;—or why it doesn't come. I couldn't have taken Gregory Newton for my husband."

"And yet he had all things to recommend him."

"I wish he had asked you, Patty!"

"Don't say that, dear, because there is in it something that annoys me. I don't think of myself in such matters, but I do hope to see you the happy wife of some happy man."

"I hope you will, with all my heart," said Clary, standing up,— "of one man, of one special, dearest, best, and brightest of all men. Oh dear! And yet I know it will never be, and I wonder at myself that I have been bold enough to tell you." And Patience, also, wondered at her sister's boldness.

Ralph Newton,—Ralph from the Priory,—did come down to the villa, and did accept the invitation to dinner which was given to him. The event was so important that Patience found it necessary to go up to London to tell her father. Mary went with her, desirous to see something of the mysteries of Southampton Buildings, while Clarissa remained at home,—waiting. After the usual skirmishes with Stemm, who began by swearing that his master was not at home, they made their way into Sir Thomas's library. "Dear, dear, dear ; this is a very awkward place to bring your cousin to," he said, frowning.

Mary would have retreated at once had it not been that Patience held her ground so boldly. "Why shouldn't she come, papa? And I had to see you. Mr. Newton is to dine with us to-morrow." To-morrow was a Saturday, and Sir Thomas became seriously displeased. Why had a Saturday been chosen? Saturday was the most awkward day in the world for the giving and receiving of dinners. It was in vain that Patience explained to him that Saturday was the only day on which Mr. Newton could come, that Sir Thomas had given his express authority for the dinner, and that no bar had been raised against Saturday. "You ought to have known," said Sir Thomas. Nevertheless, he allowed them to leave the chamber with the understanding that he would preside at his own table on the following day. "Why is it that Saturday is so distasteful to him?" Mary asked as they walked across Lincoln's Inn Fields together.

Patience was silent for awhile, not knowing how to answer the question, or how to leave it unanswered. But at last she preferred to make some reply. "He does not like going to our church, I think."

"But you like it."

"Yes;—and I wish papa did. But he doesn't." Then there was a pause. "Of course it must strike you as very odd, the way in which we live."

"I hope it is not I who drive my uncle away."

"Not in the least, Mary. Since mamma's death he has fallen into this habit, and he has got so to love solitude, that he is never happy but when alone. We ought to be grateful to him because it shows that he trusts us;—but it would be much nicer if he would come home."

"He is so different from my father."

"He was always with you."

"Well;—yes; that is, I could be always with him,—almost always. He was so fond of society that he would never be alone. We had a great rambling house, always full of people. If he could see people pleasant and laughing, that was all that he wanted. It is hard to say what is best."

"Papa is as good to us as ever he can be."

"So was my papa good to me,—in his way; but, oh dear, the people that used to come there! Poor papa! He used to say that hospitality was his chief duty. I sometimes used to think that the world would be much pleasanter and better if there was no such thing as hospitality;—if people always eat and drank alone, and lived as uncle does, in his chambers. There would not be so much money wasted, at any rate."

"Papa never wastes any money," said Patience,—"though there never was a more generous man."

Ralph Newton,—Ralph of the Priory,—came to dinner, and Miss Spooner was asked to meet him. It might have been supposed that a party so composed would not have been very bright, but the party at the villa went off very satisfactorily. Ralph made himself popular with everybody. He became very popular with Sir Thomas by the frank and easy way in which he spoke of the family difficulties at Newton. "I wish my namesake knew my father," he said, when he was alone with the lawyer after dinner. He never spoke of either of these Newtons as his cousins, though to Gregory, whom he knew well and loved dearly, he would declare that from him he felt entitled to exact all the dues of cousinship.

"It would be desirable," said Sir Thomas.

"I never give it up. You know my father, I dare say. He thought his brother interfered with him, and I suppose he did. But a more affectionate or generous man never lived. He is quite as fond of Gregory as he is of me, and would do anything on earth that Gregory told him. He is rebuilding the chancel of the church just because Gregory wishes it. Some day I hope they may be reconciled."

"It is hard to get over money difficulties," said Sir Thomas.

"I don't see why there should be money difficulties," said Ralph. "As far as I am concerned there need be none."

"Ralph Newton has made money difficulties," said Sir Thomas. "If he had been careful with his own fortune there would have been no question as to the property between him and your father."

"I can understand that;—and I can understand also my father's anxiety, though I do not share it. It would be better that my namesake should have the estate. I can see into these matters quite well enough to know that were it to be mine there would occur exactly that which my father wishes to avoid. I should be the owner of Newton Priory, and people would call me Mr. Newton. But I shouldn't be Newton of Newton. It had better go to Ralph. I should live elsewhere, and people would not notice me then."

Sir Thomas, as he looked up at the young man, leaning back in his arm-chair and holding his glass half full of wine in his hand, could not but tell himself that the greater was the pity. This off-shoot of the Newton stock, who declared of himself that he never could be Newton of Newton, was a fine, manly fellow to look at,—not handsome as was Ralph the heir, not marked by that singular mixture of gentleness, intelligence, and sweetness which was written, not only on the countenance, but in the demeanour and very step of Gregory; but he was a bigger man than either of them, with a broad chest, and a square brow, and was not without that bright gleam of the Newton blue eye, which characterised all the family. And there was so much of the man in him;—whereas, in manhood, Ralph the heir had certainly been deficient. "Ralph must lie on the bed that he has made," said Sir Thomas. "And you, of course, will accept the good things that come in your way. As far as I can see at present it will be best for Ralph that your father should redeem from him a portion, at least, of the property. The girls are waiting for us to go out, and perhaps you will like a cigar on the lawn."

It was clear to every one there to see that this other Newton greatly admired the West Indian cousin. And Mary, with this new-comer, seemed to talk on easier terms than she had ever done before since she had been at Fulham. She smiled, and listened, and was gracious, and made those pleasant little half-affected sallies which girls do make to men when they know that they are admired, and are satisfied that it should be so. All the story had been told to her, and it might be that the poor orphan felt that she was better fitted to associate with the almost nameless one than with the true heir of the family. Mr. Newton, when he got up to leave them, asked permission to come again, and left them all with a pleasant air of intimacy. Two boats had passed them, racing on the river, almost close to the edge of their lawn, and Newton had offered to bet with Mary as to which would first reach the bridge. "I wish you had taken my wager, Miss Bonner," he said, "because then I should have been bound to come back at once to pay you." "That's all very well, Mr. Newton," said Mary, "but I have heard of gentlemen who are never seen again when they lose." "Mr. Newton is unlike that, I'm sure," said Clary; "but I hope he'll come again at any rate." Newton promised that he would, and was fully determined to keep his promise when he made it.

"Wouldn't it be delightful if they were to fall in love with each other and make a match of it?." said Clary to her sister.

"I don't like to plot and plan such things," said Patience.

"I don't like to scheme, but I don't see any harm in planning. He is ever so nice,—isn't he?"

"I thought him very pleasant."

"Such an open-spoken, manly, free sort of fellow. And he'll be very well off, you know."

"I don't know;—but I dare say he will," said Patience.

"Oh yes, you do. Poor Ralph, our Ralph, is a spendthrift, and I shouldn't wonder if this one were to have the property after all. And then his father is very rich. I know that because Gregory told me. Dear me! wouldn't it be odd if we were all three to become Mrs. Newtons?"

"Clary, what did I tell you?"

"Well; I won't. But it would be odd,—and so nice, at least I think so. Well;—I dare say I ought not to say it. But then I can't help thinking it,—and surely I may tell you what I think."

"I would think it as little as I could, dear."

" Ah, that's very well. A girl can be a hypocrite if she pleases, and perhaps she ought. Of course I shall be a hypocrite to all the world except you. I tell you what it is, Patty ;—you make me tell you everything, and say that of course you and I are to tell everything,— and then you scold me. Don't you want me to tell you everything ? "

" Indeed I do ;—and I won't scold you. Dear Clary, do I scold you ? Wouldn't I give one of my eyes to make you happy ? "

" That's quite a different thing," said Clarissa.

Three days afterwards Mr. Ralph Newton ;—it is hoped that the reader may understand the attempts which are made to designate the two young men ;—Mr. Ralph Newton appeared again at Popham Villa. He came in almost with the gait of an old friend, and brought some fern leaves, which he had already procured from Hampshire, in compliance with a promise which he had made to Patience Underwood. " That's what we call the hart's tongue," said he, " though I fancy they give them all different names in different places."

" It's the same plant as ours, Mr. Newton,—only yours is larger."

" It's the ugliest of all the ferns," said Clary.

" Even that's a compliment," said Newton. " It's no use trans-planting them in this weather, but I'll send you a basket in October. You should come down to Newton and see our ferns. We think we're very pretty, but because we're so near, nobody comes to see us." Then he fell a-talking with Mary Bonner, and stayed at the villa nearly all the afternoon. For a moment or two he was alone with Clarissa, and at once expressed his admiration. " I don't think I ever saw such perfect beauty as your cousin's," he said.

" She is handsome."

" And then she is so fair, whereas everybody expects to see dark eyes and black hair come from the West Indies."

" But Mary wasn't born there."

" That doesn't matter. The mind doesn't travel back as far as that. A negro should be black, and an American thin, and a French woman should have her hair dragged up by the roots, and a German should be broad-faced, and a Scotchman red-haired,—and a West Indian beauty should be dark and languishing."

" I'll tell her you say so, and perhaps she'll have herself altered."

" Whatever you do, don't let her be altered," said Mr. Newton. " She can't be changed for the better."

" I am quite sure he is over head and ears in love," said Clarissa to Patience that evening.

CHAPTER XVI.

THE CHESHIRE CHEESE.

" LABOUR is the salt of the earth, and Capital is the sworn foe to Labour." Hear, hear, hear, with the clattering of many glasses, and the smashing of certain pipes ! Then the orator went on. " That Labour should be the salt of the earth has been the purpose of a beneficent Creator ;—that Capital should be the foe to Labour has been man's handywork. The one is an eternal decree, which nothing can change,—which neither the good nor the evil done by man can affect. The other is an evil ordinance, the fruit of man's ignorance and within the scope of man's intellect to annul." Mr. Ontario Moggs was the orator, and he was at this moment addressing a crowd of sympathising friends in the large front parlour of the Cheshire Cheese. Of all those who were listening to Ontario Moggs there was not probably one who had reached a higher grade in commerce than that of an artizan working for weekly wages ;—but Mr. Moggs was especially endeared to them because he was not an artizan working for weekly wages, but himself a capitalist. His father was a master bootmaker on a great scale ;—for none stood much higher in the West-end trade than Booby and Moggs ; and it was known that Ontario was the only child and heir, and as it were sole owner of the shoulders on which must some day devolve the mantle of Booby and Moggs. Booby had long been gathered to his fathers, and old Moggs was the stern opponent of strikes. What he had lost by absolutely refusing to yield a point during the last strike among the shoemakers of London no one could tell. He had professed aloud that he would sooner be ruined, sooner give up his country residence at Shepherd's Bush, sooner pull down the honoured names of Booby and Moggs from over the shop-window in Old Bond Street, than allow himself to be driven half an inch out of his course by men who were attempting to dictate to him what he should do with his own. In these days of strikes Moggs would look even upon his own workmen with the eyes of a Coriolanus glaring upon the disaffected populace of Rome. Mr. Moggs senior would stand at his shop-door, with his hand within his waistcoat, watching the men out on strike who were picketing the streets round his shop, and would feel himself every inch a patrician, ready to die for his order. Such was Moggs senior. And Moggs junior, who was a child of Capital, but whose heirship depended entirely on his father's will, harangued his father's workmen and other workmen at the Cheshire Cheese, telling them that Labour was the salt of the earth, and that Capital was the foe to Labour ! Of course they loved him. The demagogue who is of all demagogues the most popular, is the demagogue who is a demagogue in opposition to his apparent nature. The radical Earl, the free-thinking parson, the squire who won't preserve, the tenant who defies his landlord, the capitalist with a theory for dividing profits, the Moggs who loves a strike,—these are the men whom the working men delight to follow. Ontario Moggs, who was at any rate honest in his philanthropy, and who did in truth believe that it was better that twenty real bootmakers should eat beef daily than that one so-called bootmaker should live in a country residence,—who believed this and acted on his belief, though he was himself not of the twenty, but rather the one so-called bootmaker who would suffer by the propagation of such a creed,—was beloved and almost worshipped by the denizens of the Cheshire Cheese. How far the real philanthropy of the man may have been marred by an uneasy and fatuous ambition ; how far he was carried away by a feeling that it was better to make speeches at the Cheshire Cheese than to apply for payment of money due to his father, it would be very hard for us to decide. That there was an alloy even in Ontario Moggs is probable ;—but of this alloy his hearers knew nothing. To them he was a perfect specimen of that combination, which is so grateful to them, of the rich man's position with the poor man's sympathies. Therefore they clattered their glasses, and broke their pipes, and swore that the words he uttered were the kind of stuff they wanted.

"The battle has been fought since man first crawled upon the earth," continued Moggs, stretching himself to his full height and pointing to the farthest confines of the inhabited globe ;—"since man first crawled upon the earth." There was a sound in that word "crawl" typical of the abject humility to which working shoemakers were subjected by their employers, which specially aroused the feelings of the meeting. "And whence comes the battle?" The orator paused, and the glasses were jammed upon the table. "Yes, —whence comes the battle, in fighting which hecatombs of honest labourers have been crushed till the sides of the mountains are white with their bones, and the rivers run foul with their blood? From the desire of one man to eat the bread of two?" "That's it," said a lean, wizened, pale-faced little man in a corner, whose trembling hand was resting on a beaker of gin and water. "Yes, and to wear two men's coats and trousers, and to take two men's bedses and the wery witals out of two men's bodies. D—— them!" Ontario, who understood something of his trade as an orator, stood with his hand still stretched out, waiting till this ebullition should be over. "No, my friend," said he, "we will not damn them. I for one will damn no man. I will simply rebel. Of all the sacraments given to us, the sacrament of rebellion is the most holy." Hereupon the landlord of

the Cheshire Cheese must have feared for his tables, so great was
the applause and so tremendous the thumping ;—but he knew his
business, no doubt, and omitted to interfere. " Of Rebellion, my
friends," continued Ontario, with his right hand now gracefully laid
across his breast, " there are two kinds,—or perhaps we may say
three. There is the rebellion of arms, which can avail us nothing
here." " Perhaps it might tho'," said the little wizened man in a
corner, whose gin and water apparently did not comfort him. To
this interruption Ontario paid no attention. " And there is the
dignified and slow rebellion of moral resistance ;—too slow I fear for
us." This point was lost upon the audience, and though the speaker
paused, no loud cheer was given. " It's as true as true," said one
man ; but he was a vain fellow, simply desirous of appearing wiser
than his comrades. " And then there is the rebellion of the Strike ; "
now the clamour of men's voices, and the kicking of men's feet, and
the thumping with men's fists became more frantic than ever ;
" —— the legitimate rebellion of Labour against its tyrant. Gentlemen, of all efforts this is the most noble. It is a sacrifice of self, a
martyrdom, a giving up on the part of him who strikes of himself,
his little ones, and his wife, for the sake of others who can only thus
be rescued from the grasp of tyranny. Gentlemen, were it not for
strikes, this would be a country in which no free man could live. By
the aid of strikes we will make it the Paradise of the labourer, an
Elysium of industry, an Eden of artizans." There was much more
of it,—but the reader might be fatigued were the full flood of Mr.
Moggs's oratory to be let loose upon him. And through it all there
was a germ of truth and a strong dash of true, noble feeling ;—but
the speaker had omitted as yet to learn how much thought must be
given to a germ of truth before it can be made to produce fruit for
the multitude. And then, in speaking, grand words come so easily,
while thoughts,—even little thoughts,—flow so slowly !

But the speech, such as it was, sufficed amply for the immediate
wants of the denizens of the Cheshire Cheese. There were men there
who for the half-hour believed that Ontario Moggs had been born
to settle all the difficulties between labourers and their employers,
and that he would do so in such a way that the labourers, at least,
should have all that they wanted. It would be, perhaps, too much to
say that any man thought this would come in his own day,—that
he so believed as to put a personal trust in his own belief ; but they
did think for a while that the good time was coming, and that Ontario
Moggs would make it come. " We'll have 'im in parl'ament any
ways," said a sturdy, short, dirty-looking artizan, who shook his
head as he spoke to show that, on that matter, his mind was quite
made up. " I dunno no good as is to cum of sending sich as him to
parl'ament," said another. " Parl'ament ain't the place. When it

comes to the p'int they won't 'ave 'em. There was Odgers, and Mr.
Beale. I don't b'lieve in parl'ament no more." " Kennington
Oval's about the place," said a third. " Or Primrose 'ill," said a
fourth. " Hyde Park!" screamed the little wizen man with the gin
and water. " That's the ticket;—and down with them gold railings.
We'll let 'em see!" Nevertheless they all went away home in the
quietest way in the world, and,—as there was no strike in hand,—
got to their work punctually on the next morning. Of all those who
had been loudest at the Cheshire Cheese there was not one who was
not faithful, and, in a certain way, loyal to his employer.

As soon as his speech was over and he was able to extricate himself from the crowd, Ontario Moggs escaped from the public-house
and strutted off through certain narrow, dark streets in the neighbourhood, leaning on the arm of a faithful friend. " Mr. Moggs, you did
pitch it rayther strong, to-night," said the faithful friend.

" Pitch it rather strong;—yes. What good do you think can ever
come from pitching any thing weak? Pitch it as strong as you will,
and it don't amount to much."

" But about rebellion, now, Mr. Moggs? Rebellion ain't a good
thing, surely, Mr. Moggs."

" Isn't it? What was Washington, what was Cromwell, what was
Rienzi, what was,—was,—; but never mind," said Ontario, who
could not at the moment think of the name of his favourite Pole.

" And you think as the men should be rebels again' the masters?"

" That depends on who the masters are, Waddle."

" What good 'd cum of it if I rebelled again' Mr. Neefit, and told
him up to his face as I wouldn't make up the books? He'd only
sack me. I find thirty-five bob a week, with two kids and their
mother to keep on it, tight enough, Mr. Moggs. If I 'ad the fixing
on it, I should say forty bob wasn't over the mark;—I should
indeed. But I don't see as I should get it."

" Yes you would;—if you earned it, and stuck to your purpose.
But you're a single stick, and it requires a faggot to do this work."

" I never could see it, Mr. Moggs. All the same I do like to hear
you talk. It stirs one up, even though one don't just go along with
it. You won't let on, you know, to Mr. Neefit as I was there."

" And why not?" said Ontario, turning sharp upon his companion.

" The old gen'leman hates the very name of a strike. He's a'most
as bad as your own father, Mr. Moggs."

" You have done his work to-day. You have earned your bread.
You owe him nothing."

" That I don't, Mr. Moggs. He'll take care of that."

" And yet you are to stay away from this place, or go to that, to
suit his pleasure. Are you Neefit's slave?"

" I'm just the young man in his shop,—that's all."

" As long as that is all, Waddle, you are not worthy to be called a man."

" Mr. Moggs, you're too hard. As for being a man, I am a man. I've a wife and two kids. I don't think more of my governor than another ;—but if he sacked me, where 'd I get thirty-five bob a-week ? "

" I beg your pardon, Waddle ;—it's true. I should not have said it. Perhaps you do not quite understand me, but your position is one of a single stick, rather than of the faggot. Ah me ! She hasn't been at the shop lately ? "

" She do come sometimes. She was there the day before yesterday."

" And alone ? "

" She come alone, and she went home with the governor."

" And he ? "

" Mr. Newton, you mean ? "

" Has he been there ? "

" Well ;—yes ; he was there once last week."

" Well ? "

" There was words ;—that's what there was. It ain't going smooth, and he ain't been out there no more,—not as I knows on. I did say a word once or twice as to the precious long figure as he stands for on our books. Over two hundred for breeches is something quite stupendous. Isn't it, Mr. Moggs ? "

" And what did Neefit say ? "

" Just snarled at me. He can show his teeth, you know, and look as bitter as you like. It ain't off, because when I just named the very heavy figure in such a business as ours,—he only snarled. But it ain't on, Mr. Moggs. It ain't what I call,—on." After this they walked on in silence for a sort way, when Mr. Waddle made a little proposition. " He's on your books, too, Mr. Moggs, pretty tight, as I'm told. Why ain't you down on him ? "

" Down on him ? " said Moggs.

" I wouldn't leave him an hour, if I was you."

" D'you think that's the way I would be down on,—a rival ? " and Moggs, as he walked along, worked both his fists closely in his energy. " If I can't be down on him other gait than that, I'll leave him alone. But, Waddle, by my sacred honour as a man, I'll not leave him alone ! " Waddle started, and stood with his mouth open, looking up at his friend. " Base, mercenary, false-hearted loon ! What is it that he wants ? "

" Old Neefit's money. That's it, you know."

" He doesn't know what love means, and he'd take that fair creature, and drag her through the dirt, and subject her to the scorn of hardened aristocrats, and crush her spirits, and break her heart,

—just because her father has scraped together a mass of gold. But I,—I wouldn't let the wind blow on her too harshly. I despise her father's money. I love her. Yes ;—I'll be down upon him somehow. Good-night, Waddle. To come between me and the pride of my heart for a little dirt! Yes ; I'll be down upon him." Waddle stood and admired. He had read of such things in books, but here it was brought home to him in absolute life. He had a young wife whom he loved, but there had been no poetry about his marriage. One didn't often come across real poetry in the world,—Waddle felt ; —but when one did, the treat was great. Now Ontario Moggs was full of poetry. When he preached rebellion it was very grand,— though at such moments Waddle was apt to tell himself that he was precluded by his two kids from taking an active share in such poetry as that. But when Moggs was roused to speak of his love, poetry couldn't go beyond that. "He'll drop into that customer of ours," said Waddle to himself, "and he'll mean it when he's a doing of it. But Polly 'll never 'ave 'im." And then there came across Waddle's mind an idea which he could not express,—that of course no girl would put up with a bootmaker who could have a real gentleman. Real gentlemen think a good deal of themselves, but not half so much as is thought of them by men who know that they themselves are of a different order.

Ontario Moggs, as he went homewards by himself, was disturbed by various thoughts. If it really was to be the case that Polly Neefit wouldn't have him, why should he stay in a country so ill-adapted to his manner of thinking as this ? Why remain in a paltry island while all the starry west, with its brilliant promises, was open to him ? Here he could only quarrel with his father, and become a rebel, and perhaps live to find himself in a jail. And then what could he do of good ? He preached and preached, but nothing came of it. Would not the land of the starry west suit better such a heart and such a mind as his ? But he wouldn't stir while his fate was as yet unfixed in reference to Polly Neefit. Strikes were dear to him, and oratory, and the noisy applauses of the Cheshire Cheese ; but nothing was so dear to him as Polly Neefit. He went about the world with a great burden lying on his chest, and that burden was his love for Polly Neefit. In regard to strikes and the ballot he did in a certain way reason within himself and teach himself to believe that he had thought out those matters ; but as to Polly he thought not at all. He simply loved her, and felt himself to be a wild, frantic man, quarrelling with his father, hurrying towards jails and penal settlements, rushing about the streets half disposed to suicide, because Polly Neefit would have none of him. He had been jealous, too, of the gasfitter, when he had seen his Polly whirling round the room in the gasfitter's arms ;—but the gasfitter was no gentleman, and the battle had been even. In spite of the whirling he still had a chance against the gasfitter. But the introduction of the purple and fine linen element into his affairs was maddening to him. With all his scorn for gentry, Ontario Moggs in his heart feared a gentleman. He thought that he could make an effort to punch Ralph Newton's head if they two were ever to be brought together in a spot convenient for such an operation; but of the man's standing in the world, he was afraid. It seemed to him to be impossible that Polly should prefer him, or any one of his class, to a suitor whose hands were always clean, whose shirt was always white, whose words were soft and well-chosen, who carried with him none of the stain of work. Moggs was as true as steel in his genuine love of Labour,—of Labour with a great L,—of the People with a great P,—of Trade with a great T,—of Commerce with a great C; but of himself individually,—of himself, who was a man of the people, and a tradesman, he thought very little when he compared himself to a gentleman. He could not speak as they spoke; he could not walk as they walked; he could not eat as they ate. There was a divinity about a gentleman which he envied and hated.

Now Polly Neefit was not subject to this idolatry. Could Moggs have read her mind, he might have known that success, as from the bootmaker against the gentleman, was by no means so hopeless an affair. What Polly liked was a nice young man, who would hold up his head and be true to her,—and who would not make a fool of himself. If he could waltz into the bargain, that also would Polly like.

On that night Ontario walked all the way out to Alexandria Cottage, and spent an hour leaning upon the gate, looking up at the window of the breeches-maker's bedroom;—for the chamber of Polly herself opened backwards. When he had stood there an hour, he walked home to Bond Street.

CHAPTER XVII.

RALPH NEWTON'S DOUBTS.

THAT month of August was a very sad time indeed for Ralph the heir. With him all months were, we may say, idle months; but, as a rule, August was of all the most idle. Sometimes he would affect to shoot grouse, but hunting, not grouse-shooting, was his passion as a sportsman. He would leave London, and spend perhaps a couple of days with Mr. Horsball looking at the nags. Then he would run down to some sea-side place, and flirt and laugh and waste his time

upon the sands. Or he would go abroad as far as Dieppe, or perhaps
Biarritz, and so would saunter through the end of the summer. It
must not be supposed of him that he was not fully conscious that
this manner of life was most pernicious. He knew it well, knew
that it would take him to the dogs, made faint resolves at improvement which he hardly for an hour hoped to be able to keep,—and
was in truth anything but happy. This was his usual life ;—and so
for the last three or four years had he contrived to get through this
month of August. But now the utmost sternness of business had
come upon him. He was forced to remain in town, found himself
sitting day after day in his lawyer's anteroom, was compelled to seek
various interviews with Sir Thomas, in which it was impossible that
Sir Thomas should make himself very pleasant ; and,—worst of all,
—was at last told that he must make up his own mind !

Squire Newton was also up in London ; and though London was
never much to his taste, he was in these days by no means so
wretched as his nephew. He was intent on a certain object, and he
began to hope, nay to think, that his object might be achieved. He
had not once seen his nephew, having declared his conviction very
strongly that it would be better for all parties that they should remain
apart. His own lawyer he saw frequently, and Ralph's lawyer once,
and Sir Thomas more than once or twice. There was considerable
delay, but the Squire would not leave London till something was, if
not settled, at any rate arranged, towards a settlement. And it was
the expression of his will conveyed through the two lawyers which
kept Ralph in London. What was the worth of Ralph's interest in
the property ? That was one great question. Would Ralph sell that
interest when the price was fixed ? That was the second question.
Ralph, to whom the difficulty of giving an answer was as a labour of
Hercules, staved off the evil day for awhile by declaring that he must
know what was the price before he could say whether he would sell
the article. The exact price could not be fixed. The lawyers combined in saying that the absolute sum of money to include all Ralph's
interest in the estate could not be named that side of Christmas.
It was not to be thought of that any actuary, or valuer, or lawyer,
or conveyancer, should dispose of so great a matter by a month's
work. But something approaching to a settlement might be made.
A sum might be named as a minimum. And a compact might be
made, subject to the arbitration of a sworn appraiser. A sum was
named. The matter was carried so far, that Ralph was told that he
could sign away all his rights by the middle of September,—sign
away the entire property,—and have his pockets filled with ample
funds for the Moonbeam, and all other delights. He might pay off
Moggs and Neefit, and no longer feel that Polly,—poor dear Polly,—
was a millstone round his neck. And he would indeed, in this event,

be so well provided, that he did not for a moment doubt that, if he chose so to circumscribe himself, Clarissa Underwood might be his wife. All the savings of the Squire's life would be his,—enough, as the opposing lawyer told him with eager pressing words, to give him an estate of over a thousand a year at once. "And it may be more,—probably will be more," said the lawyer. But at the very least a sum approaching to thirty thousand pounds would be paid over to him at once. And he might do what he pleased with this. There was still a remnant of his own paternal property sufficient to pay his debts.

But why should a man whose encumbrances were so trifling, sacrifice prospects that were so glorious? Could he not part with a portion of the estate,—with the reversion of half of it, so that the house of Newton, Newton Priory, with its grouse and paddocks and adjacent farms, might be left to him? If the whole were saleable, surely so also must be the half. The third of the money offered to him would more than suffice for all his wants. No doubt he might sell the half,—but not to the Squire, nor could he effect such sale immediately as he would do if the Squire bought it, nor on such terms as were offered by the Squire. Money he might raise at once, certainly; but it became by degrees as a thing certain to him, that if once he raised money in that way, the estate would fly from him. His uncle was a hale man, and people told him that his own life was not so much better than his uncle's. His uncle had a great object, and if Ralph chose to sell at all, that fact would be worth thousands to him. But his uncle would not buy the reversion of half or of a portion of the property. The Squire at last spoke his mind freely on this matter to Sir Thomas. "It shall never be cast in my son's teeth," he said, "that his next neighbour is the real man. Early in life I made a mistake, and I have had to pay for it ever since. I am paying for it now, and must pay for it to the end. But my paying for it will be of small service if my boy has to pay for it afterwards." Sir Thomas understood him and did not press the point.

Ralph was nearly driven wild with the need of deciding. Moggs's bill at two months was coming due, and he knew that he could expect no mercy there. To Neefit's establishment in Conduit Street he had gone once, and had had words,—as Waddle had told to his rival. Neefit was still persistent in his wishes,—still urgent that Newton should go forth to Hendon like a man, and " pop " at once. " I'll tell you what, Captain," said he ;—he had taken to calling Ralph Captain, as a goodly familiar name, feeling, no doubt, that Mister was cold between father-in-law and son-in-law, and not quite daring to drop all reverential title ;—" if you're a little hard up, as I know you are, you can have three or four hundred if you want it." Ralph did want it sorely. " I know how you stand with old Moggs," said Neefit, " and I'll see you all right there." Neefit was very urgent. He too had heard something of these dealings among the lawyers. To have his Polly Mrs. Newton of Newton Priory! The prize was worth fighting for. " Don't let them frighten you about a little ready money, Captain. If it comes to that, other folk has got ready money besides them."

" Your trust in me surprises me," said Ralph. " I already owe you money which I can't pay you."

" I know where to trust, and I know where not to trust. If you'll once say as how you'll pop the question to Polly, fair and honest, on the square, you shall have five hundred ;—bless me, if you shan't. If she don't take you after all, why then I must look for my money by-and-bye. If you're on the square with me, Captain, you'll never find me hard to deal with."

" I hope I shall be on the square, at any rate."

" Then you step out to her and pop." Hereupon Ralph made a long and intricate explanation of his affairs, the object of which was to prove to Mr. Neefit that a little more delay was essential. He was so environed by business and difficulties at the present moment that he could take no immediate step such as Mr. Neefit suggested,—no such step quite immediately. In about another fortnight, or in a month at the furthest, he would be able to declare his purpose. " And how about Moggs ? " said Neefit, putting his hands into his breeches-pocket, pulling down the corners of his mouth, and fixing his saucer eyes full upon the young man's face. So he stood for some seconds, and then came the words of which Waddle had spoken. Neefit could not disentangle the intricacies of Ralph's somewhat fictitious story ; but he had wit enough to know what it meant. " You ain't on the square, Captain. That's what you ain't," he said at last. It must be owned that the accusation was just, and it was made so loudly that Waddle did not at all exaggerate in saying that there had been words. Nevertheless, when Ralph left the shop Neefit relented. " You come to me, Captain, when Moggs's bit of stiff comes round."

A few days after that Ralph went to Sir Thomas, with the object of declaring his decision ;—at least Sir Thomas understood that such was to be the purport of the visit. According to his ideas there had been quite enough of delay. The Squire had been liberal in his offer; and though the thing to be sold was in all its bearings so valuable, though it carried with it a value which, in the eyes of Sir Thomas,—and, indeed, in the eyes of all Englishmen,—was far beyond all money price, though the territorial position was, for a legitimate heir, almost a principality ; yet, when a man cannot keep a thing, what can he do but part with it ? Ralph had made his bed, and he must lie upon it. Sir Thomas had done what he could, but it had all amounted to nothing. There was this young man a beggar,—but for this reversion which he had now the power of selling. As for that mode of extrication by marrying the breeches-maker's daughter,—that to Sir Thomas was infinitely the worst evil of the two. Let Ralph accept his uncle's offer and he would still be an English gentleman, free to live as such, free to marry as such, free to associate with friends fitting to his habits of life. And he would be a gentleman, too, with means sufficing for a gentleman's wants. But that escape by way of the breeches-maker's daughter would, in accordance with Sir Thomas's view of things, destroy everything.

" Well, Ralph," he said, sighing, almost groaning, as his late ward took the now accustomed chair opposite to his own.

" I wish I'd never been born," said Ralph, " and that Gregory stood in my place."

" But you have been born, Ralph. We must take things as we find them." Then there was a long silence. . " I think, you know, that you should make up your mind one way or the other. Your uncle of course feels that as he is ready to pay the money at once he is entitled to an immediate answer."

" I don't see that at all," said Ralph. " I am under no obligation to my uncle, and I don't see why I am to be bustled by him. He is doing nothing for my sake."

" He has, at any rate, the power of retracting."

" Let him retract."

" And then you'll be just where you were before,—ready to fall into the hands of the Jews. If you must part with your property you cannot do so on better terms."

" It seems to me that I shall be selling £7,000 a year in land for about £1,200 a year in the funds."

" Just so ;—that's about it, I suppose. But can you tell me when the land will be yours,—or whether it will ever be yours at all ? What is it that you have got to sell ? But, Ralph, it is no good going over all that again."

" I know that, Sir Thomas."

" I had hoped you would have come to some decision. If you can save the property of course you ought to do so. If you can live on what pittance is left to you—— "

" I can save it."

" Then do save it."

" I can save it by—marrying."

" By selling yourself to the daughter of a man who makes —— breeches ! I can give you advice on no other point ; but I do advise you not to do that. I look upon an ill-assorted marriage as the very worst kind of ruin. I cannot myself conceive any misery greater than that of having a wife whom I could not ask my friends to meet."

Ralph when he heard this blushed up to the roots of his hair. He remembered that when he had first mentioned to Sir Thomas his suggested marriage with Polly Neefit he had said that as regarded Polly herself he thought that Patience and Clarissa would not object to her. He was now being told by Sir Thomas himself that his daughters would certainly not consent to meet Polly Neefit, should Polly Neefit become Mrs. Newton. He, too, had his ideas of his own standing in the world, and had not been slow to assure himself that the woman whom he might choose for his wife would be a fit companion for any lady,—as long as the woman was neither vicious nor disagreeable. He could make any woman a lady ; he could, at any rate, make Polly Neefit a lady. He rose from his seat, and prepared to leave the room in disgust. "I won't trouble you by coming here again," he said.

"You are welcome, Ralph," said Sir Thomas. "If I could assist you, you would be doubly welcome."

"I know I have been a great trouble to you,—a thankless, fruitless, worthless trouble. I shall make up my mind, no doubt, in a day or two, and I will just write you a line. I need not bother you by coming any more. Of course I think a great deal about it."

"No doubt," said Sir Thomas.

"Unluckily I have been brought up to know the value of what it is I have to throw away. It is a kind of thing that a man doesn't do without some regrets."

"They should have come earlier," said Sir Thomas.

"No doubt ;—but they didn't, and it is no use saying anything more about it. Good-day, sir." Then he flounced out of the room, impatient of that single word of rebuke which had been administered to him.

Sir Thomas, as soon as he was alone, applied himself at once to the book which he had reluctantly put aside when he was disturbed. But he could not divest his mind of its trouble, as quickly as his chamber had been divested of the presence of its troubler. He had said an ill-natured word, and that grieved him. And then,—was he not taking all this great matter too easily ? If he would only put his shoulder to the wheel thoroughly might he not do something to save this friend,—this lad, who had been almost as his own son,—from destruction ? Would it not be a burden on his conscience to the last day of his life that he had allowed his ward to be ruined, when by some sacrifice of his own means he might have saved him ? He sat and thought of it, but did not really resolve that anything could be done. He was wont to think in the same way of his own children, whom he neglected. His conscience had been pricking him all his life, but it hardly pricked him sharp enough to produce consequences.

During those very moments in which Ralph was leaving Southampton Buildings he had almost made up his mind to go at once to Alexandria Cottage, and to throw himself and the future fate of Newton Priory at the feet of Polly Neefit. Two incidents in his late interview with Sir Thomas tended to drive him that way. Sir Thomas had told him that should he marry the daughter of a man who made —— breeches, no lady would associate with his wife. Sir Thomas also had seemed to imply that he must sell his property. He would show Sir Thomas that he could have a will and a way of his own. Polly Neefit should become his wife; and he would show the world that no proudest lady in the land was treated with more delicate consideration by her husband than the breeches-maker's daughter should be treated by him. And when it should please Providence to decide that the present squire of Newton had reigned long enough over that dominion, he would show the world that he had known something of his own position and the value of his own prospects. Then Polly should be queen in the Newton dominions, and he would see whether the ordinary world of worshippers would not come and worship as usual. All the same, he did not on that occasion go out to Alexandria Cottage.

When he reached his club he found a note from his brother.

"Newton Peele, September 8th, 186—.

" My dear Ralph,—

"I have been sorry not to have had an answer from you to the letter which I wrote to you about a month ago. Of course I hear of what is going on. Ralph Newton up at the house tells me everything. The Squire is still in town, as, of course, you know; and there has got to be a report about here that he has, as the people say, bought you out. I still hope that this is not true. The very idea of it is terrible to me ;—that you should sell for an old song, as it were, the property that has belonged to us for centuries ! It would not, indeed, go out of the name, but, as far as you and I are concerned, that is the same. I will not refuse, myself, to do anything that you may say is necessary to extricate yourself from embarrassment; but I can hardly bring myself to believe that a step so fatal as this can be necessary.

" If I understand the matter rightly your difficulty is not so much in regard to debts as in the want of means of livelihood. If so, can you not bring yourself to live quietly for a term of years. Of course you ought to marry, and there may be a difficulty there ; but almost anything would be better than abandoning the property. As I told you before, you are welcome to the use of the whole of my share of the London property. It is very nearly £400 a year. Could you not live on that till things come round ?

"Our cousin Ralph knows that I am writing to you, and knows what my feelings are. It is not he that is so anxious for the purchase. Pray write and tell me what is to be done.

"Most affectionately yours,

"GREGORY NEWTON.

"I wouldn't lose a day in doing anything you might direct about the Holborn property."

Ralph received this at his club, and afterwards dined alone, considering it. Before the evening was over he thought that he had made up his mind that he would not, under any circumstances, give up his reversionary right. "They couldn't make me do it, even though I went to prison," he said to himself. Let him starve till he died, and then the property would go to Gregory! What did it matter? The thing that did matter was this,—that the estate should not be allowed to depart out of the true line of the Newton family. He sat thinking of it half the night, and before he left the club he wrote the following note to his brother;—

"September 9th, 186—.

"DEAR GREG.,—

"Be sure of this,—that I will not part with my interest in the property. I do not think that I can be forced, and I will never do it willingly. It may be that I may be driven to take advantage of your liberality and prudence. If so, I can only say that you shall share the property with me when it comes.

"Yours always,

"R. N."

This he gave to the porter of the club as he passed out; and then, as he went home, he acknowledged to himself that it was tantamount to a decision on his part that he would forthwith marry Polly Neefit.

CHAPTER XVIII.

WE WON'T SELL BROWNRIGGS.

ON the 10th of September the Squire was informed that Ralph Newton demanded another ten days for his decision, and that he had undertaken to communicate it by letter on the 20th. The Squire had growled, thinking that his nephew was unconscionable, and had threatened to withdraw his offer. The lawyer, with a smile, assured him that the matter really was progressing very quickly, that things of that kind could rarely be carried on so expeditiously; and that, in short, Mr. Newton had no fair ground of complaint. "When a man pays through the nose for his whistle, he ought to get it!" said the Squire, plainly showing that his idea as to the price fixed was very different from that entertained by his nephew. But he did not retract his offer. He was too anxious to accomplish the purchase to do that. He would go home, he said, and wait till the 20th. Then he would return to London. And he did go home.

On the first evening he said very little to his son. He felt that his son did not quite sympathise with him, and he was sore that it should be so. He could not be angry with his son. He knew well that this want of sympathy arose from a conviction on this son's part that, let what might be done in regard to the property, nothing could make him, who was illegitimate, capable of holding the position in the country which of right belonged to Newton of Newton. But the presence of this feeling in the mind of the son was an accusation against himself which was very grievous to him. Almost every act of his latter life had been done with the object of removing the cause for such accusation. To make his boy such as he would have been in every respect had not his father sinned in his youth, had been the one object of the father's life. And nobody gainsayed him in this but that son himself. Nobody told him that all his bother about the estate was of no avail. Nobody dared to tell him so. Parson Gregory, in his letters to his brother, could express such an opinion. Sir Thomas, sitting alone in his chamber, could feel it. Ralph, the legitimate heir, with an assumed scorn, could declare to himself that, let what might be sold, he would still be Newton of Newton. The country people might know it, and the farmers might whisper it one to another. But nobody said a word of this to the Squire. His own lawyer never alluded to such a matter, though it was of course in his thoughts. Nevertheless, the son, whom he loved so well, would tell him from day to day,—indirectly, indeed, but with words that were plain enough,—that the thing was not to be done. Men and women called him Newton, because his father had chosen so to call him ;—as they would have called him Tomkins or Montmorenci, had he first appeared before them with either of those names ; but he was not a Newton, and nothing could make him Newton of Newton Priory,—not even the possession of the whole parish, and an habitation in the Priory itself. "I wish you wouldn't think about it," the son would say to the father ;—and the expression of such a wish would contain the whole accusation. What other son would express a desire that the father would abstain from troubling himself to leave his estate entire to his child?

On the morning after his return the necessary communication was made. But it was not commenced in any set form. The two were out together, as was usual with them, and were on the road which divided the two parishes, Bostock from Newton. On the left of them was Walker's farm, called the Brownriggs ; and on the right, Darvell's farm, which was in their own peculiar parish of Newton. "I was talking to Darvell while you were away," said Ralph.

"What does he say for himself?"

"Nothing. It's the old story. He wants to stay, though he knows he'd be better away."

"Then let him stay. Only I must have the place made fit to look at. A man should have a chance of pulling through."

"Certainly, sir. I don't want him to go. I was only thinking it would be better for his children that there should be a change. As for making the place fit to look at, he hasn't the means. It's Walker's work, at the other side, that shames him."

"One can't have Walkers on every farm," said the Squire. "No; —if things go, as I think they will go, we'll pull down every stick and stone at Brumby's,"—Brumby's was the name of Darvell's farm, —"and put it up all ship-shape. The house hasn't been touched these twenty years." Ralph said nothing. He knew well that his father would not talk of building unless he intended to buy before he built. Nothing could be more opposed to the Squire's purposes in life than the idea of building a house which, at his death, would become the property of his nephew. And, in this way, the estate was being starved. All this Ralph understood thoroughly; and, understanding it, had frequently expressed a desire that his father and the heir could act in accord together. But now the Squire talked of pulling down and building up as though the property were his own, to do as he liked with it. "And I think I can do it without selling Brownriggs," continued the Squire. "When it came to black and white, the value that he has in it doesn't come to so much as I thought." Still Ralph said nothing,—nothing, at least, as to the work that had been done up in London. He merely made some observation as to Darvell's farm;—suggesting that a clear half year's rent should be given to the man. "I have pretty well arranged it all in my mind," continued the Squire. "We could part with Twining. It don t lie so near as Brownriggs."

Ralph felt that it would be necessary that he should say something. "Lord Fitzadam would be only too glad to buy it. He owns every acre in the parish except Ingram's farm."

"There'll be no difficulty about selling it,—when we have the power to sell. It'll fetch thirty years' purchase. I'd give thirty years' purchase for it, at the present rent myself, if I had the money. Lord Fitzadam shall have it, if he pleases, of course. There's four hundred acres of it."

"Four hundred and nine," said Ralph.

"And it's worth over twelve thousand pounds. It would have gone against the grain with me to part with any of the land in Bostock; but I think we can squeeze through without that."

" Is it arranged, sir ?" asked the son at last.

"Well ;—no ; I can't say it is. He is to give me his answer on the 20th. But I cannot see that he has any alternative. He must pay his debts, and he has no other way of paying them. He must live, and he has nothing else to live on. A fellow like that will have money, if he can lay his hands on it, and he can't lay his hands on it elsewhere. Of course he could get money ; but he couldn't get it on such terms as I have offered him. He is to have down thirty thousand pounds, and then,—after that,—I am to pay him whatever more than that they may think the thing is worth to him. Under no circumstances is he to have less. It's a large sum of money, Ralph."

' Yes, indeed ;—though not so much as you had expected, sir."

' Well,—no ; but then there are drawbacks. However, I shall only be too glad to have it settled. I don't think, Ralph, you have ever realised what it has been for me not to be able to lay out a shilling on the property, as to which I was not satisfied that I should see it back again in a year or two."

"And yet, sir, I have thought much about it."

"Thought! By heavens, I have thought of nothing else. As I stand here, the place has hardly been worth the having to me, because of such thinking. Your uncle, from the very first, was determined to make it bitter enough. I shall never forget his coming to me when I cut down the first tree. Was I going to build houses for a man's son who begrudged me the timber I wanted about the place ?"

" He couldn't stop you there."

"But he said he could,—and he tried. And if I wanted to change a thing here or there, was it pleasant, do you think, to have to go to him ? And what pleasure could there be in doing anything when another was to have it all? But you have never understood it, Ralph. Well ;—I hope you'll understand it some day. If this goes right, nobody shall ever stop you in cutting a tree. You shall be free to do what you please with every sod, and every branch, and every wall, and every barn. I shall be happy at last, Ralph, if I think that you can enjoy it." Then there was again a silence, for tears were in the eyes both of the father and of the son. "Indeed," continued the Squire, as he rubbed the moisture away, " my great pleasure, while I remain, will be to see you active about the place. As it is now, how is it possible that you should care for it ?"

" But I do care for it, and I think I am active about it."

"Yes,—making money for that idiot, who is to come after me. But I don't think he ever will come. I dare say he won't be ashamed to shoot your game and drink your claret, if you'll allow him. For the matter of that, when the thing is settled he may come and drink my wine if he pleases. I'll be his loving uncle then, if he don't object. But as it is now;—as it has been, I couldn't have borne him."

Even yet there had been no clear statement as to what had been done between father and son. There was so much of clinging, trusting, perfect love in the father's words towards the son, that the latter could not bear to say a word that should produce sorrow. When the Squire declared that Ralph should have it all, free,—to do just as he pleased with it, with all the full glory of ownership, Ralph could not bring himself to throw a doubt upon the matter. And yet he did doubt;—more than doubted;—felt almost certain that his father was in error. While his father had remained alone up in town he had been living with Gregory, and had known what Gregory thought and believed. He had even seen his namesake's letter to Gregory, in which it was positively stated that the reversion would not be sold. Throughout the morning the Squire went on speaking of his hopes, and saying that this and that should be done the very moment that the contract was signed; at last Ralph spoke out, when, on some occasion, his father reproached him for indifference. "I do so fear that you will be disappointed," he said.

"Why should I be disappointed?"

"It is not for my own sake that I fear, for in truth the arrangement, as it stands, is no bar to my enjoyment of the place."

"It is a most absolute bar to mine," said the Squire.

"I fear it is not settled."

"I know that;—but I see no reason why it should not be settled. Do you know any reason?"

"Gregory feels sure that his brother will never consent."

"Gregory is all very well. Gregory is the best fellow in the world. Had Gregory been in his brother's place I shouldn't have had a chance. But Gregory knows nothing about this kind of thing, and Gregory doesn't in the least understand his brother."

"But Ralph has told him so."

"Ralph will say anything. He doesn't mind what lies he tells."

"I think you are too hard on him," said the son.

"Well;—we shall see. But what is it that Ralph has said? And when did he say it?" Then the son told the father of the short letter which the parson had received from his brother, and almost repeated the words of it. And he told the date of the letter, only a day or two before the Squire's return. "Why the mischief could he not be honest enough to tell me the same thing, if he had made up his mind?" said the Squire, angrily. "Put it how you will, he is lying either to me or to his brother;—probably to both of us. His word either on one side or on the other is worth nothing. I believe he will take my money because he wants money, and because he likes money. As for what he says, it is worth nothing. When he has once written his name, he cannot go back from it, and there will be comfort in that." Ralph said nothing more. His father had talked himself into a passion, and was quite capable of becoming angry, even with him. So he suggested something about the shooting for next day, and proposed that the parson should be asked to join them. "He may come if he likes," said the Squire, "but I give you my word if this goes on much longer, I shall get to dislike even the sight of him." On that very day the parson dined with them, and early in the evening the Squire was cold, and silent, and then snappish. But he warmed afterwards under the double influence of his own port-wine, and the thorough sweetness of his nephew's manner. His last words as Gregory left him that night in the hall were as follows:— "Bother about the church. I'm half sick of the church. You come and shoot to-morrow. Don't let us have any new fads about not shooting."

"There are no new fads, uncle Greg., and I'll be with you by twelve o'clock," said the parson.

"He is very good as parsons go," said the Squire as he shut the door.

"He's as good as gold," said the Squire's son.

CHAPTER XIX.

POLLY'S ANSWER

MOGGS'S bill became due before the 20th of September, and Ralph Newton received due notice,—as of course he had known that he would do,—that it had not been cashed at his banker's. How should it be cashed at his banker's, seeing that he had not had a shilling there for the last three months? Moggs himself, Moggs senior, came to Ralph, and made himself peculiarly disagreeable. He had never heard of such a thing on the part of a gentleman! Not to have his bill taken up! To have his paper dishonoured! Moggs spoke of it as though the heavens would fall; and he spoke of it, too, as though, even should the heavens not fall, the earth would be made a very tumultuous and unpleasant place for Mr. Newton, if Mr. Newton did not see at once that these two hundred and odd pounds were forth-coming. Moggs said so much that Ralph became very angry, turned him out of the room, and told him that he should have his dirty money on the morrow. On the morrow the dirty money was paid, Ralph having borrowed the amount from Mr. Neefit. Mr. Moggs was quite content. His object had been achieved, and, when the cash was paid, he was quite polite. But Ralph Newton was **not** happy as he made the payment. He had declared to himself, after writing that letter to his brother, that the thing was settled by the very declaration made by him therein. When he assured his brother that he would not sell his interest in the property, he did, in fact, resolve that he would make Polly Neefit his wife. And he did no more than follow up that resolution when he asked Neefit for a small additional advance. His due would not be given to the breeches-maker if it were not acknowledged that on this occasion he behaved very well. He had told Ralph to come to him when Moggs's " bit of stiff " came round. Moggs's " bit of stiff " did come round, and " the Captain " did as he had been desired to do. Neefit wrote out the cheque without saying a word about his daughter. " Do you just run across to Argyle Street, Captain," said the breeches-maker, " and get the stuff in notes." For Mr. Neefit's bankers held an establishment in Argyle Street. " There ain't no need, you know, to let on, Captain ; is there ? " said the breeches-maker. Ralph Newton, clearly seeing that there was no need to " let on," did as he was bid, and so the account was settled with Mr. Moggs. But now as to settling the account with Mr. Neefit ? Neefit had his own idea of what was right between gentlemen. As the reader knows, he could upon an occasion make his own views very clearly intelligible. He was neither reticent nor particularly delicate. But there was something within him which made him give the cheque to Ralph without a word about Polly. That something, let it be what it might, was not lost upon Ralph.

Any further doubt on his part was quite out of the question. If his mind had not been made up before it must, at least, be made up now. He had twice borrowed Mr. Neefit's money, and on this latter occasion had taken it on the express understanding that he was to propose to Mr. Neefit's daughter. And then, in this way, and in this way only, he could throw over his uncle and save the property. As soon as he had paid the money to Moggs, he went to his room and dressed himself for the occasion. As he arranged his dress with some small signs of an intention to be externally smart, he told himself that it signified nothing at all, that the girl was only a breeches-maker's daughter, and that there was hardly a need that he should take a new pair of gloves for such an occasion as this. In that he was probably right. An old pair of gloves would have done just as well, though Polly did like young men to look smart.

He went out in a hansom of course. A man does not become economical because he is embarrassed. And as for embarrassment, he need not trouble himself with any further feelings on that score. When once he should be the promised husband of Polly Neefit, he would have no scruple about the breeches-maker's money. Why should he, when he did the thing with the very view of getting it ?

They couldn't expect him to be married till next spring at the earliest, and he would take another winter out of himself at the Moonbeam. As the sacrifice was to be made he might as well enjoy all that would come of the sacrifice. Then as he sat in the cab he took to thinking whether, after any fashion at all, he did love Polly Neefit. And from that he got to thinking,—not of poor Clary,—but of Mary Bonner. If his uncle could at once be translated to his fitting place among the immortals, oh,—what a life might be his ! But his uncle was still mortal, and,—after all,—Polly Neefit was a very jolly girl.

When he got to the house he asked boldly for Miss Neefit. He had told himself that no repulse could be injurious to him. If Mrs. Neefit were to refuse him admission into the house, the breeches-maker would be obliged to own that he had done his best. But there was no repulse. In two minutes he found himself in the parlour, with Polly standing up to receive him. " Dear me, Mr. Newton ; how odd ! You might have come weeks running before you'd find me here and mother out. She's gone to fetch father home. She don't do it,— not once a month." Ralph assured her that he was quite contented as it was, and that he did not in the least regret the absence of Mrs. Neefit. " But she'll be ever so unhappy. She likes to see gentlemen when they call."

" And you dislike it ? " asked Ralph.

" Indeed I don't then," said Polly.

And now in what way was he to do it ? Would it be well to allude to her father's understanding with himself ? In the ordinary way of love-making Ralph was quite as much at home as another. He had found no difficulty in saying a soft word to Clarissa Underwood, and in doing more than that. But with Polly the matter was different. There was an inappropriateness in his having to do the thing at all, which made it difficult to him,—unless he could preface what he did by an allusion to his agreement with her father. He could hardly ask Polly to be his wife without giving her some reason for the formation of so desperate a wish on his own part. " Polly," he said at last, " that was very awkward for us all,—that evening when Mr. Moggs was here."

" Indeed it was, Mr. Newton. Poor Mr. Moggs ! He shouldn't have stayed ;—but mother asked him."

" Has he been here since ? "

" He was then, and he and I were walking together. There isn't a better fellow breathing than Ontario Moggs,—in his own way. But he's not company for you, Mr. Newton, of course."

Ralph quailed at this. To be told that his own boot-maker wasn't " company " for him,—and that by the young lady whom he intended to make his wife ! " I don't think he is company for you either Polly," he said.

" Why not, Mr. Newton ?   He's as good as me.   What's the difference between him and father ? "   He wondered whether, when she should be his own, he would be able to teach her to call Mr. Neefit her papa.   " Mr. Newton, when you know me better, you'll know that I'm not one to give myself airs.   I've known Mr. Moggs all my life, and he's equal to me, anyways,—only he's a deal better."

" I hope there's nothing more than friendship, Polly."

" What business have you to hope ? "

Upon that theme he spoke, and told her in plain language that his reason for so hoping was that he trusted to be able to persuade her to become his own wife.   Polly, when the word was spoken, blushed ruby red, and trembled a little.   The thing had come to her, and, after all, she might be a real lady if she pleased.   She blushed ruby red, and trembled, but she said not a word for a while.   And then, having made his offer, he began to speak of love.   In speaking of it, he was urgent enough, but his words had not that sort of suasiveness which they would have possessed had he been addressing himself to Clary Underwood.   "Polly," he said, "I hope you can love me.   I will love you very dearly, and do all that I can to make you happy.   To me you shall be the first woman in the world.   Do you think that you can love me, Polly ? "

Polly was, perhaps, particular.   She had not quite approved of the manner in which Ontario had disclosed his love, though there had been something of the eloquence of passion even in that ;—and now she was hardly satisfied with Ralph Newton.   She had formed to herself, perhaps, some idea of a soft, insinuating, coaxing whisper, something that should be half caress and half prayer, but something that should at least be very gentle and very loving.   Ontario was loving, but he was not gentle.   Ralph Newton was gentle, but then she doubted whether he was loving.   " Will you say that it shall be so ? " he asked, standing over her, and looking down upon her with his most bewitching smile.

Polly amidst her blushing and her trembling made up her mind that she would say nothing of the kind at this present moment.   She would like to be a lady though she was not ashamed of being a tradesman's daughter ;—but she would not buy the privilege of being a lady at too dear a price.   The price would be very high indeed were she to give herself to a man who did not love her, and perhaps despised her.   And then she was not quite sure that she could love this man herself, though she was possessed of a facility for liking nice young men.   Ralph Newton was well enough in many ways.   He was good looking, he could speak up for himself, he did not give himself airs,—and then, as she had been fully instructed by her father, he must ultimately inherit a large property.   Were she to marry him her position would be absolutely that of one of the ladies of the land. But then she knew,—she could not but know,—that he sought her because he was in want of money for his present needs. To be made a lady of the land would be delightful; but to have a grand passion,—in regard to which Polly would not be satisfied unless there were as much love on one side as on the other,—would be more delightful. That latter was essentially necessary to her. The man must take an absolute pleasure in her company, or the whole thing would be a failure. So she blushed and trembled, and thought and was silent. "Dear Polly, do you mean that you cannot love me?" said Ralph.

"I don't know," said Polly.

"Will you try?" demanded Ralph.

"And I don't know that you can love me."

"Indeed, indeed, I can."

"Ah, yes;—you can say so, I don't doubt. There's a many of them as can say so, and yet it's not in 'em to do it. And there's men as don't know hardly how to say it, and yet it's in their hearts all the while." Polly must have been thinking of Ontario as she made this latter oracular observation.

"I don't know much about saying it; but I can do it, Polly."

"Oh, as for talking, you can talk. You've been brought up that way. You've had nothing else much to do."

She was very hard upon him, and so he felt it. "I think that's not fair, Polly. What can I say to you better than that I love you, and will be good to you?"

"Oh, good to me! People are always good to me. Why shouldn't they?"

"Nobody will be so good as I will be,—if you will take me. Tell me, Polly, do you not believe me when I say I love you?"

"No;—I don't."

"Why should I be false to you?"

"Ah;—well;—why? It's not for me to say why. Father's been putting you up to this. That's why."

"Your father could put me up to nothing of the kind if it were not that I really loved you."

"And there's another thing, Mr. Newton."

"What's that, Polly?"

"I'm not at all sure that I'm so very fond of you."

"That's unkind."

"Better be true than to rue," said Polly. "Why, Mr. Newton, we don't know anything about each other,—not as yet. I may be, oh, anything bad, for what you know. And for anything I know you may be idle, and extravagant, and a regular man flirt." Polly had a way of speaking the truth without much respect to persons.

"And then, Mr. Newton, I'm not going to be given away by father just as he pleases. Father thinks this and that, and he means it all for the best. I love father dearly. But I don't mean to take anybody as I don't feel I'd pretty nigh break my heart if I wasn't to have him. I ain't come to breaking my heart for you yet, Mr. Newton."

"I hope you never will break your heart."

"I don't suppose you understand, but that's how it is. Let it just stand by for a year or so, Mr. Newton, and see how it is then. Maybe we might get to know each other. Just now, marrying you would be like taking a husband out of a lottery." Ralph stood looking at her, passing his hand over his head, and not quite knowing how to carry on his suit. "I'll tell father what you was saying to me and what I said to you," continued Polly, who seemed quite to understand that Ralph had done his duty by his creditor in making the offer, and that justice to him demanded that this should be acknowledged by the whole family.

"And is that to be all, Polly?" asked Ralph in a melancholy voice.

"All at present, Mr. Newton."

Ralph, as he returned to London in his cab, felt more hurt by the girl's refusal of him than he would before have thought to be possible. He was almost disposed to resolve that he would at once renew the siege and carry it on as though there were no question of twenty thousand pounds, and of money borrowed from the breeches-maker. Polly had shown so much spirit in the interview, and had looked so well in showing it, had stood up such a perfect specimen of healthy, comely, honest womanhood, that he thought that he did love her. There was, however, one comfort clearly left to him. He had done his duty by old Neefit. The money due must of course be paid ;—but he had in good faith done that which he had pledged himself to do in taking the money.

As to the surrender of the estate there were still left to him four days in which to think of it.

CHAPTER XX.

THE CONSERVATIVES OF PERCYCROSS.

EARLY in this month of September there had come a proposition to Sir Thomas, which had thoroughly disturbed him, and made him for a few days a most miserable man. By the tenth of the month, however, he had so far recovered himself as to have made up his mind in regard to the proposition with some feeling of triumphant expectation. On the following day he went home to Fulham, and communicated his determination to his eldest daughter in the following words; "Patience, I am going to stand for the borough of Percycross."

"Papa!"

"Yes. I dare say I'm a fool for my pains. It will cost me some money which I oughtn't to spend; and if I get in I don't know that I can do any good, or that it can do me any good. I suppose you think I'm very wrong?"

"I am delighted,—and so will Clary be. I'm so much pleased! Why shouldn't you be in Parliament? I have always longed that you should go back to public life, though I have never liked to say so to you."

"It is very kind of you to say it now, my dear."

"And I feel it." There was no doubt of that, for, as she spoke, the tears were streaming from her eyes. "But will you succeed? Is there to be anybody against you?"

"Yes, my dear; there is to be somebody against me. In fact, there will be three people against me; and probably I shall not succeed. Men such as I am do not have seats offered to them without a contest. But there is a chance. I was down at Percycross for two days last week, and now I've put out an address. There it is." Upon which he handed a copy of a placard to his daughter, who read it, no doubt, with more enthusiasm than did any of the free and independent electors to whom it was addressed.

The story in regard to the borough of Percycross was as follows. There were going forward in the country at this moment preparations for a general election, which was to take place in October. The readers of this story have not as yet been troubled on this head, there having been no connection between that great matter and the small matters with which our tale has concerned itself. In the Parliament lately dissolved, the very old borough of Percycross,— or Percy St. Cross, as the place was properly called,—had displayed no political partiality, having been represented by two gentlemen, one of whom always followed the conservative leader, and the other the liberal leader, into the respective lobbies of the House of Commons. The borough had very nearly been curtailed of the privilege in regard to two members in the great Reform Bill which had been initiated and perfected and carried through as a whole by the almost unaided intellect and exertions of the great reformer of his age; but it had had its own luck, as the Irishmen say, and had been preserved intact. Now the wise men of Percycross, rejoicing in their salvation, and knowing that there might still be danger before them should they venture on a contest,—for bribery had not been unknown in previous contests at Percycross, nor petitions consequent upon bribery; and some men had marvelled that the borough should have escaped so long; and there was now supposed to be abroad a spirit of assumed virtue in regard to such matters under which Percycross might still be sacrificed if Percycross did not look very sharp after itself;—thinking of all this, the wise men at Percycross had concluded that it would be better, just for the present, to let things run smoothly, and to return their two old members. When the new broom which was to sweep up the dirt of corruption was not quite so new, they might return to the old game,—which was, in truth, a game very much loved in the old town of Percycross. So thought the wise men, and for a while it seemed that the wise men were to have their own way. But there were men at Percycross who were not wise, and who would have it that such an arrangement as this showed lack of spirit. The conservative foolish men at Percycross began by declaring that they could return two members for the borough if they pleased, and that they would do so, unless this and that were conceded to them. The liberal foolish men swore that they were ready for the battle. They would concede nothing, and would stand up and fight if the word concession were named to them. They would not only have one member, but would have half the aldermen, half the town-councillors, half the mayor, half the patronage in beadles, bell-ringers and bumbledom in general. Had the great reformer of the age given them household suffrage for nothing? The liberal foolish men of Percycross declared, and perhaps thought, that they could send two liberal members to Parliament. And so the borough grew hot. There was one very learned pundit in those parts, a pundit very learned in political matters, who thus prophesied to one of the proposed candidates;—" You'll spend a thousand pounds in the election. You won't get in, of course, but you'll petition. That'll be another thousand. You'll succeed there, and disfranchise the borough. It will be a great career, and no doubt you'll find it satisfactory. You mustn't show yourself in Percycross afterwards;—that's all." But the spirit was afloat, and the words of the pundit were of no avail. The liberal

spirit had been set a going, and men went to work with the new
lists of borough voters. By the end of August it was seen that
there must be a contest. But who should be the new candidates?

The old candidates were there,—one on each side: an old Tory
and a young Radical. In telling our tale we will not go back to the
old sins of the borough, or say aught but good of the past career of
the members. Old Mr. Griffenbottom, the Tory, had been very
generous with his purse, and was beloved, doubtless, by many in
the borough. It is so well for a borough to have some one who is
always ready with a fifty-pound note in this or that need! It is so
comfortable in a borough to know that it can always have its subscription lists well headed! And the young Radical was popular
throughout the county. No one could take a chair at a mechanics'
meeting with better grace or more alacrity, or spin out his half-hour's
speech with greater ease and volubility. And then he was a born
gentleman, which is so great a recommendation for a Radical. So
that, in fact, young Mr. Westmacott, though he did not spend so
much money as old Griffenbottom, was almost as popular in the
borough. There was no doubt about Griffenbottom and Westmacott,—if only the borough would have listened to its wise men and
confined itself to the political guardianship of such excellent representatives! But the foolish men prevailed over the wise men, and it
was decided that there should be a contest.

It was an evil day for Griffenbottom when it was suggested to him
that he should bring a colleague with him. Griffenbottom knew what
this meant almost as well as the learned pundit whose words we have
quoted. Griffenbottom had not been blessed with uncontested
elections, and had run through many perils. He had spent what he
was accustomed to call, when speaking of his political position
among his really intimate friends, "a treasure" in maintaining the
borough. He must often have considered within himself whether
his whistle was worth the price. He had petitioned and been
petitioned against, and had had evil things said of him, and had gone
through the very heat of the fire of political warfare. But he had
kept his seat, and now at last,—so he thought,—the ease and
comfort of an unopposed return was to repay him for everything.
Alas! how all this was changed; how his spirits sank within him,
when he received that high-toned letter from his confidential agent,
Mr. Trigger, in which he was invited to suggest the name of a
colleague! "I'm sure you'll be rejoiced to hear, for the sake of the
old borough," said Mr. Trigger, "that we feel confident of carrying
the two seats." Could Mr. Trigger have heard the remarks which
his patron made on reading that letter, Mr. Trigger would have
thought that Mr. Griffenbottom was the most ungrateful member of
Parliament in the world. What did not Mr. Griffenbottom owe to the

borough of Percycross ? Did he not owe all his position in the world,
all his friends, the fact that he was to be seen on the staircases of
Cabinet Ministers, and that he was called "honourable friend" by the
sons of dukes,—did he not owe it all to the borough of Percycross ?
Mr. Trigger and other friends of his, felt secure in their conviction that
they had made a man of Mr. Griffenbottom. Mr. Griffenbottom
understood enough of all this to answer Mr. Trigger without inserting
in his letter any of those anathemas which he uttered in the privacy
of his own closet. He did, indeed, expostulate, saying, that he
would of course suggest a colleague, if a colleague were required ;
but did not Mr. Trigger and his other friends in the dear old borough
think that just at the present moment a pacific line of action would
be best for the interests of the dear old borough ? Mr. Trigger
answered him very quickly, and perhaps a little sharply. The
Liberals had decided upon having two men in the field, and therefore
a pacific line of action was no longer possible. Mr. Griffenbottom
hurried over to the dear old borough, still hoping,—but could do
nothing. The scent of the battle was in the air, and the foolish men
of Percycross were keen for blood. Mr. Griffenbottom smiled and
promised, and declared to himself that there was no peace for the
politician on this side the grave. He made known his desires,—or
the desire rather of the borough,—to a certain gentleman connected
with a certain club in London, and the gentleman in question on the
following day waited upon Sir Thomas. Sir Thomas had always
been true "to the party,"—so the gentleman in question was good
enough to say. Everybody had regretted the loss of Sir Thomas
from the House. The present opportunity of returning to it was
almost unparalleled, seeing that thing was so nearly a certainty.
Griffenbottom had always been at the top of the poll, and the large
majority of the new voters were men in the employment of conservative masters. The gentleman in question was very clear in his
explanation that there was a complete understanding on this matter
between the employers and employed at Percycross. It was the
nature of the Percycross artizan to vote as his master voted. They
made boots, mustard, and paper at Percycross. The men in the
mustard and paper trade were quite safe ;—excellent men, who went
in a line to the poll, and voted just as the master paper-makers and
master mustard-makers desired. The gentleman from the club
acknowledged that there was a difficulty about the boot-trade. All
the world over, boots do affect radical sentiments. The master
bootmakers,—there were four in the borough,—were decided ; but
the men could not be got at with any certainty.

"Why should you wish to get at them ?" demanded Sir Thomas.

"No ;—of course not ; one doesn't wish to get at them," said the
gentleman from the club,—"particularly as we are safe without

them." Then he went into statistics, and succeeded in proving to Sir Thomas that there would be a hard fight. Sir Thomas, who was much pressed as to time, took a day to consider. "Did Mr. Griffen-bottom intend to fight the battle with clean hands?" The gentleman from the club was eager in declaring that everything would be done in strict accordance with the law. He could give no guarantee as to expenses, but presumed it would be about £300,—perhaps £400,—certainly under £500. The other party no doubt would bribe. They always did. And on their behalf,—on behalf of Westmacott and Co.,—there would be treating, and intimidation, and subornation, and fictitious voting, and every sin to which an election is subject. It always was so with the Liberals at Percycross. But Sir Thomas might be sure that on his side everything would be—"serene." Sir Thomas at last consented to go down to Percycross, and see one or two of his proposed supporters.

He did go down, and was considerably disgusted. Mr. Trigger took him in hand and introduced him to three or four gentlemen in the borough. Sir Thomas, in his first interview with Mr. Trigger, declared his predilection for purity. "Yes, yes; yes, yes; of course," said Mr. Trigger. Mr. Trigger, seeing that Sir Thomas had come among them as a stranger to whom had been offered the very great honour of standing for the borough of Percycross,—offered to him before he had subscribed a shilling to any of the various needs of the borough,—was not disposed to listen to dictation. But Sir Thomas insisted. "It's as well that we should understand each other at once," said Sir Thomas. "I should throw up the contest in the middle of it,—even if I were winning,—if I suspected that money was being spent improperly." How often has the same thing been said by a candidate, and what candidate ever has thrown up the sponge when he was winning? Mr. Trigger was at first dis-posed to tell Sir Thomas that he was interfering in things beyond his province. Had it not been that the day was late, and that the Liberals were supposed to be hard at work,—that the candidate was wanted at once, Mr. Trigger would have shown his spirit. As it was he could only assent with a growl, and say that he had supposed all that was to be taken as a matter of course.

"But I desire to have it absolutely understood by all those who act with me in this matter," said Sir Thomas. "At any rate I will not be petitioned against."

"Petitions never come to much at Percycross," said Mr. Trigger. He certainly ought to have known, as he had had to do with a great many of them. Then they started to call upon two or three of the leading conservative gentlemen. "If I were you, I wouldn't say anything about that, Sir Thomas."

"About what?"

"Well;—bribery and petitions, and the rest of it. Gentlemen when they're consulted don't like to be told of those sort of things. There has been a little of it, perhaps. Who can say?" Who, indeed, if not Mr. Trigger,—in regard to Percycross? "But it's better to let all that die out of itself. It never came to much in Percycross. I don't think there was ever more than ten shillings to be had for a vote. And I've known half-a-crown a piece buy fifty of 'em," he added emphatically. "It never was of much account, and it's best to say nothing about it."

"It's best perhaps to make one's intentions known," said Sir Thomas mildly. Mr. Trigger hummed and hawed, and shook his head, and put his hands into his trousers pockets;—and in his heart of hearts he despised Sir Thomas.

On that day Sir Thomas was taken to see four gentlemen of note in Percycross,—a mustard-maker, a paper-maker, and two boot-makers. The mustard-maker was very cordial in offering his support. He would do anything for the cause. Trigger knew him. The men were all right at his mills. Then Sir Thomas said a word. He was a great foe to intimidation;—he wouldn't for worlds have the men coerced. The mustard-maker laughed cheerily. "We know what all that comes to at Percycross; don't we, Trigger? We shall all go straight from this place;—shan't we, Trigger? And he needn't ask any questions;—need he, Trigger?" "Lord 'a mercy, no," said Trigger, who was beginning to be disgusted. Then they went on to the paper-maker's.

The paper-maker was a very polite gentleman, who seemed to take great delight in shaking Sir Thomas by the hand, and who agreed with energy to every word Sir Thomas said. Triggers tood a little apart at the paper-maker's, as soon as the introduction had been performed,—perhaps disapproving in part of the paper-maker's principles. "Certainly not, Sir Thomas; not for the world, Sir Thomas. I'm clean against anything of that kind, Sir Thomas," said the paper-maker. Sir Thomas assured the paper-maker that he was glad to hear it;—and he was glad. As they went to the first bootmaker's, Mr. Trigger communicated to Sir Thomas a certain incident in the career of Mr. Spiveycomb, the paper-maker. "He's got a contract for paper from the 'Walhamshire Herald,' Sir Thomas;—the largest circulation anywhere in these parts. Griffenbottom gets him that; and if ere a man of his didn't vote as he bade 'em, he wouldn't keep 'em, not a day. I don't know that we've a man in Percycross so stanch as old Spiveycomb." This was Mr. Trigger's revenge.

The first bootmaker had very little to say for himself, and hardly gave Sir Thomas much opportunity of preaching his doctrine of purity. "I hope you'll do something for our trade, Sir Thomas," said the first bootmaker. Sir Thomas explained that he did not at present see his way to the doing of anything special for the boot-makers; and then took his leave. "He's all right," said Mr. Trigger. "He means it. He's all right. And he'll say a word to his men too, though I don't know that much 'll come of it. They're a rum lot. If they're put out here to-day, they can get in there to-morrow. They're a cankery independent sort of chaps, are bootmakers. Now we'll go and see old Pile. He'll have to second one of you,—will Pile. He's a sort of father of the borough in the way of Conservatives. And look here, Sir Thomas;—let him talk. Don't you say much to him. It's no use in life talking to old Pile." Sir Thomas said nothing, but he determined that he would speak to old Pile just as freely as he had to Mr. Trigger himself.

"Eh;—ah;"—said old Pile; "you're Sir Thomas Underwood, are you? And you wants to go into Parliament?"

"If it please you and your townsmen to send me there."

"Yes;—that's just it. But if it don't please?"

"Why, then I'll go home again."

"Just so;—but the people here ain't what they are at other places, Sir Thomas Underwood. I've seen many elections here, Sir Thomas."

"No doubt you have, Mr. Pile."

"Over a dozen;—haven't you, Mr. Pile?" said Trigger.

"And carried on a deal better than they have been since you meddled with them," said Mr. Pile, turning upon Trigger. "They used to do the thing here as it should be done, and nobody wasn't extortionate, nor yet cross-grained. They're changing a deal about these things, I'm told; but they're changing all for the worse. They're talking of purity,—purity,—purity; and what does it all amount to? Men is getting greedier every day."

"We mean to be pure at this election, Mr. Pile," said Sir Thomas. Mr. Pile looked him hard in the face. "At least I do, Mr. Pile. I can answer for myself." Mr. Pile turned away his face, and opened his mouth, and put his hand upon his stomach, and made a grimace, as though,—as though he were not quite as well as he might be. And such was the case with him. The idea of purity of election at Percy-cross did in truth make him feel very sick. It was an idea which he hated with his whole heart. There was to him something absolutely mean and ignoble in the idea of a man coming forward to represent a borough in Parliament without paying the regular fees. That some-body, somewhere, should make a noise about it,—somebody who was impalpable to him, in some place that was to him quite another world,—was intelligible. It might be all very well in Manchester and such-like disagreeable places. But that candidates should come down to Percycross and talk about purity there, was a thing abominable to him. He had nothing to get by bribery. To a certain extent he was willing to pay money in bribery himself. But that a stranger should come to the borough and want the seat without paying for it was to him so distasteful, that this assurance from the mouth of one of the candidates did make him very sick.

"I think you'd better go back to London, Sir Thomas," said Mr. Pile, as soon as he recovered himself sufficiently to express his opinion.

"You mean that my ideas as to standing won't suit the borough."

"No, they won't, Sir Thomas. I don't suppose anybody else will tell you so,—but I'll do it. Why should, a poor man lose his day's wages for the sake of making you a Parliament man? What have you done for any of 'em?"

"Half an hour would take a working man to the poll and back," argued Sir Thomas.

"That's all you know about elections. That's not the way we manage matters here. There won't be any place of business agait that day." Then Mr. Trigger whispered a few words to Mr. Pile. Mr. Pile repeated the grimace which he had made before, and turned on his heel although he was in his own parlour, as though he were going to leave them. But he thought better of this, and turned again. "I always vote Blue myself," said Mr. Pile, "and I don't suppose I shall do otherwise this time. But I shan't take no trouble. There's a many things that I don't like, Sir Thomas. Good morning, Sir Thomas. It's all very well for Mr. Trigger. He knows where the butter lies for his bread."

"A very disagreeable old man," said Sir Thomas, when they had left the house, thinking that as Mr. Trigger had been grossly insulted by the bootmaker he would probably coincide in this opinion.

But Mr. Trigger knew his townsman well, and was used to him. "He's better than some of 'em, Sir Thomas. He'll do as much as he says, and more. Now there was that chap Spicer at the mustard works. They say Westmacott people are after him, and if they can make it worth his while he'll go over. There's some talk about Apothecary's Hall;—I don't know what it is. But you couldn't buy old Pile if you were to give him the Queen and all the Royal family to make boots for."

This was to have been the last of Sir Thomas's preliminary visits among the leading Conservatives of the borough, but as they were going back to the "Percy Standard,"—for such was the name of the Blue inn in the borough,—Mr. Trigger saw a gentleman in black standing at an open hall door, and immediately proposed that they should just say a word or two to Mr. Pabsby. "Wesleyan minister," whispered the Percycross bear-leader into the ear of his bear;—"and has a deal to say to many of the men, and more to the women. Can't say what he'll do;—split his vote, probably." Then he introduced the two men, explaining the cause of Sir Thomas's presence in the borough. Mr. Pabsby was delighted to make the acquaintance of Sir Thomas, and asked the two gentlemen into the house. In truth he was delighted. The hours often ran heavily with him, and here there was something for him to do. "You'll give us a help, Mr. Pabsby?" said Mr. Trigger. Mr. Pabsby smiled and rubbed his hands, and paused and laid his head on one side.

"I hope he will," said Sir Thomas, "if he is of our way of thinking, otherwise I should be sorry to ask him." Still Mr. Pabsby said nothing;—but he smiled very sweetly, and laid his head a little lower.

"He knows we're on the respectable side," said Mr. Trigger. "The Wesleyans now are most as one as the Church of England,— in the way of not being roughs and rowdies." Sir Thomas, who did not know Mr. Pabsby, was afraid that he would be offended at this; but he showed no sign of offence as he continued to rub his hands. Mr. Pabsby was meditating his speech.

"We're a little hurried, Mr. Pabsby," said Mr. Trigger; "perhaps you'll think of it."

But Mr. Pabsby was not going to let them escape in that way. It was not every day that he had a Sir Thomas, or a candidate for the borough, or even a Mr. Trigger, in that little parlour. The fact was that Mr. Trigger, who generally knew what he was about, had made a mistake. Sir Thomas, who was ready enough to depart, saw that an immediate escape was impossible. "Sir Thomas," began Mr. Pabsby, in a soft, greasy voice,—a voice made up of pretence, politeness and saliva,—"if you will give me three minutes to express myself on this subject I shall be obliged to you."

"Certainly," said Sir Thomas, sitting bolt upright in his chair, and holding his hat as though he were determined to go directly the three minutes were over.

"A minister of the Gospel in this town is placed in a peculiar position, Sir Thomas," said Mr. Pabsby very slowly, "and of all the ministers of religion in Percycross mine is the most peculiar. In this matter I would wish to be guided wholly by duty, and if I could see my way clearly I would at once declare it to you. But, Sir Thomas, I owe much to the convictions of my people."

"Which way do you mean to vote?" asked Mr. Trigger.

Mr. Pabsby did not even turn his face at this interruption. "A private man, Sir Thomas, may follow the dictates of—of—of his own heart, perhaps." Here he paused, expecting to be encouraged by some words. But Sir Thomas had acquired professionally a knowledge that to such a speaker as Mr. Pabsby any rejoinder or argument was like winding up a clock. It is better to allow such clocks to run down. "With me, I have to consider every possible point. What will my people wish? Some of them are eager in the cause of reform, Sir Thomas; and some others——"

"We shall lose the train," said Mr. Trigger, jumping up and putting on his hat.

"I'm afraid we shall," said Sir Thomas rising, but not putting on his.

"Half a minute," said Mr. Pabsby pleading, but not rising from his chair. "Perhaps you will do me the honour of calling on me when you are again here in Percycross. I shall have the greatest pleasure in discussing a few matters with you, Sir Thomas; and then, if I can give you my poor help, it will give me and Mrs. Pabsby the most sincere pleasure." Mrs. Pabsby had now entered the room, and was introduced; but Trigger would not sit down again, nor take off his hat. He boldly marshalled the way to the door, while Sir Thomas followed, subject as he came to the eloquence of Mr. Pabsby. "If I can only see my way clearly, Sir Thomas," were the last words which Mr. Pabsby spoke.

"He'll give one to Griffenbottom, certainly," said Mr. Trigger. "Westmacott 'll probably have the other. I thought perhaps your title might have gone down with him, but it didn't seem to take."

All this was anything but promising, anything but comfortable; and yet before he went to bed that night Sir Thomas had undertaken to stand. In such circumstances it is very hard for a man to refuse. He feels that a certain amount of trouble has been taken on his behalf, that retreat will be cowardly, and that the journey for nothing will be personally disagreeable to his own feelings. And then, too, there was that renewed ambition in his breast,—an ambition which six months ago he would have declared to be at rest for ever,—but which prompted him, now as strongly as ever, to go forward and do something. It is so easy to go and see;—so hard to retreat when one has seen. He had not found Percycross to be especially congenial to him. He had felt himself to be out of his element there, —among people with whom he had no sympathies; and he felt also that he had been unfitted for this kind of thing by the life which he had led for the last few years. Still he undertook to stand.

"Who is coming forward on the other side?" he asked Mr. Trigger late at night, when this matter had been decided in regard to himself.

"Westmacott, of course," said Trigger, "and I'm told that the real Rads of the place have got hold of a fellow named Moggs."

"Moggs!" ejaculated Sir Thomas.

"Yes;—Moggs. The Young Men's Reform Association is bringing him forward. He's a Trades' Union man, and a Reform Leaguer, and all that kind of thing. I shouldn't be surprised if he got in. They say he's got money."

CHAPTER XXI.

THE LIBERALS OF PERCYCROSS.

YES ;—Ontario Moggs was appalled, delighted, exalted, and nearly frightened out of his wits by an invitation, conveyed to him by certain eager spirits of the town, to come down and stand on the real radical interest for the borough of Percycross. The thing was not suggested to him till a day or two after Sir Thomas had been sounded, and he was then informed that not an hour was to be lost. The communication was made in the little back parlour of the Cheshire Cheese, and Moggs was expected to give an answer then and there. He stood with his hand on his brow for five minutes, and then asked that special question which should always come first on such occasions. Would it cost any money ? Well ;—yes. The eager spirits of Percycross thought that it would cost something. They were forced to admit that Percycross was not one of those well-arranged boroughs in which the expenses of an election are all defrayed by the public spirit of the citizens. It soon became clear that the deputation had waited upon Moggs, not only because Moggs was a good Radical, but because also Moggs was supposed to be a Radical with a command of money. Ontario frowned and expressed an opinion that all elections should be made absolutely free to the candidates. "And everybody ought to go to 'eaven, Mr. Moggs," said the leading member of the deputation, "but everybody don't, 'cause things ain't as they ought to be." There was no answer to be made to this. Ontario could only strike his forehead and think. It was clear to him that he could not give an affirmative answer that night, and he therefore, with some difficulty, arranged an adjournment of the meeting till the following afternoon at 2 P.M. "We must go down by the 4.45 express to-morrow," said the leading member of the deputation, who even by that arrangement would subject himself to the loss of two days' wages,—for he was a foreman in the establishment of Mr. Spicer the mustard-maker,—and whose allowance for expenses would not admit of his sleeping away from home a second night. Ontario departed, promising to be ready with his answer by 2 P.M. on the following day.

How bright with jewels was the crown now held before his eyes, and yet how unapproachable, how far beyond his grasp ! To be a member of Parliament, to speak in that august assembly instead of wasting his eloquence on the beery souls of those who frequented the Cheshire Cheese, to be somebody in the land at his early age,—something so infinitely superior to a maker of boots ! A member of Parliament was by law an esquire, and therefore a gentleman. Ralph Newton was not a member of Parliament ;—not half so great a fellow as a member of Parliament. Surely if he were to go to Polly Neefit as a member of Parliament Polly would reject him no longer! And to what might it not lead? He had visions before his eyes of very beautiful moments in his future life, in which, standing, as it were, on some well-chosen rostrum in that great House, he would make the burning thoughts of his mind, the soaring aspirations of his heart, audible to all the people. How had Cobden begun his career,—and Bright? Had it not been in this way? Why should not he be as great, —greater than either;—greater, because in these coming days a man of the people would be able to wield a power more extensive than the people had earned for themselves in former days? And then, as he walked alone through the streets, he took to making speeches,— some such speeches as he would make when he stood up in his place in the House of Commons as the member for Percycross. The honourable member for Percycross! There was something ravishing in the sound. Would not that sound be pleasant to the ears of Polly Neefit?

But then, was not the thing as distant as it was glorious? How could he be member for Percycross, seeing that in all matters he was subject to his father? His father hated the very name of the Cheshire Cheese, and was, in every turn and feeling of his life, diametrically opposed to his son's sentiments. He would, nevertheless, go to his father and demand assistance. If on such an occasion as this his father should give him a stone when he asked for bread, he and his father must be two! "If, when such a prospect as this is held out to his son, he cannot see it," said Ontario, "then he can see nothing!" But yet he was sure that his father wouldn't see it.

To his extreme astonishment Mr. Moggs senior did see it. It was some time before Mr. Moggs senior clearly understood the proposition which was made to him, but when he did he became alive to the honour,—and perhaps profit,—of having a member of his firm in Parliament. Of politics in the abstract Mr. Moggs senior knew very little. Nor, indeed, did he care much. In matters referring to trade he was a Conservative, because he was a master. He liked to be able to manage his people, and to pay 5s. 3d. instead of 5s. 8d. for the making of a pair of boots. He hated the Cheshire Cheese because his son went there, and because his son entertained strange and injurious ideas which were propagated at that low place. But if the Cheshire Cheese would send his son to Parliament, Mr. Moggs did not know but what the Cheshire Cheese might be very well. At any rate, he undertook to pay the bills, if Ontario, his son, were brought forward as a candidate for the borough. He lost his head so completely in the glory of the thing, that it never occurred to him to ask what might be the probable amount of the expenditure. "There ain't no father in all London as 'd do more for his son than I would, if only

I see'd there was something in it," said Moggs senior, with a tear in his eye. Moggs junior was profuse in gratitude, profuse in obedience, profuse in love. Oh, heavens, what a golden crown was there now within his grasp !

All this occurred between the father and son early in the morning at Shepherd's Bush, whither the son had gone out to the father after a night of feverish longing and ambition. They went into town together, on the top of the omnibus, and Ontario felt that he was being carried heavenwards. What a heaven had he before him, even in that fortnight's canvass which it would be his glory to undertake ! What truths he would tell to the people, how he would lead them with him by political revelations that should be almost divine, how he would extract from them bursts of rapturous applause ! To explain to them that labour is the salt of the earth ;—that would be his mission. And then, how sweet to teach them the value, the inestimable value, of the political privilege lately accorded to them,—or, as Ontario would put it, lately wrested on their behalf from the hands of an aristocracy which was more timid even than it was selfish ;—how sweet to explain this, and then to instruct them, afterwards, that it was their duty now, having got this great boon for themselves, to see at once that it should be extended to those below them. " Let the first work of household suffrage be a demand for manhood suffrage." This had been enunciated by Ontario Moggs with great effect at the Cheshire Cheese ;—and now, as the result of such enunciation, he was going down to Percycross to stand as a candidate for the borough ! He was almost drunk with delight as he sat upon the knife-board of the Shepherd's Bush omnibus, thinking of it all.

He, too, went down to Percycross, making a preliminary journey,— as had done Sir Thomas Underwood,—timing his arrival there a day or two after the departure of the lawyer. Alas, he, also, met much to disappoint him even at that early period of the contest. The people whom he was taken to see were not millionaires and tradesmen in a large way of business, but leading young men of warm political temperaments. This man was president of a mechanics' institute, that secretary to an amalgamation of unions for general improvement, and a third chairman of the Young Men's Reform Association. They were delighted to see him, and were very civil ; but he soon found that they were much more anxious to teach him than they were to receive his political lessons. When he began, as unfortunately he did very early in his dealings with them, to open out his own views, he soon found that they had views also to open out. He was to represent them,—that is to say, become the mouth piece of their ideas. He had been selected because he was supposed to have some command of money. Of course he would have to address the people in the Mechanics' Hall ; but the chairman of the

Young Men's Reform Association was very anxious to tell him what to say on that occasion. " I am accustomed to addressing people," said Ontario Moggs, with a considerable accession of dignity.

He had the satisfaction of addressing the people, and the people received him kindly. But he thought he observed that the applause was greater when the secretary of the Amalgamation-of-Improvement-Unions spoke, and he was sure that the enthusiasm for the Young Men's chairman mounted much higher than had done any ardour on his own behalf. And he was astonished to find that these young men were just as fluent as himself. He did think, indeed, that they did not go quite so deep into the matter as he did, that they had not thought out great questions so thoroughly, but they had a way of saying things which,—which would have told even at the Cheshire Cheese. The result of all this was, that at the end of three days,—though he was, no doubt, candidate for the borough of Percycross, and in that capacity a great man in Percycross,—he did not seem to himself to be so great as he had been when he made the journey down from London. There was a certain feeling that he was a cat's-paw, brought there for certain objects which were not his objects, —because they wanted money, and some one who would be fool enough to fight a losing battle ! He did not reap all that meed of personal admiration for his eloquence which he expected.

And, then, during these three days there arose another question, the discussion of which embarrassed him not a little. Mr. Westmacott was in the town, and there was a question whether he and Mr. Westmacott were to join forces. It was understood that Mr. Westmacott and Mr. Westmacott's leading friends objected to this ; but the chairmen of the young men, and the presidents and the secretaries on the Radical side put their heads together, and declared that if Mr. Westmacott were proud they would run their horse alone ;—they would vote for Moggs, and for Moggs only. Or else,—as it was whispered,—they would come to terms with Griffenbottom, and see that Sir Thomas was sent back to London. The chairmen, and the presidents, and the secretaries were powerful enough to get the better of Mr. Westmacott, and large placards were printed setting forward the joint names of Westmacott and Moggs. The two liberal candidates were to employ the same agent, and were to canvass together. This was all very well,—was the very thing which Moggs should have desired. But it was all arranged without any consultation with him, and he felt that the objection which had been raised was personal to himself. Worse than all, when he was brought face to face with Mr. Westmacott he had not a word to say for himself ! He tried it and failed. Mr. Westmacott had been a member of Parliament, and was a gentleman. Ontario, for aught he himself knew, might have called upon Mr. Westmacott for the amount of Mr. Westmacott's little bill. He caught himself calling Mr. Westmacott, sir, and almost wished that he could bite out his own tongue. He felt that he was a nobody in the interview, and that the chairmen, the secretaries, and the presidents were regretting their bargain, and saying among themselves that they had done very badly in bringing down Ontario Moggs as a candidate for their borough. There were moments before he left Percycross in which he was almost tempted to resign.

But he left the town the accepted candidate of his special friends, and was assured, with many parting grasps of the hand on the platform, that he would certainly be brought in at the top of the poll. Another little incident should be mentioned. He had been asked by the electioneering agent for a small trifle of some hundred pounds towards the expenses, and this, by the generosity of his father, he had been able to give. " We shall get along now like a house on fire," said the agent, as he pocketed the cheque. Up to that moment there may have been doubts upon the agent's mind.

As he went back to London he acknowledged to himself that he had failed hitherto,—he had failed in making that impression at Percycross which would have been becoming to him as the future member of Parliament for the borough ; but he gallantly resolved that he would do better in the future. He would speak in such a way that the men of Percycross should listen to him and admire. He would make occasion for himself. He thought that he could do better than Mr. Westmacott,—put more stuff in what he had got to say. And, whatever might happen to him, he would hold up his head. Why should he not be as good a man as Westmacott ? It was the man that was needed,—not the outside trappings. Then he asked himself a question whether, as trappings themselves were so trivial, a man was necessarily mean who dealt in trappings. He did not remember to have heard of a bootmaker in Parliament. But there should be a bootmaker in Parliament soon ;—and thus he plucked up his courage.

On his journey down to Percycross he had thought that immediately on his return to London he would go across to Hendon, and take advantage of his standing as a candidate for the borough ; but as he returned he resolved that he would wait till the election was over. He would go to Polly with all his honours on his head.

CHAPTER XXII.

RALPH NEWTON'S DECISION.

ONTARIO MOGGS was at Percycross when Ralph Newton was making his formal offer to Polly Neefit. Ralph when he had made his offer returned to London with mixed feelings. He had certainly been oppressed at times by the conviction that he must make the offer even though it went against the grain with him to do so ;—and at these moments he had not failed to remind himself that he was about to make himself miserable for life because he had been weak enough to take pecuniary assistance in the hour of his temporary necessities from the hands of Polly's father. Now he had made his offer ; it had not been accepted, and he was still free. He could see his way out of that dilemma without dishonour. But then that dilemma became very much smaller to his sight when it was surmounted,—as is the nature with all dilemmas ; and the other dilemma, which would have been remedied had Polly accepted him, again loomed very large. And as he looked back at the matrimonial dilemma which he had escaped, and at Polly standing before him, comely, healthy, and honest, such a pleasant armful, and so womanly withal,—so pleasant a girl if only she was not to be judged and sentenced by others beside himself,—he almost thought that that dilemma was one which he could have borne without complaint. But Polly's suggestion that they should allow a year to run round in order that they might learn to know each other was one which he could not entertain. He had but three days in which to give an answer to his uncle, and up to this time two alternatives had been open to him,—the sale of his reversion and independence, or Polly and the future lordship of Newton. He had thought that there was nothing but to choose. It had not occurred to him that Polly would raise any objection. He had felt neither fear nor hope in that direction. It followed as a consequence now that the lordship must go: He would not, however, make up his mind that it should go till the last moment.

On the following morning he was thinking that he might as well go to the shop in Conduit Street, feeling that he could encounter Neefit without any qualms of conscience, when Mr. Neefit came to him. This was certainly a better arrangement. It was easier to talk of his own affairs sitting at ease in his own arm-chair, than to carry on the discussion among the various sporting garments which adorned Mr. Neefit's little back room, subject to interruption from customers, and possibly within the hearing of Mr. Waddle and Herr Bawwah. Neefit, seated at the end of the sofa in Ralph's comfortable room, looking out of his saucer eyes with all his energy, was in a certain degree degrading,—but was not quite so degrading as Neefit at his own barn-door in Conduit Street. "I was just coming to you," he said, as he made the breeches-maker welcome.

"Well;—yes; but I thought I'd catch you here, Captain. Them men of mine has such long ears! That German who lets on that he don't understand only just a word or two of English, hears everything through a twelve-inch brick wall. Polly told me as you'd been with her."

"I suppose so, Mr. Neefit."

"Oh, she ain't one as 'd keep anything from me. She's open and straightforward, anyways."

"So I found her."

"Now look here, Captain. I've just one word to say about her. Stick to her." Ralph was well aware that he must explain the exact circumstances in which he stood to the man who was to have been his father-in-law, but hardly knew how to begin his explanation. "She ain't nowise again you," continued Mr. Neefit. "She owned as much when I put her through her facings. I did put her through her facings pretty tightly. 'What is it that you want, Miss?' said I. 'D' you want to have a husband, or d' you want to be an old maid?' They don't like that word old maid;—not as used again themselves, don't any young woman."

"Polly will never be an old maid," said Ralph.

"She owned as she didn't want that. 'I suppose I'll have to take some of 'em some day,' she said. Lord, how pretty she did look as she said it;—just laughing and crying, smiling and pouting all at once. She ain't a bad 'un to look at, Captain?"

"Indeed she is not."

"Nor yet to go. Do you stick to her. Them's my words. 'D' you want to have that ugly bootmaker?' said I. 'He ain't ugly,' said she. 'D' you want to have him, Miss?' said I. 'No, I don't,' said she. 'Well!' said I. 'But I do know him,' said Polly, 'and I don't know Mr. Newton no more than Adam!' Them were her very words, Captain. Do you stick to her, Captain. I'll tell you what. Let's all go down to Margate together for a week." That was Mr. Neefit's plan of action.

Then Ralph got up from his easy-chair and began his explanation. He couldn't very well go down to Margate, delightful as it would be to sit upon the sands with Polly. He was so situated that he must at once decide as to the sale of his property at Newton. Mr. Neefit put his hands in his pockets, and sat perfectly silent, listening to his young friend's explanation. If Polly would have accepted him at once, Ralph went on to explain, everything would have been straight; but, as she would not do so, he must take his uncle's offer. He had no other means of extricating himself from his embarrassments. "Why, Mr. Neefit, I could not look you in the face unless I were prepared to pay you your money," he said.

"Drat that," replied Neefit, and then again he listened.

Ralph went on. He could not go on long in his present condition. His bill for £500 to Mr. Horsball of the Moonbeam was coming round. He literally had not £20 in his possession to carry on the war. His uncle's offer would be withdrawn if it were not accepted the day after to-morrow. Nobody else would give half so much. The thing must be done, and then;—why, then he would have nothing to offer to Polly worthy of her acceptance. "Bother," said Mr. Neefit, who had not once taken his eyes off Ralph's face. Ralph said that that might be all very well, but such were the facts. "You ain't that soft that you're going to let 'em rob you of the estate ?" said the breeches-maker in a tone of horror. Ralph raised his hands and his eyebrows together. Yes;—that was what he intended to do.

"There shan't be nothing of the kind," said the breeches-maker. "What ! £7,000 a year, ain't it ? All in land, ain't it ? And it must be your own, let 'em do what they will; mustn't it ?" He paused a moment, and Ralph nodded his head. "What you have to do is to get a wife,—and a son before any of 'em can say Jack Robinson. Lord bless you ! Just spit at 'em if they talks of buying it. S'pose the old gent was to go off all along of apperplexy the next day, how'd you feel then ? Like cutting your throat ;—wouldn't you, Captain ?"

"But my uncle's life is very good."

"He ain't got no receipt against kingdom come, I dare say." Ralph was surprised by his tradesman's eloquence and wit. "You have a chick of your own, and then you'll know as it'll be yours some way or other. If I'd the chance I'd sooner beg, borrow, starve, or die, before I'd sell it ;—let alone working, Captain." There was satire too as well as eloquence in the breeches-maker. "No ;—you must run your chance, somehow."

"I don't see my way," said Ralph.

"You have got something, Captain ;—something of your own ?"

"Well ;—just enough to pay my debts, if all were sold, and buy myself a rope to hang myself."

"I'll pay your debts, Captain."

"I couldn't hear of it, Mr. Neefit."

"As for not hearing of it,—that's bother. You do hear of it now. And how much more do you want to keep you ? You shall have what you want. You meant honest along of Polly yesterday, and you mean honest now." Ralph winced, but he did not deny what Neefit said, nor aught that was implied in the saying. "We'll bring you and Polly together, and I tell you she'll come round." Ralph shook his head. "Anyways you shall have the money;—there now. We'll have a bit of a paper, and if this marriage don't come off there'll be the money to come back, and five per cent. when the old gent dies."

"But I might die first."

"We'll insure your life, Captain. Only we must be upon the square."

"Oh, yes," said Ralph.

"I'd rather a'most lose it all than think such a chance should be missed. £7,000 a year, and all in land? When one knows how hard it is to get, to think of selling it!"

Ralph made no positive promise, but when Mr. Neefit left him there was,—so at least thought Mr. Neefit,—an implied understanding that "the Captain" would at once put an end to this transaction between him and his uncle. And yet Ralph didn't feel quite certain. The breeches-maker had been generous,—very generous, and very trusting; but he hated the man's generosity and confidence. The breeches-maker had got such a hold of him that he seemed to have lost all power of thinking and acting for himself. And then such a man as he was, with his staring round eyes, and heavy face, and dirty hands, and ugly bald head! There is a baldness that is handsome and noble, and a baldness that is peculiarly mean and despicable. Neefit's baldness was certainly of the latter order. Now Moggs senior, who was grey and not bald, was not bad looking,—at a little distance. His face when closely inspected was poor and greedy, but the general effect at a passing glance was not contemptible. Moggs might have been a banker, or an officer in the Commissariat, or a clerk in the Treasury. A son-in-law would have had hopes of Moggs. But nothing of the kind was possible with Neefit. One would be forced to explain that he was a respectable tradesman in Conduit Street in order that he might not be taken for a dealer in potatoes from Whitechapel. He was hopeless. And yet he had taken upon himself the absolute management of all Ralph Newton's affairs!

Ralph was very unhappy, and in his misery he went to Sir Thomas's chambers. This was about four o'clock in the day, at which hour Sir Thomas was almost always in his rooms. But Stemm with much difficulty succeeded in making him believe that the lawyer was not at home. Stemm at this time was much disturbed by his master's terrible resolution to try the world again, to stand for a seat in Parliament, and to put himself once more in the way of work and possible promotion. Stemm had condemned the project,—but, nevertheless, took glory in it. What if his master should become,— should become anything great and magnificent. Stemm had often groaned in silence,—had groaned unconsciously, that his master should be nothing. He loved his master thoroughly,—loving no one else in the whole world,—and sympathised with him acutely. Still he had condemned the project. "There's so many of them, Sir Thomas, as is only wanting to put their fingers into somebody's eyes." "No doubt, Stemm, no doubt," said Sir Thomas; "and as well into mine as another's." "That's it, Sir Thomas." "But I'll just run down and see, Stemm." And so it had been settled. Stemm, who had always hated Ralph Newton, and who now regarded his master's time as more precious than ever, would hardly give any answer at all to Ralph's enquiries. His master might be at home at Fulham,— probably was. Where should a gentleman so likely be as at home,— that is, when he wasn't in chambers? "Anyways, he's not here," said Stemm, bobbing his head, and holding the door ready to close it. Ralph was convinced, then dined at his club, and afterwards went down to Fulham. He had heard nothing from Stemm, or elsewhere, of the intended candidature.

Sir Thomas was not at Fulham, nor did the girls know aught of his whereabouts. But the great story was soon told. Papa was going to stand for Percycross. "We are so glad," said Mary Bonner, bursting out into enthusiasm. "We walk about the garden making speeches to the electors all day. Oh dear, I do wish we could do something."

"Glad is no word," said Clarissa. "But if he loses it!"

"The very trying for it is good," said Patience. "It is just the proper thing for papa."

"I shall feel so proud when uncle is in Parliament again," said Mary Bonner. "A woman's pride is always vicarious;—but still it is pride."

Ralph also was surprised, — so much surprised that for a few minutes his own affairs were turned out of his head. He, too, had thought that Sir Thomas would never again do anything in the world, —unless that book should be written of which he had so often heard hints,—though never yet, with any accuracy, its name or subject. Sir Thomas, he was told, had been at Percycross, but was not supposed to be there now. "Of course he was in his chambers," said Clarissa. "Old Stemm does know how to tell lies so well!" It was, however, acknowledged that, having on his hands a piece of business so very weighty, Sir Thomas might be almost anywhere without any fault on his part. A gentleman in the throbs of an election for Parliament could not be expected to be at home. Even Patience did not feel called upon to regret his absence.

Before he went back to town Ralph found himself alone with Mary for a few minutes. "Mr. Newton," she said, "why don't you stand for Parliament?"

"I have not the means."

" You have great prospects. I should have thought you were just the man who ought to make it the work of your life to get into Parliament." Ralph began to ask himself what had been the work of his life. " They say that to be of real use a man ought to begin young."

" Nobody ought to go into the House without money," said Ralph.

" That means, I suppose, that men shouldn't go in who want their time to earn their bread. But you haven't that to do. If I were a man such as you are I would always try to be something. I am sure Parliament was meant for men having estates such as you will have.".

" When I've got it, I'll think about Parliament, Miss Bonner."

" Perhaps it will be too late then. Don't you know that song of ' Excelsior,' Mr. Newton ? You ought to learn to sing it."

Yes ;—he was learning to sing it after a fine fashion ;—borrowing his tradesman's money, and promising to marry his tradesman's daughter ! He was half inclined to be angry with this interference from Mary Bonner ;—and yet he liked her for it. Could it be that she herself felt an interest in what concerned him ? " Ah me,"—he said to himself,—" how much better would it have been to have learned something, to have fitted myself for some high work; and to have been able to choose some such woman as this for my wife !" And all that had been sacrificed to horses at the Moonbeam, and little dinners with Captain Fooks and Lieutenant Cox ! Every now and again during his life Phœbus had touched his trembling ears, and had given him to know that to sport with the tangles of Naæra's hair was not satisfactory as the work of a man's life. But, alas, the god had intervened but to little purpose. The horses at the Moonbeam, which had been two, became four, and then six ; and now he was pledged to marry Polly Neefit,—if only he could induce Polly Neefit to have him. It was too late in the day for him to think now of Parliament and Mary Bonner.

And then, before he left them, poor Clary whispered a word into his ear,—a cousinly, brotherly word, such as their circumstances authorised her to make. " Is it settled about the property, Ralph ? " For she, too, had heard that this question of a sale was going forward.

" Not quite, Clary."

" You won't sell it ; will you ? "

" I don't think I shall."

" Oh, don't ;—pray don't. Anything will be better than that. It is so good to wait." She was thinking only of Ralph, and of his interests, but she could not forget the lesson which she was daily teaching to herself.

" If I can help it, I shall not sell it."

" Papa will help you ;—will he not ? If I were you they should drag me in pieces before I would part with my birthright;—and such a birthright!" It had occurred to her once that Ralph might feel that, after what had passed between them one night on the lawn, he was bound not to wait, that it was his duty so to settle his affairs that he might at once go to her father and say,—"Though I shall never be Mr. Newton of Newton, I have still such and such means of support-ing your daughter." Ah! if he would only be open with her, and tell her everything, he would soon know how unnecessary it was to make a sacrifice for her. He pressed her hand as he left her, and said a word that was a word of comfort. "Clary, I cannot speak with certainty, but I do not think that it will be sold."

"I am so glad!" she said. "Oh, Ralph, never, never part with it." And then she blushed, as she thought of what she had said. Could it be that he would think that she was speaking for her own sake;—because she looked forward to reigning some day as mistress of Newton Priory? Ah, no, Ralph would never misinterpret her thoughts in a manner so unmanly as that!

The day came, and it was absolutely necessary that the answer should be given. Neefit came to prompt him again, and seemed to sit on the sofa with more feeling of being at home than he had dis-played before. He brought his cheque-book with him, and laid it rather ostentatiously upon the table. He had good news, too, from Polly. "If Mr. Newton would come down to Margate, she would be ever so glad." That was the message as given by Mr. Neefit, but the reader will probably doubt that it came exactly in those words from Polly's lips. Ralph was angry, and shook his head in wrath. "Well, Captain, how's it to be?" asked Mr. Neefit.

"I shall let my uncle know that I intend to keep my property," said Ralph, with as much dignity as he knew how to assume.

The breeches-maker jumped up and crowed,—actually crowed, as might have crowed a cock. It was an art that he had learned in his youth. "That's my lad of wax," he said, slapping Ralph on the shoulder. "And now tell us how much it's to be," said he, opening the cheque-book. But Ralph declined to take money at the present moment, endeavouring to awe the breeches-maker back into sobriety by his manner. Neefit did put up his cheque-book, but was not awed back into perfect sobriety. "Come to me, when you want it, and you shall have it, Captain. Don't let that chap as 'as the 'orses be any way disagreeable. You tell him he can have it all when he wants it. And he can;—be blowed if he can't. We'll see it through, Captain. And now, Captain, when'll you come out and see Polly?" Ralph would give no definite answer to this,—on account of business, but was induced at last to send his love to Miss Neefit. "That man will drive me into a lunatic asylum at last," he said to himself, as he threw himself into his arm-chair when Neefit had departed.

Nevertheless, he wrote his letter to his uncle's lawyer, Mr. Carey, as follows :—

"———— Club, 20 Sept., 186—.

" DEAR SIR,—

"After mature consideration I have resolved upon declining the offer made to me by my uncle respecting the Newton property.

"Faithfully yours,

" RALPH NEWTON.

"Richard Carey, Esq."

It was very short, but it seemed to him to contain all that there was to be said. He might, indeed, have expressed regret that so much trouble had been occasioned ;—but the trouble had been taken not for his sake, and he was not bound to denude himself of his property because his uncle had taken trouble.

When the letter was put into the Squire's hands in Mr. Carey's private room, the Squire was nearly mad with rage. In spite of all that his son had told him, in disregard of all his own solicitor's cautions, in the teeth of his nephew Gregory's certainty, he had felt sure that the thing would be done. The young man was penniless, and must sell; and he could sell nowhere else with circumstances so favourable. And now the young man wrote a letter as though he were declining to deal about a horse ! "It's some sham, some falsehood," said the Squire. " Some low attorney is putting him up to thinking that he can get more out of me."

" It's possible," said Mr. Carey; " but there's nothing more to be done." The Squire when last in London had asserted most positively that he would not increase his bid.

" But he's penniless," said the Squire.

" There are those about him that will put him in the way of raising money," said the lawyer.

" And so the property will go to the hammer,—and I can do nothing to help it ! " Mr. Carey did not tell his client that a gentleman had no right to complain because he could not deal with effects which were not his own; but that was the line which his thoughts took. The Squire walked about the room, lashing himself in his rage. He could not bear to be beaten. "How much more would do it ? " he said at last. It would be terribly bitter to him to be made to give way, to be driven to increase the price; but even that would be less bitter than failure.

" I should say nothing,—just at present, if I were you," said Mr. Carey. The Squire still walked about the room. "If he raises money on the estate we shall hear of it. And so much of his rights as pass from him we can purchase. It will be more prudent for us to wait."

" Would another £5,000 do it at once ? " said the Squire.

" At any rate I would not offer it," said Mr. Carey.

" Ah ;—you don't understand. You don't feel what it is that I want. What would you say if a man told you to wait while your hand was in the fire ? "

" But you are in possession, Mr. Newton."

" No ;—I'm not. I'm not in possession. I'm only a lodger in the place. I can do nothing. I cannot even build a farm-house for a tenant."

" Surely you can, Mr. Gregory."

" What ;—for him ! You think that would be one of the delights of possession ? Put my money into the ground like seed, in order that the fruit may be gathered by him ! I'm not good enough Christian, Mr. Carey, to take much delight in that. I'll tell you what it is, Mr. Carey. The place is a hell upon earth to me, till I can call it my own." At last he left his lawyer, and went back to Newton Priory, having given instructions that the transaction should be re-opened between the two lawyers, and that additional money, to the extent of £5,000, should by degrees be offered.

CHAPTER XXIII.

"I'LL BE A HYPOCRITE IF YOU CHOOSE.'

THERE could hardly be a more unhappy man than was the Squire
on his journey home. He had buoyed himself up with hope till
he had felt certain that he would return to Newton Priory its real and
permanent owner, no longer a lodger in the place, as he had called
himself to the lawyer, but able to look upon every tree as his own,
with power to cut down every oak upon the property; though, as he
knew very well, he would rather spill blood from his veins than cut
down one of them. But in that case he would preserve the oaks,—
preserve them by his own decision,—because they were his own, and
because he could give them to his own son. His son should cut them
down if he pleased. And then the power of putting up would be
quite as sweet to him as the power of pulling down. What pleasure
would he have in making every deficient house upon the estate
efficient, when he knew that the stones as he laid them would not
become the property of his enemy. He was a man who had never
spent his full income. The property had been in his hands now for
some fifteen years, and he had already amassed a considerable sum of
money,—a sum which would have enabled him to buy out his nephew
altogether, without selling an acre,—presuming the price already fixed
to have been sufficient. He had determined to sell something, knowing
that he could not do as he would do with the remainder if his hands
were empty. He had settled it all in his mind;—how Ralph, his
Ralph, must marry, and have a separate income. There would be no
doubt about his Ralph's marriage when once it should be known that
his Ralph was the heir to Newton. The bar sinister would matter
but little then;—would be clean forgotten. His mind had been full
of all this as he had come up to London. It had all been settled.
He had decided upon ignoring altogether those cautions which his son
and nephew and lawyer had croaked into his ears. This legitimate
heir was a ruined spendthrift, who had no alternative but to raise
money, no ambition but to spend money, no pursuit but to waste
money. His temperament was so sanguine that when he entered
Mr. Carey's office he had hardly doubted. Now everything had been
upset, and he was cast down from triumph into an abyss of despon-
dency by two lines from this wretched, meaningless, poor-spirited
spendthrift! "I believe he'd take a pleasure in seeing the property
going to the dogs, merely to spite me," said the Squire to his son, as
soon as he reached home,—having probably forgotten his former idea,

that his nephew was determined, with the pertinacity of a patient, far-sighted Jew money-lender, to wring from him the last possible shilling.

Ralph, who was not the heir, was of his nature so just, that he could not hear an accusation which he did not believe to be true, without protesting against it. The Squire had called the heir a spiritless spendthrift, and a malicious evil-doer, intent upon ruining the estate, and a grasping Jew, all in the same breath.

" I think you are hard upon him, sir," said the son to the father.

" Of course you think so. At any rate you'll say so," said the Squire. " One would suppose I was thinking only of myself to hear you talk."

" I know what you're thinking of," said Ralph slowly ; " and I know how much I owe you."

" I sometimes think that you ought to curse me," said the Squire.

After this, at this moment, with such words ringing in his ears, Ralph found it to be impossible to expostulate with his father. He could only take his father's arm, and whisper a soft feminine word or two. He would be as happy as the day was long, if only he could see his father happy.

" I can never be happy till I have placed you where you would have been," said the Squire. " The gods are just, and our pleasant vices make instruments to scourge us." He did not quote the line to himself, but the purport of it hung heavy on him. And yet he thought it hard that because he had money in his pocket he could not altogether make himself free of the scourge.

On the following morning he was less vituperative and less unreasonable, but he was still intent upon the subject. After breakfast he got his son into his own room,—the room in which he did his magistrate's work, and added up his accounts, and kept his spuds and spurs,—and seriously discussed the whole matter. What would it be wise that they should do next ? " You don't mean to tell me that you don't wish me to buy it ?" said the Squire. No ; Ralph would not say that. If it were in the market, to be bought, and if the money were forthcoming, of course such a purchase would be expedient. " The money is forthcoming," said the Squire. " We can make it up one way or another. What matter if we did sell Brownriggs ? What matter if we sold Brownriggs and Twining as well ?" Ralph quite acceded to this. As far as buying and selling were concerned he would have acceded to anything that would have made his father happy. " I won't say a word against this fellow, since you are so fond of him," continued the Squire. Ralph, though his father paused, made no reply to the intended sarcasm. " But you must allow that he had a reason for writing such a letter as he did."

" Of course he had a reason," said Ralph.

" Well ;—we'll say that he wants to keep it."

" That's not unnatural."

" Not at all. Everybody likes to keep what he's got, and to get as much as he can. That's nature. But a man can't eat his cake and have it. He has been slow to learn that, no doubt ; but I suppose he has learned it. He wouldn't have gone to Sir Thomas Underwood, in the way he did, crying to be helped,—if he hadn't learned it. Remember, Ralph, I didn't go to him first ;—he came to me. You always forget that. What was the meaning then of Sir Thomas writing to me in that pitiful way,—asking me to do something for him ;—and he who had I don't know how much, something like £800 a year, I take it, the day he came of age ?"

" Of course he has been imprudent."

" He cannot eat his cake and have it. He wants to eat it, and I want to have it. I am sure it may be managed. I suppose you mean to go up and see him."

" See Ralph ? "

" Why not ? You are not afraid of him." The son smiled, but made no answer. " You might find out from him what it is he really wants ;—what he will really do. Those attorneys don't understand. Carey isn't a bad fellow, and as for honesty, I'd trust him with anything. I've known him and his father all my life, and in any ordinary piece of business there is no one whose opinion I would take so soon. But he talks of my waiting, telling me that the thing will come round after a few years,—as if what one wanted was merely an investment for one's money. It isn't that."

" No, sir ;—it isn't that."

" Not that at all. It's the feeling of the thing. Your lawyer may be the best man in the world to lay out your money in a speculation, but he doesn't dare to buy contentment for you. He doesn't see it, and one hardly dares to try and make him see it. I'd give the half of it all to have the other half, but I cannot tell him that. I'd give one half so long as that fellow wasn't to be the owner of the other. We'll have no opposition Newton in the place."

The Squire's son was of course willing enough to go up to London. He would see the heir at any rate, and endeavour to learn what were the wishes of the heir. " You may say what money you like," said the Squire. " I hardly care what I pay, so long as it is possible to pay it. Go up to £10,000 more, if that will do it."

" I don't think I can bargain," said the son.

" But he can," said the father. " At any rate you can find out whether he will name a price. I'd go myself, but I know I should quarrel with him."

Ralph prepared himself for the journey, and, as a matter of course,

took the parson into his confidence ; not telling the parson anything
of the absolute sum named, but explaining that it was his purpose to
become acquainted with the heir, and if possible to learn his views.
" You'll find Ralph a very different fellow from what my uncle thinks
him," said the parson. " I shall be much mistaken if he does not
tell you quite openly what he intends. He is careless about money,
but he never was greedy." And then they got to other matters.
" You will of course see the girls at Fulham," said the parson.

" Yes ;—I shall manage to get down there."

The story of Gregory's passion for Clarissa was well known to the
other. Gregory, who would not for worlds have spoken of such a
matter among his general acquaintance, who could not have brought
himself to mention it in the presence of two hearers, had told it all
to the one companion who was nearest and dearest to him,—" I wish
I were going with you," said the parson.

" Why not come with me then ?"

"And yet I don't wish it. If I were in London I doubt whether I
would go there. There could be no use in it."

" It is one of those things," said Ralph, " in which a man should
never despair as long as there is a possibility."

"Ah, yes ; people say so. I don't believe in that kind of perseverance myself ;—at any rate not with her. She knows her own
mind,—as well as I know mine. I think I promised her that I would
trouble her no more."

" Promises like that are mere pie-crusts," said Ralph.

" Give her my love ;—that's all. And don't do that unless you
are alone with her. I shall live it down some day, no doubt, but to
tell the truth I have made up my mind not to marry. I'm half
inclined to think that a clergyman shouldn't marry. There are
some things which our ancestors understood pretty well, although we
think they were such fools. I should like to see the new cousin,
certainly."

Ralph said nothing more about the new cousin ; and was perhaps
hardly aware how greatly the idea of again seeing the new cousin
had enhanced the pleasure of his journey to London. About a week
after this he started, having devoted nearly all the afternoon before
he went to the packing of a large basket of ferns,—to each root or
small bundle of which was appended a long name in Latin,—as an
offering to Patience Underwood. And yet he did not care very much
for Patience Underwood.

It was just the end of September,—the last day of September,
when he reached London. Ralph the heir was out of town, and the
servant at his lodging professed she did not know where he was.
She thought it probable that he was " at Mr. 'Orsball's,—Mr. 'Orsball
of the Moonbeam, Barnfield, — a looking after his 'orses." She

suggested this, not from any knowledge in her possession, but because Ralph was always believed to go to the Moonbeam when he left town. He would, however, be back next week. His namesake, therefore, did not consider that it would be expedient for him to follow the heir down to the Moonbeam.

But the Underwood girls would certainly be at Fulham, and he started at once with his ferns for Popham Villa. He found them at home, and, singular to say, he found Sir Thomas there also. On the very next morning Sir Thomas was to start for Percycross, to commence the actual work of his canvass. The canvass was to occupy a fortnight, and on Monday the sixteenth the candidates were to be nominated. Tuesday the seventeenth was the day of the election. The whole household was so full of the subject that at first there was hardly room for the ferns. " Oh, Mr. Newton, we are so much obliged to you. Papa is going to stand for Percycross." That, or nearly that, was the form in which the ferns were received. Newton was quite contented. An excuse for entering the house was what he had wanted, and his excuse was deemed ample. Sir Thomas, who was disposed to be very civil to the stranger, had not much to say about his own prospects. To a certain degree he was ashamed of Percycross, and had said very little about it even to Stemm since his personal acquaintance had been made with Messrs. Spiveycomb, Pile, and Pabsby. But the girls were not ashamed of Percycross. To them as yet Percycross was the noblest of all British boroughs. Had not the Conservatives of Percycross chosen their father to be their representative out of all British subjects ? Sir Thomas had tried, but had tried quite in vain, to make them understand the real fashion of the selection. If Percycross would only send him to Parliament, Percycross should be divine. " What d'you think ?" said Clary ; " there's a man of the name of ——. I wish you'd guess the name of this man who is going to stand against papa, Mr. Newton."

" The name won't make much difference," said Sir Thomas.

" Ontario Moggs !" said Clary. " Do you think it possible, Mr. Newton, that Percycross,—the town where one of the Percys set up a cross in the time of the Crusaders,—didn't he, papa ?——"

" I shall not consider myself bound to learn all that unless they elect me," said Sir Thomas ; " but I don't think there were Percys in the days of the Crusaders."

" At any rate, the proper name is Percy St. Cross," said Clary. " Could such a borough choose Ontario Moggs to be one of its members, Mr. Newton ?"

" I do like the name," said Mary Bonner.

" Perhaps papa and Ontario Moggs may be the two members," said Clary, laughing. " If so, you must bring him down here, papa. Only he's a shoemaker."

" That makes no difference in these days," said Sir Thomas.

The ferns were at last unpacked, and the three girls were profuse in their thanks. Who does not know how large a space a basket of ferns will cover when it is unpacked and how large the treasure looms. " They'll cover the rocks on the other side," said Mary. It seemed to Newton that Mary Bonner was more at home than she had been when he had seen her before, spoke more freely of what concerned the house, and was beginning to become one of the family. But still she was, as it were, overshadowed by Clarissa. In appearance, indeed, she was the queen among the three, but in active social life she did not compete with Clary. Patience stood as a statue on a pedestal, by no means unobserved and ignored ; beautiful in form, but colourless. Newton, as he looked at the three, wondered that a man so quiet and gentle as the young parson should have chosen such a love as Clary Underwood. He remained half the day at the villa, dining there at the invitation of Sir Thomas. " My last dinner," said Sir Thomas, " unless I am lucky enough to be rejected. Men when they are canvassing never dine ;—and not often after they're elected."

The guest had not much opportunity of ingratiating himself specially with the beauty ; but the beauty did so far ingratiate herself with him,—unconsciously on her part,—that he half resolved that should her father be successful in his present enterprise, he would ask Mary Bonner to be the Queen of Newton Priory. His father had often urged him to marry,—never suggesting that any other quality beyond good looks would be required in his son's wife. He had never spoken of money, or birth, or name. " I have an idea," he had said, laughing, " that you'll marry a fright some day. I own I should like to have a pretty woman about the house. One doesn't expect much from a woman, but she is bound to be pretty." This woman was at any rate pretty. Pretty, indeed ! Was it possible that any woman should be framed more lovely than this one ? But he must bide his time. He would not ask any girl to marry him till he should know what position he could ask her to fill. But though he spoke little to Mary, he treated her as men do treat women whom they desire to be allowed to love. There was a tone in his voice, a worship in his eye, and a flush upon his face, and a hesitation in his manner, which told the story, at any rate to one of the party there. " He didn't come to bring you the ferns," said Clarissa to Patience.

" He brought them for all of us," said Patience.

" Young men don't go about with ferns for the sake of the ferns," said Clary. " They were merely an excuse to come and see Mary."

" Why shouldn't he come and see Mary ? "

" He has my leave, Patty. I think it would be excellent. Isn't it odd that there should be two Ralph Newtons. One would be Mrs. Newton and the other Mrs. Ralph."

" Clarissa, Clarissa ! " said Patience, almost in a tone of agony.

" I'll be a hypocrite if you choose, Patty," said Clarissa, " or I'll be true. But you can't have me both at once." Patience said nothing further then. The lesson of self-restraint which she desired to teach was very hard of teaching.

There was just a word spoken between Sir Thomas and Newton about the property. " I intend to see Ralph Newton, if I can find him," said Ralph who was not the heir.

" I don't think he is far from town," said Sir Thomas.

" My father thinks that we might come to an understanding."

" Perhaps so," said Sir Thomas.

" I have no strong anxiety on the subject myself," said Newton ; " but my father thinks that if he does wish to sell his reversion——"

" He doesn't wish it. How can a man wish it ? "

" Under the circumstances it may be desirable."

" You had better see him, and I think he will tell you," said Sir Thomas. " You must understand that a man thinks much of such a position. Pray come to us again. We shall always be glad to see you when you are in town."

CHAPTER XXIV.

" I FIND I MUST."

RALPH the heir had, after all, gone to Margate. Mr. Neefit had got such a hold upon him that he had no help for it. He found himself forced to go to Margate. When he was asked the second and third time, with all the energy of Mr. Neefit's eloquence, he was unable to resist. What reason could he give that he should not go to Margate, seeing that it was a thing quite understood that he was to endeavour to persuade Polly to be his wife. Neefit came to him two mornings running, catching him each morning just as he was smoking his cigar after breakfast, and was very eloquent. He already owed Mr. Neefit over five hundred pounds, and the debt on the first of these mornings was made up to one thousand pounds, a receipt being given for the shop debt on one side, and a bond for the whole money, with 5 per cent. interest, being taken in return for it. " You'd better pay off what little things you owes, Captain," said the generous breeches-maker, " and then, when the time comes, we'll settle with the gent about the 'orses." Neefit played his game very well. He said not a word about selling the horses, or as to any restriction on his young " Captain's " amusements. If you pull at your fish too hard you only break your line. Neefit had a very fine fish on his hook, and he meant to land it. Not a word was said about Margate on that occasion, till the little pecuniary transaction was completed. Then the Captain was informed that the Neefit family would certainly spend the next week at that marine Paradise, and that Polly expected " the Captain's " company. " Them's the places," said Neefit, " where a girl grows soft as butter." This he said when the door-handle was in his hand, so that " the Captain " had no chance of answering him. Then he came again the next morning, and returned to the subject as though " the Captain " had already consented. There was a near approach to anger on one side and determined opposition on the other during this interview, but it ended in acquiescence on the Captain's side. Then Mr. Neefit was once more as gracious as possible. The graciousness of such men in acknowledging their own inferiority is sometimes wonderful. " You needn't be seen about with me, you know," said Mr. Neefit. This was said after Ralph had positively declared that he would not go actually with the Neefits and occupy the same apartments. " It would be altogether wrong,—for Polly's sake," said Ralph, looking very wise and very moral. To this view Neefit assented, not being quite sure how far " the Captain " might be correct in his ideas of morality.

" They've been and fixed young Newton for Polly," said Mr. Waddle that morning, to his friend Herr Bawwah, when he was told to mark off Ralph's account in the books as settled. " Dashed if they 'aven't," the German grunted. " Old Neverfit's a-playing at 'igh game, ain't he ? " Such was the most undeserved nickname by which this excellent tradesman was known in his own establishment. " I don't see nodin about 'igh," said the German. " He ain't got no money. I call it low." Waddle endeavoured to explain the circumstances, but failed. " De peoples should be de peoples, and de nobles should be de nobles," said Herr Bawwah ;—a doctrine which was again unintelligible to Mr. Waddle.

Ralph having overcome an intense desire to throw over his engagement, to sell his horses, and to start for Jerusalem, did go down to Margate. He put himself up at an hotel there, eat his dinner, lighted a cigar, and went down upon the sands. It was growing dusk, and he thought that he should be alone,—or, at least, uninterrupted in a crowd. The crowd was there, and nobody in the place would know him,—except the Neefits. He had not been on the sands two minutes before he encountered Mr. Neefit and his daughter. The breeches-maker talked loud, and was extremely happy. Polly smiled, and was very pretty. In two minutes Neefit saw, or pretended to see, a friend, and Ralph was left with his lady-love. There never was so good-natured a father ! " You'll bring her home to tea, Captain," said the father, as he walked off.

On that occasion, Ralph abstained from all direct love-making, and Polly, when she found that it was to be so, made herself very pleasant. "The idea of your being at Margate, Mr. Newton," said Polly.

"Why not I, as well as another?"

"Oh, I don't know. Brighton, or some of those French places, or any where all about the world, would be more likely for you, I should think."

"Margate seems to be very jolly."

"Oh, I like it. But then we are not swells, you know. Have you heard the news? Ontario Moggs is going to stand to be 'member of Parliament' for Percycross."

"My rival!" That was the only word he uttered approaching to the subject of love.

"I don't know anything about that, Mr. Newton. But it's true."

"Why, Sir Thomas Underwood is going to stand."

"I don't know anything about anybody else, but Ontario Moggs is going to stand. I do so hope he'll get in. They say he speaks quite beautiful. Did you ever hear him?"

"I never heard him."

"Ah, you may laugh. But a bootmaker can make a speech sometimes as well as,—as well as a peer of Parliament. Father says that old Mr. Moggs has given him ever so much money to do it. When a man is in Parliament, Mr. Newton, doesn't that make him a gentleman?"

"No."

"What then?"

"Nothing on earth can make a man a gentleman. You don't understand Latin, Polly?"

"No. I hope that isn't necessary for a young woman."

"By no means. But a poet is born, and can't be made."

"I'm not talking of poets. Ontario Moggs is a poet. But I know what you mean. There's something better even than to be a gentleman."

"One may be an angel,—as you are, Polly."

"Oh,—me;—I'm not thinking of myself. I'm thinking of Ontario Moggs,—going into Parliament. But then he is so clever!"

Ralph was not minded to be cut out by Moggs, junior, after coming all the way to Margate after his lady-love. The thing was to be done, and he would do it. But not to-night. Then he took Polly home, and eat prawns with Mr. and Mrs. Neefit. On the next day they all went out together in a boat.

The week was nearly over, and Ralph had renewed his suit more than once, when the breeches-maker proceeded to "put him through his facings." "She's a-coming round, ain't she, Captain?" said Mr.

Neefit. By this time Ralph hated the sight of Neefit so thoroughly, that he was hardly able to repress the feeling. Indeed, he did not repress it. Whether Neefit did not see it, or seeing it chose to ignore the matter, cannot be said. He was, at any rate, as courteous as ever. Mrs. Neefit, overcome partly by her husband's authority, and partly induced to believe that as Ontario Moggs was going into Parliament he was no longer to be regarded as a possible husband, had yielded, and was most polite to the lover. When he came in of an evening, she always gave him a double allowance of prawns, and hoped that the tea was to his liking. But she said very little more than this, standing somewhat in awe of him. Polly had been changeable, consenting to walk with him every day, but always staving the matter off when he asked her whether she thought that she yet knew him well enough to be his wife. "Oh, not half well enough," she would say. "And then, perhaps, you know, I'm not over fond of the half that I do know." And so it was up to the last evening, when the father put him through his facings. In respect of "the Captain's" behaviour to Polly, the father had no just ground of complaint, for Ralph had done his best. Indeed, Ralph was fond enough of Polly. And it was hard for a man to be much with her without becoming fond of her. "She's a-coming round, ain't she, Captain?" said Mr. Neefit.

"I can't say that she is," said Ralph, turning upon his heel near the end of the pier.

"You don't stick to her fast enough, Captain."

This was not to be borne. "I'll tell you what it is, Mr. Neefit," said Ralph, "you'd better let me alone, or else I shall be off."

"You'd only have to come back, Captain, you know," said Neefit. "Not as I want to interfere. You're on the square, I see that. As long as you're on the square, there ain't nothing I won't do. I ain't a-blaming you,—only stick to her." "Damn it all!" said Ralph, turning round again in the other direction. But there was Neefit still confronting him. "Only stick to her, Captain, and we'll pull through. I'll put her through her facings to-night. She's thinking of that orkard lout of a fellow just because he's standing to be a Parl'ament gent." This did not improve matters, and Ralph absolutely ran away,—ran away, and escaped to his hotel. He would try again in the morning, would still make her his wife if she would have him! And then swore a solemn oath that in such case he would never see his father-in-law again.

Polly was not at all averse to giving him opportunities. They were together on the sands on the next morning, and he then asked her very seriously whether she did not think that there had been enough of this, that they might make up their minds to love each other, and be married as it were out of hand. Her father and mother wished it, and what was there against it? "You cannot doubt that I am in earnest now, Polly?" he said.

"I know you are in earnest well enough," she answered.

"And you do not doubt that I love you?"

"I doubt very much whether you love father," said Polly. She spoke this so sharp and quickly that he had no reply ready. "If you and I were to be married, where should we live? I should want to have father and mother with me. You'd mean that, I suppose?" The girl had read his thoughts, and he hadn't a word to say for himself. "The truth is, you despise father, Mr. Newton."

"No, indeed."

"Yes, you do. I can see it. And perhaps it's all right that you should. I'm not saying—Of course, he's not like you and your people. How should he be? Only I'm thinking, like should marry like."

"Polly, you're fit for any position in which a man could place you."

"No, I'm not. I'm not fit for any place as father wouldn't be fit for too. I'd make a better hand at it than father, I dare say,—because I'm younger. But I won't go anywhere where folk is to be ashamed of father. I'd like to be a lady well enough;—but it'd go against the very grain of my heart if I had a house and he wasn't to be made welcome to the best of everything."

"Polly, you're an angel!"

"I'm a young woman who knows who's been good to me. He's to give me pretty nigh everything. You wouldn't be taking me if it wasn't for that. And then, after all, I'm to turn my back on him because he ain't like your people. No; never; Mr. Newton! You're well enough, Mr. Newton; more than good enough for me, no doubt. But I won't do it. I'd cut my heart out if I was turning my back upon father." She had spoken out with a vengeance, and Ralph didn't know that there was any more to be said. He couldn't bring himself to assure her that Mr. Neefit would be a welcome guest in his house. At this moment the breeches-maker was so personally distasteful to him that he had not force enough in him to tell a lie upon the matter. They were now at the entrance of the pier, at which their ways would separate. "Good-bye, Mr. Newton," said she. "There had better be an end of it;—hadn't there?" "Good-bye, Polly," he said, pressing her hand as he left her.

Polly walked up home with a quick step, with a tear in her eye, and with grave thoughts in her heart. It would have been very nice. She could have loved him, and she felt the attraction, and the softness, and the sweet-smelling delicateness of gentle associations. It would have been very nice. But she could not sever herself from her father. She could understand that he must be distasteful to such a man as Ralph Newton. She would not blame Ralph. But the fact that it was so, shut for her the door of that Elysium. She knew that she could not be happy were she to be taken to such a mode of life as would force her to accuse herself of ingratitude to her father. And so Ralph went back to town without again seeing the breeches-maker.

The first thing he found in his lodgings was a note from his namesake.

" DEAR SIR,—

"I am up in town, and am very anxious to see you in respect of the arrangements which have been proposed respecting the property. Will you fix a meeting as soon as you are back ?

" Yours always,

" RALPH NEWTON.

"Charing Cross Hotel, 2 Oct., 186—."

Of course he would see his namesake. Why not ? And why not take his uncle's money, and pay off Neefit, and have done with it ? Neefit must be paid off, let the money come from where it would. He called at the hotel, and not finding his cousin, left a note asking him to breakfast on the following morning ; and then he spent the remainder of that day in renewed doubt. He was so sick of Neefit,— whose manner of eating shrimps had been a great offence added to other offences ! And yet one of his great sorrows was that he should lose Polly. Polly in her way was perfect, and he felt almost sure, now, that Polly loved him. Girls had no right to cling to their fathers after marriage. There was Scripture warranty against it. And yet the manner in which she had spoken of her father had greatly added to his admiration.

The two Ralphs breakfasted together, not having met each other since they were children, and having even then scarcely known each other. Ralph the heir had been brought up a boy at the parsonage of Newton Peele, but the other Ralph had never been taken to Newton till after his grandfather's death. The late parson had died within twelve months of his father,—a wretched year, during which the Squire and the parson had always squabbled,—and then Ralph who was the heir had been transferred to the guardianship of Sir Thomas Underwood. It was only during the holidays of that one year that the two Ralphs had been together. The " Dear Sir " will probably be understood by the discerning reader. The Squire's son had never allowed himself to call even Gregory his cousin. Ralph the heir in writing back had addressed him as " Dear Ralph." The Squire's son thought that that was very well, but chose that any such term of familiarity should come first from him who was in truth a Newton.

He felt his condition, though he was accustomed to make so light of it to his father.

The two young men shook hands together cordially, and were soon at work upon their eggs and kidneys. They immediately began about Gregory and the parsonage and the church, and the big house. The heir to the property, though he had not been at Newton for fourteen years, remembered well its slopes, and lawns, and knolls, and little valleys. He asked after this tree and that, of this old man and that old woman, of the game, and the river fishery, and the fox coverts, and the otters of which three or four were reputed to be left when he was there. Otters it seems were gone, but the foxes were there in plenty. " My father would be half mad if they drew the place blank," said the Squire's son.

" Does my uncle hunt much ?"

" Every Monday and Saturday, and very often on the Wednesday."

" And you ?"

" I call myself a three-day man, but I often make a fourth. Garth must be very far off if he don't see me. I don't do much with any other pack."

" Does my uncle ride ?"

" Yes ; he goes pretty well ;—he says he don't. If he gets well away I think he rides as hard as ever he did. He don't like a stern chace."

" No more do I," said Ralph the heir. " But I'm often driven to make it. What can a fellow do ? An old chap turns round and goes home, and doesn't feel ashamed of himself ; but we can't do that. That's the time when one ruins his horses." Then he told all about the Moonbeam and the B & B, and his own stud. The morning was half gone, and not a word had been said about business.

The Squire's son felt that it was so, and rushed at the subject all in a hurry. " I told you what I have come up to town about."

" Oh, yes ; I understand."

" I suppose I may speak plainly," said the Squire's son.

" Why not ?" said Ralph the heir.

" Well ; I don't know. Of course it's best. You wrote to Carey, you know."

" Yes ; I wrote the very moment I had made up my mind."

" You had made up your mind, then ?"

Ralph had certainly made up his mind when he wrote the letter of which they were speaking, but he was by no means sure but that his mind was not made up now in another direction. Since he had become so closely intimate with Mr. Neefit, and since Polly had so clearly explained to him her ideas as to paternal duty, his mind had veered round many points. " Yes," said he. " I had made up my mind."

"I don't suppose it can be of any use for you and me to be bargaining together," said the other Ralph.

"Not in the least."

"Of course it's a great thing to be heir to Newton. It's a nice property, and all that. Only my father thought——"

"He thought that I wanted money," said Ralph the heir.

"Just that."

"So I do. God knows I do. I would tell you everything. I would indeed. As to screwing a hard bargain, I'm the last man in London who would do it. I thought that your father might be willing to buy half the property."

"He won't do that. You see the great thing is the house and park. We should both want that;—shouldn't we? Of course it must be yours; and I feel—I don't know how I feel in asking you whether you want to sell it."

"You needn't mind that, Ralph."

"If you don't think the sum the lawyers and those chaps fixed is enough,——"

Then Ralph the heir, interrupting him, rose from his chair and spoke out. "My uncle has never understood me, and never will. He thinks hardly of me, and if he chooses to do so, I can't help it. He hasn't seen me for fourteen years, and of course he is entitled to think what he pleases. If he would have seen me the thing might have been easier."

"Don't let us go back to that, Ralph," said the Squire's son.

"I don't want to go back to anything. When it comes to a fellow's parting with such prospects as mine, it does come very hard upon him. Of course it's my own fault. I might have got along well enough;—only I haven't. I am hard up for money,— very hard up. And yet,—if you were in my place, you wouldn't like to part with it."

"Perhaps not," said the Squire's son, not knowing what to say.

"As to bargaining, and asking so much more, and all the rest of it, that's out of the question. Somebody fixed a price, and I suppose he knew what he was at."

"That was a minimum price."

"I understand. It was all fair, I don't doubt. It didn't seem a great deal; but your father might live for thirty years."

"I hope he will," said the Squire's son.

"As for standing off for more money, I never dreamed of such a thing. If your father thinks that, he has wronged me. But I believe he always does wrong me. And about the building, and the trees, and the leases, and the house, he might do just as he pleased for me. I have never said a word, and never shall. I must say I sometimes think he has been hard upon me. In fourteen years he has never

Mr. Pabsby smiled and rubbed his hands, and paused and laid his head
on one side. *(See page 153)*

He sat there alone in the little upstairs parlour, thinking of his speech for the evening,—thinking, too, of Polly Neefit. *(See page 197)*

asked me to set my foot upon the estate, that I might see the place which must one day be mine."

This was an accusation which the Squire's son found it very difficult to answer. It could not be answered without a reference to his own birth, and it was almost impossible that he should explain his father's feelings on the subject. " If this were settled, we should be glad that you would come," he said.

"Yes," said Ralph the heir; " yes,—if I consented to give up everything that is mine by right. Do you think that a fellow can bring himself to abandon all that so easily ? It's like tearing a fellow's heart out of him. If I'll do that, my uncle will let me come and see what it is that I have lost ! That which would induce him to welcome me would make it impossible that I should go there. It may be that I shall sell it. I suppose I shall. But I will never look at it afterwards." As it came to this point, the tears were streaming down his cheeks, and the eyes of the other Ralph were not dry.

" I wish it could be made pleasant for us all," said the Squire's son. The wish was well enough, but the expression of it was hardly needed, because it must be so general.

" But all this is rot and nonsense," said Ralph the heir, brushing the tears away from his eyes, " and I am only making an ass of myself. Your father wants to know whether I will sell the reversion to Newton Priory. I will. I find I must. I don't know whether I wouldn't sooner cut my throat; but unless I cut my throat I must sell it. I had a means of escape, but that has gone by. When I wrote that letter there was a means of escape. Now there's none."

" Ralph," said the other.

" Well; speak on. I've about said all I've got to say. Only don't think I want to ballyrag about the money. That's right enough, no doubt. If there's more to come, the people that have to look to it will say so. I'm not going to be a Jew about it."

" Ralph; I wouldn't do anything in a hurry. I won't take your answer in a hurry like this."

" It's no good, my dear fellow, I must do it. I must have £5,000 at once."

" You can get that from an insurance office."

"And then I should have nothing to live on. I must do it. I have no way out of it,—except cutting my throat."

The Squire's son paused a moment, thinking. " I was told by my father," said he, " to offer you more money."

" If it's worth more the people will say so," said Ralph the heir, impetuously; " I do not want to sell it for more than it's worth. Ask them to settle it immediately. There are people I must pay money to at once."

And so the Squire's son had done the Squire's errand. When he reported his success to Mr. Carey, that gentleman asked him whether he had the heir's consent in writing. At this the successful buyer was almost disposed to be angry ; but Mr. Carey softened him by an acknowledgment that he had done more than could have been expected. " I'll see his lawyer to-morrow," said Mr. Carey, "and then, unless he changes his mind again, we'll soon have it settled." After that the triumphant negotiator sent a telegram home to his father, " It is settled, and the purchase is made."

CHAPTER XXV.

" MR. GRIFFENBOTTOM."

ON Monday, the 16th of October, Sir Thomas Underwood went down to Percycross, and the first information given him was that Mr. Westmacott and Ontario Moggs had arrived on the Saturday, and were already at work. Mr. Griffenbottom was expected early on the Tuesday. " They've stolen a march on us, then," said Sir Thomas to Mr. Trigger.

" Give 'em rope enough, and they'll hang themselves," replied the managing agent. " There was Moggs spouting to them on his own hook on Saturday night, and Westmacott's chaps are ready to eat him. And he wanted to be doing it yesterday, Sunday ; only some of them got a hold of him and wouldn't let him loose. Moggs is a great card for us, Sir Thomas. There's nothing like one of them spouting fellows to overset the coach."

" Mr. Westmacott is fond of that too," said Sir Thomas.

" He understands. He's used to it. He does it in the proper place. Westmacott wasn't a bad member for the place ;—wasn't perhaps quite free enough with his money, but Westmacott was very decent." Sir Thomas could not help feeling that Trigger spoke of it as though he wished that the two old members might be returned. Ah, well! had it been possible, Mr. Trigger would have wished it. Mr. Trigger understood the borough, knew well the rocks before them, and would have wished it,—although he had been so imperative with Mr. Griffenbottom as to the second conservative candidate. And now Mr. Griffenbottom had sent them a man who would throw all the fat in the fire by talking of purity of election ! " And Moggs has been making a fool of himself in another direction," said Trigger, thinking that no opportunity for giving a valuable hint should be lost. " He's been telling the working men already that they'll be scoundrels and knaves if they take so much as a glass of beer without paying for it."

" Scoundrel is a strong word," said Sir Thomas, " but I like him for that."

" Percycross won't like him. Men would rather have all that left to their own feelings. They who want beer or money certainly won't thank him ; and they who don't want it don't like to be suspected."

" Every one will take it as addressed to his neighbour and not to himself."

" We are very fond of our neighbours here, Sir Thomas, and that kind of thing won't go down." This was on the evening of the candidate's arrival, and the conversation was going on absolutely while Sir Thomas was eating his dinner. He had asked Mr. Trigger to join him, and Mr. Trigger had faintly alleged that he had dined at three ; but he soon so far changed his mind as to be able to express an opinion that he could " pick a bit," and he did pick a bit. After which he drank the best part of a bottle of port,—having assured Sir Thomas that the port at the Percy Standard was a sort of wine that one didn't get every day. And as he drank his port, he continued to pour in lessons of wisdom. Sir Thomas employed his mind the while in wondering when Mr. Trigger would go away, and forecasting whether Mr. Trigger would desire to drink port wine at the Percy Standard every evening during the process of canvassing. About nine o'clock the waiter announced that a few gentlemen below desired to see Sir Thomas. " Our friends," said Mr. Trigger. " Just put chairs, and bring a couple of bottles of port, John. I'm glad they're come, Sir Thomas, because it shows that they mean to take to you." Up they were shown, Messrs. Spiveycomb, Spicer, Pile, Roodylands, —the bootmaker who has not yet been named,—Pabsby, and seven or eight others. Sir Thomas shook hands with them all. He observed that Mr. Trigger was especially cordial in his treatment of Spicer, the mustard-maker,—as to whose defection he had been so fearful in consequence of certain power which Mr. Westmacott might have in the wholesale disposal of mustard. " I hope you find yourself better," said Mr. Pile, opening the conversation. Sir Thomas assured his new friend that he was pretty well. " 'Cause you seemed rayther down on your luck when you was here before," said Mr. Pile.

" No need for that," said Spicer, the man of mustard. " Is there, Trigger ?" Trigger sat a little apart, with one bottle of port wine at his elbow, and took no part in the conversation. He was aware that his opportunities were so great that the outside supporters ought to have their time. " Any objection to this, Sir Thomas ?" he said, taking a cigar-case out of his pocket. Sir Thomas, who hated tobacco, of course gave permission. Trigger rang the bell, ordered cigars for the party, and then sat apart with his port wine. In ten minutes Sir Thomas hardly knew where he was, so dense was the cloud of smoke.

"Sir Thomas," began Mr. Pabsby,—"if I could only clearly see my way——"

"You'll see it clear enough before nomination-day," said Mr. Pile.

"Any ways, after election," said a conservative grocer. Both these gentlemen belonged to the Established Church and delighted in snubbing Mr. Pabsby. Indeed, Mr. Pabsby had no business at this meeting, and so he had been told very plainly by one or two as he had joined them in the street. He explained, however, that his friend Sir Thomas had come to him the very first person in Percycross, and he carried his point in joining the party. But he was a mild man, and when he was interrupted he merely bided another opportunity.

"I hope, Sir Thomas, your mind is made up to do something for our trade," said Mr. Roodylands.

"What's the matter with your trade?" said Spiveycomb, the paper-maker.

"Well;—we ain't got no jobs in it;—that's the matter," said Mr. Pile.

"As for jobs, what's the odds?" said a big and burly loud-mouthed tanner. "All on us likes a good thing when it comes in our way. Stow that, and don't let's be told about jobs. Sir Thomas, here's your health, and I wish you at the top of the poll,—that is, next to Mr. Griffenbottom." Then they all drank to Sir Thomas's health, Mr. Pabsby filling himself a bumper for the occasion.

It was eleven before they went away, at which time Mr. Pabsby had three times got as far as a declaration of his wish to see things clearly. Further than this he could not get; but still he went away in perfect good humour. He would have another opportunity, as he took occasion to whisper when he shook hands with the candidate. Trigger stayed even yet for half-an-hour. "Don't waste your time on that fellow, Pabsby," he said. "No, I won't," said Sir Thomas. "And be very civil to old Pile." "He doesn't seem disposed to return the compliment," said Sir Thomas. "But he doesn't want your interest in the borough," said Trigger, with the air of a man who had great truths to teach. "In electioneering, Sir Thomas, it's mostly the same as in other matters. Nothing's to be had for nothing. If you were a retail seller of boots from Manchester old Pile would be civil enough to you. You may snub Spicer as much as you please, because he'll expect to get something out of you." "He'll be very much deceived," said Sir Thomas. "I'm not so sure of that," said Trigger;—"Spicer knows what he's about pretty well." Then, at last, Mr. Trigger went, assuring Sir Thomas most enthusiastically that he would be with him before nine the next morning.

Many distressing thoughts took possession of Sir Thomas as he lay in bed. He had made up his mind that he would in no way break the law, and he didn't know whether he had not broken it already by giving these people tobacco and wine. And yet it would have been impossible for him to have refused Mr. Trigger permission to order the supply. Even for the sake of the seat,—even for the sake of his reputation, which was so much dearer to him than the seat,—he could not have bidden guests, who had come to him in his own room, to go elsewhere if they required wine. It was a thing not to be done, and yet, for aught he knew, Mr. Trigger might continue to order food and wine, and beer and tobacco, to be supplied ad libitum, and whenever he chose. How was he to put an end to it, otherwise than by throwing up the game, and going back to London? That now would be gross ill-usage to the Conservatives of Percycross, who by such a step would be left in the lurch without a candidate. And then was it to be expected that he should live for a week with Mr. Trigger, with no other relief than that which would be afforded by Messrs. Pile, Spiveycomb, and Co. Everything about him was reeking of tobacco. And then, when he sat down to breakfast at nine o'clock there would be Mr. Trigger!

The next morning he was out of bed at seven, and ordered his breakfast at eight sharp. He would steal a march on Trigger. He went out into the sitting-room, and there was Trigger already seated in the arm-chair, studying the list of the voters of Percycross! Heavens, what a man! "I thought I'd look in early, and they told me you were coming out or I'd have just stepped into your room." Into his very bed-room! Sir Thomas shuddered as he heard the proposition. "We've a telegram from Griffenbottom," continued Trigger, " and he won't be here till noon. We can't begin till he comes."

" Ah ;—then I can just write a few letters," said Sir Thomas.

" I wouldn't mind letters now if I was you. If you don't mind, we'll go and look up the parsons. There are four or five of 'em, and they like to be seen ;—not in the way of canvassing. They're all right, of course. And there's two of 'em won't leave a stone unturned in the outside hamlets. But they like to be seen, and their wives like it." Whereupon Mr. Trigger ordered breakfast,—and eat it. Sir Thomas reminded himself that a fortnight was after all but a short duration of time. He might live through a fortnight,—probably,—and then when Mr. Griffenbottom came it would be shared between two.

At noon he returned to the Percy Standard, very tired, there to await the coming of Mr. Griffenbottom. Mr. Griffenbottom didn't come till three, and then bustled up into the sitting-room, which Sir Thomas had thought was his own, as though all Percycross belonged to him. During the last three hours supporters had been in and out continually, and Mr. Pabsby had made an ineffectual attempt or two to catch Sir Thomas alone. Trigger had been going up and down between the Standard and the station. Various men, friends and supporters of Griffenbottom and Underwood, had been brought to him. Who were paid agents, who were wealthy townsmen, who were canvassers and messengers, he did not know. There were bottles on the sideboard the whole time. Sir Thomas, in a speculative manner, endeavouring to realise to himself the individuality of this and that stranger, could only conceive that they who helped themselves were wealthy townsmen, and that they who waited till they were asked by others were paid canvassers and agents. But he knew nothing, and could only wish himself back in Southampton Buildings.

At last Mr. Griffenbottom, followed by a cloud of supporters, bustled into the room. Trigger at once introduced the two candidates. "Very glad to meet you," said Griffenbottom. "So we're going to fight this little battle together. I remember you in the House, you know, and I dare say you remember me. I'm used to this kind of thing. I suppose you ain't. Well, Trigger, how are things looking? I suppose we'd better begin down Pump Lane. I know my way about the place, Honeywood, as well as if it was my bed-room. And so I ought, Trigger."

"I suppose you've seen the inside of pretty nearly every house in Percycross," said Trigger.

"There's some I don't want to see the inside of any more. I can tell you that. How are these new householders going to vote?"

"Betwixt and between, Mr. Griffenbottom."

"I never thought we should find much difference. It don't matter what rent a man pays, but what he does. I could tell you how nineteen out of twenty men here would vote, if you'd tell me what they did, and who they were. What's to be done about talking to 'em?"

"To-morrow night we're to be in the Town Hall, Mr. Griffenbottom, and Thursday an open-air meeting, with a balcony in the market-place."

"All right. Come along. Are you good at spinning yarns to them, Honeywood?"

"I don't like it, if you mean that," said Sir Thomas.

"It's better than canvassing. By George, anything is better than that. Come along. We may get Pump Lane, and Petticoat Yard, and those back alleys done before dinner. You've got cards, of course, Trigger." And the old, accustomed electioneerer led the way out to his work.

Mr. Griffenbottom was a heavy hale man, over sixty, somewhat inclined to be corpulent, with a red face, and a look of assured impudence about him which nothing could quell or diminish. The kind of life which he had led was one to which impudence was essentially necessary. He had done nothing for the world to justify him in assuming the airs of a great man,—but still he could assume them, and many believed in him. He could boast neither birth, nor talent, nor wit,—nor, indeed, wealth in the ordinary sense of the word. Though he had worked hard all his life at the business to which he belonged, he was a poorer man now than he had been thirty years ago. It had all gone in procuring him a seat in Parliament. And he had so much sense that he never complained. He had known what it was that he wanted, and what it was that he must pay for it. He had paid for it, and had got it, and was, in his fashion, contented. If he could only have continued to have it without paying for it again, how great would have been the blessing! But he was a man who knew that such blessings were not to be expected. After the first feeling of disgust was over on the receipt of Trigger's letter, he put his collar to the work again, and was prepared to draw his purse,— intending, of course, that the new candidate should bear as much as possible of this drain. He knew well that there was a prospect before him of abject misery;—for life without Parliament would be such to him. There would be no salt left for him in the earth if he was ousted. And yet no man could say why he should have cared to sit in Parliament. He rarely spoke, and when he did no one listened to him. He was anxious for no political measures. He was a favourite with no section of a party. He spent all his evenings at the House, but it can hardly be imagined that those evenings were pleasantly spent. But he rubbed his shoulders against the shoulders of great men, and occasionally stood upon their staircases. At any rate, such as was the life, it was his life; and he had no time left to choose another. He considered himself on this occasion pretty nearly sure to be elected. He knew the borough and was sure. But then there was that accursed system of petitioning, which according to his idea was un-English, ungentlemanlike, and unpatriotic—" A stand-up fight, and if you're licked—take it." That was his idea of what an election should be.

Sir Thomas, who only just remembered the appearance of the man in the House, at once took an extravagant dislike to him. It was abominable to him to be called Underwood by a man who did not know him. It was nauseous to him to be forced into close relations with a man who seemed to him to be rough and ill-mannered. And, judging from what he saw, he gave his colleague credit for no good qualities. Now Mr. Griffenbottom had good qualities. He was possessed of pluck. He was in the main good-natured. And though he could resent an offence with ferocity, he could forgive an offence with ease. " Hit him hard, and then have an end of it!" That was Mr. Griffenbottom's mode of dealing with the offenders and the offences with which he came in contact.

In every house they entered Griffenbottom was at home, and Sir Thomas was a stranger of whom the inmates had barely heard the name. Griffenbottom was very good at canvassing the poorer classes. He said not a word to them about politics, but asked them all whether they didn't dislike that fellow Gladstone, who was one thing one day and another thing another day. "By G——, nobody knows what he is," swore Mr. Griffenbottom over and over again. The women mostly said that they didn't know, but they liked the blue. "Blues allays was gallanter nor the yellow," said one of 'em. They who expressed an opinion at all hoped that their husbands would vote for him, "as 'd do most for 'em." "The big loaf;—that's what we want," said one mother of many children, taking Sir Thomas by the hand. There were some who took advantage of the occasion to pour out their tales of daily griefs into the ears of their visitors. To these Griffenbottom was rather short and hard. "What we want, my dear, is your husband's vote and interest. We'll hear all the rest another time." Sir Thomas would have lingered and listened; but Griffenbottom knew that 1,400 voters had to be visited in ten days, and work as they would they could not see 140 a day. Trigger explained it all to Sir Thomas. "You can't work above seven hours, and you can't do twenty an hour. And much of the ground you must do twice over. If you stay to talk to them you might as well be in London. Mr. Griffenbottom understands it so well, you'd better keep your eye on him." There could be no object in the world on which Sir Thomas was less desirous of keeping his eye.

The men, who were much more difficult to find than the women, had generally less to say for themselves. Most of them understood at once what was wanted, and promised. For it must be understood that on this their first day the conservative brigade was moving among its firm friends. In Petticoat Yard lived paper-makers in the employment of Mr. Spiveycomb, and in Pump Lane the majority of the inhabitants were employed by Mr. Spicer, of the mustard works. The manufactories of both these men were visited, and there the voters were booked much quicker than at the rate of twenty an hour. Here and there a man would hold some peculiar opinion of his own. The Permissive Bill was asked for by an energetic teetotaller; and others, even in these Tory quarters, suggested the ballot. But they all,—or nearly all of them,—promised their votes. Now and again some sturdy fellow, seeming to be half ashamed of himself in opposing all those around him, would say shortly that he meant to vote for Moggs, and pass on. "You do,—do you?" Sir Thomas heard Mr. Spicer say to one such man. "Yes, I does," said the man. Sir

Thomas heard no more, but he felt how perilous was the position on which a candidate stood under the present law.

As regarded Sir Thomas himself, he felt, as the evening was coming on, that he had hardly done his share of the work. Mr. Griffenbottom had canvassed, and he had walked behind. Every now and then he had attempted a little conversation, but in that he had been immediately pulled up by the conscientious and energetic Mr. Trigger. As for asking for votes, he hardly knew, when he had been carried back into the main street through a labyrinth of alleys at the back of Petticoat Yard, whether he had asked any man for his vote or not. With the booking of the votes he had, of course, nothing to do. There were three men with books;—and three other men to open the doors, show the way, and make suggestions on the expediency of going hither or thither. Sir Thomas would always have been last in the procession, had there not been one silent, civil person, whose duty it seemed to be to bring up the rear. If ever Sir Thomas lingered behind to speak to a poor woman, there was this silent, civil person lingering too. The influence of the silent, civil person was so strong that Sir Thomas could not linger much.

As they came into the main street they encountered the opposition party, Mr. Westmacott, Ontario Moggs, and their supporters. " I'll introduce you," said Mr. Griffenbottom to his colleague. "Come along. It's the thing to do." Then they met in the middle of the way. Poor Ontario was hanging behind, but holding up his head gallantly, and endeavouring to look as though he were equal to the occasion. Griffenbottom and Westmacott shook hands cordially, and complained with mutual sighs that household suffrage had made the work a deal harder than ever. "And I'm only a week up from the gout," said Griffenbottom. Then Sir Thomas and Westmacott were introduced, and at last Ontario was brought forward. He bowed and attempted to make a little speech; but nobody in one army or in the other seemed to care much for poor Ontario. He knew that it was so, but that mattered little to him. If he were destined to represent Percycross in Parliament, it must be by the free votes and unbiassed political aspirations of the honest working men of the borough. So remembering he stood aloof, stuck his hand into his breast, and held up his head something higher than before. Though the candidates had thus greeted each other at this chance meeting, the other parties in the contending armies had exhibited no courtesies.

The weariness of Sir Thomas when this first day's canvass was over was so great that he was tempted to go to bed and ask for a bowl of gruel. Nothing kept him from doing so but amazement at the courage and endurance of Mr. Griffenbottom. "We could get at a few of those chaps who were at the works, if we went out at eight," said Griffenbottom. Trigger suggested that Mr. Griffenbottom would be very tired. Trigger himself was perhaps tired. "Oh, tired," said Griffenbottom; "a man has to be tired at this work." Sir Thomas perceived that Griffenbottom was at least ten years his senior, and that he was still almost lame from the gout. "You'll be ready, Underwood?" said Griffenbottom. Sir Thomas felt himself bound to undertake whatever might be thought necessary. "If we were at it day and night, it wouldn't be too much," said Griffenbottom, as he prepared to amuse himself with one of the poll-books till dinner should be on the table. "Didn't we see Jacob Pucky?" asked the energetic candidate, observing that the man's name wasn't marked. "To be sure we did. I was speaking to him myself. He was one of those who didn't know till the day came. We know what that means; eh, Honeywood?" Sir Thomas wasn't quite sure that he did know; but he presumed that it meant something dishonest. Again Mr. Trigger dined with them, and as soon as ever their dinner was swallowed they were out again at their work, Sir Thomas being dragged from door to door, while Griffenbottom asked for the votes.

And this was to last yet for ten days more!

CHAPTER XXVI.

MOGGS, PURITY, AND THE RIGHTS OF LABOUR.

MR. TRIGGER had hinted that Ontario Moggs would be a thorn in the flesh of Mr. Westmacott's supporters at Percycross, and he had been right. Ontario was timid, hesitating, and not unfrequently brow-beaten in the social part of his work at the election. Though he made great struggles he could neither talk, nor walk, nor eat, nor sit, as though he were the equal of his colleague. But when they came to politics and political management, there was no holding him. He would make speeches when speeches were not held to be desirable by his committee, and he was loud upon topics as to which it was thought that no allusion whatever should have been made. To talk about the ballot had from the first been conceded to Moggs. Mr. Westmacott was, indeed, opposed to the ballot; but it had been a matter of course that the candidate of the people should support that measure. The ballot would have been a safety-valve. But Moggs was so cross-grained, ill-conditioned, and uncontrollable that he would not let the ballot suffice him. The ballot was almost nothing to him. Strikes and bribery were his great subjects; the beauty of the one and the ugliness of the other. The right of the labourer to combine with his brother labourers to make his own terms for his labour, was the great lesson he taught. The suicidal iniquity of the labourer in selling that political power which he should use to protect his labour was the source of his burning indignation. That labour was the salt of the earth he told the men of Percycross very often;—and he told them as often that manliness and courage were necessary to make that salt productive. Gradually the men of Percycross,—some said that they were only the boys of Percycross,—clustered round him, and learned to like to listen to him. They came to understand something of the character of the man who was almost too shame-faced to speak to them while he was being dragged round to their homes on his canvas, but whom nothing could repress when he was on his legs with a crowd before him. It was in vain that the managing agent told him that he would not get a vote by his spouting and shouting. On such occasions he hardly answered a word to the managing agent. But the spouting and shouting went on just the same, and was certainly popular among the bootmakers and tanners. Mr. Westmacott was asked to interfere, and did do so once in some mild fashion; but Ontario replied that having been called to this sphere of action he could only do his duty according to his own

lights. The young men's presidents, and secretaries, and chairmen
were for awhile somewhat frightened, having been assured by the
managing men of the liberal committee that the election would be
lost by the furious insanity of their candidate. But they decided
upon supporting Moggs, having found that they would be deposed
from their seats if they discarded him. At last, when the futile efforts
to control Moggs had been maintained with patience for something
over a week, when it still wanted four or five days to the election, an
actual split was made in the liberal camp. Moggs was turned adrift
by the Westmacottian faction. Bills were placarded about the town
explaining the cruel necessity for such action, and describing Moggs
as a revolutionary firebrand. And now there were three parties in the
town. Mr. Trigger rejoiced over this greatly with Mr. Griffenbottom.
" If they haven't been and cut their throats now it is a wonder," he
said over and over again. Even Sir Thomas caught something of the
feeling of triumph, and began almost to hope that he might be successful. Nevertheless the number of men who could not quite make
up their minds as to what duty required of them till the day of the
election was considerable, and Mr. Pile triumphantly whispered into
Mr. Trigger's ear his conviction that " after all, things weren't going
to be changed at Percycross quite so easily as some people supposed."

When Moggs was utterly discarded by the respectable leaders of
the liberal party in the borough,—turned out of the liberal inn at
which were the head-quarters of the party, and refused the right of
participating in the liberal breakfasts and dinners which were there
provided, Moggs felt himself to be a triumphant martyr. His port-
manteau and hat-box were carried by an admiring throng down to the
Cordwainers' Arms,—a house not, indeed, of the highest repute in
the town,—and here a separate committee was formed. Mr. Westmacott did his best to avert the secession ; but his supporters were inex-
orable. The liberal tradesmen of Percycross would have nothing to
do with a candidate who declared that inasmuch as a man's mind
was more worthy than a man's money, labour was more worthy than
capital, and that therefore the men should dominate and rule their
masters. That was a doctrine necessarily abominable to every master
tradesman. The men were to decide how many hours they would
work, what recreation they would have, in what fashion and at what
rate they would be paid, and what proportion of profit should be
allowed to the members, and masters, and creators of the firm !
That was the doctrine that Moggs was preaching. The tradesmen of
Percycross, whether liberal or conservative, did not understand
much in the world of politics, but they did understand that such a
doctrine as that, if carried out, would take them to a very Gehenna
of revolutionary desolation. And so Moggs was banished from the

Northern Star, the inn at which Mr. Westmacott was living, and was forced to set up his radical staff at the Cordwainers' Arms.

In one respect he certainly gained much by this persecution. The record of his election doings would have been confined to the columns of the "Percycross Herald" had he carried on his candidature after the usual fashion ; but, as it was now, his doings were blazoned in the London newspapers. The "Daily News" reported him, and gave him an article all to himself ; and even the "Times" condescended to make an example of him, and to bring him up as evidence that revolutionary doctrines were distasteful to the electors of the country generally. The fame of Ontario Moggs certainly became more familiar to the ears of the world at large than it would have done had he continued to run in a pair with Mr. Westmacott. And that was everything to him. Polly Neefit must hear of him now that his name had become a household word in the London newspapers.

And in another respect he gained much. All personal canvassing was now at an end for him. There could be no use in his going about from to house asking for votes. Indeed, he had discovered that to do so was a thing iniquitous in itself, a demoralising practice tending to falsehood, intimidation, and corruption,—a thing to be denounced. And he denounced it. Let the men of Percycross hear him, question him in public, learn from his spoken words what were his political principles,—and then vote for him if they pleased. He would condescend to ask a vote as a favour from no man. It was for them rather to ask him to bestow upon them the gift of his time and such ability as he possessed. He took a very high tone indeed in his speeches, and was saved the labour of parading the streets. During these days he looked down from an immeasurable height on the truckling, mean, sordid doings of Griffenbottom, Honeywood, and Westmacott. A huge board had been hoisted up over the somewhat low frontage of the Cordwainers' Arms, and on this was painted in letters two feet high a legend which it delighted him to read, MOGGS, PURITY, AND THE RIGHTS OF LABOUR. Ah, if that could only be understood, there was enough in it to bring back an age of gold to suffering humanity! No other Reform would be needed. In that short legend everything necessary for man was contained.

Mr. Pile and Mr. Trigger stood together one evening looking at the legend from a distance. "Moggs and purity!" said Mr. Pile, in that tone of disgust, and with that peculiar action which had become common to him in speaking of this election.

"He hasn't a ghost of a chance," said Mr. Trigger, who was always looking straight at the main point ;—"nor yet hasn't Westmacott."

"There's worse than Westmacott," said Mr. Pile.

"But what can we do ?" said Trigger.

"Purity! Purity!" said the old man. "It makes me that sick that I wish there weren't such a thing as a member of Parliament. Purity and pickpockets is about the same. When I'm among 'em I buttons up my breeches-pockets."

"But what can we do?" asked Mr. Trigger again, in a voice of woe. Mr. Trigger quite sympathised with his elder friend; but, being a younger man, he knew that these innovations must be endured.

Then Mr. Pile made a speech, of such length that he had never been known to make the like before;—so that Mr. Trigger felt that things had become very serious, and that, not impossibly, Mr. Pile might be so affected by this election as never again to hold up his head in Percycross. "Purity! Purity!" he repeated. "They're a going on that way, Trigger, that the country soon won't be fit for a man to live in. And what's the meaning of it all? It's just this,—that folks wants what they wants without paying for it. I hate Purity, I do. I hate the very smell of it. It stinks. When I see the chaps as come here and talk of Purity, I know they mean that nothing ain't to be as it used to be. Nobody is to trust no one. There ain't to be nothing warm, nor friendly, nor comfortable any more. This Sir Thomas you've brought down is just as bad as that shoemaking chap;—worse if anything. I know what's a going on inside him. I can see it. If a man takes a glass of wine out of his bottle, he's a asking hisself if that ain't bribery and corruption! He's got a handle to his name, and money, I suppose, and comes down here without knowing a chick or a child. Why isn't a poor man, as can't hardly live, to have his three half-crowns or fifteen shillings, as things may go, for voting for a stranger such as him? I'll tell you what it is, Trigger, I've done with it. Things have come to that in the borough, that I'll meddle and make no more." Mr. Trigger, as he listened to this eloquence, could only sigh and shake his head. "I did think it would last my time," added Mr. Pile, almost weeping.

Moggs would steal out of the house in the early morning, look up at the big bright red letters, and rejoice in his very heart of hearts. He had not lived in vain, when his name had been joined, in the public view of men, with words so glorious. Purity and the Rights of Labour! "It contains just everything," said Moggs to himself as he sat down to his modest, lonely breakfast. After that, sitting with his hands clasped upon his brow, disdaining the use of pen and paper for such work, he composed his speech for the evening,—a speech framed with the purpose of proving to his hearers that Purity and the Rights of Labour combined would make them as angels upon the earth. As for himself, Moggs, he explained in his speech,—

analysing the big board which adorned the house,—it mattered little whether they did or did not return him. But let them be always persistent in returning on every possible occasion Purity and the Rights of Labour, and then all other good things would follow to them. He enjoyed at any rate that supreme delight which a man feels when he thoroughly believes his own doctrine.

But the days were very long with him. When the evening came, when his friends were relieved from their toil, and could assemble here and there through the borough to hear him preach to them, he was happy enough. He had certainly achieved so much that they preferred him now to their own presidents and chairmen. There was an enthusiasm for Moggs among the labouring men of Percycross, and he was always happy while he was addressing them. But the hours in the morning were long, and sometimes melancholy. Though all the town was busy with these electioneering doings, there was nothing for him to do. His rivals canvassed, consulted, roamed through the town,—as he could see,—filching votes from him. But he, too noble for such work as that, sat there alone in the little upstairs parlour of the Cordwainers' Arms, thinking of his speech for the evening,— thinking, too, of Polly Neefit. And then, of a sudden, it occurred to him that it would be good to write a letter to Polly from Percycross. Surely the fact that he was waging this grand battle would have some effect upon her heart. So he wrote the following letter, which reached Polly about a week after her return home from Margate.

Cordwainers' Arms Inn, Percycross,
"14 October, 186—.

" MY DEAR POLLY,—

"I hope you won't be angry with me for writing to you. I am here in the midst of the turmoil of a contested election, and I cannot refrain from writing to tell you about it. Out of a full heart they say the mouth speaks, and out of a very full heart I am speaking to you with my pen. The honourable prospect of having a seat in the British House of Parliament, which I regard as the highest dignity that a Briton can enjoy, is very much to me, and fills my mind, and my heart, and my soul ; but it all is not so much to me as your love, if only I could win that seat. If I could sit there, in your heart, and be chosen by you, not for a short seven years, but for life, I should be prouder and happier of that honour than of any other. It ought not, perhaps, to be so, but it is. I have to speak here to the people very often ; but I never open my mouth without thinking that if I had you to hear me I could speak with more energy and spirit. If I could gain your love and the seat for this borough together, I should have done more then than emperor, or conqueror, or high priest ever accomplished.

"I don't know whether you understand much about elections. When I first came here I was joined with a gentleman who was one of the old members ;—but now I stand alone, because he does not comprehend or sympathise with the advanced doctrines which it is my mission to preach to the people. Purity and the Rights of Labour; —those are my watchwords. But there are many here who hate the very name of Purity, and who know nothing of the Rights of Labour. Labour, dear Polly, is the salt of the earth ; and I hope that some day I may have the privilege of teaching you that it is so. For myself I do not see why ladies should not understand politics as well as men ; and I think that they ought to vote. I hope you think that women ought to have the franchise.

"We are to be nominated on Monday, and the election will take place on Tuesday. I shall be nominated and seconded by two electors who are working men. I would sooner have their support than that of the greatest magnate in the land. But your support would be better for me than anything else in the world. People here, as a rule, are very lukewarm about the ballot, and they seemed to know very little about strikes till I came among them. Without combination and mutual support the working people must be ground to powder. If I am sent to Parliament I shall feel it to be my duty to insist upon this doctrine in season and out of season,—whenever I can make my voice heard. But, oh Polly, if I could do it with you for my wife, my voice would be so much louder.

"Pray give my best respects to your father and mother. I am afraid I have not your father's good wishes, but perhaps if he saw me filling the honourable position of member of Parliament for Percy-cross he might relent. If you would condescend to write me one word in reply I should be prouder of that than of anything. I suppose I shall be here till Wednesday morning. If you would say but one kind word to me, I think that it would help me on the great day.

"I am, and ever shall be,

"Your most affectionate admirer,

"ONTARIO MOGGS."

Polly received this on the Monday, the day of the nomination, and though she did answer it at once, Ontario did not get her reply till the contest was over, and that great day had done its best and its worst for him. But Polly's letter shall be given here. To a well-bred young lady, living in good society, the mixture of politics and love which had filled Ontario's epistle might perhaps have been unacceptable. But Polly thought that the letter was a good letter ; and was proud of being so noticed by a young man who was standing for Parliament. She sympathised with his enthusiasm ; and thought that she should like to be taught by him that Labour was the Salt of the Earth,—if only he were not so awkward and long, and if his hands were habitually a little cleaner. She could not, however, take upon herself to give him any hope in that direction, and therefore confined her answer to the Parliamentary prospects of the hour.

"DEAR MR. MOGGS,"—she wrote,—"I was very much pleased when I heard that you were going to stand for a member of Parliament, and I wish with all my heart that you may be successful. I shall think it a very great honour indeed to know a member of Parliament, as I have known you for nearly all my life. I am sure you will do a great deal of good, and prevent the people from being wicked. As for ladies voting, I don't think I should like that myself, though if I had twenty votes I would give them to you,—because I have known you so long.

"Father and mother send their respects, and hope you will be successful.

"Yours truly,

"MARYANNE NEEFIT.

"Alexandra Cottage, Monday."

When Moggs received this letter he was, not unnaturally, in a state of great agitation in reference to the contest through which he had just passed; but still he thought very much of it, and put it in his breast, where it would lie near his heart. Ah, if only one word of warmth had been allowed to escape from the writer, how happy could he have been. "Yes," he said scornfully,—"because she has known me all her life!" Nevertheless, the paper which her hand had pressed, and the letters which her fingers had formed, were placed close to his heart.

CHAPTER XXVII.

THE MOONBEAM.

RALPH the heir had given his answer, and the thing was settled. He had abandoned his property for ever, and was to be put into immediate possession of a large sum of money,—of a sum so large that it would seem at once to make him a rich man. He knew, however, that if he should spend this money he would be a pauper for life; and he knew also how great was his facility for spending. There might, however, be at least a thousand a year for him and for his heirs after him, and surely it ought to be easy for him to live upon a thousand a year.

As he thought of this he tried to make the best of it. He had at any rate rescued himself out of the hands of Neefit, who had become intolerable to him. As for Polly, she had refused him twice. Polly was a very sweet girl, but he could not make it matter of regret to himself that he should have lost Polly. Had Polly been all alone in the world she would have been well enough,—but Polly with papa and mamma Neefit must have been a mistake. It was well for him, at any rate, that he was out of that trouble. As regarded the Neefits, it would be simply necessary that he should pay the breeches-maker the money that he owed them, and go no more either to Conduit Street or to Hendon.

And then what else should he do,—or leave undone? In what other direction should he be active or inactive? He was well aware that hitherto he had utterly wasted his life. Born with glorious prospects, he had now so dissipated them that there was nothing left for him but a quiet and very unambitious mode of life. Of means he had sufficient, if only he could keep that sufficiency. But he knew himself,—he feared that he knew himself too well to trust himself to keep that which he had unless he altogether changed his manner of living. To be a hybrid at the Moonbeam for life,—half hero and half dupe, among grooms and stable-keepers, was not satisfactory to him. He could see and could appreciate better things, and could long for them; but he could not attain to anything better unless he were to alter altogether his mode of life. Would it not be well for him to get a wife? He was rid of Polly, who had been an incubus to him, and now he could choose for himself.

He wrote to his brother Gregory, telling his brother what he had done. The writing of letters was ever a trouble to him, and on this occasion he told his tidings in a line or two. "Dear Greg, I have accepted my uncle's offer. It was better so. When I wrote to you before things were different. I need not tell you that my heart is sore for the old place. Had I stuck to it, however, I should have beggared you and disgraced myself. Yours affectionately, R. N." That was all. What more was to be said which, in the saying, could be serviceable to any one? The dear old place! He would never see it again. Nothing on earth should induce him to go there, now that it could under no circumstances be his own. It would still belong to a Newton, and he would try and take comfort in that. He might at any rate have done worse with it. He might have squandered his interest among the Jews, and so have treated his inheritance that it must have been sold among strangers.

He was very low in spirits for two or three days, thinking of all this. He had been with his lawyer, and his lawyer had told him that it must yet be some weeks before the sale would be perfected. "Now that it is done, the sooner the better," said Ralph. The lawyer told him that if he absolutely wanted ready money for his present needs

he could have it ; but that otherwise it would be better for him to
wait patiently,—say for a month. He was not absolutely in want of
money, having still funds which had been supplied to him by the
breeches-maker. But he could not remain in town. Were he to
remain in town, Neefit would be upon him ; and, in truth, though he
was quite clear in his conscience in regard to Polly, he did not wish to
have to explain personally to Mr. Neefit that he had sold his interest in
Newton Priory. The moment the money was in his hands he would
pay Mr. Neefit ; and then——— ; why then he thought that he would
be entitled to have Mr. Neefit told that he was not at home should
Mr. Neefit trouble him again.

He would marry and live somewhere very quietly ;—perhaps take
a small farm and keep one hunter. His means would be sufficient
for that, even with a wife and family. ·Yes ;—that would be the
kind of life most suited for him. He would make a great change.
He would be simple in his habits, domestic, and extravagant in
nothing. To hunt once a week from his own little country house
would be delightful. Who should be the mistress of that home ?
That of all questions was now the most important.

The reader may remember a certain trifling incident which took
place some three or four months since on the lawn at Popham Villa.
It was an incident which Clary Underwood had certainly never
forgotten. It is hardly too much to say that she thought of it every
hour. She thought of it as a great sin ;—but as a sin which had been
forgiven, and, though a grievous sin, as strong evidence of that
which was not sinful, and which if true would be so full of joy. Clary
had never forgotten this incident ;—but Ralph had forgotten it nearly
altogether. That he had accompanied the incident by any assurance
of his love, by any mention of love intended to mean anything, he
was altogether unaware. He would have been ready to swear that
he had never so committed himself. Little tender passages of course
there had been. Such are common,—so he thought,—when young
ladies and young gentlemen know each other well and are fond of each
other's company. But that he owed himself to Clarissa Underwood,
and that he would sin grievously against her should he give himself
to another, he had no idea. It merely occurred to him that there
might be some slight preparatory embarrassment were he to offer his
hand to Mary Bonner. Yet he thought that of all the girls in the
world Mary Bonner was the one to whom he would best like to offer
it. It might indeed be possible for him to marry some young woman
with money ; but in his present frame of mind he was opposed to
any such effort. Hitherto things with him had been all worldly,
empty, useless, and at the same time distasteful. He was to have
married Polly Neefit for her money, and he had been wretched ever
since he had entertained the idea. Love and a cottage were, he

knew, things incompatible; but the love and the cottage implied in those words were synonymous with absolute poverty. Love with thirty thousand pounds, even though it should have a cottage joined with it, need not be a poverty-stricken love. He was sick of the world,—of the world such as he had made it for himself, and he would see if he could not do something better. He would first get Mary Bonner, and then he would get the farm. He was so much delighted with the scheme which he thus made for himself, that he went to his club and dined there pleasantly, allowing himself a bottle of champagne as a sort of reward for having made up his mind to so much virtue. He met a friend or two, and spent a pleasant evening, and as he walked home to his lodgings in the evening was quite in love with his prospects. It was well for him to have rid himself of the burden of an inheritance which might perhaps not have been his for the next five-and-twenty years. As he undressed himself he considered whether it would be well for him at once to throw himself at Mary Bonner's feet. There were two reasons for not doing this quite immediately. He had been told by his lawyer that he ought to wait for some form of assent or agreement from the Squire before he took any important step as consequent upon the new arrangement in regard to the property, and then Sir Thomas was still among the electors at Percycross. He wished to do everything that was proper, and would wait for the return of Sir Thomas. But he must do something at once. To remain in his lodgings and at his club was not in accord with that better path in life which he had chalked out for himself.

Of course he must go down to the Moonbeam. He had four horses there, and must sell at least three of them. One hunter he intended to allow himself. There were Brag, Banker, Buff, and Brewer; and he thought that he would keep Brag. Brag was only six years old, and might last him for the next seven years. In the meantime he could see a little cub-hunting, and live at the Moonbeam for a week at any rate as cheaply as he could in London. So he went down to the Moonbeam, and put himself under the charge of Mr. Horsball.

And here he found himself in luck. Lieutenant Cox was there, and with the lieutenant a certain Fred Pepper, who hunted habitually with the B and B. Lieutenant Cox had soon told his little tale. He had sold out, and had promised his family that he would go to Australia. But he intended to "take one more winter out of himself," as he phrased it. He had made a bargain to that effect with his governor. His debts had been paid, his commission had been sold, and he was to be shipped for Queensland. But he was to have one more winter with the B and B. An open, good-humoured, shrewd youth was Lieutenant Cox, who suffered nothing from false shame, and was intelligent enough to know that life at the rate of £1,200 a year, with £400 to spend, must come to an end. Fred

Pepper was a young man of about forty-five, who had hunted with the B and B, and lived at the Moonbeam from a time beyond which the memory of Mr. Horsball's present customers went not. He was the father of the Moonbeam, Mr. Horsball himself having come there since the days in which Fred Pepper first became familiar with its loose boxes. No one knew how he lived or how he got his horses. He had, however, a very pretty knack of selling them, and certainly paid Mr. Horsball regularly. He was wont to vanish in April, and would always turn up again in October. Some people called him the dormouse. He was good-humoured, good-looking after a horsey fashion, clever, agreeable, and quite willing to submit himself to any nickname that could be found for him. He liked a rubber of whist, and was supposed to make something out of bets with bad players. He rode very carefully, and was altogether averse to ostentation and bluster in the field. But he could make a horse do anything when he wanted to sell him, and could on an occasion give a lead as well as any man. Everybody liked him, and various things were constantly said in his praise. He was never known to borrow a sovereign. He had been known to lend a horse. He did not drink. He was a very safe man in the field. He did not lie outrageously in selling his horses. He did not cheat at cards. As long as he had a drop of drink left in his flask, he would share it with any friend. He never boasted. He was much given to chaff, but his chaff was good-humoured. He was generous with his cigars. Such were his virtues. That he had no adequate means of his own and that he never earned a penny, that he lived chiefly by gambling, that he had no pursuit in life but pleasure, that he never went inside a church, that he never gave away a shilling, that he was of no use to any human being, and that no one could believe a word he said of himself,—these were specks upon his character. Taken as a whole Fred Pepper was certainly very popular with the gentlemen and ladies of the B and B.

Ralph Newton when he dropped down upon the Moonbeam was made loudly welcome. Mr. Horsball, whose bill for £500 had been honoured at its first day of maturity, not a little, perhaps, to his own surprise, treated Ralph almost as a hero. When Ralph made some reference to the remainder of the money due, Mr. Horsball expressed himself as quite shocked at the allusion. He had really had the greatest regret in asking Mr. Newton for his note of hand, and would not have done it, had not an unforeseen circumstance called upon him suddenly to make up a few thousands. He had felt very much obliged to Mr. Newton for his prompt kindness. There needn't be a word about the remainder, and if Mr. Newton wanted something specially good for the next season,—as of course he would,—Mr. Horsball had just the horse that would suit him. "You'll about want a couple more, Mr. Newton," said Mr. Horsball.

Then Ralph told something of his plans to this Master of the Studs,—something, but not much. He said nothing of the sale of his property, and nothing quite definite as to that one horse with which his hunting was to be done for the future. " I'm going to turn over a new leaf, Horsball," he said.

" Not going to be spliced, squire ? "

" Well ;—I can't say that I am, but I won't say that I ain't. But I'm certainly going to make a change which will take me away from your fatherly care."

" I'm sorry for that, squire. We think we've always taken great care of you here."

" The very best in the world ;—but a man must settle down in the world some day, you know. I want a nice bit of land, a hundred and fifty acres, or something of that sort."

" To purchase, squire ? "

" I don't care whether I buy it or take it on lease. But it mustn't be in this county. I am too well known here, and should always want to be out when I ought to be looking after the stock."

" You'll take the season out of yourself first, at any rate," said Mr. Horsball. Ralph shook his head, but Mr. Horsball felt nearly sure of his customer for the ensuing winter. It is not easy for a man to part with four horses, seven or eight saddles, an establishment of bridles, horsesheets, spurs, rollers, and bandages, a pet groom, a roomful of top boots, and leather breeches beyond the power of counting. This is a wealth which it is easy to increase, but of which it is very difficult to get quit.

" I think I shall sell," said Ralph.

" We'll talk about that in April," said Mr. Horsball.

He went out cub-hunting three or four times, and spent the inter- mediate days playing dummy whist with Fred Pepper and Cox,—who was no longer a lieutenant. Ralph felt that this was not the sort of beginning for his better life which would have been most appropriate ; but then he hardly had an opportunity of beginning that better life quite at once. He must wait till something more definite had been done about the property,—and, above all things, till Sir Thomas should be back from canvassing. He did, however, so far begin his better life as to declare that the points at whist must be low,—shilling points, with half-a-crown on the rubber. " Quite enough for this kind of thing," said Fred Pepper. " We only want just something to do." And Ralph, when at the end of the week he had lost only a matter of fifteen pounds, congratulated himself on having begun his better life. Cox and Fred Pepper, who divided the trifle between them, laughed at the bagatelle.

But before he left the Moonbeam things had assumed a shape which, when looked at all round, was not altogether pleasant to him.

Before he had been three days at the place he received a letter from
his lawyer, telling him that his uncle had given his formal assent to
the purchase, and had offered to pay the stipulated sum as soon
as Ralph would be willing to receive it.   As to any further sum
that might be forthcoming, a valuer should be agreed upon at once.
The actual deed of sale and transfer would be ready by the middle of
November ; and the lawyer advised Ralph to postpone his acceptance
of the money till that deed should have been executed.   It was
evident from the letter that there was no need on his part to hurry
back to town.   This letter he found waiting for him on his return one
day from hunting.   There had been a pretty run, very fast, with a
kill, as there will be sometimes in cub-hunting in October,—though
as a rule, of all sports, cub-hunting is the sorriest.   Ralph had ridden
his favourite horse Brag, and Mr. Pepper had taken out,—just to try
him,—a little animal of his that he had bought, as he said, quite at
haphazard.   He knew nothing about him, and was rather afraid that
he had been done.   But the little horse seemed to have a dash of
pace about him, and in the evening there was some talk of the animal.
Fred Pepper thought that the little horse was faster than Brag.   Fred
Pepper never praised his own horses loudly ; and when Brag's merits
were chaunted, said that perhaps Ralph was right.   Would Ralph throw
his leg over the little horse on Friday and try him ?   On the Friday
Ralph did throw his leg over the little horse, and there was another
burst.   Ralph was obliged to confess, as they came home together in
the afternoon, that he had never been better carried.   " I can see
what he is now," said Fred Pepper ;—" he is one of those little horses
that one don't get every day.   He's up to a stone over my weight,
too."   Now Ralph and Fred Pepper each rode thirteen stone and
a half.

On that day they dined together, and there was much talk as to
the future prospects of the men.   Not that Fred Pepper said anything of his future prospects.   No one ever presumed him to have a
prospect, or suggested to him to look for one.   But Cox had been
very communicative and confidential, and Ralph had been prompted
to say something of himself.   Fred Pepper, though he had no future
of his own, could be pleasantly interested about the future of another,
and had quite agreed with Ralph that he ought to settle himself.   The
only difficulty was in deciding the when.   Cox intended to settle
himself too, but Cox was quite clear as to the wisdom of taking
another season out of himself.   He was prepared to prove that it
would be sheer waste of time and money not to do so.   " Here I
am," said Cox, " and a fellow always saves money by staying where
he is."   There was a sparkle of truth in this which Ralph Newton
found himself unable to deny.

" You'll never have another chance," said Pepper.

"That's another thing," said Cox. "Of course I shan't. I've turned it round every side, and I know what I'm about. As for horses, I believe they sell better in April than they do in October. Men know what they are then." Fred Pepper would not exactly back this opinion, but he ventured to suggest that there was not so much difference as some men supposed.

"If you are to jump into the cold water," said Ralph, "you'd better take the plunge at once."

"I'd sooner do it in summer than winter," said Fred Pepper.

"Of course," said Cox. "If you must give up hunting, do it at the end of the season, not at the beginning. There's a time for all things. Ring the bell, Dormouse, and we'll have another bottle of claret before we go to dummy."

"If I stay here for the winter," said Ralph, "I should want another horse. Though I might, perhaps, get through with four."

"Of course you might," said Pepper, who never spoilt his own market by pressing.

"I'd rather give up altogether than do it in a scratch way," said Ralph. "I've got into a fashion of having a second horse, and I like it."

"It's the greatest luxury in the world," said Cox.

"I never tried it," said Pepper; "I'm only too happy to get one." It was admitted by all men that Fred Pepper had the art of riding his horses without tiring them.

They played their rubber of whist and had a little hot whisky and water. On this evening Mr. Horsball was admitted to their company and made a fourth. But he wouldn't bet. Shilling points, he said, were quite as much as he could afford. Through the whole evening they went on talking of the next season, of the absolute folly of giving up one thing before another was begun, and of the merits of Fred Pepper's little horse. "A clever little animal, Mr. Pepper," said the great man, "a very clever little animal; but I wish you wouldn't bring so many clever un's down here, Mr. Pepper."

"Why not, Horsball?" asked Cox.

"Because he interferes with my trade," said Mr. Horsball, laughing. It was supposed, nevertheless, that Mr. Horsball and Mr. Pepper quite understood each other. Before the evening was over, a price had been fixed, and Ralph had bought the little horse for £130. Why shouldn't he take another winter out of himself? He could not marry Mary Bonner and get into a farm all in a day,—nor yet all in a month. He would go to work honestly with the view of settling himself; but let him be as honest about it as he might, his winter's hunting would not interfere with him. So at last he assured himself. And then he had another argument strong in his favour. He might hunt all the winter and yet have this thirty thousand pounds,—nay, more than thirty thousand pounds at the end of it. In fact, imprudent and foolish as had been his hunting in all previous winters, there would not even be any imprudence in this winter's hunting. Fortified by all these unanswerable arguments he did buy Mr. Fred Pepper's little horse.

On the next morning, the morning of the day on which he was to return to town, the arguments did not seem to be so irresistible, and he almost regretted what he had done. It was not that he would be ruined by another six months' fling at life. Situated as he now was so much might be allowed to him almost without injury. But then how can a man trust in his own resolutions before he has begun to keep them,—when, at the very moment of beginning, he throws them to the winds for the present, postponing everything for another hour? He knew as well as any one could tell him that he was proving himself to be unfit for that new life which he was proposing to himself. When one man is wise and another foolish, the foolish man knows generally as well as does the wise man in what lies wisdom and in what folly. And the temptation often is very slight. Ralph Newton had hardly wished to buy Mr. Pepper's little horse. The balance of desire during the whole evening had lain altogether on the other side. But there had come a moment in which he had yielded, and that moment governed all the other minutes. We may almost say that a man is only as strong as his weakest moment.

But he returned to London very strong in his purpose. He would keep his establishment at the Moonbeam for this winter. He had it all laid out and planned in his mind. He would at once pay Mr. Horsball the balance of the old debt, and count on the value of his horses to defray the expense of the coming season. And he would, without a week's delay, make his offer to Mary Bonner. A dim idea of some feeling of disappointment on Clary's part did cross his brain, —a feeling which seemed to threaten some slight discomfort to himself as resulting from want of sympathy on her part; but he must assume sufficient courage to brave this. That he would in any degree be an evil-doer towards Clary,—that did not occur to him. Nor did it occur to him as at all probable that Mary Bonner would refuse his offer. In these days men never expect to be refused. It has gone forth among young men as a doctrine worthy of perfect faith, that young ladies are all wanting to get married,—looking out for lovers with an absorbing anxiety, and that few can dare to refuse any man who is justified in proposing to them.

CHAPTER XXVIII.

THE NEW HEIR COUNTS HIS CHICKENS.

THE Squire was almost lost in joy when he received his son's letter, telling him that Ralph the heir had consented to sell everything. The one great wish of his life was to be accomplished at last! The property was to be his own, so that he might do what he liked with it, so that he might leave it entire to his own son, so that for the remainder of his life he might enjoy it in that community with his son which had always appeared to him to be the very summit of human bliss. From the sweet things which he had seen he had been hitherto cut off by the record of his own fault, and had spent the greater part of his life in the endurance of a bitter punishment. He had been torn to pieces, too, in contemplating the modes of escape from the position in which his father's very natural will had placed him. He might of course have married, and at least have expected and have hoped for children. But in that there would have been misery. His son was the one human being that was dear to him above all others, and by such a marriage he would have ruined his son. Early in life, comparatively early, he had made up his mind that he would not do that ;—that he would save his money, and make a property for the boy he loved. But then it had come home to him as a fact, that he could be happy in preparing no other home for his son than this old family house of his, with all its acres, woods, and homesteads. The acres, woods, and homesteads gave to him no delight, feeling as he did every hour of his life that they were not his own for purposes of a real usufruct. Then by degrees he had heard of his nephew's follies, and the idea had come upon him that he might buy his nephew out. Ralph, his own Ralph, had told him that the idea was cruel ; but he could not see the cruelty. " What a bad man loses a good man will get," he said ; " and surely it must be better for all those who are to live by the property that a good man should be the master of it." He would not interfere, nor would he have any power of interfering, till others would interfere were he to keep aloof. The doings would be the doings of that spendthrift heir, and none of his. When Ralph would tell him that he was cruel, he would turn away in wrath ; but hiding his wrath, because he loved his son. But now everything was set right, and his son had had the doing of it.

He was nearly mad with joy throughout that day as he thought of the great thing which he had accomplished. He was alone in the house, for his son was still in London, and during the last few months guests had been unfrequent at the Priory. But he did not wish to have anybody with him now. He went out, roaming through the park, and realising to himself the fact that now, at length, the very trees were his own. He gazed at one farmhouse after another, not seeking the tenants, hardly speaking to them if he met them, but with his brain full of plans of what should be done. He saw Gregory for a moment, but only nodded at him smiling, and passed on. He was not in a humour just at present to tell his happiness to any one. He walked all round Darvell's premises, the desolate, half-ruined house of Brumbys, telling himself that very shortly it should be desolate and half-ruined no longer. Then he crossed into the lane, and stood with his eyes fixed upon Brownriggs,—Walker's farm, the pearl of all the farms in those parts, the land with which he thought he could have parted so easily when the question before him was that of becoming in truth the owner of any portion of the estate. But now, every acre was ten times dearer to him than it had been then. He would never part with Brownriggs. He would even save Ingram's farm, in Twining, if it might possibly be saved. He had not known before how dear to him could be every bank, every tree, every sod. Yes;—now in very truth he was lord and master of the property which had belonged to his father, and his father's fathers before him. He would borrow money, and save it during his lifetime. He would do anything rather than part with an acre of it, now that the acres were his own to leave behind him to his son.

On the following day Ralph arrived. We must no longer call him Ralph who was not the heir. He would be heir to everything from the day that the contract was completed! The Squire, though he longed to see the young man as he had never longed before, would not go to the station to meet the welcome one. His irrepressible joy was too great to be exhibited before strangers. He remained at home, in his own room, desiring that Mr. Ralph might come to him there. He would not even show himself in the hall. And yet when Ralph entered the room he was very calm. There was a bright light in his eyes, but at first he spoke hardly a word. "So, you've managed that little job," he said, as he took his son's hand.

"I managed nothing, sir," said Ralph, smiling.

"Didn't you? I thought you had managed a good deal. It is done, anyway."

"Yes, sir, it's done. At least, I suppose so." Ralph, after sending his telegram, had of course written to his father, giving him full particulars of the manner in which the arrangement had been made.

"You don't mean that there is any doubt," said the Squire. with almost an anxious tone.

"Not at all, as far as I know. The lawyers seem to think that it is all right. Ralph is quite in earnest."

"He must be in earnest," said the Squire.

"He has behaved uncommonly well," said the namesake. "So well that I think you owe him much. We were quite mistaken in supposing that he wanted to drive a sharp bargain." He himself had never so supposed, but he found this to be the best way of speaking of that matter to his father.

"I will forgive him everything now," said the Squire, "and will do anything that I can to help him."

Ralph said many things in praise of his namesake. He still almost regretted what had been done. At any rate he could see the pity of it. It was that other Ralph who should have been looked to as the future proprietor of Newton Priory, and not he, who was hardly entitled to call himself a Newton. It would have been more consistent with the English order of things that it should be so. And then there was so much to say in favour of this young man who had lost it all, and so little to say against him! And it almost seemed to him for whose sake the purchase was being made, that advantage,—an unscrupulous if not an unfair advantage,—was being taken of the purchaser. He could not say all this to his father; but he spoke of Ralph in such a way as to make his father understand what he thought. "He is such a pleasant fellow," said Ralph, who was now the heir.

"Let us have him down here as soon as the thing is settled."

"Ah;—I don't think he'll come now. Of course he's wretched enough about it. It is not wonderful that he should have hesitated at parting with it."

"Perhaps not," said the Squire, who was willing to forgive past sins; "but of course there was no help for it."

"That was what he didn't feel so sure about when he declined your first offer. It was not that he objected to the price. As to the price he says that of course he can say nothing about it. When I told him that you were willing to raise your offer, he declared that he would take nothing in that fashion. If those who understood the matter said that more was coming to him, he supposed that he would get it. According to my ideas he behaved very well, sir."

In this there was something that almost amounted to an accusation against the Squire. At least so the Squire felt it; and the feeling for the moment robbed him of something of his triumph. According to his own view there was no need for pity. It was plain that to his son the whole affair was pitiful. But he could not scold his son;—at any rate not now. "I feel this, Ralph," he said;—"that from this moment everybody connected with the property, every tenant

on it and every labourer, will be better off than they were a month
ago. I may have been to blame. I say nothing about that. But I
do say that in all cases it is well that a property should go to the
natural heir of the life-tenant. Of course it has been my fault," he
added after a pause ; " but I do feel now that I have in a great
measure remedied the evil which I did." The tone now had become
too serious to admit of further argument. Ralph, feeling that this
was so, pressed his father's hand and then left him. " Gregory is
coming across to dinner," said the Squire as Ralph was closing the
door behind him.

At that time Gregory had received no intimation of what had been
done in London, his brother's note not reaching him till the following morning. Ralph met him before the Squire came down,
and the news was soon told. " It is all settled," said Ralph, with
a sigh.

" Well ? "

" Your brother has agreed to sell."

" No ! "

" I have almost more pain than pleasure in it myself, because I
know it will make you unhappy."

" He was so confident when he wrote to me ! "

" Yes ;—but he explained all that. He had hoped then that he
could have saved it. But the manner of saving it would have been
worse than the loss. He will tell you everything, no doubt. No
man could have behaved better." As it happened, there was still
some little space of time before the Squire joined them,—a period
perhaps of five minutes. But the parson spoke hardly a word. The
news which he now heard confounded him. He had been quite sure
that his brother had been in earnest, and that his uncle would fail.
And then, though he loved the one Ralph nearly as well as he did the
other,—though he must have known that Ralph the base-born was
in all respects a better man than his own brother, more of a man than
the legitimate heir,—still to his feelings that legitimacy was everything. He too was a Newton of Newton ; but it may be truly said
of him that there was nothing selfish in his feelings. To be the
younger brother of Newton of Newton, and parson of the parish
which bore the same name as themselves, was sufficient for his
ambition. But things would be terribly astray now that the right
heir was extruded. Ralph, this Ralph whom he loved so well, could
not be the right Newton to own the property. The world would not
so regard him. The tenants would not so think of him. The county
would not so repute him. To the thinking of parson Gregory, a great
misfortune had been consummated. As soon as he had realised it,
he was silent and could speak no more.

Nor did Ralph say a word. Not to triumph in what had been done on his behalf,—or at least not to seem to triumph,—that was the lesson which he had taught himself. He fully sympathised with Gregory; and therefore he stood silent and sad by his side. That there must have been some triumph in his heart it is impossible not to imagine. It could not be but that he should be alive to the glory of being the undoubted heir to Newton Priory. And he understood well that his birth would interfere but little now with his position. Should he choose to marry, as he would choose, it would of course be necessary that he should explain his birth; but it was not likely, he thought, that he should seek a wife among those who would reject him, with all his other advantages, because he had no just title to his father's name. That he should take joy in what had been done on his behalf was only natural; but as he stood with Gregory, waiting for his father to come to them, he showed no sign of joy. At last the Squire came. There certainly was triumph in his eye, but he did not speak triumphantly. It was impossible that some word should not be spoken between them as to the disposition of the property. "I suppose Ralph has told you," he said, "what he has done up in London?"

"Yes;—he has told me," said Gregory.

"I hope there will now be an end of all family ill-feeling among us," said the uncle. "Your brother shall be as welcome at the old place as I trust you have always found yourself. If he likes to bring his horses here, we shall be delighted."

The parson muttered something as to the kindness with which he had ever been treated, but what he said was said with an ill grace. He was almost broken-hearted, and thoroughly wished himself back in his own solitude. The Squire saw it all, and did not press him to talk;—said not a word more of his purchase, and tried to create some little interest about parish matters;—asked after the new building in the chancel, and was gracious about this old man and that young woman. But Gregory could not recover himself,—could not recall his old interests, or so far act a part as to make it seem that he was not thinking of the misfortune which had fallen upon the family. In every look of his eyes and every tone of his voice he was telling the son that he was a bastard, and the father that he was destroying the inheritance of the family. But yet they bore with him, and endeavoured to win him back to pleasantness. Soon after the cloth was taken away he took his leave. He had work to do at home, he said, and must go. His uncle went out with him into the hall, leaving Ralph alone in the parlour. "It will be for the best in the long run," said the Squire, with his hand on his nephew's shoulder.

"Perhaps it may, sir. I am not pretending to say. Good night." As he walked home across the park, through the old trees which he had known since he was an infant, he told himself that it could not be for the best that the property should be sent adrift, out of the proper line. The only thing to be desired now was that neither he nor his brother should have a child, and that there should no longer be a proper line.

The Squire's joy was too deep and well founded to be in any way damped by poor Gregory's ill-humour, and was too closely present to him for him to be capable of restraining it. Why should he restrain himself before his son? "I am sorry for Greg," he said, "because he has old-fashioned ideas. But of course it will be for the best. His brother would have squandered every acre of it." To this Ralph made no answer. It might probably have been as his father said. It was perhaps best for all who lived in and by the estate that he should be the heir. And gradually the feeling of exultation in his own position was growing upon him. It was natural that it should do so. He knew himself to be capable of filling with credit, and with advantage to all around him, the great place which was now assigned to him, and it was impossible that he should not be exultant. And he owed it to his father to show him that he appreciated all that had been done for him. "I think he ought to have the £35,000 at least," said the Squire.

"Certainly," said Ralph.

"I think so. As for the bulk sum, I have already written to Carey about that. No time ought to be lost. There is no knowing what might happen. He might die."

"He doesn't look like dying, sir."

"He might break his neck out hunting. There is no knowing. At any rate there should be no delay. From what I am told I don't think that with the timber and all they'll make it come to another £5,000; but he shall have that. As he has behaved well, I'll show him that I can behave well too. I've half a mind to go up to London, and stay till it's all through."

"You'd only worry yourself."

"I should worry myself, no doubt. And do you know, I love the place so much better than I did, that I can hardly bear to tear myself away from it. The first mark of my handiwork, now that I can work, shall be put upon Darvell's farm. I'll have the old place about his ears before I am a day older."

"You'll not get it through before winter."

"Yes, I will. If it costs me an extra £50 I shan't begrudge it. It shall be a sort of memorial building, a farmhouse of thanksgiving. I'll make it as snug a place as there is about the property. It has made me wretched for these two years."

"I hope all that kind of wretchedness will be over now."

"Thank God;—yes. I was looking at Brownriggs to-day,—and

Ingram's. I don't think we'll sell either. I have a plan, and I think we can pull through without it. It is so much easier to sell than to buy."

" You'd be more comfortable if you sold one of them."

" Of course I must borrow a few thousands ;—but why not? I doubt whether at this moment there's a property in all Hampshire so free as this. I have always lived on less than the income, and I can continue to do so easier than before. You are provided for now, old fellow."

" Yes, indeed ;—and why should you pinch yourself ?"

"I shan't be pinched. I haven't got a score of women about me, as you'll have before long. There's nothing in the world like having a wife. I am quite sure of that. But if you want to save money, the way to do it is not to have a nursery. You'll marry, of course, now ?"

" I suppose I shall some day."

" The sooner the better. Take my word for it."

" Perhaps you'd alter your opinion if I came upon you before Christmas for your sanction."

" No, by Jove ; that I shouldn't. I should be delighted. You don't mean to say you've got anybody in your eye. There's only one thing I ask, Ralph ;—open out-and-out confidence."

" You shall have it, sir."

" There is somebody, then."

" Well; no ; there isn't anybody. It would be impudence in me to say there was."

" Then I know there is." Upon this encouragement Ralph told his father that on his two last visits to London he had seen a girl whom he thought that he would like to ask to be his wife. He had been at Fulham on three or four occasions,—it was so he put it, but his visits had, in truth, been only three,—and he thought that this niece of Sir Thomas Underwood possessed every charm that a woman need possess,—" except money," said Ralph. " She has no fortune, if you care about that."

"I don't care about money," said the Squire. " It is for the man to have that ;—at any rate for one so circumstanced as you." The end of all this was that Ralph was authorised to please himself. If he really felt that he liked Miss Bonner well enough, he might ask her to be his wife to-morrow.

" The difficulty is to get at her," said Ralph.

" Ask the uncle for his permission. That's the manliest and the fittest way to do it. Tell him everything. Take my word for it he won't turn his face against you. As for me, nothing on earth would make me so happy as to see your children. If there were a dozen, I would not think them one too many. But mark you this, Ralph ; it

will be easier for us,—for you and me, if I live,—and for you without
me if I go, to make all things clear and square and free while the
bairns are little, than when they have to go to school and college, or
perhaps want to get married."

"Ain't we counting our chickens before they are hatched?" said
Ralph laughing.

When they parted for the night, which they did not do till after
the Squire had slept for an hour on his chair, there was one other
speech made,—a speech which Ralph was likely to remember to the
latest day of his life. His father had taken his candlestick in his
right hand, and had laid his left upon his son's collar. "Ralph,"
said he, "for the first time in my life I can look you in the face, and
not feel a pang of remorse. You will understand it when you have
a son of your own. Good-night, my boy." Then he hurried off
without waiting to hear a word, if there was any word that Ralph
could have spoken.

On the next morning they were both out early at Darvell's farm,
surrounded by bricklayers and carpenters, and before the week was
over the work was in progress. Poor Darvell, half elated and half
troubled, knew but little of the cause of this new vehemence. Something we suppose he did know, for the news was soon spread over
the estate that the Squire had bought out Mr. Ralph, and that this
other Mr. Ralph was now to be Mr. Ralph the heir. That the old
butler should not be told,—the butler who had lived in the house
when the present Squire was a boy,—was out of the question; and
though the communication had been made in confidence, the confidence was not hermetical. The Squire after all was glad that it
should be so. The thing had to be made known,—and why not after
this fashion? Among the labourers and poor there was no doubt as
to the joy felt. That other Mr. Ralph, who had always been up in
town, was unknown to them, and this Mr. Ralph had ever been
popular with them all. With the tenants the feeling was perhaps
more doubtful. "I wish you joy, Mr. Newton, with all my heart,"
said Mr. Walker, who was the richest and the most intelligent among
them. "The Squire has worked for you like a man, and I hope it
will come to good."

"I will do my best," said Ralph.

"I am sure you will. There will be a feeling, you know. You
mustn't be angry at that."

"I understand," said Ralph.

"You won't be vexed with me for just saying so." Ralph promised that he would not be vexed, but he thought very much of what
Mr. Walker had said to him. After all, such a property as Newton
does not in England belong altogether to the owner of it. Those
who live upon it, and are closely concerned in it with reference

to all that they have in the world, have a part property in it. They make it what it is, and will not make it what it should be, unless in their hearts they are proud of it. "You know he can't be the real squire," said one old farmer to Mr. Walker. "They may hugger-mugger it this way and that; but this Mr. Ralph can't be like t'other young gentleman."

Nevertheless the Squire himself was very happy. These things were not said to him, and he had been successful. He took an interest in all things keener than he had felt for years past. One day he was in the stables with his son, and spoke about the hunting for the coming season. He had an Irish horse of which he was proud, an old hunter that had carried him for the last seven years, and of which he had often declared that under no consideration would he part with it. "Dear old fellow," he said, putting his hand on the animal's neck, "you shall work for your bread one other winter, and then you shall give over for the rest of your life."

"I never saw him look better," said Ralph.

"He's like his master;—not quite so young as he was once. He never made a mistake yet that I know of."

Ralph when he saw how full of joy was his father, could not but rejoice also that the thing so ardently desired had been at last accomplished.

CHAPTER XXIX.

THE ELECTION.

THE day of the nomination at Percycross came at last, and it was manifest to everybody that there was a very unpleasant feeling in the town. It was not only that party was arrayed against party. That would have been a state of things not held to be undesirable, and at any rate would have been natural. But at present things were so divided that there was no saying which were the existing parties. Moggs was separated from Westmacott quite as absolutely as was Westmacott from the two Conservative candidates. The old Liberals of the borough were full of ridicule for poor Moggs, of whom all absurd stories were told by them both publicly and privately. But still he was there, the darling of the workmen. It was, indeed, asserted by the members of Mr. Westmacott's committee that Moggs's popularity would secure for him but very few votes. A great proportion of the working men of Percycross were freemen of the borough, —old voters who were on the register by right of their birth and family connection in the place, independent of householdership and rates,—and quite accustomed to the old ways of manipulation. The younger of these men might be seduced into listening to Moggs. The excitement was pleasant to them. But they were too well trained to be led away on the day of election. Moggs would give them no beer, and they had always been accustomed to their three half-crowns a head in consideration for the day's work. Not a dozen freemen of the borough would vote for Moggs. So said Mr. Kirkham, Mr. Westmacott's managing man, and no man knew the borough quite so well as did Mr. Kirkham. "They'll fight for him at the hustings," said Mr. Kirkham; "but they'll take their beer and their money, and they'll vote for us and Griffenbottom."

This might be true enough as regarded the freemen,—the men who had been, as it were, educated to political life;—but there was much doubt as to the new voters. There were about a thousand of these in the borough, and it had certainly not been the intention of either party that these men should have the half-crowns. It was from these men and their leaders,—the secretaries and chairmen and presidents, —that had come the cry for a second liberal candidate, and the consequent necessity of putting forward two Conservatives. They were equally odious to the supporters of Westmacott and of Griffenbottom. "They must have the half-crowns," Trigger had said to old Pile, the bootmaker. Pile thought that every working man was

entitled to the three half-crowns, and said as much very clearly. "I
suppose old Griff ain't going to turn Hunks at this time o' day," said
Mr. Pile. But the difficulties were endless, and were much better
understood by Mr. Trigger than by Mr. Pile. The manner of con-
veying the half-crowns to the three hundred and twenty-four freemen,
who would take them and vote honestly afterwards for Griffenbottom
and Honeywood, was perfectly well understood. But among that
godless, riotous, ungoverned and ungovernable set of new householders, there was no knowing how to act. They would take the
money and then vote wrong. They would take the money and then
split. The freemen were known. Three hundred and twenty-four
would take Griffenbottom's beer and half-crowns. Two hundred and
seventy-two would be equally complaisant with Mr. Westmacott. But
of these householders nothing was known. They could not be
handled. Some thirty or forty of them would probably have the
turning of the election at the last hour, must then be paid at their
own prices, and after that would not be safe! Mr. Trigger, in his
disgust, declared that things had got into so vile a form that he
didn't care if he never had anything to do with an election in Percycross again.

And then there was almost as much ill-feeling between the old-
fashioned Griffenbottomites and the Underwooders as there was
between Westmacott's Liberals and Moggs's Radicals. The two
gentlemen themselves still eat their breakfasts and dinners together,
and still paraded the streets of Percycross in each other's company.
But Sir Thomas had made himself very odious even to Mr. Griffenbottom himself. He was always protesting against beer which he
did see, and bribery which he did not see but did suspect. He
swore that he would pay not a shilling, as to which the cause of the
expenditure was not explained to him. Griffenbottom snarled at him,
and expressed an opinion that Sir Thomas would of course do the
same as any other gentleman. Mr. Trigger, with much dignity in his
mien as he spoke, declared that the discussion of any such matter at
the present moment was indecorous. Mr. Pile was for sending Sir
Thomas back to town, and very strongly advocated that measure.
Mr. Spicer, as to whom there was a story abroad in the borough in
respect of a large order for mustard, supposed to have reached him
from New York through Liverpool by the influence of Sir Thomas
Underwood, thought that the borough should return the two conservative candidates. Sir Thomas might be a little indiscreet; but,
upon the whole, his principles did him honour. So thought Mr.
Spicer, who, perhaps, believed that the order for the mustard was
coming. We need hardly say that the story, at any rate in so far as
it regarded Sir Thomas Underwood, was altogether untrue. "Yes;
principles!" said Mr. Pile. "I think we all know Sam Spicer's

principles. All for hisself, and nothing for a poor man. That's Sam Spicer." Of Mr. Pile, it must be acknowledged that he was not a pure-minded politician. He loved bribery in his very heart. But it is equally true that he did not want to be bribed himself. It was the old-fashioned privilege of a poor man to receive some small consideration for his vote in Percycross, and Mr. Pile could not endure to think that the poor man should be robbed of his little comforts.

In the meantime, Sir Thomas himself was in a state of great misery. From hour to hour he was fluctuating between a desire to run away from the accursed borough, and the shame of taking such a step. The desire for the seat which had brought him to Percycross had almost died out amidst the misery of his position. Among all the men of his party with whom he was associating, there was not one whom he did not dislike, and by whom he was not snubbed and contradicted. Griffenbottom, who went through his canvass under circumstances of coming gout and colchicum with a courage and pertinacity that were heroic, was painfully cross to every one who was not a voter. "What's the use of all that d——d nonsense, now?" he said to Sir Thomas the evening before the nomination day. There were half-a-dozen leading Conservatives in the room, and Sir Thomas was making a final protest against bribery. He rose from his chair when so addressed, and left the room. Never in his life before had he been so insulted. Trigger followed him to his bedroom, knowing well that a quarrel at this moment would be absolutely suicidal. "It's the gout, Sir Thomas," said Mr. Trigger. "Do remember what he's going through." This was so true that Sir Thomas returned to the room. It was almost impossible not to forgive anything in a man who was suffering agonies, but could still wheedle a voter. There were three conservative doctors with Mr. Griffenbottom, each of them twice daily; and there was an opinion prevalent through the borough that the gout would be in his stomach before the election was over. Sir Thomas did return to the room, and sat himself down without saying a word. "Sir Thomas," said Mr. Griffenbottom, "a man with the gout is always allowed a little liberty."

"I admit the claim," said Sir Thomas, bowing.

"And believe me, I know this game better than you do. It's of no use saying these things. No man should ever foul his own nest. Give me a little drop more brandy, Trigger, and then I'll get myself to bed." When he was gone, they all sang Griffenbottom's praises. In staunch pluck, good humour, and manly fighting, no man was his superior. "Give and take,—the English bull-dog all over. I do like old Griffenbottom," said Spiveycomb, the paper-maker.

On the day of nomination Griffenbottom was carried up on the hustings. This carrying did him good in the borough; but it should be acknowledged on his behalf that he did his best to walk. In the extreme agony of his attack he had to make his speech, and he made it. The hustings stood in the market-square, and straight in front of the wooden erection, standing at right angles to it, was a stout rail dividing the space for the distance of fifty or sixty yards, so that the supporters of one set of candidates might congregate on one side, and the supporters of the other candidates on the other side. In this way would the weaker part, whichever might be the weaker, be protected from the violence of the stronger. On the present occasion it seemed that the friends of Mr. Westmacott congregated with the Conservatives. Moggs's allies alone filled one side of the partition. There were a great many speeches made that day from the hustings,—thirteen in all. First the mayor, and then the four proposers and four seconders of the candidates. During these performances, though there was so much noise from the crowd below that not a word could be heard, there was no violence. When old Griffenbottom got up, supporting himself by an arm round one of the posts, he was loudly cheered from both sides. His personal popularity in the borough was undoubted, and his gout made him almost a demi-god. Nobody heard a word that he said; but then he had no desire to be heard. To be seen standing up there, a martyr to the gout, but still shouting for Percycross, was enough for his purpose. Sir Thomas encountered a very different reception. He was received with yells, apparently from the whole crowd. What he said was of no matter, as not a word was audible; but he did continue to inveigh against bribery. Before he had ceased a huge stone was thrown at him, and hit him heavily on the arm. He continued speaking, however, and did not himself know till afterwards that his arm was broken between the shoulder and the elbow. Mr. Westmacott was very short and good-humoured. He intended to be funny about poor Moggs;—and perhaps was funny. But his fun was of no avail. The Moggite crowd had determined that no men should be heard till their own candidate should open his mouth.

At last Ontario's turn had come. At first the roar from the crowd was so great that it seemed that it was to be with him as it had been with the others. But by degrees, though there was still a roar,—as of the sea,—Moggs's words became audible. The voices of assent and dissent are very different, even though they be equally loud. Men desirous of interrupting, do interrupt. But cheers, though they be continuous and loud as thunder, are compatible with a hearing. Moggs by this time, too, had learned to pitch his voice for an out-of-door multitude. He preached his sermon, his old sermon, about the Rights of Labour and the Salt of the Earth, the Tyranny of Capital and the Majesty of the Workmen, with an enthusiasm that made him for the moment supremely happy. He was certainly the hero of the hour in Percycross, and he allowed himself to believe,—just for that hour,—that he was about to become the hero of a new doctrine throughout England. He spoke for over half an hour, while poor Griffenbottom, seated in a chair that had been brought to him, was suffering almost the pains of hell. During this speech Sir Thomas, who had also suffered greatly, but had at first endeavoured to conceal that he was suffering, discovered the extent of his misfortune, and allowed himself to be taken out from the hustings to his inn. There was an effort made to induce Mr. Griffenbottom to retire at the same time ; but Mr. Griffenbottom, not quite understanding the extent of his colleague's misfortune, and thinking that it became him to remain and to endure, was obdurate, and would not be moved. He did not care for stones or threats,—did not care even for the gout. That was his place till after the show of hands, and there he would remain. The populace, seeing this commotion on the hustings, began to fear that there was an intention to stop the oratory of their popular candidate, and called loudly upon Moggs to go on. Moggs did go on,—and was happy.

At last there came the show of hands. It was declared to be in favour of Moggs and Westmacott. That it was very much in favour of Moggs,—in favour of Moggs by five to one, there was no doubt. Among the other candidates there was not perhaps much to choose. A poll was, of course, demanded for the two Conservatives ; and then the mayor, complimenting the people on their good behaviour,— in spite of poor Sir Thomas's broken arm,—begged them to go away. That was all very well. Of course they would go away ; but not till they had driven their enemies from the field. In half a minute the dividing rail,—the rail that had divided the blue from the yellow,— was down, and all those who had dared to show themselves there as supporters of Griffenbottom and Underwood were driven ignominiously from the market-place. They fled at all corners, and in a few seconds not a streak of blue ribbon was to be seen in the square. "They'll elect that fellow Moggs to-morrow," said Mr. Westmacott to Kirkham.

" No a bit of it," said Kirkham. " I could spot all the ringleaders in the row. Nine or ten of them are Griffenbottom's old men. They take his money regularly,—get something nearly every year, join the rads at the nomination, and vote for the squire at the poll. The chaps who hollow and throw stones always vote t'other side up."

Mr. Griffenbottom kept his seat till he could be carried home in safety through the town, and was then put to bed. The three conservative doctors, who had all been setting Sir Thomas's arm, sat in consultation upon their old friend ; and it was acknowledged on every side that Mr. Griffenbottom was very ill indeed. All manner of rumours went through the town that night. Some believed that both Griffenbottom and Sir Thomas were dead,—and that the mayor had

now no choice but to declare Moggs and Westmacott elected. Then
there arose a suspicion that the polls would be kept open on the
morrow on behalf of two defunct candidates, so that a further election
on behalf of the conservative party might be ensured. Men swore
that they would break into the bedrooms of the Standard Inn, in
order that they might satisfy themselves whether the two gentlemen
were alive or dead. And so the town was in a hubbub.

On that evening Moggs was called upon again to address his
friends at the Mechanics' Institute, and to listen to the speeches of
all the presidents and secretaries and chairmen; but by ten o'clock
he was alone in his bedroom at the Cordwainers' Arms. Down-
stairs men were shouting, singing, and drinking,—shouting in his
honour, though not drinking at his expense. He was alone in his
little comfortless room, but felt it to be impossible that he should lie
down and rest. His heart was swelling with the emotions of the day,
and his mind was full of his coming triumph. It was black night,
and there was a soft drizzling rain;—but it was absolutely necessary
for his condition that he should go out. It seemed to him that his
very bosom would burst, if he confined himself in that narrow space.
His thoughts were too big for so small a closet. He crept down-
stairs and out, through the narrow passage, into the night. Then,
by the light of the solitary lamp that stood before the door of the
public-house, he could still see those glorious words, " Moggs, Purity,
and the Rights of Labour." Noble words, which had sufficed to bind
to him the whole population of that generous-hearted borough! Purity
and the Rights of Labour! Might it not be that with that cry, well
cried, he might move the very world! As he walked the streets of
the town he felt a great love for the borough grow within his bosom.
What would he not owe to the dear place which had first recognised
his worth, and had enabled him thus early in life to seize hold of
those ploughshares which it would be his destiny to hold for all
his coming years? He had before him a career such as had graced
the lives of the men whom he had most loved and admired,—of men
who had dared to be independent, patriotic, and philanthropical,
through all the temptations of political life. Would he be too vain if
he thought to rival a Hume or a Cobden? Conceit, he said to
himself, will seek to justify itself. Who can rise but those who
believe their wings strong enough for soaring? There might be shipwreck of course,—but he believed that he now saw his way. As to
the difficulty of speaking in public,—that he had altogether overcome.
Some further education as to facts, historical and political, might be
necessary. That he acknowledged to himself;—but he would not
spare himself in his efforts to acquire such education. He went
pacing through the damp, muddy, dark streets, making speeches that
were deliciously eloquent to his own ears. That night he was certainly

the happiest man in Percycross, never doubting his success on the morrow,—not questioning that. Had not the whole town greeted him with loudest acclamation as their chosen member? He was deliciously happy;—while poor Sir Thomas was suffering the double pain of his broken arm and his dissipated hopes, and Griffenbottom was lying in his bed, with a doctor on one side and a nurse on the other, hardly able to restrain himself from cursing all the world in his agony.

At a little after eleven a tall man, buttoned up to his chin in an old great coat, called at the Percy Standard, and asked after the health of Mr. Griffenbottom and Sir Thomas. "They ain't neither of them very well then," replied the waiter. "Will you say that Mr. Moggs called to inquire, with his compliments," said the tall man. The respect shown to him was immediately visible. Even the waiter at the Percy Standard acknowledged that for that day Mr. Moggs must be treated as a great man in Percycross. After that Moggs walked home and crept into bed;—but it may be doubted whether he slept a wink that night.

And then there came the real day,—the day of the election. It was a foul, rainy, muddy, sloppy morning, without a glimmer of sun, with that thick, pervading, melancholy atmosphere which forces for the time upon imaginative men a conviction that nothing is worth anything. Griffenbottom was in bed in one room at the Percy Standard, and Underwood in the next. The three conservative doctors moving from one chamber to another, watching each other closely, and hardly leaving the hotel, had a good time of it. Mr. Trigger had already remarked that in one respect the breaking of Sir Thomas's arm was lucky, because now there would be no difficulty as to paying the doctors out of the common fund. Every half-hour the state of the poll was brought to them. Early in the morning Moggs had been in the ascendant. At half-past nine the numbers were as follows:—

Moggs	193
Westmacott	172
Griffenbottom	162
Underwood	147

At ten, and at half-past ten, Moggs was equally in advance, but Westmacott had somewhat receded. At noon the numbers were considerably altered, and were as follows:—

Griffenbottom	892
Moggs	777
Westmacott	752
Underwood	678

These at least were the numbers as they came from the conservative books. Westmacott was placed nearer to Moggs by his own tellers. For Moggs no special books were kept. He was content to abide by the official counting.

Griffenbottom was consulted privately by Trigger and Mr. Spivey-comb as to what steps should be taken in this emergency. It was suggested in a whisper that Underwood should be thrown over altogether. There would be no beating Moggs,—so thought Mr. Spiveycomb,—and unless an effort were made it might be possible that Westmacott would creep up. Trigger in his heart considered that it would be impossible to get enough men at three half-crowns a piece to bring Sir Thomas up to a winning condition. But Griffen-bottom, now that the fight was forward, was unwilling to give way a foot. " We haven't polled half the voters," said he.

" More than half what we shall poll," answered Trigger.

" They always hang back," growled Griffenbottom. " Fight it out. I don't believe they'll ever elect a shoemaker here." The order was given, and it was fought out.

Moggs, early in the morning, had been radiant with triumph, when he saw his name at the head of the lists displayed from the two inimical committee rooms. As he walked the streets, with a chairman on one side of him and a president on the other, it seemed as though his feet almost disdained to touch the mud. These were two happy hours, during which he did not allow himself to doubt of his triumph. When the presidents and the chairmen spoke to him, he could hardly answer them, so rapt was he in contemplation of his coming great-ness. His very soul was full of his seat in Parliament ! But when Griffenbottom approached him on the lists, and then passed him, there came a shadow upon his brow. He still felt sure of his election, but he would lose that grand place at the top of the poll to which he had taught himself to look so proudly. Soon after noon a cruel speech was made to him. " We've about pumped our side dry," said a secretary of a Young Men's Association.

" Do you mean we've polled all our friends ? " asked Moggs.

" Pretty nearly, Mr. Moggs. You see our men have nothing to wait for, and they came up early." Then Ontario's heart sank within him, and he began to think of the shop in Bond Street.

The work of that afternoon in Percycross proved how correct Mr. Griffenbottom had been in his judgment. He kept his place at the top of the poll. It was soon evident that that could not be shaken. Then Westmacott passed by Moggs, and in the next half-hour Sir Thomas did so also. This was at two, when Ontario betook himself to the privacy of his bedroom at the Cordwainers' Arms. His pluck left him altogether, and he found himself unable to face the town as a losing candidate. Then for two hours there was a terrible struggle between Westmacott and Underwood, during

which things were done in the desperation of the moment, as to
which it might be so difficult to give an account, should any subsequent account be required. We all know how hard it is to sacrifice
the power of winning, when during the heat of the contest the power
of winning is within our reach. At four o'clock the state of the poll
was as follows :—

Griffenbottom	1402
Underwood	1007
Westmacott	984
Moggs	821

When the chairmen and presidents waited upon Moggs, telling
him of the final result, and informing him that he must come to the
hustings and make a speech, they endeavoured to console him by an
assurance that he, and he alone, had fought the fight fairly. "They'll
both be unseated, you know, as sure as eggs," said the president.
"It can't be otherwise. They've been busy up in a little room
in Petticoat Court all the afternoon, and the men have been getting
as much as fifteen shillings a head !" Moggs was not consoled, but
he did make his speech. It was poor and vapid ;—but still there
was just enough of manhood left in him for that. As soon as his
speech had been spoken he escaped up to London by the night mail
train. Westmacott also spoke ; but announcement was made on
behalf of the members of the borough that they were, both of them,
in their beds.

CHAPTER XXX.

"MISS MARY IS IN LUCK."

THE election took place on a Tuesday,—Tuesday, the 17th of
October. On the following day one of the members received a
visit in his bedroom at the Percy Standard which was very pleasant
to him. His daughter Patience had come down to nurse Sir Thomas
and take him back to Fulham. Sir Thomas had refused to allow any
message to be sent home on the day on which the accident had
occurred. On the following morning he had telegraphed to say that
his arm had been broken, but that he was doing very well. And on
the Wednesday Patience was with him.

In spite of the broken arm it was a pleasant meeting. For the
last fortnight Sir Thomas had not only not seen a human being with
whom he could sympathise, but had been constrained to associate
with people who were detestable to him. His horror of Griffenbottom, his disgust at Trigger, his fear of Mr. Pabsby's explanations,

and his inability to cope with Messrs. Spicer and Roodylands when they spoke of mustard and boots, had been almost too much for him. The partial seclusion occasioned by his broken arm had been a godsend to him. In such a state he was prepared to feel that his daughter's presence was an angel's visit. And even to him his success had something of the pleasure of a triumph. Of course he was pleased to have won the seat. And though whispers of threats as to a petition had already reached him, he was able in these, the first hours of his membership, to throw his fears on that head behind him. The man must be of a most cold temperament who, under such circumstances, cannot allow himself some short enjoyment of his new toy. It was his at least for the time, and he probably told himself that threatened folk lived long. That Patience should take glory in the victory was a matter of course. "Dear papa," she said, "if you can only get your arm well again!"

"I don't suppose there is any cause for fear as to that."

"But a broken arm is a great misfortune," said Patience.

"Well;—yes. One can't deny that. And three Percycross doctors are three more misfortunes. I must get home as soon as I can."

"You mustn't be rash, papa, even to escape from Percycross. But, oh, papa; we are so happy and so proud. It is such an excellent thing that you should be in Parliament again."

"I don't know that, my dear."

"We feel it so,—Clary and I,—and so does Mary. I can't tell you the sort of anxiety we were in all day yesterday. First we got the telegram about your arm,—and then Stemm came down at eight and told us that you were returned. Stemm was quite humane on the occasion."

"Poor Stemm!—I don't know what he'll have to do."

"It won't matter to him, papa;—will it? And then he told me another piece of news."

"What is it?"

"You won't like it, papa. We didn't like it at all."

"What is it, my dear?"

"Stemm says that Ralph has sold all the Newton Priory estate to his uncle."

"It is the best thing he could do."

"Really, papa?"

"I think so. He must have done that or made some disreputable marriage."

"I don't think he would have done that," said Patience.

"But he was going to do it. He had half-engaged himself to some tailor's daughter. Indeed, up to the moment of your telling me this I thought he would marry her." Poor Clary! So Patience said to herself as she heard this. "He had got himself into such a mess that the best thing he could do was to sell his interest to his uncle. The estate will go to a better fellow, though out of the proper line."

Then Patience told her father that she had brought a letter for him which had been given to her that morning by Stemm, who had met her at the station.

" I think," she said, " that it comes from some of the Newton family because of the crest and the Basingstoke postmark." Then the letter was brought ;—and as it concerns much the thread of our story, it shall be given to the reader ;—

"Newton Priory, October 17, 186—.

" MY DEAR SIR THOMAS UNDERWOOD,—

" I write to you with the sanction, or rather at the instigation, of my father to ask your permission to become a suitor to your niece, Miss Bonner. You will probably have heard, or at least will hear, that my father has made arrangements with his nephew Ralph, by which the reversion of the Newton property will belong to my father. It is his intention to leave the estate to me, and he permits me to tell you that he will consent to any such settlement in the case of my marriage, as would have been usual, had I been his legitimate heir. I think it best to be frank about this, as I should not have ventured to propose such a marriage either to you or to Miss Bonner, had not my father's solicitude succeeded in placing me in circumstances which may, perhaps, be regarded as in part compensating the great misfortune of my birth.

" It may probably be right that I should add that I have said no word on this subject to Miss Bonner. I have hitherto felt myself constrained by the circumstances to which I have alluded from acting as other men may act. Should you be unwilling to concede that the advantages of fortune which have now fallen in my way justify me in proposing to myself such a marriage, I hope that you will at least excuse my application to yourself.

" Very faithfully yours,
" RALPH NEWTON."

Sir Thomas read the letter twice before he spoke a word to his daughter. Then, after pausing with it for a moment in his hand, he threw it to her across the bed. " Miss Mary is in luck," he said :— " in very great luck. It is a magnificent property, and as far as I can see, one of the finest young fellows I ever met. You understand about his birth ? "

" Yes," said Patience, almost in a whisper.

" It might be a hindrance to him in some circumstances ; but not here. It is nothing here. Did you know of this ? "

" No, indeed."

" Nor Mary ? "

" It will be quite a surprise to her. I am sure it will."

" You think, then, that there has been nothing said,—not a word about it ? "

" I am sure there has not, papa. Clarissa had some joke with Mary,—quite as a joke."

" Then there has been a joke ? "

" It meant nothing. And as for Mr. Newton, he could not have dreamed of anything of the kind. We all liked him."

" So did I. The property will be much better with him than with the other. Mary is a very lucky girl. That's all I can say. As for the letter, it's the best letter I ever read in my life."

There was some delay before Sir Thomas could write an answer to young Newton. It was, indeed, his left arm that had suffered ; but even with so much of power abstracted, writing is not an easy task. And this was a letter the answering of which could not be deputed to any secretary. On the third day after its receipt Sir Thomas did manage with much difficulty to get a reply written.

" DEAR MR. NEWTON,—

" I have had my left arm broken in the election here. Hence the delay. I can have no objection. Your letter does you infinite honour. I presume you know that my niece has no fortune.

" Yours, most sincerely,

" THOMAS UNDERWOOD."

" What a pity it is," said Sir Thomas, " that a man can't have a broken arm in answering all letters. I should have had to write ever so much had I been well. And yet I could not have said a word more that would have been of any use."

Sir Thomas was kept an entire week at the Percycross Standard after his election was over before the three doctors and the inn-keeper between them would allow him to be moved. During this time there was very much discussion between the father and daughter as to Mary's prospects ; and a word or two was said inadvertently which almost opened the father's eyes as to the state of his younger daughter's affections. It is sometimes impossible to prevent the betrayal of a confidence, when the line between betrayal and non-betrayal is finely drawn. It was a matter of course that there should be much said about that other Ralph, the one now disinherited and dispossessed, who had so long and so intimately been known to them ; and it was almost impossible for Patience not to show the cause of her great grief. It might be, as her father said, that the property would be better in the hands of this other young man ;

but Patience knew that her sympathies were with the spendthrift, and with the dearly-loved sister who loved the spendthrift. Since Clarissa had come to speak so openly of her love, to assert it so loudly, and to protest that nothing could or should shake it, Patience had been unable not to hope that the heir might at last prove himself worthy to be her sister's husband. Then they heard that his inheritance was sold. "It won't make the slightest difference to me," said Clary almost triumphantly, as she discussed the matter with Patience the evening before the journey to Percycross. "If he were a beggar it would be the same." To Patience, however, the news of the sale had been a great blow. And now her father told her that this young man had been thinking of marrying another girl, a tailor's daughter;—that such a marriage had been almost fixed. Surely it would be better that steps should be taken to wean her sister from such a passion ! But yet she did not tell the secret. She only allowed a word to escape her, from which it might be half surmised that Clarissa would be a sufferer. "What difference will it make to Clary ?" asked Sir Thomas.

"I have sometimes thought that he cared for her," said Patience cunningly. "He would hardly have been so often at the villa, unless there had been something."

"There must be nothing of that kind," said Sir Thomas. "He is a spendthrift, and quite unworthy of her. I will not have him at the villa. He must be told so. If you see anything of that kind, you must inform me. Do you understand, Patience ?" Patience understood well enough, but knew not what reply to make. She could not tell her sister's secret. And if there were faults in the matter, was it not her father's fault ? Why had he not lived with them, so that he might see these things with his own eyes ? "There must be nothing of that kind," said Sir Thomas, with a look of anger in his eyes.

When the week was over, the innkeeper and the doctors submitting with but a bad grace, the member for Percycross returned to London with his arm bound up in a sling. The town was by this time quite tranquil. The hustings had been taken down, and the artizans of the borough were back at their labours, almost forgetting Moggs and his great doctrines. That there was to be a petition was a matter of course. It was at least a matter of course that there should be threats of a petition. The threat of course reached Sir Thomas's ears, but nothing further was said to him. When he and his daughter went down to the station in the Standard fly, it almost seemed that he was no more to the borough than any other man might be with a broken arm. "I shall not speak of this to Mary," he said on his journey home. "Nor should you, I think, my dear."

"Of course not, papa."

"He should have the opportunity of changing his mind after receiving my letter, if he so pleases. For her sake I hope he will not." Patience said nothing further. She loved her cousin Mary, and certainly had felt no dislike for this fortunate young man. But she could not so quickly bring herself to sympathise with interests which seemed to be opposed to those of her sister.

CHAPTER XXXI.

IT IS ALL SETTLED.

IN the last half of this month of October the Squire at Newton was very pressing on his lawyers up in London to settle the affairs of the property. He was most anxious to make a new will, but could not do so till his nephew had completed the sale, and till the money had been paid. He had expressed a desire to go up to London and remain there till all was done; but against this his son had expostulated, urging that his father could not hasten the work up in London by his presence, but would certainly annoy and flurry everybody in the lawyer's office. Mr. Carey had promised that the thing should be done with as little delay as possible, but Mr. Carey was not a man to be driven. Then again the Squire would be a miserable man up in London, whereas at the Priory he might be so happy among the new works which he had already inaugurated. The son's arguments prevailed,—especially that argument as to the pleasure of the Squire's present occupations,—and the Squire consented to remain at home.

There seemed to be an infinity of things to be done, and to the Squire himself the world appeared to require more of happy activity than at any previous time of his life. He got up early, and was out about the place before breakfast. He had endless instructions to give to everybody about the estate. The very air of the place was sweeter to him than heretofore. The labourers were less melancholy at their work. The farmers smiled oftener. The women and children were more dear to him. Everything around him had now been gifted with the grace of established ownership. His nephew Gregory, after that last dinner of which mention was made, hardly came near him during the next fortnight. Once or twice the Squire went up to the church during week days that he might catch the parson, and even called at the parsonage. But Gregory was unhappy, and would not conceal his unhappiness. "I suppose it will wear off," said the Squire to his son.

"Of course it will, sir."

"It shall not be my fault if it does not. I wonder whether it would have made him happier to see the property parcelled out and sold to the highest bidder after my death."

"It is not unnatural, if you think of it," said Ralph.

"Perhaps not; and God forbid that I should be angry with him because he cannot share my triumph. I feel, however, that I have done my duty, and that nobody has a right to quarrel with me."

And then there were the hunters. Every sportsman knows, and the wives and daughters of all sportsmen know, how important a month in the calendar is the month of October. The real campaign begins in November; and even for those who do not personally attend to the earlier work of the kennel,—or look after cub-hunting, which during the last ten days of October is apt to take the shape of genuine hunting,—October has charms of its own and peculiar duties. It is the busiest month in the year in regard to horses. Is physic needed? In the Squire's stables physic was much eschewed, and the Squire's horses were usually in good condition. But it is needful to know, down to a single line on the form, whether this or that animal wants more exercise,—and if so, of what nature. We hold that for hunters which are worked regularly throughout the season, and which live in loose boxes summer and winter, but little exercise is required except in the months of September and October. Let them have been fed on oats throughout the year, and a good groom will bring them into form in two months. Such at least was the order at the Newton stables; and during this autumn,—especially during these last days of October,—this order was obeyed with infinite alacrity, and with many preparations for coming joys. And there are other cares, less onerous indeed, but still needful. What good sportsman is too proud, or even too much engaged, to inspect his horse's gear,—and his own? Only let his horses' gear stand first in his mind! Let him be sure that the fit of a saddle is of more moment than the fit of a pair of breeches;—that in riding the length, strength, and nature of the bit will avail more,—should at least avail more,—than the depth, form, and general arrangement of the flask; that the question of boots, great as it certainly is, should be postponed to the question of shoes; that a man's seat should be guarded by his girths rather than by his spurs; that no run has ever been secured by the brilliancy of the cravat, though many a run has been lost by the insufficiency of a stirrup-leather. In the stables and saddle-room, and throughout the whole establishment of the house at Newton, all these matters were ever sedulously regarded; but they had never been regarded with more joyful zeal than was given to them during this happy month. There was not a stable-boy about the place who did not know and feel that their Mr. Ralph was now to take his place in the hunting-field as the heir to Newton Priory.

And there were other duties at Newton of which the crowd of riding-men know little or nothing. Were there foxes in the coverts? The Squire had all his life been a staunch preserver, thinking more of a vixen with her young cubs than he would of any lady in the land with her first-born son. During the last spring and summer, how-ever, things had made him uncomfortable; and he had not personally inquired after the well-being of each nursery in the woods as had been his wont. Ralph, indeed, had been on the alert, and the keepers had not become slack;—but there had been a whisper about the place that the master didn't care so much about the foxes as he used to do. They soon found out that he cared enough now. The head-keeper opened his eyes very wide when he was told that the Squire would take it as a personal offence if the coverts were ever drawn blank. It was to be understood through the county that at Newton Priory everything now was happy and prosperous. "We'll get up a breakfast and a meet on the lawn before the end of the month," said the Squire to his son. "I hate hunt breakfasts myself, but the farmers like them." From all which the reader will perceive that the Squire was in earnest.

Ralph hunted all through the latter days of October, but the Squire himself would not go out till the first regular day of the season. "I like a law, and I like to stick to it," he said. "Five months is enough for the horses in all conscience." At last the happy day arrived,—Wednesday, the 2nd of November,—and the father and son started together for the meet in a dog-cart on four wheels with two horses. On such occasions the Squire always drove himself, and professed to go no more than eight miles an hour. The meet was over in the Berkshire county in the neighbourhood of Swallowfield, about twelve miles distant, and the Squire was in his seat precisely at half-past nine. Four horses had gone on in the charge of two grooms, for the Squire had insisted on Ralph riding with a second horse. "If you don't, I won't," he had said; and Ralph of course had yielded. Just at this time there had grown up in the young man's mind a feeling that his father was almost excessive in the exuberance of his joy,—that he was displaying too ostensibly to the world at large the triumph which he had effected. But the checking of this elation was almost impossible to the son on whose behalf it was exhibited. Therefore, to Ralph's own regret, the two horses had on this morning been sent on to Barford Heath. The Squire was not kept waiting a moment. Ralph lit his cigar and jumped in, and the Squire started in all comfort and joy. The road led them by Darvell's farm, and for a moment the carriage was stopped that a word might be spoken to some workman. "You'd better have a couple more men, Miles. It won't do to let the frost catch us," said the Squire. Miles touched his hat, and assented. "The house will look very well from here," said the Squire, pointing down through a line of trees. Ralph assented cheerily; and yet he thought that his father was spending more money than Darvell's house need to have cost him.

They reached Barford Heath a few minutes before eleven, and there was a little scene upon the occasion. It was the first recognised meet of the season, and the Squire had not been out before. It was now known to almost every man there that the owner of Newton Priory had at last succeeded in obtaining the reversion of the estate for his own son; and though the matter was one which hardly admitted of open congratulation, still there were words spoken and looks given, and a little additional pressure in the shaking of hands,—all of which seemed to mark a triumph. That other Ralph had not been known in the county. This Ralph was very popular; and though of course there was existent some amount of inner unexpressed feeling that the proper line of an old family was being broken, that for the moment was kept in abeyance, and all men's faces wore smiles as they were turned upon the happy Squire. He hardly carried himself with as perfect a moderation as his son would have wished. He was a little loud,—not saying much to any one openly about the property, uttering merely a word or two in a low voice in answer to the kind expressions of one or two specially intimate friends; but in discussing other matters,—the appearance of the pack, the prospects of the season, the state of the county,—he was not quite like himself. In his ordinary way he was a quiet man, not often heard at much distance, and contented to be noted as Newton of Newton rather than as a man commanding attention by his conduct before other men. There certainly was a difference to-day, and it was of that kind which wine produces on some who are not habitual drinkers. The gases of his life were in exuberance, and he was as a balloon insufficiently freighted with ballast. His buoyancy, unless checked, might carry him too high among the clouds. All this Ralph saw, and kept himself a little aloof. If there were aught amiss, there was no help for it on his part; and, after all, what was amiss was so very little amiss.

"We'll draw the small gorses first," said the old master, addressing himself specially to Mr. Newton, "and then we'll go into Barford Wood."

"Just so," said the Squire; "the gorses first by all means. I remember when there was always a fox at Barford Gorse. Come along. I hate to see time wasted. You'll be glad to hear we're full of foxes at Newton. There were two litters bred in Bostock Spring; —two, by Jove! in that little place. Dan,"—Dan was his second horseman,—"I'll ride the young one this morning. You have Paddywhack fresh for me about one." Paddywhack was the old Irish horse which had carried him so long, and has been mentioned before. There was nothing remarkable in all this. There was no word spoken that might not have been said with a good grace by any old sportsman, who knew the men around him, and who had long preserved foxes for their use ;—but still it was felt that the Squire was a little loud. Ralph the son, on whose behalf all this triumph was felt, was silenter than usual, and trotted along at the rear of the long line of horsemen.

One specially intimate friend of his,—a man whom he really loved, —hung back with the object of congratulating him. "Ralph," said George Morris, of Watheby Grove, a place about four miles from the Priory, "I must tell you how glad I am of all this."

"All right, old fellow."

"Come; you might show out a little to me. Isn't it grand? We shall always have you among us now. Don't tell me that you are indifferent."

"I think enough about it, God knows, George. But it seems to me that the less said about it the better. My father has behaved nobly to me, and of course I like to feel that I've got a place in the world marked out for me. But——"

"But what?"

"You understand it all, George. There shouldn't be rejoicing in a family because the heir has lost his inheritance."

"I can't look at it in that line."

"I can't look at it in any other," said Ralph. "Mind you, I'm not saying that it isn't all right. What has happened to him has come of his own doings. I only mean that we ought to be quiet about it. My father's spirits are so high, that he can hardly control them."

"By George, I don't wonder at it," said George Morris.

There were three little bits of gorse about half-a-mile from Barford Wood, as to which it seemed that expectation did not run high, but from the last of which an old fox broke before the hounds were in it. It was so sudden a thing that the pack was on the scent and away before half-a-dozen men had seen what had happened. Our Squire had been riding with Cox, the huntsman, who had ventured to say how happy he was that the young squire was to be the Squire some day. "So am I, Cox; so am I," said the Squire. "And I hope he'll be a friend to you for many a year."

"By the holy, there's Dick a-hallooing," said Cox, forgetting at once the comparatively unimportant affairs of Newton Priory in the breaking of this unexpected fox. "Golly ;—if he ain't away, Squire." The hounds had gone at once to the whip's voice, and were in full cry in less time than it has taken to tell the story of "the find." Cox was with them, and so was the Squire. There were two or three others, and one of the whips. The start, indeed, was not much, but the burst was so sharp, and the old fox ran so straight, that it sufficed to enable those who had got the lead to keep it. "Tally-ho!" shouted the Squire, as he saw the animal making across a stubble field before the hounds, with only one fence between him and the quarry. "Tally-ho!" It was remarked afterwards that the Squire had never been known to halloo to a fox in that way before. "Just like one of the young 'uns, or a fellow out of the town," said Cox, when expressing his astonishment.

But the Squire never rode a run better in his life. He gave a lead to the field, and he kept it. "I wouldn't 'a spoilt him by putting my nose afore 'is, were it ever so," said Cox afterwards. "He went as straight as a schoolboy at Christmas, and the young horse he rode never made a mistake. Let men say what they will, a young horse will carry a man a brush like that better than an old one. It was very short. They had run their fox, pulled him down, broken him up, and eaten him within half an hour. Jack Graham, who is particular about those things, and who was, at any rate, near enough to see it all, said that it was exactly twenty-two minutes and a half. He might be right enough in that, but when he swore that they had gone over four miles of ground, he was certainly wrong. They killed within a field of Heckfield church, and Heckfield church can't be four miles from Barford Gorse. That they went as straight as a line everybody knew. Besides, they couldn't have covered the ground in the time. The pace was good, no doubt; but Jacky Graham is always given to exaggeration."

The Squire was very proud of his performance, and, when Ralph came up, was loud in praise of the young horse. "Never was carried so well in my life,—never," said he. "I knew he was good, but I didn't know he would jump like that. I wouldn't take a couple of hundred for him." This was still a little loud; but the Squire at this moment had the sense of double triumph within, and was to be forgiven. It was admitted on all sides that he had ridden the run uncommonly well. "Just like a young man, by Jove," said Jack Graham. "Like what sort of a young man?" asked George Harris, who had come up at the heel of the hunt with Ralph.

"And where were you, Master Ralph?" said the Squire to his son.

"I fancy I just began to know they were running by the time you were killing your fox," said Ralph.

"You should have your eyes better about you, my boy; shouldn't he, Cox?"

"The young squire ain't often in the wrong box," said the huntsman.

"He wasn't in the right one to-day," said the Squire. This was still a little loud. There was too much of that buoyancy which might have come from drink; but which, with the Squire, was the effect of that success for which he had been longing rather than hoping all his life.

From Heckfield they trotted back to Barford Wood, the master resolving that he would draw his country in the manner he had proposed to himself in the morning. There was some little repining at this, partly because the distance was long, and partly because Barford Woods were too large to be popular. "Hunting is over for the day," said Jack Graham. To this view of the case the Squire, who had now changed his horse, objected greatly. "We shall find in Barford big wood as sure as the sun rises," said he. "Yes," said Jack, "and run into the little wood and back to the big wood, and so on till we hate every foot of the ground. I never knew anything from Barford Woods yet for which a donkey wasn't as good as a horse." The Squire again objected, and told the story of a run from Barford Woods twenty years ago which had taken them pretty nearly on to Ascot Heath. "Things have changed since that," said Jack Graham. "Very much for the better," said the Squire. Ralph was with him then, and still felt that his father was too loud. Whether he meant that hunting was better now than in the old days twenty years ago, or that things as regarded the Newton estate were better, was not explained; but all who heard him speak imagined that he was alluding to the latter subject.

Drawing Barford Woods is a very different thing than drawing Barford Gorses. Anybody may see a fox found at the gorses who will simply take the trouble to be with the hounds when they go into the covert; but in the wood it becomes a great question with a sportsman whether he will stick to the pack or save his horse and loiter about till he hears that a fox has been found. The latter is certainly the commoner course, and perhaps the wiser. And even when the fox has been found it may be better for the expectant sportsman to loiter about till he breaks, giving some little attention to the part of the wood in which the work of hunting may be progressing. There are those who systematically stand still or roam about very slowly;—others, again, who ride and cease riding by spurts, just as they become weary or impatient;—and others who, with dogged perseverance, stick always to the track of the hounds. For years past the Squire was to have been found among the former and more prudent set of riders, but on this occasion he went gallantly through the thickest of the underwood, close at the huntsman's heels. "You'll find it rather nasty, Mr. Newton, among them brakes," Cox had said to him. But the Squire had answered that he hadn't got his Sunday face on, and had persevered.

They were soon on a fox in Barford Wood;—but being on a fox in Barford Wood was very different from finding a fox in Barford Gorse.

Out of the gorse a fox must go ; but in the big woods he might choose to remain half the day. And then the chances were that he would either beat the hounds at last, or else be eaten in covert. "It's a very pretty place to ride about and smoke and drink one's friend's sherry." That was Jack Graham's idea of hunting in Barford Woods, and a great deal of that kind of thing was going on to-day. Now and then there was a little excitement, and cries of "away" were heard. Men would burst out of the wood here and there, ride about for a few minutes, and then go in again. Cox swore that they had thrice changed their fox, and was beginning to be a little short in his temper; the whips' horses were becoming jaded, and the master had once or twice answered very crossly when questioned. "How the devil do you suppose I'm to know," he had said to a young gentleman who had inquired, "where they were ?" But still the Squire kept on zealously, and reminded Ralph that some of the best things of the season were often lost by men becoming slack towards evening. At that time it was nearly four o'clock, and Cox was clearly of opinion that he couldn't kill a fox in Barford Woods that day.

But still the hounds were hunting. "Darned if they ain't back to the little wood again," said Cox to the Squire. They were at that moment in an extreme corner of an outlying copse, and between them and Barford Little Wood was a narrow strip of meadow, over which they had passed half-a-dozen times that day. Between the copse and the meadow there ran a broad ditch with a hedge,—a rotten made-up fence of sticks and bushes, which at the corner had been broken down by the constant passing of horses, till, at this hour of the day, there was hardly at that spot anything of a fence to be jumped. "We must cross with them again, Cox," said the Squire. At that moment he was nearest to the gap, and close to him were Ralph and George Morris, as well as the huntsman. But Mr. Newton's horse was standing sideways to the hedge, and was not facing the passage. He, nevertheless, prepared to pass it first, and turned his horse sharply at it ; as he did so, some bush or stick caught the animal in the flank, and he, in order to escape the impediment, clambered up the bank sideways, not taking the gap, and then balanced himself to make his jump over the ditch. But he was entangled among the sticks and thorns and was on broken ground, and jumping short, came down into the ditch. The Squire fell heavily head-long on to the field, and the horse, with no further effort of his own, but unable to restrain himself, rolled over his master. It was a place as to which any horseman would say that a child might ride through if on a donkey without a chance of danger, and yet the three men who saw it knew at once that the Squire had had a bad fall. Ralph was first through the gap, and was off his own horse as the old Irish hunter, with a groan, collected himself and got upon his legs. In rising, the animal was very careful not to strike his late rider with his feet; but it was too evident to Cox that the beast in his attempt to rise had given a terrible squeeze to the prostrate Squire with his saddle.

In a moment the three men were on their knees, and it was clear that Mr. Newton was insensible. "I'm afraid he's hurt," said Morris. Cox merely shook his head, as he gently attempted to raise the Squire's shoulder against his own. Ralph, as pale as death, held his father's hand in one of his own, and with the other endeavoured to feel the pulse of the heart. Presently, before any one else came up to them, a few drops of blood came from between the sufferer's lips. Cox again shook his head. "We'd better get him on to a gate, Mr. Ralph, and into a house," said the huntsman. They were quickly surrounded by others, and the gate was soon there, and within twenty minutes a surgeon was standing over our poor old friend. "No; he wasn't dead," the surgeon said; "but ——." "What is it?" asked Ralph, impetuously. The surgeon took the master of the hunt aside and whispered into his ear that Mr. Newton was a dead man. His spine had been so injured by the severity of his own fall, and by the weight of the horse rolling on him while he was still doubled up on the ground, that it was impossible that he should ever speak again. So the surgeon said, and Squire Newton never did speak again.

He was carried home to the house of a gentleman who lived in those parts, in order that he might be saved the longer journey to the Priory;—but the length of the road mattered but little to him. He never spoke again, nor was he sensible for a moment. Ralph remained with him during the night,—of course,—and so did the surgeon. At five o'clock on the following morning his last breath had been drawn, and his life had passed away from him. George Morris also had remained with them,—or rather had come back to the house after having ridden home and changed his clothes, and it was by him that the tidings were at last told to the wretched son. "It is all over, Ralph!" "I suppose so!" said Ralph, hoarsely. "There has never been a doubt," said George, "since we heard of the manner of the accident." "I suppose not," said Ralph. The young man sat silent, and composed, and made no expression of his grief. He did not weep, nor did his face even wear that look of woe which is so common to us all when grief comes to us. They two were still in the room in which the body lay, and were standing close together over the fire. Ralph was leaning on his elbow upon the chimneypiece, and from time to time Morris would press his arm. They had been standing together thus for some twenty minutes when Morris asked a question.

"The affair of the property had been settled, Ralph?"

"Don't talk of that now," said the other angrily. Then, after a pause, he put up his face and spoke again. "Nothing has been settled," he said. "The estate belongs to my cousin Ralph. He should be informed at once,—at once. He should be telegraphed to, to come to Newton. Would you mind doing it? He should be informed at once."

"There is time enough for that," said George Morris.

"If you will not I must," replied Ralph.

The telegram was at once sent in duplicate, addressed to that other Ralph,—Ralph who was declared by the Squire's son to be once more Ralph the heir,—addressed to him both at his lodgings in London and at the Moonbeam. When the messenger had been sent to the nearest railway station with the message, Ralph and his friend started for Newton Priory together. Poor Ralph still wore his boots and breeches and the red coat in which he had ridden on the former fatal day, and in which he had passed the night by the side of his dying father's bed. On their journey homeward they met Gregory, who had heard of the accident, and had at once started to see his uncle.

"It is all over!" said Ralph. Gregory, who was in his gig, dropped the reins and sat in silence. "It is all done. Let us get on, George. It is horrid to me to be in this coat. Get on quickly. Yes, indeed; everything is done now."

He had lost a father who had loved him dearly, and whom he had dearly loved,—a father whose opportunities of showing his active love had been greater even than fall to the lot of most parents. A father gives naturally to his son, but the Squire had been almost unnatural in his desire to give. There had never been a more devoted father, one more intensely anxious for his son's welfare;—and Ralph had known this, and loved his father accordingly. Nevertheless, he could not keep himself from remembering that he had now lost more than a father. The estate as to which the Squire had been so full of interest,—as to which he, Ralph, had so constantly endeavoured to protect himself from an interest that should be too absorbing,—had in the last moment escaped him. And now, in this sad and solemn hour, he could not keep himself from thinking of that loss. As he had stood in the room in which the dead body of his father had been lying, he had cautioned himself against this feeling. But still he had known that it had been present to him. Let him do what he would with his own thoughts, he could not hinder them from running back to the fact that by his father's sudden death he had lost the possession of the Newton estate. He hated himself for remembering such a fact at such a time, but he could not keep himself from remembering it. His father had fought a life-long battle to make him the heir of Newton, and had perished in the moment of his victory,—but before his victory was achieved. Ralph had borne his success well while he had thought that his success was certain; but now——! He knew that all such subjects should be absent from his mind with such cause for grief as weighed upon him at this moment,—but he could not drive away the reflection. That other Ralph Newton had won upon the post. He would endeavour to bear himself well, but he could not but remember that he had been beaten. And there was the father who had loved him so well lying dead!

When he reached the house, George Morris was still with him. Gregory, to whom he had spoken hardly a word, did not come beyond the parsonage. Ralph could not conceal from himself, could hardly conceal from his outward manner, the knowledge that Gregory must be aware that his cause had triumphed. And yet he hated himself for thinking of these things, and believed himself to be brutal in that he could not conceal his thoughts. " I'll send over for a few things, and stay with you for a day or two," said George Morris. " It would be bad that you should be left here alone." But Ralph would not permit the visit. " My father's nephew will be here to-morrow," he said, " and I would rather that he should find me alone." In thinking of it all, he remembered that he must withdraw his claims to the hand of Mary Bonner, now that he was nobody. He could have no pretension now to offer his hand to any such girl as Mary Bonner!

CHAPTER XXXII.

SIR THOMAS AT HOME.

SIR THOMAS UNDERWOOD was welcomed home at the villa with a double amount of sympathy and glory,—that due to him for his victory being added to that which came to him on the score of his broken arm. A hero is never so much a hero among women as when he has been wounded in the battle. The very weakness which throws him into female hands imparts a moiety of his greatness to the women who for the while possess him, and creates a partnership in heroism, in which the feminine half delights to make the most of its own share. During the week at Percycross and throughout the journey Patience had had this half all to herself; and there had arisen to her considerable enjoyment from it as soon as she found that her father would probably be none the worse for his accident after a few weeks. She saw more of him now than she had done for years, and was able, after a fashion, to work her quiet, loving, female will with him, exacting from him an obedience to feminine sway such as had not been exercised on him since his wife's death. He himself had been humbled, passive, and happy. He had taken his gruel, grumbled with modesty, and consoled himself with constantly reflecting that he was member of Parliament for the borough of Percycross.

During their journey, although Patience was urgent in requiring from her father quiescence, lest he should injure himself by too much exertion, there were many words spoken both as to Clarissa and Mary Bonner. As to poor Clary, Sir Thomas was very decided that if there were any truth in the suspicion which had been now roused in his mind as to Ralph the heir, the thing must be put an end to at once. Ralph who had been the heir was now in possession of that mess of pottage for which he had sold his inheritance,—so said Sir Thomas to his daughter,—and would undoubtedly consume that, as he had consumed the other mess which should have lasted him till the inheritance was his own. And he told to Patience the whole story as to Polly Neefit,—the whole story, at least, as he had heard it. Ralph had declared to Sir Thomas, when discussing the expedience of his proposed marriage with the daughter of the breeches-maker, that he was attached to Polly Neefit. Sir Thomas had done all he could to dissuade the young man from a marriage which, in his eyes, was disgraceful; but he could not bring himself to look with favour on affections transferred so quickly from the breeches-maker's daughter to his own. There must be no question of a love affair between Clary and the foolish heir who had disinherited himself by his folly. All this was doubly painful to Patience. She suffered first for her sister, the violence of whose feelings were so well known to her, and so completely understood ; and then on her own account she was obliged to endure the conviction that she was deceiving her father. Although she had allowed something of the truth to escape from her, she had not wilfully told her sister's secret. But looking at the matter from her father's point of view, and hearing all that her father now said, she was brought in guilty of hypocrisy in the court of her own conscience.

In that other matter as to Mary Bonner there was much more of pleasantness. There could be no possible reason why that other man, to whom Fortune was going to be so good, should not marry Mary Bonner, if Mary could bring herself to take him into her good graces. And of course she would. Such at least was Sir Thomas's opinion. How was it possible that a girl like Mary, who had nothing of her own, should fail to like a lover who had everything to recommend him,—good looks, good character, good temper, and good fortune. Patience did make some protest against this, for the sake of her sex. She didn't think, she said, that Mary had ever thought of Mr. Newton in that light. " There must be a beginning to such thoughts, of course," said Sir Thomas. Patience explained that she had nothing to say against Mr. Newton. It would all be very nice and proper, no doubt,—only perhaps Mary might not care for Mr. Newton. "Psha !" said Sir Thomas. Sir Thomas seemed to think that the one girl was as much bound to fall in love as the other was to abstain from so doing. Patience continued her protest, —but very mildly, because her father's arm was in a sling. Then there arose the question whether Mary should be told of the young man's letter. Patience thought that the young man should be allowed to come and speak for himself. Sir Thomas made no objection to the young man's coming. The young man might come when he pleased. But Sir Thomas thought it would be well that Mary should know what the young man had written. And so they reached home.

To be glorified by one worshipping daughter had been pleasant to the wounded hero, but to be glorified by two daughters and a niece was almost wearisome. On the first evening nothing was said about the love troubles or love prospects of the girls. Sir Thomas permitted to himself the enjoyment of his glory, with some few signs of impatience when the admiration became too strong. He told the whole story of his election, lying back among his cushions on the sofa, although Patience, with mild persistence, cautioned him against exertion.

"It is very bad that you should have your arm broken, papa," said Clarissa.

"It is a bore, my dear."

"Of course it is,—a dreadful bore. But as it is doing so well, I am so glad that you went down to Percycross. It is such a great thing that you should be in the House again. It does give so much colour to our lives here."

"I hope they were not colourless before."

"You know what I mean. It is so nice to feel that you are in Parliament."

"It is quite on the cards that I may lose the seat by petition."

"They never can be so cruel," said Mary.

"Cruelty!" said Sir Thomas laughing. "In politics men skin each other without the slightest feeling. I do not doubt that Mr. Westmacott would ruin me with the most perfect satisfaction, if by doing so he could bring the seat within his own reach again; and yet I believe Mr. Westmacott to be a kind-hearted, good sort of man. There is a theory among Englishmen that in politics no man need spare another. To wish that your opponent should fall dead upon the hustings is not an uncharitable wish at an election."

"Oh, papa!" exclaimed Patience.

"At any rate you are elected," said Clary.

"And threatened folk live long, uncle," said Mary Bonner.

"So they say, my dear. Well, Patience, don't look at me with so much reprobation in your eyes, and I will go to bed at once. Being here instead of at the Percy Standard does make one inclined to take a liberty."

"Oh, papa, it is such a delight to have you," said Clary, jumping up and kissing her father's forehead. All this was pleasant enough, and the first evening came to an end very happily.

The next morning Patience, when she was alone with her father, made a request to him with some urgency. "Papa," she said, "do not say anything to Clary about Ralph."

"Why not?"

"If there is anything in it, let it die out of itself.'

"But is there?"

"How am I to say? Think of it, papa. If I knew it, I could hardly tell,—even you."

"Why not? If I am not to hear the truth from you who is to tell me?"

"Dear papa, don't be angry. There may be a truth which had better not be told. What we both want is that Clary shouldn't suffer. If you question her she will suffer. You may be sure of this,—that she will obey your wishes."

"How can she obey them, unless she knows them?"

"She shall know them," said Patience. But Sir Thomas would give no promise.

On that same day Sir Thomas sent for his niece into his room, and there read to her the letter which he had received from the Squire's son. It was now the last week of October,—that short blessed morsel of time which to the poor Squire at Newton was the happiest of his life. He was now cutting down trees and building farm-houses, and looking after his stud in all the glory of his success. Ralph had written his letter, and had received his answer,—and he also was successful and glorious. That fatal day on which the fox would not break from Barford Woods had not yet arrived. Mary Bonner heard the letter read, and listened to Sir Thomas's speech without a word, without a blush, and without a sign. Sir Thomas began his speech very well, but became rather misty towards the end, when he found himself unable to reduce Mary to a state of feminine confusion. "My dear," he began, "I have received a letter which I think it is my duty to read to you."

"A letter, uncle?"

"Yes, my dear. Sit down while I read it. I may as well tell you at once that it is a letter which has given me very great satisfaction. It is from a young gentleman;"—upon hearing this announcement Mary's face assumed a look of settled, collected strength, which never left it for a moment during the remainder of the interview,—"yes; from a young gentleman, and I may say that I never read a letter which I thought to be more honourable to the writer. It is from Mr. Ralph Newton,—not the Ralph with whom you have found us to be so intimate, but from the other who will some day be Mr. Newton of Newton Priory." Then Sir Thomas looked into his niece's face, hoping to see there something of the flutter of expectant triumph. But there was neither flutter nor triumph in Mary's countenance. He read the letter, sitting up in his bed, with his left arm in a sling, and then he handed it to her. "You had better look at it yourself, my dear." Mary took the letter, and sat as though she were reading it. It seemed to Sir Thomas that she was reading it with the cold accuracy of a cautious attorney;—but in truth her eyes did not follow a single word of the letter. There was neither flutter nor triumph in her face, or in the movement of her limbs, or in the quiet, almost motionless carriage of her body; but, nevertheless, the pulses of her heart beat so strongly, that had all depended on it she could not have read a word of the letter. "Well, my dear," said Sir Thomas, when he thought that ample time had been given for the perusal. Mary simply folded the paper together and returned it into his hands. "I have told him, as I was bound to do, my dear, that as far as I was concerned, I should be happy to receive him; but that for any other answer, I must refer him to you. Of

In a moment the three men were on their knees, and it was clear that Mr. Newton was insensible.

(*See page 238*)

Ralph, for the first time since the accident, burst out into a flood of tears.

(See page 257)

course it will be for you to give him what answer your heart dictates. But I may say this,—and it is my duty to say it as your guardian and nearest relative ;—the way in which he has put forward his request shows him to be a most honourable man ; all that I have ever heard of him is in his favour ; he is a gentleman every inch of him ; and as for his prospects in life, they are such that they entitle him to address almost any lady in the land. Of course you will follow the dictates of your own heart, as I said ; but I cannot myself fancy any greater good fortune that could come in the way of a young woman than the honest affections of such a man as this Ralph Newton." Then Sir Thomas paused for some reply, but Mary had none ready for him. "Of course I have no questions to ask," he said, and then again paused. But still Mary did not speak. "I dare say he will be here before long, and I hope that he may meet with a happy reception. I at least shall be glad to see him, for I hold him in great honour. And as I look upon marriage as the happiest lot for all women, and as I think that this would be a happy marriage, I do hope,—I do hope—— But as I said before, all that must be left to yourself. Mary, have you nothing to say ?"

"I trust, uncle, you are not tired of me."

"Tired of you ! Certainly not. I have not been with you since you have been here as much as I should have wished because,—indeed for various reasons. But we all like you, and nobody wants to get rid of you. But there is a way in which young ladies leave their own homes, which is generally thought to be matter of congratulation. But, as I said before, nobody shall press you."

"Dear uncle, I am so full of thanks to you for your kindness."

"But it is of course my duty as your guardian to tell you that in my opinion this gentleman is entitled to your esteem."

After that Mary left him without another word, and taking her hat and cloak as she passed through the hall went at once out into the garden. It was a fine autumn morning, almost with a touch of summer in it. We do not know here that special season which across the Atlantic is called the Indian summer,—that last glow of the year's warmth which always brings with it a half melancholy conviction of the year's decay, —which in itself is so delightful, would be so full of delight, were it not for the consciousness which it seems to contain of being the immediate precursor of winter with all its horrors. There is no sufficient constancy with us of the recurrence of such a season, to make any special name needful. But now and again there comes a day, when the winds of the equinox have lulled themselves, and the chill of October rains have left the earth, and the sun gives a genial, luxurious warmth, with no power to scorch, with strength only to comfort. But here, as elsewhere, this luxury is laden with melancholy, because it tells us of decay, and is the harbinger of death. This was such a day, and Mary Bonner, as she hurried into a shrubbery walk, where she could wander unseen, felt both the sadness and the softness of the season. There was a path which ran from the front gate of the villa grounds through shrubs and tall evergreens down to the river, and was continued along the river-bank up through the flower-garden to windows opening from the drawing-room. Here she walked alone for more than an hour, turning as she came to the river in order that she might not be seen from the house.

Mary Bonner, of whose character hitherto but little has been said, was, at any rate, an acute observer. Very soon after her first introduction to Ralph the heir,—Ralph who had for so many years been the intimate friend of the Underwood family,—she perceived something in the manner of that very attractive young man which conveyed to her a feeling that, if she so pleased, she might count him as an admirer of her own. She had heard then, as was natural, much of the brilliance of his prospects, and but little,—as was also natural,—of what he had done to mar them. And she also perceived, or fancied that she perceived, that her cousin Clary gave many of her thoughts to the heir. Now Mary Bonner understood the importance to herself of a prosperous marriage, as well as any girl ever did understand its great significance. She was an orphan, living in fact on the charity of her uncle. And she was aware that having come to her uncle's house when all the weakness and attractions of her childhood were passed, she could have no hold on him or his such as would have been hers had she grown to be a woman beneath his roof. There was a thoughtfulness too about her,—a thoughtfulness which some, perhaps, may call worldliness,—which made it impossible for her not to have her own condition constantly in her mind. In her father's lifetime she had been driven by his thoughtlessness and her own sterner nature to think of these things; and in the few months that had passed between her father's death and her acceptance in her uncle's house she had taught herself to regard the world as an arena in which she must fight a battle by her own strength with such weapons as God had given to her. God had, indeed, given to her many weapons, but she knew but of one. She did know that God had made her very beautiful. But she regarded her beauty after an unfeminine fashion,—as a thing of value, but as a chattel of which she could not bring herself to be proud. Might it be possible that she should win for herself by her beauty some position in the world less burdensome, more joyous than that of a governess, and less dependent than that of a daily recipient of her uncle's charity?

She had had lovers in the West Indies,—perhaps a score of them, but they had been nothing to her. Her father's house had been so constituted that it had been impossible for her to escape the very plainly spoken admiration of captains, lieutenants, and Colonial secretaries. In the West Indies gentlemen do speak so very plainly, on, or without, the smallest encouragement, that ladies accept such speaking much as they do in England the attention of a handkerchief lifted or an offer for a dance. It had all meant nothing to Mary Bonner, who from her earliest years of girlhood had been accustomed to captains, lieutenants, and even to midshipmen. But, through it all, she had grown up with serious thoughts, and something of a conviction that love-making was but an ugly amusement. As far as it had been possible she had kept herself aloof from it, and though run after for her beauty, had been unpopular as being a "proud, cold, meaningless minx." When her father died she would speak to no one; and then it had been settled among the captains, lieutenants, and Colonial secretaries that she was a proud, cold, meaningless minx. And with this character she left the island. Now there came to her, naturally I say, this question;—What lovers might she find in England, and, should she find lovers, how should she deal with them? There are among us many who tell us that no pure-minded girl should think of finding a lover,—should only deal with him, when he comes, as truth, and circumstances, and parental control may suggest to her. If there be girls so pure, it certainly seems that no human being expects to meet them. Such was not the purity of Mary Bonner,— if pure she was. She did think of some coming lover,—did hope that there might be for her some prosperity of life as the consequence of the love of some worthy man whom she, in return, might worship. And then there had come Ralph Newton the heir.

Now to Mary Bonner,—as also to Clarissa Underwood, and to Patience, and to old Mrs. Brownlow, and a great many others, Ralph the heir did not appear in quite those colours which he probably will in the reader's eyes. These ladies, and a great many other ladies and gentlemen who reckoned him among their acquaintance, were not accurately acquainted with his transactions with Messrs. Neefit, Moggs, and Horsball; nor were they thoroughly acquainted with the easy nature of our hero's changing convictions. To Clarissa he certainly was heroic; to Patience he was very dear; to old Mrs. Brownlow he was almost a demigod; to Mr. Poojean he was an object of envy. To Mary Bonner, as she first saw him, he was infinitely more fascinating than the captains and lieutenants of West Indian regiments, or than Colonial secretaries generally.

It was during that evening at Mrs. Brownlow's that Mary Bonner resolutely made up her mind that she would be as stiff and cold to Ralph the heir as the nature of their acquaintance would allow. She had seen Clarissa without watching, and, without thinking, she had resolved. Mr. Newton was handsome, well to do, of good address, and clever;—he was also attractive; but he should not be attractive for her. She would not, as her first episode in her English life, rob a cousin of a lover. And so her mind was made up, and no word was spoken to any one. She had, no confidences. There was no one in whom she could confide. Indeed, there was no need for confidence. As she left Mrs. Brownlow's house on that evening she slipped her arm through that of Patience, and the happy Clarissa was left to walk home with Ralph the heir,—as the reader may perhaps remember.

Then that other Ralph had come, and she learned in half-pronounced ambiguous whispers what was the nature of his position in the world. She did not know,—at that time her cousins did not know,—how nearly successful were the efforts made to dispossess the heir of his inheritance in order that this other Newton might possess it. But she saw, or thought that she saw, that this was the gallanter man of the two. Then he came again, and then again, and she knew that her own beauty was of avail. She encouraged him not at all. It was not in her nature to give encouragement to a man's advances. It may, perhaps, be said of her that she had no power to do so. What was in her of the graciousness of feminine love, of the leaning, clinging, flattering softness of woman's nature, required some effort to extract, and had never hitherto been extracted. But within her own bosom she told herself that she thought that she could give it, if the asking for it were duly done. Then came the first tidings of his heirship, of his father's success,—and then, close upon the heels of those tidings, this heir's humbly expressed desire to be permitted to woo her. There was all the flutter of triumph in her bosom, as that letter was read to her, and yet there was no sign of it in her voice or in her countenance.

Nor could it have been seen had she been met walking in the shade of that shrubbery. And yet she was full of triumph. Here was the man to whom her heart had seemed to turn almost at first sight, as it had never turned to man before. She had deigned to think of him as of one she could love;—and he loved her. As she paced the walk it was also much to her that this man who was so generous in her eyes should have provided for him so noble a place in the world. She quite understood what it was to be the wife of such a one as the Squire of Newton. She had grieved for Clary's sake when she heard that the former heir should be heir no longer,— suspecting Clary's secret. But she could not so grieve as to be insensible of her own joy. And then there was something in the very manner in which the man approached her, which gratified her pride while it touched her heart. About that other Ralph there was a tone of sustained self-applause, which seemed to declare that he had only to claim any woman and to receive her. There was an old-fashioned mode of wooing of which she had read and dreamed, that implied a homage which she knew that she desired. This homage her Ralph was prepared to pay.

For an hour she paced the walk, not thinking, but enjoying what she knew. There was nothing in it requiring thought. He was to come, and till he should come there was nothing that she need either say or do. Till he should come she would do nothing and say nothing. Such was her determination when Clarissa's step was heard, and in a moment Clarissa's arm was round her waist. " Mary," she said, " you must come out with me. Come and walk with me. I am going to Mrs. Brownlow's. You must come."

" To walk there and back ? " said Mary, smiling.

" We will return in an omnibus ; but you must come. Oh, I have so much to say to you."

CHAPTER XXXIII.

" TELL ME AND I'LL TELL YOU."

" PAPA has told me all about it," were Clarissa's first words as soon as they were out of the gate on the road to Mrs. Brownlow's.

" All about what, Clary ? "

" Oh you know ;—or rather it was Patience told me, and then I asked papa. I am so glad."

Mary had as yet hardly had time to think whether the coming of this letter to her uncle would or would not be communicated to her cousins ; but had she thought, she would have been almost sure that Sir Thomas would be more discreet. The whole matter was to her so important, so secret, almost so solemn, that she could hardly imagine that it should be discussed among the whole household. And yet she felt a strong longing within herself to be able to talk of it to some one. Of the two cousins Clary was certainly her favourite, and had she been forced to consult any one, she would have consulted Clary. But an absolute confidence in such a matter with a chosen friend, the more delightful it might appear, was on that very account the more difficult of attainment. It was an occasion for thought, for doubt, and almost for dismay ; and now Clary rushed into it as though everything could be settled in a walk from Fulham to Parson's Green ! " It is very good of you to be glad, Clary," said the other,—hardly knowing why she said this, and yet meaning it. If in truth Clary was glad, it was good of her. For this man to whom Clary was alluding had won from her own lover all his inheritance.

" I like him so much. You will let me talk about him ; won't you ? "

"Oh, yes," said Mary.

"Do; pray do. There are so many reasons why we should tell each other everything." This elicited no promise from Mary. "If I thought that you would care, I would tell you all."

"I care about everything that concerns you, Clary."

"But I didn't bring you out to talk about myself now. I want to tell you how much I like your Ralph Newton."

"But he isn't mine."

"Yes he is;—at any rate, if you like to have him. And of course you will like. Why should you not? He is everything that is nice and good;—and now he is to be the owner of all the property. What I want to tell you is this; I do not begrudge it to you."

Why should Clarissa begrudge or not begrudge the property? Mary understood it all, but nothing had been said entitling her to speak as though she understood it. "I don't think you would begrudge me anything that you thought good for me," said Mary.

"And I think that Mr. Ralph Newton,—this Mr. Ralph Newton, is very good for you. Nothing could be so good. In the first place would it not be very nice to have you mistress of Newton Priory? Only that shouldn't come properly first."

"And what should come first, Clary?"

"Oh,—of course that you should love him better than anything in the world. And you do,—don't you?"

"It is too sudden to say that yet, Clary."

"But I am sure you will. Don't you feel that you will? Come, Mary, you should tell me something."

"There is so little to tell."

"Then you are afraid of me. I wanted to tell you everything."

"I am not afraid of you. But, remember, it is hardly more than an hour ago since I first heard of Mr. Newton's wishes, and up to that moment nothing was further from my dreams."

"I was sure of it, ever so long ago," said Clarissa.

"Oh, Clary!"

"I was. I told Patience how it was to be. I saw it in his eyes. One does see these things. I knew it would be so; and I told Patience that we three would be three Mrs. Newtons. But that of course was nonsense."

"Nonsense, indeed."

"I mean about Patience."

"And what about yourself, Clary?" Clarissa made no answer, and yet she was burning to tell her own story. She was most anxious to tell her own story, but only on the condition of reciprocal confidence. The very nature of her story required that the confidence should be reciprocal. "You said that you wanted to tell me everything," said Mary.

"And so I do."

"You know how glad I shall be to hear."

"That is all very well, but,——" And then Clarissa paused.

"But what, dear?"

"You do mean to accept Mr. Newton?"

Now it was time for Mary to pause. "If I were to tell you my whole heart," she said, "I should be ashamed of what I was saying; and yet I do not know that there is any cause for shame."

"There can be none," said Clary. "I am sure of that."

"My acquaintance with Mr. Newton is very, very slight. I liked him,—oh, so much. I thought him to be high-spirited, manly, and a fine gentleman. I never saw any man who so much impressed me."

"Of course not," said Clarissa, making a gesture as though she would stop on the high road and clasp her hands together, in which, however, she was impeded by her parasol and her remembrance of her present position.

"But it is so much to say that one will love a man better than all the world, and go to him, and belong to him, and be his wife."

"Ah;—but if one does love him!"

"I can hardly believe that love can grow so quickly."

"Tell the truth, Mary; has it not grown?"

"Indeed I cannot say. There; you shall have the whole truth. When he comes to me,——and I suppose he will come."

"There isn't much doubt of that."

"If he does come ----"

"Well?"

"I hardly know what I shall say to him. I shall try to—to love him."

"Of course you will love him,—better than all the world."

"I know that he is paying me the greatest compliment that a man can pay to a woman. And there is no earthly reason why I should not be proud to accept all that he offers me. I have nothing of my own to bestow in return."

"But you are so beautiful."

Mary would make no pretence of denying this. It was true that that one great feminine possession did belong to her. "After all," she said, "how little does beauty signify! It attracts, but it can make no man happy. He has everything to give to a wife, and he ought to have much in return for what he gives."

"You don't mean that a girl should refuse a rich man because she has no fortune of her own?"

"No; not quite that. But she ought to think whether she can be of use to him."

"Of course you will be of use, my dear;—of the greatest use in

the world. That's his affair, and he is the best judge of what
will be of use. You will love him, and other men will envy him,
and that will be everything. Oh dear, I do so hope he will come
soon."

" And I,—I almost hope he will not. I shall be so afraid to see
him. The first meeting will be so awful. I shall not dare to look
him in the face."

" But it is all settled."

" No ;—not settled, Clary."

" Yes ; it is settled. And now I will tell you what I mean when I
say I do not begrudge him to you. That is——; I do not know
whether you will care to be told."

"I care very much, Clary. I should be very unhappy if you did
begrudge me anything."

" Of course you know that our Ralph Newton, as we call him,
ought to have been the heir."

" Oh, yes."

" I needn't explain it all ; only,—only—— "

" Only he is everything to you. Is it that, Clary ? "

" Yes ; it is that. He is everything to me. I love him——. Oh,
yes, I do love him ! But, Mary, I am not such a happy girl as you
are. Sometimes I think he hardly cares for me."

" But he has asked you to care for him ? "

" Well ;—I don't know. I think he has. He has told me, I
know, that he loved me dearly,—better than any one."

" And what answer did you make to him, Clary ? "

Clarissa had the whole scene on the lawn at Popham Villa so
clearly impressed upon her memory, that an eternity of years, as she
thought, could obliterate no one of its incidents and render doubtful
no tone of his voice, no word that her lover had spoken. His conduct had at that time been so violent that she had answered him
only with tears and protestations of undying anger. But her tears
had been dried, and her anger had passed away ;—while the love
remained. Ralph, her Ralph, of course knew well enough that the
tears were dry and the anger gone. She could understand that he
would understand that. But the love which he had protested, if it
were real love, would remain. And why should she doubt him ?
The very fact that he was so dear to her, made such doubts almost
disgraceful. And yet there was so much cause for doubt. Patience
doubted. She knew herself that she feared more than she hoped.
She had resolved gallantly that she would be true to her own heart,
even though by such truth she should be preparing for herself a life
of disappointment. She had admitted the passion, and she would
stand by it. In all her fears, too, she consoled herself by the
reflection that her lover was hindered, not by want of earnestness

or want of truth,—but by the state of his affairs. While he was still in debt, striving to save his inheritance, but tormented by the growing certainty that it must pass away from him, how could he give himself up to love-making and preparations for marriage ? Clary made excuses for him which no one else would have made, and so managed to feed her hopes. " I made him no answer," she said at last.

" And yet you knew you loved him."

" Yes ; I knew that. I can tell you, and I told Patience. But I could not tell him." She paused a moment thinking whether she could describe the whole scene ; but she found that she could not do that. " I shall tell him, perhaps, when he comes again ; that is, if he does come."

" If he loves you he will come."

" I don't know. He has all these troubles on him, and he will be very poor ;—what will seem to him to be very poor. It would not be poor for me, but for him it would."

" Would that hinder him ? "

" How can I say ? There are so many things a girl cannot know. He may still be in debt, and then he has been brought up to want so much. But it will make no more difference in me. And now you will understand why I should tell you that I will never begrudge you your good fortune. If all should come right, you shall give us a little cottage near your grand house, and you will not despise us." Poor Clary, when she spoke of her possible future lord, and the little cottage on the Newton demesne, hardly understood the feelings with which a disinherited heir must regard the property which he has lost.

" Dear, dearest Clary," said Mary Bonner, pressing her cousin's arm.

They had now reached Mrs. Brownlow's house, and the old lady was delighted to receive them. Of course she began to discuss at once the great news. Sir Thomas had had his arm broken, and was now again a member of Parliament. Mrs. Brownlow was a thorough-going Tory, and was in an ecstasy of delight that her old friend should have been successful. The success seemed to be so much the greater in that the hero had suffered a broken bone. And then there were many questions to be asked ? Would Sir Thomas again be Solicitor-General by right of his seat in Parliament ?—for on such matters Mrs. Brownlow was rather hazy in her conceptions as to the working of the British Constitution. And would he live at home ? Clarissa would not say that she and Patience expected such a result. All that she could suggest of comfort on this matter was that there would be now something of a fair cause for excusing their father's residence at his London chambers.

But there was a subject more enticing to the old lady even than

Sir Thomas's triumphs; a subject as to which there could not be any triumph,—only dismay; but not, on that account, the less interesting. Ralph Newton had sold his inheritance. " I believe it is all settled," said Clarissa, demurely.

"Dear, dear, dear, dear!" groaned the old lady. And while she groaned Clarissa furtively cast a smile upon her cousin. "It is the saddest thing I ever knew," said Mrs. Brownlow. " And, after all, for a young man who never can be anybody, you know."

" Oh yes," said Clarissa, " he can be somebody."

" You know what I mean, my dear. I think it very shocking, and very wrong. Such a fine estate, too!"

" We all like Mr. Newton very much indeed," said Clarissa. " Papa thinks he is a most charming young man. I never knew papa taken with any one so much. And so do we all,—Patience and I,— and Mary."

" But, my dear," began Mrs. Brownlow,—Mrs. Brownlow had always thought that Ralph the heir would ultimately marry Clarissa Underwood, and that it was a manifest duty on his part to do so. She had fancied that Clarissa had expected it herself, and had believed that all the Underwoods would be broken-hearted at this transfer of the estate. " I don't think it can be right," said Mrs. Brownlow; "and I must say that it seems to me that old Mr. Newton ought to be ashamed of himself. Just because this young man happens to be, in a sort of a way, his own son, he is going to destroy the whole family. I think that it is very wicked." But she had not a word of censure for the heir who had consumed his mess of pottage.

" Wasn't she grand?" said Clary, as soon as they were out again upon the road. "She is such a dear old woman, but she doesn't understand anything. I couldn't help giving you a look when she was abusing our friend. When she knows it all, she'll have to make you such an apology."

" I hope she will not do that."

" She will if she does not forget all about it. She does forget things. There is one thing I don't agree with her in at all. I don't see any shame in your Ralph having the property; and, as to his being nobody, that is all nonsense. He would be somebody, wherever he went, if he had not an acre of property. He will be Mr. Newton, of Newton Priory, just as much as anybody else could be. He has never done anything wrong." To all which Mary Bonner had very little to say. She certainly was not prepared to blame the present Squire for having so managed his affairs as to be able to leave the estate to his own son.

The two girls were very energetic, and walked back the whole way to Popham Villa, regardless of a dozen omnibuses that passed them.

" I told her all about our Ralph,—my Ralph,"—said Clary to her sister afterward. " I could not help telling her now."

"Dear Clary," said Patience, " I wish you could help thinking of it always."

"That's quite impossible," said Clarissa, cheerily.

CHAPTER XXXIV.

ALONE IN THE HOUSE.

YOUNG Newton at last found himself alone in the house at Newton Priory after his father's death. He had sent George Morris away, becoming very stern in his demand to be left to his solitude as long as opposition was made to him. Gregory had come down to him from the parsonage, and had also been dismissed. "Your brother will be here probably to-day," said Ralph, " and then I will send for you."

"I am thinking more of you than of my brother, just now," answered the parson.

" Yes, I know,—and though I cannot talk to you, I know how good you are. I want to see nobody but him. I shall be better alone." Then Gregory had returned to the parsonage.

As soon as Ralph was alone he crept up to the room in which his father's body was lying, and stood silently by the bedside for above an hour. He was struggling to remember the loss he had had in the man, and to forget the loss in wealth and station. No father had ever been better to a son than his father had been to him. In every affair of life his happiness, his prosperity, and his future condition had given motives to his father's conduct. No lover ever worshipped a mistress more thoroughly than his father had idolised him. There had never been love to beat it, never solicitude more perfect and devoted. And yet, as he had been driven home that day, he had allowed his mind to revert to the property, and his regrets to settle themselves on his lost position. It should not be so any longer. He could not keep his mind from dwelling on the thing, but he would think of it as a trifle,—as of a thing which he could afford to lose without sorrow. Whereas he had also lost that which is of all things the most valuable and most impossible to replace,—a friend whose love was perfect.

But then there was another loss. He bitterly blamed himself for having written that letter to Sir Thomas Underwood, before he was actually in a position to do as he had proposed. It must all be unwritten now. Every resolution hitherto taken as to his future life must be abandoned. He must begin again, and plan a new life for himself. It had all come upon him so suddenly that he was utterly at a loss to think what he would do with himself or with his days. There was nothing for him but to go away, and be utterly without occupation, altogether without friends. Friends, indeed, he had,—dear, intimate, loving friends. Gregory Newton and George Morris were his friends. Every tenant on the Newton property was his friend. There was not a man riding with the hunt, worth having as a friend, who was not on friendly terms with him. But all these he must leave altogether. In whatever spot he might find for himself a future residence, that spot could not be at Peele Newton. After what had occurred he could not remain there, now that he was not the heir. And then, again, his thoughts came back from his lost father to his lost inheritance, and he was very wretched.

Between three and four o'clock he took his hat and walked out. He sauntered down along a small stream, which, after running through the gardens, bordered one of the coverts which came up near to the house. He took this path because he knew that he would be alone there, unseen. It had occurred to him already that it would be well that he should give orders to stop the works which his father had commenced, and there had been a moment in which he had almost told one of the servants in the house to do so. But he had felt ashamed at seeming to remember so small a thing. The owner would be there soon, probably in an hour or two, and could stop or could continue what he pleased. Then, as he thought of the ownership of the estate, he reflected that, as the sale had been in truth effected by his namesake, the money promised by his father would be legally due;—would not now be his money. As to the estate itself, that, of course, would go to his namesake as his father's heir. No will had been made leaving the estate to him, and his namesake would be the heir-at-law. Thus he would be utterly beggared. It was not that he actually believed that this would be the case; but his thoughts were morbid, and he took an unwholesome delight in picturing to himself circumstances in their blackest hue. Then he would strike the ground with his stick, in his wrath, because he thought of such things at all. How was it that he was base enough to think of them while the accident, which had robbed him of his father, was so recent?

As the dusk grew on, he emerged out of the copse into the park, and, crossing at the back of the home paddocks, came out upon the road near to Darvell's farm. He passed a few yards up the lane, till at a turn he could discern the dismantled house. As far as he could see through the gloom of the evening, there were no workmen near the place. Some one, he presumed, had given directions that nothing further should be done on a day so sad as this. He stood for awhile looking and listening, and then turned round to enter the park again.

It might be that the new squire was already at the house, and it would be thought that he ought not to be absent. The road from the station to the Priory was not that on which he was standing, and Ralph might have arrived without his knowledge. He wandered slowly back, but, before he could turn in at the park-gate, he was met by a man on the road. It was Mr. Walker, the farmer of Brownriggs, an old man over seventy, who had lived on the property all his life, succeeding his father in the same farm. Walker had known young Newton since he had first been brought to the Priory as a boy, and could speak to him with more freedom than perhaps any other tenant on the estate. "Oh, Mr. Ralph," he said, "this has been a dreary thing!" Ralph, for the first time since the accident, burst out into a flood of tears. "No wonder you take on, Mr. Ralph. He was a good father to you, and a fine gentleman, and one we all respected." Ralph still sobbed, but put his hand on the old man's arm and leaned upon him. "I hope, Mr. Ralph, that things was pretty well settled about the property." Ralph shook his head, but did not speak. "A bargain is a bargain, Mr. Ralph, and I suppose that this bargain was made. The lawyers would know that it had been made."

"It don't matter about that, Mr. Walker," said Ralph; "but the estate would go to my father's nephew as his heir." The farmer started as though he had been shot. "You will have another landlord, Mr. Walker. He can hardly be better than the one you have lost."

"Then, Mr. Ralph, you must bear it manly."

"I think that I can say that I will do that. It is not for the property that I am crying. I hope you don't think that of me, Mr. Walker."

"No, no, no."

"I can bear that;—though it is hard the having to go away and live among strange people. I think I shall get a farm somewhere, and see if I can take a lesson from you. I don't know anything else that I can do."

"You could have the Mordykes, Mr. Ralph," said Mr. Walker, naming a holding on the Newton property as to which there were rumours that it would soon be vacant.

"No, Mr. Walker, it mustn't be here. I couldn't stand that. I must go away from this,—God knows where. I must go away from this, and I shall never see the old place again!"

"Bear it manly, Mr. Ralph," said the farmer.

"I think I shall, after a bit. Good evening, Mr. Walker. I expect my father's nephew every hour, and I ought to be up at the house when he comes. I shall see you again before I go."

"Yes, yes; that's for certain," said the farmer. They were both thinking of the day on which they would follow the old Squire to his grave in Newton Peele churchyard.

Ralph re-entered the park, and hurried across to the house as though he were afraid that he would be too late to receive the heir; but there had been no arrival, nor had there come any message from the other Ralph. Indeed up to this hour the news had not reached the present owner of Newton Priory. The telegram had been duly delivered at the Moonbeam, where the fortunate youth was staying; but he was hunting on this day, riding the new horse which he had bought from Mr. Pepper, and, up to this moment, did not know anything of that which chance had done for him. Nor did he get back to the Moonbeam till late at night, having made some engagement for dinner after the day's sport. It was not till noon on the following day, the Friday, that a message was received from him at the Priory, saying that he would at once hurry down to Hampshire.

Ralph sat down to dinner all alone. Let what will happen to break hearts and ruin fortunes, dinner comes as long as the means last for providing it. The old butler waited upon him in absolute silence, fearing to speak a word, lest the word at such a time should be ill-spoken. No doubt the old man was thinking of the probable expedience of his retiring upon his savings; feeling, however, that it became him to show, till the last, every respect to all who bore the honoured name of Newton. When the meat had been eaten, the old servant did say a word. "Won't you come round to the fire, Mr. Ralph?" and he placed comfortably before the hearth one of the heavy arm-chairs with which the corners of the broad fire-place were flanked. But Ralph only shook his head, and muttered some refusal. There he sat, square to the table, with the customary bottle of wine before him, leaning back with his hands in his pockets, thinking of his condition in life. The loneliness of the room, the loneliness of the house, were horrible to him. And yet he would not that his solitude should be interrupted. He had been so sitting, motionless, almost overcome by the gloom of the big dark room, for so long a period that he hardly knew whether it was night or not, when a note was brought to him from Gregory. "Dear Ralph,—Shall I not come down to you for an hour?—G. N." He read the note, and sent back a verbal message. "Tell Mr. Gregory that I had rather not." And so he sat motionless till the night had really come, till the old butler brought him his candlestick and absolutely bade him betake himself to bed. He had watched during the whole of the previous night, and now had slumbered in his chair from time to time. But his sleeping had been of that painful, wakeful nature which brings with it no refreshment. It had been full of dreams, in all of which there had been some grotesque reference to the property, but in none of them had there been any memory of the Squire's terrible death. And yet, as he woke and woke and woke again, it can hardly be said that the truth had come back upon him as a new blow. Through such dreams there seems to exist a double memory, and a second identity. The misery of his isolated position never for a moment left him; and yet there were repeated to him over and over again those bungling, ill-arranged, impossible pictures of trivial transactions about the place, which the slumber of a few seconds sufficed to create in his brain. "Mr. Ralph, you must go to bed;—you must indeed, sir," said the old butler, standing over him with a candle during one of these fitful dreamings.

"Yes, Grey;—yes, I will; directly. Put it down. Thank you. Don't mind sitting up," said Ralph, rousing himself in his chair.

"It's past twelve," Mr. Ralph.

"You can go to bed, you know, Grey."

"No, sir;—no. I'll see you to bed first. It'll be better so. Why, Mr. Ralph, the fire's all out, and you're sitting here perished. You wasn't in bed last night, and you ought to be there now. Come, Mr. Ralph."

Then Ralph rose from his chair and took the candlestick. It was true enough that he had better be in bed. As he shook himself, he felt that he had never been so cold in his life. And then as he moved there came upon him that terrible feeling that everything was amiss with him, that there was no consolation on any side. "That'll do, Grey; good night," he said, as the old man prepared to follow him up-stairs. But Grey was not to be shaken off. "I'll just see you to your room, Mr. Ralph." He wanted to accompany his young master past the door of that chamber in which was lying all that remained of the old master. But Ralph would open the door. "Not to-night, Mr. Ralph," said Grey. But Ralph persisted, and stood again by the bedside. "He would have given me his flesh and blood;—his very life," said Ralph to the butler. "I think no father ever so loved a son. And yet, what has it come to?" Then he stooped down, and put his lips to the cold clay-blue forehead.

"It ain't come to much surely," said old Grey to himself as he crept away to his own room; "and I don't suppose it do come to much mostly when folks go wrong."

Ralph was out again before breakfast, wandering up and down the banks of the stream where the wood hid him, and then he made up his mind that he would at once write again to Sir Thomas Underwood. He must immediately make it understood that that suggestion which he had made in his ill-assumed pride of position must be abandoned. He had nothing now to offer to that queenly princess worthy of the acceptance of any woman. He was a base-born son, about to be turned out of his father's house because of the disgrace of his birth. In the eye of the law he was nobody. The law allowed to him not even a name ;—certainly allowed to him the possession of no relative; denied to him the possibility of any family tie. His father had succeeded within an ace of giving him that which would have created for him family ties, relatives, name and all. The old Squire had understood well how to supersede the law, and to make the harshness of man's enactments of no avail. Had the Squire quite succeeded, the son would have stood his ground, would have called himself Newton of Newton, and nobody would have dared to tell him that he was a nameless bastard. But now he could not even wait to be told. He must tell it himself, and must vanish. He had failed to understand it all while his father was struggling and was yet alive ; but he understood it well now. So he came in to his breakfast, resolved that he would write that letter at once.

And then there were orders to be given ;—hideous orders. And there was that hideous remembrance that legally he was entitled to give no orders. Gregory came down to him as he sat at breakfast, making his way into the parlour without excuse. " My brother cannot have been at home at either place," he said.

" Perhaps not," said Ralph. " I suppose not."

" The message will be sent after him, and you will hear to-day no doubt."

" I suppose I shall," said Ralph.

Then Gregory in a low voice made the suggestion in reference to which he had come across from the parsonage. " I think that perhaps I and Larkin had better go over to Basingstoke." Larkin was the steward. Ralph again burst out into tears, but he assented; and in this way those hideous orders were given.

As soon as Gregory was gone he took himself to his desk, and did write to Sir Thomas Underwood. His letter, which was perhaps somewhat too punctilious, ran as follows :—

" Newton Priory, 4th November, 186—.

" MY DEAR SIR,—

" I do not know whether you will have heard before this of the accident which has made me fatherless. The day before yesterday my father was killed by a fall from his horse in the hunting-field. I should not have ventured to trouble you with a letter on this subject, nor should I myself have been disposed to write about it at present, were it not that I feel it to be an imperative duty to refer without delay to my last letter to you, and to your very flattering reply. When I wrote to you it was true that my father had made arrangements for purchasing on my behalf the reversion to the property.

That it was so you doubtless were aware from your own personal knowledge of the affairs of Mr. Ralph Newton. Whether that sale was or was not legally completed I do not know. Probably not ;—and in regard to my own interests it is to be hoped that it was not completed. But in any event the whole Newton property will pass to your late ward, as my father certainly made no such will as would convey it to me even if the sale were complete.

" It is a sad time for explaining all this, when the body of my poor father is still lying unburied in the house, and when, as you may imagine, I am ill-fitted to think of matters of business; but, after what has passed between us, I conceive myself bound to explain to you that I wrote my last letter under a false impression, and that I can make no such claim to Miss Bonner's favour as I then set up. I am houseless and nameless, and for aught I yet know to the contrary, absolutely penniless. The blow has hit me very hard. I have lost my fortune, which I can bear; I have lost whatever chance I had of gaining your niece's hand, which I must learn to bear; and I have lost the kindest father a man ever had,—which is unbearable.

" Yours very faithfully,
" RALPH NEWTON (so called)."

If it be thought that there was something in the letter which should have been suppressed,—the allusion, for instance, to the possible but most improbable loss of his father's private means, and his morbid denial of his own right to a name which he had always borne, a right which no one would deny him,—it must be remembered that the circumstances of the hour bore very heavily on him, and that it was hardly possible that he should not nurse the grievance which afflicted him. Had he not been alone in these hours he might have carried himself more bravely. As it was, he struggled hard to carry himself well. If no one had ever been told how nearly successful the Squire had been in his struggle to gain the power of leaving the estate to his son, had there been nothing of the triumph of victory, he could have left the house in which he had lived and the position which he had filled almost without sorrow,—certainly without lamentation. In the midst of calamities caused by the loss of fortune, it is the knowledge of what the world will say that breaks us down ;—not regret for those enjoyments which wealth can give, and which had been long anticipated.

At two o'clock on this day he got a telegram. " I will be at the parsonage this evening, and will come down at once." Ralph the heir, on his return home late at night, had heard the news, and early on the following morning had communicated with his brother and with his namesake. In the afternoon, after his return from Basingstoke, Gregory again came down to the house, desiring to know whether

Ralph would prefer that the meeting should be at the Priory or at the parsonage, and on this occasion his cousin bore with him. "Why should not your brother come to his own house?" asked Ralph.

"I suppose he feels that he should not claim it as his own."

"That is nonsense. It is his own, and he knows it. Does he think that I am likely to raise any question against his right?"

"I do not suppose that my brother has ever looked at the matter in that light," said the parson. "He is the last man in the world to do so. For the present, at any rate, you are living here and he is not. In such an emergency, perhaps, he feels that it would be better that he should come to his brother than intrude here."

"It would be no intrusion. I should wish him to feel that I am prepared to yield to him instantly. Of course the house cannot be very pleasant for him as yet. He must suffer something of the misery of the occasion before he can enjoy his inheritance. But it will only be for a day or so."

"Dear Ralph," said the parson, "I think you somewhat wrong my brother."

"I endeavour not to do so. I think no ill of him, because I presume he should look for enjoyment from what is certainly his own. He and my father were not friends, and this, which has been to me so terrible a calamity in every way, cannot affect him with serious sorrow. I shall meet him as a friend; but I would sooner meet him here than at the parsonage."

It was at last settled that the two brothers should come down to the great house,—both Ralph the heir, and Gregory the parson; and that the three young men should remain there, at any rate, till the funeral was over. And when this was arranged, the two who had really been fast friends for so many years, were able to talk to each other in true friendship. The solitude which he had endured had been almost too much for the one who had been made so desolate; but at last, warmed by the comfort of companionship, he resumed his manhood, and was able to look his affairs in the face, free from the morbid feeling which had oppressed him. Gregory had his own things brought down from the parsonage, and in order that there might be no hesitation on his brother's part, sent a servant with a note to the station desiring his brother to come at once to the Priory. They resolved to wait dinner for him till after the arrival of a train leaving London at five P.M. By that train the heir came, and between seven and eight he entered the house which he had not seen since he was a boy, and which was now his own.

The receipt of the telegram at the Moonbeam had affected Ralph, who was now in truth the Squire, with absolute awe. He had returned late from a somewhat jovial dinner, in company with his friend Cox, who was indeed more jovial than was becoming. Ralph was not given to drinking more wine than he could carry decently; but his friend, who was determined to crowd as much enjoyment of life as was possible into the small time allowed him before his disappearance from the world that had known him, was noisy and rollicking. Perhaps it may be acknowledged in plain terms that he was tipsy. They both entered together the sitting-room which Ralph used, and Cox was already calling for brandy and water, when the telegram was handed to Newton. He read it twice before he understood it. His uncle dead! —suddenly dead! And the inheritance all his own! In doing him justice, however, we must admit that he did not at the time admit this to be the case. He did perceive that there must arise some question; but his first feeling, as regarded the property, was one of intense remorse that he should have sold his rights at a moment in which they would so soon have been realised in his own favour. But the awe which struck him was occasioned by the suddenness of the blow which had fallen upon his uncle. " What's up now, old fellow? " hiccupped Mr. Cox.

I wonder whether any polite reader, into whose hands this story may fall, may ever have possessed a drunken friend, and have been struck by some solemn incident at the moment in which his friend is exercising the privileges of intoxication. The effect is not pleasant, nor conducive of good-humour. Ralph turned away in disgust, and leaned upon the chimney-piece, trying to think of what had occurred to him. "What ish it, old chap? Shomebody wants shome tin? I'll stand to you, old fellow."

" Take him away," said Ralph. " He's drunk." Then, without waiting for further remonstrance from the good-natured but now indignant Cox, he went off to his own room.

On the following morning he started for London by an early train, and by noon was with his lawyer. Up to that moment he believed that he had lost his inheritance. When he sent those two telegrams to his brother and to his namesake, he hardly doubted but that the entire property now belonged to his uncle's son. The idea had never occurred to him that, even were the sale complete, he might still inherit the property as his uncle's heir-at-law,—and that he would do so unless his uncle had already bequeathed it to his son. But the attorney soon put him right. The sale had not been yet made. He, Ralph, had not signed a single legal document to that effect. He had done nothing which would have enabled his late uncle to make a will leaving the Newton estate to his son. " The letters which have been written are all waste-paper," said the lawyer. " Even if they were to be taken as binding as agreements for a covenant, they would operate against your cousin,—not in his favour. In such case you would demand the specified price and still inherit."

"That is out of the question," said the heir.

"Quite out of the question," said the attorney. "No doubt Mr. Newton left a will, and under it his son will take whatever property the father had to leave."

And so Ralph the heir found himself to be the owner of it all just at the moment in which he thought that he had lost all chance of the inheritance as the result of his own folly. When he walked out of the lawyer's office he was almost wild with amazement. This was the prize to which he had been taught to look forward through all his boyish days, and all his early manhood;—but to look forward to it, as a thing that must be very distant, so distant as almost to be lost in the vagueness of the prospect. Probably his youth would have clean passed from him, and he would have entered upon the downhill course of what is called middle life before his inheritance would come to him. He had been unable to wait, and had wasted everything,—nearly everything; had, at any rate, ruined all his hopes before he was seven-and-twenty; and yet, now, at seven-and-twenty, it was, as his lawyer assured him, all his own. How nearly had he lost it all! How nearly had he married the breeches-maker's daughter! How close upon the rocks he had been. But now all was his own, and he was in truth Newton of Newton, with no embarrassments of any kind which could impose a feather's weight upon his back.

CHAPTER XXXV.

" SHE'LL ACCEPT YOU, OF COURSE."

WE will pass over the solemn sadness of the funeral at Newton and the subsequent reading of the old Squire's will. As to the latter, the will was as it had been made some six or seven years ago. The Squire had simply left all that he possessed to his illegitimate son Ralph Newton. There was no difficulty about the will. Nor was there any difficulty about the estate. The two lawyers came down to the funeral. Sir Thomas Underwood would have come but that he was prevented by the state of his arm. A statement showing all that had been done in the matter was prepared for him, but it was agreed on all sides that the sale had not been made, and that the legitimate heir must succeed to the property. No one was disposed to dispute the decision. The Squire's son had never for a moment supposed that he could claim the estate. Nor did Ralph the heir suppose for a moment that he could surrender it after the explanation which he had received from the lawyer in London.

The funeral was over, and the will had been read, and at the end of November the three young men were still living together in the great house at Newton. The heir had gone up to London once or twice, instigated by the necessity of the now not difficult task of raising a little ready money. He must at once pay off all his debts. He must especially pay that which he owed to Mr. Neefit; and he must do so with many expressions of his gratitude,—perhaps with some expressions of polite regret at the hardness of Polly's heart towards him. But he must do so certainly without any further entreaty that Polly's heart might be softened. Ah,—with what marvellous good fortune had he escaped from that pitfall! For how much had he not to be thankful to some favouring goddess who must surely have watched over him from his birth! From what shipwrecks had he not escaped! And now he was Squire of Newton, with wealth and all luxuries at command, hampered with no wife, oppressed by no debts, free from all cares. As he thought of his perfect freedom in these respects, he remembered his former resolution as to Mary Bonner. That resolution he would carry out. It would be well for him now to marry a wife, and of all the women he had ever seen Mary Bonner was certainly the most beautiful. With Newton all his own, with such a string of horses as he would soon possess, and with such a wife at the head of his table, whom need he envy, and how many were there who would not envy him?

Throughout November he allowed his horses to remain at the Moonbeam, being somewhat in doubt whether or no he would return to that fascinating hostelrie. He received one or two most respectful letters from Mr. Horsball, in which glowing accounts were given of the sport of the season, and the health of his horses, and offers made of most disinterested services. Rooms should be ready for him at a moment's notice if he liked at any time to run over for a week's hunting. It was quite evident that in the eyes of Mr. Horsball Newton of Newton was a great man. And there came congratulations from Mr. Cox, in which no allusion whatever was made to the Squire's somewhat uncivil conduct at their last meeting. Mr. Cox trusted that his dearest friend would come over and have another spell at the Moonbeam before he settled down for life;—and then hinted in language that was really delicate in the niceness of its expression, that if he, Cox, were but invited to spend a week or two at Newton Priory before he banished himself for life to Australia, he would be able to make his way over the briny deep with a light heart and an uncomplaining tongue. "You know, old fellow, how true I've always been to you," wrote Cox, in language of the purest friendship. "As true as steel,—to sausages in the morning and brandy and soda at night," said Ralph to himself as he read this.

He behaved with thorough kindness to his cousin. The three men lived together for a month, and their intercourse was as pleasant as was possible under the circumstances. Of course there was no hunting during this month at Newton. Nor indeed did the heir see a hound till December, although, as the reader is aware, he was not particularly bound to revere his uncle's memory. He made many overtures to his namesake. He would be only too happy if his cousin, —he always called the Squire's son his cousin,—would make Newton his home for the next twelvemonth. It was found that the Squire had left behind him something like forty thousand pounds, so that the son was by no means to be regarded as a poor man. It was his idea at present that he would purchase in some pleasant county as much land as he might farm himself, and there set up his staff for life. "And get about two-and-a-half per cent. for your money," said the heir, who was beginning to consider himself learned in such matters, and could talk of land as a very serious thing in the way of a possession.

"What else am I to do?" said the other. "Two-and-a-half per cent. with an occupation is better than five per cent. with none. I should make out the remainder, too, by farming the land myself. There is nothing else in the world that I could do."

As for remaining twelve months at Newton, that was of course out of the question. Nevertheless, when December came he was still living in the house, and had consented to remain there till Christmas should have passed. He had already heard of a farm in Norfolk. "The worst county for hunting in England," the heir had said. "Then I must try and live without hunting," said Ralph who was not the heir. During all this time not a horse was sent to the meet from the Newton stables. The owner of Newton was contented to see the animals exercised in the park, and to amuse himself by schooling them over hurdles, and by high jumping at the bar.

During the past month the young Squire had received various letters from Sir Thomas Underwood, and the other Ralph had received one. With Sir Thomas's caution, advice, and explanations to his former ward, the story has no immediate concern; but his letter to him who was to have been Mary Bonner's suitor may concern us more nearly. It was very short, and the reader shall have it entire.

"Popham Villa, 10th November, 186—.

" My Dear Mr. Newton,—

"I have delayed answering your letter for a day or two in order that it may not disturb you till the last sad ceremony be over. I do not presume to offer you consolation in your great sorrow. Such tenders should only be made by the nearest and the dearest. Perhaps you will permit me to say that what little I have seen of you and what further I have heard of you assure to you my most perfect sympathy.

" On that other matter which gave occasion for your two letters to me I shall best perhaps discharge my duty by telling you that I showed them both to my niece; and that she feels, as do I, that they are both honourable to you, and of a nature to confer honour upon her. The change in your position, which I acknowledge to be most severe, undoubtedly releases you, as it would have released her,— had she been bound and chose to accept such release.

" Whenever you may be in this neighbourhood we shall be happy to see you.

" The state of my arm still prevents me from writing with ease.

" Yours very faithfully,

" Thomas Underwood."

Newton, when he received this letter, struggled hard to give to it its proper significance, but he could bring himself to no conclusion respecting it. Sir Thomas had acknowledged that he was released,— and that Mary Bonner would also have been released had she placed herself under any obligation; but Sir Thomas did not say a word from which his correspondent might gather whether in his present circumstances he might still be regarded as an acceptable suitor. The letter was most civil, most courteous, almost cordial in its expression of sympathy; but yet it did not contain a word of encouragement.

It may be said that the suitor had himself so written to the lady's uncle, as to place himself out of the way of all further encouragement;—as to have put it beyond the power of his correspondent to write a word to him that should have in it any comfort. Certainly he had done so. He had clearly shown in his second letter that he had abandoned all idea of making the match as to which he had shown so much urgent desire in his first letter. He had explained that the marriage would now be impossible, and had spoken of himself as a ruined, broken man, all whose hopes were shipwrecked. Sir Thomas could hardly have told him in reply that Mary Bonner would still be pleased to see him. And yet Mary Bonner had almost said so. She had been very silent when the letter was read to her. The news of Mr. Newton's death had already reached the family at Popham Villa, and had struck them all with awe. How it might affect the property even Sir Thomas had not absolutely known at first; though he was not slow to make it understood that in all probability this terrible accident would be ruinous to the hopes which his niece had been justified in entertaining. At that hour Mary had spoken not a word;—nor could she be induced to speak respecting it either by Patience or Clarissa. Even to them she could not bring herself to say that if the man really loved her he would still come to her and say so. There was a feeling of awe upon her which made her mute, and stern, and altogether unplastic in the hands of her friends. It seemed even to Patience that Mary was struck by a stunning sorrow at the ruin which had come upon her lover's prospects. But it was not so at all. The thought wronged her utterly. What stunned her was this,—that she could not bring herself to express a passion for a man whom she had seen so seldom, with whom her conversation had been so slight, from whom personally she had received no overtures of attachment,—even though he were ruined. She could not bring herself to express such a passion;—but yet it was there. When Clarissa thought that she might obtain if not a word, at least a tear, Mary appeared to be dead to all feeling, though crushed by what she had lost. She was thinking the while whether it might be possible for such a one as her to send to the man and to tell him that that which had now occurred had of a sudden made him really dear to her. Thoughts of maiden boldness flitted across her mind, but she could not communicate them even to the girls who were her friends. Yet in silence and in solitude she resolved that the time should come in which she would be bold.

Then young Newton's second letter reached the house, and that also had been read to her. "He is quite right," said Sir Thomas. "Of course it releases both of you."

"There was nothing to release," said Mary, proudly.

"I mean to say that having made such a proposition as was

contained in his first letter, he was bound to explain his altered position."

" I suppose so," said Mary.

" Of course he was. He had made his offer believing that he could make you mistress of Newton Priory,—and he had made it thinking that he himself could marry in that position. And he would have been in that position had not this most unforeseen and terrible calamity have occurred."

" I do not see that it makes any difference," said Mary, in a whisper.

" What do you mean, my dear ? "

" I hardly know, uncle."

" Try to explain yourself, Mary."

" If I had accepted any man when he was rich, I should not go back when he was poor,—unless he wanted it." This also she said in a whisper.

" But you had not accepted him."

" No," said Mary, still in a whisper. Sir Thomas, who was perhaps not very good at such things, did not understand the working of her mind. But had she dared, she would have asked her uncle to tell Mr. Newton to come and see her. Sir Thomas, having some dim inkling of what perhaps might be the case, did add a paragraph to his letter in which he notified to his correspondent that a personal visit would be taken in good part.

By the end of the first week in December things were beginning to settle into shape at the Priory. The three young men were still living together at the great house, and the tenants on the estate had been taught to recognise the fact that Ralph, who had ever been the heir, was in truth the owner. Among the labourers and poorer classes there was no doubt much regret, and that regret was expressed. The tenants, though they all liked the Squire's son, were not upon the whole ill-pleased. It was in proper conformity with English habits and English feelings that the real heir should reign. Among the gentry the young Squire was made as welcome as the circumstances of the heir would admit. According to their way of thinking, personally popular as was the other man, it was clearly better that a legitimate descendant of the old family should be installed at Newton Priory. The old Squire's son rode well to hounds, and was loved by all ; but nothing that all the world could do on his behalf would make him Newton of Newton. If only he would remain in the neighbourhood and take some place suited to his income, every house would be open to him. He would be received with no diminution of attachment or respect. Overtures of this nature were made to him. This house could be had for him, and that farm could be made comfortable. He might live among them as a general favourite ; but he could not under any circumstances have been,—Newton of Newton.

Nothing, however, was clearer to himself than this;—that as he could not remain in the county as the master of Newton Priory, he would not remain in the county at all.

As things settled down and took shape he began to feel that even in his present condition he might possibly make himself acceptable to such a girl as Mary Bonner. In respect of fortune there could be no reason whatever why he should not offer her his hand. He was in truth a rich man, whereas she had nothing, By birth he was nobody, —absolutely nobody; but then also would he have been nobody had all the lands of Newton belonged to him. When he had written that second letter, waiving all claim to Mary's hand because of the inferiority of his position, he was suffering from a morbid view which he had taken of his own affairs. He was telling himself then,—so assuring himself, though he did not in truth believe the assurance,— that he had lost not only the estate, but also his father's private fortune. At that moment he had been unstrung, demoralized, and unmanned,—so weak that a feather would have knocked him over. The blow had been so sudden, the solitude and gloom of the house so depressing, and his sorrow so crushing, that he was ready to acknowledge that there could be no hope for him in any direction. He had fed himself upon his own grief, till the idea of any future success in life was almost unpalatable to him. But things had mended with him now, and he would see whether there might not yet be joys for him in the world. He would first see whether there might not be that one great joy which he had promised to himself.

And then there came another blow. The young Squire had resolved that he would not hunt before Christmas in the Newton country. It was felt by him and by his brother that he should abstain from doing so out of respect to the memory of his uncle, and he had declared his purpose. Of course there was neither hunting nor shooting in these days for the other Ralph. But at the end of a month the young Squire began to feel that the days went rather slowly with him, and he remembered his stud at the Moonbeam. He consulted Gregory; and the parson, though he would fain have induced his brother to remain, could not say that there was any real objection to a trip to the B and B's. Ralph would go there on the 10th of December, and be back at his own house before Christmas. When Christmas was over, the other Ralph was to leave Newton,—perhaps for ever.

The two Ralphs had become excellent friends, and when the one that was to go declared his intention of going with no intention of returning, the other pressed him warmly to think better of it, and to look upon the Priory at any rate as a second home. There were reasons why it could not be so, said the namesake; but in the close confidence of friendship which the giving and the declining of the offer generated came this further blow. They were standing together

leaning upon a gate, and looking at the exhumation of certain vast
roots, as to which the trees once belonging to them had been made
to fall in consequence of the improvements going on at Darvell's farm.
"I don't mind telling you," said Ralph the heir, "that I hope soon
to have a mistress here."

"And who is she?"

"That would be mere telling;—would it not?"

"Clarissa Underwood?" asked the unsuspecting Ralph.

There did come some prick of conscience, some qualm of an injury
done, upon the young Squire as he made his answer. "No; not
Clarissa;—though she is the dearest, sweetest girl that ever lived, and
would make a better wife perhaps than the girl I think of."

"And who is the girl you think of?"

"She is to be found in the same house."

"You do not mean the elder sister?" said the unfortunate one.
He had known well that his companion had not alluded to Patience
Underwood; but in his agony he had suggested to himself that mode
of escape.

"No; not Patience Underwood. Though, let me tell you, a man
might do worse than marry Patience Underwood. I have always
thought it a pity that Patience and Gregory would not make a match
of it. He, however, would fall in love with Clary, and she has too
much of the rake in her to give herself to a parson. I was thinking
of Mary Bonner, who, to my mind, is the handsomest woman I ever
saw in my life."

"I think she is," said Ralph, turning away his face.

"She hasn't a farthing, I fancy," continued the happy heir, "but
I don't regard that now. A few months ago I had a mind to marry
for money; but it isn't the sort of thing that any man should do. I
have almost made up my mind to ask her. Indeed, when I tell you,
I suppose I have quite made up my mind."

"She'll accept you,—of course."

"I can say nothing about that, you know. A man must take his
chance. I can offer her a fine position, and a girl, I think, should
have some regard to money when she marries, though a man should
not. If there's nobody before me I should have a chance, I suppose."

His words were not boastful, but there was a tone of triumph in
his voice. And why should he not triumph? thought the other
Ralph. Of course he would triumph. He had everything to recommend him. And as for himself,—for him, the dispossessed one,—any
particle of a claim which he might have secured by means of that
former correspondence had been withdrawn by his own subsequent
words. "I dare say she'll take you," he said, with his face still
averted.

Ralph the heir did indeed think that he would be accepted, and he went on to discuss the circumstances of their future home, almost as though Mary Bonner were already employed in getting together her wedding garments. His companion said nothing further, and Ralph the heir did not discover that anything was amiss.

On the following day Ralph the heir went across the country to the Moonbeam in Buckinghamshire.

CHAPTER XXXVI.

NEEFIT MEANS TO STICK TO IT.

THERE was some business to be done as a matter of course before the young Squire could have all his affairs properly settled. There were debts to be paid, among which Mr. Neefit's stood certainly first. It was first in magnitude, and first in obligation; but it gave Ralph no manner of uneasiness. He had really done his best to get Polly to marry him, and, luckily for him,—by the direct interposition of some divine Providence, as it now seemed to Ralph,—Polly had twice refused him. It seemed to him, indeed, that divine Providence looked after him in a special way, breaking his uncle's neck in the very nick of time, and filling a breeches-maker's daughter's mind with so sound a sense of the propriety of things, as to induce her to decline the honour of being a millstone round his neck, when positively the offer was pressed upon her. As things stood there could be no difficulty with Mr. Neefit. The money would be paid, of course, with all adjuncts of accruing interest, and Mr. Neefit should go on making breeches for him to the end of the chapter. And for raising this money he had still a remnant of the old property which he could sell, so that he need not begin by laying an ounce of ,encumbrance on his paternal estates. He was very clear in his mind at this period of his life that there should never be any such encumbrance in his days. That remnant of property should be sold, and Neefit, Horsball, and others, should be paid. But it certainly did occur to him in regard to Neefit, that there had been that between them which made it expedient that the matter should be settled with some greater courtesy than would be shown by a simple transaction through his man of business. Therefore he wrote a few lines to Mr. Neefit on the day before he left the Priory,—a few lines which he thought to be very civil.

"Newton, 9th December, 186—.

"My Dear Mr. Neefit,—

"You have probably heard before this of the accident which has happened in my family. My uncle has been killed by a fall from his horse, and I have come into my property earlier than I expected. As soon as I could begin to attend to matters of business, I thought of my debt to you, and of all the obligation I owe you. I think the debt is £1,000; but whatever it is it can be paid now. The money will be ready early in the year, if that will do for you,—and I am very much obliged to you. Would you mind letting Mr. Carey know how much it is, interest and all. He is our family lawyer.

"Remember me very kindly to Miss Polly. I hope she will always think of me as a friend. Would you tell Bawwah to put three pairs of breeches in hand for me,—leather.

"Yours very truly,

"RALPH NEWTON."

The wrath of Mr. Neefit on receiving this letter at his shop in Conduit Street was almost divine. He had heard from Polly an account of that last interview at Ramsgate, and Polly had told her story as truly as she knew how to tell it. But the father had never for a moment allowed himself to conceive that therefore the thing was at an end, and had instructed Polly that she was not to look upon it in that light. He regarded his young customer as absolutely bound to him, and would not acknowledge to himself that such obligation could be annulled by Polly's girlish folly. And he did believe that young Newton intended to act, as he called it, "on the square." So believing, he was ready to make almost any sacrifice of himself; but that Newton should now go back, after having received his hard money, was to him a thing quite out of the question. He scolded Polly with some violence, and asked whether she wanted to marry such a lout as Moggs. Polly replied with spirit that she wouldn't marry any man till she found that she could love him, and that the man loved her. "Ain't he told you as he loves you ever so often?" said Neefit. "I know what I'm doing of, father," said Polly, "and I'm not going to be drove." Nevertheless Mr. Neefit had felt certain that if young Newton would still act upon the square, things would settle themselves rightly. There was the money due, and, as Neefit constantly said to himself, "money was a thing as was not to be got over."

Then had come upon the tradesman the tidings of the old Squire's death. They were read to him out of a newspaper by his shopman, Waddle. "I'm blessed if he ain't been and tumbled all at once into his uncle's shoes," said Waddle. The paragraph in question was one which appeared in a weekly newspaper some two days after the Squire's death. Neefit, who at the moment was turning over the pages of his ledger, came down from his desk and stood for about ten minutes in the middle of his shop, while the Herr ceased from his cutting, and Waddle read the paragraph over and over again.

Neefit stood stock still, with his hands in his breeches pockets, and his great staring eyes fixed upon vacancy. "I'm blessed if it ain't true," said Waddle, convinced by the repetition of his own reading. News had previously reached the shop that the Squire had had a fall. Tidings as to troubles in the hunting-field were quick in reaching Mr. Neefit's shop;—but there had been no idea that the accident would prove to be fatal. Neefit, when he went home that night, told his wife and daughter. "That will be the last of young Newton," said Mrs. Neefit. "I'm d—— if it will!" said the breeches-maker. Polly maintained a discreet silence as to the heir, merely remarking that it was very sad for the old gentleman. Polly at that time was very full of admiration for Moggs,—in regard, that is, to the political character of her lover. Moggs had lost his election, but was about to petition.

Neefit was never called upon, in the way of his own trade, to make funereal garments. Men, when they are bereaved of their friends, do not ride in black breeches. But he had all a tailor's respect for a customer with a dead relation. He felt that it would not become him to make an application to the young Squire on a subject connected with marriage, till the tombstone over the old Squire should have been properly adjusted. He was a patient man, and could wait. And he was a man not good at writing letters. His customer and future son-in-law would turn up soon; or else, the expectant father-in-law might drop down upon him at the Moonbeam or elsewhere. As for a final escape, Polly Neefit's father hardly feared that any such attempt would be made. The young man had acted on the square, and had made his offer in good faith.

Such was Mr. Neefit's state of mind when he received the young Squire's letter. The letter almost knocked him down. There was a decision about it, a confidence that all was over between them except the necessary payment of the money, an absence of all doubt as to "Miss Polly," which he could not endure. And then that order for more breeches, included in the very same paragraph with Polly, was most injurious. It must be owned that the letter was a cruel, heart-rending, bad letter. For an hour or so it nearly broke Mr. Neefit's heart. But he resolved that he was not going to be done. The young Squire should marry his daughter, or the whole transaction should be published to the world. He would do such things and say such things that the young Squire should certainly not have a good time of it. He said not a word to Polly of the letter that night, but he did speak of the young Squire. "When that young man comes again, Miss Polly," he said, "I shall expect you to take him."

"I don't know anything about that, father," said Polly. "He's had his answer, and I'm thinking he won't ask for another." Upon this the breeches-maker looked at his daughter, but made no other reply.

During the two or three following days Neefit made some inquiries, and found that his customer was at the Moonbeam. It was now necessary that he should go to work at once, and, therefore, with many misgivings, he took Waddle into his confidence. He could not himself write such a letter as then must be written ;—but Waddle was perfect at the writing of letters. Waddle shrugged his shoulders, and clearly did not believe that Polly would ever get the young Squire. Waddle indeed went so far as to hint that his master would be lucky in obtaining payment of his money,—but, nevertheless, he gave his mind to the writing of the letter. The letter was written as follows :—

"Conduit Street, 14th December, 186—.

"DEAR SIR,—

"Yours of the 9th instant has come to hand, and I beg to say with compliments how shocked we were to hear of the Squire's accident. It was terribly sudden, and we all felt it very much ; as in the way of our business we very often have to.

"As to the money that can stand. Between friends such things needn't be mentioned. Any accommodation of that kind was and always will be ready when required. As to that other matter, a young gentleman like you won't think that a young lady is to be taken at her first word. A bargain is a bargain, and honourable is honourable, which nobody knows as well as you who was always disposed to be upon the square. Our Polly hasn't forgotten you,— and isn't going." It should be acknowledged on Mr. Waddle's behalf, that that last assurance was inserted by the unassisted energy of Mr. Neefit himself. "We shall expect to see you without delay, here or at Hendon, as may best suit ; but pray remember that things stand just as they was. Touching other matters, as needn't be named here, orders will be attended to as usual if given separate.

"Yours very truly and obedient,

"THOMAS NEEFIT."

This letter duly reached the young Squire, and did not add to his happiness at the Moonbeam. That he should ever renew his offer to Polly Neefit was, he well knew, out of the question ; but he could see before him an infinity of trouble should the breeches-maker be foolish enough to press him to do so. He had acted " on the square." In compliance with the bargain undoubtedly made by him, he had twice proposed to Polly, and had Polly accepted his offer on either of these occasions, there would,—he now acknowledged to himself,—have been very great difficulty in escaping from the difficulty. Polly had thought fit to refuse him, and of course he was free. But, nevertheless, there might be trouble in store for him. He had hardly begun to ask himself in what way this trouble might next show itself,

when Neefit was at the Moonbeam.   Three days after the receipt of
his letter, when he rode into the Moonbeam yard on his return from
hunting, there was Mr. Neefit waiting to receive him.

He certainly had not answered Mr. Neefit's letter, having told himself that he might best do so by a personal visit in Conduit Street;
but now that Neefit was there, the personal intercourse did not seem
to him to be so easy.   He greeted the breeches-maker very warmly,
while Pepper, Cox, and Mr. Horsball, with sundry grooms and helpers,
stood by and admired.   Something of Mr. Neefit's money, and of
Polly's charms as connected with the young Squire, had already
reached the Moonbeam by the tongue of Rumour; and now Mr.
Neefit had been waiting for the last four hours in the little parlour
within the Moonbeam bar.   He had eaten his mutton chop, and drunk
three or four glasses of gin and water, but had said nothing of his
mission.   Mrs. Horsball, however, had already whispered her
suspicions to her husband's sister, a young lady of forty, who dis-
pensed rum, gin, and brandy, with very long ringlets and very small
glasses.

" You want to have a few words with me, old fellow," said Ralph
to the breeches-maker, with a cheery laugh.   It was a happy idea
that of making them all around conceive that Neefit had come after
his money.   Only it was not successful.   Men are not dunned so
rigorously when they have just fallen into their fortunes.   Neefit,
hardly speaking above his breath, with that owlish, stolid look, which
was always common to him except when he was measuring a man
for a pair of breeches, acknowledged that he did.   " Come along, old
fellow," said Ralph, taking him by the arm.   " But what'll you take
to drink first?"   Neefit shook his head, and accompanied Ralph into
the house.   Ralph had a private sitting-room of his own, so that there
was no difficulty on that score.   " What's all this about?" he said,
standing with his back to the fire, and still holding Neefit by the arm.
He did it very well, but he did not as yet know the depth of Neefit's
obstinacy.

" What's it all about?" asked Neefit in disgust.

" Well; yes.   Have you talked to Polly herself about this, old
fellow?"

" No, I ain't; and I don't mean."

" Twice I went to her, and twice she refused me.   Come, Neefit,
be reasonable.   A man can't be running after a girl all his life, when
she won't have anything to say to him.   I did all that a man could
do; and upon my honour I was very fond of her.   But, God bless
my soul,—there must be an end to everything."

" There ain't to be no end to this, Mr. Newton."

" I'm to marry the girl whether she will or not?"

" Nohow," said Mr. Neefit, oracularly.   " But when a young

gentleman asks a young lady as whether she'll have him, she's not a-going to jump down his throat. You knows that, Mr. Newton. And as for money, did I ask for any settlement? I'd a' been ashamed to mention money. When are you a-coming to see our Polly, that's the question?"

"I shall come no more, Mr. Neefit."

"You won't?"

"Certainly not, Mr. Neefit. I've been twice rejected."

"And that's the kind of man you are; is it? You're one of them sort, are you?" Then he looked out of his saucer eyes upon the young Squire with a fishy ferocity, which was very unpleasant. It was quite evident that he meant war. "If that's your game, Mr. Newton, I'll be even with you."

"Mr. Neefit, I'll pay you anything that you say I owe you."

"Damn your money!" said the breeches-maker, walking out of the room. When he got down into the bar he told them all there that young Newton was engaged to his daughter, and that, by G——, he should marry her.

"Stick to that, Neefit," said Lieutenant Cox.

"I mean to stick to it," said Mr. Neefit. He then ordered another glass of gin and water, and was driven back to the station.

CHAPTER XXXVII.

"HE MUST MARRY HER."

ON the day following that on which Mr. Neefit made his journey to the Moonbeam, Sir Thomas Underwood was at his chambers in London. It was now eight weeks since his bone had been broken, and though he still carried his arm in a sling, he declared of himself that he was able to go about as usual;—which assertion was taken at the villa as meaning that he was now able to live in Southampton Buildings without further assistance from women. When Patience reminded him, with tears in her eyes, that he could not as yet put on his own coat, he reminded her that Stemm was the most careful of men. Up to London he went with a full understanding that he was not at any rate to be expected home on that night. He had business on hand of great importance, which, as he declared, made his presence in town imperative. Mr. Trigger, from Percycross, was to be up with reference to the pestilent petition which had been presented against the return of Griffenbottom and himself. Moggs had petitioned on his own behalf, and two of the Liberals of the borough had also petitioned in the interest of Mr. Westmacott. The two Liberal parties who had quarrelled during the contest had now again joined forces in reference to the petition, and there was no doubt that the matter would go on before the judge. Mr. Trigger was coming up to London with reference to the defence. Sir Thomas gave Stemm to understand that Mr. Trigger would call at one o'clock.

Exactly at one o'clock the bell was rung at Sir Thomas's outside door, and Stemm was on the alert to give entrance to Mr. Trigger. When the door was opened who should present himself but our unfortunate friend Neefit. He humbly asked whether Sir Thomas was within, and received a reply which, as coming from Stemm, was courteous in the extreme. "Mr. Trigger, I suppose ;—walk in, Mr. Trigger." Neefit, not at all understanding why he was called Trigger, did walk in. Stemm, opening the door of his master's sanctum, announced Mr. Trigger. Neefit advanced into the middle of the room. Sir Thomas, with some solicitude as to the adjustment of his arm, rose to greet his agent from Percycross. "This isn't Mr. Trigger," said Sir Thomas. "He told me he was, anyhow," said Stemm. "I didn't tell you nothing of the kind," said Neefit. "But you come from Percycross ?" said Sir Thomas. "No I don't; I comes from Conduit Street," said Neefit. "You must go away," said Stemm, leaving the door open, and advancing into the room as though to turn the enemy's flank.

But Neefit, having made good his point so far, did not intend to be dislodged without a struggle on his own part. "I've something to say to Sir Thomas about Mr. Newton, as I wants to say very particular." "You can't say it now," said Stemm. "Oh, but I can," said Neefit, "and it won't take three minutes. "Wouldn't another day do for it, as I am particularly busy now ?" pleaded Sir Thomas. "Well, Sir Thomas ;—to tell the truth, it wouldn't," said Mr. Neefit, standing his ground. Then there came another ring at the bell. "Ask Mr. Trigger to sit down in the other room for two minutes, Stemm," said Sir Thomas. And so Mr. Neefit had carried his point. "And now, sir," said Sir Thomas, "as I am particularly engaged, I will ask you to be as quick as possible."

"My name is Neefit," began the breeches-maker,—and then paused. Sir Thomas, who had heard the name from Ralph, but had forgotten it altogether, merely bowed his head. "I am the breeches-maker of Conduit Street," continued Mr. Neefit, with a proud conviction that he too had ascended so high in his calling as to be justified in pre- suming that he was known to mankind. Sir Thomas again bowed. Neefit went on with his story. "Mr. Newton is a-going to behave to me very bad."

"If he owes you money, he can pay you now," said Sir Thomas.

"He do owe me money ;—a thousand pound he owe me."

"A thousand pounds for breeches !"

"No, Sir Thomas. It's most for money lent; but it's not along of that as I'd trouble you. I know how to get my money, or to put up with the loss if I don't. A thousand pound ain't here nor there,—not in what I've got to say. I wouldn't demean myself to ring at your bell, Sir Thomas;—not in the way of looking for a thousand pounds."

"In God's name, then, what is it? Pray be quick."

"He's going back from his word as he's promised to my daughter. That's what it is." As Neefit paused again, Sir Thomas remembered Ralph's proposition, made in his difficulties, as to marrying a trades-man's daughter for money, and at once fell to the conclusion that Mr. and Miss Neefit had been ill-used. "Sir Thomas," continued the breeches-maker, "I've been as good as a father to him. I gave him money when nobody else wouldn't."

"Do you mean that he has had money from you?"

"Yes; in course he has; ever so much. I paid for him a lot of money to 'Orsball, where he 'unts. Money! I should think so. Didn't I pay Moggs for him, the bootmaker? The very money as is rattling in his pocket now is my money."

"And he engaged himself to your daughter?"

"He engaged hisself to me to marry her. He won't say no other-wise himself. And he asked her twice. Why, Sir Thomas, he was all on the square about it till the old gentleman broke his neck. He hadn't nowhere else to go to for a shilling. But now the estate's come in like, he's for behaving dishonourable. He don't know me yet; that's what he don't. But I'll make him know me, Sir Thomas."

Then the door was opened, and Stemm's head appeared. "Mr. Trigger says as he's in the greatest possible haste, Sir Thomas." The reader, however, may as well be informed that this was pure invention on the part of Mr. Stemm.

Sir Thomas tore his hair and rubbed his face. He couldn't bid Neefit to call again, as he certainly did not desire to have a second visit. "What can I do for you, Mr. Neefit? I have no doubt the money will be paid, if owing. I will guarantee that for you."

"It ain't the money. I knows how to get my money."

"Then what can I do for you?"

"Make him go upon the square, Sir Thomas."

"How can I make him? He's twenty-six years old, and he's nothing to me. I don't think he should marry the young lady. He's not in her rank of life. If he has done her an injury, he must pay for it."

"Injury!" shouted Neefit, upon whose mind the word produced an unintended idea. "No, no! Our Polly ain't like that. By G——, I'd eat him, if it was that way! There ain't a duchess in the land as 'd 've guv' him his answer more ready than Polly had he ever spoke to her that way."

"If he has given rise to hopes which through him will be disappointed," said Sir Thomas, gravely, "he is bound to make what compensation may be in his power."

"Compensation be d—— !" said Neefit. "He must marry her."

"I don't think he will do that."

"You didn't think he would take my money, I suppose ; but he did. You didn't think he'd come and spend his Sundays out at my cottage, but he did. You didn't think as he'd come after our Polly down to Ramsgate, but he did. You didn't think as he'd give me his word to make her his wife, but he did." At every assertion that he made, the breeches-maker bobbed forward his bullet head, stretched open his eyes, and stuck out his under lip. During all this excited energy, he was not a man pleasant to the eye. "And now how is it to be, Sir Thomas ? That's what I want to know."

"Mr. Newton is nothing to me, Mr. Neefit."

"Oh ;—that's all. Nothing to you, ain't he ? Wasn't he brought up by you just as a son like ? And now he ain't nothing to you ! Do you mean to say as he didn't ought to marry my girl ? "

"I think he ought not to marry her."

"Not arter his promise ? "

Sir Thomas was driven very hard, whereas had the sly old breeches-maker told all his story, there would have been no difficulty at all. "I think such a marriage would lead to the happiness of neither party. If an injury has been done,—as I fear may be too probable,—I will advise my young friend to make any reparation in his power—short of marriage. I can say nothing further, Mr. Neefit."

"And that's your idea of being on the square, Sir Thomas ? "

"I can say nothing further, Mr. Neefit. As I have an appointment made, I must ask you to leave me." As Sir Thomas said this, his hand was upon the bell.

"Very well ;—very well. As sure as my name's Neefit, he shall hear of me. And so shall you, Sir Thomas. Don't you be poking at me in that way, old fellow. I don't choose to be poked at." These last words were addressed to Stemm, who had entered the room, and was holding the door open for Mr. Neefit's exit with something more than the energy customary in speeding a parting guest. Mr. Neefit, however, did take his departure, and Sir Thomas joined Mr. Trigger in the other room.

We will not be present at that interview. Sir Thomas had been in a great hurry to get rid of Mr. Neefit, but it may be doubted whether he found Mr. Trigger much better company. Mr. Trigger's business chiefly consisted in asking Sir Thomas for a considerable sum of money, and in explaining to him that the petition would certainly cost a large sum beyond this,—unless the expenses could be saddled on Westmacott and Moggs, as to which result Mr. Trigger seemed to have considerable doubt. But perhaps the bitterest part of Mr. Trigger's communication consisted in the expression of his opinion that Mr. Griffenbottom should be held by Sir Thomas free from any expense as to the petition, on the ground that Griffenbottom, had he stood alone, would certainly have carried one of the seats without any fear of a petition. " I don't think I can undertake that, Mr. Trigger," said Sir Thomas. Mr. Trigger simply shrugged his shoulders.

Sir Thomas, when he was alone, was very uncomfortable. While at Percycross he had extracted from Patience an idea that Ralph the heir and Clarissa were attached to each other, and he had very strongly declared that he would not admit an engagement between them. At that time Ralph was supposed to have sold his inheritance, and did not stand well in Sir Thomas's eyes. Then had come the Squire's death and the altered position of his late ward. Sir Thomas would be injured, would be made subject to unjust reproach if it were thought of him that he would be willing to give his daughter to a young man simply because that young man owned an estate. He had no such sordid feeling in regard to his girls. But he did feel that all that had occurred at Newton had made a great difference. Ralph would now live at the Priory, and there would be enough even for his extravagance. Should the Squire of Newton ask him for his girl's hand with that girl's consent, he thought that he could hardly refuse it. How could he ask Clarissa to abandon so much seeming happiness because the man had failed to keep out of debt upon a small income ? He could not do so. And then it came to pass that he was prepared to admit Ralph as a suitor to his child should Ralph renew his request to that effect. They had all loved the lad as a boy, and the property was wholly unencumbered. Of course he said nothing to Clarissa ; but should Ralph come to him there could be but one answer. Such had been the state of his mind before Mr. Neefit's visit.

But the breeches-maker's tale had altered the aspect of things very greatly. Under no circumstances could Sir Thomas recommend the young Squire to marry the daughter of the man who had been with him ; but if Ralph Newton had really engaged himself to this girl, and had done so with the purport of borrowing money from the father, that might be a reason why, notwithstanding the splendour of his prospects, he should not be admitted to further intimacy at the villa. To borrow money from one's tradesman was, in the eyes of Sir Thomas, about as inexcusable an offence as a young man could commit. He was too much disturbed in mind to go home on the following day, but on the Thursday he returned to the villa. The following Sunday would be Christmas Day.

CHAPTER XXXVIII.

FOR TWO REASONS.

THE young Squire, as soon as Neefit had left him in his own sitting-room at the Moonbeam, sat himself down and began to think over his affairs seriously. One thing was certain to him;—nothing on earth should induce him to offer his hand again to Polly Neefit. He had had a most miraculous escape, and assuredly would run no further risk in that direction. But though he had escaped, he could perceive that there was considerable trouble before him,—considerable trouble and perhaps some disgrace. It certainly could not be proved against him that he had broken any promise, as there had been no engagement; but it could be made public that he had twice offered himself to Polly, and could also be made public that he had borrowed the breeches-maker's money. He kept himself alone on that evening; and though he hunted on the following day, he was not found to be a lively companion either by Cox or Pepper. The lieutenant was talking about Neefit and Neefit's daughter all day: but Mr. Pepper, who was more discreet, declined to canvass the subject. " It's nothing to me who a man marries and who he don't," said Mr. Pepper. " What sort of horses he rides;—that's what I look at." During this day and the next Ralph did consider the state of his affairs very closely, and the conclusion he came to was this, that the sooner he could engage himself to marry Mary Bonner the better. If he were once engaged, the engagement would not then be broken off because of any previous folly with Miss Neefit; and, again, if he were once engaged to Mary Bonner, Neefit would see the absurdity of torturing him further in regard to Polly. On the Wednesday evening he went up to town, and on the Thursday morning he put himself into a cab and ordered the man to drive him to Popham Villa.

It was about noon when he started from town; and though he never hesitated,—did not pause for a moment after he had made up his mind as to the thing that he would do, still he felt many misgivings as he was driven down to Fulham. How should he begin his story to Mary Bonner, and how should he look Clary Underwood in the face? And yet he had not an idea that he was in truth going to behave badly to Clarissa. There had no doubt been a sort of tenderness in the feeling that had existed between them,—a some-thing just a little warmer than brotherly regard. They had been thrown together and had liked each other. And as he was driven nearer to the villa, he remembered distinctly that he had kissed her on the lawn. But did any one suppose that a man was bound to marry the first girl he kissed,—or if not the first, then why the second, or the third ? Clarissa could have no fair ground of complaint against him ; and yet he was uneasy as he reflected that she too must know the purport of his present visit to the villa.

And he was not quite easy about Mary. The good things which he carried in his hand were so many that he did not conceive that Mary would refuse him ; but yet he wished that the offer had been made, and had been accepted. Hitherto he had taken pleasure in his intercourse with young ladies, and had rather enjoyed the excitement of those moments which to some men are troublesome and even painful. When he had told Clarissa that she was dearer than any one else, he had been very happy while he was telling her. There had been nothing of embarrassment to him in the work of proposing to Polly Neefit. There may perhaps have been other passages in his life of the same nature, and he certainly had not feared them beforehand or been ashamed of them afterwards. But now he found himself endeavouring to think what words he would use to Mary Bonner, and in what attitude he would stand or sit as he used them. " The truth is," he said to himself, " a man should do these kind of things without premeditation," But not the less was he resolved, and at the gate he jumped out of his cab with a determination to have it over as soon as possible. He desired the cabman to wait for him at the nearest stables, remarking that he might be there for a few minutes, or for a few hours, and then turned to the gate. As he did so, he saw Sir Thomas walking from the direction of Fulham Bridge. Sir Thomas had come down by the railway on the other side of the river, and was now walking home. A sudden thought struck the young Squire. He would begin his work by telling his tale to Sir Thomas. There could be nothing so fitting as that he should obtain the uncle's leave to address the niece.

The two men greeted each other, and there were many things to be said. Sir Thomas had not seen his ward since the old Squire's death, and Ralph had not seen Sir Thomas since the election at Percycross and the accident of the broken arm. Sir Thomas was by far too reticent, too timid, and too reflective a man to begin at once whatever observations he might have to make ultimately in regard to Miss Polly Neefit. He was somewhat slow of speech, unless specially aroused, and had hardly received the congratulations of his young friend respecting the election, and expressed with some difficult decency his sorrow for the old Squire's death as combined with his satisfaction that the estate had not been sacrificed, when Ralph stopped him just as they had reached the front door, and, with much solemnity of manner, declared his wish to make a very particular private communication to Sir Thomas. " Certainly," said Sir Thomas, "certainly. Come into my room." But there was some delay before this privacy could be achieved, for in the hall they were met by the three girls, and of course there were many things to be said by them. Clarissa could hardly repress the flutter of her heart. When the reader last saw her flutter, and last heard her words as she spoke of her love to her cousin, she was taking an opportunity of declaring to Mary Bonner that she did not begrudge the brilliance of Mary's present prospects, —though the grand estate which made them brilliant was in a measure taken from her own hopes. And she had owned at the same time that she did not dare to feel confidence in her own love, because her lover would now be too poor in his own esteem to indulge himself with the luxury of a wife. All this Mary had accepted from her, certainly with no expression of triumph, but certainly with some triumph in her heart. Now this was entirely changed,—and here was her lover, with his fortune restored to him, once more beneath her father's roof! She gave him her hand the first of the three. She could not repress herself. He took it with a smile, and pressed it warmly. But he turned to Patience and took hers as rapidly as he was able. Then came Mary's turn. "I hope you also are glad to see me once again?" he said. Clarissa's heart sank within her as she heard the words. The appreciation of a woman in such matters is as fine as the nose of a hound, and is all but unintelligible to a man. "Oh, yes, Mr. Newton," said Mary smiling. "But if he asks her, she'll take him." No such words as these were formed even in Clarissa's mind; but after some fashion such was the ejaculation of her heart. Mary's "Oh, yes," had meant little enough, but could Mary withstand such chances if they were offered to her?

Sir Thomas led the way into his private room, and Ralph followed him. "You won't be long, papa," said Patience.

"I hope not," said Sir Thomas.

"Remember, Ralph, you will be keeping lunch waiting," said Patience.

Then the two men were alone. Sir Thomas's mind had recurred to Neefit at the first moment of Ralph's request. The young man was going to consult him as to the best mode of getting rid of that embarrassment. But in the hall another idea had come upon him. He was to be asked for his consent regarding Clarissa. As he seated himself in one chair and asked Ralph to take another, he had not quite made up his mind as to the answer he would give. There must at any rate be some delay. The reader will of course remember that Sir Thomas was persuaded that Ralph had engaged himself to marry Polly Neefit.

Ralph rushed boldly at his subject at once. "Sir Thomas," he said, "I am going to make a proposition, and I wish to ask you for your consent. I have made up my mind that the sooner I marry in my present condition the better." Sir Thomas smiled and assented. "And I want to know whether you will object to my asking Miss Bonner to be my wife."

"Miss Bonner!" said Sir Thomas, throwing up both his hands.

"Yes, sir;—is there any objection on your part?"

Sir Thomas hardly knew how to say whether there was or was not an objection on his part. In the first place he had made up his mind that the other Ralph was to marry Mary,—that he would do so in spite of that disclaimer which had been made in the first moment of the young man's disinheritance. He, Sir Thomas, however, could have no right to object on that score. Nor could he raise any objection on the score of Clarissa. It did seem to him that all the young people were at cross purposes, that Patience must have been very stupid and Clarissa most addlepated, or else that this Ralph was abominably false; but still, he could say nothing respecting that. No tale had reached his ears which made it even possible for him to refer to Clarissa. But yet he was dissatisfied with the man, and was disposed to show it. "Perhaps I ought to tell you," said Sir Thomas, "that a man calling himself Neefit was with me yesterday."

"Oh, yes; the breeches-maker."

"I believe he said that such was his trade. He assured me that you had borrowed large sums of money from him."

"I do owe him some money."

"A thousand pounds, I think he said."

"Certainly as much as that."

"Not for breeches,—which I suppose would be impossible, but for money advanced."

"Part one and part the other," said Ralph.

"And he went on to tell me that you were engaged,—to marry his daughter."

"That is untrue."

"Were you never engaged to her?"

"I was never engaged to her, Sir Thomas."

"And it was all a lie on the part of Mr. Neefit? Was there no foundation for it? You had told me yourself that you thought of such a marriage."

"There is nothing to justify him in saying that I was ever engaged to the young lady. The truth is that I did ask her and she,—refused me."

"You did ask her?"

"I did ask her," said Ralph.

"In earnest?"

"Well; yes;—certainly in earnest. At that time I thought it the only way to save the property. I need not tell you how wretched I was at the time. You will remember what you yourself had said to me. It is true that I asked her, and that I did so by agreement with her father. She refused me,—twice. She was so good, so sensible, and so true, that she knew she had better not make herself a party to such a bargain. Whatever you may think of my own conduct I shall not have behaved badly to Miss Neefit."

Sir Thomas did think very ill of Ralph's conduct, but he believed him. After a while the whole truth came out, as to the money lent and as to Neefit's schemes. It was of course understood by both of them that Ralph was required neither by honesty nor by honour to renew his offer. And then under such circumstances was he or was he not to be allowed to propose to Mary Bonner? At first Ralph had been much dismayed at having the Neefit mine sprung on him at such a moment; but he collected himself very quickly, and renewed his demand as to Mary. Sir Thomas could not mean to say that because he had been foolish in regard to Polly Neefit, that therefore he was to be debarred from marrying! Sir Thomas did not exactly say that; but, nevertheless, Sir Thomas showed his displeasure. "It seems," said he, "particularly easy to you to transfer your affections."

"My affection for Miss Neefit was not strong," said Ralph. "I did, and always shall, regard her as a most excellent young woman."

"She showed her sense in refusing you," said Sir Thomas.

"I think she did," said Ralph.

"And I doubt much whether my niece will not be equally—sensible."

"Ah,—I can say nothing as to that."

"Were she to hear this story of Miss Neefit I am sure she would refuse you."

"But you would not tell it to her,—as yet! If all goes well with me I will tell it to her some day. Come, Sir Thomas, you don't mean to be hard upon me at last. It cannot be that you should really regret that I have got out of that trouble."

"But I regret much that you should have borrowed a tradesman's money, and more that you should have offered to pay the debt by marrying his daughter." Through it all, however, there was a feeling present to Sir Thomas that he was, in truth, angry with the Squire of Newton, not so much for his misconduct in coming to propose to Mary so soon after the affair with Polly Neefit, but because he had not come to propose to Clarissa. And Sir Thomas knew that such a feeling, if it did really exist, must be overcome. Mary was entitled to her chance, and must make the best of it. He would not refuse his sanction to a marriage with his niece on account of Ralph's misconduct, when he would have sanctioned a marriage with his own daughter in spite of that misconduct. The conversation was ended by Sir Thomas leaving the room with a promise that Miss Bonner should be sent to fill his place. In five minutes Miss Bonner was there. She entered the room very slowly, with a countenance that was almost savage, and during the few minutes that she remained there she did not sit down.

"Sir Thomas has told you why I am here?" he said, advancing towards her, and taking her hand.

"No; that is;—no. He has not told me."

"Mary——"

"Mr. Newton, my name is Miss Bonner."

"And must it between us be so cold as that?" He still had her by the hand, which she did not at the moment attempt to withdraw. "I have come to tell you, at the first moment that was possible to me after my uncle's death, that of all women in the world I love you the best."

Then she withdrew her hand. "Mr. Newton, I am sorry to hear you say so;—very sorry."

"Why should you be sorry? If you are unkind to me like this, there may be reason why I should be sorry. I shall, indeed, be very sorry. Since I first saw you, I have hoped that you would be my wife."

"I never can be your wife, Mr. Newton."

"Why not? Have I done anything to offend you? Being here as one of the family you must know enough of my affairs to feel sure, —that I have come to you the first moment that was possible. I did not dare to come when I thought that my position was one that was not worthy of you."

"It would have been the same at any time," said Mary.

"And why should you reject me,—like this; without a moment's thought?"

"For two reasons," said Mary, slowly, and then she paused, as though doubting whether she would continue her speech, or give the two reasons which now guided her. But he stood, looking into her face, waiting for them. "In the first place," she said, "I think you are untrue to another person." Then she paused again, as though asking herself whether that reason would not suffice. But she resolved that she would be bold, and give the other. "In the next place, my heart is not my own to give."

"Is it so?" asked Ralph.

"I have said as much as can be necessary,—perhaps more, and I would rather go now." Then she left the room with the same slow, stately step, and he saw her no more on that day.

Then in those short five minutes Sir Thomas had absolutely told her the whole story about Polly Neefit, and she had come to the conclusion that because in his trouble he had offered to marry a tradesman's daughter, therefore he was to be debarred from ever receiving the hand of a lady! That was the light in which he looked upon Mary's first announcement. As to the second announcement he was absolutely at a loss. There must probably, he thought, have been some engagement before she left Jamaica. Not the less on that account was it an act of unpardonable ill-nature on the part of Sir Thomas,—that telling of Polly Neefit's story to Mary Bonner at such a moment.

He was left alone for a few minutes after Mary's departure, and then Patience came to him. Would he stay for dinner? Even Patience was very cold to him. Sir Thomas was fatigued and was lying down, but would see him, of course, if he wished it. "And where is Clarissa?" asked Ralph. Patience said that Clarissa was not very well. She also was lying down. "I see what it is," said Ralph, turning upon her angrily. "You are, all of you, determined to quarrel with me because of my uncle's death."

"I do not see why that should make us quarrel," said Patience. "I do not know that any one has quarrelled with you."

Of course he would not wait for dinner, nor would he have any lunch. He walked out on to the lawn with something of a bluster in his step, and stood there for three or four minutes looking up at the house and speaking to Patience. A young man when he has been rejected by one of the young ladies of a family has rather a hard time of it till he gets away. "Well, Patience," he said at last, "make my farewells for me." And then he was gone.

CHAPTER XXXIX.

HORSELEECHES.

THE honour of representing the borough of Percycross in Parliament was very great, and Sir Thomas, no doubt, did enjoy it after a fashion; but it was by no means an unalloyed pleasure. While he was still in bed with his broken arm at the Percy Standard, many applications for money had been made to him. This man wanted a sovereign, that man a five-pound-note, and some poor starving wretch a half-a-crown; and they all came to him with notes from Trigger, or messages from Spicer or Spiveycomb, to the effect that as the election was now over, the money ought to be given. The landlord of the Percy Standard was on such occasions very hard upon him. "It really will do good, Sir Thomas." "It is wanted, Sir Thomas." "It will make a good feeling in the town, Sir Thomas, and we don't know how soon we may have to go to work again." Sir Thomas was too weak in health to refuse. He gave the sovereigns, the five-pound-notes, and the half-crowns, and hurried back home as quickly as he was able.

But things were almost worse with him at home than at Percycross. The real horseleeches felt that they could hardly get a good hold of him while he was lying at the Percycross inn. Attacks by letter were, they well knew, more fatal than those made personally, and they waited. The first that came was from Mr. Pabsby. Mr. Pabsby had at last seen his way clear, and had voted for Underwood and Westmacott, absolutely throwing away his vote as far as the cause was concerned. But Mr. Pabsby had quarrelled with Griffenbottom, who once, when pressed hard for some favours, had answered the reverend gentleman somewhat roughly. "You may go and be ——," said Mr. Griffenbottom in his wrath, "and tell everybody in Percycross that I said so." Mr. Pabsby had smiled, had gone away, and had now voted for Mr. Westmacott. Mr. Pabsby was indeed a horseleech of the severest kind. There had been some outward show of reconciliation between Griffenbottom and Pabsby; but Pabsby had at last voted for Underwood and Westmacott. Sir Thomas had not been home two days before he received a letter from Mr. Pabsby. "It had been with infinite satisfaction,"—so Mr. Pabsby now said,—"that he had at length seen his way clearly, and found himself able to support his friend Sir Thomas. And he believed that he might take upon himself to say that when he once had seen his way clearly, he had put his shoulder to the wheel gallantly." In fact, it was to be inferred from the contents of Mr.

Pabsby's letter that Sir Thomas's return had been due altogether to Mr. Pabsby's flock, who had, so said Mr. Pabsby, been guided in the matter altogether by his advice. Then he sent a list of his "hearers," who had voted for Sir Thomas. From this the slight change of subject needed to bring him to the new chapel which he was building, and his desire that Sir Thomas should head the subscription-list in so good a cause, was easy enough. It might be difficult to say in what Mr. Pabsby's strength lay, but it certainly was the case that the letter was so written as to defy neglect and almost to defy refusal. Such is the power of horseleeches. Sir Thomas sent Mr. Pabsby a cheque for twenty pounds, and received Mr. Pabsby's acknowledgment, thanking him for his "first" subscription. The thanks were not very cordial, and it was evident that Mr. Pabsby had expected a good deal more than twenty pounds in return for all that he had done.

Mr. Pabsby was simply the first. Before Christmas had come, it seemed to Sir Thomas that there was not a place of divine worship in the whole of Percycross that was not falling to the ground in ruins. He had not observed it when he was there, but now it appeared that funds were wanted for almost every such edifice in the borough. And the schools were in a most destitute condition. He was informed that the sitting member had always subscribed to all the schools, and that if he did not continue such subscription the children would literally be robbed of their education. One gentleman, whose name he did not even remember to have heard, simply suggested to him that he would, as a matter of course, continue to give " the £50 " towards the general Christmas collection on behalf of the old women of the borough. The sitting members had given it time out of mind. Mr. Roodiland had a political project of his own, which in fact, if carried out, would amount to a prohibition on the import of French boots, and suggested that Sir Thomas should bring in a bill to that effect on the meeting of Parliament. If Sir Thomas would not object to the trouble of visiting Amiens, Lille, Beauvais, and three or four other French towns which Mr. Roodilands mentioned, he would be able to ascertain how much injury had been done to Percycross by the Cobden treaty. Mr. Spiveycomb had his own ideas about Italian rags,—Mr. Spiveycomb being in the paper line,—and wrote a very long letter to Sir Thomas, praying the member to make himself master of a subject so vitally important to the borough which he represented. Mr. Spicer also communicated to him the astounding fact that some high official connected with the army was undoubtedly misbehaving himself in regard to mustard for the troops. The mustard contracts were not open as they should be open. The mustard was all supplied by a London house, and Mr. Spicer was very anxious that Sir Thomas should move for a committee to inquire of the members of that London firm as to the manner in which the contracts were obtained by them. Mr. Spicer was disposed to think that this was the most important matter that would be brought forward in the next session of Parliament.

Mr. Pabsby had got his cheque before the other applications were received; but when they came in shoals, Sir Thomas thought that it might be well to refer them to Mr. Trigger for advice. Sir Thomas had not loved Griffenbottom during the election, and was not inclined to ask his colleague for counsel. Griffenbottom had obtained a name for liberality in Percycross, and had shown symptoms,—so thought Sir Thomas,—of an intention to use his reputation as a means of throwing off further burdens from his own shoulders. "I have spent a treasure in the borough. Let my colleague begin now." Words spoken by Mr. Griffenbottom in that strain had been repeated to Sir Thomas; and, after many such words, Sir Thomas could not go to Mr. Griffenbottom for advice as to what he should give, or refuse to give. He doubted whether better reliance could be placed on Mr. Trigger;—but to some one he must go for direction. Were he once to let it be known in Percycross that demands made would be satisfied, he might sign cheques to the extent of his whole fortune, during his first session. He did write to Mr. Trigger, enclosing the various Percycross applications; and Mr. Trigger duly replied to him. Mr. Trigger regretted that money had been given to Mr. Pabsby. Mr. Pabsby had been of no use, and could be of no use. Mr. Griffenbottom, who knew the borough better than any one else, had understood this well when on one occasion he had been "a little short" with Mr. Pabsby. Sir Thomas ought not to have sent that cheque to Mr. Pabsby. The sending it would do infinite harm, and cause dissensions in the borough, which might require a considerable expenditure to set right. As to the other clerical demands, it seemed to Sir Thomas that Mr. Trigger was of opinion that they should all be gratified. He had, in fact, sent his money to the only person in Percycross who ought not to have received money. The £50 for the old women was a matter of course, and would not be begrudged, as it was the only payment which was absolutely annual. In regard to the schools, Sir Thomas could do what he pleased; but the sitting members had always been liberal to the schools. Schools were things to which sitting members were, no doubt, expected to subscribe. As to the question of French boots, Mr. Trigger thought that there was something in it, and said that if Sir Thomas could devote his Christmas holidays to getting up the subject in Lille and Amiens, it would have a good effect in the borough, and show that he was in earnest. This might be the more desirable, as there was no knowing as yet what might be done about the petition. There no doubt was a strong feeling in the borough as to the Cobden treaty, and Sir

Thomas would probably feel it to be his duty to get the question up. In regard to the mustard, Mr. Trigger suggested that though there was probably nothing in it, it might be as well to ask the Secretary at War a question or two on the subject. Mr. Spicer was, no doubt, a moving man in Percycross. Sir Thomas could at any rate promise that he would ask such questions, as Mr. Spicer certainly had friends who might be conducive to the withdrawal of the petition. Sir Thomas could at any rate put himself into correspondence with the War Office. Mr. Trigger also thought that Sir Thomas might judiciously study the subject of Italian rags, in reference to the great paper trade of the country. No doubt the manufacture of paper was a growing business at Percycross. Mr. Trigger returned all the applications, and ended his letter by hinting that the cheques might as well be sent at once. Mr. Trigger thought that "a little money about the borough," would do good at the present moment.

It need hardly be said that this view of things was not pleasant to the sitting member, who was still confined to his house at Fulham by an arm broken in the cause. Sir Thomas had at once sent the £50 towards the Christmas festivities for the poor of the borough, and had declared his purpose of considering the other matters. Then had come a further letter from Mr. Trigger, announcing his journey to London, and Mr. Trigger and Sir Thomas had their first meeting after the election, immediately upon Mr. Neefit's departure from the chambers. "And is it to be?" asked Stemm, as soon as he had closed the door behind Mr. Trigger's back.

"Is what to be?"

"Them petitions, Sir Thomas? Petitions costs a deal of money they tell me, Sir Thomas." Sir Thomas winced. "I suppose you must go on now as your hand is in," continued Stemm.

"I don't know that at all," said Sir Thomas.

"You'll find as you must. There ain't no way out of it;—not now as you are the sitting member."

"I am not going to ruin myself, Stemm, for the sake of a seat in Parliament."

"I don't know how that may be, Sir Thomas. I hope not, Sir Thomas. But I don't see how you're not to go on now, Sir Thomas. If it wasn't for petitions, one wouldn't mind."

"There must be petitions, of course; and if there be good cause for them, they should succeed."

"No doubt, Sir Thomas. They say the bribery at Percycross was tremenjous;—but I suppose it was on the other side."

"If it was on our side, Stemm, it was not so with my knowledge. I did all I could to prevent it. I spoke against it whenever I opened my mouth. I would not have given a shilling for a single vote, though it would have got me the election."

" But they were not all that way, Sir Thomas ;—was they ? "

" How can I tell ? No ;—I know that they were not. I fear they were not. I cannot say that money was given, but I fear it."

" You must go on now, Sir Thomas, any way," said Stemm with a groan that was not reassuring.

" I wish I had never heard the name of Percycross," said Sir Thomas.

" I dare say," replied Stemm.

" I went there determined to keep my hands clean."

" When one puts one's hand into other people's business, they won't come out clean," said the judicious Stemm. " But you must go on with it now, any way, Sir Thomas."

" I don't know what I shall do," said the unhappy member.

On the next morning there came another application from Percycross. The postmaster in that town had died suddenly, and the competitors for the situation, which was worth about £150 per annum, were very numerous. There was a certain Mr. O'Blather, only known in Percycross as cousin to one Mrs. Givantake, the wife of a liberal solicitor in the borough. Of Mr. O'Blather the worst that could be said was that at the age of forty he had no income on which to support himself. Mrs. Givantake was attached to her cousin, and Mr. Givantake had become sensible of a burden. That the vacant office was just the thing for him appeared at a glance to all his friends. Mrs. Givantake, in her energy on the subject, expressed an opinion that the whole Cabinet should be impeached if the just claims of Mr. O'Blather were not conceded. But it was felt that the justice of the claims would not prevail without personal interest. The liberal party was in power, and application, hot and instant, was made to Mr. Westmacott. Mr. Westmacott was happy enough to have his answer ready. The Treasury had nothing to do with the matter. It was a Post Office concern ; and he, simply as the late liberal member, and last liberal candidate for the borough, was not entitled to intrude, even in a matter of patronage, upon the Postmaster-General, with whom he was not acquainted. But Mr. Westmacott was malicious as well as secure. He added a postscript to his letter, in which he said that he believed the present sitting member, Sir Thomas Underwood, was intimately acquainted with the noble lord who presided at the Post Office. There were various interests at Percycross moved, brought together, weighed against each other, and balanced to a grain, and finally dovetailed. If Sir Thomas Underwood would prevail on Lord ―― to appoint Mr. O'Blather to the vacant office, then all the Givantake influence at Percycross should be used towards the withdrawal of the petition. Such was the communication now made to Sir Thomas by a gentleman who signed his name as Peter Piper, and who professed himself authorised to act on behalf of Mr. Givantake. Sir Thomas's answer was as follows ;—

"Southampton Buildings, December 21, 186—.

"SIR,—

"I can have nothing to do with Mr. O'Blather and the post-office at Percycross.

"I am,

"Your obedient servant,

"THOMAS UNDERWOOD.

"MR. PETER PIPER, Post-office, Percycross."

Christmas had passed,—and had passed uncomfortably enough at Popham Villa, in which retreat neither of the three young ladies was at present very happy,—when Sir Thomas was invited by Mr. Trigger to take further steps with reference to the petitions. It was thought necessary that there should be a meeting in the conservative interest, and it was suggested that this meeting should take place in Sir Thomas's chambers. Mr. Trigger in making the proposition seemed to imply that a great favour was thereby conferred on Sir Thomas,— as that country is supposed to be most honoured which is selected as the meeting-ground for plenipotentiaries when some important international point requires to be settled. Sir Thomas could not see the arrangement in that light, and would have shuffled out of the honour had it been possible. But it was not possible. At this period of the year Mr. Griffenbottom had no house in town, and Mr. Trigger explained that it was inexpedient that such meetings should take place at hotels. There was no place so fitting as a lawyer's chambers. Sir Thomas, who regarded as a desecration the entrance of one such man as Mr. Trigger into his private room, and who was particularly anxious not to fall into any intimacy with Mr. Griffenbottom, was driven to consent, and at one o'clock on the 29th, Stemm was forced to admit the deputation. The deputation from Percycross consisted of Mr. Trigger, Mr. Spicer, and Mr. Pile ; but with them came also the senior sitting member. At first they were all very grave, and Sir Thomas asked them, indiscreetly, whether they would take a glass of sherry. Pile and Spicer immediately acceded to this proposition, and sherry was perhaps efficacious in bringing about speedy conversation.

"Well, Underwood," said Mr. Griffenbottom, "it seems that after all we are to have these d—— petitions." Sir Thomas lifted his left foot on his right knee, and nursed his leg,—but said nothing. On one point he was resolved ;—nothing on earth should induce him to call his colleague Griffenbottom.

"No doubt about that, Mr. Griffenbottom," said Mr. Pile, "—that is, unless we can make Westmacott right. 'Tother chap wouldn't be of much account."

"Mr. Pile, you're going a little too fast," said Trigger.

"No, I ain't," said Mr. Pile. But for the moment he allowed himself to be silenced.

"We don't like the looks of it at Percycross," said Mr. Spicer.

"And why don't we like the looks of it?" asked Sir Thomas.

"I don't know what your idea of pleasure is," said Mr. Griffen-bottom, "but I don't take delight in spending money for nothing. I have spent enough, I can tell you, and I don't mean to spend much more. My seat was as safe as the Church."

"But they have petitioned against that as well as mine," said Sir Thomas.

"Yes;—they have. And now what's to be done?"

"I don't know whether Sir Thomas is willing to take the whole cost of the defence upon himself," said Mr. Trigger, pouring out for himself a second glass of sherry.

"No, I am not," said Sir Thomas. Whereupon there was a pause, during which Pile and Spicer also took second glasses of sherry. "Why should I pay the cost of defending Mr. Griffenbottom's seat?"

"Why should I pay it?" said Griffenbottom. "My seat was safe enough. The fact is, if money was paid,—as to which I know nothing,—it was paid to get the second seat. Everybody knows that. Why should any one have paid money for me? I was safe. I never have any difficulty; everybody knows that. I could come in for Percycross twenty times running, without buying a vote. Isn't that true, Trigger?"

"I believe you could, Mr. Griffenbottom."

"Of course I could. Look here, Underwood——"

"I beg your pardon for one moment, Mr. Griffenbottom," said Sir Thomas. "Will you tell me, Mr. Trigger, whether votes were bought on my behalf?" Mr. Trigger smiled, and put his head on one side, but made no answer. "I wish I might be allowed to hear the truth," continued Sir Thomas. Whereupon Spicer grinned, and Mr. Pile looked as though he were about to be sick. How was it that a set of gentlemen, who generally knew their business so well as did the political leaders at Percycross, had got themselves into the same boat with a man silly enough to ask such a question as that?

"I shan't spend money," said Griffenbottom; "it's out of the question. They can't touch me. I've spent my money, and got my article. If others want the article, they must spend theirs."

Mr. Trigger thought it might be as well to change the subject for a moment, or, at any rate, to pass on to another clause of the same bill. "I was very sorry, Sir Thomas," said he, "that you wrote that letter to Mr. Givantake."

"I wrote no letter to Mr. Givantake. A man named Piper addressed me."

"Well, well, well; that's the same thing. It was Givantake, though of course he isn't going to sign his name to everything. If you could just have written a line to your friend the Postmaster-General, I really think we could have squared it all."

" I wouldn't have made a request so improper for all Percycross," said Sir Thomas.

"Patronage is open to everybody," suggested Mr. Griffenbottom.

" Those sort of favours are asked every day," said Trigger.

" We live in a free country," said Spicer.

" Givantake is a d—— scoundrel all the same," said Mr. Pile; " and as for his wife's Irish cousin, I should be very sorry to leave my letters in his hands."

"It wouldn't have come off, Mr. Pile," said Trigger, " but the request might have been made. If Sir Thomas will allow me to say as much, the request ought to have been made."

" I will allow nothing of the kind, Mr. Trigger," said Sir Thomas, with an assumption of personal dignity which caused every one in the room to alter his position in his chair. " I understand these things are given by merit." Mr. Trigger smiled, and Mr. Griffenbottom laughed outright. " At any rate, they ought to be, and in this office I believe they are." Mr. Griffenbottom, who had had the bestowal of some local patronage, laughed again.

" The thing is over now, at any rate," said Mr. Trigger.

"I saw Givantake yesterday," said Spicer. " He won't stir a finger now."

" He never would have stirred a finger," said Mr. Pile; " and if he'd stirred both his fistesses, he wouldn't have done a ha'porth of good. Givantake, indeed! He be blowed!" There was a species of honesty about Mr. Pile which almost endeared him to Sir Thomas.

" Something must be settled," said Trigger.

" I thought you'd got a proposition to make," said Spicer.

" Well, Sir Thomas," began Mr. Trigger, as it were girding his loins for the task before him, " we think that your seat wouldn't stand the brunt. We've been putting two and two together and that's what we think." A very black cloud came over the brow of Sir Thomas Underwood, but at the moment he said nothing. " Of course it can be defended. If you choose to fight the battle you can defend it. It will cost about £1,500,—or perhaps a little more. That is, the two sides, for both will have to be paid." Mr. Trigger paused again, but still Sir Thomas said not a word. " Mr. Griffenbottom thinks that he should not be asked to take any part of this cost."

" Not a shilling," said Mr. Griffenbottom.

" Well," continued Mr. Trigger, " that being the case, of course we have got to see what will be our best plan of action. I suppose, Sir Thomas, you are not altogether indifferent about the money."

" By no means," said Sir Thomas.

" I don't know who is. Money is money all the world over."

" You may say that," put in Mr. Spicer.

"Just let me go on for a moment, Mr. Spicer, till I make this thing clear to Sir Thomas. That's how we stand at present. It will cost us,—that is to say you,—about £1,500, and we should do no good. I really don't think we should do any good. Here are these judges, and you know that new brooms sweep clean. I suppose we may allow that there was a little money spent somewhere. They do say now that a glass of beer would lose a seat."

Sir Thomas could not but remember all that he had said to prevent there being even a glass of beer, and the way in which he had been treated by all the party in that matter, because he had so endeavoured. But it was useless to refer to all that at the present moment. "It seems to me," he said, "that if one seat be vacated, both must be vacated."

"It doesn't follow at all," said Mr. Griffenbottom.

"Allow me just for a moment longer," continued Trigger, who rose from his seat as he came to the real gist of his speech. "A proposition has been made to us, Sir Thomas, and I am able to say that it is one which may be trusted. Of course our chief anxiety is for the party. You feel that, Sir Thomas, of course." Sir Thomas would not condescend to make any reply to this. "Now the Liberals will be content with one seat. If we go on it will lead to disfranchising the borough, and we none of us want that. It would be no satisfaction to you, Sir Thomas, to be the means of robbing the borough of its privilege after all that the borough has done for you."

"Go on, Mr. Trigger," said Sir Thomas.

"The Liberals only want one seat. If you'll undertake to accept the Hundreds, the petition will be withdrawn, and Mr. Westmacott will come forward again. In that case we shouldn't oppose. Now, Sir Thomas, you know what the borough thinks will be the best course for all of us to pursue."

Sir Thomas did know. We may say that he had known for some minutes past. He had perceived what was coming, and various recollections had floated across his mind. He especially remembered that £50 for the poor old women which Mr. Trigger only a week since had recommended that he should give,—and he remembered also that he had given it. He recollected the sum which he had already paid for his election expenses, as to which Mr. Trigger had been very careful to get the money before this new proposition was made. He remembered Mr. Pabsby and his cheque for £20. He remembered his broken arm, and that fortnight of labour and infinite vexation in the borough. He remembered all his hopes, and his girls' triumph. But he remembered also that he had told himself a dozen times since his return that he wished that he might rid himself altogether of Percycross and the seat in Parliament. Now a proposition that would have this effect was made to him.

" Well, Sir Thomas, what do you think of it ?" asked Mr. Trigger.

Sir Thomas required the passing of a few moments that he might think of it, and yet there was a feeling strong at his heart telling him that it behoved him not even to seem to doubt. He was a man not deficient in spirit when roused as he now was roused. He knew that he was being ill used. From the first moment of his entering Percycross he had felt that the place was not fit for him, that it required a method of canvassing of which he was not only ignorant, but desirous to remain ignorant,—that at Percycross he would only be a catspaw in the hands of other men. He knew that he could not safely get into the same boat with Mr. Griffenbottom, or trust himself to the steering of such a coxswain as Mr. Trigger. He had found that there could be no sympathy between himself and any one of those who constituted his own party in the borough. And yet he had persevered. He had persevered because in such matters it is so difficult to choose the moment in which to recede. He had persevered,—and had attained a measure of success. As far as had been possible for him to do so, he had fought his battle with clean hands, and now he was member of Parliament for Percycross. Let what end there might come to this petition,—even though his seat should be taken from him,—he could be subjected to no personal disgrace. He could himself give evidence, the truth of which no judge in the land would doubt, as to the purity of his own intentions, and as to the struggle to be pure which he had made. And now they asked him to give way in order that Mr. Griffenbottom might keep his seat !

He felt that he and poor Moggs had been fools together. At this moment there came upon him a reflection that such men as he and Moggs were unable to open their mouths in such a borough as Percycross without having their teeth picked out of their jaws. He remembered well poor Moggs's legend, " Moggs, Purity, and the Rights of Labour ;" and he remembered thinking at the time that neither Moggs nor he should have come to Percycross. And now he was told of all that the borough had done for him, and was requested to show his gratitude by giving up his seat,—in order that Griffenbottom might still be a member of Parliament, and that Percycross might not be disfranchised ! Did he feel any gratitude to Percycross or any love to Mr. Griffenbottom ? In his heart he desired that Mr. Griffenbottom might be made to retire into private life, and he knew that it would be well that the borough should be disfranchised.

These horrid men that sat around him,—how he hated them ! He could get rid of them now, now and for ever, by acceding to the proposition made to him. And he thought that in doing so he could speak a few words which would be very agreeable to him in the speaking. And then all that Mr. Trigger had said about the £1,500 had been doubtless true. If he defended his seat money must be spent, and he did not know how far he might be able to compel Mr. Griffenbottom to share the expense. He was not so rich but what he was bound to think of the money, for his children's sake. And he did believe Mr. Trigger, when Mr. Trigger told him that the seat could not be saved.

Yet he could not bring himself to let these men have their way with him. To have to confess that he had been their tool went so much against the grain with him that anything seemed to him to be preferable to that. The passage across his brain of all these thoughts had not required many seconds, and his guests seemed to acknowledge by their silence that some little space of time should be allowed to him. Mr. Pile was leaning forward on his stick with his eyes fixed upon Sir Thomas's face. Mr. Spicer was amusing himself with a third glass of sherry. Mr. Griffenbottom had assumed a look of absolute indifference, and was sitting with his eyes fixed upon the ceiling. Mr. Trigger, with a pleasant smile on his face, was leaning back in his chair with his hands in his trousers pockets. He had done his disagreeable job of work, and upon the whole he thought that he had done it well.

"I shall do nothing of the kind," said Sir Thomas at last.

"You'll be wrong, Sir Thomas," said Mr. Trigger.

"You'll disfranchise the borough," said Mr. Spicer.

"You'll not be able to keep your seat," said Mr. Trigger.

"And there'll be all the money to pay," said Mr. Spicer.

"Sir Thomas don't mind that," said Mr. Griffenbottom.

"As for paying the money, I do mind it very much," said Sir Thomas. "As for disfranchising the borough, I cannot say that I regard it in the least. As to your seat, Mr. Griffenbottom——"

"My seat is quite safe," said the senior member.

"As to your seat, which I am well aware must be jeopardised if mine be in jeopardy, it would have been matter of more regret to me, had I experienced from you any similar sympathy for myself. As it is, it seems that each of us is to do the best he can for himself, and I shall do the best I can for myself. Good morning."

"What then do you mean to do?" said Mr. Trigger.

"On that matter I shall prefer to converse with my friends."

"You mean," said Mr. Trigger, "that you will put it into other hands."

"You have made a proposition to me, Mr. Trigger, and I have given you my answer. I have nothing else to say. What steps I may take I do not even know at present."

"You will let us hear from you," said Mr. Trigger.

"I cannot say that I will."

"This comes of bringing a gentleman learned in the law down into the borough," said Mr. Griffenbottom.

"Gentlemen, I must ask you to leave me," said Sir Thomas, rising from his chair and ringing the bell.

"Look here, Sir Thomas Underwood," said Mr. Griffenbottom. "This to me is a very important matter."

"And to me also," said Sir Thomas.

"I do not know anything about that. Like a good many others, you may like to have a seat in Parliament, and may like to get it without any trouble and without any money. I have sat for Percycross for many years, and have spent a treasure, and have worked myself off my legs. I don't know that I care much for anything except for keeping my place in the House. The House is everything to me,—meat and drink; employment and recreation; and I can tell you I'm not going to lose my seat if I can help it. You came in for the second chance, Sir Thomas; and a very good second chance it was if you'd just have allowed others who knew what they were about to manage matters for you. That chance is over now, and according to all rules that ever I heard of in such matters, you ought to surrender. Isn't that so, Mr. Trigger?"

"Certainly, Mr. Griffenbottom, according to my ideas," said Mr. Trigger.

"That's about it," said Mr. Spicer.

Sir Thomas was still standing. Indeed they were all standing now. "Mr. Griffenbottom," he said, "I have nothing further that I can say at the present moment. To the offer made to me by Mr. Trigger I at present positively decline to accede. I look upon that offer as unfriendly, and can therefore only wish you a good morning."

"Unfriendly," said Mr. Griffenbottom with a sneer.

"Good-bye, Sir Thomas," said Mr. Pile, putting out his hand. Sir Thomas shook hands with Mr. Pile cordially. "It's my opinion that he's right," said Mr. Pile. "I don't like his notions, but I do like his pluck. Good-bye, Sir Thomas." Then Mr. Pile led the way out of the room, and the others followed him.

"Oh!" said Stemm, as soon as he had shut the door behind their backs. "That's a deputation from Percycross, is it, Sir Thomas? You were saying as how you didn't quite approve of the Percycrossians." To this, however, Sir Thomas vouchsafed no reply.

CHAPTER XL.

WHAT SIR THOMAS THOUGHT ABOUT IT.

SIR THOMAS UNDERWOOD had been engaged upon a very great piece of work ever since he had been called to the Bar in the twenty-fifth year of his life. He had then devoted himself to the writing of a life of Lord Verulam, and had been at it ever since. But as yet he had not written a word. In early life, that is, up to his fortieth year, he had talked freely enough about his opus magnum to those of his compeers with whom he had been intimate; but of late Bacon's name had never been on his lips. Patience, at home, was aware of the name and nature of her father's occupation, but Clarissa had not yet learned to know that he who had been the great philosopher and little Lord Chancellor was not to be lightly mentioned. To Stemm the matter had become so serious, that in speaking of books, papers, and documents he would have recourse to any periphrasis rather than mention in his master's hearing the name of the fallen angel. And yet Sir Thomas was always talking to himself about Sir Francis Bacon, and was always writing his life.

There are men who never dream of great work, who never realise to themselves the need of work so great as to demand a lifetime, but who themselves never fail in accomplishing those second-class tasks with which they satisfy their own energies. Men these are who to the world are very useful. Some few there are, who seeing the beauty of a great work and believing in its accomplishment within the years allotted to man, are contented to struggle for success, and struggling, fail. Here and there comes one who struggles and succeeds. But the men are many who see the beauty, who adopt the task, who promise themselves the triumph, and then never struggle at all. The task is never abandoned; but days go by and weeks; and then months and years,—and nothing is done. The dream of youth becomes the doubt of middle life, and then the despair of age. In building a summer-house it is so easy to plant the first stick, but one does not know where to touch the sod when one begins to erect a castle. So it had been with Sir Thomas Underwood and his life of Bacon. It would not suffice to him to scrape together a few facts, to indulge in some fiction, to tell a few anecdotes, and then to call his book a biography. Here was a man who had risen higher and was reported to have fallen lower,— perhaps than any other son of Adam. With the finest intellect ever given to a man, with the purest philanthropy and the most enduring energy, he had become a by-word for greed and injustice. Sir Thomas had resolved that he would tell the tale as it had never yet been told, that he would unravel facts that had never seen the light, that he would let the world know of what nature really had been this man,—and that he would write a book that should live. He had never abandoned his purpose; and now at sixty years of age, his purpose remained with him, but not one line of his book was written.

And yet the task had divorced him in a measure from the world. He had not been an unsuccessful man in life. He had made money, and had risen nearly to the top of his profession. He had been **in**

Parliament, and was even now a member. But yet he had been divorced from the world, and Bacon had done it. By Bacon he had justified to himself,—or rather had failed to justify to himself,—a seclusion from his family and from the world which had been intended for strenuous work, but had been devoted to dilettante idleness. And he had fallen into those mistakes which such habits and such pursuits are sure to engender. He thought much, but he thought nothing out, and was consequently at sixty still in doubt about almost everything. Whether Christ did or did not die to save sinners was a question with him so painfully obscure that he had been driven to obtain what comfort he might from not thinking of it. The assurance of belief certainly was not his to enjoy ;—nor yet that absence from fear which may come from assured unbelief. And yet none who knew him could say that he was a bad man. He robbed no one. He never lied. He was not self-indulgent. He was affectionate. But he had spent his life in an intention to write the life of Lord Verulam, and not having done it, had missed the comfort of self-respect. He had intended to settle for himself a belief on subjects which are, of all, to all men the most important ; and, having still postponed the work of inquiry, had never attained the security of a faith. He was for ever doubting, for ever intending, and for ever despising himself for his doubts and unaccomplished intentions. Now, at the age of sixty, he had thought to lessen these inward disturbances by returning to public life, and his most unsatis-factory alliance with Mr. Griffenbottom had been the result.

They who know the agonies of an ambitious, indolent, doubting, self-accusing man,—of a man who has a skeleton in his cupboard as to which he can ask for sympathy from no one,—will understand what feelings were at work within the bosom of Sir Thomas when his Percycross friends left him alone in his chamber. The moment that he knew that he was alone he turned the lock of the door, and took from out a standing desk a whole heap of loose papers. These were the latest of his notes on the great Bacon subject. For though no line of the book had ever been written,—nor had his work even yet taken such form as to enable him to write a line,—nevertheless, he always had by him a large assemblage of documents, notes, queries, extracts innumerable, and references which in the course of years had become almost unintelligible to himself, upon which from time to time he would set himself to work. Whenever he was most wretched he would fly at his papers. When the qualms of his conscience became very severe, he would copy some passage from a dusty book, hardly in the belief that it might prove to be useful, but with half a hope that he might cheat himself into so believing. Now, in his misery, he declared that he would bind himself to his work and never leave it. There, if anywhere, might consolation be found.

With rapid hands he moved about the papers, and tried to fix his eyes upon the words. But how was he to fix his thoughts? He could not even begin not to think of those scoundrels who had so misused him. It was not a week since they had taken £50 from him for the poor of Percycross, and now they came to him with a simple statement that he was absolutely to be thrown over! He had already paid £900 for his election, and was well aware that the account was not closed. And he was a man who could not bear to speak about money, or to make any complaint as to money. Even though he was being so abominably misused, still he must pay any further claim that might be made on him in respect of the election that was past. Yes;—he must pay for those very purchased votes, for that bribery, as to which he had so loudly expressed his abhorrence, and by reason of which he was now to lose his seat with ignominy.

But the money was not the worst of it. There was a heavier sorrow than that arising from the loss of his money. He alone had been just throughout the contest at Percycross; he alone had been truthful, and he alone straightforward! And yet he alone must suffer! He began to believe that Griffenbottom would keep his seat. That he would certainly lose his own, he was quite convinced. He might lose it by undergoing an adverse petition, and paying ever so much more money,—or he might lose it in the manner that Mr. Trigger had so kindly suggested. In either way there would be disgrace, and contumely, and hours of the agony of self-reproach in store for him!

What excuse had he for placing himself in contact with such filth? Of what childishness had he not been the victim when he allowed himself to dream that he, a pure and scrupulous man, could go among such impurity as he had found at Percycross, and come out, still clean and yet triumphant? Then he thought of Griffenbottom as a member of Parliament, and of that Legislation and that Constitution to which Griffenbottoms were thought to be essentially necessary. That there are always many such men in the House he had always known. He had sat there and had seen them. He had stood shoulder to shoulder with them through many a division, and had thought about them,—acknowledging their use. But now that he was brought into personal contact with such an one, his very soul was aghast. The Griffenbottoms never do anything in politics. They are men of whom in the lump it may be surmised that they take up this or that side in politics, not from any instructed conviction, not from faith in measures or even in men, nor from adherence either through reason or prejudice to this or that set of political theories,— but simply because on this side or on that there is an opening. That gradually they do grow into some shape of conviction from the moulds in which they are made to live, must be believed of them;

but these convictions are convictions as to divisions, convictions as to patronage, convictions as to success, convictions as to Parliamentary management; but not convictions as to the political needs of the people. So said Sir Thomas to himself as he sat thinking of the Griffenbottoms. In former days he had told himself that a pudding cannot be made without suet or dough, and that Griffenbottoms were necessary if only for the due adherence of the plums. Whatever most health-bestowing drug the patient may take would bestow anything but health were it taken undiluted. It was thus in former days Sir Thomas had apologised to himself for the Griffenbottoms in the House;—but no such apology satisfied him now. This log of a man, this lump of suet, this diluting quantity of most impure water,—'twas thus that Mr. Griffenbottom was spoken of by Sir Thomas to himself as he sat there with all the Bacon documents before him,—this politician, whose only real political feeling consisted in a positive love of corruption for itself, had not only absolutely got the better of him, who regarded himself at any rate as a man of mind and thought, but had used him as a puppet, and had compelled him to do dirty work. Oh,—that he should have been so lost to his own self-respect as to have allowed himself to be dragged through the dirt of Percycross!

But he must do something;—he must take some step. Mr. Griffenbottom had declared that he would put himself to no expense in defending the seat. Of course he, Sir Thomas, could do the same. He believed that it might be practicable for him to acknowledge the justice of the petition, to declare his belief that his own agents had betrayed him, and to acknowledge that his seat was indefensible. But, as he thought of it, he found that he was actually ignorant of the law in the matter. That he would make no such bargain as that suggested to him by Mr. Trigger,—of so much he thought that he was sure. At any rate he would do nothing that he himself knew to be dishonourable. He must consult his own attorney. That was the end of his self-deliberation,—that, and a conviction that under no circumstances could he retain his seat.

Then he struggled hard for an hour to keep his mind fixed on the subject of his great work. He had found an unknown memoir respecting Bacon, written by a German pen in the Latin language, published at Leipzig shortly after the date of Bacon's fall. He could translate that. It is always easiest for the mind to work in such emergencies, on some matter as to which no creative struggles are demanded from it.

CHAPTER XLI.

A BROKEN HEART.

IT was very bad with Clarissa when Ralph Newton was closeted with Mary at Popham Villa. She had suspected what was about to take place, when Sir Thomas and Ralph went together into the room; but at that moment she said nothing. She endeavoured to seem to be cheerful, and attempted to joke with Mary. The three girls were sitting at the table on which lunch was spread,—a meal which no one was destined to eat at Popham Villa on that day,—and thus they remained till Sir Thomas joined them. "Mary," he had said, "Ralph Newton wishes to speak to you. You had better go to him."

"To me, uncle?"

"Yes, to you. You had better go to him."

"But I had rather not."

"Of course you must do as you please, but I would advise you to go to him." Then she had risen very slowly and had gone.

All of them had understood what it meant. To Clarissa the thing was as certain as though she already heard the words spoken. With Patience even there was no doubt. Sir Thomas, though he had told nothing, did not pretend that the truth was to be hidden. He looked at his younger daughter sorrowfully, and laid his hand upon her head caressingly. With her there was no longer the possibility of retaining any secret, hardly the remembrance that there was a secret to retain. "Oh, papa," she said;—"oh, papa!" and burst into tears.

"My dear," he said, "believe me that it is best that it should be so. He is unworthy." Patience said not a word, but was now holding Clarissa close to her bosom. "Tell Mary," continued Sir Thomas, "that I will see her when she is at liberty. Patience, you can ask Ralph whether it will suit him to stay for dinner. I am ̶i̶red and will go up-stairs myself." And so the two girls were left ̶ ̶her.

̶ ̶tty, take me away," said Clarissa. "I must never see him ̶ ̶ever!—nor her."

̶ ̶ll not accept him, Clary."

̶ ̶will. I know she will. She is a sly, artful creature. ̶ ̶en so good to her."

̶ ̶—I think not;—but what does it matter? He is ̶ ̶can be nothing to you now. Papa was right. He is

̶ ̶ng for that. I only care for him. Oh, Patty, take ̶ ̶uld not bear to see them when they come out."

Then Patience took her sister up to their joint room, and laid the poor sufferer on the bed, and throwing herself on her knees beside the bed, wept over her sister and caressed her. That argument of Ralph's unworthiness was nothing to Clarissa. She did not consider herself to be so worthy but what she might forgive any sin, if only the chance of forgiving such sin were given to her. At this moment in her heart of hearts her anger was more against her rival than against the man. She had not yet taught herself to think of all his baseness to her,—had only as yet had time to think that that evil had come upon her which she had feared from the first moment of her cousin's arrival.

Presently Patience heard the door opened of the room down-stairs and heard Mary's slow step as she crossed the hall. She understood well that some one should be below, and with another single word of affection to her sister, she went down-stairs. "Well, Mary," she said, looking into her cousin's face.

"There is nothing particular to tell," said Mary, with a gentle smile.

"Of course we all knew what he wanted."

"Then of course you all knew what I should say to him."

"I knew," said Patience.

"I am sure that Clary knew," said Mary. "But he is all alone there, and will not know what to do with himself. Won't you go to him?"

"You will go up to Clary?" Mary nodded her head, and then Patience crossed the hall to liberate the rejected suitor. Mary stood for awhile thinking. She already knew from what Patience had said, that Clarissa had suspected her, and she felt that there should have been no such suspicion. Clarissa had not understood, but ought to have understood. For a moment she was angry, and was disposed to go to her own room. Then she remembered all her cousin's misery, and crept up-stairs to the door. She had come so softly, that though the door was hardly closed, nothing had been heard of her approach. "May I come in, dear?" she said very gently.

"Well, Mary; tell me all," said Clarissa.

"There is nothing to tell, Clary;—only this, that I fear ▊ ton is not worthy of your love."

"He asked you to take him?"

"Never mind, dearest. We will not talk of that. ▊ Clary, if I only could make you happy."

"But you have refused him?"

"Don't you know me better than to ask me? ▊ where my heart is? We will carry our burdens ▊ and then they will be lighter."

"But he will come to you again;—that other one ▊

"Clary, dear; we will not think about it. There are things which should not be thought of. We will not talk of it, but we will love each other so dearly." Clarissa, now that she was assured that her evil fortune was not to be aggravated by any injury done to her by her cousin, allowed herself to be tranquillised if not comforted. There was indeed something in her position that did not admit of comfort. All the family knew the story of her unrequited love, and treated her with a compassion which, while its tenderness was pleasant to her, was still in itself an injury. A vain attachment in a woman's heart must ever be a weary load, because she can take no step of her own towards that consummation by which the burden may be converted into a joy. A man may be active, may press his suit even a tenth time, may do something towards achieving success. A woman can only be still and endure. But Clarissa had so managed her affairs that even that privilege of being still was hardly left to her. Her trouble was known to them all. She doubted whether even the servants in the house did not know the cause of her woe. How all this had come to pass she could not now remember. She had told Patience,—as though in compliance with some compact that each should ever tell the other all things. And then circumstances had arisen which made it so natural that she should be open and candid with Mary. The two Ralphs were to be their two lovers. That to her had been a delightful dream during the last few months. He, whose inheritance at that moment was supposed to have been gone, had, as Clarissa thought, in plainest language told his love to her. "Dear, dear Clary, you know I love you." The words to her sense had been so all-important, had meant so much, had seemed to be so final, that they hardly wanted further corroboration. Then, indeed, had come the great fault,—the fault which she had doubted whether she could ever pardon; and she, because of the heinousness of that offence, had been unable to answer the question that had been asked. But the offence, such as it was, had not lightened the solemnity of her assurance, as far as love went, that Ralph ought to be her own after the speaking of such words as he had spoken. There were those troubles about money, but yet she was entitled to regard him as her own. Then had come the written offer from the other Ralph to Mary,—the offer written in the moment of his believed prosperity; and it had been so natural that Clarissa should tell her cousin that as regarded the splendour of position there should be no jealousy between them. Clarissa did not herself think much of a lover who wrote letters instead of coming and speaking,— had perhaps an idea that open speech, even though offence might follow, was better than formal letters; but all that was Mary's affair. This very respectful Ralph was Mary's lover, and if Mary were satisfied, she would not quarrel with the well-behaved young man. She would not even quarrel with him because he was taking from her own Ralph the inheritance which for so many years had been believed to be his own. Thus in the plenitude of her affection and in the serenity of her heart she had told everything to her cousin. And now also her father knew it all. How this had come to pass she did not think to inquire. She suspected no harm from Patience. The thing had been so clear, that all the world might see it. Ralph, that false one, knew it also. Who could know it so well as he did? Had not those very words been spoken by him,—been repeated by him? Now she was as one stricken, where wounds could not be hidden.

On that day Ralph was driven back to town in his cab, in a rather disheartened condition, and no more was seen or heard of him for the present at Popham Villa. His late guardian had behaved very ill to him in telling Mary Bonner the story of Polly Neefit. That was his impression,—feeling sure that Mary had alluded to the unfortunate affair with the breeches-maker's daughter, of which she could have heard tidings only from Sir Thomas. As to Clarissa, he had not exactly forgotten the little affair on the lawn; but to his eyes that affair had been so small as to be almost overlooked amidst larger matters. Mary, he thought, had never looked so beautiful as she had done while refusing him. He did not mean to give her up. Her heart, she had told him, was not her own. He thought he had read of young ladies in similar conditions, of young ladies who had bestowed their hearts and had afterwards got them back again for the sake of making second bestowals. He was not sure but that such an object would lend a zest to life. There was his brother Gregory in love with Clarissa, and still true to her. He would be true to Mary, and would see whether, in spite of that far-away lover, he might not be more successful than his brother. At any rate he would not give her up,—and before he had gone to bed that night he had already concocted a letter to her in his brain, explaining the whole of that Neefit affair, and asking her whether a man should be condemned to misery for life because he had been led by misfortune into such a mistake as that. He dined very well at his club, and on the following morning went down to the Moonbeam by an early train, for that day's hunting. Thence he returned to Newton Priory in time for Christmas, and as he was driven up to his own house, through his own park, meeting one or two of his own tenants, and encountering now and then his own obsequious labourers, he was not an unhappy man in spite of Mary Bonner's cruel answer. It may be doubted whether his greatest trouble at this moment did not arise from his dread of Neefit. He had managed to stay long enough in London to give orders that Neefit's money should be immediately paid. He knew that Neefit could not harm him at law; but it would not be

agreeable if the old man were to go about the country telling every-
one that he, Ralph Newton of Newton, had twice offered to marry
Polly. For the present we will leave him, although he is our hero,
and will return to the girls at Popham Villa.

"It is all very well talking, Patience, but I don't mean to try to
change," Clarissa said. This was after that visit of the Percycross
deputation to Sir Thomas, and after Christmas. More than a week
had now passed by since Ralph had rushed down to Fulham with his
offer, and the new year had commenced. Sir Thomas had been at
home for Christmas,—for the one day,—and had then returned to
London. He had seen his attorney respecting the petition, who was
again to see Mr. Griffenbottom's London attorney and Mr. Trigger.
In the meantime Sir Thomas was to remain quiet for a few days.
The petition was not to be tried till the end of February, and there
was still time for deliberation. Sir Thomas just now very often took
out that great heap of Baconian papers, but still not a word of the
biography was written. He was, alas! still very far from writing
the first word. "It is all very well, Patience, but I do not mean to
try to change," said Clarissa.

Poor Patience could make no answer, dreadful as was to her such
an assertion from a young woman. "There is a man who clearly
does not want to marry you, who has declared in the plainest way
that he does want to marry some one else, who has grossly deceived
you, and who never means to think of you again; and yet you say
that you will wilfully adhere to your regard for him!" Such would
have been the speech which Patience would have made, had she
openly expressed her thoughts. But Clarissa was ill, and weak, and
wretched; and Patience could not bring herself to say a word that
should distress her sister.

"If he came to me to-morrow, of course I should forgive him,"
Clarissa said again. These conversations were never commenced by
Patience, who would rather have omitted any mention of that base
young man. "Of course I should. Men do do those things. Men
are not like women. They do all manner of things and everybody
forgives them. I don't say anything about hoping. I don't hope
for anything. I am not happy enough to hope. I shouldn't care if
I knew I were going to die to-morrow. But there can be no change.
If you want me to be a hypocrite, Patience, I will; but what will be
the use? The truth will be the same."

The two girls let her have her way, never contradicted her, coaxed
her, and tried to comfort her;—but it was in vain. At first she
would not go out of the house, not even to church, and then she
took to lying in bed. This lasted into the middle of January, and
still Sir Thomas did not come home. He wrote frequently, short
notes to Patience, sending money, making excuses, making promises,

always expressing some word of hatred or disgust as to Percycross; but still he did not come. At last, when Clarissa declared that she preferred lying in bed to getting up, Patience went up to London and fetched her father home. It had gone so far with Sir Thomas now that he was unable even to attempt to defend himself. He humbly said that he was sorry that he had been away so long, and returned with Patience to the villa.

"My dear," said Sir Thomas, seating himself by Clarissa's bedside, "this is very bad."

"If I had known you were coming, papa, I would have got up."

"If you are not well, perhaps you are better here, dear."

"I don't think I am quite well, papa."

"What is it, my love?" Clarissa looked at him out of her large tear-laden eyes, but said nothing. "Patience says that you are not happy."

"I don't know that anybody is happy, papa."

"I wish that you were with all my heart, my child. Can your father do anything that will make you happy?"

"No, papa."

"Tell me, Clary. You do not mind my asking you questions?"

"No, papa."

"Patience tells me that you are still thinking of Ralph Newton."

"Of course I think of him."

"I think of him too;—but there are different ways of thinking. We have known him, all of us, a long time."

"Yes, papa."

"I wish with all my heart that we had never seen him. He is not worthy of our solicitude."

"You always liked him. I have heard you say you loved him dearly."

"I have said so, and I did love him. In a certain way I love him still."

"So do I, papa."

"But I know him to be unworthy. Even if he had come here to offer you his hand I doubt whether I could have permitted an engagement. Do you know that within the last two months he has twice offered to marry another young woman, and I doubt whether he is not at this moment engaged to her?"

"Another?" said poor Clarissa.

"Yes, and that without a pretence of affection on his part, simply because he wanted to get money from her father."

"Are you sure, papa?" asked Clarissa, who was not prepared to believe, and did not believe this enormity on the part of the man she loved.

"I am quite sure. The father came to me to complain of him,

and I had the confession from Ralph's own lips, the very day that he came here with his insulting offer to Mary Bonner."

"Did you tell Mary?"

"No. I knew that it was unnecessary. There was no danger as to Mary. And who do you think this girl was? The daughter of a tailor, who had made some money. It was not that he cared for her, Clary;—no more than I do! Whether he meant to marry her or not I do not know."

"I'm sure he didn't, papa," said Clarissa, getting up in bed.

"And will that make it better? All that he wanted was the tradesman's money, and to get that he was willing either to deceive the girl, or to sell himself to her. I don't know which would have been the baser mode of traffic. Is that the conduct of a gentleman, Clary?"

Poor Clarissa was in terrible trouble. She hardly believed the story, which seemed to tell her of a degree of villany greater than ever her imagination had depicted to her;—and yet, if it were true, she would be driven to look for means of excusing it. The story as told was indeed hardly just to Ralph, who in the course of his transactions with Mr. Neefit had almost taught himself to believe that he could love Polly very well; but it was not in this direction that Clarissa looked for an apology for such conduct. "They say that men do all manner of things," she said, at last.

"I can only tell you this," said Sir Thomas very gravely, "what men may do I will not say, but no gentleman can ever have acted after this fashion. He has shown himself to be a scoundrel."

"Papa, papa; don't say that!" screamed Clarissa.

"My child, I can only tell you the truth. I know it is hard to bear. I would save you if I could; but it is better that you should know."

"Will he always be bad, papa?"

"Who can say, my dear? God forbid that I should be too severe upon him. But he has been so bad now that I am bound to tell you that you should drive him from your thoughts. When he told me, all smiling, that he had come down here to ask your cousin Mary to be his wife, I was almost minded to spurn him from the door. He can have no feeling himself of true attachment, and cannot know what it means in others. He is heartless,—and unprincipled."

"Oh, papa, spare him. It is done now."

"And you will forget him, dearest?"

"I will try, papa. But I think that I shall die. I would rather die. What is the good of living when nobody is to care for anybody, and people are so bad as that?"

"My Clarissa must not say that nobody cares for her. Has any person ever been false to you but he? Is not your sister true to you?"

"Yes, papa."

"And Mary?"

"Yes, papa." He was afraid to ask her whether he also had not been true to her? Even in that moment there arose in his mind a doubt, whether all this evil might not have been avoided, had he contented himself to live beneath the same roof with his children. He said nothing of himself, but she supplied the want. "I know you love me, papa, and have always been good to me. I did not mean that. But I never cared for any one but him,——in that way."

Sir Thomas, in dealing with the character of his late ward, had been somewhat too severe. It is difficult, perhaps, to say what amount of misconduct does constitute a scoundrel, or justifies the critic in saying that this or that man is not a gentleman. There be those who affirm that he who owes a debt for goods which he cannot pay is no gentleman, and tradesmen when they cannot get their money are no doubt sometimes inclined to hold that opinion. But the opinion is changed when the money comes at last,—especially if it comes with interest. Ralph had never owed a shilling which he did not intend to pay, and had not property to cover. That borrowing of money from Mr. Neefit was doubtless bad. No one would like to know that his son had borrowed money from his tailor. But it is the borrowing of the money that is bad, rather than the special dealing with the tradesman. And as to that affair with Polly, some excuse may be made. He had meant to be honest to Neefit, and he had meant to be true to Neefit's daughter. Even Sir Thomas, high-minded as he was, would hardly have passed so severe a sentence, had not the great sufferer in the matter been his own daughter.

But the words that he spoke were doubtless salutary to poor Clarissa. She never again said to Patience that she would not try to make a change, nor did she ever again declare that if Ralph came back again she would forgive him. On the day after the scene with her father she was up again, and she made an effort to employ herself about the house. On the next Sunday she went to church, and then they all knew that she was making the necessary struggle. Ralph's name was never mentioned, nor for a time was any allusion made to the family of the Newtons. "The worst of it, I think, is over," said Patience one day to Mary.

"The worst of it is over," said Mary; "but it is not all over. It is hard to forget when one has loved."

CHAPTER XLII.

NOT BROKEN-HEARTED.

CHRISTMAS had come and gone at Newton Priory, and the late Squire's son had left the place,—protesting as he did so that he left it for ever. To him also life in that particular spot of earth was impossible, unless he could live there as the lord and master of all. Everybody throughout that and neighbouring parishes treated him not only with kindness, but with the warmest affection. The gentry, the farmers, and the labourers, all men who had known him in the hunting-field, in markets, on the bench, or at church, men, women and children, joined together in forming plans by means of which he could remain at Newton. The young Squire asked him to make the house his home, at any rate for the hunting season. The parson offered half the parsonage. His friend Morris, who was a bachelor, suggested a joint home and joint stables between them. But it was all of no avail. Had it not been for the success which had so nearly crowned the late Squire's efforts during the last six months, it might have been that his friends would have prevailed with him. But he had been too near being the master to be able to live at Newton in any other capacity. The tenants had been told that they were to be his tenants. The servants had been told that they were to be his servants. During a few short weeks, he had almost been master, so absolute had been the determination of the old Squire to show to all around him that his son, in spite of the blot upon the young man's birth, was now the heir in all things, and possessed of every privilege which would attach itself to an elder son. He himself while his father lived had taken these things calmly, had shown no elation, had even striven to moderate the vehemence of his father's efforts on his behalf ;—but not the less had he been conscious of the value of what was being done for him. To be the promised future owner of the acres on which he had lived, of the coverts through which he had ridden, of every tree and bank which he had known from his boyhood, had been to him a source of gratified pride not the less strong because he had concealed it. The disappointment did hit him sorely. His dreams had been of parliament, of power in the county, of pride of place, and popularity. He now found that they were to be no more than dreams ;—but with this additional sorrow, that all around him knew that they had been dreamed. No ;—he could not stay at Newton even for the sake of living with friends who loved him so dearly. He said little or nothing of this to any one. Not even to Gregory Newton or to his friend Morris did he tell much of his feeling. He was not proud of his dreamings, and it seemed to himself that his punishment was just. Nor could he speak to either of them or to any man of his past ambition, or of what hopes might remain to him in reference to Mary Bonner. The young Squire had gone forth with the express purpose of wooing her, had declared his purpose of doing so, and had returned to Newton at any rate without any ready tale of triumph on his tongue. What had been his fortune the rival would not ask; and while the two remained together at the priory no further word was spoken of Mary Bonner. He, Ralph the dispossessed one, while he believed himself to be the heir, had intended to bring her home as a fitting queen to share his throne. It might be that she would consent to be his without a throne to share; but in thinking of her he could not but remember what his ambition had been, and he could hardly bring himself now to offer to her that which was comparatively so little worth the having. To suppose that she should already " be fond of him," should already long for him as he longed for her, was contrary to his nature. Hitherto when he had been in her presence, he had stood there as a man whose position in life was almost contemptible; and though it would be unjust to him to say that he had hoped to win her by his acres, still he had felt that his father's success on his behalf might justify him in that which would otherwise be unjustifiable. For the present, however, he could take no steps in that direction. He could only suggest to himself what had already been her answer, or what at some future time might be the answer she would make to his rival. He had lost a father between whom and himself there had existed ties, not only of tender love, but of perfect friendship, and for awhile he must bewail his loss. That he could not bewail his lost father without thinking of his lost property, and of the bride that had never been won, was an agony to his soul.

He had found a farm down in Norfolk, near to Swaffham, which he could take for twelve months, with the option of purchase at the expiration of that time, and thither he betook himself. There were about four hundred acres, and the place was within his means. He did not think it likely that Mary Bonner would choose to come and live upon a Norfolk farm; and yet what other work in life was there for which he was fit? Early in January he went down to Beamingham Hall, as the place was called, and there we will leave him for the present, consoling himself with oil-cake, and endeavouring to take a pride in a long row of stall-fed cattle.

At this time the two brothers were living at Newton Priory. Ralph the heir had bought some of his uncle's horses, and had commenced hunting with the hounds around him; though he had not as yet withdrawn his stud from the Moonbeam. He was not altogether at his ease, as he had before the end of February received three or four letters from Neefit, all of them dictated by Waddle, in which his conduct was painted not in the most flattering colours. Neefit's money had been repaid, but Neefit would not understand that the young heir's obligations to him had by any means been acquitted by that very ordinary process. He had risked his money when payment was very doubtful, and now he intended to have something beyond cash in return for all that he had done. "There are debts of honour which a real gentleman feels himself more bound to pay than any bills," Waddle had written. And to such dogmatic teachings as these Neefit would always add something out of his own head. "There ain't nobody who shan't know all about it, unless you're on the square again." Ralph had written one reply since he had been at Newton, in which he explained at some length that it was impossible that he should renew his addresses to a young lady who had twice rejected them, and who had assured him that she did not love him. He professed the greatest respect for Miss Neefit, a respect which had, if possible, been heightened by her behaviour in this matter,— but it must now be understood that the whole affair was at an end. Neefit would not understand this, but Neefit's further letters, which had not been unfrequent, were left unanswered. Ralph had now told the whole story to his brother, and had written his one reply from Newton in conformity with his brother's advice. After that they both thought that no further rejoinder could be of any service.

The parsonage was for the time deserted, Gregory having for the present consented to share his brother's house. In spite of that little thorn in the flesh which Neefit was, Ralph was able to enjoy his life very thoroughly. He went on with all the improvements about the place which the Squire had commenced, and was active in making acquaintance with every one who lived upon his land. He was not without good instincts, and understood thoroughly that respectability had many more attractions than a character for evil living. He was, too, easily amenable to influence from those around him ; and under Gregory's auspices, was constant at his parish church. He told himself at once that he had many duties to per- form, and he attempted to perform them. He did not ask Lieu- tenant Cox or Captain Fooks to the Priory, and quite prepared himself for the character of Henry V. in miniature, as he walked about his park, and rode about his farms, and talked with the wealthier farmers on hunting mornings. He had a full conception of his own dignity, and some not altogether inaccurate idea of the manner in which it would become him to sustain it. He was, perhaps, a little too self-conscious, and over-inclined to suppose that people were regarding his conduct because he was Newton of Newton ; —Newton of Newton with no blot on his shield, by right of his birth, and subject to no man's reproach.

He had failed grievously in one matter on which he had set his heart; but as to that he was, as the reader knows, resolved to try again. He had declared his passion to the other Ralph, but his rival had not made the confidence mutual. But hitherto he had said nothing on the subject to his brother. He had put it by, as it were, out of his mind for awhile, resolving that it should not trouble him immediately, in the middle of his new joys. It was a thing that would keep,—a thing, at any rate, that need not overshadow him night and morning. When Neefit continued to disturb him with threats of publicity in regard to Polly's wrongs, he did tell himself that in no way could he so effectually quiet Mr. Neefit as by marrying somebody else, and that he would, at some very early date, have recourse to this measure; but, in the meantime, he would enjoy himself without letting his unrequited passion lie too heavily as a burden on his heart. So he eat and drank, and rode and prayed, and sat with his brother magistrates on the bench, and never ceased to think of his good fortune, in that he had escaped from the troubles of his youth, unscathed and undegraded.

Then there came a further letter from Mr. Neefit, from which there arose some increase of confidence among the brothers. There was nothing special in this letter. These letters, indeed, were very like to each other, and, as had now come to be observed, were always received on a Tuesday morning. It was manifest to them that Neefit spent the leisure hours of his Sundays in meditating upon the hardness of his position; and that, as every Monday morning came, he caused a new letter to be written. On this particular Tuesday, Ralph had left home before the post had come, and did not get the breeches-maker's epistle till his return from hunting. He chucked it across the table to Gregory when he came down to dinner, and the parson read it. There was no new attack in it; and as the servant was in the room, nothing was then said about it. But after dinner the subject was discussed.

"I wish I knew how to stop the fellow's mouth," said the elder brother.

"I think I should get Carey to see him," suggested Gregory. "He would understand a lawyer when he was told that nothing could come of it but trouble to himself and his daughter."

"She has no hand in it, you know."

"But it must injure her."

"One would think so. But she is a girl whom nothing can injure. You can't imagine how good and how great she is;—great in her way, that is. She is as steady as a rock; and nobody who knows her will ever imagine her to be a party to her father's folly. She may pick and choose a husband any day she pleases. And the men about her won't mind this kind of thing as we should. No doubt all their friends joke him about it, but no one will think of blaming Polly."

"It can't do her any good," said Gregory.

"It cannot do her any harm. She has a strength of her own that even her father can't lessen."

"All the same, I wish there were an end of it."

"So do I, for my own sake," said Ralph. As he spoke he filled his glass, and passed the bottle, and then was silent for a few moments. "Neefit did help me," he continued, "and I don't want to speak against him; but he is the most pig-headed old fool that ever existed. Nothing will stop him but Polly's marriage, or mine."

"I suppose you will marry soon now. You ought to be married," said Gregory, in a melancholy tone, in which was told something of the disappointment of his own passion.

"Well;—yes. I believe I might as well tell you a little secret, Greg."

"I suppose I can guess it," said Gregory, with still a deeper sound of woe.

"I don't think you can. It is quite possible you may, however. You know Mary Bonner;—don't you?"

The cloud upon the parson's brow was at once lightened. "No," said he. "I have heard of her, of course."

"You have never seen Mary Bonner?"

"I have not been up in town since she came. What should take me up? And if I were there, I doubt whether I should go out to Fulham. What is the use of going?" But still, though he spoke thus, there was something less of melancholy in his voice than when he had first spoken. Ralph did not immediately go on with his story, and his brother now asked a question. "But what of Mary Bonner? Is she to be the future mistress of the Priory?"

"God only knows."

"But you mean to ask her?"

"I have asked her."

"And you are engaged?"

"By no means. I wish I were. You haven't seen her, but I suppose you have heard of her?"

"Ralph spoke of her,—and told me that she was very lovely."

"Upon my word, I don't think that even in a picture I ever saw anything approaching to her beauty. You've seen that thing at Dresden. She is more like that than anything I know. She seems almost too grand for a fellow to speak to, and yet she looks as if she didn't know it. I don't think she does know it." Gregory said not a word, but looked at his brother, listening. "But, by George there's a dignity about her, a sort of self-possession, a kind of noli me tangere, you understand, which makes a man almost afraid to come near her. She hasn't sixpence in the world."

"That needn't signify to you now."

"Not in the least. I only just mention it to explain. And her father was nobody in particular,—some old general who used to wear a cocked hat and keep the niggers down out in one of the colonies. She herself talked of coming home here to be a governess ;—by Jove! yes, a governess. Well, to look at her, you'd think she was born a countess in her own right."

"Is she so proud ? "

"No ;—it's not that. I don't know what it is. It's the way her head is put on. Upon my word, to see her turn her neck is the grandest thing in the world. I never saw anything like it. I don't know that she's proud by nature,—though she has got a dash of that too. Don't you know there are some horses show their breeding at a glance ? I don't suppose they feel it themselves ; but there it is on them, like the Hall-mark on silver. I don't know whether you can understand a man being proud of his wife."

"Indeed I can."

"I don't mean of her personal qualities, but of the outside get up. Some men are proud of their wives' clothes, or their jewels, or their false hair. With Mary nothing of that sort could have any effect ; but to see her step, or move her head, or lift her arm, is enough to make a man feel,—feel,—feel that she beats every other woman in the world by chalks."

"And she is to be mistress here ? "

"Indeed she should,—to-morrow, if she'd come."

"You did ask her ? "

"Yes,—I asked her."

"And what did she say ? "

"Nothing that I cared to hear. She had just been told all this accursed story about Polly Neefit. I'll never forgive Sir Thomas,— never." The reader will be pleased to remember that Sir Thomas did not mention Miss Neefit's name, or any of the circumstances of the Neefit contract, to his niece.

"He could hardly have wished to set her against you."

"I don't know ; but he must have told her. She threw it in my teeth that I ought to marry Polly."

"Then she did not accept you ? "

"By George! no ;—anything but that. She is one of those women who, as I fancy, never take a man at the first offer. It isn't that they mean to shilly and shally and make a fuss, but there's a sort of majesty about them which instinctively declines to yield itself. Unconsciously they feel something like offence at the suggestion that a man should think enough of himself to ask for such a possession. They come to it, after a time."

" And she will come to it, after a time ? "

" I didn't mean to say that. I don't intend, however, to give it up." Ralph paused in his story, considering whether he would tell his brother what Mary had confessed to him as to her affection for some one else, but he resolved, at last, that he would say nothing of that. He had himself put less of confidence in that assertion than he did in her rebuke with reference to the other young woman to whom she chose to consider that he owed himself. It was his nature to think rather of what absolutely concerned himself, than of what related simply to her. " I shan't give her up. That's all I can say," he continued. " I'm not the sort of fellow to give things up readily." It did occur to Gregory at that moment that his brother had not shown much self-confidence on that question of giving up the property. " I'm pretty constant when I've set my mind on a thing. I'm not going to let any woman break my heart for me, but I shall stick to it."

He was not going to let any woman break his heart for him! Gregory, as he heard this, knew that his brother regarded him as a man whose heart was broken, and he could not help asking himself whether or not it was good for a man that he should be able to suffer as he suffered, because a woman was fair and yet not fair for him. That his own heart was broken,—broken after the fashion of which his brother was speaking,—he was driven to confess to himself. It was not that he should die, or that his existence would be one long continued hour of misery to him. He could eat and drink, and do his duty and enjoy his life. And yet his heart was broken. He could not piece it so that it should be fit for any other woman. He could not teach himself not to long for that one woman who would not love him. The romance of his life had formed itself there, and there it must remain. In all his solitary walks it was of her that he still thought. Of all the bright castles in the air which he still continued to build, she was ever the mistress. And yet he knew that she would never make him happy. He had absolutely resolved that he would not torment her by another request. But he gave himself no praise for his constancy, looking on himself as being somewhat weak in that he could not overcome his longing. When Ralph declared that he would not break his heart, but that, nevertheless, he would stick to the girl, Gregory envied him, not doubting of his success, and believing that it was to men of this calibre that success in love is generally given. " I hope with all my heart that you may win her," he said.

" I must run my chance like another. There's no ' Veni, vidi, vici,' about it, I can tell you ; nor is it likely that there should be with such a girl as Mary Bonner. Fill your glass, old fellow. We needn't sit mumchance because we're thinking of our loves."

" I had thought,——" began Gregory very slowly.

" What did you think ? "

" I had thought once that you were thinking of—Clarissa."

" What put that into your head ? "

" If you had I should never have said a word, nor fancied any wrong. Of course she'll marry some one. And I don't know why I should ever wish that it should not be you."

" But what made you think of it ? "

" Well; I did. It was just a word that Patience said in one of her letters."

" What sort of word ? " asked Ralph, with much interest.

" It was nothing, you know. I just misunderstood her. When one is always thinking of a thing everything turns itself that way. I got it into my head that she meant to hint to me that as you and Clary were fond of each other, I ought to forget it all. I made up my mind that I would ;—but it is so much easier to make up one's mind than to do it." There came a tear in each eye as he spoke, and he turned his face towards the fire that his brother might not see them. And there they remained hot and oppressive, because he would not raise his hand to rub them away.

" I wonder what it was she said," asked Ralph.

" Oh, nothing. Don't you know how a fellow has fancies ? "

" There wasn't anything in it," said Ralph.

" Oh ;—of course not."

" Patience might have imagined it," said Ralph. " That's just like such a sister as Patience."

" She's the best woman that ever lived," said Gregory.

" As good as gold," said Ralph. " I don't think, however, I shall very soon forgive Sir Thomas."

" I don't mind saying now that I am glad it is so," said Gregory ; " though as regards Clary that seems to be cruel. But I don't think I could have come much here had she become your wife."

" Nothing shall ever separate us, Greg."

" I hope not ;—but I don't know whether I could have done it. I almost think that I oughtn't to live where I should see her ; and I did fear it at one time."

" She'll come to the parsonage yet, old fellow, if you'll stick to her," said Ralph.

" Never," said Gregory. Then that conversation was over.

CHAPTER XLIII.

ONCE MORE.

AT the end of February Ralph declared his purpose of returning to the Moonbeam, for the rest of the hunting season. "I'm not going to be such an ass," he said to his brother, "as to keep two sets of horses going. I bought my uncle's because it seemed to suit just at the time; and there are the others at Horsball's, because I've not had time to settle down yet. I'll go over for March, and take a couple with me; and, at the end of it, I'll get rid of those I don't like. Then that'll be the end of the Moonbeam, as far as I am concerned." So he prepared to start, and on the evening before he went his brother declared that he would go as far as London with him. "That's all right," said Ralph, "but what's taking you up now?" The parson said that he wanted to get a few things, and to have his hair cut. He shouldn't stay above one night. Ralph asked no more questions, and the two brothers went up to London together.

We fear that Patience Underwood may not have been in all respects a discreet preserver of her sister's secrets. But then there is nothing more difficult of attainment than discretion in the preservation of such mysteries. To keep a friend's secret well the keeper of it should be firmly resolved to act upon it in no way,—not even for the advantage of the owner of it. If it be confided to you as a secret that your friend is about to make his maiden speech in the House, you should not even invite your acquaintances to be in their places, —not if secrecy be the first object. In all things the knowledge should be to you as though you had it not. Great love is hardly capable of such secrecy as this. In the fulness of her love Patience had allowed her father to learn the secret of poor Clary's heart; and in the fulness of her love she had endeavoured to make things smooth at Newton. She had not told the young clergyman that Clarissa had given to his brother that which she could not give to him; but, meaning to do a morsel of service to both of them, if that might be possible, she had said a word or two, with what effect the reader will have seen from the conversation given in the last chapter.

"She'll come to the parsonage yet," Ralph had said; and Gregory in one word had implied his assured conviction that any such coming was a thing not to be hoped for,—an event not even to be regarded as possible. Nevertheless, he made up his mind that he would go up to London,—to have his hair cut. In so making up his mind he did not for a moment believe that it could be of any use to him. He was not quite sure that when in London he would go to Popham Villa. He was quite sure that if he did go to Popham Villa he would make no further offer to Clarissa. He knew that his journey was foolish, simply the result of an uneasy, restless spirit,—that it would be better for him to remain in his parish and move about among the old women and bed-ridden men; but still he went. He would dine at his club, he said, and perhaps he might go down to Fulham on the following morning. And so the brothers parted. Ralph, as a man of property, with many weighty matters on hand, had, of course, much to do. He desired to inspect some agricultural implements, and a new carriage,—he had ever so many things to say to Carey, the lawyer, and wanted to order new harnesses for the horses. So he went to his club, and played whist all the afternoon.

Gregory, as soon as he had secured a bed at a quiet inn, walked off to Southampton Buildings. From the direct manner in which this was done, it might have been argued that he had come up to London with the purpose of seeing Sir Thomas; but it was not so. He turned his steps towards the place where Clary's father was generally to be found, because he knew not what else to do. As he went he told himself that he might as well leave it alone;—but still he went. Stemm at once told him, with a candour that was almost marvellous, that Sir Thomas was out of town. The hearing of the petition was going on at Percycross, and Sir Thomas was there, as a matter of course. Stemm seemed to think it rather odd that an educated man, such as was the Rev. Gregory Newton, should have been unaware that the petition against the late election at Percycross was being carried on at this moment. "We've got Serjeant Burnaby, and little Mr. Joram down, to make a fight of it," said Mr. Stemm; "but, as far as I can learn, they might just as well have remained up in town. It's only sending good money after bad." The young parson hardly expressed that interest in the matter which Stemm had expected, but turned away, thinking whether he had not better have his hair cut at once, and then go home.

But he did go to Popham Villa on the same afternoon, and,—such was his fortune,—he found Clarissa alone. Since her father had seen her in bed, and spoken to her of what he had called the folly of her love, she had not again given herself up to the life of a sick-room. She dressed herself and came down to breakfast of a morning, and then would sit with a needle in her hand till she took her book, and then with a book till she took her needle. She tried to work, and tried to read, and perhaps she did accomplish a little of each. And then, when Patience would tell her that exercise was necessary, she would put on her hat and creep out among the paths. She did make some kind of effort to get over the evil that had come upon her; but still no one could watch her and not know that she was a wounded deer. "Miss Clarissa is at home," said the servant, who well knew that the young clergyman was one of the rejected suitors. There had been hardly a secret in the house in reference to Gregory Newton's love. The two other young ladies, the girl said, had gone to London, but would be home to dinner. Then, with a beating heart, Gregory was ushered into the drawing-room. Clarissa was sitting near the window, with a novel in her lap, having placed herself there with the view of getting what was left of the light of the early spring evening; but she had not read a word for the last quarter of an hour. She was thinking of that word scoundrel, with which her father had spoken of the man she loved. Could it be that he was in truth so bad as that? And, if it were true, would she not take him, scoundrel as he was, if he would come to her? He might be a——scoundrel in that one thing, on that one occasion, and yet be good to her. He might repent his scoundrelism, and she certainly would forgive it. Of one thing she was quite sure;—he had not looked like a scoundrel when he had given her that assurance on the lawn! And so she thought of young men in general. It was very easy to call a young man a scoundrel, and yet to forgive him all his iniquities when it suited to do so. Young men might get in debt, and gamble, and make love wherever they pleased, and all at once,—and yet be forgiven. All these things were very bad. It might be just to call a man a scoundrel because he could not pay his debts, or because he made bets about horses. Young men did a great many things which would be horrid indeed were a girl to do them. Then one papa would call such a man a scoundrel, because he was not wanted to come to the house; while another papa would make him welcome, and give him the best of everything. Ralph Newton might be a scoundrel; but if so,—as Clarissa thought,—there were a great many good-looking scoundrels about in the world, as to whom their scoundrelism did very little to injure them in the esteem of all their friends. It was thus that Clarissa was thinking over her own affairs when Gregory Newton was shown into the room.

The greeting on both sides was at first formal and almost cold. Clary had given a little start of surprise, and had then subsided into a most demure mode of answering questions. Yes; papa was at Percycross. She did not know when he was expected back. Mary and Patience were in London. Yes;—she was at home all alone. No; she had not seen Ralph since his uncle's death. The question which elicited this answer had been asked without any design, and Clary endeavoured to make her reply without emotion. If she displayed any, Gregory, who had his own affairs upon his mind, did not see it. No;—they had not seen the other Mr. Newton as he passed through town. They had all understood that he had been very much disturbed by his father's horrible accident and death. Then Gregory paused in his questions, and Clarissa expressed a hope that there might be no more hunting in the world.

It was very hard work, this conversation, and Gregory was beginning to think that he had done no good by coming, when on a sudden he struck a chord from whence came a sound of music. "Ralph and I have been living together at the Priory," he said.

"Oh;—indeed; yes;—I think I heard Patience say that you were at the Priory."

"I suppose I shall not be telling any secret to you in talking about him and your cousin Mary?"

Clarissa felt that she was blushing up to her brow, but she made a great effort to compose herself. "Oh, no," she said, "we all know of it."

"I hope he may be successful," said Gregory.

"I do not know. I cannot tell."

"I never knew a man more thoroughly in love than he is."

"I don't believe it," said Clarissa.

"Not believe it! Indeed you may, Clary. I have never seen her, but from what he says of her I suppose her to be most beautiful."

"She is,—very beautiful." This was said with a strong emphasis.

"And why should you not believe it?"

"It will not be of the slightest use, Mr. Newton; and you may tell him so. Though I suppose it is impossible to make a man believe that."

"Are we both so unfortunate?" he asked.

The poor girl with her wounded love, and every feeling sore within her, had not intended to say anything that should be cruel or injurious to Gregory himself, and it was not till the words were out of her mouth that she herself perceived their effect. "Oh, Mr. Newton, I was only thinking of him," she said, innocently. "I only meant that Ralph is one of those who always think they are to have everything they want."

"I am not one of those, Clarissa. And yet I am one who seem never to be tired of asking for that which is not to be given to me. I said to myself when last I went from here that I would never ask again;—that I would never trouble you any more." She was sitting with the book in her hand, looking out into the gloom, and now she made no attempt to answer him. "And yet you see here I am," he continued. She was still silent, and her head was still turned away from him; but he could see that tears were streaming down her cheeks. "I have not the power not to come to you while yet there is a chance," he said. "I can live and work without you, but I can have no life of my own. When I first saw you I made a picture to myself of what my life might be, and I cannot get that moved from before my eyes. I am sorry, however, that my coming should make you weep."

"Oh, Mr. Newton, I am so wretched!" she said, turning round sharply upon him. For a moment she had thought that she would tell him everything, and then she checked herself, and remembered how ill-placed such a confidence would be.

"What should make you wretched, dearest?"

"I do not know. I cannot tell. I sometimes think the world is bad altogether, and that I had better die. People are so cruel and so hard, and things are so wrong. But you may tell your brother that he need not think of my cousin, Mary. Nothing ever would move her. H——sh——. Here they are. Do not say that I was crying."

He was introduced to the beauty, and as the lights came, Clarissa escaped. Yes;—she was indeed most lovely; but as he looked on her, Gregory felt that he agreed with Clarissa that nothing on earth would move her. He remained there for another half-hour; but Clarissa did not return, and then he went back to London.

CHAPTER XLIV.

THE PETITION.

THE time for hearing the petition at Percycross had at length come, and the judge had gone down to that ancient borough. The day fixed was Monday, the 27th, and Parliament had then been sitting for three weeks. Mr. Griffenbottom had been as constant in his place as though there had been no sword hanging over his head; but Sir Thomas had not as yet even taken the oaths. He had made up his mind that he would not even enter the house while this bar against him as a legislator existed, and he had not as yet even been seen in the lobby. His daughters, his colleague, Mr. Trigger, and Stemm had all expostulated with him on the subject, assuring him that he should treat the petition with the greatest contempt, at any rate till it should have proved itself by its success to be a matter not contemptible; but to these counsellors he gave no ear, and when he went down to give his evidence before the judge at Percycross his seat had as yet availed him nothing.

Mr. Griffenbottom had declared that he would not pay a shilling towards the expense of the petition, maintaining that his own seat was safe, and that any peril incurred had been so incurred simply on behalf of Sir Thomas. Nothing, according to Mr. Griffenbottom's views, could be more unjust than to expect that he should take any part in the matter. Trigger, too, had endeavoured to impress this

upon Sir Thomas more than once or twice.   But this had been all
in vain; and Sir Thomas, acting under the advice of his own
attorney, had at last compelled Mr. Griffenbottom to take his share
in the matter.   Mr. Griffenbottom did not scruple to say that he was
very ill-used, and to hint that any unfair practices which might
possibly have prevailed during the last election at Percycross, had all
been adopted on behalf of Sir Thomas, and in conformity with Sir
Thomas's views.   It will, therefore, be understood that the two
members did not go down to the borough in the best humour with
each other.   Mr. Trigger still nominally acted for both; but it had
been almost avowed that Sir Thomas was to be treated as a Jonah, if
by such treatment any salvation might be had for the ship of which
Griffenbottom was to be regarded as the captain.

Mr. Westmacott was also in Percycross,—and so was Moggs, re-
instated in his old room at the Cordwainers' Arms.   Moggs had not
been summoned, nor was his presence there required for any purpose
immediately connected with the inquiry to be made; but Purity and
the Rights of Labour may always be advocated; and when better
than at a moment in which the impurity of a borough is about to be
made the subject of public condemnation?   And Moggs, moreover,
had now rankling in his bosom a second cause of enmity against the
Tories of the borough.   Since the election he had learned that his
rival, Ralph Newton, was in some way connected with the sitting
member, Sir Thomas, and he laid upon Sir Thomas's back the weight
of his full displeasure in reference to the proposed marriage with
Polly Neefit.   He had heard that Polly had raised some difficulty,—
had, indeed, rejected her aristocratic suitor, and was therefore not
without hope; but he had been positively assured by Neefit himself
that the match would be made, and was consequently armed with a
double purpose in his desire to drive Sir Thomas ignominiously out
of Percycross.

Sir Thomas had had more than one interview with Serjeant Burnaby
and little Mr. Joram, than whom two more astute barristers in such
matters were not to be found at that time practising,—though
perhaps at that time the astuteness of the Serjeant was on the wane;
while that of Jacky Joram, as he was familiarly called, was daily
rising in repute.   Sir Thomas himself, barrister and senior to these
two gentlemen, had endeavoured to hold his own with them, and to
impress on them the conviction that he had nothing to conceal; that
he had personally endeavoured, as best he knew how, to avoid
corruption, and that if there had been corruption on the part of his
own agents, he was himself ready to be a party in proclaiming it.
But he found himself to be absolutely ignored and put out of court
by his own counsel.   They were gentlemen with whom professionally
he had had no intercourse, as he had practised at the Chancery, and

they at the Common Law Bar. But he had been Solicitor-General, and was a bencher of his Inn, whereas Serjeant Burnaby was only a Serjeant, and Jacky Joram still wore a stuff gown. Nevertheless, he found himself to be "nowhere" in discussing with them the circumstances of the election. Even Joram, whom he seemed to remember having seen only the other day as an ugly shame-faced boy about the courts, treated him, not exactly with indignity, but with patronising good-nature, listening with an air of half-attention to what he said, and then not taking the slightest heed of a word of it. Who does not know this transparent pretence of courtesies, which of all discourtesies is the most offensive? "Ah, just so, Sir Thomas; just so. And now, Mr. Trigger, I suppose Mr. Puffer's account hasn't yet been settled." Any word from Mr. Trigger was of infinitely greater value with Mr. Joram than all Sir Thomas's pro- testations. Sir Thomas could not keep himself from remembering that Jacky Joram's father was a cheesemonger at Gloucester, who had married the widow of a Jew with a little money. Twenty times Sir Thomas made up his mind to retire from the business altogether; but he always found himself unable to do so. When he mentioned the idea, Griffenbottom flung up his hands in dismay at such treachery on the part of an ally,—such treachery and such cowardice! What! —had not he, Sir Thomas, forced him, Griffenbottom, into all this ruinous expenditure? And now to talk of throwing up the sponge! It was in vain that Sir Thomas explained that he had forced nobody into it. It was manifestly the case that he had refused to go on with it by himself, and on this Mr. Griffenbottom and Mr. Trigger insisted so often and with so much strength that Sir Thomas felt him- self compelled to stand to his guns, bad as he believed those guns to be.

If Sir Thomas meant to retreat, why had he not retreated when a proposition to that effect was made to him at his own chambers? Of all the weak, vacillating, ill-conditioned men that Mr. Griffen- bottom had ever been concerned with, Sir Thomas Underwood was the weakest, most vacillating, and most ill-conditioned. To have to sit in the same boat with such a man was the greatest misfortune that had ever befallen Mr. Griffenbottom in public life. Mr. Griffenbottom did not exactly say these hard things in the hearing of Sir Thomas, but he so said them that they became the common property of the Jorams, Triggers, Spiveycombs, and Spicers; and were repeated piecemeal to the unhappy second member.

He had secured for himself a separate sitting-room at the "Percy Standard," thinking that thus he would have the advantage of being alone; but every one connected with his party came in and out of his room as though it had been specially selected as a chamber for public purposes. Even Griffenbottom came into it to have interviews there with Trigger, although at the moment Griffenbottom and Sir Thomas were not considered to be on speaking terms. Griffenbottom in these matters seemed to have the hide of a rhinoceros. He had chosen to quarrel with Sir Thomas. He had declared that he would not speak to a colleague whose Parliamentary ideas and habits were so repulsive to him. He had said quite aloud, that Trigger had never made a greater mistake in his life than in bringing Sir Thomas to the borough, and that, let the petition go as it would, Sir Thomas should never be returned for the borough again. He had spoken all these things, almost in the hearing of Sir Thomas. And yet he would come to Sir Thomas's private room, and sit there half the morning with a cigar in his mouth! Mr. Pile would come in, and make most unpleasant speeches. Mr. Spicer called continually, with his own ideas about the borough. The thing could be still saved if enough money were spent. If Mr. Givantake were properly handled, and Mr. O'Blather duly provided for, the two witnesses upon whom the thing really hung would not be found in Percycross when called upon to-morrow. That was Mr. Spicer's idea; and he was very eager to communicate it to Serjeant Burnaby. Trigger, in his energy, told Mr. Spicer to go and be ——. All this occurred in Sir Thomas's private room. And then Mr. Pabsby was there constantly, till he at last was turned out by Trigger. In his agony, Sir Thomas asked for another sitting-room; but was informed that the house was full. The room intended for the two members was occupied by Griffenbottom; but nobody ever suggested that the party might meet there when Sir Thomas's vain request was made for further accommodation. Griffenbottom went on with his cigar, and Mr. Pile sat picking his teeth before the fire, and making unpleasant little speeches.

The judge, who had hurried into Percycross from another town, and who opened the commission on the Monday evening, did not really begin his work till the Tuesday morning. Jacky Joram had declared that the inquiry would last three days, he having pledged himself to be at another town early on the following Friday. Serjeant Burnaby, whose future services were not in such immediate demand, was of opinion that they would not get out of Percycross till Saturday night. Judge Crumbie, who was to try the case, and who had been trying similar cases ever since Christmas, was not due at his next town till the Monday; but it was understood by everybody that he intended if possible to spend his Saturday and Sunday in the bosom of his family. Trigger, however, had magnificent ideas. "I believe we shall carry them into the middle of next week," he said, "if they choose to go on with it." Trigger thoroughly enjoyed the petition; and even Griffenbottom, who was no longer troubled by gout, and was not now obliged to walk about the borough, did not seem to dislike it. But to poor Sir Thomas it was indeed a purgatory.

The sitting members were of course accused, both as regarded themselves and their agents, of every crime known in electioneering tactics. Votes had been personated. Votes had been bought. Votes had been obtained by undue influence on the part of masters and landlords, and there had been treating of the most pernicious and corrupt description. As to the personating of votes, that according to Mr. Trigger, had been merely introduced as a pleasant commencing fiction common in Parliamentary petitions. There had been nothing of the kind, and nobody supposed that there had, and it did not signify. Of undue influence,—what purists choose to call undue influence,—there had of course been plenty. It was not likely that masters paying thousands a year in wages were going to let these men vote against themselves. But this influence was so much a matter of course that it could not be proved to the injury of the sitting members. Such at least was Mr. Trigger's opinion. Mr. Spicer might have been a little imprudent with his men; but no case could be brought up in which a man had been injured. Undue influence at Percycross was—" gammon." So said Mr. Trigger, and Jacky Joram agreed with Mr. Trigger. Serjeant Burnaby rubbed his hands, and would give no opinion till he had heard the evidence. That votes had been bought during the day of the election there was no doubt on earth. On this matter great secrecy prevailed, and Sir Thomas could not get a word spoken in his own hearing. It was admitted, however, that votes had been bought. There were a dozen men, perhaps more than a dozen, who would prove that one Glump had paid them ten shillings a piece between one and two on the day of the election. There was a general belief that perhaps over a hundred had been bought at that rate. But Trigger was ready to swear that he did not know whence Glump had got the money, and Glump himself was,—nobody knew where Glump was, but strange whispers respecting Glump were floating about the borough. Trigger was disposed to believe that they, on their side, could prove that Glump had really been employed by Westmacott's people to vitiate the election. He was quite sure that nothing could connect Glump with him as an agent on behalf of Griffenbottom and Underwood. So Mr. Trigger asserted with the greatest confidence; but what was in the bottom of Mr. Trigger's mind on this subject no one pretended to know. As for Glump himself he was a man who would certainly take payment from anybody for any dirty work. It was the general impression through the borough that Glump had on this occasion been hired by Trigger, and Trigger certainly enjoyed the prestige which was thus conferred upon him.

As to the treating,—there could be no doubt about that. There had been treating. The idea of conducting an election at Percycross without beer seemed to be absurd to every male and female Percycrossian. Of course the publicans would open their taps and then send in their bills for beer to the electioneering agents. There was a prevailing feeling that any interference with so ancient a practice was not only un-English, but unjust also ;—that it was beyond the power of Parliament to enforce any law so abominable and unnatural. Trigger was of opinion that though there had been a great deal of beer, no attempt would be made to prove that votes had been influenced by treating. There had been beer on both sides, and Trigger hoped sincerely that there might always be beer on both sides as long as Percycross was a borough.

Sir Thomas found that his chance of success was now spoken of in a tone very different from that which had been used when the matter was discussed in his own chamber. He had been then told that it was hardly possible that he should keep his seat ;—and he had in fact been asked to resign it. Though sick enough of Percycross, this he would not do in the manner then proposed to him. Now he was encouraged in the fight ;—but the encouragement was of a nature which gave him no hope, which robbed him even of the wish to have a hope. It was all dirt from beginning to end. Whatever might be the verdict of the judge,—from the judge the verdict was now to come,—he should still believe that nothing short of absolute disfranchisement would meet the merits of the case.

The accusation with regard to the personation of votes was abandoned,—Serjeant Burnaby expressing the most extreme disgust that any such charge should have been made without foundation,—although he himself at the borough which he had last left had brought forward the same charge on behalf of his then clients, and had abandoned it in the same way. Then the whole of the remaining hours of the Tuesday and half the Wednesday were passed in showing that Messrs. Spicer, Spiveycomb, and Roodiland had forced their own men to vote blue. Mr. Spicer had dismissed one man and Mr. Spiveycomb two men ; but both these gentlemen swore that the men dismissed were not worth their salt, and had been sent adrift upon the world by no means on account of their politics. True : they had all voted for Moggs ; but then they had done that simply to spite their late master. On the middle of Wednesday, when the matter of intimidation had been completed,—the result still lying in the bosom of Baron Crumbie,—Mr. Trigger thought that things were looking up. That was the report which he brought to Mr. Griffenbottom, who was smoking his midday cigar in Sir Thomas's armchair, while Sir Thomas was endeavouring to master the first book of Lord Verulam's later treatise " De dignitate scientiarum," seated in a cane-bottomed chair in a very small bed-room up-stairs.

By consent the question of treating came next. Heaven and earth were being moved to find Glump. When the proposition was made that the treating should come before the bribery Trigger stated in court that he was himself doing his very best to find the man. There might yet be a hope, though, alas, the hope was becoming slighter every hour. His own idea was that Glump had been sent away to Holland by,—well, he did not care to name the parties by whom he believed that Glump had been expatriated. However, there might be a chance. The counsel on the other side remarked that there might, indeed, be a chance. Baron Crumbie expressed a hope that Mr. Glump might make his appearance,—for the sake of the borough, which might otherwise fare badly; and then the great beer question was discussed for two entire days.

There was no doubt about the beer. Trigger, who was examined after some half-score of publicans, said openly that thirsty Conservative souls had been allowed to slake their drought at the joint expense of the Conservative party in the borough,—as thirsty Liberal souls had been encouraged to do on the other side. When reminded that any malpractice in that direction on the part of a beaten candidate could not affect the status of the elected members, he replied that all the beer consumed in Percycross during the election had not, to the best of his belief, affected a vote. The Percycrossians were not men to vote this way or that because of beer! He would not believe it even in regard to a Liberal Percycrossian. It might be so in other boroughs, but of other boroughs he knew absolutely nothing. Who paid for the beer? Mr. Trigger at once acknowledged that it was paid for out of the general funds provided for the election. Who provided those funds? There was not a small amount of fencing on this point, during the course of which Mr. Joram snapped very sharply and very frequently at the counsel on the other side,—hoping thereby somewhat to change the issue. But at last there came out these two facts, that there was a general fund, to which all Conservatives might subscribe, and that the only known subscribers to this fund were Mr. Griffenbottom, Sir Thomas Underwood, and old Mr. Pile, who had given a £10 note,—apparently with the view of proving that there was a fund. It was agreed on all hands that treating had been substantiated; but it was remarked by some that Baron Crumbie had not been hard upon treating in other boroughs. After all, the result would depend upon what the Baron thought about Mr. Glump. It might be that he would recommend further inquiry, under a special commission, into the practices of the borough, because of the Glump iniquities, and that he should, nevertheless, leave the seats to the sitting members. That seemed to be Mr. Trigger's belief on the evening of the Thursday, as he took his brandy and water in Sir Thomas's private sitting-room.

There is nothing in the world so brisk as the ways and manners of lawyers when in any great case they come to that portion of it which they know to be the real bone of the limb and kernel of the nut. The doctor is very brisk when after a dozen moderately dyspeptic patients he comes on some unfortunate gentleman whose gastric apparatus is gone altogether. The parson is very brisk when he reaches the minatory clause in his sermon. The minister is very brisk when he asks the House for a vote, telling his hoped-for followers that this special point is absolutely essential to his government. Unless he can carry this, he and all those hanging on to him must vacate their places. The horse-dealer is very brisk when, after four or five indifferent lots, he bids his man bring out from the stable the last thorough-bred that he bought, and the very best that he ever put his eye on. But the briskness of none of these is equal to the briskness of the barrister who has just got into his hands for cross-examination him whom we may call the centre witness of a great case. He plumes himself like a bull-finch going to sing. He spreads himself like a peacock on a lawn. He perks himself like a sparrow on a paling. He crows amidst his attorneys and all the satellites of the court like a cock among his hens. He puts his hands this way and that, settling even the sunbeams as they enter, lest a moat should disturb his intellect or dull the edge of his subtlety. There is a modesty in his eye, a quiescence in his lips, a repose in his limbs, under which lie half-concealed,—not at all concealed from those who have often watched him at his work,—the glance, the tone, the spring, which are to tear that unfortunate witness into pieces, without infringing any one of those conventional rules which have been laid down for the guidance of successful well-mannered barristers.

Serjeant Burnaby, though astute, was not specially brisk by nature; but on this Friday morning Mr. Joram was very brisk indeed. There was a certain Mr. Cavity, who had acted as agent for Westmacott, and who,—if anybody on the Westmacott side had been so guilty,—had been guilty in the matter of Glump's absence. Perhaps we should not do justice to Mr. Joram's acuteness were we to imagine him as believing that Glump was absent under other influence than that used on behalf of the conservative side; but there were subsidiary points on which Mr. Cavity might be made to tell tales. Of course there had been extensive bribery for years past in Percycross on the liberal as well as on the conservative side, and Mr. Joram thought that he could make Mr. Cavity tell a tale. And then, too, he could be very brisk in that affair of Glump. He was pretty nearly sure that Mr. Glump could not be connected by evidence with either of the sitting members or with any of their agents. He would prove that Glump was neutral ground, and that as such his services could not be traced to his friend, Mr. Trigger. Mr. Joram on this occasion was very brisk indeed.

A score of men were brought up, ignorant, half-dumb, heavy-browed men, all dressed in the amphibious garb of out-o'-door town labourers,—of whom there exists a class of hybrids between the rural labourer and the artizan,—each one of whom acknowledged that after noon on the election day he received ten shillings, with instructions to vote for Griffenbottom and Underwood. And they did vote for Griffenbottom and Underwood. At all elections in Percycross they had, as they now openly acknowledged, waited till about the same hour on the day of election, and then somebody had bought their votes for somebody. On this occasion the purchase had been made by Mr. Glump. There was a small empty house up a little alley in the town, to which there was a back door opening on a vacant space in the town known as Grinder's Green. They entered this house by one door, leaving it by the other, and as they passed through, Glump gave to each man half a sovereign with instructions, entering their names in a small book;—and then they went in a body and voted for Griffenbottom and Underwood. Each of the twenty knew nearly all the other twenty, but none of them knew any other men who had been paid by Glump. Of course none of them had the slightest knowledge of Glump's present abode. It was proved that at the last election Glump had acted for the Liberals; but it was also proved that at the election before he had been active in bribing for the Conservatives. Very many things were proved,—if a thing be proved when supported by testimony on oath. Trigger proved that twenty votes alone could have been of no service, and would not certainly have been purchased in a manner so detrimental. According to Trigger's views it was as clear as daylight that Glump had not been paid by them. When asked whether he would cause Mr. Glump to be repaid that sum of ten pounds, should Mr. Glump send in any bill to that effect, he simply stated that Mr. Glump would certainly send no such bill to him. He was then asked whether it might not be possible that the money should be repaid by Messrs. Griffenbottom and Underwood through his hands, reaching Glump again by means of a further middleman. Mr. Trigger acknowledged that were such a claim made upon him by any known agent of his party, he would endeavour to pass the ten pounds through the accounts, as he thought that there should be a certain feeling of honour in these things; but he did not for a moment think that any one acting with him would have dealings with Glump. On the Saturday morning, when the case was still going on, to the great detriment of Baron Crumbie's domestic happiness, Glump had not yet been caught. It seemed that the man had no wife, no relative, no friend. The woman at whose house he lodged declared that he often went and came after this fashion. The respect with which Glump's name was mentioned, as his persistency in disobeying the law and his capability for intrigue were thus proved, was so great, that it was a pity he could not have been there to enjoy it. For the hour he was a great man in Percycross,—and the greater because Baron Crumbie did not cease to threaten him with terrible penalties.

Much other bribery was alleged, but none other was distinctly brought home to the agents of the sitting members. As to bringing bribery home to Mr. Griffenbottom himself;—that appeared to be out of the question. Nobody seemed even to wish to do that. The judge, as it appeared, did not contemplate any result so grave and terrible as that. There was a band of freemen of whom it was proved that they had all been treated with most excessive liberality by the corporation of the town; and it was proved, also, that a majority of the corporation were supporters of Mr. Griffenbottom. A large number of votes had been so secured. Such, at least, was the charge made by the petitioners. But this allegation Jacky Joram laughed to scorn. The corporation, of course, used the charities and privileges of the town as they thought right; and the men voted,—as they thought right. The only cases of bribery absolutely proved were those manipulated by Glump, and nothing had been adduced clearly connecting Glump and the Griffenbottomites. Mr. Trigger was in ecstasies; but Mr. Joram somewhat repressed him by referring to these oracular words which had fallen from the Baron in respect to the corporation. " A corporation may be guilty as well as an individual," the Baron had said. Jacky Joram had been very eager in assenting to the Baron, but in asserting at the same time that the bribery must be proved. "It won't be assumed, my lord, that a corporation has bribed because it has political sympathies." "It should have none," said the Baron. "Human nature is human nature, my lord,—even in corporations," said Jacky Joram. This took place just before luncheon,—which was made a solemn meal on all sides, as the judge had declared his intention of sitting till midnight, if necessary.

Immediately after the solemn meal Mr. Griffenbottom was examined. It had been the declared purpose of the other side to turn Mr. Griffenbottom inside out. Mr. Griffenbottom and his conduct had on various former occasions been the subject of parliamentary petitions under the old form; but on such occasions the chief delinquent himself was never examined. Now Mr. Griffenbottom would be made to tell all that he knew, not only of his present, but of his past, iniquities. And yet Mr. Griffenbottom told very little; and it certainly did seem to the bystanders, that even the opposing counsel, even the judge on the bench, abstained from their prey because he was a member of Parliament. It was notorious to all the world that Griffenbottom had debased the borough; had so used its venal tendencies as to make that systematic which had before been too frequent indeed, but yet not systematized ; that he had trained the rising generation of Percycross politicians to believe in political corruption ;—and yet he escaped that utter turning inside out of which men had spoken.

The borough had cost him a great deal of money certainly ; but as far as he knew the money had been spent legally. It had at least always been his intention before an election was commenced that nothing illegal should be done. He had no doubt always afterwards paid sums of money the use of which he did not quite understand, and as to some of which he could not but fear that it had been doubtfully applied. The final accounts as to the last election had not reached him, but he did not expect to be charged with improper expenses. There no doubt would be something for beer, but that was unavoidable. As to Mr. Glump he knew literally nothing of the man,—nor had he wanted any such man's assistance. Twenty votes indeed ! Let them look at his place upon the poll. There had been a time in the day when twenty votes this way or that might be necessary to Sir Thomas. He had been told that it was so. On the day of the election his own position on the poll had been so certain to him, that he should not have cared,—that is, for himself,— had he heard that Glump was buying votes against him. He considered it to be quite out of the question that Glump should have bought votes for him,—with any purpose of serving him. And so Mr. Griffenbottom escaped from the adverse counsel and from the judge.

There was very little in the examination of Sir Thomas Underwood to interest any one. No one really suspected him of corrupt practices. In all such cases the singular part of the matter is that everybody, those who are concerned and those who are not concerned, really know the whole truth which is to be investigated ; and yet, that which everybody knows cannot be substantiated. There were not five men in court who were not certain that Griffenbottom was corrupt, and that Sir Thomas was not ; that the borough was rotten as a six-months-old egg ; that Glump had acted under one of Trigger's aides-de-camp ; that intimidation was the law of the borough ; and that beer was used so that men drunk might not fear that which sober they had not the courage to encounter. All this was known to everybody ; and yet, up to the last, it was thought by many in Percycross that corruption, acknowledged, transparent, egregious corruption, would prevail even in the presence of a judge. Mr. Trigger believed it to the last.

But it was not so thought by the Jacky Jorams or by the Serjeant Burnabys. They made their final speeches,—the leading lawyer on each side, but they knew well what was coming. At half-past seven, for to so late an hour had the work been continued, the judge retired to get a cup of tea, and returned at eight to give his award. It was as follows :—

As to the personation of votes, there should have been no allegation made. In regard to the charge of intimidation it appeared that the system prevailed to such an extent as to make it clear to him that Percycross was unfit to return representatives to Parliament. In the matter of treating he was not quite prepared to say that had no other charge been made he should have declared this election void, but of that also there had been sufficient to make him feel it to be his duty to recommend to the Speaker of the House of Commons that further inquiry should be made as to the practices of the borough. And as to direct bribery, though he was not prepared to say that he could connect the agents of the members with what had been done, —and certainly he could not connect either of the two members themselves,—still, quite enough had been proved to make it imperative upon him to declare the election void. This he should do in his report to the Speaker, and should also advise that a commission be held with the view of ascertaining whether the privilege of returning members of Parliament should remain with the borough. With Griffenbottom he dealt as tenderly as he did with Sir Thomas, sending them both forth to the world, unseated indeed, but as innocent, injured men.

There was a night train up to London at 10 p.m., by which on that evening Sir Thomas Underwood travelled, shaking off from his feet as he entered the carriage the dust of that most iniquitous borough.

CHAPTER XLV.

" NEVER GIVE A THING UP."

MR. NEEFIT'S conduct during this period of disappointment was not exactly what it should have been, either in the bosom of his family or among his dependents in Conduit Street. Herr Bawwah, over a pot of beer in the public-house opposite, suggested to Mr. Waddle that "the governor might be ——," in a manner that affected Mr. Waddle greatly. It was an eloquent and energetic expression of opinion,—almost an expression of a settled purpose as coming from the German as it did come ; and Waddle was bound to admit that cause had been given. " Fritz," said Waddle pathetically, " don't think about it. You can't better the wages." Herr Bawwah looked up from his pot of beer and muttered a German oath. He had been told that he was beastly, skulking, pig-headed, obstinate, drunken, with some other perhaps stronger epithets which may be omitted,— and he had been told that he was a German. In that had lain the venom. There was the word that rankled. He had another pot of beer, and though it was then only twelve o'clock on a Monday morning Herr Bawwah swore that he was going to make a day of it, and that old Neefit might cut out the stuff for himself if he pleased. As they were now at the end of March, which is not a busy time of the year in Mr. Neefit's trade, the great artist's defalcation was of less immediate importance ; but, as Waddle knew, the German was given both to beer and obstinacy when aroused to wrath ; and what would become of the firm should the obstinacy continue ?

" Where's that pig-headed German brute ? " asked Mr. Neefit, when Mr. Waddle returned to the establishment. Mr. Waddle made no reply ; and when Neefit repeated the question with a free use of the epithets previously omitted by us, Waddle still was dumb, leaning over his ledger as though in that there were matters so great as to absorb his powers of hearing. " The two of you may go and be —— together ! " said Mr. Neefit. If any order requiring immediate obedience were contained in this, Mr. Waddle disobeyed that order. He still bent himself over the ledger, and was dumb. Waddle had been trusted with his master's private view in the matter of the Newton marriage, and felt that on this account he owed a debt of forbearance to the unhappy father.

The breeches-maker was in truth very unhappy. He had accused his German assistant of obstinacy, but the German could hardly have been more obstinate than his master. Mr. Neefit had set his heart upon making his daughter Mrs. Newton, and had persisted in declaring that the marriage should be made to take place. The young man had once given him a promise, and should be compelled to keep the promise so given. And in these days Mr. Neefit seemed to have lost that discretion for which his friends had once given him credit. On the occasion of his visit to the Moonbeam early in the hunting season he had spoken out very freely among the sportsmen there assembled; and from that time all reticence respecting his daughter seemed to have been abandoned. He had paid the debts of this young man, who was now lord of wide domains, when the young man hadn't " a red copper in his pocket,"—so did Mr. Neefit explain the matter to his friends,—and he didn't intend that the young man should be off his bargain. " No ;—he wasn't going to put up with that ;—not if he knew it." All this he declared freely to his general acquaintance. He was very eloquent on the subject in a personal interview which he had with Mr. Moggs senior, in consequence of a visit made to Hendon by Mr. Moggs junior, during which he feared that Polly had shown some tendency towards yielding to the young politician. Mr. Moggs senior might take this for granted ;—that if Moggs junior made himself master of Polly, it would be of Polly pure and simple, of Polly without a shilling of dowry. " He'll have to take her in her smock." That was the phrase in which Mr. Neefit was pleased to express his resolution. To all of which Mr. Moggs senior answered never a word. It was on returning from Mr. Moggs's establishment in Bond Street to his own in Conduit Street that Mr. Neefit made himself so very unpleasant to the unfortunate German. When Ontario put on his best clothes, and took himself out to Hendon on the previous Sunday, he did not probably calculate that, as one consequence of that visit, the Herr Bawwah would pass a whole week of intoxication in the little back parlour of the public-house near St. George's Church.

It may be imagined how very unpleasant all this must have been to Miss Neefit herself. Poor Polly indeed suffered many things ; but she bore them with an admirable and a persistent courage. Indeed, she possessed a courage which greatly mitigated her sufferings. Let her father be as indiscreet as he might, he could not greatly lower her, as long as she herself was prudent. It was thus that Polly argued with herself. She knew her own value, and was not afraid that she should ever lack a lover when she wanted to find a husband. Of course it was not a nice thing to be thrown at a man's head, as her father was constantly throwing her at the head of young Newton ; but such a man as she would give herself to at last would understand all that. Ontario Moggs, could she ever bring herself to accept Ontario, would not be less devoted to her because of her father's ill-arranged ambition. Polly could be obstinate too, but with her obstinacy there was combined a fund of feminine strength which, as we think, quite justified the devotion of Ontario Moggs.

Amidst all these troubles Mrs. Neefit also had a bad time of it ; so bad a time that she was extremely anxious that Ontario should at once carry off the prize ;—Ontario, or the gasfitter, or almost anybody. Neefit was taking to drink in the midst of all this confusion, and was making himself uncommonly unpleasant in the bosom of his family. On the Sunday,—the Sunday before the Monday on which the Herr decided that his wisest course of action would be to abstain from work and make a beast of himself, in order that he might spite his master,—Mr. Neefit had dined at one o'clock, and had insisted on his gin-and-water and pipe immediately after his dinner. Now Mr. Neefit, when he took too much, did not fall into the extreme sins which disgraced his foreman. He simply became very cross till he fell asleep, very heavy while sleeping, and more cross than ever when again awake. While he was asleep on this Sunday afternoon Ontario Moggs came down to Hendon dressed in his Sunday best. Mrs. Neefit whispered a word to him before he was left alone with Polly. " You be round with her, and run your chance about the money." " Mrs. Neefit," said Ontario, laying his hand upon his heart, " all the bullion in the Bank of England don't make a feather's weight in the balance." " You never was mercenary, Mr. Ontario," said the lady. " My sweetheart is to me more than a coined hemisphere," said Ontario. The expression may have been absurd, but the feeling was there.

Polly was not at all coy of her presence,—was not so, though she had been specially ordered by her father not to have anything to say to that long-legged, ugly fool. " Handsome is as handsome does," Polly had answered. Whereupon Mr. Neefit had shown his teeth and growled ;—but Polly, though she loved her father, and after a fashion respected him, was not afraid of him ; and now, when her mother left her alone with Ontario, she was free enough of her conversation. " Oh, Polly," he said, after a while, " you know why I'm here."

" Yes ; I know," said Polly.

" I don't think you do care for that young gentleman."

" I'm not going to break my heart about him, Mr. Moggs."

" I'd try to be the death of him, if you did."

" That would be a right down tragedy, because then you'd be hung,—and so there'd be an end of us all. I don't think I'd do that, Mr. Moggs."

" Polly, I sometimes feel as though I didn't know what to do."

" Tell me the whole story of how you went on down at Percy-cross. I was so anxious you should get in."

" Were you now ? "

"Right down sick at heart about it;—that I was. Don't you think we should all be proud to know a member of Parliament?"

"Oh; if that's all——"

"I shouldn't think anything of Mr. Newton for being in Parliament. Whether he was in Parliament or out would be all the same. Of course he's a friend, and we like him very well; but his being in Parliament would be nothing. But if you were there——!"

"I don't know what's the difference," said Moggs despondently.

"Because you're one of us."

"Yes; I am," said Moggs, rising to his legs and preparing himself for an oration on the rights of labour. "I thank my God that I am no aristocrat." Then there came upon him a feeling that this was not a time convenient for political fervour. "But, I'll tell you something, Polly," he said, interrupting himself.

"Well;—tell me something, Mr. Moggs."

"I'd sooner have a kiss from you than be Prime Minister."

"Kisses mean so much, Mr. Moggs," said Polly.

"I mean them to mean much," said Ontario Moggs. Whereupon Polly, declining further converse on that delicate subject, and certainly not intending to grant the request made on the occasion, changed the subject.

"But you will get in still;—won't you, Mr. Moggs? They tell me that those other gentlemen ain't to be members any longer, because what they did was unfair. Oughtn't that to make you member?"

"I think it ought, if the law was right;—but it doesn't."

"Doesn't it now? But you'll try again;—won't you? Never give a thing up, Mr. Moggs, if you want it really." As the words left her lips she understood their meaning,—the meaning in which he must necessarily take them,—and she blushed up to her forehead. Then she laughed as she strove to recall the encouragement she had given him. "You know what I mean, Mr. Moggs. I don't mean any silly nonsense about being in love."

"If that is silly, I am the silliest man in London."

"I think you are sometimes;—so I tell you fairly."

In the meantime Mr. Neefit had woke from his slumbers. He was in his old arm-chair in the little back room, where they had dined, while Polly with her lover was in the front parlour. Mrs. Neefit was seated opposite to Mr. Neefit, with an open Bible in her lap, which had been as potent for sleep with her as had been the gin-and-water with her husband. Neefit suddenly jumped up and growled. "Where's Polly?" he demanded.

"She's in the parlour, I suppose," said Mrs. Neefit doubtingly.

"And who is with her?"

"Nobody as hadn't ought to be," said Mrs. Neefit.

"Who's there, I say?" But without waiting for an answer, he stalked into the front room. "It's no use in life your coming here," he said, addressing himself at once to Ontario; "not the least. She ain't for you. She's for somebody else. Why can't one word be as good as a thousand?" Moggs stood silent, looking sheepish and confounded. It was not that he was afraid of the father; but that he feared to offend the daughter should he address the father roughly. "If she goes against me she'll have to walk out of the house with just what she's got on her back."

"I should be quite contented," said Ontario.

"But I shouldn't;—so you may just cut it. Anybody who wants her without my leave must take her in her smock."

"Oh, father!" screamed Polly.

"That's what I mean,—so let's have done with it. What business have you coming to another man's house when you're not welcome? When I want you I'll send for you; and till I do you have my leave to stay away."

"Good-bye, Polly," said Ontario, offering the girl his hand.

"Good-bye, Mr. Moggs," said Polly; "and mind you get into Parliament. You stick to it, and you'll do it."

When she repeated this salutary advice, it must have been that she intended to apply to the double event. Moggs at any rate took it in that light. "I shall," said he, as he opened the door and walked triumphantly out of the house.

"Father," said Polly, as soon as they were alone, "you've behaved very bad to that young man."

"You be blowed," said Mr. Neefit.

"You have, then. You'll go on till you get me that talked about that I shall be ashamed to show myself. What's the good of me trying to behave, if you keep going on like that?"

"Why didn't you take that chap when he came after you down to Margate?"

"Because I didn't choose. I don't care enough for him; and it's all no use of you going on. I wouldn't have him if he came twenty times. I've made up my mind, so I tell you."

"You're a very grand young woman."

"I'm grand enough to have a will of my own about that. I'm not going to be made to marry any man, I know."

"And you mean to take that long-legged shoemaker's apprentice."

"He's not a shoemaker's apprentice any more than I'm a breeches-maker's apprentice." Polly was now quite in earnest, and in no mood for picking her words. "He is a bootmaker by his trade; and I've never said anything about taking him."

"You've given him a promise."

"No; I've not."

"And you'd better not, unless you want to walk out of this house with nothing but the rags on your back. Ain't I doing it all for you? Ain't I been sweating my life out these thirty years to make you a lady?" This was hard upon Polly, as she was not yet one-and-twenty.

"I don't want to be a lady; no more than I am just by myself, like. If I can't be a lady without being made one, I won't be a lady at all."

"You be blowed."

"There are different kinds of ladies, father. I want to be such a one as neither you nor mother shall ever have cause to say I didn't behave myself."

"You'd talk the figures off a milestone," said Mr. Neefit, as he returned to his arm-chair, to his gin-and-water, to his growlings, and before long to his slumbers. Throughout the whole evening he was very unpleasant in the bosom of his family,—which consisted on this occasion of his wife only, as Polly took the opportunity of going out to drink tea with a young lady friend. Neefit, when he heard this, suggested that Ontario was drinking tea at the same house, and would have pursued his daughter but for mingled protestations and menaces which his wife used for preventing such a violation of parental authority. "Moggs don't know from Adam where she is; and you never knowed her do anything of that kind. And you'll go about with your mad schemes and jealousies till you about ruin the poor girl; that's what you will. I won't have it. If you go, I'll go too, and I'll shame you. No; you shan't have your hat. Of course she'll be off some day, if you make the place that wretched that she can't live in it. I know I would,—with the fust man as'd ask me." By these objurgations, by a pertinacious refusal as to his hat, and a little yielding in the matter of gin-and-water, Mr. Neefit was at length persuaded to remain at home.

On the following morning he said nothing before he left home, but as soon as he had opened his letters and spoken a few sharp things to the two men in Conduit Street, he went off to Mr. Moggs senior. Of the interview between Mr. Neefit and Mr. Moggs senior sufficient has already been told. Then it was, after his return to his own shop, that he so behaved as to drive the German artist into downright mutiny and unlimited beer. Through the whole afternoon he snarled at Waddle; but Waddle sat silent, bending over the ledger. One question Waddle did answer.

"Where's that pig-headed German gone?" asked Mr. Neefit for the tenth time.

"I believe he's cutting his throat about this time," said Mr. Waddle.

"He may wait till I come and sew it up," said the breeches-maker.

All this time Mr. Neefit was very unhappy. He knew, as well as did Mr. Waddle or Polly, that he was misbehaving himself. He was by no means deficient in ideas of duty to his wife, to his daughter, and to his dependents. Polly was the apple of his eye; his one jewel;—in his estimation the best girl that ever lived. He admired her in all her moods, even though she would sometimes oppose his wishes with invincible obstinacy. He knew in his heart that were she to marry Ontario Moggs he would forgive her on the day of her marriage. He could not keep himself from forgiving her though she were to marry a chimney-sweep. But, as he thought, a great wrong was being done him. He could not bring himself to believe that Polly would not marry the young Squire, if the young Squire would only be true to his undertaking; and then he could not endure that the young Squire should escape from him, after having been, as it were, saved from ruin by his money, without paying for the accommodation in some shape. He had some inkling of an idea that in punishing Ralph by making public the whole transaction, he would be injuring his daughter as much as he injured Ralph. But the inkling did not sufficiently establish itself in his mind to cause him to desist. Ralph Newton ought to be made to repeat his offer before all the world; even though he should only repeat it to be again refused. The whole of that evening he sat brooding over it, so that he might come to some great resolution.

CHAPTER XLVI.

MR. NEEFIT AGAIN.

THE last few days in March and the first week in April were devoted by Ralph the heir to a final visit to the Moonbeam. He had resolved to finish the hunting season at his old quarters, and then to remove his stud to Newton. The distinction with which he was welcomed by everybody at the Moonbeam must have been very gratifying to him. Though he had made no response whatever to Lieutenant Cox's proposition as to a visit to Newton, that gentleman received him as a hero. Captain Fooks also had escaped from his regiment with the sole object of spending these last days with his dear old friend. Fred Pepper too was very polite, though it was not customary with Mr. Pepper to display friendship so enthusiastic as that which warmed the bosoms of the two military gentlemen. As to Mr. Horsball, one might have thought from his manner that he hoped to engage his customer to remain at the Moonbeam for the rest of his life. But it was not so. It was in Mr. Horsball's nature to be civil to a rich hunting country gentleman; and it was the fact also that

Ralph had ever been popular with the world of the Moonbeam,—
even at times when the spasmodic, and at length dilatory, mode of
his payment must have become matter for thought to the master of
the establishment. There was no doubt about the payments now,
and Ralph's popularity was increased fourfold. Mrs. Horsball got out
from some secluded nook a special bottle of orange-brandy in his
favour,—which Lieutenant Cox would have consumed on the day of
its opening, had not Mrs. Horsball with considerable acrimony declined
to supply his orders. The sister with ringlets smiled and smirked
whenever the young Squire went near the bar. The sister in ringlets
was given to flirtations of this kind, would listen with sweetest com-
placency to compliments on her beauty, and would return them with
interest. But she never encouraged this sort of intimacy with gentlemen who did not pay their bills, or with those whose dealings with
the house were not of a profitable nature. The man who expected
that Miss Horsball would smile upon him because he ordered a glass
of sherry and bitters or half-a-pint of pale ale was very much mistaken;
but the softness of her smiles for those who consumed the Moonbeam
champagne was unbounded. Love and commerce with her ran
together, and regulated each other in a manner that was exceedingly
advantageous to her brother. If I were about to open such a house
as the Moonbeam the first thing I should look for would be a discreet,
pleasant-visaged lady to assist me in the bar department, not much
under forty, with ringlets, having no particular leaning towards
matrimony, who knew how to whisper little speeches while she made
a bottle of cherry-brandy serve five-and-twenty turns at the least.
She should be honest, patient, graceful, capable of great labour,
grasping,—with that wonderful capability of being greedy for the
benefit of another which belongs to women,—willing to accept plentiful meals and a power of saving £20 a year as sufficient remunera-
tion for all hardships, with no more susceptibility than a milestone,
and as indifferent to delicacy in language as a bargee. There are
such women, and very valuable women they are in that trade. Such
a one was Miss Horsball, and in these days the sweetest of her
smiles were bestowed upon the young Squire.

Ralph Newton certainly liked it, though he assumed an air of
laughing at it all. " One would think that old Hossy thought that I
am going to go on with this kind of thing," he said one morning to
Mr. Pepper as the two of them were standing about near the stable
doors with pipes in their mouths. Old Hossy was the affectionate
nickname by which Mr. Horsball was known among the hunting men
of the B. B. Mr. Pepper and Ralph had already breakfasted, and
were dressed for hunting except that they had not yet put on their
scarlet coats. The meet was within three miles of their head-
quarters; the captain and the lieutenant were taking advantage

of the occasion by prolonged slumbers ; and Ralph had passed the morning in discussing hunting matters with Mr. Pepper.

" He don't think that," said Mr. Pepper, taking a very convenient little implement out of his pocket, contrived for purposes of pipe-smoking accommodation. He stopped down his tobacco, and drew the smoke, and seemed by his manner to be giving his undivided attention to his pipe. But that was Mr. Pepper's manner. He was short in speech, but always spoke with a meaning.

" Of course he doesn't really," said Ralph. " I don't suppose I shall ever see the old house again after next week. You see when a man has a place of one's own, if there be hunting there, one is bound to take it ; if there isn't, one can go elsewhere and pick and choose."

" Just so," said Mr. Pepper.

" I like this kind of thing amazingly, you know."

" It has its advantages."

" Oh dear, yes. There is no trouble, you know. Everything done for you. No servants to look after,—except just the fellow who brings you your breeches and rides your second horse." Mr. Pepper never had a second horse, or a man of his own to bring him his breeches, but the allusion did not on that account vex him. "And then you can do what you like a great deal more than you can in a house of your own."

" I should say so," remarked Mr. Pepper.

" I tell you what it is, Fred," continued Ralph, becoming very confidential. " I don't mind telling you, because you are a man who understands things. There isn't such a great pull after all in having a property of your own."

" I shouldn't mind trying it,—just for a year or so," said Mr. Pepper.

" I suppose not," said Ralph, chuckling in his triumph. "And yet there isn't so much in it. What does it amount to when it's all told ? You keep horses for other fellows to ride, you buy wine for other fellows to drink, you build a house for other fellows to live in. You've a deal of business to do, and if you don't mind it you go very soon to the dogs. You have to work like a slave, and everybody gets a pull at you. The chances are you never have any ready money, and become as stingy as an old file. You have to get married because of the family, and the place, and all that kind of thing. Then you have to give dinners to every old fogy, male and female, within twenty miles of you, and before you know where you are you become an old fogy yourself. That's about what it is."

" You ought to know," said Mr. Pepper.

" I've been expecting it all my life,—of course. It was what I was born to, and everybody has been telling me what a lucky fellow I am since I can remember. Now I've got it, and I don't find it

comes to so very much. I shall always look back upon the dear old
Moonbeam, and the B B, and Hossy's wonderful port wine with
regret. It hasn't been very swell, you know, but it's been uncommonly cosy. Don't you think so?"

"You see I wasn't born to anything better," said Mr. Pepper.

Just at this moment Cox and Fooks came out of the house. They
had not as yet breakfasted, but had thought that a mouthful of air in
the stable-yard might enable them to get through their toast and
red herrings with an amount of appetite which had not as yet been
vouchsafed to them. Second and third editions of that wonderful
port had been produced on the previous evening, and the two
warriors had played their parts with it manfully. Fooks was
bearing up bravely as he made his way across the yard; but Cox
looked as though his friends ought to see to his making that journey
to Australia very soon if they intended him to make it at all. "I'm
blessed if you fellows haven't been and breakfasted," said Captain
Fooks.

"That's about it," said the Squire.

"You must be uncommon fond of getting up early."

"Do you know who gets the worm?" asked Mr. Pepper.

"Oh, bother that," said Cox.

"There's nothing I hate so much as being told about that nasty
worm," said Captain Fooks. "I don't want a worm."

"But the early birds do," said Mr. Pepper.

Captain Fooks was rather given to be cross of mornings. "I
think, you know, that when fellows say over night they'll breakfast
together, it isn't just the sort of thing for one or two to have all
the things brought up at any unconscionable hour they please.
Eh, Cox?"

"I'm sure I don't know," said Cox. "I shall just have another
go of soda and brandy with a devilled biscuit. That's all I want."

"Fooks had better go to bed again, and see if he can't get out
the other side," said Ralph.

"Chaff doesn't mean anything," said Captain Fooks.

"That's as you take it," said Mr. Pepper.

"I shall take it just as I please," said Captain Fooks.

Just at this moment Mr. Horsball came up to them, touching his
hat cheerily in sign of the commencement of the day. "You'll ride
Mr. Pepper's little 'orse, I suppose, sir?" he said, addressing himself
to the young Squire.

"Certainly,—I told Larking I would."

"Exactly, Mr. Newton. And Banker might as well go out as
second."

"I said Brewer. Banker was out on Friday."

"That won't be no odds, Mr. Newton. The fact is, Brewer's legs
is a little puffed."

" All right," said the Squire.

" Well, old Hossy," said Lieutenant Cox, summing up all his energy in an attempt at matutinal joviality as he slapped the land- lord on the back, " how are things going with you ? "

Mr. Horsball knew his customers, and did not like being slapped on the back with more than ordinary vigour by such a customer as Lieutenant Cox. " Pretty well, I thank you, Mr. Cox," said he. " I didn't take too much last night, and I eat my breakfast 'earty this morning."

" There is one for you, young man," said Captain Fooks. Where- upon the Squire laughed heartily. Mr. Horsball went on nodding his head, intending to signify his opinion that he had done his work thoroughly ; Mr. Pepper, standing on one foot with the other raised on a horse-block, looked on without moving a muscle of his face. The lieutenant was disgusted, but was too weak in his inner man to be capable of instant raillery ;—when, on a sudden, the whole aspect of things was changed by the appearance of Mr. Neefit in the yard.

" D———tion ! " exclaimed our friend Ralph. The apparition had been so sudden that the Squire was unable to restrain himself. Mr. Neefit, as the reader will perhaps remember, had been at the Moonbeam before. He had written letters which had been answered, and then letters,—many letters,—to which no reply had been given. In respect of the Neefit arrangements Ralph Newton felt himself to be peculiarly ill-used by persecutions such as these, because he had honestly done his best to make Polly his wife. No doubt he acknow- ledged that fortune had favoured him almost miraculously, in first saving him from so injurious a marriage by the action of the young lady, and then at once bestowing upon him his estate. But the escape was the doing of fortune and Polly Neefit combined, and had not come of any intrigue on his own part. He was in a position,— so he thought,—absolutely to repudiate Neefit, and to throw himself upon facts for his protection ;—but then it was undoubtedly the case that for a year or two Mr. Neefit could make his life a burden to him. He would have bought off Neefit at a considerable price, had Neefit been purchaseable. But Neefit was not in this matter greedy for himself. He wanted to make his daughter a lady, and he thought that this was the readiest way to accomplish that object. The Squire, in his unmeasurable disgust, uttered the curse aloud ; but then, remembering himself, walked up to the breeches-maker with his extended hand. He had borrowed the man's money. " What's in the wind now, Mr. Neefit ? " he said.

" What's in the wind, Captain ? Oh, you know. When are you coming to see us at the cottage ? "

" I don't think my coming would do any good. I'm not in favour with the ladies there." Ralph was aware that all the men standing round him had heard the story, and that nothing was to be gained by an immediate attempt at concealment. It behoved him, above all things, to be upon his metal, to put a good face upon it, and to be at any rate equal to the breeches-maker in presence of mind and that kind of courage which he himself would have called " cheek."

" My money was in favour with you, Captain, when you promised as how you would be on the square with me in regard to our Polly."

" Mr. Neefit," said Ralph, speaking in a low voice, but still clearly, so that all around him could hear him, " your daughter and I can never be more to each other than we are at present. She has decided that. But I value her character and good name too highly to allow even you to injure them by such a discussion in a stable-yard." And, having said this, he walked away into the house.

" My Polly's character ! " said the infuriated breeches-maker, turning round to the audience, and neglecting to follow his victim in his determination to vindicate his daughter. " If my girl's character don't stand higher nor his or any one's belonging to him I'll eat it ! "

" Mr. Newton meant to speak in favour of the young lady, not against her," said Mr. Pepper.

" Then why don't he come out on the square ? Now, gents, I'll tell you just the whole of it. He came down to my little box, where I, and my missus, and my girl lives quiet and decent, to borrow money; —and he borrowed it. He won't say as that wasn't so."

" And he's paid you the money back again," said Mr. Pepper.

" He have ;—but just you listen. I know you, Mr. Pepper, and all about you ; and do you listen. He have paid it back. But when he come there borrowing money, he saw my girl; and, says he,— ' I've got to sell that 'eritance of mine for just what it 'll fetch.' ' That's bad, Captain,' says I. ' It is bad,' says he. Then says he again, ' Neefit, that girl of yours there is the sweetest girl as ever I put my eyes on.' And so she is,—as sweet as a rose, and as honest as the sun, and as good as gold. I says it as oughtn't; but she is. ' It's a pity, Neefit,' says he, ' about the 'eritance; ain't it ? ' ' Captain,' says I,—I used to call him Captain 'cause he come down quite familiar like to eat his bit of salmon and drink his glass of wine. Laws,—he was glad enough to come then, mighty grand as he is now."

" I don't think he's grand at all," said Mr. Horsball.

" Well ;— do you just listen, gents. ' Captain,' says I, ' that 'eritance of yourn mustn't be sold no how. I says so. What's the figure as is wanted ? ' Well; then he went on to say as how Polly was the sweetest girl he ever see ;—and so we came to an understanding. He was to have what money he wanted at once, and then £20,000 down when he married Polly. He did have a thousand. And, now,—see what his little game is."

" But the young lady wouldn't have anything to say to him," suggested Captain Fooks, who, even for the sake of his breakfast, could not omit to hear the last of so interesting a conversation.

"Laws, Captain Fooks, to hear the likes of that from you, who is an officer and a gentleman by Act of Parliament! When you have anything sweet to say to a young woman, does she always jump down your throat the first go off?"

"If she don't come at the second time of asking I always go elsewhere," said Captain Fooks.

"Then it's my opinion you have a deal of travelling to do," said Mr. Neefit, "and don't get much at the end of it. It's because he's come in for his 'eritance, which he never would have had only for me, that he's demeaning himself this fashion. It ain't acting the gentleman; it ain't the thing; it's off the square. Only for me and my money there wouldn't be an acre his this blessed minute;—d——d if there would! I saved it for him, by my ready money,—just that I might see my Polly put into a station as she'd make more genteel than she found it. That's what she would;—she has that manners, not to talk of her being as pretty a girl as there is from here to,—to anywheres. He made me a promise, and he shall keep it. I'll worry the heart out of him else. Pay me back my money! Who cares for the money? I can tell guineas with him now, I'll be bound. I'll put it all in the papers,—I will. There ain't a soul shan't know it. I'll put the story of it into the pockets of every pair of breeches as leaves my shop. I'll send it to every M. F. H. in the kingdom."

"You'll about destroy your trade, old fellow," said Mr. Pepper.

"I don't care for the trade, Mr. Pepper. Why have I worked like a 'orse? It's only for my girl."

"I suppose she's not breaking her heart for him?" said Captain Fooks.

"What she's a doing with her heart ain't no business of yours, Captain Fooks. I'm her father, and I know what I'm about. I'll make that young man's life a burden to him, if 'e ain't on the square with my girl. You see if I don't. Mr. 'Orsball, I want a 'orse to go a 'unting on to-day. You lets 'em. Just tell your man to get me a 'orse. I'll pay for him."

"I didn't know you ever did anything in that way," said Mr. Horsball.

"I may begin if I please, I suppose. If I can't go no other way, I'll go on a donkey, and I'll tell every one that's out. Oh, 'e don't know me yet,—don't that young gent."

Mr. Neefit did not succeed in getting any animal out of Mr. Horsball's stables, nor did he make further attempt to carry his last threat into execution on that morning. Mr. Horsball now led the way into the house, while Mr. Pepper mounted his nag. Captain Fooks and Lieutenant Cox went in to their breakfast, and the unfortunate father followed them. It was now nearly eleven o'clock, and it was found that Ralph's horses had been taken round to the other door, and that he had already started. He said very little to any one during the day, though he was somewhat comforted by information conveyed to him by Mr. Horsball in the course of the afternoon that Mr. Neefit had returned to London. " You send your lawyer to him, Squire," said Mr. Horsball. " Lawyers cost a deal of money, but they do make things straight." This suggestion had also been made to him by his brother Gregory.

On the following day Ralph went up to London, and explained all the circumstances of the case to Mr. Carey. Mr. Carey undertook to do his best to straighten this very crooked episode in his client's life.

CHAPTER XLVII.

THE WAY WHICH SHOWS THAT THEY MEAN IT.

IF this kind of thing were to go on, life wouldn't be worth having. That was the feeling of Ralph, the squire of Newton, as he returned on that Saturday from London to the Moonbeam ; and so far Mr. Neefit had been successful in carrying out his threat. Neefit had sworn that he would make the young man's life a burden to him, and the burden was already becoming unbearable. Mr. Carey had promised to do something. He would, at any rate, see the infatuated breeches-maker of Conduit Street. In the meantime he had suggested one remedy of which Ralph had thought before,—" If you were married to some one else he'd give it up," Mr. Carey had suggested. That no doubt was true.

Ralph completed his sojourn at the Moonbeam, leaving that place at the end of the first week in April, took a run down to his own place, and then settled himself up to London for the season. His brother Gregory had at this time returned to the parsonage at Newton ; but there was an understanding that he was to come up to London and be his brother's guest for the first fortnight in May. Ralph the heir had taken larger rooms, and had a spare chamber. When Ralph had given this invitation, he had expressed his determination of devoting his spring in town to an assiduous courtship of Mary Bonner. At the moment in which he made that assertion down at Newton, the nuisance of the Neefit affair was less intolerable to him than it had since become. He had spoken cheerily of his future prospects, declaring himself to be violently in love with Mary, though he declared at the same time that he had no idea of breaking his heart for any young woman. That last assertion was probably true.

As for living in the great house at the Priory all alone, that he had declared to be impossible. Of course he would be at home for the hunting next winter; but he doubted whether he should be there much before that time, unless a certain coming event should make it necessary for him to go down and look after things. He thought it probable that he should take a run abroad in July; perhaps go to Norway for the fishing in June. He was already making arrangements with two other men for a move in August. He might be at home for partridge shooting about the middle of September, but he shouldn't " go into residence " at Newton before that. Thus he had spoken of it in describing his plans to his brother, putting great stress on his intention to devote the spring months to the lovely Mary. Gregory had seen nothing wrong in all this. Ralph was now a rich man, and was entitled to amuse himself. Gregory would have wished that his brother would at once make himself happy among his own tenants and dependents, but that, no doubt, would come soon. Ralph did spend two nights at Newton after the scene with Neefit in the Moonbeam yard,—just that he might see his nags safe in their new quarters,—and then went up to London. He was hardly yet strong in heart, because such a trouble as that which vexed him in regard to Polly does almost make a man's life a burden. Ralph was gifted with much aptitude for throwing his troubles behind, but he hardly was yet able to rid himself of this special trouble. That horrid tradesman was telling his story to everybody. Sir Thomas Underwood knew the story; and so, he thought, did Mary Bonner. Mary Bonner, in truth, did not know it; but she had thrown in Ralph's teeth, as an accusation against him, that he owed himself and his affections to another girl; and Ralph, utterly forgetful of Clarissa and that now long-distant scene on the lawn, had believed, and still did believe, that Mary had referred to Polly Neefit. On the 10th of April he established himself at his new rooms in Spring Gardens, and was careful in seeing that there was a comfortable little bedroom for his brother Greg. His uncle had now been dead just six months, but he felt as though he had been the owner of the Newton estate for years. If Mr. Carey could only settle for him that trouble with Mr. Neefit, how happy his life would be to him. He was very much in love with Mary Bonner, but his trouble with Mr. Neefit was of almost more importance to him than his love for Mary Bonner.

In the meantime the girls were living, as usual, at Popham Villa, and Sir Thomas was living, as usual, in Southampton Buildings. He and his colleague had been unseated, but it had already been decided by the House of Commons that no new writ should be at once issued, and that there should be a commission appointed to make extended inquiry at Percycross in reference to the contemplated disfranchisement of the borough. There could be no possible connexion between this inquiry and the expediency of Sir Thomas living at home; but, after some fashion, he reconciled further delay to his conscience by the fact that the Percycross election was not even yet quite settled. No doubt it would be necessary that he should again go to Percycross during the sitting of the Commission.

The reader will remember the interview between Gregory Newton and Clarissa, in which poor Clary had declared with so much emphasis her certainty that his brother's suit to Mary must be fruitless. This she had said, with artless energy, in no degree on her own behalf. She was hopeless now in that direction, and had at last taught herself to feel that the man was unworthy. The lesson had reached her, though she herself was ignorant not only of the manner of the teaching, but of the very fact that she had been taught. She had pleaded, more than once, that men did such things, and were yet held in favour and forgiven, let their iniquities have been what they might. She had hoped to move others by the doctrine; but gradually it had ceased to be operative, even on herself. She could not tell how it was that her passion faded and died away. It can hardly be said that it died away; but it became to herself grievous and a cause of soreness, instead of a joy and a triumph. She no longer said, even to herself, that he was to be excused. He had come there, and had made a mere plaything of her,—wilfully. There was no earnestness in him, no manliness, and hardly common honesty. A conviction that it was so had crept into her poor wounded heart, in spite of those repeated assertions which she had made to Patience as to the persistency of her own affection. First dismay and then wrath had come upon her when the man who ought to be her lover came to the very house in which she was living, and there offered his hand to another girl, almost in her very presence. Had the sin been committed elsewhere, and with any rival other than her own cousin, she might have still clung to that doctrine of forgiveness, because the sinner was a man, and because it is the way of the world to forgive men. But the insult had been too close for pardon; and now her wrath was slowly changing itself to contempt. Had Mary accepted the man's offer this phase of feeling would not have occurred. Clarissa would have hated the woman, but still might have loved the man. But Mary had treated him as a creature absolutely beneath her notice, had evidently despised him, and Mary's scorn communicated itself to Clarissa. The fact that Ralph was now Newton of Newton, absolutely in harbour after so many dangers of shipwreck, assisted her in this. "I would have been true to him, though he hadn't had a penny," she said to herself: "I would never have given him up though all the world had been against him." Debts, difficulties, an inheritance squandered, idle habits, even profligacy, should not have torn him from her heart, had he possessed the one virtue of meaning what he said when he told her that he loved her. She remembered the noble triumph she had felt when she declared to Mary that that other Ralph, who was to have been Mary's lover, was welcome to the fine property. Her sole ambition had been to be loved by this man; but the man had been incapable of loving her. She herself was pretty, and soft, bright on occasions, and graceful. She knew so much of herself; and she knew, also, that Mary was far prettier than herself, and more clever. This young man to whom she had devoted herself possessed no power of love for an individual,—no capability of so joining himself to another human being as to feel, that in spite of any superiority visible to the outside world, that one should be esteemed by him superior to all others,—because of his love. The young man had liked prettiness and softness and grace and feminine nicenesses; and seeing one who was prettier and more graceful,—all which poor Clary allowed, though she was not so sure about the softness and niceness,—had changed his aim without an effort! Ah, how different was poor Gregory!

She thought much of Gregory, reminding herself that as was her sorrow in regard to her own crushed hopes, so were his. His hopes, too, had been crushed, because she had been so obdurate to him. But she had never been false. She had never whispered a word of love to Gregory. It might be that his heart was as sore, but he had not been injured as she had been injured. She despised the owner of Newton Priory. She would scorn him should he come again to her and throw himself at her feet. But Gregory could not despise her. She had, indeed, preferred the bad to the good. There had been lack of judgment. But there had been on her side no lack of truth. Yes;—she had been wrong in her choice. Her judgment had been bad. And yet how glorious he had looked as he lay upon the lawn, hot from his rowing, all unbraced, brown and bold and joyous as a young god, as he bade her go and fetch him drink to slake his thirst! How proud, then, she had been to be ordered by him, as though their mutual intimacies and confidences and loves were sufficient, when they too were alone together, to justify a reversal of those social rules by which the man is ordered to wait upon the woman. There is nothing in the first flush of acknowledged love that is sweeter to the woman than this. All the men around her are her servants; but in regard to this man she may have the inexpressibly greater pleasure of serving him herself. Clarissa had now thought much of these things, and had endeavoured to define to herself what had been those gifts belonging to Ralph which had won from her her heart. He was not, in truth, handsomer than his brother Gregory, was certainly less clever, was selfish in small things from habit, whereas Gregory had no thought for his own comfort. It had all come from this,—that a black coat and a grave manner of life and serious pursuits had been less alluring to her idleness and pleasure. It had suited her that her young god should be joyous.

unbraced, brown, bold, and thirsty. She did not know Pope's famous line, but it all lay in that. She was innocent, pure, unknowing in the ways of vice, simple in her tastes, conscientious in her duties, and yet she was a rake at heart,—till at last sorrow and disappointment taught her that it is not enough that a man should lie loose upon the grass with graceful negligence and call for soda-water with a pleasant voice. Gregory wore black clothes, was sombre, and was a parson;—but, oh, what a thing it is that a man should be true at heart!

She said nothing of her changing feelings to Mary, or even to Patience. The household at this time was not very gay or joyous. Sir Thomas, after infinite vexation, had lost the seat of which they had all been proud. Mary Bonner's condition was not felt to be deplorable, as was that of poor Clary, and she certainly did not carry herself as a lovelorn maiden. Of Mary Bonner it may be said that no disappointment of that kind would affect her outward manner; nor would she in any strait of love be willing to make a confidence or to discuss her feelings. Whatever care of that kind might be present to her would be lightened, if not made altogether as nothing, by her conviction that such loads should be carried in silence, and without any visible sign to the world that the muscles are overtaxed. But it was known that the banished Ralph had, in the moment of his expected prosperity, declared his purpose of giving all that he had to give to this beauty, and it was believed that she would have accepted the gift. It had, therefore, come to pass that the name of neither Ralph could be mentioned at the cottage, and that life among these maidens was sober, sedate, and melancholy. At last there came a note from Sir Thomas to Patience. "I shall be home to dinner to-morrow. I found the enclosed from R. N. this morning. I suppose he must come. Affectionately, T. U." The enclosed note was as follows:—
"Dear Sir Thomas, I called this morning, but old Stemm was as hard as granite. If you do not object I will run down to the villa to-morrow. If you are at home I will stay and dine. Yours ever, Ralph Newton."

The mind of Sir Thomas when he received this had been affected exactly as his words described. He had supposed that Ralph must come. He had learned to hold his late ward in low esteem. The man was now beyond all likelihood of want, and sailing with propitious winds; but Sir Thomas, had he been able to consult his own inclinations, would have had no more to do with him. And yet the young Squire had not done anything which, as Sir Thomas thought, would justify him in closing his doors against one to whom he had been bound in a manner peculiarly intimate. However, if his niece should choose at last to accept Ralph, the match would be very brilliant; and the uncle thought that it was not his duty to interfere between her and so great an advantage. Sir Thomas, in truth, did not as yet understand Mary Bonner,—knew very little of her character; but he did know that it was incumbent on him to give her some opportunity of taking her beauty to market. He wrote a line to Ralph, saying that he himself would dine at home on the day indicated.

"Impossible!" said Clary, when she was first told.

"You may be sure he's coming," said Patience.

"Then I shall go and spend the day with Mrs. Brownlow. I cannot stand it."

"My dear, he'll know why you are away."

"Let him know," said Clarissa. And she did as she said she would. When Sir Thomas came home at about four o'clock on the Thursday which Ralph had fixed,—Thursday, the fourteenth of April,—he found that Clarissa had flown. The fly was to be sent for her at ten, and it was calculated that by the time she returned, Ralph would certainly have taken his leave. Sir Thomas expressed neither anger nor satisfaction at this arrangement,—"Oh; she has gone to Mrs. Brownlow's, has she? Very well. I don't suppose it will make much difference to Ralph." "None in the least," said Patience, severely. "Nothing of that kind will make any difference to him." But at that time Ralph had been above an hour in the house.

We will now return to Ralph and his adventures. He had come up to London with the express object of pressing his suit upon Mary Bonner; but during his first day or two in London had busied himself rather with the affairs of his other love. He had been with Mr. Carey, and Mr. Carey had been with Mr. Neefit. "He is the maddest old man that I ever saw," said Mr. Carey. "When I suggested to him that you were willing to make any reasonable arrangement,—meaning a thousand pounds, or something of that kind,—I couldn't get him to understand me at all."

"I don't think he wants money," said Ralph.

"'Let him come down and eat a bit of dinner at the cottage,' said he, 'and we'll make it all square.' Then I offered him a thousand pounds down."

"What did he say?"

"Called to a fellow he had there with a knife in his hand, cutting leather, to turn me out of the shop. And the man would have done it, too, if I hadn't gone."

This was not promising, but on the following morning Ralph received a letter which put him into better heart. The letter was from Polly herself, and was written as follows :—

"Alexandra Cottage, Hendon,
April 10th, 186—.

"MY DEAR SIR,

"Father has been going on with all that nonsense of his, and I think it most straightforward to write a letter to you at once, so that things may be understood and finished. Father has no right to be angry with you, anyway not about me. He says somebody has come and offered him money. I wish they hadn't, but perhaps you didn't send them. There's no good in father talking about you and me. Of course it was a great honour, and all that, but I'm not at all sure that anybody should try to get above themselves, not in the way of marrying. And the heart is everything. So I've told father. If ever I bestow mine, I think it will be to somebody in a way of business,—just like father. So I thought I would just write to say that there couldn't be anything between you and me, were it ever so ; only that I was very much honoured by your coming down to Margate. I write this to you, because a very particular friend advises me, and I don't mind telling you at once,—it is Mr. Moggs. And I shall show it to father. That is, I have written it twice, and shall keep the other. It's a pity father should go on so, but he means it for the best. And as to anything in the way of money,—oh, Mr. Newton, he's a deal too proud for that.

" Yours truly,
" Maryanne Neefit."

As to which letter the little baggage was not altogether true in one respect. She did not keep a copy of the whole letter, but left out of that which she showed to her father the very material passage in which she referred to the advice of her particular friend, Mr. Moggs. Ralph, when he received this letter, felt really grateful to Polly, and wrote to her a pretty note, in which he acknowledged her kindness, and expressed his hope that she might always be as happy as she deserved to be. Then it was that he made up his mind to go down at once to Popham Villa, thinking that the Neefit nuisance was sufficiently abated to enable him to devote his time to a more pleasurable pursuit.

He reached the villa between three and four, and learned from the gardener's wife at the lodge that Sir Thomas had not as yet returned. He did not learn that Clarissa was away, and was not aware of that fact till they all sat down to dinner at seven o'clock. Much had been done and much endured before that time came. He sauntered slowly up the road, and looked about the grounds, hoping to find the young ladies there, as he had so often done during his summer visits ; but there was no one to be seen, and he was obliged to knock at the door. He was shown into the drawing-room, and in a few minutes Patience came to him. There had been no arrangement between her and Mary as to the manner in which he should be received. Mary on a previous occasion had given him an answer, and really did believe that that would be sufficient. He was, according to her thinking, a light, inconstant man, who would hardly give himself the labour necessary for perseverance in any suit. Patience at once began to ask him after his brother and the doings at the Priory. He had been so intimate at the house, and so dear to them all, that in spite of the disapprobation with which he was now regarded by them, it was impossible that there should not be some outer kindness. "Ah," said he, "I do so look forward to the time when you will all be down there. I have been so often welcome at your house, that it will be my greatest pleasure to make you welcome there."

"We go so little from home," said Patience.

"But I am sure you will come to me. I know you would like to see Greg's parsonage and Greg's church."

"I should indeed."

"It is the prettiest church, I think, in England, and the park is very nice. The whole house wants a deal of doing to, but I shall set about it some day. I don't know a pleasanter neighbourhood anywhere." It would have been so natural that Patience should tell him that he wanted a mistress for such a home; but she could not say the words. She could not find the proper words, and soon left him, muttering something as to directions for her father's room.

He had been alone for twenty minutes when Mary came into the room. She knew that Patience was not there; and had retreated up-stairs. But there seemed to be a cowardice in such retreating, which displeased herself. She, at any rate, had no cause to be afraid of Mr. Newton. So she collected her thoughts, and arranged her gait, and went down, and addressed him with assumed indifference,—as though there had never been anything between them beyond simple acquaintance. "Uncle Thomas will be here soon, I suppose," she said.

"I hope he will give me half-an-hour first," Ralph answered. There was an ease and grace always present in his intercourse with women, and a power of saying that which he desired to say,—which perhaps arose from the slightness of his purposes and the want of reality in his character.

"We see so little of him that we hardly know his hours," said Mary. "Uncle Thomas is a sad truant from home."

"He always was, and I declare I think that Patience and Clary have been the better for it. They have learned things of which they would have known nothing had he been with them every morning and evening. I don't know any girls who are so sweet as they are. You know they have been like sisters to me."

"So I have been told."

"And when you came, it would have been like another sister coming; only——"

"Only what?" said Mary, assuming purposely a savage look.

"That something else intervened."

"Of course it must be very different,—and it should be different. You have only known me a few months."

"I have known you enough to wish to know you more closely than anybody else for the rest of my life."

"Mr. Newton, I thought you had understood me before."

"So I did." This he said with an assumed tone of lachrymose complaint. "I did understand you,—thoroughly. I understood that I was rebuked, and rejected, and disdained. But a man, if he is in earnest, does not give over on that account. Indeed, there are things which he can't give over. You may tell a man that he shouldn't drink, or shouldn't gamble; but telling will do no good. When he has once begun, he'll go on with it."

"What does that mean?"

"That love is as strong a passion, at any rate, as drinking or gambling. You did tell me, and sent me away, and rebuked me because of that tradesman's daughter."

"What tradesman's daughter?" asked Mary. "I have spoken of no tradesman's daughter. I gave you ample reason why you should not address yourself to me."

"Of course there are ample reasons," said Ralph, looking into his hat, which he had taken from the table. "The one,—most ample of all, is that you do not care for me."

"I do not," said Mary resolutely.

"Exactly;—but that is a sort of reason which a man will do his best to conquer. Do not misunderstand me. I am not such a fool as to think that I can prevail in a day. I am not vain enough to think that I can prevail at all. But I can persist."

"It will not be of the slightest use; indeed, it cannot be allowed. I will not allow it. My uncle will not allow it."

"When you told me that I was untrue to another person——; I think that was your phrase."

"Very likely."

"I supposed you had heard that stupid story which had got round to my uncle,—about a Mr. Neefit's daughter."

"I had heard no stupid story."

"What then did you mean?"

Mary paused a moment, thinking whether it might still be possible that a good turn might be done for her cousin. That Clarissa had loved this man with her whole heart she had herself owned to Mary. That the man had professed his love for Clary, Clary had also let her know. And Clary's love had endured even after the blow it had received from Ralph's offer to her cousin. All this that cousin knew; but she did not know how that love had now turned to simple soreness. "I have heard nothing of the man's daughter," said Mary.

"Well then?"

"But I do know that before I came here at all you had striven to gain the affections of my cousin."

"Clarissa!"

"Yes; Clarissa. Is it not so?" Then she paused, and Ralph remembered the scene on the lawn. In very truth it had never been forgotten. There had always been present with him when he thought of Mary Bonner a sort of remembrance of the hour in which he had played the fool with dear Clary. He had kissed her. Well; yes; and with some girls kisses mean so much,—as Polly Neefit had said to her true lover. But then with others they mean just nothing. "If you want to find a wife in this house you had better ask her. It is certainly useless that you should ask me."

"Do you mean quite useless?" asked Ralph, beginning to be somewhat abashed.

"Absolutely useless. Did I not tell you something else,—something that I would not have hinted to you, had it not been that I desired to prevent the possibility of a renewal of anything so vain? But you think nothing of that! All that can be changed with you at a moment, if other things suit."

"That is meant to be severe, Miss Bonner, and I have not deserved it from you. What has brought me to you but that I admire you above all others?"

"You shouldn't admire me above others. Is a man to change as he likes because he sees a girl whose hair pleases him for the moment better than does hers to whom he has sworn to be true?" Ralph did not forget at this moment to whisper to himself for his own consolation, that he had never sworn to be true to Clarissa. And, indeed, he did feel, that though there had been a kiss, the scene on the lawn was being used unfairly to his prejudice. "I am afraid you are very fickle, Mr. Newton, and that your love is not worth much."

"I hope we may both live till you learn that you have wronged me."

"I hope so. If my opinion be worth anything with you, go back to her from whom you have allowed yourself to stray in your folly. To me you must not address yourself again. If you do, it will be an insult." Then she rose up, queenly in her beauty, and slowly left the room.

There must be an end of that. Such was Ralph's feeling as she left the room, in spite of those protestations of constancy and persistence which he had made to himself. "A fellow has to go on with it, and be refused half a dozen times by one of those proud ones," he had said; "but when they do knuckle under, they go in harness better than the others." It was thus that he had thought of Mary Bonner, but he did not so think of her now. No, indeed. There was an end of that. "There is a sort of way of doing it, which shows that they mean it." Such was his inward speech; and he did believe that Miss Bonner meant it. "By Jove, yes; if words and looks ever can mean anything." But how about Clarissa? If it was so, as Mary Bonner had told him, would it be the proper kind of thing for him to go back to Clarissa? His heart, too,—for he had a heart,—was very soft. He had always been fond of Clarissa, and would not, for worlds, that she should be unhappy. How pretty she was, and how soft, and how loving! And how proudly happy she would be to be driven about the Newton grounds by him as their mistress. Then he remembered what Gregory had said to him, and how he had encouraged Gregory to persevere. If anything of that kind were to happen, Gregory must put up with it. It was clear that Clarissa couldn't marry Gregory if she were in love with him. But how would he look Sir Thomas in the face? As he thought of this he laughed. Sir Thomas, however, would be glad enough to give his daughter, not to the heir but to the owner of Newton. Who could be that fellow whom Mary Bonner preferred to him—with all Newton to back his suit? Perhaps Mary Bonner did not know the meaning of being the mistress of Newton Priory.

After a while the servant came to show him to his chamber. Sir Thomas had come and had gone at once to his room. So he went upstairs and dressed, expecting to see Clarissa when they all assembled before dinner. When he went down, Sir Thomas was there, and Mary, and Patience,—but not Clarissa. He had summoned back his courage and spoke jauntily to Sir Thomas. Then he turned to Patience and asked after her sister. "Clarissa is spending the day with Mrs. Brownlow," said Patience, "and will not be home till quite late."

"Oh, how unfortunate!" exclaimed Ralph. Taking all his difficulties into consideration, we must admit that he did not do it badly.

After dinner Sir Thomas sat longer over his wine than is at present usual, believing, perhaps, that the young ladies would not want to see much more of Ralph on the present occasion. The conversation was almost entirely devoted to the affairs of the late election, as to which Ralph was much interested and very indignant. "They cannot do you any harm, sir, by the investigation," he said.

"No; I don't think they can hurt me."

"And you will have the satisfaction of knowing that you have been the means of exposing corruption, and of helping to turn such a man as Griffenbottom out of the House. Upon my word, I think it has been worth while."

"I am not sure that I would do it again at the same cost, and with the same object," said Sir Thomas.

Ralph did have a cup of tea given to him in the drawing-room, and then left the villa before Clarissa's fly had returned.

CHAPTER XLVIII.

MR. MOGGS WALKS TOWARDS EDGEWARE.

THE judges' decision in Percycross as to the late election was no sooner known than fresh overtures were made to Ontario Moggs by the Young Men's Association. A letter of triumph was addressed to him at the Cheshire Cheese, in which he was informed that Intimidation and Corruption had been trodden under food in the infamous person of Mr. Griffenbottom, and that Purity and the Rights of Labour were still the watchwords of that wholesome party in the borough which was determined to send Mr. Moggs to Parliament. Did not Mr. Moggs think it best that he should come down at once to the borough and look after his interests ? Now Mr. Moggs junior, when he received this letter, had left the borough no more than three or four days since, having been summoned there as a witness during the trial of the petition ;—and such continued attendance to the political interests of a small and otherwise uninteresting town, without the advantage of a seat in Parliament, was felt by Mr. Moggs senior to be a nuisance. The expense in all these matters fell of course upon the shoulders of the father. " I don't believe in them humbugs no longer," said Mr. Moggs senior. Moggs junior, who had felt the enthusiasm of the young men of Percycross, and who had more to get and less to lose than his father, did believe. Although he had been so lately at Percycross, he went down again, and again made speeches to the young men at the Mechanics' Institute. Nothing could be more triumphant than his speeches, nothing more pleasant than his popularity ; but he could not fail to become aware, after a further sojourn of three days at Percycross, of two things. The first was this,— that if the borough were spared there would be a compromise between the leading men on the two sides, and Mr. Westmacott would be returned together with a young Griffenbottom. The second conviction forced upon him was that the borough would not be spared. There was no comfort for him at Percycross,—other than what arose from a pure political conscience. On the very morning on which he left, he besought his friends, the young men,—though they were about to be punished, degraded, and disfranchised for the sins of their elders, though it might never be allowed to them again to stir themselves for the political welfare of their own borough,— still to remember that Purity and the Rights of Labour were the two great wants of the world, and that no man could make an effort, however humble, in a good cause without doing something towards bringing nearer to him that millennium of political virtue which was so much wanted, and which would certainly come sooner or later. He was cheered to the echo, and almost carried down to the station on the shoulders of a chairman, or president, and a secretary; but he left Percycross with the conviction that that borough would never confer upon him the coveted honour of a seat in Parliament.

All this had happened early in March, previous to that Sunday on which Mr. Neefit behaved so rudely to him at the cottage. "I think as perhaps you'd better stick to business now a bit," said old Moggs. At that moment Ontario was sitting up at a high desk behind the ledger which he hated, and was sticking to business as well as he knew how to stick to it. "No more Cheshire Cheeses, if you please, young man," said the father. This was felt by the son to be unfair, cruel, and even corrupt. While the election was going on, as long as there was a hope of success at Percycross, Moggs senior had connived at the Cheshire Cheese, had said little or nothing about business, had even consented on one occasion to hear his son make a speech advocating the propriety of combination among workmen. "It ain't my way of thinking," Moggs senior had said; "but then, perhaps, I'm old." To have had a member of the firm in Parliament would have been glorious even to old Moggs, though he hardly knew in what the glory would have consisted. But as soon as he found that his hopes were vain, that the Cheshire Cheese had been no stepping-stone to such honour, and that his money had been spent for nothing, his mind reverted to its old form. Strikes became to him the work of the devil, and unions were once more the bane of trade.

"I suppose," said Ontario, looking up from his ledger, "if I work for my bread by day, I may do as I please with my evenings. At any rate I shall," he continued to say after pausing awhile. "It's best we should understand each other, father." Moggs senior growled. At a word his son would have been off from him, rushing about the country, striving to earn a crust as a political lecturer. Moggs knew his son well, and in truth loved him dearly. There was, too, a Miss Moggs at home, who would give her father no peace if Ontario were turned adrift. There is nothing in the world so cruel as the way in which sons use the natural affections of their fathers, obtaining from these very feelings a power of rebelling against authority! "You must go to the devil if you please, I suppose," said Moggs senior.

"I don't know why you say that. What do I do devilish?"

"Them Unions is devilish."

"I think they're Godlike," said Moggs junior.

After that they were silent for a while, during which Moggs senior was cutting his nails with a shoemaker's knife by the fading light of the evening, and Moggs junior was summing up an account against a favoured aristocrat, who seemed to have worn a great many boots, but who was noticeable to Ontario, chiefly from the fact that he represented in Parliament the division of the county in which Percycross was situated. "I thought you was going to make it all straight by marrying that girl," said Moggs senior.

Here was a subject on which the father and the son were in unison; —and as to which the romantic heart of Miss Moggs, at home at Shepherd's Bush, always glowed with enthusiasm. That her brother was in love, was to her, of whom in truth it must be owned that she was very plain, the charm of her life. She was fond of poetry, and would read to her brother aloud the story of Juan and Haidee, and the melancholy condition of the lady who was loved by the veiled prophet. She sympathised with the false Queen's passion for Launcelot, and, being herself in truth an ugly old maid very far removed from things romantic, delighted in the affairs of the heart when they did not run smooth. "O Ontario," she would say, "be true to her;—if it's for twenty years." "So I will;—but I'd like to begin the twenty years by making her Mrs. Moggs," said Ontario. Now Mr. Moggs senior knew to a penny what money old Neefit could give his daughter, and placed not the slightest trust in that threat about the smock in which she stood upright. Polly would certainly get the better of her father as Ontario always got the better of him. Ontario made no immediate reply to his father, but he found himself getting all wrong among the boots and shoes which had been supplied to that aristocratic young member of Parliament. "You don't mean as it's all off?" asked Moggs senior.

"No; it isn't all off."

"Then why don't you go in at it?"

"Why don't I go in at it?" said Ontario, closing the book in hopeless confusion of mind and figures. "I'd give every pair of boots in this place, I'd give all the business, to get a kind word from her."

"Isn't she kind?"

"Kind;—yes, she's kind enough in a way. She's everything just what she ought to be. That's what she is. Don't you go on about it, father. I'm as much in earnest as you can be. I shan't give it up till she calls somebody else her husband; and then,——; why then I shall just cut it, and go off to uncle in Canada. I've got my mind made up about all that." And so he left the shop, somewhat uncourteously perhaps. But he had worked his way back into his father's good graces by his determination to stick to Neefit's girl. A young man ought to be allowed to attend trades' unions, or any other meetings, if he will marry a girl with twenty thousand pounds. That evening Ontario Moggs went to the Cheshire Cheese, and was greater than ever.

It has been already told how, on a Sunday subsequent to this, he managed to have himself almost closeted with Polly, and how he was working himself into her good graces, when he was disturbed by Mr. Neefit and turned out of the house. Polly's heart had been yielding during the whole of that interview. There had come upon her once a dream that it would be a fine thing to be the lady of Newton ;— and the chance had been hers. But when she set herself to work to weigh it all, and to find out what it was that young Newton really wanted,—and what he ought to want, she shook off from herself that dream before it had done her any injury. She meant to be married certainly. As to that she had no doubt. But then Ontario Moggs was such a long-legged, awkward, ugly, shambling fellow, and Moggs as a name was certainly not euphonious. The gasfitter was handsome, and was called Yallolegs, which perhaps was better than Moggs. He had proposed to her more than once ; but the gasfitter's face meant nothing, and the gasfitter himself hadn't much meaning in him. As to outside appearance, young Newton's was just what he ought to be,—but that was a dream which she had shaken off. Onty Moggs had some meaning in him, and was a man. If there was one thing, too, under the sun of which Polly was quite sure, it was this, —that Onty Moggs did really love her. She knew that in the heart, and mind, and eyes of Onty Moggs she possessed a divinity which made the ground she stood upon holy ground for him. Now that is a conviction very pleasant to a young woman.

Ontario was very near his victory on that Sunday. When he told her that he would compass the death of Ralph Newton if Ralph Newton was to cause her to break her heart, she believed that he would do it, and she felt obliged to him,—although she laughed at him. When he declared to her that he didn't know what to do because of his love, she was near to telling him what he might do. When he told her that he would sooner have a kiss from her than be Prime Minister, she believed him, and almost longed to make him happy. Then she had tripped, giving him encouragement which she did not intend,—and had retreated, telling him that he was silly. But as she said so she made up her mind that he should be perplexed not much longer. After all, in spite of his ugliness, and awkwardness, and long legs, this was to be her man. She recognised the fact, and was happy. It is so much for a girl to be sure that she is really loved ! And there was no word which fell from Ontario's mouth which Polly did not believe. Ralph Newton's speeches were very pretty, but they conveyed no more than his intention to be civil. Ontario's speeches really brought home to her all that the words could mean. When he told her father that he was quite contented to take her just as she was, without a shilling, she knew that he would do so with the utmost joy. Then it was that she resolved that he should have her, and that for the future all doubtings, all flirtations, all coyness, should be over. She had been won, and she lowered her flag. "You stick to it, and you'll do it," she said;—and this time she meant it. "I shall," said Ontario;—and he walked all the way back to London, with his head among the clouds, disregarding Percycross utterly, forgetful of all the boots and aristocrats' accounts, regardless almost of the Cheshire Cheese, not even meditating a new speech in defence of the Rights of Labour. He believed that on that day he had gained the great victory. If so, life before him was one vista of triumph. That he himself was what the world calls romantic, he had no idea,—but he had lived now for months on the conviction that the only chance of personal happiness to himself was to come from the smiles and kindness and love of a certain human being whom he had chosen to beatify. To him Polly Neefit was divine, and round him also there would be a halo of divinity if this goddess would consent to say that she would become his wife.

It was impossible that many days should be allowed to pass before he made an effort to learn from her own lips, positively, the meaning of those last words which she had spoken to him. But there was a difficulty. Neefit had warned him from the house, and he felt unwilling to knock at the door of a man in that man's absence, who, if present, would have refused to him the privilege of admittance. That Mrs. Neefit would see him, and afford him opportunity of pleading his cause with Polly, he did not doubt ;—but some idea that a man's house, being his castle, should not be invaded in the owner's absence, restrained him. That the man's daughter might be the dearer and the choicer, and the more sacred castle of the two, was true enough ; but then Polly was a castle which, as Moggs thought, ought to belong to him rather than to her father. And so he resolved to waylay Polly

His weekdays, from nine in the morning till seven in the evening, were at this time due to Booby and Moggs, and he was at present paying that debt religiously, under a conviction that his various absences at Percycross had been hard upon his father. For there was, in truth, no Booby. Moggs senior, and Moggs junior, constituted the whole firm ;—in which, indeed, up to this moment Moggs junior, had no recognised share,—and if one was absent, the other must be present. But Sunday was his own, and Polly Neefit always went to church. Nevertheless, on the first Sunday he failed. He failed, though he saw her, walking with two other ladies, and though, to the best of his judgment, she also saw him. On the second Sunday he was at Hendon from ten till three, hanging about in the lanes, sitting on gates, whiling away the time with a treatise on political economy which he had brought down in his pocket, thinking of Polly while he strove to confine his thoughts to the great subject of man's productive industry. Is there any law of Nature,—law of

God, rather,—by which a man has a right to enough of food, enough of raiment, enough of shelter, and enough of recreation, if only he will work? But Polly's cheeks, and Polly's lips, the eager fire of Polly's eye as she would speak, and all the elastic beauty of Polly's gait as she would walk, drove the great question from his mind. Was he ever destined to hold Polly in his arms,—close, close to his breast? If not, then the laws of Nature and the laws of God, let them be what they might, would not have been sufficient to protect him from the cruellest wrong of all.

It was as she went to afternoon church that he hoped to intercept her. Morning church with many is a bond. Afternoon church is a virtue of supererogation,—practised often because there is nothing else to do. It would be out of the question that he should induce her to give up the morning service; but if he could only come upon her in the afternoon, a little out of sight of others, just as she would turn down a lane with which he was acquainted, near to a stile leading across the fields towards Edgeware, it might be possible that he should prevail. As the hour came near, he put the useless volume into his pocket, and stationed himself on the spot which he had selected. Almost at the first moment in which he had ventured to hope for her presence, Polly turned into the lane. It was six months after this occurrence that she confessed to him that she had thought it just possible that he might be there. "Of course you would be there,—you old goose; as if Jemima hadn't told me that you'd been about all day. But I never should have come, if I hadn't quite made up my mind." Then Ontario administered to her one of those bear's hugs which were wont to make Polly declare that he was an ogre. It was thus that Polly made her confession after the six months, as they were sitting very close to each other on some remote point of the cliffs down on the Kentish coast. At that time the castle had been altogether transferred out of the keeping of Mr. Neefit.

But Polly's conduct on this occasion was not at all of a nature to make it supposed that Jemima's eyes had been so sharp. "What, Mr. Moggs!" she said. "Dear me, what a place to find you in! Are you coming to church?"

"I want you just to take a turn with me for a few minutes, Polly."

"But I'm going to church."

"You can go to church afterwards;—that is, if you like. I can't come to the house now, and I have got something that I must say to you."

"Something that you must say to me!" And then Polly followed him over the stile.

They had walked the length of nearly two fields before Ontario had commenced to tell the tale which of necessity must be told; but

Polly, though she must have known that her chances of getting back to church were becoming more and more remote, waited without impatience. "I want to know," he said, at last, "whether you can ever learn to love me."

"What's the use, Mr. Moggs?"

"It will be all the use in the world to me."

"Oh, no it won't. It can't signify so very much to anybody."

"Nothing, I sometimes think, can ever be of any use to me but that."

"As for learning to love a man,—I suppose I could love a man without any learning if I liked him."

"But you don't like me, Polly?"

"I never said I didn't like you. Father and mother always used to like you."

"But you, Polly?"

"Oh, I like you well enough. Don't, Mr. Moggs.'

"But do you love me?" Then there was a pause, as they stood leaning upon a gateway. "Come, Polly; tell a fellow. Do you love me?"

"I don't know." Then there was another pause; but he was in a seventh heaven, with his arm round her waist. "I suppose I do; a little," whispered Polly.

"But better than anybody else?"

"You don't think I mean to have two lovers;—do you?"

"And I am to be your lover?"

"There's father, you know. I'm not going to be anybody's wife because he tells me; but I wouldn't like to vex him, if we could help it."

"But you'll never belong to any one else?"

"Never," said she solemnly.

"Then I've said what I've got to say, and I'm the happiest man in all the world, and you may go to church now if you like." But his arm was still tight round her waist.

"It's too late," said Polly, in a melancholy tone,—"and it's all your doing."

The walk was prolonged not quite to Edgeware; but so far that Mr. Neefit was called upon to remark that the parson was preaching a very long sermon. Mrs. Neefit, who perhaps had also had communication with Jemima, remarked that it was not to be expected, but that Polly should take a ramble with some of her friends. "Why can't she ramble where I want her to ramble?" said Mr. Neefit.

Many things were settled during that walk. Within five minutes of the time in which she had declared that it was too late for her to go to church, she had brought herself to talk to him with all the delightful confidence of a completed engagement. She made him understand at once that there was no longer any doubt. " A girl must have time to know," she said, when he half-reproached her with the delay. A girl wasn't like a man, she said, who could just make up his mind at once,—a girl had to wait and see. But she was quite sure of this,—that having once said the word she would never go back from it. She didn't quite know when she had first begun to love him, but she thought it was when she heard that he had made up his mind to stand for Percycross. It seemed to her to be such a fine thing,—his going to Percycross. " Then," said Ontario, gallantly, " Percycross has done ten times more for me than it would have done, had it simply made me a member of Parliament." Once, twice, and oftener he was made happier than he could have been had fortune made him a Prime Minister. For Polly, now that she had given her heart and promised her hand, would not coy her lips to the man she had chosen.

Many things were settled between them. Polly told her lover all her trouble about Ralph Newton, and it was now that she received that advice from her " very particular friend, Mr. Moggs," which she followed in writing to her late suitor. The letter was to be written and posted that afternoon, and then shown to her father. We know already that in making the copy for her father she omitted one clause, —having resolved that she would tell her mother of her engagement, and that her mother should communicate it to her father. As for naming any day for their marriage, " That was out of the question," she said. She did not wish to delay it ; but all that she could do was to swear to her father that she would never marry anybody else. " And he'll believe me too," said Polly. As for eloping, she would not hear of it. " Just that he might have an excuse to give his money to somebody else," she said.

" I don't care for his money," protested Moggs.

" That's all very well ; but money's a good thing in its way. I hate a man who'd sell himself ; he's a mean fellow ;—or a girl either. Money should never be first. But as for pitching it away just because you're in a hurry, I don't believe in that at all. I'm not going to be an old woman yet, and you may wait a few months very well." She walked with him direct up to the gate leading up to their own house, —so that all the world might see her, if all the world pleased ; and then she bade him good-bye. " Some day before very long, no doubt," she said when, as he left her, he asked as to their next meeting.

And so Polly had engaged herself. I do not know that the matter seemed to her to be of so much importance as it does to many girls. It was a piece of business which had to be done some day, as she had well known for years past ; and now that it was done, she was quite contented with the doing of it. But there was not

much of that ecstasy in her bosom which was at the present moment
sending Ontario Moggs bounding up to town, talking, as he went, to
himself,—to the amazement of passers by, and assuring himself that
he had triumphed like an Alexander or a Cæsar. She made some
steady resolves to do her duty by him, and told herself again and
again that nothing should ever move her now that she had decided.
As for beauty in a man;—what did it signify? He was honest. As
for awkwardness;—what did it matter? He was clever. And in
regard to being a gentleman; she rather thought that she liked him
better because he wasn't exactly what some people call a gentleman.
Whatever sort of a home he would give her to live in, nobody would
despise her in it because she was not grand enough for her place.
She was by no means sure that a good deal of misery of that kind
might not have fallen to her lot had she become the mistress of
Newton Priory. "When the beggar woman became a queen, how
the servants must have snubbed her," said Polly to herself.

That evening she showed her letter to her father. "You haven't
sent it, you minx?" said he.

"Yes, father. It's in the iron box."

"What business had you to write to a young man?"

"Come, father. I had a business."

"I believe you want to break my heart," said old Neefit.

That evening her mother asked her what she had been doing that
afternoon. "I just took a walk with Ontario Moggs," said Polly.

"Well?"

"And I've just engaged myself straight off, and you had better
tell father. I mean to keep to it, mother, let anybody say anything.
I wouldn't go back from my promise if they were to drag me. So
father may as well know at once."

CHAPTER XLIX.

AMONG THE PICTURES.

NORFOLK is a county by no means devoted to hunting, and Ralph
Newton,—the disinherited Ralph as we may call him,—had been
advised by some of his friends round Newton to pitch his tent elsewhere,—because of his love of that sport. "You'll get a bit of land just
as cheap in the shires," Morris had said to him. "And, if I were you,
I wouldn't go among a set of fellows who don't think of anything in
the world except partridges." Mr. Morris, who was a very good
fellow in his way, devoted a considerable portion of his mental and
physical energies to the birth, rearing, education, preservation, and
subsequent use of the fox,—thinking that in so doing he employed

himself nobly as a country gentleman; but he thoroughly despised a county in which partridges were worshipped.

"They do preserve foxes," pleaded Ralph.

"One man does, and the next don't. You ought to know what that means. It's the most heart-breaking kind of thing in the world. I'd sooner be without foxes altogether, and ride to a drag;—I would indeed." This assertion Mr. Morris made in a sadly solemn tone, such as men use when they speak of some adversity which fate and fortune may be preparing for them. "I'd a deal rather die than bear it," says the melancholy friend; or,—"I'd much sooner put up with a crust in a corner." "I'd rather ride to a drag;—I would indeed," said Mr. Morris, with a shake of the head, and a low sigh. As for life without riding to hounds at all, Mr. Morris did not for a moment suppose that his friend contemplated such an existence.

But Ralph had made up his mind that, in going out into the world to do something, foxes should not be his first object. He had to seek a home certainly, but more important than his home was the work to which he should give himself; and, as he had once said, he knew nothing useful that he could do except till the land. So he went down into Norfolk among the intermittent fox preservers, and took Beamingham Hall.

Almost every place in Norfolk is a "ham," and almost every house is a hall. There was a parish of Beamingham, four miles from Swaffham, lying between Tillham, Soham, Reepham, and Grindham. It's down in all the maps: It's as flat as a pancake; it has a church with a magnificent square tower, and a new chancel; there is a resident parson, and there are four or five farmers in it; it is under the plough throughout, and is famous for its turnips; half the parish belongs to a big lord, who lives in the county, and who does preserve foxes, but not with all his heart; two other farms are owned by the yeomen who farm them,—men who have been brought up to shoot, and who hate the very name of hunting. Beamingham Hall was to be sold, and by the beginning of May Ralph Newton had bought it. Beamingham Little Wood belonged to the estate, and, as it contained about thirty acres, Ralph determined that he would endeavour to have a fox there.

By the middle of May he had been four months in his new home. The house itself was not bad. It was spacious; and the rooms, though low, were large. And it had been built with considerable idea of architectural beauty. The windows were all set in stone and mullioned,—long, low windows, very beautiful in form, which had till some fifteen years back been filled with a multitude of small diamond panes;—but now the diamond panes had given way to plate glass. There were three gables to the hall, all facing an old-fashioned large garden, in which the fruit trees came close up to the house, and that which perhaps ought to have been a lawn was almost an orchard.

But there were trim gravel walks, and trim flower-beds, and a trim fish-pond, and a small walled kitchen-garden, with very old peaches, and very old apricots, and very old plums. The plums, however, were at present better than the peaches or the apricots. The fault of the house, as a modern residence, consisted in this,—that the farm-yard, with all its appurtenances, was very close to the back door. Ralph told himself when he first saw it that Mary Bonner would never consent to live in a house so placed.

For whom was such a house as Beamingham Hall originally built, —a house not grand enough for a squire's mansion, and too large for a farmer's homestead ? Such houses throughout England are much more numerous than Englishmen think,—either still in good repair, as was Beamingham Hall, or going into decay under the lessened domestic wants of the present holders. It is especially so in the eastern counties, and may be taken as one proof among many that the broad-acred squire, with his throng of tenants, is comparatively a modern invention. The country gentleman of two hundred years ago farmed the land he held. As years have rolled on, the strong have swallowed the weak,—one strong man having eaten up half-a-dozen weak men. And so the squire has been made. Then the strong squire becomes a baronet and a lord,—till he lords it a little too much, and a Manchester warehouseman buys him out. The strength of the country probably lies in the fact that the change is ever being made, but is never made suddenly.

To Ralph the great objection to Beamingham Hall lay in that fear, —or rather certainty,—that it could not be made a fitting home for Mary Bonner. When he first decided on taking it, and even when he decided on buying it, he assured himself that Mary Bonner's taste might be quite indifferent to him. In the first place, he had himself written to her uncle to withdraw his claim as soon as he found that Newton would never belong to him ; and then he had been told by the happy owner of Newton that Mary was still to be asked to share the throne of that principality. When so told he had said nothing of his own ambition, but had felt that there was another reason why he should leave Newton and its neighbourhood. For him, as a bachelor, Beamingham Hall would be only too good a house. He, as a farmer, did not mean to be ashamed of his own dunghill.

By the middle of May he had heard nothing either of his name-sake or of Mary Bonner. He did correspond with Gregory Newton, and thus received tidings of the parish, of the church, of the horses, —and even of the foxes ; but of the heir's matrimonial intentions he heard nothing. Gregory did write of his own visits to the metropolis, past and future, and Ralph knew that the young parson would again singe his wings in the flames that were burning at Popham Villa ; but nothing was said of the heir. Through March and April that trouble respecting Polly Neefit was continued, and Gregory in his letter of course did not speak of the Neefits. At last May was come, and Ralph from Beamingham made up his mind that he also would go up to London. He had been hard at work during the last four months doing all those wonderfully attractive things with his new property which a man can do when he has money in his pocket,—knocking down hedges, planting young trees or preparing for the planting of them, buying stock, building or preparing to build sheds, —and the rest of it. There is hardly a pleasure in life equal to that of laying out money with a conviction that it will come back again. The conviction, alas, is so often ill founded,—but the pleasure is the same. In regard to the house itself he would do nothing, not even form a plan—as yet. It might be possible that some taste other than his own should be consulted.

In the second week in May he went up to London, having heard that Gregory would be there at the same time ; and he at once found himself consorting with his namesake almost as much as with the parson. It was now a month since the heir had been dismissed from Popham Villa, and he had not since that date renewed his visit. Nor from that day to the present had he seen Sir Thomas. It cannot be said with exact truth that he was afraid of Sir Thomas or ashamed to see the girls. He had no idea that he had behaved badly to anybody; and, if he had, he was almost disposed to make amends for such sin by marrying Clarissa ; but he felt that should he ultimately make up his mind in Clarissa's favour, a little time should elapse for the gradual curé of his former passion. No doubt he placed reliance on his position as a man of property, feeling that by his strength in that direction he would be pulled through all his little difficulties ; but it was an unconscious reliance. He believed that he was perfectly free from what he himself would have called the dirt and littleness of purse-pride—or acre-pride, and would on some occasions assert that he really thought nothing of himself because he was Newton of Newton. And he meant to be true. Nevertheless, in the bottom of his heart, there was a confidence that he might do this and that because of his acres, and among the things which might be thus done, but which could not otherwise have been done, was this return to Clarissa after his little lapse in regard to Mary Bonner.

He was delighted to welcome Ralph from Norfolk to all the pleasures of the metropolis. Should he put down Ralph's name at the famous Carlton, of which he had lately become a member ? Ralph already belonged to an old-fashioned club, of which his father had been long a member, and declined the new honour. As for balls, evening crushes, and large dinner-parties, our Norfolk Ralph thought himself to be unsuited for them just at present, because of his father's death. It was not for the nephew of the dead man to tell the son that eight months of mourning for a father was more than the world now required. He could only take the excuse, and suggest the play, and a little dinner at Richmond, and a small party to Maidenhead as compromises. "I don't know that there is any good in a fellow being so heavy in hand because his father is dead," the Squire said to his brother.

"They were so much to each other," pleaded Gregory in return. The Squire accepted the excuse, and offered his namesake a horse for the park. Would he make one of the party for the moors in August? The Squire asserted that he had room for another gun, without entailing any additional expense upon himself. This indeed was not strictly true, as it had been arranged that the cost should be paid per gun; but there was a vacancy still, and Ralph the heir, being quite willing to pay for his cousin, thought no harm to cover his generosity under a venial falsehood. The disinherited one, however, declined the offer, with many thanks. "There is nothing, old fellow, I wouldn't do for you, if I knew how," said the happy heir. Whereupon the Norfolk Ralph unconsciously resolved that he would accept nothing,—or as little as possible,—at the hands of the Squire.

All this happened during the three or four first days of his sojourn in London, in which, he hardly knew why, he had gone neither to the villa nor to Sir Thomas in Southampton Buildings. He meant to do so, but from day to day he put it off. As regarded the ladies at the villa the three young men now never spoke to each other respecting them. Gregory believed that his brother had failed, and so believing did not recur to the subject. Gregory himself had already been at Fulham once or twice since his arrival in town; but had nothing to say,—or at least did say nothing,— of what happened there. He intended to remain away from his parish for no more than the parson's normal thirteen days, and was by no means sure that he would make any further formal offer. When at the villa he found that Clarissa was sad and sober, and almost silent; and he knew that something was wrong. It hardly occurred to him to believe that after all he might perhaps cure the evil.

One morning, early, Gregory and Ralph from Norfolk were together at the Royal Academy. Although it was not yet ten when they entered the gallery, the rooms were already so crowded that it was difficult to get near the line, and almost impossible either to get into or to get out of a corner. Gregory had been there before, and knew the pictures. He also was supposed by his friends to understand something of the subject; whereas Ralph did not know a Cooke from a Hook, and possessed no more than a dim idea that Landseer painted all the wild beasts, and Millais all the little children. "That's a fine picture," he said, pointing up at an enormous portrait of the Master of the B B, in a red coat, seated square on a seventeen-hand high horse, with his hat off, and the favourite hounds of his pack around him. "That's by Grant," said Gregory. "I don't know that I care for that kind of thing." "It's as like as it can stare," said Ralph, who appreciated the red coat, and the well-groomed horse, and the finely-shaped hounds. He backed a few steps to see the picture better, and found himself encroaching upon a lady's dress. He turned round and found that the lady was Mary Bonner. Together with her were both Clarissa and Patience Underwood.

The greetings between them all were pleasant, and the girls were unaffectedly pleased to find friends whom they knew well enough to accept as guides and monitors in the room. "Now we shall be told all about everything," said Clarissa, as the young parson shook hands first with her sister and then with her. "Do take us round to the best dozen, Mr. Newton. That's the way I like to begin." Her tone was completely different from what it had been down at the villa.

"That gentleman in the red coat is my cousin's favourite," said Gregory.

"I don't care a bit about that." said Clarissa.

"That's because you don't hunt," said Ralph.

"I wish I hunted," said Mary Bonner.

Mary, when she first saw the man, of whom she had once been told that he was to be her lover, and, when so told, had at least been proud that she was so chosen,—felt that she was blushing slightly ; but she recovered herself instantly, and greeted him as though there had been no cause whatever for disturbance. He was struck almost dumb at seeing her, and it was her tranquillity which restored him to composure. After the first greetings were over he found himself walking by her side without any effort on her part to avoid him, while Gregory and the two sisters went on in advance. Poor Ralph had not a word to say about the pictures. "Have you been long in London?" she asked.

"Just four days."

"We heard that you were coming, and did think that perhaps you and your cousin might find a morning to come down and see us ; —your cousin Gregory, I mean."

"Of course I shall come."

"My uncle will be so glad to see you ;—only, you know, you can't always find him at home. And so will Patience. You are a great favourite with Patience. You have gone down to live in Norfolk,—haven't you?"

"Yes—in Norfolk."

"You have bought an estate there?"

"Just one farm that I look after myself. It's no estate, Miss Bonner;—just a farm-house, with barns and stables, and a horse-pond, and the rest of it." This was by no means a fair account of the place, but it suited him so to speak of it. "My days for having an estate were quickly brought to a close;—were they not?" This he said with a little laugh, and then hated himself for having spoken so foolishly.

"Does that make you unhappy, Mr. Newton?" she asked. He did not answer her at once, and she continued, "I should have thought that you were above being made unhappy by that."

"Such disappointments carry many things with them of which people outside see nothing."

"That is true, no doubt."

"A man may be separated from every friend he has in the world by such a change of circumstances."

"I had not thought of that. I beg your pardon," said she, looking into his face almost imploringly.

"And there may be worse than that," he said. Of course she knew what he meant, but he did not know how much she knew. "It is easy to say that a man should stand up against reverses,—but there are some reverses a man cannot bear without suffering." She had quite made up her mind that the one reverse of which she was thinking should be cured; but she could take no prominent step towards curing it yet. But that some step should be taken sooner or later she was resolved. It might be taken now, indeed, if he would only speak out. But she quite understood that he would not speak out now because that house down in Norfolk was no more than a farm. "But I didn't mean to trouble you with all that nonsense," he said.

"It doesn't trouble me at all. Of course you will tell us everything when you come to see us."

"There is very little to tell,—unless you care for cows and pigs, and sheep and horses."

"I do care for cows and pigs, and sheep and horses," she said.

"All the same, they are not pleasant subjects of conversation. A man may do as much good with a single farm as he can with a large estate; but he can't make his affairs as interesting to other people." There was present to his own mind the knowledge that he and his rich namesake were rivals in regard to the affections of this beautiful girl, and he could not avoid allusions to his own inferiority. And yet his own words, as soon as they were spoken and had sounded in his ear, were recognised by himself as being mean and pitiful,—as whining words, and sorry plaints against the trick which fortune had played him. He did not know how to tell her boldly that he lamented this change from the estate to the farm because he had hoped that she would share the one with him, and did not dare even to ask her to share the other. She understood it all, down to the look of displeasure which crossed his face as he felt the possible effect of his own speech. She understood it all, but she could not give him much help,—as yet. There might perhaps come a moment in which she could explain to him her own ideas about farms and estates, and the reasons in accordance with which these might be selected and those rejected. "Have you seen much of Ralph Newton lately?" asked the other Ralph.

"Of your cousin?"

"Yes;—only I do not call him so. I have no right to call him my cousin."

"No; we do not see much of him." This was said in a tone of voice which ought to have sufficed for curing any anxiety in Ralph's bosom respecting his rival. Had he not been sore and nervous, and, as it must be admitted, almost stupid in the matter, he could not but have gathered from that tone that his namesake was at least no favourite with Miss Bonner. "He used to be a great deal at Popham Villa," said Ralph.

"We do not see him often now. I fancy there has been some cause of displeasure between him and my uncle. His brother has been with us once or twice. I do like Mr. Gregory Newton."

"He is the best fellow that ever lived," exclaimed Ralph with energy.

"So much nicer than his brother," said Mary;—"though perhaps I ought not to say so to you."

This at any rate could not but be satisfactory to him. "I like them both," he said; "but I love Greg dearly. He and I have lived together like brothers for years, whereas it is only quite lately that I have known the other."

"It is only lately that I have known either;—but they seem to me to be so different. Is not that a wonderfully beautiful picture, Mr. Newton? Can't you almost fancy yourself sitting down and throwing stones into the river, or dabbling your feet in it?"

"It is very pretty," said he, not caring a penny for the picture.

"Have you any river at Beamingham?"

"There's a muddy little brook that you could almost jump over. You wouldn't want to dabble in that."

"Has it got a name?"

"I think they call it the Wissey. It's not at all a river to be proud of,—except in the way of eels and water-rats."

"Is there nothing to be proud of at Beamingham?"

"There's the church tower;—that's all."

"A church tower is something;—but I meant as to Beamingham Hall."

"That word Hall misleads people," said Ralph. "It's a kind of upper-class farm-house with a lot of low rooms, and intricate passages, and chambers here and there, smelling of apples, and a huge kitchen, and an oven big enough for a small dinner-party."

"I should like the oven."

"And a laundry, and a dairy, and a cheese-house,—only we never make any cheese; and a horse-pond, and a dung-hill, and a cabbage-garden."

"Is that all you can say for your new purchase, Mr. Newton?"

"The house itself isn't ugly."

"Come;—that's better."

"And it might be made fairly comfortable, if there were any use in doing it."

"Of course there will be use."

"I don't know that there will," said Ralph. "Sometimes I think one thing, and sometimes another. One week I'm full of a scheme about a new garden and a conservatory, and a bow-window to the drawing-room; and then, the next week, I think that the two rooms I live in at present will be enough for me."

"Stick to the conservatory, Mr. Newton. But here are the girls, and I suppose it is about time for us to go."

"Mary, where have you been?" said Clarissa.

"Looking at landscapes," said Mary.

"Mr. Newton has shown us every picture worth seeing, and described everything, and we haven't had to look at the catalogue once. That's just what I like at the Academy. I don't know whether you've been as lucky."

"I've had a great deal described to me too," said Mary; "but I'm afraid we've forgotten the particular duty that brought us here." Then they parted, the two men promising that they would be at the villa before long, and the girls preparing themselves for their return home.

"That cousin of theirs is certainly very beautiful," said Gregory, after some short tribute to the merits of the two sisters.

"I think she is," said Ralph.

"I do not wonder that my brother has been struck with her."

"Nor do I." Then after a pause he continued; "She said something which made me think that she and your brother haven't quite hit it off together."

"I don't know that they have," said Gregory. "Ralph does change his mind sometimes. He hasn't said a word about her to me lately."

CHAPTER L.

ANOTHER FAILURE.

THE day after the meeting at the Academy, as Ralph, the young Squire, was sitting alone in his room over a late breakfast, a maid-servant belonging to the house opened the door and introduced Mr. Neefit. It was now the middle of May, and Ralph had seen nothing of the breeches-maker since the morning on which he had made his appearance in the yard of the Moonbeam. There had been messages, and Mr. Carey had been very busy endeavouring to persuade the father that he could benefit neither himself nor his daughter by persistence in so extravagant a scheme. Money had been offered to Mr. Neefit,— most unfortunately, and this offer had added to his wrongs. And he had been told by his wife that Polly had at last decided in regard to her own affections, and had accepted her old lover, Mr. Moggs. He had raved at Polly to her face. He had sworn at Moggs behind his back. He had called Mr. Carey very hard names;—and now he forced himself once more upon the presence of the young Squire. "Captain," he said, as soon as he had carefully closed the door behind him, " are you going to be upon the square?" Newton had given special orders that Neefit should not be admitted to his presence; but here he was, having made his way into the chamber in the temporary absence of the Squire's own servant.

"Mr. Neefit," said Newton, " I cannot allow this."

"Not allow it, Captain?"

"No;—I cannot. I will not be persecuted. I have received favours from you——"

"Yes, you have, Captain."

"And I will do anything in reason to repay them."

"Will you come out and see our Polly?"

"No, I won't."

"You won't?"

"Certainly not. I don't believe your daughter wants to see me. She is engaged to another man." So much Mr. Carey had learned from Mrs. Neefit. "I have a great regard for your daughter, but I will not go to see her."

"Engaged to another man;—is she?"

"I am told so."

"Oh;—that's your little game, is it? And you won't see me when I call,—won't you? I won't stir out of this room unless you sends for the police, and so we'll get it all into one of the courts of law. I shall just like to see how you'll look when you're being cross-hackled by one of them learned gents. There'll be a question or two about the old breeches-maker as the Squire of Newton mayn't like to see in the papers the next morning. I shall take the liberty of ringing the bell and ordering a bit of dinner here, if you don't mind. I shan't go when the police comes without a deal of row, and then we shall have it all out in the courts."

This was monstrously absurd, but at the same time very annoying. Even though he should disregard that threat of being " cross-hackled by a learned gent," and of being afterwards made notorious in the newspapers,—which it must be confessed he did not find himself able to disregard,—still, independently of that feeling, he was very unwilling to call for brute force to remove Mr. Neefit from the arm-chair in which that worthy tradesman had seated himself. He had treated the man otherwise than as a tradesman. He had borrowed the man's money, and eaten the man's dinners; visited the man at Ramsgate, and twice offered his hand to the man's daughter. " You are very welcome to dine here," he said, " only I am sorry that I cannot dine here with you."

" I won't stir from the place for a week.'

" That will be inconvenient," said Ralph.

" Uncommon inconvenient I should say, to a gent like you,— especially as I shall tell everybody that I'm on a visit to my son-in-law."

" I meant to yourself,—and to the business."

" Never you mind the business, Captain. There'll be enough left to give my girl all the money I promised her, and I don't think I shall have to ask you to keep your father-in-law neither. Sending an attorney to offer me a thousand pounds ! It's my belief I could buy you out yet, Captain, in regard to ready money."

" I daresay you could, Mr. Neefit."

" And I won't stir from here till you name a day to come and see me and my missus and Polly."

" This is sheer madness, Mr. Neefit."

" You think so ;—do you, Captain ? You'll find me madder nor you think for yet. I'm not agoing to be put upon by you, and nothing come of it. I'll have it out of you in money or marbles, as the saying is. Just order me a glass of sherry wine, will you ? I'm a thirsty talking. When you came a visiting me, I always give you lashings of drink." This was so true that Ralph felt himself compelled to ring the bell, and order up some wine. " Soda and brandy let it be, Jack," said Mr. Neefit to Mr. Newton's own man. " It'll be more comfortable like between near relations."

" Soda-water and brandy for Mr. Neefit," said the young Squire, turning angrily to the man. " Mr. Neefit, you are perfectly welcome to as much brandy as you can drink, and my man will wait upon you

while I'm away. Good morning." Whereupon Newton took up his
hat and left the room. He had not passed into the little back room,
in which he knew that the servant would be looking for soda-water,
before he heard a sound as of smashed crockery, and he was convinced that Mr. Neefit was preparing himself for forcible eviction by
breaking his ornaments. Let the ornaments go, and the mirror, and
the clock on the chimney-piece, and the windows. It was a frightful
nuisance, but anything would be better than sending for the police to
take away Mr. Neefit. " Keep your eye on that man in the front
room," said he, to his Swiss valet.

" On Mr. Neefit, saar ? "

" Yes ; on Mr. Neefit. He wants me to marry his daughter, and
I can't oblige him. Let him have what he wants to eat and drink.
Get rid of him if you can, but don't send for the police. He's
smashing all the things, and you must save as many as you can."
So saying, he hurried down the stairs and out of the house. But
what was he to do next ? If Mr. Neefit chose to carry out his threat
by staying in the rooms, Mr. Neefit must be allowed to have his own
way. If he chose to amuse himself by breaking the things, the
things must be broken. If he got very drunk, he might probably be
taken home in a cab, and deposited at the cottage at Hendon. But
what should Ralph do at this moment'? He sauntered sadly down
St. James's Street with his hands in his trousers-pockets, and finding
a crawling hansom at the palace-gate, he got into it and ordered the
man to drive him down to Fulham. He had already made up his mind
about " dear little Clary," and the thing might as well be done at
once. None of the girls were at home. Miss Underwood and Miss
Bonner had gone up to London to see Sir Thomas. Miss Clarissa
was spending the day with Mrs. Brownlow. " That will just be
right," said Ralph to himself, as he ordered the cabman to drive him
to the old lady's house on the Brompton Road.

Mrs. Brownlow had ever been a great admirer of the young Squire,
and did not admire him less now that he had come to his squireship.
She had always hoped that Clary would marry the real heir, and was
sounding his praises while Ralph was knocking at her door. " He
is not half so fine a fellow as his brother," said Clarissa.

" You did not use to think so," said Mrs. Brownlow. Then the
door was opened and Ralph was announced.

With his usual easy manner,—with that unabashed grace which
Clarissa used to think so charming,—he soon explained that he had
been to Fulham, and had had himself driven back to Bolsover House
because Clarissa was there. Clarissa, as she heard this, felt the
blood tingle in her cheeks. His manner now did not seem to her to be
so full of grace. Was it not all selfishness ? Mrs. Brownlow purred
out her applause. It was not to be supposed that he came to see an

old woman ;—but his coming to see a young woman, with adequate intentions, was quite the proper thing for such a young man to do ! They were just going to take lunch. Of course he would stop and lunch with them. He declared that he would like nothing better. Mrs. Brownlow rang the bell, and gave her little orders. Clarissa's thoughts referred quickly to various matters,—to the scene on the lawn, to a certain evening on which she had walked home with him from this very house, to the confessions which she had made to her sister, to her confidence with her cousin ;—and then to the offer that had been made to Mary, now only a few weeks since. She looked at him, though she did not seem to be looking at him, and told herself that the man was nothing to her. He had caused her unutterable sorrow, with which her heart was still sore ;—but he was nothing to her. She would eat her lunch with him, and endeavour to talk to him ; but the less she might see of him henceforth the better. He was selfish, heartless, weak, and unworthy.

The lunch was eaten, and within three minutes afterwards, Mrs. Brownlow was away. As they were returning to the little parlour in which they had been sitting during the morning, she contrived to escape, and Ralph found himself alone with his " dear, darling little Clary." In spite of his graceful ease, the task before him was not without difficulty. Clarissa, of course, knew that he had proposed to Mary, and probably knew that he had proposed to Polly. But Mary had told him that Clarissa was devoted to him,—had told him at least that which amounted to almost as much. And then it was incumbent on him to do something that might put an end to the Neefit abomination. Clarissa would be contented to look back upon that episode with Mary Bonner, as a dream that meant nothing ;— just as he himself was already learning to look at it. " Clary," he said, " I have hardly seen you to speak to you since the night we walked home together from this house."

" No, indeed, Mr. Newton," she said. Hitherto she had always called him Ralph. He did not observe the change, having too many things of his own to think of at the moment.

" How much has happened since that ! "

" Very much, indeed, Mr. Newton."

" And yet it seems to be such a short time ago,—almost yesterday. My poor uncle was alive then."

" Yes, he was."

He did not seem to be getting any nearer to his object by these references to past events. " Clary," he said, " there are many things which I wish to have forgotten, and some perhaps which I would have forgiven."

" I suppose that is so with all of us," said Clarissa.

" Just so, though I don't know that any of us have ever been so absurdly foolish as I have,—throwing away what was of the greatest value in the world for the sake of something that seemed to be precious, just for a moment." It was very difficult, and he already began to feel that the nature of the girl was altered towards him. She had suddenly become hard, undemonstrative, and almost unkind. Hitherto he had always regarded her, without much conscious thought about it, as a soft, sweet, pleasant thing, that might at any moment be his for the asking. And Mary Bonner had told him that he ought to ask. Now he was willing to beseech her pardon, to be in very truth her lover, and to share with her all his prosperity. But she would give him no assistance in his difficulty. He was determined that she should speak, and, trusting to Mrs. Brownlow's absence, he sat still, waiting for her.

"I hope you have thrown away nothing that you ought to keep," she said at last. "It seems to me that you have got everything."

"No,—not as yet everything. I do not know whether I shall ever get that which I desire the most." Of course she understood him now; but she sat hard, and fixed, and stern,—so absolutely unlike the Clarissa whom he had known since they were hardly more than children together! "You know what I mean, Clarissa."

"No;—I do not," she said.

"I fear you mean that you cannot forgive me."

"I have nothing to forgive."

"Oh yes, you have; whether you will ever forgive me I cannot say. But there is much to forgive;—very much. Your cousin Mary for a short moment ran away with us all."

"She is welcome,—for me."

"What do you mean, Clarissa?"

"Just what I say. She is welcome for me. She has taken nothing that I prize. Indeed I do not think she has condescended to take anything,—anything of the sort you mean. Mary and I love each other dearly. There is no danger of our quarrelling."

"Come, Clary," he got up as he spoke, and stood over her, close to her shoulder, "you understand well enough what I mean. We have known each other so long, and I think we have loved each other so well, that you ought to say that you will forgive me. I have been foolish. I have been wrong. I have been false, if you will. Cannot you forgive me?"

Not for a moment was there a look of forgiveness in her eye, or a sign of pardon in the lines of her face. But in her heart there was a contest. Something of the old passion remained there, though it was no more than the soreness it had caused. For half a moment she thought whether it might not be as he would have it. But if so, how could she again look any of her friends in the face and admit that she had surrendered herself to so much unworthiness? How could she tell Patience, who was beginning to be full of renewed hope for Gregory ? How could she confess such a weakness to her father ? How could she stand up before Mary Bonner ? And was it possible that she should really give herself, her whole life, and all her future hopes, to one so weak and worthless as this man ? "There is nothing to forgive," she said, " but I certainly cannot forget."

" You know that I love you," he protested.

" Love me ;—yes, with what sort of love ? But it does not matter. There need be no further talk about it. Your love to me can be nothing."

" Clarissa ! "

" And to you it will be quite as little. Your heart will never suffer much, Ralph. How long is it since you offered your hand to my cousin ? Only that you are just a boy playing at love, this would be an insult." Then she saw her old friend through the window. "Mrs. Brownlow," she said, " Mr. Newton is going, and I am ready for our walk whenever you please."

" Think of it twice, Clarissa ;—must this be the end of it ? " pleaded Ralph.

" As far as I am concerned it must be the end of it. When I get home I shall probably find that you have already made an offer to Patience." Then he got up, took his hat, and having shaken hands cordially with Mrs. Brownlow through the window, went out to his hansom cab, which was earning sixpence a quarter of an hour out on the road, while he had been so absolutely wasting his quarter of an hour within the house.

" Has he said anything, my dear ? " asked Mrs. Brownlow.

" He has said a great deal."

" Well, my dear ? "

" He is an empty, vain, inconstant man."

" Is he, Clarissa ? "

" And yet he is so good-humoured, and so gay, and so pleasant, that I do not see why he should not make a very good husband to some girl."

" What do you mean, Clarissa ? You have not refused him ? "

" I did not say he had offered ;—did I ? "

" But he has ? "

" If he did,—then I refused him. He is good-natured ; but he has no more heart than a log of wood. Don't talk about it any more, dear Mrs. Brownlow. I dare say we shall all be friends again before long, and he'll almost forget everything that he said this morning."

Throughout the afternoon she was gay and almost happy, and before she went home she had made up her mind that she would tell Patience, and then get rid of it from her thoughts for ever. Not to tell Patience would be a breach of faith between them, and would moreover render future sisterly intercourse between them very difficult. But had it been possible she would have avoided the expression of triumph without which it would be almost impossible for her to tell the story. Within her own bosom certainly there was some triumph. The man for whose love she had sighed and been sick had surrendered to her at last. The prize had been at her feet, but she had not chosen to lift it. "Poor Ralph," she said to herself; "he means to do as well as he can, but he is so feeble." She certainly would not tell Mary Bonner, nor would she say a word to her father. And when she should meet Ralph again,—as she did not doubt but that she would meet him shortly, she would be very careful to give no sign that she was thinking of his disgrace. He should still be called Ralph,—till he was a married man; and when it should come to pass that he was about to marry she would congratulate him with all the warmth of old friendship.

That night she did tell it all to Patience. "You don't mean," she said, "that I have not done right?"

"I am sure you have done quite right."

"Then why are you so sober about it, Patty?"

"Only if you do love him——! I would give my right hand, Clary, that you might have that which shall make you happy in life."

"If you were to give your right and left hand too, a marriage with Ralph Newton would not make me happy. Think of it, Patty;—to both of us within two months! He is just like a child. How could I ever have respected him, or believed in him? I could never have respected myself again. No, Patty, I did love him dearly. I fancied that life without him must all be a dreary blank. I made him into a god;—but his feet are of the poorest clay! Kiss me, dear, and congratulate me;—because I have escaped."

Her sister did kiss her and did congratulate her;—but still there was a something of regret in the sister's heart. Clarissa was, to her thinking, so fit to be the mistress of Newton Priory.

CHAPTER LI.

MUSIC HAS CHARMS

THE Commission appointed to examine into the condition of the borough of Percycross cannot exactly be said to have made short work of it, for it sat daily for many consecutive weeks, and examined half the voters in the town ; but it made sharp work, and reported to the Speaker of the House such a tale of continual corruption, that all the world knew that the borough would be disfranchised. The glory of Percycross was gone, and in regard to political influence it was to be treated as the cities of the plain, and blotted from off the face of existence. The learned gentlemen who formed the Commission had traced home to Mr. Griffenbottom's breeches-pockets large sums of money which had been expended in the borough for purposes of systematised corruption during the whole term of his connection with it ;—and yet they were not very hard upon Mr. Griffenbottom personally in their report. He had spent the money no doubt, but had so spent it that at every election it appeared that he had not expected to spend it till the bills were sent to him. He frankly owned that the borough had been ruinous to him ; had made a poor man of him,—but assured the Commission at the same time that all this had come from his continued innocence. As every new election came round, he had hoped that that would at least be pure, and had been urgent in his instructions to his agents to that effect. He had at last learned, he said, that he was not a sufficient Hercules to cleanse so foul a stable. All this created no animosity against him in Percycross during the sitting of the Commission. His old friends, the Triggers, and Piles, and Spiveycombs, clung to him as closely as ever. Every man in Percycross knew that the borough was gone, and there really seemed at last to be something of actual gratitude in their farewell behaviour to the man who had treated the place as it liked to be treated. As the end of it all, the borough was undoubtedly to be disfranchised, and Mr. Griffenbottom left it,—a ruined man, indeed, according to his own statement,—but still with his colours flying, and, to a certain extent, triumphantly. So we will leave him, trusting,—or perhaps rather hoping,—that the days of Mr. Griffenbottom are nearly at an end.

His colleague, Sir Thomas, on the occasion of his third visit to Percycross,—a visit which he was constrained to make, sorely against his will, in order that he might give his evidence before the Commission,—remained there but a very short time. But while there he made a clean breast of it. He had gone down to the borough with the most stedfast purpose to avoid corruption ; and had done his best in that direction. But he had failed. There had been corruption, for which he had himself paid in part. There had been treating of the grossest kind. Money had been demanded from him since the election, as to the actual destination of which he was profoundly ignorant. He did not, however, doubt but that this money had been spent in the purchase of votes. Sir Thomas was supposed to have betrayed the borough in his evidence, and was hooted out of the town. On this occasion he only remained there one night, and left Percycross for ever, after giving his evidence.

This happened during the second week in May. On his return to London he did not go down to Fulham, but remained at his chambers in a most unhappy frame of mind. This renewed attempt of his to enter the world and to go among men that he might do a man's work, had resulted in the loss of a great many hundred pounds, in absolute failure, and, as he wrongly told himself, in personal disgrace. He was almost ashamed to show himself at his club, and did for two days absolutely have his dinner brought to him in his chambers from an eating-house.

"I'm sure you won't like that, Sir Thomas," Stemm had said to him, expostulating, and knowing very well the nature of his master's sufferings.

"I don't know that I like anything very much," said Sir Thomas.

"I wouldn't go and not show my face because of other people's roguery," rejoined Stemm, with cruel audacity. Sir Thomas looked at him, but did not answer a word, and Stemm fetched the food.

"Stemm," said Sir Thomas the same evening, "it's getting to be fine weather now."

"It's fine enough," said Stemm.

"Do you take your nieces down to Southend for an outing. Go down on Thursday and come back on Saturday. I shall be at home. There's a five-pound note for the expenses." Stemm slowly took the note, but grunted and grumbled. The girls were nuisances to him, and he didn't want to take them an outing. They wouldn't care to go before July, and he didn't care to go at all. "You can go when you please," said Sir Thomas. Stemm growled and grumbled, and at last left the room with the money.

The morning afterwards Sir Thomas was sitting alone in his room absolutely wretched. He had so managed his life that there seemed to be nothing left to him in it worth the having. He had raised himself to public repute by his intellect and industry, and had then, almost at once, allowed himself to be hustled out of the throng simply because others had been rougher than he,—because other men had pushed and shouldered while he had been quiet and unpretending. Then he had resolved to make up for this disappointment by work of another kind,—by work which would, after all, be more congenial to him. He would go back to the dream of his youth, to the labours of former days, and would in truth write his Life of Bacon. He had then surrounded himself with his papers, had gotten his books together and read up his old notes, had planned chapters and sections, and settled divisions, had drawn up headings, and revelled in those paraphernalia of work which are so dear to would-be working men;—and then nothing had come of it. Of what use was it that he went about ever with a volume in his pocket, and read a page or two as he sat over his wine? When sitting alone in his room he did read; but when reading he knew that he was not working. He went, as it were, round and round the thing, never touching it, till the labour which he longed to commence became so frightful to him that he did not dare to touch it. To do that thing was the settled purpose of his life, and yet, from day to day and from month to month, it became more impossible to him even to make a beginning. There is a misery in this which only they who have endured it can understand. There are idle men who rejoice in idleness. Their name is legion. Idleness, even when it is ruinous, is delightful to them. They revel in it, look forward to it, and almost take a pride in it. When it can be had without pecuniary detriment, it is to such men a thing absolutely good in itself. But such a one was not Sir Thomas Underwood. And there are men who love work, who revel in that, who attack it daily with renewed energy, almost wallowing in it, greedy of work, who go to it almost as the drunkard goes to his bottle, or the gambler to his gaming-table. These are not unhappy men, though they are perhaps apt to make those around them unhappy. But such a one was not Sir Thomas Underwood. And again there are men, fewer in number, who will work though they hate it, from sheer conscience and from conviction that idleness will not suit them or make them happy. Strong men these are;—but such a one certainly was not Sir Thomas Underwood. Then there are they who love the idea of work, but want the fibre needful for the doing it. It may be that such a one will earn his bread as Sir Thomas Underwood had earned his, not flinching from routine task or even from the healthy efforts necessary for subsistence. But there will ever be present to the mind of the ambitious man the idea of something to be done over and above the mere earning of his bread;—and the ambition may be very strong, though the fibre be lacking. Such a one will endure an agony protracted for years, always intending, never performing, self-accusing through every wakeful hour, self-accusing almost through every sleeping hour. The work to be done is close there by the hand, but the tools are loathed, and the paraphernalia of it become hateful. And yet it can never be put aside. It is to be grasped to-morrow, but on every morrow the grasping of it becomes more difficult, more impossible, more revolting. There is no peace, no happiness for such a man;—and such a one was Sir Thomas Underwood.

In this strait he had been tempted to make another effort in political life, and he had made it. There had been no difficulty in this,—only that the work itself had been so disagreeable, and that he had failed in it so egregiously. During his canvass, and in all his intercourse with the Griffenbottomites, he had told himself, falsely, how pleasant to him it would be to return to his books ;—how much better for him would be a sedentary life, if he could only bring himself to do, or even attempt to do, the work which he had appointed for himself. Now he had returned to his solitude, had again dragged out his papers, his note-book, his memoranda, his dates, and yet he could not in truth get into his harness, put his neck to the collar, and attempt to drag the burden up the hill.

He was sitting alone in his room in this condition, with a book in his hand of no value to his great purpose, hating himself and wretched, when Stemm opened his door, ushering Patience and Mary Bonner into his room. "Ah, my dears," he said, "what has brought you up to London? I did not think of seeing you here." There was no expression of positive displeasure in his voice, but it was understood by them all, by the daughter, by the cousin, by old Stemm, and by Sir Thomas himself, that such a visit as this was always to be regarded more or less as an intrusion. However, he kissed them both, and handed them chairs, and was more than usually civil to them.

"We do so want to hear about Percycross, papa," said Patience.

"There is nothing to be told about Percycross."

"Are you to stand again, papa ?"

"Nobody will ever stand for Percycross again. It will lose its members altogether. The thing is settled."

"And you have had all the trouble for nothing, uncle ?" Mary asked.

"All for nothing,—and the expense. But that is a very common thing, and I have no ground of complaint beyond many others."

"It does seem so hard," said Patience.

"So very hard," said Mary. And then they were silent. They had not come without a purpose; but, as is common with young ladies, they kept their purpose for the end of the interview.

"Are you coming home, papa ?" Patience asked.

"Well, yes ; I won't settle any day now, because I am very busy just at present. But I shall be home soon,—very soon."

"I do so hope you'll stay some time with us, papa."

"My dear, you know——" And then he stopped, having been pounced upon so suddenly that he had not resolved what excuse he would for the moment put forward. "I've got my papers and things in such confusion here at present,—because of Percycross and the trouble I have had,—that I cannot leave them just now."

"But why not bring the papers with you, papa ?"

"My dear, you know I can't."

Then there was another pause. "Papa, I think you ought," said

Patience. " Indeed I do, for Clary's sake,—and ours." But even this was not the subject which had specially brought them on that morning to Southampton Buildings.

" What is there wrong with Clary ? " asked Sir Thomas.

" There is nothing wrong," said Patience

" What do you mean then ? "

" I think it would be so much more comfortable for her that you should see things as they are going on."

" I declare I don't know what she means. Do you know what she means, Mary ? "

" Clary has not been quite herself lately," said Mary.

" I suppose it's something about that scamp, Ralph Newton," said Sir Thomas.

" No, indeed, papa; I am sure she does not think of him now." On this very morning, as the reader may perhaps remember, the scamp had gone down to Fulham, and from Fulham back to Brompton, in search of Clarissa; but of the scamp's energy and renewed affections, Patience as yet knew nothing. " Gregory has been up in London and has been down at Fulham once or twice. We want him to come again before he goes back on Saturday, and we thought if you would come home on Thursday, we could ask him to dinner." Sir Thomas scratched his head, and fidgeted in his chair. " Their cousin is in London also," continued Patience.

" The other Ralph; he who has bought Beamingham Hall ? "

" Yes, papa; we saw him at the Academy. I told him how happy you would be to see him at Fulham."

" Of course I should be glad to see him; that is, if I happened to be at home," said Sir Thomas.

" But I could not name a day without asking you, papa."

" He will have gone back by this time," said Sir Thomas.

" I think not, papa."

" And what do you say, Mary ? "

" I have nothing to say at all, uncle. If Mr. Newton likes to come to the villa, I shall be glad to see him. Why should I not ? He has done nothing to offend me." There was a slight smile on her face as she spoke, and the merest hint of a blush on her cheek.

" They tell me that Beamingham Hall isn't much of a place after all," said Sir Thomas.

" From what Mr. Newton says, it must be a very ugly place," said Mary, with still the same smile and the same hint of a blush ;—" only I don't quite credit all he tells us."

" If there is anything settled you ought to tell me," said Sir Thomas.

" There is nothing settled, uncle, or in any way of being settled. It so happened that Mr. Newton did speak to me about his new house. There is nothing more."

" Nevertheless, papa, pray let us ask him to dinner on Thursday."
It was for the purpose of making this request that Patience had come
to Southampton Buildings, braving her father's displeasure. Sir
Thomas scratched his head, and rubbed his face, and yielded. Of
course he had no alternative but to yield, and yet he did it with a
bad grace. Permission, however, was given, and it was understood
that Patience would write to the two young men, Ralph of Beamingham Hall and the parson, asking them to dinner for the day but one
following. " As the time is so short, I've written the notes ready,"
said Patience, producing them from her pocket. Then the bell was
rung, and the two notes were confided to Stemm. Patience, as she
was going, found a moment in which to be alone with her father, and
to speak one more word to him. " Dear papa, it would be so much
better for us that you should come and live at home. Think of those
two, with nobody, as it were, to say a word for them." Sir Thomas
groaned, and again scratched his head; but Patience left him before
he had arranged his words for an answer.

When they were gone, Sir Thomas sat for hours in his chair
without moving, making the while one or two faint attempts at the
book before him, but in truth giving up his mind to contemplation
of the past and to conjectures as to the future, burdened by heavy
regrets, and with hopes too weak to afford him any solace. The last
words which Patience had spoken rang in his ears,—" Think of those
two, with nobody, as it were, to say a word for them." He did
think of them, and of the speaker also, and knew that he had
neglected his duty. He could understand that such a girl as his
own Clarissa did require some one "to say a word for her," some
stalwart arm to hold her up, some loving strength to support her,
some counsel to direct her. Of course those three girls were as other
girls, looking forward to matrimony as their future lot in life, and it
would not be well that they should be left to choose or to be chosen,
or left to reject and be rejected, without any aid from their remaining
parent. He knew that he had been wrong, and he almost resolved
that the chambers in Southampton Buildings should be altogether
abandoned, and his books removed to Popham Villa.

But such men do not quite resolve. Before he could lay his hand
upon the table and assure himself that the thing should be done, the
volume had been taken up again, used for a few minutes, and then
the man's mind had run away again to that vague contemplation
which is so much easier than the forming of a steady purpose. It
was one of those almost sultry days which do come to us occasionally
amidst the ordinary inclemency of a London May, and he was sitting
with his window open, though there was a fire in the grate. As he
sat, dreaming rather than thinking, there came upon his ear the
weak, wailing, puny sound of a distant melancholy flute. He had
heard it often before, and had been roused by it to evil wishes, and

sometimes even to evil words, against the musician. It was the effort of some youth in the direction of Staple's Inn to soothe with music the savageness of his own bosom. It was borne usually on the evening air, but on this occasion the idle swain had taken up his instrument within an hour or two of his early dinner. His melody was burdened with no peculiar tune, but consisted of a few low, wailing, melancholy notes, such as may be extracted from the reed by a breath and the slow raising and falling of the little finger, much, we believe, to the comfort of the player, but to the ineffable disgust of, too often, a large circle of hearers.

Sir Thomas was affected by the sound long before he was aware that he was listening to it. To-whew, to-whew; to-whew, to-whew; whew-to-to, whew-to-to, whew, to-whew. On the present occasion the variation was hardly carried beyond that; but so much was repeated with a persistency which at last seemed to burden the whole air round Southampton Buildings. The little thing might have been excluded by the closing of the window; but Sir Thomas, though he suffered, did not reflect for a while whence the suffering came. Who does not know how such sounds may serve to enhance the bitterness of remorse, to add a sorrow to the present thoughts, and to rob the future of its hopes?

There come upon us all as we grow up in years, hours in which it is impossible to keep down the conviction that everything is vanity, that the life past has been vain from folly, and that the life to come must be vain from impotence. It is the presence of thoughts such as these that needs the assurance of a heaven to save the thinker from madness or from suicide. It is when the feeling of this pervading vanity is strongest on him, that he who doubts of heaven most regrets his incapacity for belief. If there be nothing better than this on to the grave,—and nothing worse beyond the grave, why should I bear such fardels?

Sir Thomas, as he sat there listening and thinking, unable not to think and not to listen, found that the fardels were very heavy. What good had come to him of his life,—to him or to others? And what further good did he dare to promise to himself? Had it not all been vanity? Was it not all vain to him now at the present? Was not life becoming to him vainer and still vainer every day? He had promised himself once that books should be the solace of his age, and he was beginning to hate his books, because he knew that he did no more than trifle with them. He had found himself driven to attempt to escape from them back into public life; but had failed, and had been inexpressibly dismayed in the failure. While failing, he had promised himself that he would rush at his work on his return to privacy and to quiet; but he was still as the shivering coward, who stands upon the brink, and cannot plunge in among the bathers. And then there was sadness beyond this, and even deeper than this.

Why should he have dared to arrange for himself a life different from the life of the ordinary men and women who lived around him? Why had he not contented himself with having his children around him; walking with them to church on Sunday morning, taking them to the theatre on Monday evening, and allowing them to read him to sleep after tea on the Tuesday? He had not done these things, was not doing them now, because he had ventured to think himself capable of something that would justify him in leaving the common circle. He had left it, but was not justified. He had been in Parliament, had been in office, and had tried to write a book. But he was not a legislator, was not a statesman, and was not an author. He was simply a weak, vain, wretched man, who, through false conceit, had been induced to neglect almost every duty of life! To-whew, to-whew, to-whew, to-whew! As the sounds filled his ears, such were the thoughts which lay heavy on his bosom. So idle as he had been in thinking, so inconclusive, so frail, so subject to gusts of wind, so incapable of following his subject to the end, why had he dared to leave that Sunday-keeping, church-going, domestic, decent life, which would have become one of so ordinary a calibre as himself? There are men who may doubt, who may weigh the evidence, who may venture to believe or disbelieve in compliance with their own reasoning faculties,—who may trust themselves to think it out; but he, too clearly, had not been, was not, and never would be one of these. To walk as he saw other men walking around him,—because he was one of the many; to believe that to be good which the teachers appointed for him declared to be good; to do prescribed duties without much personal inquiry into the causes which had made them duties; to listen patiently, and to be content without excitement; that was the mode of living for which he should have known himself to be fit. But he had not known it, and had strayed away, and had ventured to think that he could think,—and had been ambitious. And now he found himself stranded in the mud of personal condemnation,—and that so late in life, that there remained to him no hope of escape. Whew-to-to; whew-to-to; whew,—to-whew. "Stemm, why do you let that brute go on with his cursed flute?" Stemm at that moment had opened the door to suggest that as he usually dined at one, and as it was now past three, he would go out and get a bit of something to eat.

"He's always at it, sir," said Stemm, pausing for a moment before he alluded to his own wants.

"Why the deuce is he always at it? Why isn't he indited for a nuisance? Who's to do anything with such a noise as that going on for hours together? He has nearly driven me mad."

"It's young Wobble as has the back attic, No. 17, in the Inn," said Stemm.

"They ought to turn him out," said Sir Thomas.

"I rather like it myself," said Stemm. "It suits my disposition, sir." Then he made his little suggestion in regard to his own personal needs, and of course was blown up for not having come in two hours ago to remind Sir Thomas that it was dinner-time. "It's because I wouldn't disturb you when you has the Bacon papers out, Sir Thomas," said Stemm serenely. Sir Thomas winced and shook his head; but such scenes as this were too common to have much effect. "Stemm!" he called aloud, as soon as the old clerk had closed the door; "Stemm!" Whereupon Stemm reappeared. "Stemm, have some one here next week to pack all these books."

"Pack all the books, Sir Thomas!"

"Yes;—to pack all the books. There must be cases. Now, go and get your dinner."

"New cases, Sir Thomas!"

"That will do. Go and get your dinner." And yet his mind was not quite made up.

CHAPTER LII.

GUS EARDHAM.

WHETHER Mr. Neefit broke Ralph Newton's little statuette,—a miniature copy in porcelain of the Apollo Belvidere, which stood in a corner of Ralph's room, and in the possession of which he took some pride,—from awkwardness in his wrath or of malice prepense, was never known. He told the servant that he had whisked it down with his coat tails; but Ralph always thought that the breeches-maker had intended to make a general ruin, but had been cowed by the noise of his first attack. He did, at any rate, abstain from breaking other things, and when the servant entered the room, condescended to make some careless apology. "A trifle like that ain't nothing between me and your master, Jack," said Mr. Neefit, after accounting for the accident by his coat-tails.

"I am not Jack," said the indignant valet, with a strong foreign accent. "I am named—Adolphe."

"Adolphe, are you? I don't think much of Adolphe for a name; —but it ain't no difference to me. Just pick up them bits; will you?"

The man turned a look of scorn on Mr. Neefit, and did pick up the bits. He intended to obey his master as far as might be possible, but was very unwilling to wait upon the breeches-maker. He felt that the order which had been given to him was very cruel. It was his duty,—and his pleasure to wait upon gentlemen; but this man he knew to be a tradesman who measured customers for hunting apparel in his own shop. It was hard upon him that his master should go and leave him to be insulted, ordered about, and trodden upon by a breeches-maker. "Get me a bit of steak, will you?" demanded Neefit;—"a bit of the rump, not too much done, with the gravy in it,—and an onion. What are you staring at? Didn't you hear what your master said to you?"

"Onion,—and romp-steak!"

"Yes; rump-steak and onion. I ain't going out of this till I've had a bit of grub. Your master knows all about it. I'm going to have more nor that out of him before I've done with him."

Neefit did at last succeed, and had his rump-steak and onion, together with more brandy and soda-water, eating and drinking as he sat in Ralph's beautiful new easy chair,—not very much to his own comfort. A steak at the Prince's Feathers in Conduit Street would have been very much more pleasant to him, and he would have preferred half-and-half in the pewter to brandy and soda-water;—but he felt a pride in using his power in a fashion that would be disgraceful to his host. When he had done his steak he pulled his pipe out of his pocket, and smoked. Against this Adolphe remonstrated stoutly, but quite in vain. "The Captain won't mind a little baccy-smoke out of my pipe," he said. "He always has his smoke comfortable when he comes down to me." At last, about four o'clock, he did go away, assuring Adolphe that he would repeat his visit very soon. "I means to see a deal of the Captain this season," he said. At last, however, he retreated, and Adolphe opened the door of the house for him without speaking a word. "Bye, bye," said Neefit. "I'll be here again before long."

Ralph on that afternoon came home to dress for dinner at about seven, in great fear lest Neefit should still be found in his rooms. "No, saar; he go away at last!" said Adolphe, with a melancholy shake of his head.

"Has he done much harm?"

"The Apollo gone!—and he had romp-steak,—and onions,—and a pipe. Vat vas I to do? I hope he vill never come again." And so also did Mr. Newton hope that Neefit would never come again.

He was going to dine with Lady Eardham, the wife of a Berkshire baronet, who had three fair daughters. At this period of his life he found the aristocracy of Berkshire and Hampshire to be very civil to him; and, indeed, the world at large was disposed to smile on him. But there was very much in his lot to make him unhappy. He had on that morning been utterly rejected by Clarissa Underwood. It may, perhaps, be true that he was not a man to break his heart because a girl rejected him. He was certainly one who could have sung the old song, "If she be not fair for me, what care I how fair she be." And yet Clarissa's conduct had distressed him, and had caused him to go about throughout the whole afternoon with his heart almost in his boots. He had felt her coldness to him much more severely than he had that of Mary Bonner. He had taught himself to look upon that little episode with Mary as though it had really meant nothing. She had just crossed the sky of his heaven like a meteor, and for a moment had disturbed its serenity. And Polly also had

been to him a false light, leading him astray for awhile under excep-
tional, and, as he thought, quite pardonable circumstances. But dear
little Clary had been his own peculiar star,—a star that was bound to
have been true to him, even though he might have erred for a
moment in his worship,—a star with a sweet, soft, enduring light,
that he had always assured himself he might call his own when he
pleased. And now this soft, sweet star had turned upon him and
scorched him. "When I get home," she had said to him, "I
shall find that you have already made an offer to Patience!" He
certainly had not expected such scorn from her. And then he was
so sure in his heart that if she would have accepted him; he would
have been henceforth so true to her, so good to her! He would
have had such magnanimous pleasure in showering upon her pretty
little head all the good things at his disposal, that, for her own sake,
the pity was great. When he had been five minutes in his cab,
bowling back towards his club, he was almost minded to return and
give her one more chance. She would just have suited him. And
as for her,—would it not be a heaven on earth for her if she would
only consent to forget that foolish, unmeaning little episode. Could
Clary have forgotten the episode, and been content to care little or
nothing for that easiness of feeling which made our Ralph what he
was, she might, probably, have been happy as the mistress of the
Priory. But she would not have forgotten, and would not have been
content. She had made up her little heart stoutly that Ralph the
heir should sit in it no longer, and it was well for him that he did not
go back.

He went to his club instead,—not daring to go to his rooms. The
insanity of Neefit was becoming to him a terrible bane. It was, too,
a cruelty which he certainly had done nothing to deserve. He could
lay his hand on his heart and assure himself that he had treated that
mad, pig-headed tradesman well in all respects. He knew himself to be the last man to make a promise, and then to break it
wilfully. He had certainly borrowed money of Neefit;—and at
the probable cost of all his future happiness he had, with a noble-
ness which he could not himself sufficiently admire, done his
very best to keep the hard terms which in his distress he had
allowed to be imposed upon himself. He had been loyal, even
to the breeches-maker;—and this was the return which was made
to him!

What was he to do, should Neefit cling to his threat and remain
permanently at his chambers? There were the police, and no doubt
he could rid himself of his persecutor. But he understood well the
barbarous power which some underbred, well-trained barrister would
have of asking him questions which it would be so very disagreeable

for him to answer! He lacked the courage to send for the police. Jacky Joram had just distinguished himself greatly, and nearly exterminated a young gentleman who had married one girl while he was engaged to another. Jacky Joram might ask him questions as to his little dinners at Alexandra Lodge, which it would nearly kill him to answer. He was very unhappy, and began to think that it might be as well that he should travel for twelve months. Neefit could not persecute him up the Nile, or among the Rocky Mountains. And perhaps Clary's ferocity would have left her were he to return after twelve months of glorious journeyings, still constant to his first affections. In the meantime he did not dare to go home till it would be absolutely necessary that he should dress for dinner.

In the billiard-room of his club he found Lord Polperrow,—the eldest son of the Marquis of Megavissey,—pretty Poll, as he was called by many young men, and by some young ladies, about town. Lord Polperrow had become his fast friend since the day on which his heirship was established, and now encountered him with friendly intimacy. "Halloa, Newton," said the young lord, "have you seen old Neefit lately?" There were eight or ten men in the room, and suddenly there was silence among the cues.

Ralph would have given his best horse to be able to laugh it off, but he found that he could not laugh. He became very hot, and knew that he was red in the face. "What about old Neefit?" he said.

"I've just come from Conduit Street, and he says that he has been dining with you. He swears that you are to marry his daughter."

"He be d——!" said Newton. It was a poor way of getting out of the scrape, and so Ralph felt.

"But what's the meaning of it all? He's telling everybody about London that you went down to stay with him at Margate."

"Neefit has gone mad lately," said Captain Fooks, with a good-natured determination to stand by his friend in misfortune.

"But how about the girl, Newton?" asked his lordship.

"You may have her yourself, Poll,—if she don't prefer a young shoemaker, to whom I believe she's engaged. She's very pretty, and has got a lot of money—which will suit you to a T." He tried to put a good face on it; but, nevertheless, he was very hot and red in the face.

"I'd put a stop to this if I were you," said another friend, confidentially and in a whisper. "He's not only telling everybody, but writing letters about it."

"Oh, I know," said Ralph. "How can I help what a madman does? It's a bore of course." Then he sauntered out again, feeling sure that his transactions with Mr. Neefit would form the subject of conversation in the club billiard-room for the next hour and a half. It would certainly become expedient that he should travel abroad.

He felt it to be quite a relief when he found that Mr. Neefit was

not waiting for him at his chambers. "Adolphe," he said as soon as
he was dressed, "that man must never be allowed to put his foot
inside the door again."

"Ah;—the Apollo gone! And he did it express!"

"I don't mind the figure;—but he must never be allowed to enter
the place again. I shall not stay up long, but while we are here you
must not leave the place till six. He won't come in the evening."
Then he put a sovereign into the man's hand, and went out to dine
at Lady Eardham's.

Lady Eardham had three fair daughters, with pretty necks, and
flaxen hair, and blue eyes, and pug noses, all wonderfully alike.
They ranged from twenty-seven to twenty-one, there being sons
between,—and it began to be desirable that they should be married.
Since Ralph had been in town the Eardham mansion in Cavendish
Square had been opened to him with almost maternal kindness. He
had accepted the kindness; but being fully alive to the purposes of
matronly intrigue, had had his little jokes in reference to the young
ladies. He liked young ladies generally, but was well aware that a
young man is not obliged to offer his hand and heart to every girl that
is civil to him. He and the Eardham girls had been exceedingly
intimate, but he had had no idea whatever of sharing Newton Priory
with an Eardham. Now, however, in his misery he was glad to go to
a house in which he would be received with an assured welcome.

Everybody smiled upon him. Sir George in these days was very
cordial, greeting him with that genial esoteric warmth which is
always felt by one English country gentleman with a large estate for
another equally blessed. Six months ago, when it was believed that
Ralph had sold his inheritance to his uncle, Sir George when he met
the young man addressed him in a very different fashion. As he
entered the room he felt the warmth of the welcoming. The girls,
one and all, had ever so many things to say to him. They all
hunted, and they all wanted him to look at horses for them. Lady
Eardham was more matronly than ever, and at the same time was a
little fussy. She would not leave him among the girls, and at last
succeeded in getting him off into a corner of the back drawing-room.
"Now, Mr. Newton," she said, "I am going to show you that I put
the greatest confidence in you."

"So you may," said Ralph, wondering whether one of the girls
was to be offered to him, out of hand. At the present moment he
was so low in spirits that he would probably have taken either.

"I have had a letter," said Lady Eardham, whispering the words
into his ear;—and then she paused. "Such a strange letter, and
very abominable. I've shown it to no one,—not even to Sir George.
I wouldn't let one of the girls see it for ever so much." Then there
was another pause. "I don't believe a word of it, Mr. Newton;
but I think it right to show it to you,—because it's about you."

"About me ?" said Ralph, with his mind fixed at once upon Mr. Neefit.

"Yes, indeed ;—and when I tell you it refers to my girls too, you will see how strong is my confidence in you. If either had been specially named, of course I could not have shown it." Then she handed him the letter, which poor Ralph read, as follows :—

"MY LADY,—I'm told as Mr. Ralph Newton, of Newton Priory, is sweet upon one of your ladyship's daughters. I think it my duty to tell your ladyship he's engaged to marry my girl, Maryanne Neefit.
"Yours most respectful,
'THOMAS NEEFIT,
"Breeches-Maker, Conduit Street."

"It's a lie," said Ralph.

"I'm sure it's a lie," said Lady Eardham, "only I thought it right to show it you."

Ralph took Gus Eardham down to dinner, and did his very best to make himself agreeable. Gus was the middle one of the three, and was certainly a fine girl. The Eardham girls would have no money ; but Ralph was not a greedy man,—except when he was in great need. It must not be supposed, however, that on this occasion he made up his mind to marry Gus Eardham. But, as on previous occasions, he had been able to hold all the Eardhams in a kind of subjection to himself, feeling himself to be bigger than they,—as hitherto he had been conscious that he was bestowing and they receiving,—so now, in his present misfortune, did he recognise that Gus was a little bigger than himself, and that it was for her to give and for him to take. And Gus was able to talk to him as though she also entertained the same conviction. Gus was very kind to him, and he felt grateful to her.

Lady Eardham saw Gus alone in her bedroom that night. "I believe he's a very good young man," said Lady Eardham, "if he's managed rightly. And as for all this about the horrid man's daughter, it don't matter at all. He'd live it down in a month if he were married."

"I don't think anything about that, mamma. I dare say he's had his fun,—just like other men."

"Only, my dear, he's one of that sort that have to be fixed."

"It's so hard to fix them, mamma."

"It needn't be hard to fix him,—that is, if you'll only be steady. He's not sharp and hard and callous, like some of them. He doesn't mean any harm, and if he once speaks out, he isn't one that can't be kept to time. His manners are nice. I don't think the property is involved ; but I'll find out from papa ; and he's just the man to think his wife the pink of perfection." Lady Eardham had read our hero's character not inaccurately.

CHAPTER LIII.

THE END OF POLLY NEEFIT.

RUMOURS, well-supported rumours, as to the kind of life which Mr. Neefit was leading reached Alexandra Cottage, filling Mrs. Neefit's mind with dismay, and making Polly very angry indeed. He came home always somewhat the worse for drink, and would talk of punching the heads both of Mr. Newton and of Mr. Ontario Moggs. Waddle, who was very true to his master's interests, had taken an opportunity of seeing Mrs. Neefit, and of expressing a very distinct idea that the business was going to the mischief. Mrs. Neefit was of opinion that in this emergency the business should be sold, and that they might safely remove themselves to some distant country,—to Tunbridge, or perhaps to Ware. Polly, however, would not accede to her mother's views. The evil must, she thought, be cured at once. "If father goes on like this, I shall just walk straight out of the house, and marry Moggs at once," Polly said. "Father makes no account of my name, and so I must just look out for myself." She had not as yet communicated these intentions to Ontario, but she was quite sure that she would be supported in her views by him whenever she should choose to do so.

Once or twice Ontario came down to the cottage, and when he did so, Mr. Neefit was always told of the visit. "I ain't going to keep anything from father, mother," Polly would say. "If he chooses to misbehave, that isn't my fault. I mean to have Mr. Moggs, and it's only natural I should like to see him." Neefit, when informed of these visits, after swearing that Moggs junior was a sneaking scoundrel to come to his house in his absence, would call upon Moggs senior, and swear with many threats that his daughter should have nothing but what she stood up in. Moggs senior would stand quite silent, cutting the skin on his hand with his shoemaker's knife, and would simply bid the infuriated breeches-maker good morning, when he left the shop. But, in truth, Mr. Moggs senior had begun to doubt. "I'd leave it awhile, Onty, if I was you," he said. "May be, after all, he'll give her nothing."

"I'll take her the first day she'll come to me,—money or no money," said Moggs junior.

Foiled ambition had, in truth, driven the breeches-maker to madness. But there were moments in which he was softened, melancholy, and almost penitent. "Why didn't you have him when he come down to Margate," he said, with the tears running down his cheek, that very evening after eating his rump-steak in Mr. Newton's rooms. The soda-water and brandy, with a little gin-and-water after it, had reduced him to an almost maudlin condition, so that he was unable to support his parental authority.

"Because I didn't choose, father. It wasn't his fault. He spoke fair enough,—though I don't suppose he ever wanted it. Why should he?"

"You might have had him then. He'd 've never dared to go back. I'd a killed him if he had."

"What good would it have done, father? He'd never have loved me, and he'd have despised you and mother."

"I wouldn't 've minded that," said Mr. Neefit, wiping his eyes.

"But I should have minded. What should I have felt with a husband as wouldn't have wanted me ever to have my own father in his house? Would that have made me happy?"

"It 'd 've made me happy to know as you was there."

"No, father; there would have been no happiness in it. When I came to see what he was I knew I should never love him. He was just willing to take me because of his word;—and was I going to a man like that? No, father;—certainly not." The poor man was at that moment too far gone in his misery to argue the matter further, and he lay on the old sofa, very much at Polly's mercy. "Drop it, father," she said. "It wasn't to be, and it couldn't have been. You'd better say you'll drop it." But, sick and uncomfortable as he was on that evening, he couldn't be got to say that he would drop it.

Nor could he be got to drop it for some ten days after that;—but on a certain evening he had come home very uncomfortable from the effects of gin-and-water, and had been spoken to very sensibly both by his wife and daughter.

By seven on the following morning Ontario Moggs was sitting in the front parlour of the house at Hendon, and Polly Neefit was sitting with him. He had never been there at so early an hour before, and it was thought afterwards by both Mr. and Mrs. Neefit that his appearance, so unexpected by them, had not surprised their daughter Polly. Could it have been possible that she had sent a message to him after that little scene with her father? There he was, at any rate, and Polly was up to receive him. "Now, Onty, that'll do. I didn't want to talk nonsense, but just to settle something."

"But you'll tell a fellow that you're glad to see him?"

"No, I won't. I won't tell a fellow anything he doesn't know already. You and I have got to get married."

"Of course we have."

"But we want father's consent. I'm not going to have him made unhappy, if I can help it. He's that wretched sometimes at present that my heart is half killed about him."

"The things he says are monstrous," asserted Moggs, thinking of the protestation lately made by the breeches-maker in his own hearing, to the effect that Ralph Newton should yet be made to marry his daughter.

"All the same I've got to think about him. There's a dozen or so of men as would marry me, Mr. Moggs; but I can never have another father."

"I'll be the first of the dozen any way," said the gallant Ontario.

"That depends. However, mother says so, and if father 'll consent, I won't go against it. I'll go to him now, before he's up, and I'll tell him you're here. I'll bring him to his senses if I can. I don't know whatever made him think so much about gentlemen."

"He didn't learn it from you, Polly."

"Perhaps he did, after all; and if so, that's the more reason why I'd forgive him." So saying, Polly went up-stairs upon her mission. On the landing she met her mother, and made known the fact that Ontario was in the parlour. "Don't you go to him, mother;—not yet," said Polly. Whereby it may be presumed that Mrs. Neefit had been informed of Mr. Moggs's visit before Polly had gone to him.

Mr. Neefit was in bed, and his condition apparently was not a happy one. He was lying with his head between his hands, and was groaning, not loudly, but very bitterly. His mode of life for the last month had not been of a kind to make him comfortable, and his conscience, too, was ill at ease. He had been a hard-working man, who had loved respectability and been careful of his wife and child. He had been proud to think that nobody could say anything against him, and that he had always paid his way. Up to the time of this disastrous fit of ambition on Polly's behalf he had never made himself ridiculous, and had been a prosperous tradesman, well thought of by his customers. Suddenly he had become mad, but not so mad as to be unconscious of his own madness. The failure of his hopes, joined to the inexpressibly bitter feeling that in their joint transactions young Newton had received all that had been necessary to him, whereas he, Neefit, had got none of that for which he had bargained,—these together had so upset him that he had lost his balance, had travelled out of his usual grooves, and had made an ass of himself. He knew he had made an ass of himself,—and was hopelessly endeavouring to show himself to be less of an ass than people thought him, by some success in his violence. If he could only punish young Newton terribly, people would understand why he had done all this. But drink had been necessary to give him courage for his violence, and now as he lay miserable in bed, his courage was very low.

"Father," said Polly, "shall I give you a drink?" Neefit muttered something, and took the cold tea that was offered to him. It was cold tea, with just a spoonful of brandy in it to make it acceptable. "Father, there ought to be an end of all this;—oughtn't there?"

"I don't know about no ends. I'll be down on him yet."

"No you won't, father. And why should you? He has done nothing wrong to you or me. I wouldn't have him if it was ever so."

"It's all been your fault, Polly."

"Yes;—my fault; that I wouldn't be made what you call a lady; to be taken away, so that I'd never see any more of you and mother!" Then she put her hand gently on his shoulder. "I couldn't stand that, father."

"I'd make him let you come to us."

"A wife must obey her husband, father. Mother always obeyed you."

"No, she didn't. She's again me now."

"Besides, I don't want to be a lady," said Polly, seeing that she had better leave that question of marital obedience; "and I won't be a lady. I won't be better than you and mother."

"You've been brought up better."

"I'll show my breeding, then, by being true to you, and true to the man I love. What would you think of your girl, if she was to give her hand to a——gentleman, when she'd given her heart to a ——shoemaker?"

"Oh, d—— the shoemaker!"

"No, father, I won't have it. What is there against Ontario? He's a fine-hearted fellow, as isn't greedy after money,—as 'd kiss the very ground I stand on he's that true to me, and is a tradesman as yourself. If we had a little place of our own, wouldn't Ontario be proud to have you there, and give you the best of everything; and wouldn't I wait upon you, just only trying to know beforehand every tittle as you'd like to have. And if there was to be babies, wouldn't they be brought up to love you. If I'd gone with that young man down to his fine place, do you think it would have been like that? How 'd I've felt when he was too proud to let his boy know as you was my father?" Neefit turned on his bed and groaned. He was too ill at ease as to his inner man to argue the subject from a high point of view, or to assert that he was content to be abased himself in order that his child and grandchildren might be raised in the world. "Father," said Polly, "you have always been kind to me. Be kind to me now."

"The young 'uns is always to have their own way," said Neefit.

"Hasn't my way been your way, father?"

"Not when you wouldn't take the Captain when he come to Margate."

"I didn't love him, father. Dear father, say the word. We haven't been happy lately;—have we, father?"

"I ain't been very 'appy," said Neefit, bursting out into sobs.

She put her face upon his brow and kissed it. "Father, let us be happy again. Ontario is down-stairs,—in the parlour now."

"Ontario Moggs in my parlour!" said Neefit, jumping up in bed.

" Yes, father; Ontario Moggs,—my husband, as will be; the man I honour and love; the man that will honour and love you; as true a fellow as ever made a young woman happy by taking her. Let me tell him that you will have him for a son." In truth, Neefit did not speak the word;—but when Polly left the room, which she presently did after a long embrace, Mr. Neefit was aware that his consent to the union would be conveyed to Ontario Moggs in less than five minutes.

" And now you can name the day," said Ontario.

" I cannot do any such thing," replied Polly; " and I think that quite enough has been settled for one morning. It's give an inch and take an ell with some folks."

Ontario waited for breakfast, and had an interview with his future father-in-law. It was an hour after the scene up-stairs before Mr. Neefit could descend, and when he did come down he was not very jovial at the breakfast-table. " It isn't what I like, Moggs," was the first word that he spoke when the young politician rose to grasp the hand of his future father-in-law.

" I hope you'll live to like. it, Mr. Neefit," said Ontario, who, now that he was to have his way in regard to Polly, was prepared to disregard entirely any minor annoyances.

"I don't know how that may be. I think my girl might have done better. I told her so, and I just tell you the same. She might a' done a deal better, but women is always restive."

" We like to have our own way about our young men, father," said Polly, who was standing behind her father's chair.

" Bother young men," said the breeches-maker. After that the interview passed off, if not very pleasantly, at least smoothly,—and it was understood that Mr. Neefit was to abandon that system of persecution against Ralph Newton, to which his life had been devoted for the last few weeks.

After that there was a pretty little correspondence between Polly and Ralph, with which the story of Polly's maiden life may be presumed to be ended, and which shall be given to the reader, although by doing so the facts of our tale will be somewhat anticipated. Polly, with her father's permission, communicated the fact of her engagement to her former lover.

" Hendon, Saturday.

" DEAR SIR,—

" Father thinks it best that I should tell you that I am engaged to marry Mr. Ontario Moggs,—whom you will remember. He is a most respectable tradesman, and stood once for a member of Parliament, and I think he will make me quite happy; and I'm quite sure that's what I'm fitted for." Whether Polly meant that she was fitted to be made happy, or fitted to be the wife of a tradesman who stood for Parliament, did not appear quite clearly.

" There have been things which we are very sorry for, and hope you'll forgive and forget. Father bids me say how sorry he is he broke a figure of a pretty little man in your room. He would get another, only he would not know where to go for it.

"Wishing you always may be happy, believe me to remain,

"Yours most respectfully,

"MARY ANNE NEEFIT."

Ralph's answer was dated about a fortnight afterwards ;—

"—, Cavendish Square, 1 June, 186—.

"MY DEAR POLLY,—

"I hope you will allow me to call you so now for the last time. I am, indeed, happy that you are going to be married. I believe Mr. Moggs to be a most excellent fellow. I hope I may often see him,—and sometimes you. He must allow you to accept a little present which I send you, and never be jealous if you wear it at your waist.

"The pretty little man that your father broke by accident in my rooms did not signify at all. Pray tell him so from me.

"Believe me to be your very sincere friend,

"RALPH NEWTON.

"I may as well tell you my own secret. I am going to be married, too. The young lady lives in this house, and her name is Augusta Eardham."

This letter was sent by messenger from Cavendish Square, with a very handsome watch and chain. A month afterwards, when he was preparing to leave London for Brayboro' Park, he received a little packet, with a note as follows ;—

"Linton, Devonshire, Wednesday.

"DEAR MR. NEWTON,—

"I am so much obliged for the watch, and so is Ontario, who will never be jealous, I'm sure. It is a most beautiful thing, and I shall value it, oh ! so much. I am very glad you are going to be married, and should have answered before, only I wanted to finish making with my own hand a little chain which I send you. And I hope your sweetheart won't be jealous either. We looked her out in a book, and found she is the daughter of a great gentleman with a title. That is all just as it should be. Ontario sends his respects. We have come down here for the honeymoon.

"I remain, yours very sincerely,

"MARY ANNE MOGGS."

CHAPTER LIV.

MY MARY.

BOTH the invitations sent by Patience Underwood were accepted, and Sir Thomas, on the day named, was at home to receive them. Nothing had as yet been done as to the constructing of those cases which he so suddenly ordered to be made for his books; and, indeed, Stemm had resolved to take the order as meaning nothing. It would not be for him to accelerate his master's departure from Southampton Buildings, and he knew enough of the man to be aware that he must have some very strong motive indeed before so great a change could be really made. When Sir Thomas left Southampton Buildings for Fulham, on the day named for the dinner, not a word further had been said about packing the books.

There was no company at the villa besides Sir Thomas, the three girls, and the two young men. As to Clarissa, Patience said not a word, even to her father,—that must still be left till time should further cure the wound that had been made;—but she did venture to suggest, in private with Sir Thomas, that it was a pity that he who was certainly the more worthy of the two Ralphs should not be made to understand that others did not think so much of the present inferiority of his position in the world as he seemed to think himself.

" You mean that Mary would take him ? " asked Sir Thomas.

" Why should she not, if she likes him ? He is very good."

" I can't tell him to offer to her, without telling him also that he would be accepted."

" No ;—I suppose not," said Patience.

Nevertheless, Sir Thomas did speak to Ralph Newton before dinner,—stuttering and muttering, and only half finishing his sentence. " We had a correspondence once, Mr. Newton. I dare say you remember."

" I remember it very well, Sir Thomas."

" I only wanted to tell you ;—you seem to think more about what has taken place,—I mean as to the property,—than we do ;—that is, than I do.'

" It has made a change."

" Yes ; of course. But I don't know that a large place like Newton is sure to make a man happy. Perhaps you'd like to wash your hands before dinner." Gregory, in the meantime, was walking round the garden with Mary and Clarissa.

The dinner was very quiet, but pleasant and cheerful. Sir Thomas talked a good deal, and so did Patience. Mary also was at her ease, and able to do all that was required of her. Ralph certainly was not gay. He was seated next to Clarissa, and spoke a few words now and again; but he was arranging matters in his mind; and Patience, who was observing them all, knew that he was pre-occupied. Clarissa, who now and again would forget her sorrow and revert to her former self,—as she had done in the picture-gallery,—could not now, under the eye as it were of her father, her sister, and her old lover, forget her troubles. She knew what was expected of her; but she could not do it;—she could not do it at least as yet. Nevertheless, Patience, who was the engineer in the present crisis, was upon the whole contented with the way in which things were going.

The three girls sat with the gentlemen for a quarter of an hour after the decanters were put upon the table, and then withdrew. Sir Thomas immediately began to talk about Newton Priory, and to ask questions which might interest the parson without, as he thought, hurting the feelings of the disinherited Ralph. This went on for about five minutes, during which Gregory was very eloquent about his church and his people, when, suddenly, Ralph rose from his chair and withdrew. " Have I said anything that annoyed him ? " asked Sir Thomas anxiously.

" It is not that, I think," said Gregory.

Ralph walked across the passage, opened the door of the drawing-room, in which the three girls were at work, walked up to the chair in which Mary Bonner was sitting, and said something in so low a voice that neither of the sisters heard him.

" Certainly I will," said Mary, rising from her chair. Patience glanced round, and could see that the colour, always present in her cousin's face, was heightened,—ever so little indeed; but still the tell-tale blush had told its tale. Ralph stood for a moment while Mary moved away to the door, and then followed her without speaking a word to the other girls, or bestowing a glance on either of them.

" He is going to propose to her," said Clarissa as soon as the door was shut.

" No one can be sure," said Patience.

" Only fancy,—asking a girl to go out of the room,—in that brave manner ! I shouldn't have gone because I'm a coward; but it's just what Mary will like."

" Let me get my hat, Mr. Newton," said Mary, taking the opportunity to trip up-stairs, though her hat was hanging in the hall. When she was in her room she merely stood upright there, for half a minute, in the middle of the chamber, erect and stiff, with her arms and fingers stretched out, thinking how she would behave herself. Half a minute sufficed for her to find her clue, and then she came down as quickly as her feet would carry her. He had opened the front door, and was standing outside upon the gravel, and there she joined him.

" I had no other way but this of speaking to you," he said.

"I don't dislike coming out at all," she answered. Then there was silence for a moment or two as they walked along into the gloom of the shrubbery. "I suppose you are going down to Norfolk soon?" she said.

"I do not quite know. I thought of going to-morrow."

"So soon as that?"

"But I've got something that I want to settle. I think you must know what it is." Then he paused again, almost as though he expected her to confess that she did know. But Mary was well aware that it was not for her to say another word till he had fully explained in most open detail what it was that he desired to settle. "You know a good deal of my history, Miss Newton. When I thought that things were going well with me,—much better than I had ever allowed myself to expect in early days, I,—I,—became acquainted with you." Again he paused, but she had not a word to say. "I dare say you were not told, but I wrote to your uncle then, asking him whether I might have his consent to,—just to ask you to be my wife." Again he paused, but after that he hurried on, speaking the words as quickly as he could throw them forth from his mouth. "My father died, and of course that changed everything. I told your uncle that all ground for pretension that I might have had before was cut from under me. He knew the circumstances of my birth,—and I supposed that you would know it also."

Then she did speak. "Yes, I did," she said.

"Perhaps I was foolish to think that the property would make a difference. But the truth of it is, I have not got over the feeling, and shall never get over it. I love you with all my heart,—and though it be for no good, I must tell you so."

"The property can make no difference," she said. "You ought to have known that, Mr. Newton."

"Ah;—but it does. I tried to tell you the other day something of my present home."

"Yes;—I know you did;—and I remember it all."

"There is nothing more to be said;—only to ask you to share it with me."

She walked on with him in silence for a minute; but he said nothing more to press his suit, and certainly it was her turn to speak now. "I will share it with you," she said, pressing her arm upon his.

"My Mary!"

"Yes;—your Mary,—if you please." Then he took her in his arms, and pressed her to his bosom, and kissed her lips and forehead, and threw back her hat, and put his fingers among her hair. "Why did you say that the property would make a difference?" she asked, in a whisper. To this he made no answer, but walked on silently, with his arm round her waist, till they came out from among the trees, and stood upon the bank of the river. "There are people in the boats. You must put your arm down," she said.

"I wonder how you will like to be a farmer's wife?" he asked.

"I have not an idea."

"I fear so much that you'll find it rough and hard."

"But I have an idea about something." She took his hand, and looked up into his face as she continued. "I have an idea that I shall like to be your wife." He was in a seventh heaven of happiness, and would have stood there gazing on the river with her all night, if she would have allowed him. At last they walked back into the house together,—and into the room where the others were assembled, with very little outward show of embarrassment. Mary was the first to enter the room, and though she blushed she smiled also, and every one knew what had taken place. There was no secret or mystery, and in five minutes her cousins were congratulating her. "It's all settled for you now," said Clarissa laughing.

"Yes, it's all settled for me now, and I wouldn't have it unsettled for all the world."

While this was being said in the drawing-room,—being said even in the presence of poor Gregory, who could not but have felt how hard it was for him to behold such bliss, Sir Thomas and Ralph had withdrawn into the opposite room. Ralph began to apologise for his own misfortunes,—his misfortune in having lost the inheritance, his misfortune in being illegitimate; but Sir Thomas soon cut his apologies short. "You think a great deal more of it than she does, or than I do," said Sir Thomas.

"If she does not regard it, I will never think of it again," said Ralph. "My greatest glory in what had been promised me was in thinking that it might help to win her."

"You have won her without such help as that," said Sir Thomas, with his arm on the young man's shoulder.

There was another delicious hour in store for him as they sat over their late tea. "Do you still think of going to Norfolk to-morrow?" she said to him, with that composure which in her was so beautiful, and, at the same time, so expressive.

"By an early train in the morning."

"I thought that perhaps you might have stayed another day now."

"I thought that perhaps you might want me to come back again," said Ralph;—"and, if so, I could make arrangements;—perhaps for a week or ten days."

"Do come back," she said. "And do stay."

Ralph's triumph as he returned that evening to London received Gregory's fullest sympathy; but still it must have been hard to bear. Perhaps his cousin's parting words contained for him some comfort. "Give her a little time, and she will be yours yet. I shall find it all out from Mary, and you may be sure we shall help you."

CHAPTER LV.

COOKHAM.

WE have been obliged to anticipate in some degree the course of our story by the necessity which weighed upon us of completing the history of Polly Neefit. In regard to her we will only further express an opinion,—in which we believe that we shall have the concurrence of our readers,—that Mr. Moggs junior had chosen well. Her story could not be adequately told without a revelation of that correspondence, which, while it has explained the friendly manner in which the Neefit-Newton embarrassments were at last brought to an end, has, at the same time, disclosed the future lot in life of our hero,—as far as a hero's lot in life may be said to depend on his marriage.

Mr. Neefit had been almost heart-broken, because he was not satisfied that his victim was really punished by any of those tortures which his imagination invented, and his energy executed. Even when the "pretty little man" was smashed, and was, in truth, smashed of malice prepense by a swinging blow from Neefit's umbrella, Neefit did not feel satisfied that he would thereby reach his victim's heart. He could project his own mind with sufficient force into the bosom of his enemy to understand that the onions and tobacco consumed in that luxurious chamber would cause annoyance;—but he desired more than annoyance;—he wanted to tear the very heart-strings of the young man who had, as he thought, so signally outwitted him. He did not believe that he was successful; but, in truth, he did make poor Ralph very unhappy. The heir felt himself to be wounded, and could not eat and drink, or walk and talk, or ride in the park, or play billiards at his club, in a manner befitting the owner of Newton Priory. He was so injured by Neefit that he became pervious to attacks which would otherwise have altogether failed in reaching him. Lady Eardham would never have prevailed against him as she did,—conquering by a quick repetition of small blows, — had not all his strength been annihilated for the time by the persecutions of the breeches-maker.

Lady Eardham whispered to him as he was taking his departure on the evening of the dinner in Cavendish Square. "Dear Mr. Newton,—just one word," she said, confidentially,—"that must be a very horrid man,"—alluding to Mr. Neefit.

"It's a horrid bore, you know, Lady Eardham."

"Just so;—and it makes me feel,—as though I didn't quite know whether something ought not to be done. Would you mind calling at eleven to-morrow? Of course I shan't tell Sir George,—unless you think he ought to be told." Ralph promised that he would call, though he felt at the moment that Lady Eardham was an interfering old fool. Why should she want to do anything; and why should she give even a hint as to telling Sir George? As he walked across Hanover Square and down Bond Street to his rooms he did assert to himself plainly that the "old harridan," as he called her, was at work for her second girl, and he shook his head and winked his eye as he thought of it. But, even in his solitude, he did not feel strong against Lady Eardham, and he moved along the pavement oppressed by a half-formed conviction that her ladyship would prevail against him. He did not, however, think that he had any particular objection to Gus Eardham. There was a deal of style about the girl, a merit in which either Clarissa or Mary would have been sadly deficient. And there could be no doubt in this,—that a man in his position ought to marry in his own class. The proper thing for him to do was to make the daughter of some country gentleman,—or of some noble-man, just as it might happen,—mistress of the Priory. Dear little Clary would hardly have known how to take her place properly down in Hampshire. And then he thought for a moment of Polly! Perhaps, after all, fate, fashion, and fortune managed marriage for young men better than they could manage it for themselves. What a life would his have been had he really married Polly Neefit! Though he did call Lady Eardham a harridan, he resolved that he would keep his promise for the following morning.

Lady Eardham when he arrived was mysterious, eulogistic, and beneficent. She was clearly of opinion that something should be done. "You know it is so horrid having these kind of things said." And yet she was almost equally strong in opinion that nothing could be done. "You know I wouldn't have my girl's name brought up for all the world;—though why the horrid wretch should have named her I cannot even guess." The horrid wretch had not, in truth, named any special her, though it suited Lady Eardham to presume that allusion had been made to that hope of the flock, that crowning glory of the Eardham family, that most graceful of the Graces, that Venus certain to be chosen by any Paris, her second daughter, Gus. She went on to explain that were she to tell the story to her son Marmaduke, her son Marmaduke would probably kill the breeches-maker. As Marmaduke Eardham was, of all young men about town, perhaps the most careless, the most indifferent, and the least ferocious, his mother was probably mistaken in her estimate of his resentful feelings. "As for Sir George, he would be for taking the law of the wretch for libel, and then we should be——! I don't know where we should be then; but my dear girl would die."

Of course there was nothing done. During the whole interview Lady Eardham continued to press Neefit's letter under her hand upon the table, as though it was of all documents the most precious. She handled it as though to tear it would be as bad as to tear an original document bearing the king's signature. Before the interview was over she had locked it up in her desk, as though there were something in it by which the whole Eardham race might be blessed or banned. And, though she spoke no such word, she certainly gave Ralph to understand that by this letter he, Ralph Newton, was in some mysterious manner so connected with the secrets, and the interests, and the sanctity of the Eardham family, that, whether such connection might be for weal or woe, the Newtons and the Eardhams could never altogether free themselves from the link. "Perhaps you had better come and dine with us in a family way to-morrow," said Lady Eardham, giving her invitation as though it must necessarily be tendered, and almost necessarily accepted. Ralph, not thanking her, but taking it in the same spirit, said that he would be there at half past seven. "Just ourselves," said Lady Eardham, in a melancholy tone, as though they two were doomed to eat family dinners together for ever after.

"I suppose the property is really his own?" said Lady Eardham to her husband that afternoon.

Sir George was a stout, plethoric gentleman, with a short temper and many troubles. Marmaduke was expensive, and Sir George himself had spent money when he was young. The girls, who knew that they had no fortunes, expected that everything should be done for them, at least during the period of their natural harvest,—and they were successful in having their expectations realised. They demanded that there should be horses to ride, servants to attend them, and dresses to wear; and they had horses, servants, and dresses. There were also younger children; and Sir George was quite as anxious as Lady Eardham that his daughters should become wives. "His own—of course it's his own? Who else should it belong to?"

"There was something about that other young man."

"The bastard! It was the greatest sin that ever was thought of to palm such a fellow as that off on the county;—but it didn't come to anything."

"I'm told, too, he has been very extravagant. No doubt he did get money from the,—the tailor who wants to make him marry his daughter."

"A flea-bite," said Sir George. "Don't you bother about that." Thus authorised, Lady Eardham went to the work with a clear conscience and a good will.

On the next morning Ralph received by post an envelope from Sir Thomas Underwood containing a letter addressed to him from Mr. Neefit. "Sir,—Are you going to make your ward act honourable to me and my daughter?—Yours, respectful, THOMAS NEEFIT." The reader will understand that this was prior to Polly's triumph over her father. Ralph uttered a deep curse, and made up his mind that he must either throw himself entirely among the Eardhams, or else start at once for the Rocky Mountains. He dined in Cavendish Square that day, and again took Gus down to dinner.

" I'm very glad to see you here," said Sir George, when they two were alone together after the ladies had left them. Sir George, who had been pressed upon home service because of the necessity of the occasion, was anxious to get off to his club.

" You are very kind, Sir George," said Ralph.

" We shall be delighted to see you at Brayboro', if you'll come for a week in September and look at the girls' horses. They say you're quite a pundit about horseflesh."

" Oh, I don't know," said Ralph.

" You'll like to go up to the girls now, I dare say, and I've got an engagement." Then Sir George rang the bell for a cab, and Ralph went up-stairs to the girls. Emily had taken herself away ; Josephine was playing bésique with her mother, and Gus was thus forced into conversation with the young man. " Bésique is so stupid," said Gus.

" Horribly stupid," said Ralph.

" And what do you like, Mr. Newton ? "

" I like you," said Ralph. But he did not propose on that evening. Lady Eardham thought he ought to have done so, and was angry with him. It was becoming almost a matter of necessity with her that young men should not take much time. Emily was twenty-seven, and Josephine was a most difficult child to manage,—not pretty, but yet giving herself airs and expecting everything. She had refused a clergyman with a very good private fortune, greatly to her mother's sorrow. And Gus had already been the source of much weary labour. Four eldest sons had been brought to her feet and been allowed to slip away ; and all, as Lady Eardham said, because Gus would "joke " with other young men, while the one man should have received all her pleasantry. Emily was quite of opinion that young Newton should by no means have been allotted to Gus. Lady Eardham, who had played bésique with an energy against which Josephine would have mutinied but that some promise was made as to Marshall and Snelgrove, could see from her little table that young Newton was neither abject nor triumphant in his manner. He had not received nor had he even asked when he got up to take his leave. Lady Eardham could have boxed his ears ; but she smiled upon him ineffably, pressed his hand, and in the most natural way in the world alluded to some former allusion about riding and the park.

" I shan't ride to-morrow," said Gus, with her back turned to them.

" Do," said Ralph.

" No ; I shan't."

" You see what she says, Lady Eardham," said Ralph.

" You promised you would before dinner, my dear," said Lady

Eardham, "and you ought not to change your mind. If you'll be good-natured enough to come, two of them will go." Of course it was understood that he would come.

"Nothing on earth, mamma, shall ever induce me to play bésique again," said Josephine, yawning.

"It's not worse for you than for me," said the old lady sharply.

"But it isn't fair," said Josephine, who was supposed to be the clever one of the family. "I may have to play my bésique a quarter of a century hence."

"He's an insufferable puppy," said Emily, who had come into the room, and had been pretending to be reading.

"That's because he don't bark at your bidding, my dear," said Gus.

"It doesn't seem that he means to bark at yours," said the elder sister.

"If you go on like that, girls, I'll tell your papa, and we'll go to Brayboro' at once. It's too bad, and I won't bear it."

"What would you have me do?" said Gus, standing up for herself fiercely.

Gus did ride, and so did Josephine, and there was a servant with them of course. It had been Emily's turn,—there being two horses for the three girls; but Gus had declared that no good could come if Emily went;—and Emily's going had been stopped by parental authority. "You do as you're bid," said Sir George, "or you'll get the worst of it." Sir George suffered much from gout, and had obtained from the ill-temper which his pangs produced a mastery over his daughters which some fathers might have envied.

"You behaved badly to me last night, Mr. Newton," said Gus, on horseback. There was another young man riding with Josephine, so that the lovers were alone together.

"Behaved badly to you?"

"Yes, you did, and I felt it very much,—very much indeed."

"How did I behave badly?"

"If you do not know, I'm sure that I shall not tell you." Ralph did not know;—but he went home from his ride an unengaged man, and may perhaps have been thought to behave badly on that occasion also.

But Lady Eardham, though she was sometimes despondent and often cross, was gifted with perseverance. A picnic party up the river from Maidenhead to Cookham was got up for the 30th of May, and Ralph Newton of course was there. Just at that time the Neefit persecution was at its worst. Letters directed by various hands came to him daily, and in all of them he was asked when he meant to be on the square. He knew the meaning of that picnic as well as does the reader,—as well as did Lady Eardham; but it had come to that with him that he was willing to yield. It cannot exactly be said for him that out of all the feminine worth that he had seen, he himself had chosen Gus Eardham as being the most worthy,—or even that he had chosen her as being to him the most charming. But it was evident to him that he must get married, and why not to her as well as to another? She had style, plenty of style ; and, as he told himself, style for a man in his position was more than anything else. It can hardly be said that he had made up his mind to offer to her before he started for Cookham,—though doubtless through all the remaining years of his life he would think that his mind had been so fixed,—but he had concluded, that if she were thrown at his head very hard, he might as well take her. " I don't think he ever does drink champagne," said Lady Eardham, talking it all over with Gus on the morning of the picnic.

At Cookham there is, or was, a punt,—perhaps there always will be one, kept there for such purposes ;—and into this punt either Gus was tempted by Ralph, or Ralph by Gus. " My darling child, what are you doing?" shouted Lady Eardham from the bank.

" Mr. Newton says he can take me over," said Gus, standing up in the punt, shaking herself with a pretty tremor.

" Don't, Mr. Newton; pray don't!" cried Lady Eardham, with affected horror.

Lunch was over, or dinner, as it might be more properly called, and Ralph had taken a glass or two of champagne. He was a man whom no one had ever seen the " worse for wine;" but on this occasion that which might have made others drunk had made him bold. " I will not let you out, Gus, till you have promised me one thing," said Ralph.

" What is the one thing?"

" That you will go with me everywhere, always."

" You must let me out," said Gus.

" But will you promise?" Then Gus promised; and Lady Eardham, with true triumph in her voice, was able to tell her husband on the following morning that the cost of the picnic had not been thrown away.

On the next morning early Ralph was in the square. Neither when he went to bed at night, nor when he got up in the morning, did he regret what he had done. The marriage would be quite a proper marriage. Nobody could say that he had been mercenary, and he hated a mercenary feeling in marriages. Nobody could say that the match was beneath him, and all people were agreed that Augusta Eardham was a very fine girl. As to her style, there could be no doubt about it. There might be some little unpleasantness in communicating the fact to the Underwoods,—but that could be done by letter. After all, it would signify very little to him what Sir Thomas thought about him. Sir Thomas might think him feeble ; but he himself knew very well that there had been no feebleness in it. His circumstances had been very peculiar, and he really believed that he had made the best of them. As Squire of Newton, he was doing quite the proper thing in marrying the daughter of a baronet out of the next county. With a light heart, a pleased face, and with very well got-up morning apparel, Ralph knocked the next morning at the door in Cavendish Square, and asked for Sir George Eardham. " I'll just run up-stairs for a second," said Ralph, when he was told that Sir George was in the small parlour.

He did run up-stairs, and in three minutes had been kissed by Lady Eardham and all her daughters. At this moment Gus was the " dearest child " and the " best love of a thing " with all of them. Even Emily remembered how pleasant it might be to have a room at Newton Priory, and then success always gives a new charm.

" Have you seen Sir George ? " asked Lady Eardham.

" Not as yet ;—they said he was there, but I had to come up and see her first, you know."

" Go down to him," said Lady Eardham, patting her prey on the back twice. " When you've daughters of your own, you'll expect to be consulted."

" She couldn't have done better, my dear fellow," said Sir George, with kind, genial cordiality. " She couldn't have done better, to my thinking, even with a peerage. I like you, and I like your family, and I like your property ; and she's yours with all my heart. A better girl never lived."

" Thank you, Sir George."

" She has no money, you know."

" I don't care about money, Sir George."

" My dear boy, she's yours with all my heart ; and I hope you'll make each other happy."

CHAPTER LVI.

RALPH NEWTON IS BOWLED AWAY.

A DAY or two after his engagement, Ralph did write his letter to Sir Thomas, and found when the moment came that the task was difficult. But he wrote it. The thing had to be done, and there was nothing to be gained by postponing it.

" —— Club, June 2, 186—.

" My Dear Sir Thomas,—

" You will, I hope, be glad to hear that I am engaged to be married to Augusta Eardham, the second daughter of Sir George Eardham, of Brayboro' Park, in Berkshire. Of course you will know the name, and I rather think you were in the House when Sir George sat for Berkshire. Augusta has got no money, but I have not been placed under the disagreeable necessity of looking out for a rich wife. I believe we shall be married about the end of August. As the ceremony will take place down at Brayboro', I fear that I cannot expect that you or Patience and Clarissa should come so far. Pray tell them my news, with my best love.

"Yours, most grateful for all your long kindness,

"RALPH NEWTON.

"I am very sorry that you should have been troubled by letters from Mr. Neefit. The matter has been arranged at last."

The letter when done was very simple, but it took him some time, and much consideration. Should he or should he not allude to his former loves? It was certainly much easier to write his letter without any such allusion, and he did so.

About a week after this Sir Thomas went home to Fulham, and took the letter with him. "Clary," he said, taking his youngest daughter affectionately by the waist, when he found himself alone with her. "I've got a piece of news for you."

"For me, papa?"

"Well, for all of us. Somebody is going to be married. Who do you think it is?"

"Not Ralph Newton?" said Clarissa, with a little start.

"Yes, Ralph Newton."

"How quick he arranges things!" said Clarissa. There was some little emotion, just a quiver, and a quick rush of blood into her cheeks, which, however, left them just as quickly.

"Yes;—he is quick."

"Who is it, papa?"

"A very proper sort of person,—the daughter of a Berkshire baronet."

"But what is her name?"

"Augusta Eardham."

"Augusta Eardham. I hope he'll be happy, papa. We've known him a long time."

"I think he will be happy;—what people call happy. He is not gifted,—or cursed, as it may be,—with fine feelings, and is what perhaps may be called thick-skinned; but he will love his own wife and children. I don't think he will be a spendthrift now that he has plenty to spend, and he is not subject to what the world calls vices. I shouldn't wonder if he becomes a prosperous and most respectable country gentleman, and quite a model to his neighbours."

"It doesn't seem to matter much;—does it?" said Clarissa, when she told the story to Mary and Patience.

"What doesn't matter?" asked Mary.

"Whether a man cares for the girl he's going to marry, or doesn't care at all. Ralph Newton cannot care very much for Miss Eardham."

"I think it matters very much," said Mary.

"Perhaps, after all, he'll be just as fond of his wife, in a way, as though he had been making love to her,—oh, for years," said Clarissa. This was nearly all that was said at the villa, though, no doubt, poor Clary had many thoughts on the matter, in her solitary rambles along the river. That picture of the youth, as he lay upon the lawn, looking up into her eyes, and telling her that she was dear to him, could not easily be effaced from her memory. Sir Thomas before this had written his congratulations to Ralph. They had been very short, and in them no allusion had been made to the young ladies at Popham Villa.

In the meantime Ralph was as happy as the day was long, and delighted with his lot in life. For some weeks previous to his offer he had been aware that Lady Eardham had been angling for him as for a fish, that he had been as a prey to her and to her daughter, and that it behoved him to amuse himself without really taking the hook between his gills. He had taken the hook, and now had totally forgotten all those former notions of his in regard to a prey, and a fish, and a mercenary old harridan of a mother. He had no sooner been kissed all round by the women, and paternally blessed by Sir George, than he thought that he had exercised a sound judgment, and had with true wisdom arranged to ally himself with just the woman most fit to be his wife, and the future mistress of Newton Priory. He was proud, indeed, of his success, when he read the paragraph in the "Morning Post," announcing as a fact that the alliance had been arranged, and was again able to walk about among his comrades as one of those who make circumstances subject to them, rather than become subject to circumstances. His comrades, no doubt, saw the matter in another light. "By Jove," said Pretty Poll at his club, "there's Newton been and got caught by old Eardham after all. The girl has been running ten years, and been hawked about like a second-class race-horse."

"Yes, poor fellow," said Captain Fooks. "Neefit has done that for him. Ralph for a while was so knocked off his pins by the breeches-maker, that he didn't know where to look for shelter."

Whether marriages should be made in heaven or on earth, must be a matter of doubt to observers;—whether, that is, men and women are best married by chance, which I take to be the real fashion of heaven-made marriages; or should be brought into that close link and loving bondage to each other by thought, selection, and decision. That the heavenly mode prevails the oftenest there can hardly be a doubt. It takes years to make a friendship; but a marriage may be settled in a week,—in an hour. If you desire to go into partnership with a man in business, it is an essential necessity that you should know your partner; that he be honest,—or dishonest, if such be your own tendency,—industrious, instructed in the skill required, and of

habits of life fit for the work to be done. But into partnerships
for life,—of a kind much closer than any business partnership,—men
rush without any preliminary inquiries. Some investigation and
anxiety as to means there may be, though in this respect the ordinary
parlance of the world endows men with more caution, or accuses them
of more greed than they really possess. But in other respects everything is taken for granted. Let the woman, if possible, be pretty;—
or if not pretty, let her have style. Let the man, if possible, not be
a fool; or if a fool, let him not show his folly too plainly. As for
knowledge of character, none is possessed, and none is wanted. The
young people meet each other in their holiday dresses, on holiday
occasions, amidst holiday pleasures,—and the thing is arranged.
Such matches may be said to be heaven-made.

It is a fair question whether they do not answer better than those
which have less of chance,—or less of heaven,—in their manufacture. If it be needful that a man and woman take five years to
learn whether they will suit each other as husband and wife, and that
then, at the end of the five years, they find that they will not suit,
the freshness of the flower would be gone before it could be worn in
the button-hole. There are some leaps which you must take in
the dark, if you mean to jump at all. We can all understand well
that a wise man should stand on the brink and hesitate; but we can
understand also that a very wise man should declare to himself that
with no possible amount of hesitation could certainty be achieved.
Let him take the jump or not take it,—but let him not presume to
think that he can so jump as to land himself in certain bliss. It is
clearly God's intention that men and women should live together,
and therefore let the leap in the dark be made.

No doubt there had been very much of heaven in Ralph Newton's
last choice. It may be acknowledged that in lieu of choosing at all,
he had left the matter altogether to heaven. Some attempt he had
made at choosing,—in reference to Mary Bonner; but he had found
the attempt simply to be troublesome and futile. He had spoken
soft, loving words to Clarissa, because she herself had been soft and
lovable. Nature had spoken,—as she does when the birds sing to
each other. Then, again, while suffering under pecuniary distress he
had endeavoured to make himself believe that Polly Neefit was just
the wife for him. Then, amidst the glories of his emancipation from
thraldom, he had seen Mary Bonner,—and had actually, after a
fashion, made a choice for himself. His choice had brought upon
him nothing but disgrace and trouble. Now he had succumbed at the
bidding of heaven and Lady Eardham, and he was about to be provided with a wife exactly suited for him. It may be said at the same
time that Augusta Eardham was equally lucky. She also had gotten
all that she ought to have wanted, had she known what to want.
They were both of them incapable of what men and women call love

when they speak of love as a passion linked with romance. And in one sense they were cold-hearted. Neither of them was endowed with the privilege of pining because another person had perished. But each of them was able to love a mate, when assured that that mate must continue to be mate, unless separation should come by domestic earthquake. They had hearts enough for paternal and maternal duties, and would probably agree in thinking that any geese which Providence might send them were veritable swans. Bickerings there might be, but they would be bickerings without effect; and Ralph Newton, of Newton, would probably so live with this wife of his bosom, that they, too, might lie at last pleasantly together in the family vault, with the record of their homely virtues visible to the survivors of the parish on the same tombstone. The means by which each of them would have arrived at these blessings would not redound to the credit of either; but the blessings would be there, and it may be said of their marriage, as of many such marriages, that it was made in heaven, and was heavenly.

The marriage was to take place early in September, and the first week in August was passed by Sir George and Lady Eardham and their two younger daughters at Newton Priory. On the 14th Ralph was to be allowed to run down to the moors just for one week, and then he was to be back, passing between Newton and Brayboro', signing deeds and settlements, preparing for their wedding tour, and obedient in all things to Eardham influences. It did occur to him that it would be proper that he should go down to Fulham to see his old friends once before his marriage; but he felt that such a visit would be to himself very unpleasant, and therefore he assured himself, and moreover made himself believe, that, if he abstained from the visit, he would abstain because it would be unpleasant to them. He did abstain. But he did call at the chambers in Southampton Buildings; he called, however, at an hour in which he knew that Sir Thomas would not be visible, and made no second pressing request to Stemm for the privilege of entrance.

He had great pride in showing his house and park and estate to the Eardhams, and had some delicious rambles with his Augusta through the shrubberies and down by the little brook. Ralph had an enjoyment in the prettiness of nature, and Augusta was clever enough to simulate the feeling. He was a little annoyed, perhaps, when he found that the beauty of her morning dresses did not admit of her sitting upon the grass or leaning against gates, and once expressed an opinion that she need not be so particular about her gloves in this the hour of their billing and cooing. Augusta altogether declined to remove her gloves in a place swarming, as she said, with midges, or to undergo any kind of embrace while adorned with that sweetest of all hats, which had been purchased for his especial delight. But in other respects she was good humoured, and tried to please him. She learned the names of all his horses, and was beginning to remember those of his tenants. She smiled upon Gregory, and behaved with a pretty decorum when the young parson showed her his church. Altogether her behaviour was much better than might have been expected from the training to which she had been subjected during her seven seasons in London. Lord Polperrow wronged her greatly when he said that she had been "running" for ten years.

There was a little embarrassment in Ralph's first interview with Gregory. He had given his brother notice of his engagement by letter as soon as he had been accepted, feeling that any annoyance coming to him, might be lessened in that way. Unfortunately he had spoken to his brother in what he now felt to have been exaggerated terms of his passion for Mary Bonner, and he himself was aware that that malady had been quickly cured. "I suppose the news startled you ? " he had said, with a forced laugh, as soon as he met his brother.

" Well ;—yes, a little. I did not know that you were so intimate with them."

" The truth is, I had thought a deal about the matter, and I had come to see how essential it was for the interests of us all that I should marry into our own set. The moment I saw Augusta I felt that she was exactly the girl to make me happy. She is very handsome. Don't you think so ? "

" Certainly."

" And then she has just the style which, after all, does go so far. There's nothing dowdy about her. A dowdy woman would have killed me. She attracted me from the first moment ; and, by Jove, old fellow, I can assure you it was mutual. I am the happiest fellow alive, and I don't think there is anything I envy anybody." In all this Ralph believed that he was speaking the simple truth.

" I hope you'll be happy, with all my heart," said Gregory.

" I am sure I shall ;—and so will you if you will ask that little puss once again. I believe in my heart she loves you." Gregory, though he had been informed of his brother's passion for Mary, had never been told of that other passion for Clarissa ; and Ralph could therefore speak of ground for hope in that direction without uncomfortable twinges.

There did occur during this fortnight one or two little matters, just sufficiently laden with care to ruffle the rose-leaves of our hero's couch. Lady Eardham thought that both the dining-room and drawing-room should be re-furnished, that a bow-window should be thrown out to the breakfast-parlour, and that a raised conservatory should be constructed into which Augusta's own morning sitting-room up-stairs might be made to open. Ralph gave way about the furniture with a good grace, but he thought that the bow-window would disfigure the house, and suggested that the raised conservatory would cost money. Augusta thought the bow-window was the very thing for the house, and Lady Eardham knew as a fact that a similar conservatory,—the sweetest thing in the world,—which she had seen at Lord Rosebud's had cost almost absolutely nothing. And if anything was well-known in gardening it was this, that the erection of such conservatories was a positive saving in garden expenses. The men worked under cover during the rainy days, and the hot-water served for domestic as well as horticultural purposes. There was some debate and a little heat, and the matter was at last referred to Sir George. He voted against Ralph on both points, and the orders were given.

Then there was the more important question of the settlements. Of course there were to be settlements, in the arrangement of which Ralph was to give everything and to get nothing. With high-handed magnanimity he had declared that he wanted no money, and therefore the trifle which would have been adjudged to be due to Gus was retained to help her as yet less fortunate sisters. In truth Marmaduke at this time was so expensive that Sir George was obliged to be a little hard. Why, however, he should have demanded out of such a property as that of Newton a jointure of £4,000 a year, with a house to be found either in town or country as the widow might desire, on behalf of a penniless girl, no one acting in the Newton interest could understand, unless Sir George might have thought that the sum to be ultimately obtained might depend in some degree on that demanded. Had he known Mr. Carey he would probably not have subjected himself to the rebuke which he received.

Ralph, when the sum was first named to him by Sir George's lawyer, who came down purposely to Newton, looked very blank, and said that he had not anticipated any arrangement so destructive to the property. The lawyer pointed out that there was unfortunately no dowager's house provided ; that the property would not be destroyed as the dower would only be an annuity ; that ladies now were more liberally treated in this matter than formerly ;—and that the suggestion was quite the usual thing. " You don't suppose I mean my daughter to be starved ? " said Sir George, upon whom gout was then coming. Ralph plucked up spirit and answered him. " Nor do I intend that your daughter, sir, should be starved." " Dear Ralph, do be liberal to the dear girl," said Lady Eardham afterwards, caressing our hero in the solitude of her bed-room. Mr. Carey, however, arranged the whole matter very quickly. The dower must be £2,000, out of which the widow must find her own house. Sir George must be well aware, said Mr. Carey, that the demand made was preposterous. Sir George said one or two very nasty things ; but the dower as fixed by Mr. Carey was accepted, and then everything smiled again.

When the Eardhams were leaving Newton the parting between

Augusta and her lover was quite pretty. "Dear Gus," he said, "when next I am here, you will be my own, own wife," and he kissed her. "Dear Ralph," she said, "when next I am here, you will be my own, own husband," and kissed him; "but we have Como, and Florence, and Rome, and Naples to do before that;—and won't that be nice?"

"It will be very nice to be anywhere with you," said the lover.

"And mind you have your coat made just as I told you," said Augusta. So they parted.

Early in September they were married with great éclat at Brayboro', and Lady Eardham spared nothing on the occasion. It was her first maternal triumph, and all the country round was made to know of her success. The Newtons had been at Newton for—she did not know how many hundred years. In her zeal she declared that the estate had been in the same hands from long before the Conquest. "There's no title," she said to her intimate friend, Lady Wiggham, "but there's that which is better than a title. We're mushrooms to the Newtons, you know. We only came into Berkshire in the reign of Henry VIII." As the Wigghams had only come into Buckinghamshire in the reign of George IV., Lady Wiggham, had she known the facts, would probably have reminded her dear friend that the Eardhams had in truth first been heard of in those parts in the time of Queen Anne,—the original Eardham having made his money in following Marlborough's army. But Lady Wiggham had not studied the history of the county gentry. The wedding went off very well, and the bride and bridegroom were bowled away to the nearest station with four grey post-horses from Reading in a manner that was truly delightful to Lady Eardham's motherly feelings.

And with the same grey horses shall the happy bride and bridegroom be bowled out of our sight also. The writer of this story feels that some apology is due to his readers for having endeavoured to entertain them so long with the adventures of one of whom it certainly cannot be said that he was fit to be delineated as a hero. It is thought by many critics that in the pictures of imaginary life which novelists produce for the amusement, and possibly for the instruction of their readers, none should be put upon the canvas but the very good, who by their noble thoughts and deeds may lead others to nobility, or the very bad, who by their declared wickedness will make iniquity hideous. How can it be worth one's while, such critics will say,—the writer here speaks of all critical readers, and not of professional critics,—how can it be worth our while to waste our imaginations, our sympathies, and our time upon such a one as Ralph, the heir of the Newton property? The writer, acknowledging the force of these objections, and confessing that his young heroes of romance are but seldom heroic, makes his apology as follows.

The reader of a novel,—who has doubtless taken the volume up simply for amusement, and who would probably lay it down did he suspect that instruction, like a snake in the grass, like physic beneath the sugar, was to be imposed upon him,—requires from his author chiefly this, that he shall be amused by a narrative in which elevated sentiment prevails, and gratified by being made to feel that the elevated sentiments described are exactly his own. When the heroine is nobly true to her lover, to her friend, or to her duty, through all persecution, the girl who reads declares to herself that she also would have been a Jeannie Deans had Fate and Fortune given her an Effie as a sister. The bald-headed old lawyer,—for bald-headed old lawyers do read novels,—who interests himself in the high-minded, self-devoting chivalry of a Colonel Newcombe, believes he would have acted as did the Colonel had he been so tried. What youth in his imagination cannot be as brave, and as loving, though as hopeless in his love, as Harry Esmond? Alas, no one will wish to be as was Ralph Newton! But for one Harry Esmond, there are fifty Ralph Newtons,—five hundred and fifty of them; and the very youth whose bosom glows with admiration as he reads of Harry,—who exults in the idea that as Harry did, so would he have done,—lives as Ralph lived, is less noble, less persistent, less of a man even than was Ralph Newton.

It is the test of a novel writer's art that he conceals his snake-in-the-grass; but the reader may be sure that it is always there. No man or woman with a conscience,—no man or woman with intellect sufficient to produce amusement, can go on from year to year spinning stories without the desire of teaching; with no ambition of influencing readers for their good. Gentle readers, the physic is always beneath the sugar, hidden or unhidden. In writing novels we novelists preach to you from our pulpits, and are keenly anxious that our sermons shall not be inefficacious. Inefficacious they are not, unless they be too badly preached to obtain attention. Injurious they will be unless the lessons taught be good lessons.

What a world this would be if every man were a Harry Esmond, or every woman a Jeannie Deans! But then again, what a world if every woman were a Beckie Sharp and every man a Varney or a Barry Lyndon! Of Varneys and Harry Esmonds there are very few. Human nature, such as it is, does not often produce them. The portraits of such virtues and such vices serve no doubt to emulate and to deter. But are no other portraits necessary? Should we not be taught to see the men and women among whom we really live,—men and women such as we are ourselves,—in order that we should know what are the exact failings which oppress ourselves, and thus learn to hate, and if possible to avoid in life the faults of character which in life are hardly visible, but which in portraiture of life can be made to be so transparent.

Ralph Newton did nothing, gentle reader, which would have caused thee greatly to grieve for him, nothing certainly which would have caused thee to repudiate him, had he been thy brother. And gentlest, sweetest reader, had he come to thee as thy lover, with sufficient protest of love, and with all his history written in his hand, would that have caused thee to reject his suit? Had he been thy neighbour, thou well-to-do reader, with a house in the country, would he not have been welcome to thy table? Wouldst thou have avoided him at his club, thou reader from the West-end? Has he not settled himself respectably, thou grey-haired, novel-reading pater-familias, thou materfamilias, with daughters of thine own to be married? In life would he have been held to have disgraced himself, —except in the very moment in which he seemed to be in danger? Nevertheless, the faults of a Ralph Newton, and not the vices of a Varney or a Barry Lyndon are the evils against which men should in these days be taught to guard themselves;—which women also should be made to hate. Such is the writer's apology for his very indifferent hero, Ralph the Heir.

CHAPTER LVII.

CLARISSA'S FATE.

IN the following October, while Newton of Newton and his bride were making themselves happy amidst the glories of Florence, she with her finery from Paris, and he with a newly-acquired taste for Michael Angelo and the fine arts generally, Gregory the parson again went up to London. He had, of course, "assisted" at his brother's marriage,—in which the heavy burden of the ceremony was imposed on the shoulders of a venerable dean, who was related to Lady Eardham,—and had since that time been all alone at his parsonage. Occasionally he had heard of the Underwoods from Ralph Newton of Beamingham, whose wedding had been postponed till Beamingham Hall had been made fit for its mistress; and from what he had heard Gregory was induced,—hardly to hope,—but to dream it to be possible that even yet he might prevail in love. An idea had grown upon him, springing from various sources, that Clarissa had not been indifferent to his brother, and that this feeling on her part had marred, and must continue to mar, his own happiness. He never believed that there had been fault on his brother's part; but still, if Clarissa had been so wounded,—he could hardly hope,—and perhaps should not even wish,—that she would consent to share with him his parsonage in the close neighbourhood of his brother's house. During all that September he told himself that the thing should be over, and he began to teach himself,—to try to teach himself,—that celibacy was the state in which a clergyman might best live and do his duty. But the lesson had not gone far with him before he shook himself, and determined that he would try yet once again. If there had been such a wound, why should not the wound be cured? Clarissa was at any rate true. She would not falsely promise him a heart, when it was beyond her power to give it. In October, therefore, he went again up to London.

The cases for packing the books had not even yet been made, and Sir Thomas was found in Southampton Buildings. The first words had, of course, reference to the absent Squire. The squire of one's parish, the head of one's family, and one's elder brother, when the three are united in the same personage, will become important to one, even though the personage himself be not heroic. Ralph had written home twice, and everything was prospering with him. Sir Thomas, who had become tired of his late ward, and who had thought worse of the Eardham marriage than the thing deserved, was indifferent to the joys of the Italian honeymoon. "They'll do very well, no doubt," said Sir Thomas. "I was delighted to learn that Augusta bore her journey so well," said Gregory. "Augustas always do bear their journeys well," said Sir Thomas; "though sometimes, I fancy, they find the days a little too long."

But his tone was very different when Gregory asked his leave to make one more attempt at Popham Villa. "I only hope you may succeed,—for her sake, as well as for your own," said Sir Thomas. But when he was asked as to the parson's chance of success, he declared that he could say nothing. "She is changed, I think, from what she used to be,—is more thoughtful, perhaps, and less giddy. It may be that such change will turn her towards you." "I would not have her changed in anything," said Gregory,—"except in her feelings towards myself."

He had been there twice or thrice before he found what he thought to be an opportunity fit for the work that he had on hand. And yet both Patience and Mary did for him and for her all that they knew how to do. But in such a matter it is so hard to act without seeming to act! She who can manœuvre on such a field without displaying her manœuvres is indeed a general! No man need ever attempt the execution of a task so delicate. Mary and Patience put their heads together, and resolved that they would say nothing. Nor did they manifestly take steps to leave the two alone together. It was a question with them, especially with Patience, whether the lover had not come too soon.

But Clarissa at last attacked her sister. "Patience," she said, "why do you not speak to me?"

"Not speak to you, Clary?"

"Not a word,—about that which is always on my mind. You have not mentioned Ralph Newton's name once since his marriage."

" I have thought it better not to mention it. Why should I mention it ?"

" If you think that it would pain me, you are mistaken. It pains me more that you should think that I could not bear it. He was welcome to his wife."

" I know you wish him well, Clary."

" Well! Oh, yes, I wish him well. No doubt he will be happy with her. She is fit for him, and I was not. He did quite right."

" He is not half so good as his brother," said Patience.

" Certainly he is not so good as his brother. Men, of course, will be different. But it is not always the best man that one likes the best. It ought to be so, perhaps."

" I know which I like the best," said Patience. " Oh, Clary, if you could but bring yourself to love him."

" How is one to change like that ? And I do not know that he cares for me now."

" Ah ;—I think he cares for you."

" Why should he ? Is a man to be sacrificed for always because a girl will not take him ? His heart is changed. He takes care to show me so when he comes here. I am glad that it should be changed. Dear Patty, if papa would but come and live at home, I should want nothing else."

" I want something else," said Patience.

" I want nothing but that you should love me ;—and that papa should be with us. But, Patty, do not make me feel that you are afraid to speak to me."

On the day following Gregory was again at Fulham, and he had come thither fully determined that he would now for the last time ask that question, on the answer to which, as it now seemed to him, all his future happiness must depend. He had told himself that he would shake off this too human longing for a sweet face to be ever present with him at his board, for a sweet heart to cherish him with its love, for a dear head to lie upon his bosom. But he had owned to himself that it could not be shaken off, and having so owned, was more sick than ever with desire. Mary and Clarissa were both out when he arrived, and he was closeted for a while with Patience. " How tired you must be of seeing me," he said.

" Tired of seeing you ? Oh no ! "

" I feel myself to be going about like a phantom, and I am ashamed of myself. My brother is successful and happy, and has all that he desires."

" He is easily satisfied," said Patience, with something of sarcasm in her voice.

" And my cousin Ralph is happy and triumphant. I ought not to pine, but in truth I am so weak that I am always pining. Tell me at once,—is there a chance for me ? "

Did it occur to him to think that she to whom he was speaking, ever asked herself why it was not given to her to have even a hope of that joy for which he was craving? Did she ever pine because, when others were mating round her, flying off in pairs to their warm mutual nests, there came to her no such question of mating and flying off to love and happiness? If there was such pining, it was all inward, hidden from her friends so that their mirth should not be lessened by her want of mirth, not expressed either by her eye or mouth because she knew that on the expression of her face depended somewhat of the comfort of those who loved her. A homely brow, and plain features, and locks of hair that have not been combed by Love's attendant nymphs into soft and winning tresses, seems to tell us that Love is not wanted by the bosom that owns them. We teach ourselves to regard such a one, let her be ever so good, with ever so sweet temper, ever so generous in heart, ever so affectionate among her friends, as separated alike from the perils and the privileges of that passion without which they who are blessed or banned with beauty would regard life but as a charred and muti-lated existence. It is as though we should believe that passion springs from the rind, which is fair or foul to the eye, and not in the heart, which is often fairest, freshest, and most free, when the skin is dark and the cheeks are rough. This young parson expected Patience to sympathise with him, to greet for him, to aid him if there might be aid, and to understand that for him the world would be blank and wretched unless he could get for himself a soft sweet mate to sing when he sang, and to wail when he wailed. The only mate that Patience had was this very girl that was to be thus taken from her. But she did sympathise with him, did greet for him, did give him all her aid. Knowing what she was herself and how God had formed her, she had learned to bury self absolutely and to take all her earthly joy from the joys of others. Shall it not come to pass that, hereafter, she too shall have a lover among the cherubim? "What can I say to you?" replied Patience to the young man's earnest entreaty. "If she were mine to give, I would give her to you instantly."

"Then you think there is no chance. If I thought that, why should I trouble her again?"

"I do not say so. Do you not know, Mr. Newton, that in such matters even sisters can hardly tell their thoughts to each other? How can they when they do not even know their own wishes?"

"She does not hate me then?"

"Hate you! no;—she does not hate you. But there are so many degrees between hating and that kind of love which you want from her! You may be sure of this, that she so esteems you that your persistence cannot lessen you in her regard."

He was still pleading his case with the elder sister,—very uselessly indeed, as he was aware; but having fallen on the subject of his love it was impossible for him to change it for any other,—when Clarissa came into the room swinging her hat in her hand. She had been over at Miss Spooner's house and was full of Miss Spooner's woes and complaints. As soon as she had shaken hands with her lover and spoken the few words of courtesy which the meeting demanded of her, she threw herself into the affairs of Miss Spooner as though they were of vital interest. "She is determined to be unhappy, Patty, and it is no use trying to make her not so. She says that Jane robs her, which I don't believe is true, and that Sarah has a lover,—and why shouldn't Sarah have a lover? But as for curing her grievances, it would be the cruellest thing in the world. She lives upon her grievances. Something has happened to the chimney-pot, and the landlord hasn't sent a mason. She is revelling in her chimney-pot."

"Poor dear Miss Spooner," said Patience, getting up and leaving the room as though it were her duty to look at once after her old friend in the midst of these troubles.

Clarissa had not intended this. "She's asleep now," said Clarissa. But Patience went all the same. It might be that Miss Spooner would require to be watched in her slumbers. When Patience was gone Gregory Newton got up from his seat and walked to the window. He stood there for what seemed to be an endless number of seconds before he returned, and Clarissa had time to determine that she would escape. "I told Mary that I would go to her," she said, "you won't mind being left alone for a few minutes, Mr. Newton."

"Do not go just now, Clarissa."

"Only that I said I would," she answered, pleading that she must keep a promise which she had never made.

"Mary can spare you,—and I cannot. Mary is staying with you, and I shall be gone,—almost immediately. I go back to Newton to-morrow, and who can say when I shall see you again?"

"You will be coming up to London, of course."

"I am here now at any rate," he said smiling, "and will take what advantage of it I can. It is the old story, Clarissa;—so old that I know you must be sick of it."

"If you think so, you should not tell it again."

"Do not be ill-natured to me. I don't know why it is but a man gets to be ashamed of himself, as though he were doing something mean and paltry, when he loves with persistence, as I do." Had it been possible that she should give him so much encouragement she would have told him that the mean man, and paltry, was he who could love or pretend to love with no capacity for persistency. She could not fail to draw a comparison between him and his brother, in which there was so much of meanness on the part of him who had at one time been as a god to her, and so much nobility in him to whom she was and ever had been as a goddess. "I suppose a man should take an answer and have done with it," he continued. "But how is a man to have done with it, when his heart remains the same?"

"A man should master his heart."

"I am, then, to understand that that which you have said so often before must be said again?" He had never knelt to her, and he did not kneel now; but he leaned over her so that she hardly knew whether he was on his knees or still seated on his chair. And she herself, though she answered him briskly,—almost with impertinence, —was so little mistress of herself that she knew not what she said. She would take him now,—if only she knew how to take him without disgracing herself in her own estimation. "Dear Clary, think of it. Try to love me. I need not tell you again how true is my love for you." He had hold of her hand, and she did not withdraw it, and he ought to have known that the battle was won. But he knew nothing. He hardly knew that her hand was in his. "Clary, you are all the world to me. Must I go back heart-laden, but empty-handed, with no comfort?"

"If you knew all!" she said, rising suddenly from her chair.

"All what?"

"If you knew all, you would not take me though I offered myself." He stood staring at her, not at all comprehending her words, and she perceived in the midst of her distress that it was needful that she should explain herself. "I have loved Ralph always;—yes, your brother."

"And he?"

"I will not accuse him in anything. He is married now, and it is past."

"And you can never love again?"

"Who would take such a heart as that? It would not be worth the giving or worth the taking. Oh—how I loved him!" Then he left her side, and went back to the window, while she sank back upon her chair, and, burying her face in her hands, gave way to tears and sobs. He stood there perhaps for a minute, and then returning to her, so gently that she did not hear him, he did kneel at her side. He knelt, and putting his hand upon her arm, he kissed the sleeve of her gown. "You had better go from me now," she said, amidst her sobs.

"I will never go from you again," he answered. "God's mercy can cure also that wound, and I will be his minister in healing it. Clarissa, I am so glad that you have told me all. Looking back I can understand it now. I once thought that it was so."

"Yes," she said, "yes; it was so."

Gradually one hand of hers fell into his, and though no word of acceptance had been spoken he knew that he was at last accepted.

"My own Clary," he said. "I may call you my own?" There was no answer, but he knew that it was so. "Nothing shall be done to trouble you;—nothing shall be said to press you. You may be sure of this, if it be good to be loved,—that no woman was ever loved more tenderly than you are."

"I do know it," she said, through her tears.

Then he rose and stood again at the window, looking out upon the lawn and the river. She was still weeping, but he hardly heeded her tears. It was better for her that she should weep than restrain them. And, as to himself and his own feelings,—he tried to question himself, whether, in truth, was he less happy in this great possession, which he had at last gained, because his brother had for a while interfered with him in gaining it? That she would be as true to him now, as tender and as loving, as though Ralph had never crossed her path, he did not for a moment doubt. That she would be less sweet to him because her sweetness had been offered to another he would not admit to himself,—even though the question were asked. She would be all his own, and was she not the one thing in the world which he coveted? He did think that for such a one as his Clarissa he would be a better mate than would have been his brother, and he was sure that she herself would learn to know that it was so. He stood there long enough to resolve that this which had been told him should be no drawback upon his bliss. "Clary," he said, returning to her, "it is settled?" She made him no answer. "My darling, I am as happy now as though Ralph had never seen your sweet face, or heard your dear voice. Look up at me once." Slowly she looked up into his eyes, and then stood before him almost as a suppliant, and gave him her face to be kissed. So at last they became engaged as man and wife;—though it may be doubted whether she spoke another word before he left the room.

It was, however, quite understood that they were engaged; and, though he did not see Clarissa again, he received the congratulations both of Patience and Mary Bonner before he left the house; and that very night succeeded in hunting down Sir Thomas, so that he might tell the father that the daughter had at last consented to become his wife.

CHAPTER LVIII.

CONCLUSION.

CLARISSA had found it hard to change the object of her love, so hard, that for a time she had been unwilling even to make the effort;—and she had been ashamed that those around her should think that she would make it; but when the thing was done, her second hero was dearer to her than ever had been the first. He at least was true. With him there was no need of doubt. His assurances were not conveyed in words so light that they might mean much or little. This second lover was a lover, indeed, who thought no pains too great to show her that she was ever growing in his heart of hearts. For a while,—for a week or two,—she restrained her tongue ; but when once she had accustomed herself to the coaxing kindness of her sister and her cousin, then her eloquence was loosened, and Gregory Newton was a god indeed. In the course of time she got a very pretty note from Ralph, congratulating her, as he also had congratulated Polly, and expressing a fear that he might not be home in time to be present at the wedding. Augusta was so fond of Rome that they did not mean to leave it till the late spring. Then, after a while, there came to her, also, a watch and chain, twice as costly as those given to Polly,—which, however, no persuasion from Gregory would ever induce Clarissa to wear. In after time Ralph never noticed that the trinkets were not worn.

The winter at Popham Villa went on very much as other winters had gone, except that two of the girls living there were full of future hopes, and preparing for future cares, while the third occupied her heart and mind with the cares and hopes of the other two. Patience, however, had one other task in hand, a task upon the performance of which her future happiness much depended, and in respect to which she now ventured to hope for success. Wherever her future home might be, it would be terrible to her if her father would not consent to occupy it with her. It had been settled that both the marriages should take place early in April,—both on the same day, and, as a matter of course, the weddings would be celebrated at Fulham. Christmas had come and gone, and winter was going, before Sir Thomas had absolutely promised to renew that order for the making the packing-cases for his books. " You won't go back, papa, after they are married," Patience said to her father, early in March.

" If I do it shall not be for long."

" Not for a day, papa ! Surely you will not leave me alone ? There will be plenty of room now. The air of Fulham will be better for your work than those stuffy, dark, dingy lawyers' chambers."

" My dear, all the work of my life that was worth doing was done in those stuffy, dingy rooms." That was all that Sir Thomas said, but the accusation conveyed to him by his daughter's words was very heavy. For years past he had sat intending to work, purposing to achieve a great task which he set for himself, and had done—almost nothing. Might it be yet possible that that purer air of which Patty spoke should produce new energy, and lead to better results ? The promise of it did at least produce new resolutions. It was impossible, as Patience had said, that his child should be left to dwell alone, while yet she had a father living.

"Stemm," he said, "I told you to get some packing-cases made."

"Packing-cases, Sir Thomas?"

"Yes;—packing-cases for the books. It was months ago. Are they ready?"

"No, Sir Thomas. They ain't ready."

"Why not?"

"Well, Sir Thomas;—they ain't; that's all." Then the order was repeated in a manner so formal, as to make Stemm understand that it was intended for a fact. "You are going away from this; are you, Sir Thomas?"

"I believe that I shall give the chambers up altogether at midsummer. At any rate, I mean to have the books packed at once."

"Very well, Sir Thomas." Then there was a pause, during which Stemm did not leave the room. Nor did Sir Thomas dismiss him, feeling that there might well be other things which would require discussion. "And about me, Sir Thomas?" said Stemm.

"I have been thinking about that, Stemm."

"So have I, Sir Thomas,—more nor once."

"You can come to Fulham if you like,—only you must not scold the maids."

"Very well, Sir Thomas," said Stemm, with hardly any variation in his voice, but still with less of care upon his brow.

"Mind, I will not have you scolding them at the villa."

"Not unless they deserve it, Sir Thomas," said Stemm. Sir Thomas could say nothing further. For our own part we fear that the maidens at the villa will not be the better in conduct, as they certainly will not be more comfortable in their lives, in consequence of this change.

And the books were moved in large packing-cases, not one of which had yet been opened when the two brides returned to Popham Villa after their wedding tours, to see Patience just for a day before they were taken to their new homes. Nevertheless, let us hope that the change of air and of scene may tend to future diligence, and that the magnus opus may yet be achieved. We have heard of editions of Aristophanes, of Polybius, of the Iliad, of Ovid, and what not, which have ever been forthcoming under the hands of notable scholars, who have grown grey amidst the renewed promises which have been given. And some of these works have come forth, belying the prophecies of incredulous friends. Let us hope that the great Life of Bacon may yet be written.

A CATALOGUE OF SELECTED DOVER BOOKS
IN ALL FIELDS OF INTEREST

A CATALOGUE OF SELECTED DOVER BOOKS
IN ALL FIELDS OF INTEREST

THE NOTEBOOKS OF LEONARDO DA VINCI, edited by J.P. Richter. Extracts from manuscripts reveal great genius; on painting, sculpture, anatomy, sciences, geography, etc. Both Italian and English. 186 ms. pages reproduced, plus 500 additional drawings, including studies for Last Supper, Sforza monument, etc. 860pp. 7⅞ x 10¾. USO 22572-0, 22573-9 Pa., Two vol. set $15.90

ART NOUVEAU DESIGNS IN COLOR, Alphonse Mucha, Maurice Verneuil, Georges Auriol. Full-color reproduction of Combinaisons ornamentales (c. 1900) by Art Nouveau masters. Floral, animal, geometric, interlacings, swashes — borders, frames, spots — all incredibly beautiful. 60 plates, hundreds of designs. 9⅜ x 8¹/₁₆. 22885-1 Pa. $4.00

GRAPHIC WORKS OF ODILON REDON. All great fantastic lithographs, etchings, engravings, drawings, 209 in all. Monsters, Huysmans, still life work, etc. Introduction by Alfred Werner. 209pp. 9⅛ x 12¼. 21996-8 Pa. $6.00

EXOTIC FLORAL PATTERNS IN COLOR, E.-A. Seguy. Incredibly beautiful full-color pochoir work by great French designer of 20's. Complete Bouquets et frondaisons, Suggestions pour étoffes. Richness must be seen to be believed. 40 plates containing 120 patterns. 80pp. 9⅜ x 12¼. 23041-4 Pa. $6.00

SELECTED ETCHINGS OF JAMES A. McN. WHISTLER, James A. McN. Whistler. 149 outstanding etchings by the great American artist, including selections from the Thames set and two Venice sets, the complete French set, and many individual prints. Introduction and explanatory note on each print by Maria Naylor. 157pp. 9⅜ x 12¼. 23194-1 Pa. $5.00

VISUAL ILLUSIONS: THEIR CAUSES, CHARACTERISTICS, AND APPLICATIONS, Matthew Luckiesh. Thorough description, discussion; shape and size, color, motion; natural illusion. Uses in art and industry. 100 illustrations. 252pp.
21530-X Pa. $3.00

TEN BOOKS ON ARCHITECTURE, Vitruvius. The most important book ever written on architecture. Early Roman aesthetics, technology, classical orders, site selection, all other aspects. Stands behind everything since. Morgan translation. 331pp.
20645-9 Pa. $3.75

THE CODEX NUTTALL. A PICTURE MANUSCRIPT FROM ANCIENT MEXICO, as first edited by Zelia Nuttall. Only inexpensive edition, in full color, of a pre-Columbian Mexican (Mixtec) book. 88 color plates show kings, gods, heroes, temples, sacrifices. New explanatory, historical introduction by Arthur G. Miller. 96pp. 11³/₈ x 8½. 23168-2 Pa. $7.50

CREATIVE LITHOGRAPHY AND HOW TO DO IT, Grant Arnold. Lithography as art form: working directly on stone, transfer of drawings, lithotint, mezzotint, color printing; also metal plates. Detailed, thorough. 27 illustrations. 214pp.
21208-4 Pa. $3.50

DESIGN MOTIFS OF ANCIENT MEXICO, Jorge Enciso. Vigorous, powerful ceramic stamp impressions — Maya, Aztec, Toltec, Olmec. Serpents, gods, priests, dancers, etc. 153pp. 6⅛ x 9¼.
20084-1 Pa. $2.50

AMERICAN INDIAN DESIGN AND DECORATION, Leroy Appleton. Full text, plus more than 700 precise drawings of Inca, Maya, Aztec, Pueblo, Plains, NW Coast basketry, sculpture, painting, pottery, sand paintings, metal, etc. 4 plates in color. 279pp. 8⅜ x 11¼.
22704-9 Pa. $5.00

CHINESE LATTICE DESIGNS, Daniel S. Dye. Incredibly beautiful geometric designs: circles, voluted, simple dissections, etc. Inexhaustible source of ideas, motifs. 1239 illustrations. 469pp. 6⅛ x 9¼.
23096-1 Pa. $5.00

JAPANESE DESIGN MOTIFS, Matsuya Co. Mon, or heraldic designs. Over 4000 typical, beautiful designs: birds, animals, flowers, swords, fans, geometric; all beautifully stylized. 213pp. 11⅜ x 8¼.
22874-6 Pa. $5.00

PERSPECTIVE, Jan Vredeman de Vries. 73 perspective plates from 1604 edition; buildings, townscapes, stairways, fantastic scenes. Remarkable for beauty, surrealistic atmosphere; real eye-catchers. Introduction by Adolf Placzek. 74pp. 11⅜ x 8¼.
20186-4 Pa. $3.00

EARLY AMERICAN DESIGN MOTIFS, Suzanne E. Chapman. 497 motifs, designs, from painting on wood, ceramics, appliqué, glassware, samplers, metal work, etc. Florals, landscapes, birds and animals, geometrics, letters, etc. Inexhaustible. Enlarged edition. 138pp. 8⅜ x 11¼.
22985-8 Pa. $3.50
23084-8 Clothbd. $7.95

VICTORIAN STENCILS FOR DESIGN AND DECORATION, edited by E.V. Gillon, Jr. 113 wonderful ornate Victorian pieces from German sources; florals, geometrics; borders, corner pieces; bird motifs, etc. 64pp. 9⅜ x 12¼.
21995-X Pa. $3.00

ART NOUVEAU: AN ANTHOLOGY OF DESIGN AND ILLUSTRATION FROM THE STUDIO, edited by E.V. Gillon, Jr. Graphic arts: book jackets, posters, engravings, illustrations, decorations; Crane, Beardsley, Bradley and many others. Inexhaustible. 92pp. 8⅛ x 11.
22388-4 Pa. $2.50

ORIGINAL ART DECO DESIGNS, William Rowe. First-rate, highly imaginative modern Art Deco frames, borders, compositions, alphabets, florals, insectals, Wurlitzer-types, etc. Much finest modern Art Deco. 80 plates, 8 in color. 8⅜ x 11¼.
22567-4 Pa. $3.50

HANDBOOK OF DESIGNS AND DEVICES, Clarence P. Hornung. Over 1800 basic geometric designs based on circle, triangle, square, scroll, cross, etc. Largest such collection in existence. 261pp.
20125-2 Pa. $2.75

150 MASTERPIECES OF DRAWING, edited by Anthony Toney. 150 plates, early 15th century to end of 18th century; Rembrandt, Michelangelo, Dürer, Fragonard, Watteau, Wouwerman, many others. 150pp. 8⅜ x 11¼. 21032-4 Pa. $4.00

THE GOLDEN AGE OF THE POSTER, Hayward and Blanche Cirker. 70 extraordinary posters in full colors, from Maîtres de l'Affiche, Mucha, Lautrec, Bradley, Cheret, Beardsley, many others. 9⅜ x 12¼. 22753-7 Pa. $5.95

SIMPLICISSIMUS, selection, translations and text by Stanley Appelbaum. 180 satirical drawings, 16 in full color, from the famous German weekly magazine in the years 1896 to 1926. 24 artists included: Grosz, Kley, Pascin, Kubin, Kollwitz, plus Heine, Thöny, Bruno Paul, others. 172pp. 8½ x 12¼. 23098-8 Pa. $5.00
23099-6 Clothbd. $10.00

THE EARLY WORK OF AUBREY BEARDSLEY, Aubrey Beardsley. 157 plates, 2 in color: Manon Lescaut, Madame Bovary, Morte d'Arthur, Salome, other. Introduction by H. Marillier. 175pp. 8½ x 11. 21816-3 Pa. $4.00

THE LATER WORK OF AUBREY BEARDSLEY, Aubrey Beardsley. Exotic masterpieces of full maturity: Venus and Tannhäuser, Lysistrata, Rape of the Lock, Volpone, Savoy material, etc. 174 plates, 2 in color. 176pp. 8½ x 11. 21817-1 Pa. $4.50

DRAWINGS OF WILLIAM BLAKE, William Blake. 92 plates from Book of Job, Divine Comedy, Paradise Lost, visionary heads, mythological figures, Laocoön, etc. Selection, introduction, commentary by Sir Geoffrey Keynes. 178pp. 8½ x 11. 22303-5 Pa. $4.00

LONDON: A PILGRIMAGE, Gustave Doré, Blanchard Jerrold. Squalor, riches, misery, beauty of mid-Victorian metropolis; 55 wonderful plates, 125 other illustrations, full social, cultural text by Jerrold. 191pp. of text. 8⅛ x 11. 22306-X Pa. $6.00

THE COMPLETE WOODCUTS OF ALBRECHT DÜRER, edited by Dr. W. Kurth. 346 in all: Old Testament, St. Jerome, Passion, Life of Virgin, Apocalypse, many others. Introduction by Campbell Dodgson. 285pp. 8½ x 12¼. 21097-9 Pa. $6.00

THE DISASTERS OF WAR, Francisco Goya. 83 etchings record horrors of Napoleonic wars in Spain and war in general. Reprint of 1st edition, plus 3 additional plates. Introduction by Philip Hofer. 97pp. 9⅜ x 8¼. 21872-4 Pa. $3.50

ENGRAVINGS OF HOGARTH, William Hogarth. 101 of Hogarth's greatest works: Rake's Progress, Harlot's Progress, Illustrations for Hudibras, Midnight Modern Conversation, Before and After, Beer Street and Gin Lane, many more. Full commentary. 256pp. 11 x 14. 22479-1 Pa. $7.95

PRIMITIVE ART, Franz Boas. Great anthropologist on ceramics, textiles, wood, stone, metal, etc.; patterns, technology, symbols, styles. All areas, but fullest on Northwest Coast Indians. 350 illustrations. 378pp. 20025-6 Pa. $3.75

MOTHER GOOSE'S MELODIES. Facsimile of fabulously rare Munroe and Francis "copyright 1833" Boston edition. Familiar and unusual rhymes, wonderful old woodcut illustrations. Edited by E.F. Bleiler. 128pp. 4½ x 6⅜. 22577-1 Pa. $1.50

MOTHER GOOSE IN HIEROGLYPHICS. Favorite nursery rhymes presented in rebus form for children. Fascinating 1849 edition reproduced in toto, with key. Introduction by E.F. Bleiler. About 400 woodcuts. 64pp. 6⅞ x 5¼. 20745-5 Pa. $1.50

PETER PIPER'S PRACTICAL PRINCIPLES OF PLAIN & PERFECT PRONUNCIATION. Alliterative jingles and tongue-twisters. Reproduction in full of 1830 first American edition. 25 spirited woodcuts. 32pp. 4½ x 6⅜. 22560-7 Pa. $1.25

MARMADUKE MULTIPLY'S MERRY METHOD OF MAKING MINOR MATHEMATICIANS. Fellow to Peter Piper, it teaches multiplication table by catchy rhymes and woodcuts. 1841 Munroe & Francis edition. Edited by E.F. Bleiler. 103pp. 4⅝ x 6. 22773-1 Pa. $1.25

THE NIGHT BEFORE CHRISTMAS, Clement Moore. Full text, and woodcuts from original 1848 book. Also critical, historical material. 19 illustrations. 40pp. 4⅝ x 6. 22797-9 Pa. $1.35

THE KING OF THE GOLDEN RIVER, John Ruskin. Victorian children's classic of three brothers, their attempts to reach the Golden River, what becomes of them. Facsimile of original 1889 edition. 22 illustrations. 56pp. 4⅝ x 6⅜. 20066-3 Pa. $1.50

DREAMS OF THE RAREBIT FIEND, Winsor McCay. Pioneer cartoon strip, unexcelled for beauty, imagination, in 60 full sequences. Incredible technical virtuosity, wonderful visual wit. Historical introduction. 62pp. 8⅜ x 11¼. 21347-1 Pa. $2.50

THE KATZENJAMMER KIDS, Rudolf Dirks. In full color, 14 strips from 1906-7; full of imagination, characteristic humor. Classic of great historical importance. Introduction by August Derleth. 32pp. 9¼ x 12¼. 23005-8 Pa. $2.00

LITTLE ORPHAN ANNIE AND LITTLE ORPHAN ANNIE IN COSMIC CITY, Harold Gray. Two great sequences from the early strips: our curly-haired heroine defends the Warbucks' financial empire and, then, takes on meanie Phineas P. Pinchpenny. Leapin' lizards! 178pp. 6⅛ x 8⅜. 23107-0 Pa. $2.00

ABSOLUTELY MAD INVENTIONS, A.E. Brown, H.A. Jeffcott. Hilarious, useless, or merely absurd inventions all granted patents by the U.S. Patent Office. Edible tie pin, mechanical hat tipper, etc. 57 illustrations. 125pp. 22596-8 Pa. $1.50

THE DEVIL'S DICTIONARY, Ambrose Bierce. Barbed, bitter, brilliant witticisms in the form of a dictionary. Best, most ferocious satire America has produced. 145pp. 20487-1 Pa. $1.75

THE BEST DR. THORNDYKE DETECTIVE STORIES, R. Austin Freeman. The Case of Oscar Brodski, The Moabite Cipher, and 5 other favorites featuring the great scientific detective, plus his long-believed-lost first adventure — 31 New Inn — reprinted here for the first time. Edited by E.F. Bleiler. USO 20388-3 Pa. $3.00

BEST "THINKING MACHINE" DETECTIVE STORIES, Jacques Futrelle. The Problem of Cell 13 and 11 other stories about Prof. Augustus S.F.X. Van Dusen, including two "lost" stories. First reprinting of several. Edited by E.F. Bleiler. 241pp.
20537-1 Pa. $3.00

UNCLE SILAS, J. Sheridan LeFanu. Victorian Gothic mystery novel, considered by many best of period, even better than Collins or Dickens. Wonderful psychological terror. Introduction by Frederick Shroyer. 436pp.   21715-9 Pa. $4.50

BEST DR. POGGIOLI DETECTIVE STORIES, T.S. Stribling. 15 best stories from EQMM and The Saint offer new adventures in Mexico, Florida, Tennessee hills as Poggioli unravels mysteries and combats Count Jalacki. 217pp. 23227-1 Pa. $3.00

EIGHT DIME NOVELS, selected with an introduction by E.F. Bleiler. Adventures of Old King Brady, Frank James, Nick Carter, Deadwood Dick, Buffalo Bill, The Steam Man, Frank Merriwell, and Horatio Alger — 1877 to 1905. Important, entertaining popular literature in facsimile reprint, with original covers. 190pp. 9 x 12.   22975-0 Pa. $3.50

ALICE'S ADVENTURES UNDER GROUND, Lewis Carroll. Facsimile of ms. Carroll gave Alice Liddell in 1864. Different in many ways from final Alice. Handlettered, illustrated by Carroll. Introduction by Martin Gardner. 128pp. 21482-6 Pa. $2.00

ALICE IN WONDERLAND COLORING BOOK, Lewis Carroll. Pictures by John Tenniel. Large-size versions of the famous illustrations of Alice, Cheshire Cat, Mad Hatter and all the others, waiting for your crayons. Abridged text. 36 illustrations. 64pp. 8¼ x 11.   22853-3 Pa. $1.50

AVENTURES D'ALICE AU PAYS DES MERVEILLES, Lewis Carroll. Bué's translation of "Alice" into French, supervised by Carroll himself. Novel way to learn language. (No English text.) 42 Tenniel illustrations. 196pp.   22836-3 Pa. $3.00

MYTHS AND FOLK TALES OF IRELAND, Jeremiah Curtin. 11 stories that are Irish versions of European fairy tales and 9 stories from the Fenian cycle — 20 tales of legend and magic that comprise an essential work in the history of folklore. 256pp.   22430-9 Pa. $3.00

EAST O' THE SUN AND WEST O' THE MOON, George W. Dasent. Only full edition of favorite, wonderful Norwegian fairytales — Why the Sea is Salt, Boots and the Troll, etc. — with 77 illustrations by Kittelsen & Werenskiöld. 418pp.
22521-6 Pa. $4.50

PERRAULT'S FAIRY TALES, Charles Perrault and Gustave Doré. Original versions of Cinderella, Sleeping Beauty, Little Red Riding Hood, etc. in best translation, with 34 wonderful illustrations by Gustave Doré. 117pp. 8⅛ x 11. 22311-6 Pa. $2.50

EARLY NEW ENGLAND GRAVESTONE RUBBINGS, Edmund V. Gillon, Jr. 43 photographs, 226 rubbings show heavily symbolic, macabre, sometimes humorous primitive American art. Up to early 19th century. 207pp. 8⅜ x 11¼.
21380-3 Pa. $4.00

L.J.M. DAGUERRE: THE HISTORY OF THE DIORAMA AND THE DAGUERREOTYPE, Helmut and Alison Gernsheim. Definitive account. Early history, life and work of Daguerre; discovery of daguerreotype process; diffusion abroad; other early photography. 124 illustrations. 226pp. 6⅙ x 9¼.
22290-X Pa. $4.00

PHOTOGRAPHY AND THE AMERICAN SCENE, Robert Taft. The basic book on American photography as art, recording form, 1839-1889. Development, influence on society, great photographers, types (portraits, war, frontier, etc.), whatever else needed. Inexhaustible. Illustrated with 322 early photos, daguerreotypes, tintypes, stereo slides, etc. 546pp. 6⅛ x 9¼.
21201-7 Pa. $6.00

PHOTOGRAPHIC SKETCHBOOK OF THE CIVIL WAR, Alexander Gardner. Reproduction of 1866 volume with 100 on-the-field photographs: Manassas, Lincoln on battlefield, slave pens, etc. Introduction by E.F. Bleiler. 224pp. 10¾ x 9.
22731-6 Pa. $6.00

THE MOVIES: A PICTURE QUIZ BOOK, Stanley Appelbaum & Hayward Cirker. Match stars with their movies, name actors and actresses, test your movie skill with 241 stills from 236 great movies, 1902-1959. Indexes of performers and films. 128pp. 8⅜ x 9¼.
20222-4 Pa. $3.00

THE TALKIES, Richard Griffith. Anthology of features, articles from Photoplay, 1928-1940, reproduced complete. Stars, famous movies, technical features, fabulous ads, etc.; Garbo, Chaplin, King Kong, Lubitsch, etc. 4 color plates, scores of illustrations. 327pp. 8⅜ x 11¼.
22762-6 Pa. $6.95

THE MOVIE MUSICAL FROM VITAPHONE TO "42ND STREET," edited by Miles Kreuger. Relive the rise of the movie musical as reported in the pages of Photoplay magazine (1926-1933): every movie review, cast list, ad, and record review; every significant feature article, production still, biography, forecast, and gossip story. Profusely illustrated. 367pp. 8⅜ x 11¼.
23154-2 Pa. $7.95

JOHANN SEBASTIAN BACH, Philipp Spitta. Great classic of biography, musical commentary, with hundreds of pieces analyzed. Also good for Bach's contemporaries. 450 musical examples. Total of 1799pp.
EUK 22278-0, 22279-9 Clothbd., Two vol. set $25.00

BEETHOVEN AND HIS NINE SYMPHONIES, Sir George Grove. Thorough history, analysis, commentary on symphonies and some related pieces. For either beginner or advanced student. 436 musical passages. 407pp.
20334-4 Pa. $4.00

MOZART AND HIS PIANO CONCERTOS, Cuthbert Girdlestone. The only full-length study. Detailed analyses of all 21 concertos, sources; 417 musical examples. 509pp.
21271-8 Pa. $6.00

THE FITZWILLIAM VIRGINAL BOOK, edited by J. Fuller Maitland, W.B. Squire. Famous early 17th century collection of keyboard music, 300 works by Morley, Byrd, Bull, Gibbons, etc. Modern notation. Total of 938pp. 8³⁄₈ x 11.
ECE 21068-5, 21069-3 Pa., Two vol. set $15.00

COMPLETE STRING QUARTETS, Wolfgang A. Mozart. Breitkopf and Härtel edition. All 23 string quartets plus alternate slow movement to K156. Study score. 277pp. 9³⁄₈ x 12¼. 22372-8 Pa. $6.00

COMPLETE SONG CYCLES, Franz Schubert. Complete piano, vocal music of Die Schöne Müllerin, Die Winterreise, Schwanengesang. Also Drinker English singing translations. Breitkopf and Härtel edition. 217pp. 9³⁄₈ x 12¼.
22649-2 Pa. $5.00

THE COMPLETE PRELUDES AND ETUDES FOR PIANOFORTE SOLO, Alexander Scriabin. All the preludes and etudes including many perfectly spun miniatures. Edited by K.N. Igumnov and Y.I. Mil'shteyn. 250pp. 9 x 12. 22919-X Pa. $6.00

TRISTAN UND ISOLDE, Richard Wagner. Full orchestral score with complete instrumentation. Do not confuse with piano reduction. Commentary by Felix Mottl, great Wagnerian conductor and scholar. Study score. 655pp. 8¹⁄₈ x 11.
22915-7 Pa. $11.95

FAVORITE SONGS OF THE NINETIES, ed. Robert Fremont. Full reproduction, including covers, of 88 favorites: Ta-Ra-Ra-Boom-De-Aye, The Band Played On, Bird in a Gilded Cage, Under the Bamboo Tree, After the Ball, etc. 401pp. 9 x 12.
EBE 21536-9 Pa. $6.95

SOUSA'S GREAT MARCHES IN PIANO TRANSCRIPTION: ORIGINAL SHEET MUSIC OF 23 WORKS, John Philip Sousa. Selected by Lester S. Levy. Playing edition includes: The Stars and Stripes Forever, The Thunderer, The Gladiator, King Cotton, Washington Post, much more. 24 illustrations. 111pp. 9 x 12.
USO 23132-1 Pa. $3.50

CLASSIC PIANO RAGS, selected with an introduction by Rudi Blesh. Best ragtime music (1897-1922) by Scott Joplin, James Scott, Joseph F. Lamb, Tom Turpin, 9 others. Printed from best original sheet music, plus covers. 364pp. 9 x 12.
EBE 20469-3 Pa. $7.50

ANALYSIS OF CHINESE CHARACTERS, C.D. Wilder, J.H. Ingram. 1000 most important characters analyzed according to primitives, phonetics, historical development. Traditional method offers mnemonic aid to beginner, intermediate student of Chinese, Japanese. 365pp. 23045-7 Pa. $4.00

MODERN CHINESE: A BASIC COURSE, Faculty of Peking University. Self study, classroom course in modern Mandarin. Records contain phonetics, vocabulary, sentences, lessons. 249 page book contains all recorded text, translations, grammar, vocabulary, exercises. Best course on market. 3 12" 33¹⁄₃ monaural records, book, album. 98832-5 Set $12.50

MANUAL OF THE TREES OF NORTH AMERICA, Charles S. Sargent. The basic survey of every native tree and tree-like shrub, 717 species in all. Extremely full descriptions, information on habitat, growth, locales, economics, etc. Necessary to every serious tree lover. Over 100 finding keys. 783 illustrations. Total of 986pp. 20277-1, 20278-X Pa., Two vol. set $9.00

BIRDS OF THE NEW YORK AREA, John Bull. Indispensable guide to more than 400 species within a hundred-mile radius of Manhattan. Information on range, status, breeding, migration, distribution trends, etc. Foreword by Roger Tory Peterson. 17 drawings; maps. 540pp. 23222-0 Pa. $6.00

THE SEA-BEACH AT EBB-TIDE, Augusta Foote Arnold. Identify hundreds of marine plants and animals: algae, seaweeds, squids, crabs, corals, etc. Descriptions cover food, life cycle, size, shape, habitat. Over 600 drawings. 490pp. 21949-6 Pa. $5.00

THE MOTH BOOK, William J. Holland. Identify more than 2,000 moths of North America. General information, precise species descriptions. 623 illustrations plus 48 color plates show almost all species, full size. 1968 edition. Still the basic book. Total of 551pp. 6½ x 9¼. 21948-8 Pa. $6.00

HOW INDIANS USE WILD PLANTS FOR FOOD, MEDICINE & CRAFTS, Frances Densmore. Smithsonian, Bureau of American Ethnology report presents wealth of material on nearly 200 plants used by Chippewas of Minnesota and Wisconsin. 33 plates plus 122pp. of text. 6⅛ x 9¼. 23019-8 Pa. $2.50

OLD NEW YORK IN EARLY PHOTOGRAPHS, edited by Mary Black. Your only chance to see New York City as it was 1853-1906, through 196 wonderful photographs from N.Y. Historical Society. Great Blizzard, Lincoln's funeral procession, great buildings. 228pp. 9 x 12. 22907-6 Pa. $6.95

THE AMERICAN REVOLUTION, A PICTURE SOURCEBOOK, John Grafton. Wonderful Bicentennial picture source, with 411 illustrations (contemporary and 19th century) showing battles, personalities, maps, events, flags, posters, soldier's life, ships, etc. all captioned and explained. A wonderful browsing book, supplement to other historical reading. 160pp. 9 x 12. 23226-3 Pa. $4.00

PERSONAL NARRATIVE OF A PILGRIMAGE TO AL-MADINAH AND MECCAH, Richard Burton. Great travel classic by remarkably colorful personality. Burton, disguised as a Moroccan, visited sacred shrines of Islam, narrowly escaping death. Wonderful observations of Islamic life, customs, personalities. 47 illustrations. Total of 959pp. 21217-3, 21218-1 Pa., Two vol. set $10.00

INCIDENTS OF TRAVEL IN CENTRAL AMERICA, CHIAPAS, AND YUCATAN, John L. Stephens. Almost single-handed discovery of Maya culture; exploration of ruined cities, monuments, temples; customs of Indians. 115 drawings. 892pp. 22404-X, 22405-8 Pa., Two vol. set $9.00

CONSTRUCTION OF AMERICAN FURNITURE TREASURES, Lester Margon. 344 detail drawings, complete text on constructing exact reproductions of 38 early American masterpieces: Hepplewhite sideboard, Duncan Phyfe drop-leaf table, mantel clock, gate-leg dining table, Pa. German cupboard, more. 38 plates. 54 photographs. 168pp. 8⅜ x 11¼. 23056-2 Pa. $4.00

JEWELRY MAKING AND DESIGN, Augustus F. Rose, Antonio Cirino. Professional secrets revealed in thorough, practical guide: tools, materials, processes; rings, brooches, chains, cast pieces, enamelling, setting stones, etc. Do not confuse with skimpy introductions: beginner can use, professional can learn from it. Over 200 illustrations. 306pp. 21750-7 Pa. $3.00

METALWORK AND ENAMELLING, Herbert Maryon. Generally conceded best all-around book. Countless trade secrets: materials, tools, soldering, filigree, setting, inlay, niello, repoussé, casting, polishing, etc. For beginner or expert. Author was foremost British expert. 330 illustrations. 335pp. 22702-2 Pa. $4.00

WEAVING WITH FOOT-POWER LOOMS, Edward F. Worst. Setting up a loom, beginning to weave, constructing equipment, using dyes, more, plus over 285 drafts of traditional patterns including Colonial and Swedish weaves. More than 200 other figures. For beginning and advanced. 275pp. 8¾ x 6⅜. 23064-3 Pa. $4.50

WEAVING A NAVAJO BLANKET, Gladys A. Reichard. Foremost anthropologist studied under Navajo women, reveals every step in process from wool, dyeing, spinning, setting up loom, designing, weaving. Much history, symbolism. With this book you could make one yourself. 97 illustrations. 222pp. 22992-0 Pa. $3.00

NATURAL DYES AND HOME DYEING, Rita J. Adrosko. Use natural ingredients: bark, flowers, leaves, lichens, insects etc. Over 135 specific recipes from historical sources for cotton, wool, other fabrics. Genuine premodern handicrafts. 12 illustrations. 160pp. 22688-3 Pa. $2.00

DRIED FLOWERS, Sarah Whitlock and Martha Rankin. Concise, clear, practical guide to dehydration, glycerinizing, pressing plant material, and more. Covers use of silica gel. 12 drawings. Originally titled "New Techniques with Dried Flowers." 32pp. 21802-3 Pa. $1.00

THOMAS NAST: CARTOONS AND ILLUSTRATIONS, with text by· Thomas Nast St. Hill. Father of American political cartooning. Cartoons that destroyed Tweed Ring; inflation, free love, church and state; original Republican elephant and Democratic donkey; Santa Claus; more. 117 illustrations. 146pp. 9 x 12.
22983-1 Pa. $4.00
23067-8 Clothbd. $8.50

FREDERIC REMINGTON: 173 DRAWINGS AND ILLUSTRATIONS. Most famous of the Western artists, most responsible for our myths about the American West in its untamed days. Complete reprinting of *Drawings of Frederic Remington* (1897), plus other selections. 4 additional drawings in color on covers. 140pp. 9 x 12.
20714-5 Pa. $5.00'

HOW TO SOLVE CHESS PROBLEMS, Kenneth S. Howard. Practical suggestions on problem solving for very beginners. 58 two-move problems, 46 3-movers, 8 4-movers for practice, plus hints. 171pp. 20748-X Pa. **$3.00**

A GUIDE TO FAIRY CHESS, Anthony Dickins. 3-D chess, 4-D chess, chess on a cylindrical board, reflecting pieces that bounce off edges, cooperative chess, retrograde chess, maximummers, much more. Most based on work of great Dawson. Full handbook, 100 problems. 66pp. 7⅞ x 10¾. 22687-5 Pa. **$2.00**

WIN AT BACKGAMMON, Millard Hopper. Best opening moves, running game, blocking game, back game, tables of odds, etc. Hopper makes the game clear enough for anyone to play, and win. 43 diagrams. 111pp. 22894-0 Pa. **$1.50**

BIDDING A BRIDGE HAND, Terence Reese. Master player "thinks out loud" the binding of 75 hands that defy point count systems. Organized by bidding problem—no-fit situations, overbidding, underbidding, cueing your defense, etc. 254pp. EBE 22830-4 Pa. **$3.00**

THE PRECISION BIDDING SYSTEM IN BRIDGE, C.C. Wei, edited by Alan Truscott. Inventor of precision bidding presents average hands and hands from actual play, including games from 1969 Bermuda Bowl where system emerged. 114 exercises. 116pp. 21171-1 Pa. **$2.25**

LEARN MAGIC, Henry Hay. 20 simple, easy-to-follow lessons on magic for the new magician: illusions, card tricks, silks, sleights of hand, coin manipulations, escapes, and more —all with a minimum amount of equipment. Final chapter explains the great stage illusions. 92 illustrations. 285pp. 21238-6 Pa. **$2.95**

THE NEW MAGICIAN'S MANUAL, Walter B. Gibson. Step-by-step instructions and clear illustrations guide the novice in mastering 36 tricks; much equipment supplied on 16 pages of cut-out materials. 36 additional tricks. 64 illustrations. 159pp. 6⅝ x 10. 23113-5 Pa. **$3.00**

PROFESSIONAL MAGIC FOR AMATEURS, Walter B. Gibson. 50 easy, effective tricks used by professionals —cards, string, tumblers, handkerchiefs, mental magic, etc. 63 illustrations. 223pp. 23012-0 Pa. **$2.50**

CARD MANIPULATIONS, Jean Hugard. Very rich collection of manipulations; has taught thousands of fine magicians tricks that are really workable, eye-catching. Easily followed, serious work. Over 200 illustrations. 163pp. 20539-8 Pa. **$2.00**

ABBOTT'S ENCYCLOPEDIA OF ROPE TRICKS FOR MAGICIANS, Stewart James. Complete reference book for amateur and professional magicians containing more than 150 tricks involving knots, penetrations, cut and restored rope, etc. 510 illustrations. Reprint of 3rd edition. 400pp. 23206-9 Pa. **$3.50**

THE SECRETS OF HOUDINI, J.C. Cannell. Classic study of Houdini's incredible magic, exposing closely-kept professional secrets and revealing, in general terms, the whole art of stage magic. 67 illustrations. 279pp. 22913-0 Pa. **$3.00**

THE MAGIC MOVING PICTURE BOOK, Bliss, Sands & Co. The pictures in this book move! Volcanoes erupt, a house burns, a serpentine dancer wiggles her way through a number. By using a specially ruled acetate screen provided, you can obtain these and 15 other startling effects. Originally "The Motograph Moving Picture Book." 32pp. 8¼ x 11.   23224-7 Pa. $1.75

STRING FIGURES AND HOW TO MAKE THEM, Caroline F. Jayne. Fullest, clearest instructions on string figures from around world: Eskimo, Navajo, Lapp, Europe, more. Cats cradle, moving spear, lightning, stars. Introduction by A.C. Haddon. 950 illustrations. 407pp.   20152-X Pa. $3.50

PAPER FOLDING FOR BEGINNERS, William D. Murray and Francis J. Rigney. Clearest book on market for making origami sail boats, roosters, frogs that move legs, cups, bonbon boxes. 40 projects. More than 275 illustrations. Photographs. 94pp.
20713-7 Pa $1.50

INDIAN SIGN LANGUAGE, William Tomkins. Over 525 signs developed by Sioux, Blackfoot, Cheyenne, Arapahoe and other tribes. Written instructions and diagrams: how to make words, construct sentences. Also 290 pictographs of Sioux and Ojibway tribes. 111pp. 6⅛ x 9¼.   22029-X Pa. $1.75

BOOMERANGS: HOW TO MAKE AND THROW THEM, Bernard S. Mason. Easy to make and throw, dozens of designs: cross-stick, pinwheel, boomabird, tumblestick, Australian curved stick boomerang. Complete throwing instructions. All safe. 99pp.   23028-7 Pa. $1.75

25 KITES THAT FLY, Leslie Hunt. Full, easy to follow instructions for kites made from inexpensive materials. Many novelties. Reeling, raising, designing your own. 70 illustrations. 110pp.   22550-X Pa. $1.50

TRICKS AND GAMES ON THE POOL TABLE, Fred Herrmann. 79 tricks and games, some solitaires, some for 2 or more players, some competitive; mystifying shots and throws, unusual carom, tricks involving cork, coins, a hat, more. 77 figures. 95pp.   21814-7 Pa. $1.50

WOODCRAFT AND CAMPING, Bernard S. Mason. How to make a quick emergency shelter, select woods that will burn immediately, make do with limited supplies, etc. Also making many things out of wood, rawhide, bark, at camp. Formerly titled Woodcraft. 295 illustrations. 580pp.   21951-8 Pa. $4.00

AN INTRODUCTION TO CHESS MOVES AND TACTICS SIMPLY EXPLAINED, Leonard Barden. Informal intermediate introduction: reasons for moves, tactics, openings, traps, positional play, endgame. Isolates patterns. 102pp. USO 21210-6 Pa. $1.35

LASKER'S MANUAL OF CHESS, Dr. Emanuel Lasker. Great world champion offers very thorough coverage of all aspects of chess. Combinations, position play, openings, endgame, aesthetics of chess, philosophy of struggle, much more. Filled with analyzed games. 390pp.   20640-8 Pa. $4.00

SLEEPING BEAUTY, illustrated by Arthur Rackham. Perhaps the fullest, most delightful version ever, told by C.S. Evans. Rackham's best work. 49 illustrations. 110pp. 7⅞ x 10¾. 22756-1 Pa. $2.00

THE WONDERFUL WIZARD OF OZ, L. Frank Baum. Facsimile in full color of America's finest children's classic. Introduction by Martin Gardner. 143 illustrations by W.W. Denslow. 267pp. 20691-2 Pa. $3.50

GOOPS AND HOW TO BE THEM, Gelett Burgess. Classic tongue-in-cheek masquerading as etiquette book. 87 verses, 170 cartoons as Goops demonstrate virtues of table manners, neatness, courtesy, more. 88pp. 6½ x 9¼.
22233-0 Pa. $2.00

THE BROWNIES, THEIR BOOK, Palmer Cox. Small as mice, cunning as foxes, exuberant, mischievous, Brownies go to zoo, toy shop, seashore, circus, more. 24 verse adventures. 266 illustrations. 144pp. 6⅝ x 9¼. 21265-3 Pa. $2.50

BILLY WHISKERS: THE AUTOBIOGRAPHY OF A GOAT, Frances Trego Montgomery. Escapades of that rambunctious goat. Favorite from turn of the century America. 24 illustrations. 259pp. 22345-0 Pa. $2.75

THE ROCKET BOOK, Peter Newell. Fritz, janitor's kid, sets off rocket in basement of apartment house; an ingenious hole punched through every page traces course of rocket. 22 duotone drawings, verses. 48pp. 6⅞ x 8⅜. 22044-3 Pa. $1.50

CUT AND COLOR PAPER MASKS, Michael Grater. Clowns, animals, funny faces . . . simply color them in, cut them out, and put them together, and you have 9 paper masks to play with and enjoy. Complete instructions. Assembled masks shown in full color on the covers. 32pp. 8¼ x 11. 23171-2 Pa. $1.50

THE TALE OF PETER RABBIT, Beatrix Potter. The inimitable Peter's terrifying adventure in Mr. McGregor's garden, with all 27 wonderful, full-color Potter illustrations. 55pp. 4¼ x 5½. USO 22827-4 Pa. $1.00

THE TALE OF MRS. TIGGY-WINKLE, Beatrix Potter. Your child will love this story about a very special hedgehog and all 27 wonderful, full-color Potter illustrations. 57pp. 4¼ x 5½. USO 20546-0 Pa. $1.00

THE TALE OF BENJAMIN BUNNY, Beatrix Potter. Peter Rabbit's cousin coaxes him back into Mr. McGregor's garden for a whole new set of adventures. A favorite with children. All 27 full-color illustrations. 59pp. 4¼ x 5½.
USO 21102-9 Pa. $1.00

THE MERRY ADVENTURES OF ROBIN HOOD, Howard Pyle. Facsimile of original (1883) edition, finest modern version of English outlaw's adventures. 23 illustrations by Pyle. 296pp. 6½ x 9¼. 22043-5 Pa. $4.00

TWO LITTLE SAVAGES, Ernest Thompson Seton. Adventures of two boys who lived as Indians; explaining Indian ways, woodlore, pioneer methods. 293 illustrations. 286pp. 20985-7 Pa. $3.50

HOUDINI ON MAGIC, Harold Houdini. Edited by Walter Gibson, Morris N. Young. How he escaped; exposés of fake spiritualists; instructions for eye-catching tricks; other fascinating material by and about greatest magician. 155 illustrations. 280pp. 20384-0 Pa. **$2.75**

HANDBOOK OF THE NUTRITIONAL CONTENTS OF FOOD, U.S. Dept. of Agriculture. Largest, most detailed source of food nutrition information ever prepared. Two mammoth tables: one measuring nutrients in 100 grams of edible portion; the other, in edible portion of 1 pound as purchased. Originally titled Composition of Foods. 190pp. 9 x 12. 21342-0 Pa. **$4.00**

COMPLETE GUIDE TO HOME CANNING, PRESERVING AND FREEZING, U.S. Dept. of Agriculture. Seven basic manuals with full instructions for jams and jellies; pickles and relishes; canning fruits, vegetables, meat; freezing anything. Really good recipes, exact instructions for optimal results. Save a fortune in food. 156 illustrations. 214pp. 6⅛ x 9¼. 22911-4 Pa. **$2.50**

THE BREAD TRAY, Louis P. De Gouy. Nearly every bread the cook could buy or make: bread sticks of Italy, fruit breads of Greece, glazed rolls of Vienna, everything from corn pone to croissants. Over 500 recipes altogether. including buns, rolls, muffins, scones, and more. 463pp. 23000-7 Pa. **$4.00**

CREATIVE HAMBURGER COOKERY, Louis P. De Gouy. 182 unusual recipes for casseroles, meat loaves and hamburgers that turn inexpensive ground meat into memorable main dishes: Arizona chili burgers, burger tamale pie, burger stew, burger corn loaf, burger wine loaf, and more. 120pp. 23001-5 Pa. **$1.75**

LONG ISLAND SEAFOOD COOKBOOK, J. George Frederick and Jean Joyce. Probably the best American seafood cookbook. Hundreds of recipes. 40 gourmet sauces, 123 recipes using oysters alone! All varieties of fish and seafood amply represented. 324pp. 22677-8 Pa. **$3.50**

THE EPICUREAN: A COMPLETE TREATISE OF ANALYTICAL AND PRACTICAL STUDIES IN THE CULINARY ART, Charles Ranhofer. Great modern classic. 3,500 recipes from master chef of Delmonico's, turn-of-the-century America's best restaurant. Also explained, many techniques known only to professional chefs. 775 illustrations. 1183pp. 6⅝ x 10. 22680-8 Clothbd. **$22.50**

THE AMERICAN WINE COOK BOOK, Ted Hatch. Over 700 recipes: old favorites livened up with wine plus many more: Czech fish soup, quince soup, sauce Perigueux, shrimp shortcake, filets Stroganoff, cordon bleu goulash, jambonneau, wine fruit cake, more. 314pp. 22796-0 Pa. **$2.50**

DELICIOUS VEGETARIAN COOKING, Ivan Baker. Close to 500 delicious and varied recipes: soups, main course dishes (pea, bean, lentil, cheese, vegetable, pasta, and egg dishes), savories, stews, whole-wheat breads and cakes, more. 168pp. USO 22834-7 Pa. **$2.00**

COOKIES FROM MANY LANDS, Josephine Perry. Crullers, oatmeal cookies, chaux au chocolate, English tea cakes, mandel kuchen, Sacher torte, Danish puff pastry, Swedish cookies — a mouth-watering collection of 223 recipes. 157pp.
22832-0 Pa. $2.25

ROSE RECIPES, Eleanour S. Rohde. How to make sauces, jellies, tarts, salads, potpourris, sweet bags, pomanders, perfumes from garden roses; all exact recipes. Century old favorites. 95pp.
22957-2 Pa. $1.75

"OSCAR" OF THE WALDORF'S COOKBOOK, Oscar Tschirky. Famous American chef reveals 3455 recipes that made Waldorf great; cream of French, German, American cooking, in all categories. Full instructions, easy home use. 1896 edition. 907pp. 6⅝ x 9⅜.
20790-0 Clothbd. $15.00

JAMS AND JELLIES, May Byron. Over 500 old-time recipes for delicious jams, jellies, marmalades, preserves, and many other items. Probably the largest jam and jelly book in print. Originally titled May Byron's Jam Book. 276pp.
USO 23130-5 Pa. $3.50

MUSHROOM RECIPES, André L. Simon. 110 recipes for everyday and special cooking. Champignons à la grecque, sole bonne femme, chicken liver croustades, more; 9 basic sauces, 13 ways of cooking mushrooms. 54pp.
USO 20913-X Pa. $1.25

THE BUCKEYE COOKBOOK, Buckeye Publishing Company. Over 1,000 easy-to-follow, traditional recipes from the American Midwest: bread (100 recipes alone), meat, game, jam, candy, cake, ice cream, and many other categories of cooking. 64 illustrations. From 1883 enlarged edition. 416pp.
23218-2 Pa. $4.00

TWENTY-TWO AUTHENTIC BANQUETS FROM INDIA, Robert H. Christie. Complete, easy-to-do recipes for almost 200 authentic Indian dishes assembled in 22 banquets. Arranged by region. Selected from Banquets of the Nations. 192pp.
23200-X Pa. $2.50